ON THE STEEL BREEZE

Also by Alastair Reynolds from Gollancz:

Novels
Revelation Space
Redemption Ark
Absolution Gap
Chasm City
Century Rain
Pushing Ice
The Prefect
House of Suns
Terminal World
Blue Remembered Earth

Short Story Collections:
Diamond Dogs, Turquoise Days
Galactic North
Zima Blue

ON THE STEEL BREEZE

Alastair Reynolds

GOLLANCZ

LONDON

Copyright © Alastair Reynolds 2013
All rights reserved

The right of Alastair Reynolds to be identified as the author of this work has been asserted by him in accordance with the
Copyright, Designs and Patents Act 1988.

First published in Great Britain in 2013 by Gollancz
An imprint of the Orion Publishing Group
Orion House, 5 Upper St Martin's Lane, London WC2H 9EA
An Hachette UK Company

A CIP catalogue record for this book is available
from the British Library.

ISBN 978 0 575 09045 3 (Cased)
ISBN 978 0 575 09046 0 (Export Trade Paperback)

10 9 8 7 6 5 4 3 2 1

Typeset by Input Data Services Ltd, Bridgwater, Somerset

Printed and bound by CPI Group (UK) Ltd, Croydon, CR0 4YY

The Orion Publishing Group's policy is to use papers that
are natural, renewable and recyclable products and made
from wood grown in sustainable forests. The logging and
manufacturing processes are expected to conform to the
environmental regulations of the country of origin.

www.alastairreynolds.com
www.orionbooks.co.uk
www.gollancz.co.uk

For Louise Kleba, who started it all.

'A starlit or a moonlit dome disdains
All that man is,
All mere complexities,
The fury and the mire of human veins.'
— W.B. Yeats

(lines from 'Byzantium'.)

PROLOGUE

To begin with there was one of us, and now – if the news from Crucible is to be believed – there may soon be one of us again.

Lately I have been spending more time down at the shore, watching the arrival and departure of the sailing ships. I like the sound of their wind-whipped rigging, the quick and nimble business of the sailors, the lubbers and the merfolk, united in their fearlessness and strange ways of speaking. I watch the seagulls spoiling for scraps, and listen to their squabblesome cries. Sometimes I even flatter myself that I might be on the cusp of understanding them. Very occasionally, they share the sky with a dirigible or some other flying thing.

For a long time, though, it was difficult to return to this place. It is not that I have ever felt uncomfortable in Lisbon, even after the changes. True, there were hardships. But the city has endured worse, and doubtless, given enough time, it will endure worse again. I have many friends here, and, through the classes that I have organised, the children and adults I have helped with the learning of Portuguese, a surprising number of people have come to rely on me.

No, the city itself was not the problem and I cannot say that it has been unkind to me. But there were parts of it that for long years I felt obliged to avoid, tainted as they were by unpleasant association. The Baixa and the Santa Justa elevator, the long-established café at the top of the elevator, the tower at Belém, the Monument to the Discoveries. Not because bad things happened at all these places, but because they were the points where settled lives took sudden and unexpected turns, and (it must be said) not always for the better. But without these turns, I do not suppose I would be here now, with a mouth and a voice. Looking back on the chain of events that brought me to Lisbon, I can say with some conviction that nothing is ever entirely for good or ill. The city would concur, I think. I have strode its wide thoroughfares, enjoyed the benevolent shade of its grand imperial buildings. But before the city could be relaid out like this, it had first to be consumed in one terrible

1

morning of water and fire. On another day, my sister ended the world so that the world could keep living.

I finger the charm that she gave me that morning. It is a simple wooden thing, worn around my neck on an equally simple strand of leather. Someone might look at this charm and think nothing of it, and in a sense they would be right in their assessment. It has little value and certainly no power. I am not a believer in such things, even though there is more superstition in the world than when I was a girl. People have begun to think of gods and ghosts again, although I am not one of them. But it cannot be denied that there is a small quiet miracle in the mere fact of the charm's continued existence. It has come through an astonishing amount of time, tunnelling its way through history and into my care. It was my great-grandmother's once, and that is far enough back for most people. But I suppose the charm would have seemed inscrutably old even to my great-grandmother, and just as old to *her* great-grandmother, whoever that woman was. There must have been so many times when the charm was almost lost, almost destroyed, but it slipped through those moments of crisis and somehow found its way into the present, a blessing from history.

I have been fortunate as well. By rights, I should not be standing here at all. I should have died, centuries ago, in deep space. In one sense, that is exactly what happened to me. I wagered myself against time and distance and lost the wager. Of course, I remember very little of what it was like to be me before the accident. What I remember now, or think I remember, is mostly what I was told by my sister. She spoke of a meeting under a candelabra tree, of the drawing of coloured lots, of the selecting of individual fates. Our lives decided. She was jealous of me, then. She thought my fate offered more glory than her own.

She was right, in her way, but the things that happened to us made a mockery of our plans and ambitions. Chiku Green did get to stand on Crucible and breathe the alien airs of another world. Chiku Red did reach that tiny drifting spacecraft, and she did learn something of its contents. Chiku Yellow did get to stay behind, where (it was hoped) she would stay out of harm's way, leading a life of quiet unadventurousness.

So it was, for a time. As I have said, people did not as a rule believe in ghosts in those enlightened days. But there are ghosts and there are ghosts. If it had not been for a particular haunting, Chiku Yellow would never have come to the interest of the merfolk, and if she had not snared their attention, my eventual part in this chain of events would be, to say the least, greatly diminished.

So I am not sorry about the ghost. Sorry about everything else, yes.

2

But I am glad that the phantom came to worry my sister out of her happy complacency. She had a good life, back then, if only she had known it.

But then so did everyone else.

CHAPTER ONE

She was on her way to the Santa Justa elevator when she saw the ghost again.

It was down in the Baixa, not far from the river. A street juggler had gathered onlookers, a party of tourists canopied under coloured umbrellas. When a gap opened in the group the ghost was with them, reaching out to Chiku. The ghost wore black clothes and a black hat with a wide brim. The ghost kept saying something, her expression becoming steadily more tormented. Then the tourists closed in again. The juggler did some more tricks and then made the mistake of asking for money. Disgruntled by this development, the party began to disperse. Chiku waited a moment but the ghost was gone.

Riding the iron elevator, she wondered what she was going to do about the apparitions. They were becoming more frequent. She knew the ghost could do her no harm, but that was not the same thing as accepting its presence.

'You look troubled,' a voice said. 'Why would you look troubled on such a lovely afternoon?'

The speaker was one of three merfolk jammed in next to her near the elevator's doors. They had squeezed in at the last moment, offending her with their briny smell and the hard edges of their mobility exos. She had wondered where they were going. It was said that merfolk disliked confined spaces, and heights, and being too far from the sea.

'I'm sorry?'

'I shouldn't have spoken.'

'No, you shouldn't.'

'But it *is* a lovely afternoon, isn't it? We like rain. We admire the reflectivity of wet surfaces. The particular way the sun splinters and refracts. The glossiness of things that were formerly matte. The heaviness of the sky.'

'I'm not interested in joining you. Go and recruit someone else.'

'Oh, we're not recruiting. That's not something we need to do any more. Are you going to the café?'

'What café?'

'The one at the top.'

Chiku had indeed been on her way to the café but the question had blindsided her. How did the merperson know her habits? Not everyone in the elevator would be going to the café, nor even a majority of them. They might stop there on their way back from the Carmo Convent, but the café was seldom the point of their elevation up from the Rua do Ouro.

'Who are you?' she asked.

'A friend of the family.'

'Leave me alone.'

The doors opened. Chiku shuffled out alongside the tourists and headed straight to the café, taking her usual seat near the window. She watched seagulls raucously, recklessly helter-skeltering on the updraught of a thermal. The clouds had begun to break, sunlight splintering off the tumble of wet red rooftops that ferried the eye down to the platinum ribbon of the Tagus.

She ordered coffee. She had been considering a pastry, but the ghost and the strange conversation in the elevator had taken the edge off her appetite. She wondered if she was starting to dislike Lisbon.

She had brought her book with her. It was an old looking thing, cased in marbled covers. Inside were pages and pages of handwritten text. Her letters all sloped to the right like windblown trees. Chiku saw an omission on one page and touched the nib of her fountain pen to the vellum. The inked words budged up, forming a space in which she could insert the missing word. Elsewhere she struck through two superflous lines and the text on either side of the deleted passage married itself together.

Feeling eyes on her, she glanced up.

The merfolk had entered the café, forcing the proprietor to move tables and chairs to accommodate their exos. They were sitting in a loose triangle around a small, low circular table, a big pot of tea steaming between them.

One of the merfolk met her gaze. She thought it might have been the one who had spoken to her in the elevator. The aquatic – she thought it likely now that it was a male – held a teacup in his blubbery grey fingers and elevated it to the lipless gash of his mouth. His eyes were unblinking black voids. From the cup the aquatic sipped a watery preparation. He lowered the cup to the table then employed the back of his hand to wipe a green smear from his mouth. His skin had the gleam of wet pebbles. On land they were forever rubbing oils and perfumes into themselves.

The aquatic's eyes never left hers.

Fed up, Chiku voked payment and prepared to leave. The ghost had ruined her afternoon and now the merfolk had ruined her day. She thought about walking out without saying a word. That would have been the dignified thing.

'I have no interest in you or your seasteads, and I don't care a damn about your stupid plans for colonising the universe. And you don't know me or my family.'

'Are you certain of that fact?' Definitely the one who had spoken to her before. 'Truth be told, you've been taking a definite interest in us – the United Aquatic Nations, the Panspermian Initiative. That makes us take an interest in you. Whether you like it or not.'

Beyond the merfolk, through another window, the suspension bridge glittered like a piece of brand-new jewellery. A silver spitball of reconstructive machinery had been inching its way along the ancient structure for weeks, digesting and renewing metal parts that were nearly as old as Santa Justa herself. Supervising this delicate work, towering over the bridge on their preposterous stilt-legs, were a pair of mantis-like Providers.

'Whether I like it or not? Who the hell do you think you are?'

'I am Mecufi. You have been probing our public and private history – why are you taking such an interest in the past?'

'It's none of your business.'

'This is the Surveilled World,' Mecufi said sternly, the way one might explain some exceedingly simple thing to a child. 'Everything is everyone's business in the Surveilled World. That's the point.'

Tourists strode the distant castle battlements. Along the banks of the Tagus, cyberclippers made landfall after transatlantic crossings, elegant sleek sails ruffling in a stiff river breeze. Dirigibles and airpods slid under clouds, colourful as balloons.

'What would you know about the Surveilled World? You're not even part of it.'

'Its influence extends into our realm more than we'd wish. And we're good at detecting data searches, especially when they happen to concern us.'

The odd exchange was beginning to draw the interest of the café's other customers. Chiku's skin crawled at the attention. She liked it here. She enjoyed the anonymity.

'I'm a historian. That's all.'

'Writing a private history of the Akinya clan? Eunice Akinya and all that stuff? Geoffrey and the elephants? The dusty goings-on of two hundred years ago? Is that what's in this book of yours?'

'Like I said, it's none of your business either way.'

'Well, that's a ringing denial.'

The other two made froglike chuckling sounds.

'This is harassment,' Chiku said. 'As a free citizen, I'm entitled to make any enquiries I wish. If you've got a problem with that, take it up with the Mechanism.'

Mecufi held up a placating hand. 'We might be in a position to help you. But we'll need some – shall we say reciprocity?'

'What do I need your help with?'

'The ghost, for a start – we can definitely help you with that. But we need something from you first.' Mecufi reached into a pouch in his exo and drew out a slim wooden box, the kind that might have held a collection of pencils or drawing compasses. Mecufi worked a little catch and slid out an interior compartment. It contained a dozen felt-lined partitions, in each of which nestled a coloured marble about the size of a glass eye. His hand dithered over the marbles. They were a variety of pale colours, glittering and swirling, save for one at the back, which was either a very dark purple or a pure black.

He settled on a sphere of fire-flecked amber. He held it between his fingers, closed his eyes. It took him a few seconds to achieve a clean formulation, and to make the necessary assignment.

'Take my mote,' Mecufi said.

'I don't—' Chiku began.

'Take my mote.' Mecufi pushed the amber marble into her palm and made her fingers close around the marble. 'If it convinces you of my basic good intentions, be at the Monument to the Discoveries no later than ten o' clock tomorrow morning. Then we shall visit the Atlantic seasteads. Only a small adventure – you'll be back in time for tea.'

Pedro Braga was humming quietly to himself as he cleaned brushes. His studio reeked of varnishes and lacquers. Beneath that pungency lay the permanent tang of wood shavings, sawdust, expensive traditional resins.

'Something odd happened to me today,' Chiku said.

'Odd in what way?'

'To do with the ghost. Only odder than that. I met a merman. Named Mecufi.'

Guitars, in various states of assembly, hung from the ceiling's bare rafters by their necks. Some were only embryonic outlines, bounded in crotchet-like curves. Others were nearly done save for stringing or the final touches of decorative work. It was complicated, baffling work, but the guitars sold well. In a world in which assemblers and Providers could furnish almost any artefact at almost no cost, there was a premium in imperfection.

'I didn't think you wanted anything to do with them.'

'I didn't. Mecufi made the contact, not me – in the elevator, on the way to the café. There were three of them. They knew who I was. They also knew about the ghost.'

'That *is* weird.' Pedro had finished cleaning his brushes, leaving them to dry in a wooden frame. 'Can they do something about it?'

'I don't know. They want me to go to the seasteads.'

'Lucky you. There are millions who'd kill for an invitation.'

'Good for them. I don't happen to feel that way.'

Pedro opened a bottle of wine and poured two glasses. They kissed briefly, took the glasses out onto the balcony and sat either side of a gently rusting table flaky with white paint. They could not see the sea unless they leaned out at the very end of the balcony, where it offered itself up coyly for inspection in the gap between two nearby tenements. At night, when the glow from windows and street lamps buttered the city yellow, Chiku never missed the sight of the sea.

'You really don't like them, do you?'

'They took my son. That's reason enough, isn't it?'

They had hardly ever spoken of her life before the day they met in Belém. It was what they had both agreed on, a relationship built on a solid foundation of mutual ignorance. Pedro knew of her siblings and that Chiku had a son, and that the son had joined the seasteaders – become, in effect, a member of a new species. Chiku, in turn, knew that Pedro had travelled widely before settling in Lisbon and that he had not always been a luthier. He had money she could not quite square with the modest income from his business – the studio rental alone should have been beyond his means. But she had no desire to dig for the details.

'Perhaps you need to get over it.'

'Get over it?' Feeling a flush of irritation Chiku leaned on the table, making it rock on its uneven metal legs. 'You don't get over something like that. Plus that's just the start of it – they've been messing with my family's business for far too long.'

'But if they can make the ghost go away—'

'He said "help me with that". That might mean being able to answer the ghost. To find out what Chiku Green wants.'

'Would you want that?'

'I'd like the option. I think maybe ...' But Chiku chose not to finish her sentence. She drank some wine. A woman bellowed the same three lines of *Fado* from the open doorway of one of the bars in the street below, rehearsing for an evening performance. 'I don't know if I can trust them. But Mecufi gave me this.'

She placed the little marble on the table between them.

Pedro reached out and pinched it between thumb and forefinger with a faint sneer of distaste. He did not approve, Chiku knew. He thought motes somehow short-circuited an essential element of human discourse.

'These aren't foolproof.'

She took back the amber marble. It would not work for Pedro anyway. Motes were always keyed to a specific recipient.

'I know. But I'm willing to try it.'

Chiku crushed the mote. The glassy orb shattered into harmless self-dissolving shards as the mote's payload – its cargo of emotions – unfolded inside her head like a flower. The mote spoke of caution and hopefulness and a singular desire to be trusted. There were no dark notes in the chorus.

I was right about Mecufi being a he,' Chiku decided. 'That came through clearly.'

'What else?'

'He wants me to go to the seasteads very badly. They need me at least as much as I need them. And it's not just about the ghost. There's something else.'

The woman singing *Fado* ran through the same three phrases again and her voice cracked on the last syllable. The woman laughed.

CHAPTER TWO

Belém was where she had met Pedro. It had not been long after her arrival in Lisbon. Both of them buying ice creams from the same stand and laughing as wickedly determined seagulls dived and skimmed to scoop away their purchases.

She went up onto the roof of the Monument to the Discoveries, with its sea-gazing ranks of carved navigators. It was the only place to get a decent view of the Wind Rose. It was a map of the ancient world, laid out across a wide terrace in slabs of red and blue marble. Galleons and seamonsters patrolled its fathomless seas and oceans. A kraken was hauling a ship to the depths in its tentacles. Beyond the map, arrows delineated the cardinal compass points.

'It's good that you came.'

She turned around sharply. When she had arrived there had been no merfolk on the Monument's viewing level, or at least none that she had recognised as such. It was a whisker after ten and she assumed her lateness had caused the agreement to be nullified. And yet here was Mecufi, stuffed now into an upright mobility exo.

'You mentioned the ghost. I've seen it once already this morning, on the tram.'

'Yes, it's getting worse, isn't it? But we'll talk about that later. There are a couple of other things on the agenda before that. Shall we fly?'

'Fly?'

Mecufi looked up. Chiku followed his gaze, squinting against the haze. A shape detached itself from a bright wheel of gulls and grew larger as it descended. It was a flier, about as wide across as the top of the monument.

'We have special dispensation,' Mecufi said. 'They love us in Lisbon, after we installed the tsunami baffles. They've got long memories here – 1755 was yesterday.' From the flier's broad green belly came a warm downdraught. A ramp tongued down and Mecufi directed Chiku to step

11

aboard. 'Why do you hesitate? There's no need not to trust us. I gave you the mote, didn't I?'

'Motes can be faked.'

'Everything can be faked. You'll just have to trust that it wasn't.'

'Then we're back to square one, aren't we? I have to trust that you're trustworthy?'

'Trust is a fine and paradoxical thing. I promised I'd have you home before evening – will you take me at my word?'

'We're just going to the seasteads?'

'And no further. It's a beautiful day for it. The quality of light on water, as restless as the sea itself! What better time to be alive?'

Chiku acquiesced. They escalated aboard, taking lounge seats in a generously proportioned cabin. The cabin sealed itself and the flier gathered speed as it rose. In a few breaths they were banking away from the coast. The waters were a gorgeous mingling of hues, lakes of indigo and ultramarine ink spilt into the ocean.

'Earth's quite nice, isn't it?' Mecufi's exo had deposited him in his seat like a large stuffed toy, then folded itself away for the duration of the flight.

'It was working out for me.'

'The perfect backwater to study your family history? Crumbly old Lisbon, of all places?'

'I thought I'd find some peace and quiet there. Evidently I was wrong about that.'

The flier kept low. Occasionally they passed a cyberclipper, pleasure yacht or small wooden fishing boat with a gaily painted hull. Chiku barely glimpsed the fishermen busy on deck as the flier sped past, fussing with nets and winches. They never looked up. The aircraft was tidying up after itself, dissipating its own Mach cone so that there was no sonic boom.

Its hull would have tuned itself to the colour of sky.

'Let me ask you about your counterparts,' Mecufi said.

'I'd rather you didn't.'

'And yet I must. Let's begin with the basics. Your mother and father were Sunday Akinya and Jitendra Gupta, both still living. You were born in what used to be the Descrutinised Zone, on the Moon, about two hundred years ago. Do you dispute these facts?'

'Why would I?'

Mecufi paused to smear some lavender-smelling oil onto himself from a small dispenser. 'You had a carefree and prosperous childhood. You grew up in a time of tremendous peace and beneficial social and

12

technological change. A time free of wars and poverty and nearly all illnesses. You were extraordinarily fortunate – billions of dead souls would have traded places with you in a heartbeat. And yet as you entered adulthood you detected an emptiness inside yourself. A lack of direction, an absence of moral purpose. It was hard, growing up with that name. Your parents and grandparents and great-grandparents moved mountains. Eunice opened up the solar system for deep-space settlement and exploitation. Sunday and your other relatives opened up the stars! What could you possibly do that would compare with any of that?'

Chiku folded her arms. 'Are you done?'

'Not remotely. That's the trouble with being very long-lived: there's an awful lot of life to catch up with.'

'So perhaps you should think about cutting to the chase.'

'When you were fifty years old, a new technology came to fruition and you made a momentous decision. You engaged the firm Quorum Binding to produce two clones of you using rapid phenotyping. In a few months the clones were fully formed physically, but little more than semi-conscious blank canvases. They had your face but not your memories; none of your scars, none of the marks life had left on you, nothing of your developmental or immunological history. But that was also part of the plan.

'While the clones matured, you submitted your own body to a process of structural adjustment. Medical nanomachines gorged you down to a woman-shaped core. They took apart your bones and muscles and nervous system and remade them so that they were genetically and functionally indistinguishable from those of your clone siblings. A front of neural machines tore through your brain like a wildfire. They recorded your idiosyncratic connectome – the detailed pattern of your own mental wiring. At the same time, similar machines – scriptors – wrote those same patterns into the minds of your siblings. Their minds had always been similar to your own, but now they were identical – even down to the level of memory. What you recollected, they recollected. The process was a kind of stochastic averaging. Some of the innate structures of your siblings were even transcribed back into your head. By the end of it, by the time the three of you were hauled out of the immersion vats, there was literally no way to tell you apart. You looked and thought the same. The telomeric clock of your cells had been wound back to zero. Epigenetic factors had been corrected and reversed. Since you all had access to the same memories, you could not even say for yourselves which was the original. That was precisely the point: that there should not be a favoured sibling. And the firm that had done this to you, Quorum Binding – even they didn't know which one of you was authentic. Their process was rigorously blind. Their customers expected nothing less.'

'And this would be your business, exactly, because ...?'

'You have *always* been our business, Chiku, whether you like it or not. Tell me how you selected your individual paths.'

'Why?'

'Because it's the one part of your history I can't get at.'

Six months after the procedure, the three of them had reconvened in Equatorial East Africa. It was a warm day; they decided on a picnic away from the household. They had gone out in three airpods, skimming low and fast until they found a suitable spot. She remembered the airpods resting on the ground and a table set beneath the drowsy shade of a candelabra tree. Upon some impulse they had agreed to select their individual fates by breaking bread. The loaves contained coloured paper lots, the nature of which they had agreed on beforehand. Two of the siblings would embark on different enterprises which entailed a measure of risk. The third sibling would remain in the solar system as a kind of insurance policy, the only requirement being that she live a life of relative safety. With the family's investments still growing exponentially, the third sibling would not need to work unless she wanted to.

Each secretly desired to be the third sibling. There was no dishonour in that.

Chiku remembered breaking bread three times, from the simultaneous perspective of each woman. After the breaking of the bread they had all undergone the periodic sharing of each other's memories, and of course those memories all contained the recollection of that day under the tree, seen from a different perspective. The mixture of emotions was in each case distinct, like three photographs that had been tinted in varying hues

For the sibling who broke her bread to reveal a pale-green lot, the expedition to Crucible beckoned. She experienced a sort of dizzy and delighted apprehension, like the sensation of approaching the first peak of a roller coaster. She would be leaving Earth behind and committing to a century and a half within the stone bowels of a holoship. The risks were difficult to assess: the holoships were new, untested, and such a thing had never been attempted before. But the reward at the end of that crossing – the right to set foot on a new world, orbiting a new sun – was incalculable.

For the sibling choosing to travel out into space and find the drifting hulk of the *Winter Queen* – her lot was a pinkish red – the apprehension was sharper and arrived with oboe-like undertones of dread. The risks of this expedition were much more immediately quantifiable. She would be going out alone, pushing a little spacecraft to the outer envelope of its performance. On the other hand, when she returned home with the prize, her debt to posterity would be paid. This was high risk, but maximum reward. And whereas the sibling on the holoship would share her achievement with millions, this triumph would be hers alone.

For the sibling who had to stay at home, the sibling who drew the yellow lot, the feeling was one of relief. She had drawn the easy duty. But at the same time she felt a sharp, brassy stab of resentment that she would be denied the individual glories of Crucible or the reaching of *Winter Queen*. Nonetheless, this was what they had agreed. She had no need to feel ashamed of herself. Any of them could have drawn this lot.

There was a wooden box on the table. As one, their hands moved to open it. They laughed at the awkwardness of this moment, its betrayal of their fixed behaviour. Then by some silent consensus, two of them moved their hands back into their laps and allowed the third – Chiku Yellow – to open the lid.

The box contained an assortment of Akinya heirlooms, which were few in number. There were some pencils that had belonged to Uncle Geoffrey and a pair of scuffed Ray-Ban sunglasses. There was a print of a digital photograph taken of Eunice when she was little, by her own mother Soya, when the two of them had been climate refugees in some kind of transit camp. There was a rare Samsung mobile telephone, a Swiss Army knife, a compass and a thumb-sized digital memory device in the form of a key ring. There was a tattered copy of *Gulliver's Travels* which appeared to be missing some pages. There were six wooden elephants, each fixed onto a coal-coloured plinth – bull, matriarch, two young adults and two calves. The elephants were divided between the two siblings venturing into space. This was what they had agreed.

After they had divided up the other items, the only thing remaining in the box was a simple wooden charm. It hung from a thin leather strap, a circular talisman of unguessable age. They all knew it had belonged to their great-grandmother, and that it had passed from Eunice to Soya: not the Soya who was Eunice's mother, but the daughter of Eunice's former husband Jonathan Beza. Soya had in turn gifted the charm to Sunday, during her time on Mars, and Sunday had passed the charm on to her daughter, Chiku Akinya.

Now they were three.

'It should remain here,' said Chiku Green, the version of Chiku travelling to Crucible.

'I agree,' said Chiku Red, the version of Chiku pursuing *Winter Queen*.

'We could cut it into three,' Chiku Yellow ventured, but that was an idea they had already raised and dismissed on a dozen occasions. The simple fact was that the charm belonged on Earth or near to it. It had no business leaving the solar system.

Chiku Yellow took the charm and slipped the cord around her neck. They were all riding the tramlines of different fates now, but for the first time since the drawing of the lots, she had some tangible sense of her own diminished future. She was not going out there.

'It began well,' Mecufi said.

'Most things do.'

Mecufi popped the oil dispenser back into its pouch next to his seat and picked up his potted narrative of Chiku's life. 'The idea was that the three of you would have different experiences but remain essentially the same individual. You would go off and live independent lives, but the readers and scriptors in your heads would hold your memories in strict congruence, like bookkeepers maintaining identical sets of accounts. What one of you experienced, so would the other two. It was meant to be a process of periodic realignment rather than constant synchronisation, but for one reason or another you gradually drifted apart. You remained in contact with each other, but the relationships grew distant, strained. You stopped feeling as if you had much in common. There was a catalysing event, of course—'

'I thought you had something to tell me,' Chiku said. That was how she thought of herself, not as Chiku Yellow. The colours were for keeping tabs on her siblings, not herself. She added: 'If this is all you've got, I think we need to go back to Lisbon.'

'We haven't got to the ghost yet.'

'What about it?'

'One of you is trying to re-establish contact. You have disavowed the readers and scriptors from touching your memories, so your sibling is attempting to reach you by other means. Of course, we know which one of you it has to be.'

'No prizes for that – there are only two of us left.'

16

'I understand why you drifted apart from Chiku Green. The further away she travelled, the longer the time lag became. Weeks and months were almost manageable. But years? Decades? We're not wired for that. We're not built to maintain any kind of empathic connection with someone that far from home. Especially when they begin to feel like a rival, someone living a better, more adventurous life. A life with a purpose. When you both had children, you felt a kinship – a sense of shared achievement. Chiku Green had Ndege and Mposi. You had Kanu. But when your own son turned from you—'

'He didn't turn from me. You turned him from everything he knew and loved – his family, his world, even his species.'

'Regardless, his turning brought sorrow. After that, you couldn't stand to share any part of Chiku Green's existence. It wasn't that you hated her – how could you? That would be like hating yourself. But you hated the idea that there was a version of you living a better life. As for your son – I would ask you not to blame us for the choices Kanu made.'

'I'll blame you for whatever I feel like.'

Mecufi twisted in his seat. Like a hyperactive child, he appeared easily distracted. 'Look, we're coming up on our islands!'

They were somewhere near the Azores. This, though, was no natural island chain. These were vast floating platelets, hexagonal platforms ten kilometres wide, jigsawed together in rafts and archipelagos, forming larger islands with their own angular coastlines, peninsulas, atolls and bays.

There were hundreds of distinct island aggregations in the United Aquatic Nations. The smallest were nimble microstates, formed from only a few linked platelets. Others were supercolonies composed of thousands or tens of thousands of platelets, but always in flux – platelets breaking away, reshuffling, honeycombing into new polities and federations and alliances. There were also breakaway states, independencies, fractious alliances between rogue seasteaders and the land powers. No maps existed for these nervous, jostling territories.

'Where does he live now?' she asked. 'You'd know that, wouldn't you? Even if Kanu doesn't want to talk to me?'

'Your son is still on Earth, but on the other side of Africa, in the Indian Ocean, working with krakens.'

'You've met him, then.'

'Not personally, no. But I have it on good authority that he leads a very happy and productive life. There would have been no ill will, Chiku, had you not tried to steer him from us. But you cannot blame him for shunning you now.'

'And you can't blame me for wanting to know how my son is doing.'

'Then you are equal in your blamelessness.'

They were flying lower and slower now. No two of the platelets were exactly alike. Some had been turned over to agriculture, spawning cloud-piercing vertical farms. Others were frogspawned with sealed biomes, replicating specific terrestrial ecosystems. Some were dense with dwellings, tier after tier of them, air-breathing arcologies as thriving and urban as any landbound conurbation. They hauled their own little weather systems. Others were gridded with elegant sun-tracking mirror. Some had become leisure complexes, gravid with casinos and resort hotels. Near the equator, Chiku knew, a few served as the anchorpoints for space elevators. But that was the wave of the past now, yesterday's technology. From their seasteads, the merfolk were building daunting chimney-like structures that pushed all the way out of the atmosphere, enclosing a column of vacuum. She could see one of those towers now, a glassy chimney that was all but invisible except when she looked directly at it. It rose up and up, into the zenith, never ending. A ship was rising in silence: a tiny ascending spark of solar brightness.

'Tell me what you know about the ghost.'

'Chiku Green sent her, after the normal communication channel was blocked. She's a flock of data, circling the globe, looking for somewhere to land, and such phenomena attract our attention. Do you regret what you did, with the blocking?'

'I assumed it would be reversible.'

'And now?'

'What's done is done.'

She had asked Quorum Binding to exclude her from the memory synchronisations, effectively isolating herself from her siblings. But then Quorum Binding had gone into administration during the fall of the Descrutinised Zone, and when their creditors stepped in and examined Quorum's records, they could find no way of undoing Chiku's request. A vital numeric code had been lost.

'You'd burnt your last mental bridge.'

'And your point is?'

'There's a chance we can unburn it – allow you to receive and transmit memories again, to resume contact with Chiku Green. And find out exactly what it is she so very desperately wants you to know.'

'Define "chance".'

18

'Let's just say that the omens are propitious. But we'll need a favour from you in return. We've lost touch with an old friend, and we think you can help us re-establish contact.'

CHAPTER THREE

An island rose to a false mountaintop with a snowcap of terraced white buildings that lapped over the edge of its hollow summit – balconied hotels and transformation clinics for those preparing to join the mer-folk. Between the hotels and clinics, forcing through cracks and crevices like some kind of industrial foam, was a dense eruption of rainforest. Throngs of skittish vermillion birds – parrots or parakeets – swept through the burgeoning canopy. Rainbowed cataracts thundered from beneath the hotels, tonguing out into space, raining down onto rimmed ledges, lakes and lagoons, the foundations for still more hotels and clinics, malls and restaurant districts within the mountain's hollow core. The flier sank into the false mountain, turning slowly on its axis. It was blazing bright much of the way down the shaft, sunlight tossed from mirror to mirror and splintered off where it was needed. Veils of mist rose from the bases of the cataracts.

'They keep saying demand for our services will peak,' Mecufi said. 'The truth is there's no end to it. Returning to the seas is the oldest human aspiration – much older, much less easily sated, than the simple and rather childish aspiration to fly. We were never *meant* to fly – that's the preserve of other species. But we all came from the seas.'

'Go back a bit further,' Chiku said, 'and we all came from primordial slime.'

'They tell me your great-grandmother was just as cynical when she dealt with our founder. Lin Wei was driven by a vision of human possibility, a grand dream of Panspermianism and the Green Efflorescence. Eunice was driven by no higher calling than the need to plant flags on things.'

'Your point being?'

'Let me add another name to the mix. June Wing was an old friend of your family's, wasn't she?'

'I wouldn't know.'

'Then you're not much of a historian. June Wing was – is – one of your father Jitendra's friends. They worked together on cybernetics problems. Like your father, June Wing is still alive. She's busy beetling around the solar system, collecting junk for a museum.'

'And this is relevant because?'

'June Wing, we believe, has a line of contact with Lin Wei – or Arethusa, as she's taken to calling herself. We would very much like to speak with Arethusa, our founder. But Arethusa won't return our calls and June Wing isn't exactly in a hurry to speak to us, either. But at least we know where June Wing is and what she's doing. Now all we need is for someone June trusts to speak to her on our behalf. That's where you come in.'

'I should have listened to Geoffrey.'

'And what did he tell you?'

'Never have anything to do with merpeople.'

'You expressed a similar sentiment to Kanu, and look what happened there. But tell me – from your many conversations with Geoffrey, what did he make of Arethusa?'

'We had plenty of more important things to talk about – your founder wasn't the first topic on everyone's mind, you know.'

She thought of Geoffrey, the handful of times they had met. Of course they had spoken, and of course they had spoken of Arethusa, who had once been Lin Wei but was now something very far from a human woman. But all that was ancient history.

They had reached water at the base of the shaft. Without any fuss the flier went submersible, water lapping its windows. The clinics and hotels and boutiques carried on beneath the surface, except now they were airtight and lit up with neon. Other vehicles and swimmers moved through the water, outlined in glowing colour. There Chiku glimpsed nets and canopies of marine vegetation, darting shoals of electric-blue fish, astonishing pastel-coloured coral formations. Under swimmer supervision, a huge biomechanical monster, like a cross between a lobster and a squid, helped to position prefab building parts into place. Chiku surveyed its claws and tentacles with dread, imagining the damage it could do, but the swimmers appeared unconcerned by their docile helper.

'A construction kraken,' Mecufi said, as if the monster were the most mundane thing in the universe. 'The same sort of animal that Kanu works with. They're actually very agreeable creatures, once you get to know them.'

And then they were moving horizontally along a lit tunnel, into the great vaults of the false mountain.

'We've established that the ghost is a message from your sibling on the holoship,' Mecufi said. 'Tell me about the *other* Chiku – Chiku Red, the one who never came back.'

'What's to tell?'

'Humour me.'

Chiku sighed. 'Eunice had a ship called *Winter Queen*. It was the one she'd used for all her expeditions around the solar system. Long before anyone else knew about the Chibesa Principle, she upgraded *Winter Queen*'s engine, set the ship running and headed for interstellar space. She wasn't expecting to get anywhere – it was a gesture, the throwing down of a gauntlet. Eventually they worked out where she was, how far out. But no one thought there was a hope in hell of catching up with her.'

'Except for Chiku Red.'

'There'd been some improvements in engine design that would allow a ship to reach Eunice and make it back, but everything still had to be cut to the bone – one passenger, the bare minimum of redundant systems, no backup if something went wrong. Sixty years just to reach Eunice, even longer to slow down, turn around and travel back.'

'What exactly was the mission objective? To fetch *Winter Queen* – or your great-grandmother?'

'It wasn't about bringing her home. Her body, maybe. And any secrets she might have carried with her.'

'Presumably she didn't mean for those secrets to return to Earth.'

'You didn't know my great-grandmother. She presented her family with one set of challenges from beyond the grave. Maybe this was another. We were hoping for *something*.'

'New physics, beyond even the Chibesa Principle?'

'Who knows?' Chiku shrugged, boring of this inquisition. 'The only way to know was to get out there and look.'

'And what became of Chiku Red?'

'She never made it back. Her ship – *Memphis* – sent a message to say it was on final approach to *Winter Queen* and that it had initiated the wake-up procedure for Chiku Red. Then silence. That was the last anyone heard from her.'

'Then your presumption is that she died out there?'

'My great-grandmother was a twitchy old woman. She'd already installed defences on her space station and an iceteroid, to ward against casual intruders. Something similar must have taken out Chiku Red's ship.'

'Or communications simply failed.'

The vehicle was surfacing in a dome-shaped cave half-full of water. It had been a flier, then a submarine; now it effortlessly assumed the role of boat. As it approached a jetty, another door opened in its hull, this time in the side rather than the belly. Mecufi's mobility exo reappeared, scooped him from his seat and took delicate charge of its passenger.

'Chiku Red never came home.'

'And if she had . . . how would that have changed things?'

They disembarked into moist warm air. Windows and balconies rose in overlapping circles to the dome's apex. Suspended by invisible wires and limned by spotlights, the awesome skeleton of a plesiosaur loomed over the flier, its flippers frozen in the action of paddling air.

'It's time to stop playing games,' Chiku said. 'I'm an Akinya. We don't like to be messed around.'

'Once upon a time,' Mecufi said as his exo carried him to the edge of the jetty, 'there might have been some truth in that statement.'

At the jetty's side, a translucent, ice-coloured boat with a swan's neck and head bobbed on the waves created by the flier's arrival. Mecufi slipped out of the exo into the water and vanished beneath the surface. He reappeared a few seconds later, his large dark eyes blinking, and he rubbed them with his hands. He was smiling, floating on his back like a sea otter, suddenly muscular and sleek.

'What am I meant to do?'

'Swim if you like – we're not going far – but you may prefer to take the boat.'

Chiku opted for the boat. It was a two-seater affair with very rudimentary controls – the sort of craft available for hire by the hour at civic boating lakes. Mecufi swam ahead, the boat puppying after him. A water-filled channel beside the jetty took them out of the chamber, down branching corridors with walls of glowing green. They passed another swimmer, an elderly aquatic moving in the opposite direction, but Chiku's was the only boat. She began to feel self-conscious, as if they had made special provisions for her clumsiness.

At length, they entered another chamber and Mecufi hauled himself onto a railed ledge that circled the wall at the water's edge. Chiku's boat bobbed to a halt, nodding its swan's head as she climbed out. Suspended vertically from the ceiling was a spacecraft, like some improbably ornate chandelier.

Chiku's jaw dropped as she realised exactly what she was looking at, but Mecufi spoke before she could.

'Chiku Red did come home – this is her ship, *Memphis*. As you can see, it sustained considerable damage.'

Chiku said nothing for a few moments. It was too much to take in, too much to assess and consider. Nothing she had experienced in her long life had prepared her for this.

Slowly and calmly she said: 'This is either a hoax, or an outrage.'

'We spotted the ship on its way through the system and calculated that it was travelling too quickly to be captured by the sun's gravitational field. We did you a favour and recovered it.'

'You had no right to keep this from my family.' Chiku tightened her grip on the rail, shivering with indignation. 'Anyway, how do I know it's authentic?'

'That's an excellent question – we wondered at first whether someone was playing a hoax on *us*. We brought the ship back here and examined it, piece by piece, performed every test we could devise and finally concluded that this is indeed *Memphis*, returned from deep space. It was a time-consuming process and we saw no need to rush it.'

'How long have you had this?'

'Not very long. A few years.'

Mecufi slipped back into the water and began to swim in the chamber's pool. Chiku followed him, moving carefully around the ledge.

'How many, exactly?'

'Twelve. Since we returned her to Earth. Fifteen since we found her. Scarcely any time at all compared to the hundred and twenty-two she was out there.'

'There'll be hell to pay for this.'

'I very much doubt it, once you've heard the rest. I'm afraid Chiku Red was beyond medical revival – but you always knew her voyage was a high-stakes gamble.'

Chiku studied the hanging ship, wondering if it could possibly be what Mecufi claimed. It was the right shape, and the overall design looked sufficiently antiquated. *Memphis* had been the best that money could buy, at the time of its departure – equipped with the highest-rated engine, the most modern and efficient steering, navigation and life-support systems. But all of it stripped down to the ruthless essentials, until the ship was all lean muscle and nervous system, not a surplus molecule anywhere on the thing. The life-support module was tiny, like a vestigial organ, while the engine and fuel tank assembly was hypertrophied, swollen to ugly disproportion.

It was damaged, too. Bits of the ship had been shot or blown away. There were fist-sized holes all over it. Scorch marks and buckling. It had taken a beating, and not just from the usual rigours of spaceflight.

'What about my great-grandmother?'

'No trace of her. I'll prepare a mote if you'd find that more convincing than my words.'

'How could there be no trace?'

'We found two caskets aboard *Memphis* – one for Chiku Red, the other presumably to bring Eunice home if Chiku found her. But when we recovered the ship, the second casket had never been used.'

Chiku's mind reeled again. First her sister's ship, now the news that her great-grandmother had vanished from the vessel Chiku Red had been sent to find.

'Then where is she?'

'No idea. From the damage the ship's sustained, we're fairly sure that *Memphis* made it to the vicinity of *Winter Queen* – those holes and scorch marks suggest anti-collision defences set at too twitchy a threshold. Beyond that, it's guesswork. Comms systems were damaged and there were no backup systems or spare parts aboard – when the attack took out her antenna, she had no way of replacing it.'

'You don't know for sure that *Memphis* ever docked with *Winter Queen*. Maybe it backed off as soon as the attack started and she never got to look inside.'

'That's one possibility, of course,' Mecufi said, 'but it wouldn't be very Akinya of her, would it – to come so far, and not go the last mile? I mean, be honest with yourself.'

'I don't know what to think beyond your outrageous interference with Akinya affairs. And what does any of this have to do with the reason you dragged me here in the first place? The ghost was sent by Chiku Green, not Chiku Red.'

'In my experience,' Mecufi said, 'most things turn out to be connected in the end.'

Not far from the ship was a white-walled, brightly lit and aggressively sterile chamber that made Chiku think of operating theatres and morgues. A handful of exo-clad aquatic technicians were on duty at a bank of upright consoles surrounding a hibernation casket like a ring of standing stones. The angular coffin was an early twenty-third-century design, raised on a plinth and plumbed via a gristle of tubes and cables into a temporary support chassis. On the slanted faces of the consoles were physical screens and arrays of old-fashioned tactile controls, grouped like an accordion's buttons. Merfolk were like babies in that they liked pushing and pressing things.

Chiku watched graphs and images flit across the screens, accompanied by webs of analysis. Temperature profiles, chemical gradients, neural cross-sections, zoom-ins of detailed brain anatomy, down to the synapse level.

Visible through the smoked glass lid of the casket was a sleeping form.

She bore a face Chiku knew as well as her own.

'You told me she was dead.'

'I told you she couldn't be revived,' Mecufi answered carefully. 'Not *quite* the same thing. The casket kept her in this state all the way home. She's on the edge of life or the edge of death, depending on your proclivities.'

'Why haven't you woken her?'

'She's too fragile. These neural scans ... they're only at the resolution allowed by the casket's own instruments, most of which are broken. We can't get any closer to her head without risking irreversible damage.'

'Then open the casket. Get into her head with nano. Readers and scriptors. Stabilise the structure and revive. This is *child's play*, Mecufi. Machines have already taken my head apart – it's how we became three.'

'Under controlled conditions, with an undamaged mind as the starting point. That's not the case here. She's an ice sculpture, Chiku – the slightest intervention would be like blasting her with a blowtorch.'

'She belongs to me – she *is* me. I want her back. I want custody of myself.'

'Of course she's yours, always has been. You can preserve her like this for ever, if your luck holds out. Or hers. Or you can risk bringing her back to life, when you feel confident enough.'

'That'll be for the family to decide. You've taken this way too far, you know – keeping her here like this, all this time, without telling any of us ... that's got to be a crime under someone's legislation.'

'So ask yourself why we'd tell you about her now, if doing so risks putting ourselves in legal difficulty. There has to be a reason.'

'Now would be a very good time to give me one.'

'There's a device in her head, an implant inserted by Quorum Binding that governs the readers and scriptors. It's identical to the one in your head, except the numeric key in hers is still intact. She hasn't chosen to forget it.'

Slowly, a shivery sort of understanding prickled over Chiku.

'Her key would have been the same as mine.'

'My point exactly. The ghost is a message from Chiku Green, but you can't talk to her. Chiku Red *could* – but she's frozen. Intervention might well kill her ... but if we were able to open her up and extract the implant, and do so quickly, we would stand a good chance of recovering its numeric key. Then we could transfer it to your implant and you could address the ghost from Chiku Green. It must have something very important to tell you – don't you want to know what that is?'

Chiku returned her attention to the sleeping form. 'At her expense.'

'She's not alive. You wouldn't be taking anything from her.'

'Except the possibility of ever living again.'

'She had a life. No one forced her to risk it.'

Chiku narrowed her eyes. 'Wait – you said "do so quickly". Why? Why does it have to be done in a rush?'

'The implants – hers, yours – they were installed with anti-tamper measures. If the implants *think* they're being extracted or interfered with, the codes will be deleted. We think we understand the protocols well enough to get in and out in time – but you need to understand that this won't be much like brain surgery. It'll be closer to mining.'

'You bastard, Mecufi.'

'Think things over – there's no immediate rush. Take days or weeks if you like. But not months. And definitely not years. Our patience isn't inexhaustible.'

'I want to go back to Lisbon now,' Chiku said.

By the time the flier returned her to Belém, and the tram to Pedro's studio, it was night in Lisbon, night in Portugal, night all over that sleepy hemisphere of the good Earth. Chiku imagined a tide of life and wakefulness sloshing from one face of the planet to the other. She thought about the way dolphins slept, switching conscious activity from one half of their brain to the other.

She told Pedro what had happened. She told him of the complications and the position she now found herself in. She gave more of herself to him in that one conversation than she had in the five previous years of their life together.

Pedro offered love and sympathy and understanding. But he could not make the decision for her.

'I know,' she said.

In the morning, though, it was simple enough.

She rode the Santa Justa elevator to the café, and waited, and at length Mecufi arrived. She told him to do what needed to be done. Mecufi nodded and reiterated the risks to Chiku Red, and insisted she convince him that she fully understood and accepted those risks. If she approved the procedure, it could effectively cost Chiku Red her life. At Mecufi's insistence Chiku formulated a mote which conveyed – she hoped – her state of preparedness. The merman took the mote but bowed to etiquette in not disclosing its contents in her presence.

Later, when Mecufi was gone, she returned to the Baixa and walked to the shore of the Tagus. Plump clouds stacked up high to the south, yellow-bellied with rain. Across the river stood the statue of Christ the Redeemer. Chiku wondered if the kind of redemption she was likely to need was the kind on offer, and found it doubtful. She was glad of the old statue, though. They kept talking about what do to with it, as if in some sense it embarrassed the present, a piece of the past sticking around longer than was circumspect. No one had similar problems with the suspension bridge, but it was just as old. Today it glittered like a thing made from mercury. It was a marvel. Everyone loved the suspension bridge.

She wept for what she was about to do to herself. But her mind was set.

CHAPTER FOUR

The memories hit her in a green rush. The delegation was speeding along in an open-topped monorail car, whooshing through the gaps between trees. Chiku had to keep reaching up to hold her hat on, but she was enjoying the feeling of motion, the simple pleasure of having a breeze on her face.

'So,' their host said, steepling his fingers, 'do our arrangements meet with your exacting standards, Representatives?'

Chiku was wise enough to remain politely noncommittal. 'We'll need to review our findings in depth, Representative Endozo, then make a formal report to our legislative assembly.'

'Although,' Noah said, 'what we've seen can't be faulted. Isn't that right, Gonithi?'

After Chiku and Noah, Gonithi Namboze was the third member of the *Zanzibar* Delegation. An expert in Crucible ecosystem dynamics, Namboze had accompanied them to verify that the chamber in *Malabar* was suitable for the elephants.

'I do not anticipate any difficulties,' Namboze said, although her tone betrayed her nervousness.

Noah had spoken out of turn, putting the young representative on the spot.

'Difficulties?' Endozo asked, as if the mere mention of such things was a cause for concern.

Chiku smiled tightly. 'As I said, we're here to conduct a thorough review. We can't afford to skimp on any details, not when so much is at stake.'

'Well, of course not,' Endozo said, with an equally tight smile.

They were on their way back to the shuttle dock. They should have been on their way already but Chiku had requested a second look at the prospective chamber before they returned to their holoship. It was here, in this marvellous wooded space, that the offshoot herd elephants might be accommodated.

There were no elephants here in *Malabar*, not yet, but there was a suitable biome and a stable ecology that already supported large herbivores. The introduction of elephants would need to be managed carefully – *Zanzibar*'s animals had not left their own chamber in the hundred and fifty years since departure – but Chiku saw no insurmountable problems. They had done it once before, exporting a small offshoot of the herd to *Majuli*. It had been one of the early successes of Chiku's political career.

At the shuttle dock, their boxy little craft had been serviced and readied for departure while the formalities were in progress. Although the day had gone well, Chiku was still exhausted. It had been the culmination of months of careful preparation and diligent committee work, bringing the Assembly around to her point of view.

Lately Chiku wondered if the tiredness ran deeper. It had been many decades since her last skipover. Chiku and Noah's last two applications had been declined – too valuable to the community effort, supposedly. It was flattering up to a point. And Mposi and Ndege, when the matter had been put to them, were not at all approving of the idea of being wrenched away from their friends and routine. But Chiku had heard that her next request might be looked upon more favourably. Sixty years, if they won full approval – enough to bring them out barely thirty years from their destination.

Thirty years was nothing – they could all bear that easily. And if the children disliked it, they would come round to their parents' view in time.

'I will report back to our chair,' Endozo said. 'We shall await your report on our facilities with great interest.'

They formulated motes and exchanged them as tokens of good intent. Endozo had brought two additional motes provided by senior members of his own legislation. As was customary, the motes were not to be disclosed until later.

Soon the three politicians from *Zanzibar* were on their way home, strapped into their seats as the shuttle boosted out of *Malabar*'s dock. Clear of the holoship and its buzzing armada of support craft, they accelerated quickly. Presently, the engines quietened and the cabin was weightless. There was no room in such a small ship for provision of artificial gravity.

Noah was the first to let out an enormous sigh of pent-up tension. 'Sarcastic bastard. He didn't have to rub our noses in it quite that much, did he?'

'He was just doing his job,' Chiku said, agreeing with her husband but careful not to give the wrong impression to the junior Namboze. 'We need their cooperation a lot more than they need ours and they've got excellent facilities. But they do have to meet our requirements – or I should say the elephants'. They'll be living there, not us. So for their sakes, we'd better get this right.'

'Your family name,' Namboze said hesitantly. 'That's no coincidence, is it? Your involvement with these animals?'

Chiku had been down this road enough times to know where it led.

'No, it's not a coincidence. Working with elephants is something of a family tradition.'

'Going back a long way?'

'Way back – to Africa and the work my uncle was doing there.'

'Geoffrey Akinya?'

So the eager Namboze had been doing her homework.

'Correct.' Chiku hoped the firm but polite terseness of her answer would send the right signal. She was far too worn out for a history lesson, however well-intentioned the enquiry might be.

Unfortunately, Namboze was not quite so easily discouraged.

'Did you ever meet him?'

'Once or twice.'

'In Africa?'

'In the East African Federation. That's where we lived, where we all came from. Near the old border between Tanzania and Kenya.'

'My family were from a lot further south,' Namboze said.

'Gonithi's a Zulu name, isn't it?' Chiku was hoping to change the subject. 'It's very beautiful.'

During their exchange, the holoship *Malabar* had diminished to a blue-green thumbprint, blurred at the extremities, slightly out of focus. Light spilt from the sprawl of communities and service structures wrapping the holoship's skin from pole to pole. The great asteroid vessel bristled with a fine peach-like fuzz of docking spines and service towers. Hundreds of smaller ships were in constant attendance.

Beyond *Malabar*, Chiku could make out the lights of half a dozen other holoships, most so faint they could have been mistaken for planets or stars. Other members of the local caravan were too remote to see at all. Floating labels identified them all, and the larger taxis and shuttles moving from one to the other.

Chiku had no need of these embellishments. This far into the crossing, with old rivalries and alliances long since settled, the formation of the local caravan had not shifted in decades. Nothing much would change between here and Crucible.

Only *Pemba* was absent.

They were on the deceleration phase for *Zanzibar* when Namboze decided to reopen the conversation.

'They say your uncle refused prolongation.'

'Yes, he did.'

'That's quite an unusual decision, isn't it?'

'Geoffrey still lived a long life by any reasonable human measure,' Chiku answered. 'He felt that to extend his time would be excessive, a kind of greediness.'

'I'm not sure I understand.'

Chiku thought, *I don't give a damn whether you understand or not.*

Relenting, she said, 'I didn't either, at least not to begin with. Geoffrey was only born about thirty years before me, so he could have lived for hundreds of years, if he'd wanted to.'

'Why didn't he?'

Chiku could tell she was not going to get out of this until Namboze's curiosity had been satisfied. 'Geoffrey tried to explain it to me on one of our visits. If you've looked up his biography, you'll know he was a scientist, an expert in animal cognition. That's how he ended up working with the elephants. Later in life, though, he gave all that up and became an artist instead. It's the reverse of what happened to his sister, Sunday – my mother. Geoffrey took to painting elephants instead of studying them, and Sunday became so involved in the family business that she felt she needed to understand some of the physics that had made our name – the Chibesa Principle and all that. Turned out she had a weird aptitude for it, even started coming up with this new mathematics no one had seen before. Sculpting numbers like clay. Isn't it wonderful, that a life can contain so much?'

Namboze smiled in polite acknowledgement. 'I suppose it is.'

'Anyway, Geoffrey had a little studio at the household, tucked away at the back of one of the wings. He had two paintings in particular that he wanted to show me, both of elephants from a distance, with Kilimanjaro rising beyond them. One was just a canvas, all ragged and torn around the edges, the brush-marks messy. The other was one he'd done earlier; finished and framed. Uncle Geoffrey asked me which one I preferred. I said I liked the one in the frame best, although I didn't really know why. The other one, I suppose, looked ragged and uncontained.

It didn't have a definite beginning and end. It was a thing which might never be complete.'

'Like a life.'

'That was Geoffrey's point. Birth and death frame a life, give it shape. Without that border it just becomes a kind of sprawling mess, a thing with no edge, no definition, no centre.'

'Did you agree with him?'

'To begin with, no.' Chiku said.

'And now?'

'I suppose you could say I have a bit more perspective.'

After a while, Namboze said, 'It must have been wonderful to see the elephants in their natural habitat. I can understand why you're so keen to push this through. It'll make a great deal of difference to our resource allocation if we can move some of our elephants to *Malabar*.'

'It's not just about elephants,' Chiku said. 'If it began and ended with them, I'd still be pleading our case for assistance. But my ancestors – people like Geoffrey – understood something important. We don't do this for the elephants because it benefits us, or because they'll be useful to us when we land on Crucible. It's because we owe them. We did terrible things to their kind, over many centuries. Drove them to the edge of extinction. Butchered and mutilated them for a profit. But we can be better than we were. By taking the elephants with us into space, even if it costs us, even if it forces us to make sacrifices elsewhere, we're showing that we can rise above what we once were.'

'If times turn really bad,' Namboze said, 'do you think we'll still put the elephants' well-being ahead of our own?'

'It won't come to that,' Chiku said, after a few moments' reflection on the unusually direct question. 'We'll find a way through, no matter how hard things become. That's what we've always done. Make do and mend. Muddle through. Ask for outside assistance, if we have to. We're part of a community. That's the point of travelling with a caravan.'

Chiku was done, drained of words, drained of responsibility. The day had finally taken its toll. She did not mind Namboze's curiosity, but all she wanted right now was to be back in her home, with Noah and Mposi and Ndege.

Namboze seemed on the point of answering – her mouth opened fractionally, then froze. Her face brightened. It became, for an instant, a striking negative of itself. The shuttle was flooded with hard, bleaching light that attained, at its edges, a purity beyond white.

The light snapped off. Chiku blinked at after-images.

Namboze had screwed her eyes into knots. She had been facing forward, with Noah and Chiku in the reverse-facing seats.

'Something's happened,' Namboze said.

Chiku could barely bring herself to turn around, to see what the young politician had witnessed directly.

Zanzibar was still there. It had not been ripped out of existence, the way *Pemba* had. Of course, they were too close for a *Pemba* event to be survivable. This had been nothing comparable, nothing of the same magnitude.

Nonetheless, something terrible had happened.

'Hold approach,' Noah called. 'Assume fixed station at this distance, until I say otherwise.'

The taxi obeyed Noah, as it would have obeyed Chiku or Namboze. Seat restraints and foot stirrups tightened.

'Holding station,' the taxi informed Noah.

'Are you all right, Gonithi?' Chiku asked Namboze. 'You caught whatever that blast was full on.'

'I'm all right.' She had managed to open her eyes again. 'I think the filters dropped just before it reached full brightness. What do you think it was?'

Noah had unhooked himself from the taxi's stirrups to float closer to the observation window. 'Something pretty bad.'

There was a wound, still livid, in *Zanzibar*'s skin. It was a third of the way between the trailing pole and the holoship's fat equator. The wound was weeping gases, spiralling out in a slow-winding corkscrew. Chiku lacked a clear view of the damaged area, but she guessed that it spanned several hundred metres, perhaps as much as half a kilometre. A hole in the hull wide enough to fly a shuttle through, with elbow room.

Gases were still venting. Air, water vapour, other critical volatiles ... it pained Chiku to think of how little they could afford to spare. The winding corkscrew emulated a galactic whorl, the Milky Way in miniature.

Suddenly, the gush of gases ebbed to a trickle.

'Containment control,' Noah said. 'They've sealed that chamber, whichever one just ruptured. It's bleeding dry.'

'What was in it?' Namboze asked.

'I'm not sure,' Chiku said. It was difficult to relate this external view to her mental map of the holoship's interior.

'Take us in,' Noah told the taxi. 'Minimum approach speed.'

By the time they neared the docking hub, the trickle of escaping gases had been all but staunched. Emergency crews were already at work, spilling out of hull locks and docking bays in service craft and individual vacuum suits. By now they would surely be entering the compromised chamber from within *Zanzibar* as well. Chiku watched the figures as they traversed the outer skin, tiny and beetle-bright in their luminous vacuum gear. With *Zanzibar* still rotating – Chair Utomi had yet to order a spindown, and might not judge matters serious enough to warrant such a drastic measure – the emergency crews were effectively hanging upside down, only a slip away from being snatched into space.

The coming and going of service vehicles delayed docking for thirty minutes. The shuttle waited its turn, then fell into the open maw of the polar aperture.

Zanzibar, like *Malabar*, had the proportions of a fat ellipsoid. All the holoships looked similar from the outside, and all were within a few kilometres of being the same size. Fifty kilometre walnuts, skewered on the long axis of their engines.

Chiku had seen them being born, in the year before she went to Quorum Binding. She had gone out to the birthing orbits from Triton, on a sumptuous high-burn liner the size of a small city-state. The holoships were strung out like beads on an invisible wire, all at varying stages of completion. Gravity tractors hauled in asteroids, mountains of rock and ice selected for size, composition and stability, raw matter for the shaping. They chiselled and cored the asteroids, voiding mighty chambers large enough to swallow the liner a thousand times over. They fused and glued loosely-bound rubble piles, infiltrated rock and ice with webs of spiderfibre reinforcement, until they had the integrity to withstand spin and the ferocious, barely-contained impulse of a truly monstrous Chibesa engine. They bottled and pressurised the interior chambers, then gifted them with warmth and water and ten thousand forms of plant and animal life. Then they built towns, cities and parks, schools, hospitals and seats of government, and allowed people to begin moving in, eager droves of them, in their hundreds and thousands. What had been a shell became a place.

Last of all, the Chibesa engines were lit. With the slowness of clouds the readied arks began to pull away from the birthing orbits. They went out in caravans, for mutual support. Each caravan was part of a larger flow of holoships, assigned to a particular solar system. Hundreds, for the most popular target systems. Typically a dozen or so holoships would be organised into a local caravan, with one or more light-years between each caravan.

It took years, decades, for the holoships to reach their cruising speeds. But once that had been attained – presently a whisker under thirteen per cent of the speed of light – there was no immediate requirement to re-employ their engines. Some of the holoships, like *Zanzibar*, had partially dismantled their engines so that the forward and aft polar apertures could be used for the docking of large ships. The dismantled components were moved into secondary chambers, like the pieces of an ominous puzzle.

Chiku's little vessel was now sliding into the space that would once have been occupied by the end of the Chibesa engine. Larger ships, shuttles and taxis were attached around the curving walls, linked by connecting tubes and service umbilicals. The taxi matched rotation, docked. Clamps secured and the airlock connector grappled into place.

Chiku set about loosening her restraints. 'An hour ago, our only concern was how our presentation had gone down.'

'The elephants are safe, aren't they?' Namboze asked. 'Whatever was in that chamber, that's nowhere near the elephants.'

'They should be all right,' Chiku said. 'The damage is nowhere near the main community cores, either, or the school chamber.'

They disembarked from the taxi. Chiku had been anticipating chaos in the processing area on the other side of the lock, but everything was surprisingly ordered, albeit busier than usual, and with an unmistakable air of heightened tension. Walls were alive with status reports – images and text updates, refreshing and scrolling constantly. Pulsing bars of red, outlining doors and windows, signified a shift to emergency conditions.

Chiku struggled to remember the last time this had happened. The *Pemba* loss, perhaps. Maybe the occasional emergency drill. But even those were extremely uncommon.

Chair Utomi, busy with crisis management, had tasked another Assembly member to meet the diplomatic party at the dock. Chiku was only slightly surprised to see her old colleague Sou-Chun Lo.

'Have you any idea what happened?' Namboze asked.

'Whatever it was, it doesn't seem to have gone beyond Kappa Chamber. We're hoping and praying that was the end of it.'

'Kappa Chamber,' Chiku echoed in a low voice. A weird chime of déjà vu, there and gone in a moment.

'Chiku, Noah – your children and immediate family have been accounted for and are safe,' said Sou-Chun Lo. 'Gonithi – there's no immediate reason to worry for your friends and colleagues. I doubt any of them were in Kappa, unless they had a direct connection to any of the research programmes.'

Chiku, Noah and Namboze nodded their thanks.

'You have all been working hard,' Sou-Chun Lo said, steepling her fingers in a prayer-like gesture. 'You should go home now.'

'Provided there are suits to spare,' Noah said, 'Chiku and I intend to assist with the search in Kappa.'

Chiku flicked a glance at her husband. They had discussed no such thing.

'There is no need, really,' Sou-Chun Lo said kindly. 'You have all done more than enough for the committee in recent days. Your particular commitment has been noted, Chiku.'

She wondered if that was a reference to their hopes of obtaining skipover.

'I'd still like to help,' Noah said.

Chiku shook her head. 'You can help by going and finding the children – they must be scared out of their wits. I can take care of myself here. It's important that someone from the Assembly gets their hands dirty in the rescue effort, so it may as well be me.'

'I want to help, too,' Namboze said. 'I have suit and field medical experience.'

'We're not expecting to find many alive,' Sou-Chun cautioned. 'You should be ready for that. It's going to be messy.'

'We know,' said Chiku. 'We saw the explosion.' But tired as she was, she made an effort to strike a positive note. 'Still, there's a chance a few may have survived the blast and managed to get to suits, or pressurised structures, or even into the service tunnels under the chamber. Besides, the whole place has to be searched regardless of the likelihood of finding anyone alive. We need to know what happened in there, and whether it continues to pose a risk to us.'

'There are no immediate structural concerns,' Sou-Chun said. 'The blast and pressure loss deflected our course by a very small amount, but our trimming motors can easily correct for that. Most of the citizens wouldn't have felt anything – the first they knew of the accident was when Utomi appeared in their homes.'

'What about the research programmes? Most of those were housed in Kappa, right? Thousands of scientists, engineers, all their support staff … hundreds of them must have been there at the time.'

'Including Travertine,' Noah said quietly.

That was the connection she had almost made for herself. Travertine and Kappa.

How could she not have seen it?

'The hours ve kept … how could Travertine *not* have been there?'

'Travertine?' Namboze asked, incredulous. 'The *same* Travertine?'

'There's only one Travertine,' Noah said, with a long-suffering expression.

'I thought Travertine wasn't allowed to conduct experiments any more,' Namboze said.

'Not quite,' Chiku answered. 'Travertine didn't break the old rules deliberately, they were just drawn up badly. After *Pemba* there was a mad rush to create new legislation, and it wasn't done properly.'

'I think Travertine knew full well what ve was doing,' Sou-Chun said.

'You could just as easily say ve acted in the interests of the local caravan,' replied Chiku. 'No one ever thought Travertine had been motivated by personal gain, just a desire to solve the slowdown problem. Look, can we save this for later? For all we know, ve's among the dead or dying.'

'I'll see if I can reach the children,' Noah said. Then he put a hand on Chiku's elbow. 'Be careful, please.'

'I will,' she said, and made a mental note to the effect that from this day forward she would never once complain about having an uneventful life.

CHAPTER FIVE

Chiku and Namboze went to the nearest transit point and requested pod conveyance to Kappa. When the pod arrived, it brought four
workers who would soon be suiting up and going outside. The workers disembarked and Chiku and Namboze boarded and took opposite
facing seats. The pod gathered speed, smooth-bored rock rushing past
its airtight canopy.

'You don't have to do this,' Chiku told the younger woman.

'Nor do you.'

'I'm old enough to take some risks – and some responsibility. How old
are you, Gonithi?'

'Thirty-eight.'

'In absolute years?'

'Yes. I was born thirty-eight years ago.'

'Then you've only ever known *Zanzibar*.' Chiku shook her head as if
this were some strange and miraculous condition, like the ability to part
waves or turn base metals into gold. 'No skipover intervals?'

'I haven't applied, and at my age I doubt there'd be any point.'

'I still can't get my head around the idea that there are grown-
up people walking around who've never lived anywhere but the
holoship.'

Namboze produced a shrug. 'It's normal enough to me. This is my
world, just as Crucible will be my world when we get there. What was
all that about, by the way?'

'All what?'

'Well, two things. I wasn't sure whose side to take when you started
talking about Travertine.'

'Travertine's a pretty divisive figure. Ve's a friend of mine – or was,
I suppose. When ve was last in trouble, I was one of those who pushed
for a lighter punishment. The issue split the assembly – Sou-Chun was
among those who felt we needed to make a clearer example of ver, if
only to keep the rest of the local caravan happy.'

Namboze brooded on this for a few seconds. 'Weren't you and Sou-Chun political allies at one time?'

'We're not exactly enemies, even now. I've known Sou-Chun for longer than you've been alive, and we have a lot in common. Sure, we had our differences over Travertine. And then there was that whole stupid business over what to do with the high-capacity lander – whether we should keep it or dismantle it and make room for something else. But it's nothing, really.' In her mind, she added: *You'll see how it is, when you've played at politics a little longer.* Aloud, she said, 'I still have a lot of respect for Sou-Chun.'

The pod swerved sharply into a different tunnel and Chiku's stomach tingled. They were travelling against *Zanzibar*'s spin, counteracting it to a degree.

'What if this mess turns out to be something to do with Travertine?'

'It won't. Everything that went on in Kappa was under tight control. All the research programmes. Improved energy conversion and storage, better skipover protocols, more efficient recycling and repurification techniques. Rehearsal of methods that will serve us well when we land on Crucible. Agriculture, water management, low-impact terraforming. God, I sound like a politician, don't I? But that kind of thing, anyway. Even simulations of what we can expect when we start hands-on investigation of Mandala.'

'Nothing fundamental, then?'

'After *Pemba*? Good grief, no. We're not fools, Gonithi. I'll argue to the death against stupid legislation, but some rules exist for a reason.'

Presently the pod slowed as it approached one of Kappa's access stations. It was snug in the bedrock out of which the chamber had been hollowed, and provided its automatic pressure seals had closed, there was no further risk of exposure to vacuum.

Chiku and Namboze stepped out of the pod. The atrium was as busy as the docking station, but there was also a sense of subdued resignation, of people going through the motions. And indeed as Chiku looked around, she saw rescue workers, citizen volunteers, medical teams and assembly members. But no one who looked as if they had just been pulled out the rubble, or whatever was left inside Kappa. The triage teams seemed bewildered, at loose ends.

Chiku reminded herself that the incident had really only just happened – less than an hour ago they were still in space, waiting to dock. Why, she wondered, did the brain insist on inducing this time-dilation effect during periods of intense emotional stress? Why could it not bestow equivalent favour during Mposi and Ndege's birthdays?

Chiku and Namboze found a local coordinator and volunteered their services. They were shown to a staging area where suits were being issued. Some were coming fresh out of storage; others were being recycled as work teams emerged from a stint inside Kappa. Several of the suits came equipped with an extra pair of teleoperable arms, mounted at waist level, for which special operational training was required. More suits were arriving from elsewhere in *Zanzibar*, riding the pods under autonomous control then offering themselves up for use. They walked around headless, helmets tucked under their arms.

Namboze was in her suit, ready to go, needing only trivial adjustments – a glove- and boot-swap, that was all – while Chiku was still struggling to find a torso section that did not feel too tight around the waist or chafe under her armpits. Finally she was done, helmet locked down, the visual field stripping away all unnecessary distractions. The suit's power-assist made movement effortless.

Chiku and Namboze emerged through a portcullis-like airlock into the ruins of Kappa at the top of a gently sloping ramp leading down to the chamber's true floor. In the community cores, the pod-terminal ramps were often lined with flagpoles, benches and bright-painted concessions. But not here.

Kappa was now darker than any of the thirty-five other chambers Chiku had visited in *Zanzibar*. Even at night, when the sky became a bowl of simulated stars, there would still have been lights from buildings and street lamps. Now the entire chamber had been enucleated, gouged clean like an eye socket. She might as well have been staring into the void between galaxies.

The aug dropped a faint overlay across Chiku's visual field. Compiled from *Zanzibar*'s own memory of itself, it revealed roads and structures, bridges and underpasses, subsurface tunnels and ducts, possible refuges for survivors. Everything was colour-coded and annotated. The overlay was updating constantly as the other search parties made their own reports and improved the aug's real-time picture of the chamber.

Chiku was glad of it. She had visited Kappa a few times but did not know it anywhere near as well as the residential and administrative chambers where she spent most of her days.

'How are your eyes, Gonithi?' Chiku asked.

'Fine enough now.' Namboze paused. 'Wait a moment. Adjusting my amplification.'

Chiku did likewise. It took an effort of will to remember the subvocal aug commands, so little did she use them. She swept her vision across the blackness and pointed. 'Some lights over there, moving. Must be the sweep team from the next entrance along.'

They walked down the ramp, the luminous patterning of their own suits casting two moving puddles of light as they descended. Chiku activated her crown-mounted lamp and swept the beam before her. It glanced off the sides of low, rectangular, mostly windowless buildings, reaching away on either side of a narrow thoroughfare. Some of the buildings appeared superficially intact, but many were now ruined: torn apart by the blast and decompression, or crumpled under the debris that had come raining down on them in the moments after the blowout. The thoroughfare was littered with junk: huge, scab-like chunks of wall cladding; mangled machines of unidentifiable origin; the corpses of uprooted and fallen trees; and the rubble and flattened carcasses of destroyed buildings. And nowhere a light or hint of life, save that provided by the rescue parties.

They reached the base of the ramp and began picking their way along the thoroughfare. Chiku's suit was sniffing the environment for human life-signs, taking care to ignore Namboze and the other searchers. So far, nothing. They pushed on, the thoroughfare connecting with another. They reached one of the buildings on their search list. On the overlay it was outlined in blue, pulsing gently – a white cube with doors and windows on the lowest floor, but otherwise blank. A tree, uprooted from elsewhere, impaled its roof. A mass of house-sized debris had collapsed against the aft-facing wall. Otherwise the building's integrity looked good.

'This is Chiku,' she said, calling back to the search coordinators in the pod terminal. 'Gonithi and I have reached our first target building. The door's still closed – doesn't look as if anyone's opened it before us. We're going in.'

'Tag it on your way out,' the coordinator told her. 'And watch your step in there.'

'We will,' Chiku replied.

Only a handful of buildings in Kappa were capable of retaining air in the event of decompression, so those were the first to be searched. Most of the damage appeared to have been caused by the blowout rather than the flash that preceded it. Chiku had no intention of voicing theories in the junior politician's presence, but it was beginning to look unlikely that the blast had originated inside Kappa itself. If the force of an explosion within Kappa had been sufficient to punch right through *Zanzibar*'s skin – through tens of metres of solid rock – there would be nothing left within the chamber.

Therefore the blast could only have originated in the chamber's skin.

An airlock protected the building, but it had not retained atmosphere. Chiku and Namboze searched the pitch-black interior – a maze of corridors and bioscience laboratories, judging by the glass-walled rooms they passed – until they found their way to the rear of the structure, where its shell had been pierced by debris. They found bodies on the second floor: a woman slumped in a corridor, still clutching research notes – Chiku imagined the gale tearing the air from her lungs, the life from her body, but somehow she had held on to those notes. Two people were still seated on high stools at their desks – the blast of decompression had shoved their equipment and notes to one end of the table, like a bar being cleared for a brawl, but somehow they remained upright at their posts. On the next floor, a young man lay in a corridor, not far from a lavatory. They found another person sprawled halfway down the connecting staircase, her leg broken.

Judging by their postures none of these people had been trying to get to safety. Chiku doubted that there had been more than a couple of seconds of awareness before the air roared out. Unconsciousness would have followed very swiftly, followed by death. She doubted that there had been time for fear.

Just surprise.

Chiku and Namboze tagged the bodies' locations. Dedicated medical teams would arrive in time to preserve the corpses in vacuum with immense and loving care. Non-invasive methods would be used to assess neural damage. If there was even the slightest possibility of resurrection, the bodies would be shipped downstream to one of the holoships with sufficiently advanced medical techniques to carry out the process.

They tagged the airlock as they exited and moved on.

Their route to the next building brought them fearfully close to the wound in the world. A block ahead, the thoroughfare and its lines of flanking research buildings simply ended. The ground wrenched down, cracked and fissured, arcing and steepening to vertical. The wound was circular, maybe four hundred metres across. They climbed a ramp to get a better view, and looked right down into a circle of stars and blackness.

Shafts and tunnels and service ducts threaded *Zanzibar*'s skin. They glowed in different colours on the overlay, coded for function and annotated for age, origin and destination. Many were disused or mothballed. Some were still weeping air or fluid – white or ghost-blue secretions cataracting into darkness. A tiny, trifling amount compared to the total resource load of the holoship, but it pained Chiku as much as the sight of her own blood would have.

Crucible was still a very long way off.

'What was here?' Namboze asked, indicating the missing terrain with a sweep of her lit-up arm.

Chiku knew. She had already consulted the suit's map. 'Various things. But the main one was Travertine's physics lab.'

'Are you sure?'

'I wouldn't have said it otherwise.'

Namboze was uncowed by Chiku's testy tone. 'The explosion, whatever it was, must have started down in that bedrock, don't you think?'

'What makes you say that?'

'There'd be a lot more damage to the surface structures, if it had begun above ground.'

Namboze's conclusion matched Chiku's, but that didn't make her like it any better.

'We'll leave the explanation to the specialists, Gonithi,' she said firmly. 'Our job's to look for survivors.'

She was glad that their search assignment took them no closer to the edge. They located and searched another building a few blocks from the first, standing on its own in what would have been an area of gently stepped wooded parkland, had most of the trees not been plucked from the ground. The building's peeled-back roof had allowed atmosphere to vent from most of its levels, and they found no survivors on any of the airless floors. The basement – which had maintained pressure despite the loss of the roof – contained only a mindless floor-scrubbing machine still going about its duties.

The day had already brought more bodies, more evidence of human mortality, than Chiku had confronted in her entire life. But on some numb level she knew they had been lucky. Many of Kappa's laboratories and research facilities required only a skeleton staff. Some of them, judging by the reports coming in from the other search parties, had been running on a purely automated basis. Experiments in plant nutrition, soil hydration and so on, once established, could be set to run unsupervised.

Yet the scale of destruction here was still almost unthinkable, and the loss of life might tally in the high hundreds or even low thousands once all the buildings had been searched. By any measure, this was a tragedy. But it could have been so much worse, had it happened in one of the densely populated chambers. Tens of thousands, easily. A civic catastrophe to equal almost anything that had happened since departure.

So they had been fortunate. But it was something in Kappa that had made this happen in the first place. And Travertine's research complex had been precisely at the epicentre.

Chiku felt a coiled apprehension deep inside her. She knew this was not going to end well.

For any of them.

'Where's the next structure?' Namboze asked.

'Over that way,' she said. 'Those two linked domes. I'd best check in with the coordinators, though – we're already a little behind schedule, so they may decide to pull us back in before we get too tired.'

'It's an emergency, Representative Akinya – won't they be expecting us to show some initiative?'

Privately Chiku agreed. According to the schematic, they were looking at one of the oldest structures in Kappa, dating all the way back to the years before departure. Two domes, linked together – she thought of the soap bubbles that Mposi and Ndege liked to make. From their present angle, it appeared that the building had sustained damage to only one of the two domes, where a piece of the chamber's ceiling had dropped onto it, cracking it like an eggshell. There would be airtight doors inside it, if the building was as old as the schematic claimed – they were a common feature in the older buildings, constructed when there was still a strong psychological need to defend against cavern blowout. In recent years, codes had been relaxed. The newer buildings rehearsed the architectural principles that would make sense on Crucible, rather than within a hollowed-out rock light-years from any sun.

They found a door and cycled through. There was pressure on the other side, at seven-tenths of normal atmospheric. Chiku studied the reading carefully, until it was beyond doubt that the air was slowly draining away. A rough calculation told her that the building would not be capable of supporting life for much more than twenty minutes.

'Seems unlikely that there are going to be survivors,' she said, 'but we'll look anyway. The air pressure's dropping quickly, though, so we'll need to be quick about it.'

'Can I make a suggestion, Chiku?'

'Of course, Gonithi.'

'It'll be much quicker if we search different areas. Our suits will remain in contact, so we'll know if either of us runs into trouble. We'll be able to get to each other quickly enough if there's a problem.'

'I'm not sure we should split up.'

'I'll be careful.'

Debating the point further would only waste more precious time, so they quickly agreed on a division of effort: Namboze would search the upper levels of the intact dome, Chiku the lower levels.

The building was very obviously another laboratory, and although the aug remained mute as to its precise function, they had clearly been conducting some kind of physics or chemistry experiments. The high-ceilinged rooms were full of hulking, kettle-shaped machines, fed with pipes and conduits of impressive thickness. With the right queries, Chiku's suit could probably have dug out the relevant information, but she did not need to know for her current purposes. Even in fundamental physics, there were few avenues of research that came anywhere near those prohibited by the *Pemba* Accord.

Besides, this was not where the trouble had begun.

She completed her search of the lower levels without incident. There were no survivors, nor any bodies. She checked her suit readings. Air pressure was now nudging below forty per cent.

'I've found someone,' Namboze said, grunting as she shifted position. 'Still alive, but barely conscious. I'm going to get them into the portable preserver.' Her voice was husky, on the edge of breathlessness.

'I'll be with you in a moment,' Chiku said.

'It's all right – I've got it under control. We could use another party to help us ferry the survivor back out through the chamber, though.' Namboze paused, her breathing heavy. 'Once this one's stabilised, I'll complete my search of the upper floors. We missed this one's life-signs – maybe there are more survivors.'

'I'll call for help. Don't take any risks, Gonithi – you've done well as it is.'

'Did you find anyone?'

'Empty down here so far. Pressure's still falling, though, so pretty soon it won't matter who we find. I'm going to take a look in the other dome, just in case there's an air pocket. Call me if you find any more survivors.'

The map showed Chiku a ground-floor entry point into the secondary dome, protected by a sturdy internal airlock of antique but foolproof design. The lock admitted her. Beyond was hard vacuum. She shone her light around, trying to make sense of mangled architecture. The ceiling fragment had daggered its way to the ground, crushing and buckling interior floors and partitions, and come to rest at a sharp angle. She moved around it cautiously, not sure how firmly it was embedded. Judging by the absence of machines and equipment, this part of the complex had likely been reserved for administration and supervision. There were chairs and tables, bent and squashed beyond easy recognition. A small refectory, unoccupied at the time of the accident. No survivors or bodies anywhere, as far as she could tell.

'How are you doing, Gonithi?'

The other woman sounded much more confident now. 'Got the survivor bagged and stable. I've tagged the location and am completing my search. What about you?'

'I don't think there's anyone here, but I want to make absolutely sure before we tag it as searched.'

Chiku had swept the basement of the other dome, but it had not connected through to this one. She could see into the lower level at the point where the ceiling fragment had penetrated the floor. A staircase existed, but it was now buried under the rubble of the dome's collapsed roof. The ceiling fragment itself offered a kind of makeshift ramp, if she dared trust it not to shift or collapse. The quilt of illumination elements studding the panel's uppermost face – it had flipped over at some point after falling from the ceiling – promised enough traction to enable her to climb or scramble down.

Chiku moved to the edge of the gap in the floor and stood with her toes on the very brink. It was four, maybe five metres down to a scree of rubble piled up on the basement's floor. To reach the steep slope of the ceiling fragment, she would have to leap across a good metre of clear space, and then hope that she maintained her footing. Hesitating, she bent down and scooped up a chunk of debris as large as her helmet. She hurled it at the ceiling fragment, the suit amplifying the power of her swing. The chunk shattered in a silent eruption, blooming into a blue-grey cloud. The fragment had absorbed the impact without a hint of movement. It appeared to be solidly fixed.

Chiku took a couple of paces back, then leapt across the threshold. She landed roughly, one foot slipping into empty space, but her other found a purchase. She grabbed hold of a pair of lighting elements and stabilised herself. The jump would not have fazed even Ndege or Mposi under normal circumstances, but she was alone, in a dangerous place, with only a spacesuit between her and vacuum, and for a few moments her heart surged on a rush of adrenalin and relief.

Chiku descended carefully, spidering down the quilt of lighting elements until her feet touched debris. The ground crunched, then supported her. She stepped gingerly off the ramp and turned around slowly, sweeping the beam over the jumbled and unwelcoming surroundings. Even the dust kicked up as she moved curtained back down with indecent haste.

'Chiku,' came Namboze's voice. 'I'm done here. There's no one else alive so I'm heading outside. I think I can manage the preserver on my own.'

'Good work,' Chiku said. 'I'll be with you in a few minutes.'

Leaning around a buckled metal pillar, she took cautious steps deeper into the basement. It had been subdivided into two large rooms, but the intervening wall had collapsed when the ceiling fragment came down. She stepped over and around chunks of knee-high rubble, watching where she placed her feet.

Namboze asked, 'Where are you?'

'Just completing a sweep of the secondary basement. It's open to vacuum, but I wanted to be sure. Doesn't look like there's anything down here, though.'

Chiku fell silent, heart jamming her throat. She had been about to put her foot down into what looked at first glance to be a shadowy space between two chunks of debris. An instant before committing herself, she realised it was a void, not shadow.

There was a hole in the floor.

Namboze must have heard her draw breath. 'Chiku?'

'Still here. Nearly lost my balance.'

Chiku steadied herself. She poked at one of the boulders on the edge of the void. It teetered and fell in, increasing the diameter of the void. It had been big enough to swallow her foot to begin with. Now it was big enough to swallow Chiku.

If the boulder landed on anything below, it did so without a hint of impact. She found the void troubling in a way that felt monstrously disproportionate to its size. According to the aug, no sub-levels or infra-structure pipes lay beneath this laboratory, even allowing for decades of disuse or abandonment. The overlay had proven accurate so far.

Chiku was greatly unnerved by this sudden discrepancy. *Zanzibar's* memory was as limitless and infallible as a person's was cramped and unreliable. *Zanzibar* was meant to know every wrinkle and pore of itself.

But it did not know about this hole.

Chiku took another deep, steadying breath. What was more likely: that a hole had been present where none was charted; or that the acci-dent, the violence of the collapsing ceiling, had shifted the structural foundations beneath the laboratory and revealed the opening? This rift could only have opened up today, when Kappa blew out. Given the scale of destruction Chiku had already witnessed – that four-hundred-metre-wide hole punched clean through *Zanzibar's* skin to space – a lack of additional structural shifts elsewhere within the chamber would have been more remarkable than finding this one.

But then she risked leaning far enough over the edge to allow her helmet light to spill into the void, and saw that whatever this might have been, it was not another rift.

This hole was the entrance to a shaft, and the shaft's walls were not only smoothly bored but set with recessed handholds. It curved away beneath her, out of sight and into darkness. And Chiku shivered, because such a thing had no business existing on *Zanzibar*.

A secret passage.

She looked around and her gaze chanced upon a sheet of lightweight walling material that must have come loose when the overlying floor collapsed. Moving carefully – what little faith she had had in the integrity of the floor beneath her had vanished the moment she found the void – Chiku grasped the blade-shaped fragment and levered it free. She positioned the fragment over the hole, adjusting it until she was satisfied that she had concealed her discovery as best she could. The hole's dark mouth was still visible under the fragment's edges, but to the unsuspecting eye it looked like shadow.

There was no need to tag the location.

CHAPTER SIX

From the transit station, all the way up the winding stone-walled paths to her dwelling, Chiku ran a gauntlet of questions from well-meaning citizens. They had learned from Noah about her visit to Kappa and they wanted to know what she had seen inside. Most of all, they wanted reassurance. Chair Utomi might have told everyone that *Zanzibar* was safe, but what else could he say? Chiku had first-hand information and they were eager for it. She did not have to lie to them, or bend the truth to any excessive degree, to give them what they wanted. *Things will be all right*, she assured them. *It's bad, but we'll weather it. We have the local caravan to call on. There will be no more deaths.*

Eventually she had to start telling them not to ask any more questions, that she had already told them all she knew. She directed the rest back down the path, to the people who had already interrogated her. *Talk to them, they know the picture.*

When she finally reached the house, she was surprised to see Noah sitting outside it, squatting on one of the low walls. Mposi and Ndegi were at his feet, squabbling over a game of marbles. Noah had an odd look about him – not the relief and concern she had been counting on.

'I'm glad you're safe,' he said, rising from the wall.

She had expected to find him indoors, preparing a meal, not day-dreaming out here. 'Yes, I'm safe,' she said guardedly. 'Is everything all right?'

'I'm not sure.' Noah embraced her briefly, breaking contact almost as soon as he had initiated it. 'We have ... well, it's difficult to explain. I think you need to go inside.'

'Why are you waiting out here?'

'I think you need to go inside,' Noah repeated, as if she had not heard him the first time. 'I'll wait here with the children. You can decide what we should do next.'

This was definitely more strangeness than she needed at the end of a hard day. But Noah was a good husband and not given to dramas. She nodded wordlessly, knelt down to kiss the children – tousled their hair, whispered that they should play nicely. And then – steeling herself – she entered the house.

Travertine was sitting at the kitchen table, hands before ver, fingering a wine glass.

'Hello, Chiku.'

Chiku said nothing at first. Travertine had poured the wine from the same bottle she and Noah had started the evening before their mission to *Malabar*. Chiku eased into the seat opposite Travertine and helped herself to a sip from the same glass. Then the sip became a gulp, and she carried on drinking until the glass was empty and her throat was burning.

She said: 'You shouldn't be here.'

'In the immediate sense, or the existential?'

'Dead, alive, whatever – you shouldn't be in my house. Not after whatever happened today.'

'I have no idea what happened today.'

'Whatever went wrong, it started with your laboratory. You did this. You did this and they're going to hang you for it.'

'Well, it's good to know I can turn to friends for reassurance.'

'Get out of my house.'

Travertine took the glass from her and poured more wine. 'I'm not an idiot. I expect to be arrested for this. The only reason I was able to get here in the first place was because there was so much chaos and confusion.'

'Were you in Kappa when it happened?'

'If I had been, we wouldn't be having this cosy little chat, would we?'

'I can't shelter you.'

'I'm *not* asking you to.'

'What happened? What the hell were you doing?'

'Nothing much. Just trying to save the world. And how was your day?'

'You were punished once. You were lucky they didn't lock you up then. Wasn't that lesson enough for you?'

'All it did was teach me that I needed to be cleverer.'

'Oh, please.'

'In case you haven't noticed, that little problem of ours hasn't magically vanished. Does it keep you awake at night? It really ought to. It gives me cold, shivering nightmares.'

'I won't argue with you. There'd be nothing to gain. Are you going to turn yourself in, or do I have to call the authorities?'

'You *are* the authorities, Chiku. That's rather the point.' But Travertine sighed, then. 'I am going to turn myself in – it's not as if I'd have a hope in hell of evading justice.'

'So why have you come here instead of going straight to the constables?'

'There's something we need to discuss.'

'I've heard enough of your justifications over the years. You just blew a hole in the skin of the holoship.'

'True. But you know what? It proves there's something we don't understand. *Pemba* proved it, too, but that time there was no wreckage to comb through, and no survivors to question. We had no idea what they'd been doing in there before it all went pop.'

'The same as you – meddling.'

'Meddling is what we do. It's what defines us. Meddling gave us fire and tools and civilisation and the keys to the universe. Fingers will get burnt along the way, yes. That's the way of it.' Travertine examined vis fingers. They were strong and elaborately wrinkled around the knuckles. Unlike Chiku's, they looked like they had done honest work.

'Well?' she prompted, after Travertine fell silent and appeared to be in no hurry to speak again.

'I found something. A hint of a breakthrough, a door into Post-Chibesa physics. A glimpse of the energies we'll need to decelerate, when we approach Crucible. I decided to investigate further with a simple experiment. In secret, of course – underneath my lab.'

'I think you should save all this for the hearing.'

'When you dig under something, Chiku, you often make discoveries.'

'What the hell are you talking about, Travertine?'

'I have some information that I think might interest you, both as a respected member of the Assembly and as someone with influence in the Council of Worlds.'

'And exactly how long have you had this "information"?'

'I always knew the time might come when I would need your support, so when I made my discovery, I decided not to act on it immediately.'

'You kept it back as a bargaining chip.'

Travertine pulled a face as if ve had just sucked on something sour. '*It* sounds *terribly* cynical, doesn't it? I prefer to think of it as a wise investment. I wasn't endangering the community. Whatever I'd found had been there for years and years and done no harm. I had no reason to believe that situation would change.'

'And what, exactly, did you discover?'

'Well, now, that brings us right to the nub of things, doesn't it? As I said, I'm going to turn myself in, and I have no doubt that dreadful things are going to happen to me. Even I have to acknowledge that they'll be well within their rights to push for the death penalty.'

'You might want to get to the point, then.'

'I'm going to need someone on my side. I want you to state my case, put my side of the argument to the authorities – even if that makes you unpopular at committee level. There'll be plenty of voices ready to condemn me. I need one person prepared to state that I'm not a monster. Someone who's endured the same nightmares I have.'

Chiku shook her head slowly. 'I'll tell the truth – you didn't need to bargain that out of me.'

'But I want more than neutrality. I want you to be my advocate, when no one else will stand by me.'

'You can't ask that of me.'

'I can and I will. This matters more than anything in the world, Chiku. I know you and Noah have been working very hard lately, and that you're hoping to call in some favours – four cosy skipover slots for you and your family, a one-way ticket to the future, an escape from these problems.'

Chiku stared down her friend. All this was true, but she despised Travertine for stating it so bluntly.

'What the committee makes of your request is their business – I can't influence them one way or the other.'

'Perhaps you can, perhaps you can't. Here's the thing, though – I absolutely must be allowed to continue my work. And if not me, then a team of people I'll appoint and supervise. If that doesn't happen, we're all finished.'

'And this ... information you've been hoarding?'

'When I excavated underneath my laboratory, I found tunnels in *Zanzibar*'s skin that aren't supposed to be there.'

'I know.'

Travertine's eyes narrowed in suspicion. 'That's easy to say.'

'I saw a shaft under one of the buildings while I was searching Kappa for survivors. It goes down deep, and it isn't documented.'

'Then that's *all* you know?'

'The shaft I saw was some distance from your complex. There's no reason to assume they're connected.'

'They are. I explored. I'm a scientist – what else was I going to do? I mapped a network of tunnels and shafts radiating away from the entry point under my lab. Most of them were dead ends, sealed off with fused rubble or concrete. None of them show up in the official documents, but they're obviously as old as *Zanzibar* itself. That means someone put them in deliberately, for a reason, and then decided not to tell anyone about it.'

'That's all you've got?' Chiku shook her head. 'I already knew this, Travertine. I'll be making an official report as soon as this mess is behind us.'

'Then the existence of these features isn't common knowledge yet?'

'Whether it is or not, it doesn't give you anything to bargain with.'

'Then a map of the tunnel system wouldn't be of any interest to you?'

'I can make my own map.'

'I could save you the bother. And save you the trouble of learning something else the hard way, too. I found one tunnel that leads out of Kappa altogether. But I couldn't explore that one.'

'Too scared?'

'Exploring the tunnels was a distraction, remember – I had my official work to be getting on with. Regardless, curious as I was, and even if I'd found the time, I couldn't have explored it if I'd wanted to. Not easily. But there's no reason why *you* couldn't.'

'What's so special about me?'

'You have the right name.'

'You've lost me, Travertine.'

'Then I'll make it very simple for you. There's a sort of . . . sphinxware preventing access to the deeper tunnel. My guess – and my guesses tend to be reliable – is that it's waiting for a blood Akinya to show up. Some-one of that ancient and holy lineage. Given time, I could have fooled the sphinxware, but as I said, I had other fish to fry. And I was satisfied that what I'd already learned would be useful enough, when the time came.'

'Like now, for instance?'

'Your family and its network of allies played a large role in the build-ing and launching of the holoships, Chiku. Someone connected to the family decided to smuggle a secret aboard this ship.'

'Impossible. I was alive back then, remember? I saw the holoships being assembled, I saw the first of them leaving.'

'Then maybe you weren't as close to the bosom of the family as you liked to think. Maybe there are *dark secrets* no one involved was quite willing to share with the young and feckless Chiku Akinya.' Travertine smiled for the first time. 'Now, shall we discuss my hearing again?'

'I want your map,' Chiku said.

'Is that a promise of assistance?'

Chiku said nothing. She went to Ndege's room and found a sheet of paper and some wax crayons. She brought them back to the table and set them down before Travertine.

Noah coughed gently as he entered the kitchen.

'This can't go on for much longer,' he said.

Travertine turned to look at him. 'You can call the constables whenever you like. Say I arrived in a state of distress and confusion. It'll take them a little while to get here – there'll be no suggestion that you were harbouring me.'

'We're not,' Noah said. His folded arms conveyed his distaste. Chiku and Noah had both been Travertine's friends, but Noah's scepticism had hardened after Travertine's original censure.

Travertine turned back to the paper and crayons and started to draw.

'This won't take long,' ve said.

Chair Utomi was making another public announcement. Their children now asleep, Chiku and Noah watched it from their kitchen. Both were brittle with exhaustion but anxious to hear the latest news, the latest casualty estimates, the latest hints of a political response from the rest of the local caravan.

'By now,' Utomi said, 'some of you will be aware of compelling evidence that today's accident was caused by something originating in or near Travertine's research facility. Some of you will also be aware that Travertine survived the accident. I can confirm that these rumours are correct. I can also confirm that Travertine is now in custody, having turned verself over to the administration. The Council of Worlds can be assured of our total cooperation in all matters relating to this incident. If it transpires that Travertine was involved in actions contrary to the provisions of the *Pemba* Accord, and that those actions occurred due to our oversight, we will submit to the full weight of caravan authority.'

'Why not just throw Travertine to the wolves and be done with it,' Chiku said, when Utomi was done.

'This isn't going to end well,' Noah said. 'Travertine did this while we were supposed to keep an eye on ver – how does that make us look?'

'Stupider than Travertine,' Chiku said. 'But if that was a hanging offence, we'd all be for the gallows.'

Noah nodded carefully. 'What did Travertine want to talk about anyway?'

'Ve was shocked. Who wouldn't be, under those circumstances? Travertine wanted reassurance that ve was going to get a fair hearing.'

'Ve got a fair hearing the first time.'

'It'll be a different this time.' Chiku clicked her nails against the table-top. A red circle stained the surface where the wine glass had been. 'People have died because of the experiment. It's going to be difficult to get beyond that.'

'What was Travertine drawing on that piece of paper? Ve didn't take it with ver, and you didn't show it to the constables.'

'Is this my trial, or Travertine's?'

'I'm only asking,' Noah said, and his hurt tone made her wince inside. And she had to admit that, yes, he had only asked, as he had a right to – this was his home as well. They did not normally keep secrets from one another.

'Travertine wanted to make sure there was no further risk of decompression,' Chiku said. 'The sketch shows the underground workings connected to the laboratory, in case any of them need to be sealed off or reinforced.'

This was true, as far as it went – Travertine had mentioned, in passing, that someone should double-check the tunnels and shafts, especially when they started repressurising Kappa. But that had been only an incidental concern.

Chiku did not like lying to Noah – not even by omission.

'There's something I want to investigate,' she said. 'I would have mentioned it to you sooner, but when I got home Travertine was here, and after that everything got a bit intense. Anyway, when I was in the chamber with Namboze, I saw something unusual. It's probably nothing, but I need to take a second look at it.'

'And are you going to tell me what it is?'

'Probably nothing, which is why I won't report it just yet.'

'This isn't helping.'

'Look, I was tired when I went in there. I saw what appeared to be a void under one of the buildings.' She carefully refrained from saying 'shaft', because 'shaft' implied something that led somewhere else, and that carried a whole freight of implications she did not presently care to unpack.

'Gonithi saw this, too?'

'No – she was searching a different part of the building.'

'But you told her about it.'

'I didn't see any need to. As I said, it's probably nothing, plus I don't want to make a fool of myself in front of the Assembly until I know there's definitely something worth bringing to their attention.'

'Let's not make a habit of keeping secrets, okay?'

'I hope we won't have to.' She forced a smile – it felt as if she was bending a part of her face that had never bent before. 'I'll make arrangements to return to Kappa – they're going to be sending in search parties for a while.'

'Whatever you do, don't get into trouble.'

'We're already in trouble – all of us. I can't make things much worse.'

'That's no answer.' Noah let out an exasperated, world-weary sigh. 'You're my wife, and we have Mposi and Ndege to think about. We all want skipover, and our chances are much better now than they were the last time. Whatever you think you owe *Zanzibar*, it's not more important than our family.'

'It never has been,' she said. 'And I will be careful.'

The Assembly building lay at the bottom of a bowl of gently sloping ground, hemmed by lawns, lakes and neat copses of quill-like trees. Chiku always had mixed feelings at her first view of the prospect whenever she arrived in Gamma Chamber, the administrative core. There were thirty-six chambers in Zanzibar, twenty-four of them named for the Greek alphabet, and the remaining twelve (there was no logic in terms of utilisation or population density) for the dozen months of the terrestrial calendar, January to December. The 'A'-shaped building betrayed the heavy hand of the Akinyas in the creation of *Zanzibar*. It was carefully modelled on the old family home in Equatorial East Africa, duplicated down to the last blue tile, the last white stone and ornamental wall. Chiku had visited the original household on several occasions. She had climbed nearby Kilimanjaro, a gruelling ascent without exo assistance, all the way to the chiselled snowcap where the lasers of the old ballistic launcher still stood sentinel. She had observed the Amboseli herds by airpod and on foot. She had met with patient old Geoffrey, and listened to him as he talked about painting, about the endless negotiation between art and memory.

The cab dropped her off and left to collect new passengers. She walked past the greening bronze statue of her great-grandmother, averting her gaze from that imperious frowning visage. Constables flanked the gate to the grounds. Even though they knew her there were formalities, badges and documents to be presented and scrutinised. The constables asked after Noah, and about the ongoing search effort in Kappa. They asked how her children were coping with the accident. Chiku's answers were curter than she might have wished, but the constables appeared not to mind. Everyone was on edge today, and allowances could be made.

'Just a moment,' Chiku said to them, when she noticed the time.

Overhead, bisecting the false sky from one end of the chamber to the other, was a stiff metal rail. Threaded onto this rail was a black oval about the size of a small house. This oval, a scaled-down model of *Zanzibar*, was a kind of clock. It had started out at one end when the holoship launched and now it was more than halfway across the chamber. Rather than moving continuously, it ticked along in daily increments of about a hand's width.

The movements always occurred at noon. Chiku was often coming or going from the Assembly at this hour and she always made a point of looking up at the sky clock. It was difficult to see the model move, but on occasion she had succeeded, especially when the edge of it happened to line up with a projected cloud or some other reference point.

She heard the distant chime that indicated the model had moved forward by its statutory amount. But as was often the case she saw no obvious change in the thing.

The sky clock had appeared to be a good idea, in the early days of *Zanzibar*'s crossing. A reminder that, as far away as their destination looked, they would get there eventually. It was just a question of adding up those daily chimes. Eighty thousand – fewer than the number of seconds in a single day. Put like that, it felt bearable. A human span.

She had come to hate the sky clock.

Despite her best efforts, she ended up entering the hall alongside Chair Utomi. They were both wearing formal dress, styled along traditional African lines but with a few modern concessions. Utomi was a huge, broad-shouldered man, bulky as a wrestler.

'It's an unfortunate mess. Things would be a lot simpler for all of us if Travertine had had the good grace to die along with the rest of them.'

This was an uncharacteristically callous assessment from the normally agreeable Utomi. It offered some gauge of the pressures weighing on him.

'I'm sure Travertine agrees,' Chiku said. 'It's not going to be easy for ver, going forward.'

'At least ve's a realist.'

'Travertine thinks the death penalty might be imposed. We won't sink that low, will we?'

'It's been done before. I doubt there'd be an outcry against the decision this time.'

'But Travertine didn't exactly commit cold-blooded murder.'

'And none of us has the luxury of splitting hairs. If it wasn't cold-blooded murder, it was certainly cold-blooded flaunting of our laws.'

'We need Travertine's mind. No matter what ve did, that intellect is still too valuable to waste.'

'It's not in our hands.' Under his gold-patterned formal skirt, Utomi's shoes squeaked on the waxed floor. He had a heavy, solemn stride, with a slight limp from an injury sustained in a vacuum accident many years ago, and which he'd never bothered to correct. 'This will go to the Council of Worlds. If they want the death penalty badly enough, they'll get it.'

'They'll need to demonstrate malintent.'

'That won't be terribly difficult. You can't say that the provisions of the *Pemba* Accord aren't widely known.'

'We need to hear Travertine's side of things.'

'Of course. You spoke to Travertine yesterday, when ve came to your house. How would you describe vis state of mind?'

Chiku deliberated. 'Troubled.'

'For verself, or for what ve's done to us?'

'A bit of both, I think. Look, I'm not going to pretend that Travertine is an angel, or that ve feels much beyond disdain for most of the rest of us. But ve was shocked by what happened.'

'That's odd. Knowing Travertine, I'd have expected cocky disregard.' They were nearing the heavy black doors of the Assembly chamber. 'That's the thing, though – we all know Travertine on some level. That's unavoidable in a closed community. But if you feel your relationship will affect your impartiality, you shouldn't hesitate to recuse yourself. The Assembly will accept a temporary leave of absence while this matter is settled. Get some rest, or something. You like gardening, don't you?'

'You can count on my impartiality, Chair.'

'Very good, Chiku.' Utomi hesitated in his stride, as if the limp had worsened. 'Oh – one more thing.'

'Yes, Chair?'

'Good work on *Malabar*, and in the Kappa situation. It's not gone un-noticed. I'm aware of your recent request for full-term skipover.'

'I see.'

'Obviously, nothing will be decided until we resolve this crisis. But beyond that, you might want to start making the necessary legal and educational arrangements.'

'Thank you. It's very good of you—'

'Off the record, of course.'

'Of course.'

'And your children – Ndege and ... what's the other one?'

'Mposi, Chair.'

'How old are they now?'

He meant their physiological ages. 'Ndege's twelve and Mposi's eleven.'

'How do they feel about skipover?'

'They've been through it twice during our last couple of terms. I don't suppose they remember all that much.'

'Those were only twenty-year skips, though. Plus they're older, now – they'll have friends. They won't like the thought of being torn away from them for sixty years.'

'They'll be happy, Chair. And we'll all be happy when we get to Crucible.'

Constables opened the double doors and admitted them into the chamber. It was a large dark room with a stepped floor and a fan of seats set in concentric rows. Here at least the Assembly building parted company with its counterpart back in Africa. There had been no room this grand in the original household.

There were thirty-six seats in the concentric rows, one for each of Zanzibar's chambers. The rows formed a horseshoe, with a smaller arrangement of seats pincered between the extremities. Chair Utomi's throne-like elevated position faced the elected representatives and was flanked by the chairs and desks of two record-keeping constables. Immediately in front of Utomi and the record keepers was a slablike black table. Above it floated a ghostly schematic of *Zanzibar*, as if made from many layers of coloured glass. It was an aug-generated figment, the only thing in the room not physically present.

Chiku took her seat in the front row. Only twenty-five representatives were in session, but that was not unusual, especially during a state of emergency. Once preliminaries had been attended to, Travertine was brought into the room under the supervision of a pair of constables. They sat ver down in a chair immediately in front of the image of *Zanzibar*, so that Travertine faced Utomi. Chiku could only see the side of Travertine's face.

That suited her very well. She did not want to be making eye contact today.

'What are the latest casualty figures?' Utomi asked of his record keepers, once Travertine was settled.

'Total loss of life, at the latest estimate, stands at two hundred and twelve,' reported the constable to Utomi's right. She was a pale, Nordic-looking woman with a bowl of peppery hair. 'Search-and-rescue efforts are continuing, along with preparations to stabilise the damage. There's an outside chance that there may still be one or two survivors, trapped in isolated air pockets. We may also expect to find more casualties. Accounting for all the dead – including those caught in the immediate vicinity of the explosion – may take days, possibly weeks.'

Utomi nodded gravely. This uncertainty was the price they paid for their mode of living in *Zanzibar*. On *Malabar* – in fact aboard almost any other holoship – the identities and locations of the dead would have been a matter of instantaneous public record. But here, even constables did not have the routine means to track individuals via their implants. On *Malabar*, Travertine would have found it quite impossible to hide, even for a few hours.

But we do things differently here, Chiku thought. *That's the point of the caravan. We travel in multiple holoships for mutual support and insurance against a disaster like Pemba, but also because it allows us to rehearse different modes of living, new permutations, before we reach Crucible.* What worked back home might not work on a new world, under strange and disfigured constellations.

'We were very lucky, in most respects,' the constable continued. 'Fewer people work in Kappa now than before. We lost some air and water, but not enough to cause us immediate difficulties. Our breach-containment systems proved their worth, and there were no critical systems routed through the part of the skin we lost. But the damage is still catastrophic, and if the energy release had been an order of magnitude greater, we could easily be looking at a second *Pemba*.'

No one needed to voice the silent corollary to that ominous declaration. Had this been a 'second *Pemba*', no one in or near *Zanzibar* would be in a position to look at anything at all.

Zanzibar would no longer exist.

'Our good fortune notwithstanding,' Utomi said, 'what matters is that our most serious laws – laws enacted to protect the integrity of the holoship – were ignored, treated with disdain, as if they applied to everyone else but Travertine. Do you deny this?'

There was silence in the chamber as they waited for the scientist to respond. Knowing Travertine's wilful character, Chiku would not have been remotely surprised if ve simply stared them all down in wordless defiance.

But after several seconds of silence, Travertine twisted in vis seat to look around the gathering.

'What's the point of all this?'

'A demonstration of your respect for the authority of this Assembly,' said Utomi.

'I'll respect it when you stop deluding yourselves. This isn't about me. It's not even about the Kappa accident. It's about you and your double standards – enforcing laws while hoping someone breaks them!'

'You've stated these opinions on many occasions,' Utomi said, visibly weary. 'You clearly haven't changed your mind.'

'Our situation hasn't changed, either. We're still hurtling through space at twelve-point-seven per cent of the speed of light with no means of slowing down. In fewer than ninety years, we'll sail right past our destination. That won't change until you pull your heads out of the sand and start facing reality.'

'We do not need to be reminded of our predicament,' Utomi said, 'any more than you need to be reminded that we still have many decades of flight ahead of us.'

'And when will you finally lift the *Pemba* Accord? Twenty years from now? Fifty? What if that doesn't give us enough time?'

'When the terms of the *Pemba* Accord are relaxed,' Utomi said, 'a caravan-wide research programmeme into the slowdown problem will be initiated. Hundreds, thousands of minds, with all the resources and equipment they need. A massive cooperative effort. But that's never sat very well with you, has it? You could never be part of a collective enterprise. It has to be Travertine, the lone genius.'

Travertine turned around in vis seat again and addressed the Assembly. 'I was using more energy in my lab than could ever be explained by the experiments I *claimed* to be doing. But did one of you ever have the courage to question me about it?'

'That sounds like a confession to me,' Utomi said. 'Before my constables commit it to the record for posterity, would you like to amend your statement?'

'What I did was an obligation, not a crime. My statement stands.'

'Then why did you run?' Utomi asked.

'Because I'm human. Because I know what this will mean for me.'

'Nothing is … settled,' Utomi said, as if he sought to offer this beleaguered, belligerent individual some glimmer of hope. 'The legislation is very precisely worded – it had to be, after you tested our existing laws to destruction last time. We require proof that you knowingly brought this risk upon us, that you deliberately invoked Post-Chibesa Physics rather than stumbling into it by accident, while engaged in some other line of research.'

Travertine rewarded this statement with a look of blazing contempt. 'I've never stumbled into anything in my life.'

None of the representatives had spoken so far, but Chung, the representative from Mu Chamber who was sitting a few spaces to Chiku's right, could restrain himself no longer. 'The *Pemba* Accord wasn't instigated to stifle scientific enquiry, Travertine. It was to ensure it didn't accelerate out of our control. If we wished to abandon experimentation altogether, we could easily have done so after *Pemba*. Yet we still allow it, even encourage it – but always under the assumption that those conducting the research will do so responsibly.'

'The trouble is,' said Firdausi, the representative from Sigma Chamber and who was sitting behind Chiku, 'that we know Travertine's history. There's never been anyone less likely to *accidentally* transgress the Accord.'

'That's true,' Travertine said, with blithe disregard for the consequences of this admission. 'Why would I ever deny it? We don't understand Post-Chibesa Physics, so how can we draw a fence around it and say never cross that line?'

'In time,' said Utomi, 'we will develop a much fuller understanding.'

'Yes,' Travertine replied levelly. 'And to the best of my recollection, you were saying exactly the same thing fifty years ago – everything will be all right, little children. Go to bed and stop worrying. And don't mention slowdown in polite company.'

There was truth in this, Chiku knew. Slowdown had gone from being an awkward, emotionally sensitive topic to something that was barely ever mentioned. As if, by not talking about it, the problem would somehow magic itself away.

The simple fact of it was this: the holoships were travelling too quickly. Early in their voyages, in the flush of optimism that accompanied a time of rapid technological and scientific progress, their governments had wagered against the future. Rather than take three hundred years to cross space to Crucible – the original, achievable intention – the journey could be compressed to a mere two hundred and twenty. The trick was to keep burning fuel, eating into the mountainous stocks that were supposed to be held in reserve until the holoships needed to slow down. Instead of using that fuel to slow down, they would use *something else* – some more efficient process, or an entirely new propulsion system.

Something – in other words – yet to be invented.

But that 'something else' had shown a stubborn reluctance to arrive. Many promising avenues had led to dead ends. Glimpses had revealed themselves to be mirages, hoaxes. Still the researchers forged on: theory buttressing experiment, experiment buttressing theory. The intellectual effort encompassed many holoships and stretched as far back as the solar system. The enterprise swallowed lives and dreams and spat out bitterness and dejection.

No one minded that, at least not to begin with. But gradually the will had faltered. Research lines began to be abandoned, facilities mothballed or dismantled.

Yet there were always a few mavericks, bright minds like Travertine, who were convinced that there was a solution, and that it lay close at hand. Just one more push, and the kingdom would be theirs. They forged bigger and grander experiments, and did increasingly perverse things to matter and energy and spacetime.

Finally they made a breakthrough that could not be disputed.

The energy liberated in the destruction of the holoship *Pemba*, it was calculated, demanded an explanation outside the framework of orthodox Chibesa physics. It was an 'existence proof' of PCP – the Post-Chibesa Physics. If that unwieldy power could be tamed, harnessed for propulsion, all their worries would be over. They could even move a little faster now, if they wished.

But *Pemba* had been a step too far. Ten million lives had been extinguished in an instant, the result of an experiment whose parameters were sufficiently unclear that it could never be adequately reconstructed, even if the will were there. And the risk of such a disaster happening again, taking out a second holoship, could not be sanctioned. The *Pemba* Accord had dropped like a guillotine.

So Travertine had set verself on this path, constantly testing Assembly authority, chafing against restrictions, pushing vis luck. After the last censure, ve had done well to avoid imprisonment. But Travertine always rebuilt and pushed further. And Chiku had to agree with ver here – the Assembly always knew what Travertine was up to and chose not to intervene. Because on some unspoken level they wanted ver to succeed.

If there was one positive thing to be drawn from yesterday's tragedy, Chiku thought, it was that Travertine must have been on to something.

'Your experiment in Kappa was totally destroyed,' Chiku said, seizing the opportunity to speak. 'Along with, I'm guessing, all the records relating to it. But you'll still be required to give an account of what was involved.'

'So someone else can reproduce my work?'

'So we can make sure no one comes anywhere near it,' Utomi said.

'Clearly, I made progress.' Travertine's chin was elevated now, with that familiar cocksure defiance of vis. 'And if I had the chance, I'd do it again. I ran an experiment and I got a *result*. That's more useful to us than fifty years of theorising.'

'If you intend to show contrition,' Utomi said, 'now would be an excellent place to start.'

'For what? Two hundred lives?'

'Two hundred and twelve,' a constable corrected, before glancing down. 'Make that two hundred and fourteen. They've recovered two more bodies since we went into session.'

'Make it three hundred. A thousand. You think it matters?' Travertine surveyed the appalled faces that followed this statement. 'I grieve for them, believe me. But the survival of this entire holoship depends on slowdown. That's ten million lives. Hundreds of millions in the local caravan, a billion people spread throughout all the other holoships, and not just those en route for Crucible, but also the other extrasolar worlds in other systems. If my death would guarantee the breakthrough we need, I'd kill myself now.'

'You truly believe this?' Utomi said, consternation written in his features.

Travertine's gaze was unblinking, resolute.

'Absolutely.'

Chiku studied the dismayed reactions of her fellows. She could not be sure what disturbed them the most: the fact that Travertine could make such an assertion in the one place where ve ought to be pleading for clemency; or the fact that Travertine was utterly and irrevocably sincere in vis convictions.

Perhaps a little of both.

CHAPTER SEVEN

Chiku returned to Kappa later that day. Putting on her suit, she deliberately found fault with as many components as she could without arousing suspicion. Fortunately, this was hardly a challenge since many of the suits were coming back with all sorts of minor ailments. By the time she cycled through into Kappa, Chiku's assigned search party was far ahead and not making any effort to slow down. That suited her perfectly. She told them she would rendezvous with them after they had completed a sweep of one grid, at a junction a couple of blocks astern of the breach. They agreed; it was clear from their indifferent tones that Representative Chiku Akinya could do whatever the hell she liked as far as they were concerned.

Her ruse allowed her perhaps thirty minutes to make the rendezvous, which was just enough time to return to the laboratory and the collapsed basement. If she was late meeting up with the other search party, her actions might start to attract attention.

She found her way back into the damaged structure. From its ruined heart, Chiku looked up at the chamber's distant ceiling, defined now by random constellations – the lights of repair teams lashed high above, trying to prevent more cladding from breaking loose. She turned her attention to the improvised ramp, the shard of fallen sky, which was still in place. Chiku vaulted the gap with more confidence than on her first attempt.

She started descending.

Chiku had been trepidatious before, but there was no time for that now, even with the knowledge that the floor might not be as secure as it looked. She reached the basement and moved through the rubble until she found the sheet of walling material she had placed over the hole in an effort to disguise it. It had not been disturbed. Chiku heaved the piece aside, taking care not to shatter it.

Then she stood on the edge of the hole and directed her helmet light downwards. It was just as she remembered, except that it appeared to plunge deeper than she had originally thought. At the very limit of the lamp's reach, the shaft began to curve around to a less steep angle, perhaps even to the horizontal. The recessed hand- and footholds looked intact. She could climb down them, no problem, but the real difficulty was getting to them in the first place – the aperture was only half as wide as the shaft under it.

Chiku checked the time. Twenty minutes, give or take.

She cast around for a chunk of debris and found a chest-sized boulder that would have taxed her without the suit's ampliation. She walked to the edge of the hole, raised the boulder to her sternum and thrust it down and away as hard as she could, stepping back in the same instant so that there was no risk of the boulder crushing her feet on its way down.

Her aim was true. The boulder crunched through the lip of overhanging floor, pulverising it. Chiku watched the debris rain down the shaft in perfect soundlessness. Now the hole was more or less the same diameter as the shaft. All she had to do was lower herself over the lip and start climbing.

Chiku crushed her misgivings. She knelt down with her back to the hole and began to drop her right foot into the void, maintaining balance so that the weight of her suit's life-support hump did not tip her over the edge. It did not work. Why had she ever thought it was going to? If there had been a shaft like this in a normal part of *Zanzibar*, there would have been railings, or something to hold onto, to help the transition into a climbing position. Here there was nothing, just a hole in the ground … and nothing to stop her toppling into it. She could sit with feet over the edge and somehow try and wriggle around …

Chiku spotted something that might work. It was a length of pipe or spar as thick as her wrist, one end still embedded in a chunk of debris. The pipe was perhaps three metres long, its free end terminating abruptly, as if severed.

It was madness, and she knew it, but now her actions had a momentum of their own. She carried the spar and its ragged anchor to the edge of the hole, holding it like a pole vault, and rammed the severed end into a mound of debris. It crunched, jammed, then gripped. The other end, where the chunk was still embedded, she allowed to drop between two large boulders, where it became pinned in place. The bar now ran at a tangent to the edge of the hole, half a metre from it and half a metre above the floor's level. Chiku gave it a kick, testing its fixity.

She knelt down, between the hole and the improvised railing. Now she was able to keep both hands on the bar. She lowered her right foot, scrabbled it around until it found the foothold. Placing more trust in the railing, she shifted her centre of gravity over the hole. Her left leg followed, finding another foothold. The bar shifted, then caught again.

Chiku's heart resumed beating.

She released her right hand from the bar and lowered further, a foot at a time, until her right hand located a handhold and her face was nearly level with the rim of the hole. The foot- and handholds felt safe. With an intake of breath she released the bar, and descended fully into the shaft. Now there was nothing for it but to keep going down.

She soon found a rhythm. Climbing in the suit was much easier than climbing without it, since the power-assist gave the illusion of effortlessness. Even the gloves were augmented, so that her fingers never began to tire. This illusion of weightless ease was treacherous, of course. She could still fall.

Chiku paused in her descent to catch her breath and looked up. Craning her head back as far as she dared, she saw that the ragged hole had diminished to a milky circle, a false moon glimmering with the pale lights of the rescue workers in Kappa. Chiku had given no thought as to how far she ought to go before turning back.

Further than this, certainly. She checked the time again. Her margin had diminished to ten minutes.

She resumed the descent and kept going until she felt the shaft beginning to curve and level out. The descent became easier, but she could no longer see the hole above. No milky circle now, just swallowing blackness in both directions.

Chiku paused, torn between continuing and turning back. Then she swallowed and carried on.

The shaft levelled out and she stood – it was high enough that she could stand upright. The hand- and footholds were still present; perhaps they had been installed to assist locomotion under weightlessness, before the holoship was set spinning. She crunched past the remains of some of the debris dislodged from above that had fallen down the shaft, careened around the bend and come to rest here.

She paused again and tugged Travertine's map from her thigh pocket. It had taken some nerve to smuggle it in under the scrutiny of the techs who had helped her suit-up. Not that the map was incriminating in itself – it had the look of something executed by a child – but she had no easy explanation for bringing it with her.

Travertine had identified this probable entry point and indicated how the shaft linked into the underground network ve had already begun to explore. There was a junction not far ahead, and a little way beyond that – within easy walking distance, Chiku judged – was the barrier, or impediment, that had blocked Travertine's progress.

Chiku walked another fifty metres, according to the suit, now moving horizontally, parallel to Kappa's surface, but away from the breach. The tunnel met another. As she pushed on, trusting Travertine, she checked the time. She could still make her planned rendezvous with the search party and avoid difficult explanations – but only if she turned around soon.

Then her helmet light fell on something ahead, at the limit of her vision, and she had to know what it was. The shaft widened ahead, the smooth-bored walls curving away on either side of her, and she could just make out something waiting there, dark and squat, curves and angles. Some kind of machine. It could have been a generator or water purifier.

It was neither of those things.

It was a transit pod, big enough to carry both freight and passengers, shaped like a fat, blunt-ended capsule with doors and cargo hatches in its curving, slug-back sides. Chiku's memory prickled. She had travelled in pods like this, in the early days of the voyage, but fifty or seventy-five years into the crossing, *Zanzibar*'s entire internal transit network had been ripped out and refurbished. Somehow the engineers had missed this pod along with Travertine's forgotten subterranean tunnel system.

The pod rested on triplet induction rails spaced around the widened shaft at separations of one hundred and twenty degrees. They gleamed clean and cold, stretching into the distance as far as her helmet light could illuminate. Concentric red circles glowed at intervals along the tunnel.

This was wrong. She could accept a minor detail of *Zanzibar*'s history being forgotten and omitted from the structural logs. But this tunnel was huge and the presence of a transit pod suggested that it continued for some distance. And the pod was big enough to carry almost anything Chiku could imagine.

She touched a hand to its side. Through the glove, she felt dead ages of cold and silence, as though this pod had been waiting here, biding its time with a monumental patience. She could also feel the faintest tremble of waiting power, as if it was still energised, still drawing wattage from the induction rails. They ended here, terminating in large angled buffers designed to stop a runaway pod. This one had stopped safely a couple of metres from the buffers.

Chiku walked to the end facing into the tunnel, where the converging lines of rails gleamed back in brassy tones. The pod was sealed. She brushed her hand against the faint oval outline of the forward passenger door, wondering who had last travelled in this vehicle – someone still aboard *Zanzibar*, perhaps, or one of the holoship's architects, completing their final inspection before the CP drive had been lit.

The door's outline lit up at her touch, glowing neon purple against the pod's black surface. Chiku took an involuntary step backwards as the door bulged out of its recess and slid to one side along the hull.

Chiku stared at the cabin space. Subdued lights and an arrangement of deep, plushly padded seats made the interior look warmly inviting. The tunnel was in vacuum now, but the passengers would normally have boarded in a fully pressurised environment.

Chiku could not help herself. She stepped into the glowing cabin and took one of the seats, which looked brand new. There were no controls to speak of, merely an angled console beneath the curving forward window. An illuminated three-dimensional map of the holoship's transit links appeared to hover under the console's glossy black surface. Chiku compared it against her memories. Though the basic arrangement of chambers had been fixed since launch, the interconnections had undergone several changes. Over the years, the citizens aboard *Zanzibar* had imposed workable, human solutions on the architects' scrupulously logical intentions. Major routes, designed to be vital trunks, had fallen into puzzling disuse, while a number of secondary connections had proven vastly more popular. The most direct routes between chambers were not always preferred, and over the years the map had been redrawn and simplified, pruned of surplus branches.

Chiku touched her glove to the console and one route flared to particular brightness. She tried to follow it through the confusion of connecting lines, but the knot was tangled. It led forward, though, to the holoship's leading pole. Chiku noticed some words hovering beneath the console's surface that had not been there a moment before.

Chamber Thirty-Seven.

Another phrase followed, pulsing gently.

Submit for familial genetic verification.

This, Chiku surmised, was as far as Travertine had come. Ve had found the pod but it was beyond vis ability to make it move. By intuition or investigation, Travertine had concluded that it was waiting to taste an Akinya's blood.

That might have been nothing more than an inspired guess on Travertine's part – a gambit to buy Chiku's sympathy and support in the trial, before it could be put to the test.

There was a very simple way to tell.

Chiku's finger hovered above the panel for a moment before she lowered it to within a skin's breadth of the surface. She thought it unlikely that the machine would be able to sample her DNA through the fabric of her glove, but it was not a chance she was prepared take. She lifted her hand away from the panel without touching it, warily, like a saboteur stepping back from a primed bomb.

And then stepped out of the cabin, back onto the tunnel floor. After a few seconds, sensing her egress, the door slid back into place. The outline pulsed purple and then faded into seamlessness.

Chiku remained intrigued. It would be an interesting exercise to see where the pod ended up, if it was in fact capable of moving. But one thing was clear. Wherever the pod thought it was supposed to go, it could not possibly be Chamber Thirty-Seven.

Because there was and never had been any such place. There had only ever been thirty-six chambers aboard *Zanzibar*.

Even a child knew that.

'You had me worried sick,' Noah said. He was at the school gates, leaning on the low white wall with his arms folded on top of it.

'I promised I wouldn't do anything foolish.'

'Foolish or not, you took a big risk. Was it worth it?'

'I think so.' Chiku paused for a moment, then added, 'Actually, I'm not certain. Part of me thinks I should go back, but a bigger part is telling me that might be a bad idea.'

They had arrived separately, before Ndege and Mposi were allowed out of their lessons. Chiku watched a teacher walk along a covered passage between two of the school blocks. Ve carried a potted plant, cradling the bowl while the plant tickled vis chin.

'It'd be a really bad idea to keep this a secret,' Noah said.

'I haven't decided one way or the other yet – I need to do a bit more digging before I decide. I want all the facts at my disposal before I bring this to the Assembly's attention. It's not that I don't trust them, but they don't always make the right decisions.'

'That sounds exactly like not trusting the Assembly to me.'

'You know what I mean. And in my position, you'd be doing exactly the same things.'

Noah made the low, equivocal noise she had come to recognise as grudging agreement. 'So tell me what you found.'

'Are you sure you want to know?'

'You started this, wife. The time for keeping me in the dark has passed.'

'I found a hole under one of the buildings I searched yesterday. It's actually a shaft, but it's not on any of the construction documents.'

'So you did what any normal, cautious-minded person with family and responsibilities would have done. You definitely did not climb down this shaft to see what was at the bottom of it.'

'I only went down a little way. It looked safe and I made sure I'd be able to climb out again. And at the bottom I found ... well, more tunnels, for a start. And a pod.'

'A pod.'

'Just sitting there on rails, all powered up and ready to go somewhere. Travertine told me there was something down there I'd find interesting.'

'Travertine's mixed up in this as well?' Noah tried to make light of it, but the dismay behind his smile was obvious to Chiku. 'I can't tell you how much that gladdens my heart.'

'Travertine's a minor detail in this. Ve never got further than the pod. It wouldn't work for ver – it's got a genetic lock.'

'Couldn't Travertine have walked down the tunnel?'

'Ve lost interest in the pod when ve couldn't activate it. At that point it became a distraction, only useful as a potential bargaining chip.'

'What did ve put you up to?'

'I didn't make any promises to Travertine, and Travertine didn't tell me much beyond that. So on balance, I think I've got to go back.'

'This genetic lock won't be a problem?'

'Not if it's waiting for someone like me. An Akinya, I mean.'

'Not everything in the known universe has to revolve around that name of yours.'

'Given the significant role my family played in making the holoships, we were in a good position to put something inside *Zanzibar* that isn't on the maps.'

Chiku wasn't sure whether Noah was humouring her, or whether his own curiosity had got the better of him. 'Have you any idea where the pod might go?'

'Somewhere that doesn't exist – Chamber Thirty-Seven. Obviously, there's no such place.'

'Obviously,' Noah affirmed.

'But I'd still like to find out where it goes.'

'Surely this is a matter for the Assembly now, Chiku.'

She took her time answering. 'I really don't know.'

'It's simple,' Noah said. 'You've made your preliminary investigation and found something much more significant than a hole in the ground. You can't keep this to yourself any longer.'

She forced a conciliatory smile, hoping it would placate him. 'I'm sharing it with you, aren't I?'

Children were coming out of the school. Normally they would have spilt out in an exuberant mass, tripping over themselves in their eagerness to leave the classrooms. Today they were earnest in their solemnity, as if they had all suffered a collective scolding. They would have been told more about what had happened yesterday, including the fact that more than two hundred people had died in the accident.

It was probably the first time most of these children had been confronted with the notion of human mortality. Animals died, machines very occasionally malfunctioned or broke down – this they understood. But most of the time, people just kept on living. Of the citizens aboard *Zanzibar* upon departure, remarkably few had died, and over such a long span of time that most of these children would have missed it.

Today, though, they had been touched by death, and it would take up permanent residence in their psyches. Chiku did not envy the teachers the supremely difficult questions they would have been faced with. It was not as if the teachers had much experience of death themselves.

She spotted their children near the back of the exodus.

'You're not going down there again,' Noah said. He paused a beat before adding, 'Not without me, anyway.'

She shook her head in flat refusal. 'Out of the question.'

'And that response tells me it might not be as safe as you're implying. The truth, now, Chiku – is it risky or not?'

'I can't guess what's at the end of the tunnel, so yes, there is risk involved – but it's a small one. Plus in spite of all your misgivings, I know you're almost as curious as I am to find out where the pod wants to take me.' She glanced over the wall and lowered her voice when she saw that Ndege and Mposi were almost within earshot. 'For their sakes, we can't both go down there. It has to be one or the other. And since I'm the Akinya—'

'When?' he asked quietly.

'Tomorrow, if I can.'

'Then promise me something. When you come back, you either hand this over to the Assembly, or we never speak of it again. And you never go back to the shaft. Not now, not in a hundred years.'

'That sounds reasonable,' Chiku said.

CHAPTER EIGHT

The following day, work took Chiku beyond *Zanzibar*. She was summoned to accompany a delegation of Assembly members and constables to escort Travertine to the Council of Worlds. She wanted to tell Travertine that this outing had not been her idea, but she could think of no way of saying it that would not sound as if she were shifting the blame onto her colleagues.

They went out in a high-capacity shuttle and made a slow orbit around their own holoship before powering up for deeper space. The breach slid into view: a gash on the holoship's side that widened to a yawning void. Construction teams hemmed the wound's edge, defining it with the blue-white blaze of floodlights and the yellow glow of temporary living modules and equipment shacks. Small ships and robots hovered 'below' the wound from Chiku's perspective, holding station with thrust or impact-tethers. More evidence of consolidation and repair was visible through the rupture itself. False stars spangled back from the distant concavity of Kappa's sky.

Zanzibar was huge, but at a steady half-gee of thrust it diminished rapidly to the size of a pebble. Holoships only felt big when you were inside them, Chiku reflected. Viewed from outside, it was quite absurd to imagine ten million busy lives squeezed into the interstices of that little rock, infiltrating it like some kind of endolithic bacteria.

She had been to *Malabar* recently, but this time the destination was *New Tiamaat*. From the outside, it resembled the other holoships. It had the same rocky hide, barnacled with human industry; the same docking ports studding the surface, with wider apertures at the leading and trailing poles. Fat bumble-bee ships and transports congested its airspace. Congregations of drones and suited people flitted around them like tiny golden sparks. There were many people outside *Zanzibar* at the moment, but only because of the accident. *New Tiamaat* was always like this. Blisters and domes bulged from the surface as the citizens sought new habitable space. They had slowed their world's rotation and hollowed out most of its interior.

Chiku did not quite trust the inhabitants of *New Tiamaat*. They were Panspermians, to begin with, and Panspermians had decidedly odd ideas about lots of things. They had set their holoship on a course for Crucible, but lately there was talk of not making landfall when they arrived. They would continue to live in *New Tiamaat*, orbiting Crucible. Or they might even carry on into deeper space, having already achieved perfect adaptation to interstellar conditions. They liked it out here, sliding between stars. When the terms of the *Pemba* Accord were drafted, the people of *New Tiamaat* had pushed for the strictest legislation. They had no real interest in solving the slowdown problem.

Lacking spin and no longer under thrust, there was no sense of up and down in New Tiamaat. When they demolished their connecting walls, the rubble – a portion of it, anyway – had been fused into fantastic spires and outcroppings, spirals and arcs and buttresses, jutting from the floor, ceiling, walls – projecting into open space, providing the foundation and bedrock for dreamlike sky palaces and aerial citadels. Buildings, towers erupted out in every direction, growing like crystal or coral. Jagged promontories of glass, blocky extrusions of windowed stone, nets and nests, like traps or filters, and frogspawn clumps of pastel spheres. Tiny flying things – citizens of *New Tiamaat*, air-swimming through the weightless spaces – came and went in all directions. It was an explosion of possibility, an architectural expression of the Pans' cherished Green Efflorescence.

But in embracing one set of possibilities, another was denied. These structures were as lacy as sugar sculptures. Slowdown – the application of even a hundredth of a gee of thrust – would court disaster. The citizens knew that, of course. They had sanctioned these marvellous palaces and cities in precisely that knowledge.

The *Zanzibar* delegation was escorted to the core of one of the city complexes. Flute-shaped towers burst in all directions from an anchoring foundation of green-matted rock. Some way inside was spherical courtroom. It was white and bony, like a monstrous hollowed-out skull. Airy light seeped in through cunning ducts and channels. Functionaries and delegates stationed themselves around the incurving walls, clinging to studs and handholds, gargoyling from warty outgrowths.

Chalky struts buttressed a central platform to the walls. Upon the platform, big as a throne and rife with carved ornamentation, was a strap-in chair in which constables and *New Tiamaat* functionaries secured Travertine. A ring of smaller and less impressive seats than Travertine's surrounded the platform and accommodated the representatives of the eleven democratic Assemblies of the local caravan, together with the empty chairs that would have been occupied by the *Pemba* delegation.

The Council of Worlds was brought to session by *New Tiamaat*'s senior representative, Chair Teslenko. An aquatic born in one of Earth's seastead communities, the stern Teslenko had long ago forsaken oceans for space. The whiskered, seal-like representative wheezed a lot and his skin needed to be moisturised with oils at regular intervals.

Chiku knew Teslenko well enough. He had never made much secret of his dislike for the way they did things on *Zanzibar*, with its lax approach to public scrutiny. Travertine would have had to work very hard to find a worse foe.

The preliminary business proceeded rapidly, motes formulated and exchanged as tokens of good intent. Chiku was required to do very little except witness and nod. Travertine's identity was formally established with evidence offered to prove that ve was who *Zanzibar*'s delegation claimed ver to be. Travertine disputed neither the delegation's identification nor their accusation that ve was responsible for what had happened in Kappa.

'I know what I did, and I'd take the same risks a second time, and a third. Can I go now?'

'Of course not,' Teslenko rumbled through his whiskers.

'It was actually a rhetorical question.'

'You offered no defence in your earlier account,' said another of the *New Tiamaat* delegates. 'Do you wish to amend your statement?'

'I've said everything that needs to be said.'

'You display no contrition, no hint of remorse,' commented Representative Endozo, the *Malabar* politician Chiku had recently liaised with regarding the matter of elephants.

'When you permit someone to do something,' Travertine said, 'when you secretly *want* them to do it, contrition's not required.'

'Are you saying that this work of yours had tacit approval from *Zanzibar*'s Assembly?' enquired one of the delegates from the holoship *Cheju*, with sharp, sceptical interest. 'That's an astonishing claim, Travertine.'

'And one we refute, absolutely,' said Utomi, glancing at Chiku and her fellow delegates for support. 'We most certainly did not authorise this work. Travertine went to great pains to make sure none of us was aware of it. There was no "tacit approval".'

Chiku spoke up. 'I know Travertine at least as well as anyone else in this room. We were friends, once – I won't deny that. Ve certainly has a streak of intellectual vanity a mile wide. I recognise it because I've seen it in many of us, myself included. That's not a crime, and neither is honesty. I believe Travertine states vis position accurately. Ve won't admit to making a simple blunder because that would be a lie. But I also know this: Travertine would never have done anything unless ve believed it was for the best, for all of us.'

'This isn't the time to debate the *Pemba* Accord,' Teslenko said, to murmurs of agreement from around the chamber.

Chiku forged on. 'But we can't discuss Travertine's actions as if they occurred in a vacuum. Time and again, good people have attempted to use legitimate political channels to challenge the Accord. Time and again, they've been rebuffed. But Travertine's conscience wouldn't let ver just stand by and do nothing.'

'Are you trying to justify what happened?' Endozo asked.

Chiku shook her head forcefully. 'Travertine's actions were wrong – but that doesn't make them inhuman.'

Teslenko turned to face Chair Utomi. 'No one has offered a plausible defence of Travertine's actions. Under your internal system of governance, what would be the appropriate response?'

Of course, Teslenko knew exactly the range of penalties available in *Zanzibar*, and the limits of their severity.

'We have no death penalty,' Utomi said.

'Regardless, Travertine's crime must be among the worst you've faced,' Teslenko said.

'Ve didn't set out to commit murder,' Utomi answered.

'And you have no form of punishment more severe than incarceration, yet less severe than execution?' Teslenko asked.

'You know we do,' Utomi said, 'but it's one we're disinclined to use. Historically, it's only ever been a tool of absolute last resort. It has come to acquire a stigma worse than execution itself.'

Teslenko settled his gaze on Travertine. His eyes were liquid, dark, like black gems pushed into the mottled clay of his face. 'You are aware of this punishment – the denial of prolongation?'

'Of course,' Travertine replied.

'And would you not regard it as a kindness, if the alternative were execution?' Teslenko asked.

'The alternative isn't execution,' Chiku protested, in as firm a tone as she dared. 'It's house arrest, or a hundred other disciplinary measures.'

'Under *Zanzibar* law, perhaps,' Teslenko said. 'But this is a Council matter, and we have a range of options open to us. If *Zanzibar* exercises responsible judgement, the Council will have no need to impose a sentence of execution. The Council would also be inclined to adopt a sympathetic position with regard to any further sanctions, such as the imposition of external administration. And Travertine's ... condition would serve as a continued reminder to those who might contemplate challenging the *Pemba* Accord in the future.'

Chiku saw it then, with acid clarity. There would be the illusion of debate, a façade of procedural give and take. But Travertine's fate was already determined. *Zanzibar* would snatch at this chance to close the whole sorry business at the earliest opportunity. No escalation to higher levels of justice, no reprisals, no threat of takeover by another holoship.

'The decision need not be made immediately,' Teslenko said. 'Shall we say ... three days?'

Three seconds would have been enough, Chiku thought.

CHAPTER NINE

The pod was such an anomaly that it would not have surprised her to find it gone, vanished back into the tunnel in the two days since she had last seen it. But there it was, still waiting, pinned in the wavering light of her helmet. As before, the door opened obligingly and she stepped apprehensively into the plush interior. Everything was the way she remembered it. The system map still hung under the glossy surface of the console in its three-dimensional complexity. And the pod was still offering to convey her to Chamber Thirty-Seven.

Submit for familial genetic verification.

She had come this far. There was no going back.

She touched the console with her gloved hand, wondering as before if that might be sufficient to establish her genetic credentials. But instead of moving, the pod's door slid closed behind her and her suit registered an inrush of air. As soon as the air pressure equalised, she removed her glove and pressed her hand against the glass. Something prickled against her palm, like static electricity.

Genetic verification complete. Journey commencing.

Chiku put her glove back on.

The pod lurched gently, levitating away from its induction rails, and began to move, accelerating as smoothly and surely as if it was only moments since it had last carried a passenger. Chiku eased into the forward-facing seat as well as her suit allowed. Speed built up quickly, then levelled out. The pod had no forward lights, but periodically an illuminated ring of red interrupted the tunnel's smooth bore, probably demarking some maintenance hatch or service duct. For a long while the red circles were perfectly concentric, but then the tunnel began to bend, gently at first, and then more sharply. Where was it taking her? Forward, according to the suit's inertial compass – closer to the leading cone of *Zanzibar*'s elongated profile. The suit estimated that their velocity was somewhere between one hundred and fifty and two hundred kilometres per hour. No point trying to make herself more comfortable, in that case. Wherever they were going, they would arrive soon enough.

Fear spiked. If the tunnel came to an abrupt end, would the pod actually stop? At the speed they were racing, Chiku would only have a few moments to react. She stiffened involuntarily and braced a hand against the console.

But the pod sped on, and there was no dead-end. Chiku forced herself to relax again, trusting to fate. The tunnel curved and straightened, hair-pinned and kinked, then straightened again. The red hoops rushed by. And after fifteen minutes of travel she felt the pod commencing a smooth, unhurried deceleration.

It came to a halt. On the console it read:

Chamber Thirty Seven. Arrived. Please stand by for environment exchange.

The air returned to its reservoir. When vacuum had again been reached, the door opened. Chiku extracted herself from the seat and disembarked from the pod.

It had indeed reached the limit of travel. Ahead, the three rails terminated in angled blocks, as they had under Kappa. As in Kappa, the tunnel was wider here, to allow movement around all sides of the pod. Needing reassurance that she had a ride home, Chiku walked to the other end of the pod. She opened the door and climbed in. An identical arrangement of seats and console awaited her.

The console read:

Chamber Kappa. Proceed?

She was almost ready to touch it. Perhaps she had done enough for today. But she stilled her hand and exited the compartment. Reviewing her suit systems again – all functioning optimally, reserves all close to their maximum values – she set off into the tunnel beyond the pod, glancing back every few dozen paces to assure herself that the pod was still there.

She walked along the gently curving tunnel for a hundred paces, at which point it widened further. Blue lights shone from the floor, strips of pale green higher up the walls. Chiku searched for foot- or handprints, evidence that someone else had been this way, but the surfaces were flawless.

Ahead, outlined in green on one wall, stood the upright rectangle of a door. At Chiku's touch, the green lines pulsed and brightened as the door sank back into its recess and slid aside. A soft amber glow greeted her. Stairs, as sharp edged as if recently lasered from marble, climbed away. Continuing down the tunnel felt by far the less risky option, but Chiku had to know where the stairs led.

She climbed. The staircase was a gentle spiral. She counted three complete turns before she reached a rectangular enclosure at the top, about the size of a small bathroom. Another door was set into one of the walls. Confidence rising, Chiku opened it and stepped through into the narrow little space beyond.

She was in an airlock.

After the door behind her had sealed, air began to flood the chamber. The lock soon completed its work, and she stepped through the outer door at the one end of a short, rough-hewn rock-walled corridor. Beyond was a curtain of greenery penetrated by a hard blue light.

Chiku walked forwards, leaning and stooping to avoid damaging her suit against the rock's sharp edges. The tunnel's floor was compacted dirt or soil, and vegetation flourished abundantly all around her. She brushed aside the loose-hanging curtain – a tangle of branches and leaves that had grown across the opening – and stepped out into the full glory of daylight.

She did not know this place.

That was wrong, and impossible, but there it was. She was not just seeing an existing chamber from a novel vantage point. This was somewhere she had never been before.

The chamber was not particularly large by *Zanzibar* standards, but it was by no means small by any human measure – it was still an easy two or three kilometres to the other side of the the steep-sloped valley rift she was now overlooking. The chamber was considerably longer than it was wide and the ceiling was a curving surface sewn with facets of false sky. Patches of squared-off darkness signified where bits of the sky had stopped working or fallen to the ground.

There was no sign of civilisation: no towns, hamlets or roads. But there was a kind of rough, meandering path zigzagging down from the covered entrance through thickets of trees and overgrowth toward the valley floor some two or three hundred metres below.

After checking her suit functions again – all was well – Chiku began to pick her way down the path, watching her footing all the while. There was a steep drop to her left.

The patches of missing sky – cryptic daytime constellations – suggested decay, but most of the sky was still functioning, and there were trees in this chamber. Rain must still fall occasionally, misting down from the fine grid of ceiling ducts. The mere fact that there was a ecosystem here proved that temperatures could not become uncomfortably cold or warm. It was a marvel of both robust design philosophies and the basic tenacity of living organisms. That this place endured was a tribute

82

to both human skill and the natural resilience of trees and plants and soil ecologies.

A few paces ahead, where the path kinked around a small rocky out-cropping, something exploded from the ground. The shock of it had her teetering, wheeling her arms for balance as her heart thundered in her chest. Then she began to laugh. The thing had been a bird, breaking cover. Regaining her balance, her footing secure again, she watched it wheel against the black-patterned sky. Some kind of plump ground-nesting thing.

So the ecology in Chamber Thirty-Seven went beyond plants and trees. Many birds were insectivores, of course. She wondered how iso-lated this place really was; whether it had been hermetically sealed since departure.

Her composure regained, Chiku resumed a cautious descent as the bird gyred overhead. Though the valley floor was densely forested, there were also clearings and wider tracts of open ground. As her angle of view changed, she glimpsed the muddy mirror of a small lake or pond, hemmed by trees. Further away, she could see an odd, slightly unnatu-ral-looking conjunction of semicircular clearing and sheer rock face, the rock as smooth and flat-faced as a tombstone. From the corner of her eye, she glimpsed something vanishing into the cover of trees.

Slow and ponderous and grey, like a boulder on legs.

She blinked. There was no doubt in her mind. She had seen an elephant.

Chiku grinned, shaking her head in both wonder and disbelief.

'Really, though, you shouldn't have bothered,' she said aloud in a delighted half-whisper. 'We already have more elephants than we know what to do with.'

Chiku made a decision. The presence of an elephant proved that the air was breathable. She wanted to taste it, gulp it into her lungs, com-pare it with the air she had been breathing since departure. She reached up and released the equalisation valve on the side of her neck ring. There was a hiss, followed by a painless pop in one ear. Chiku lifted the helmet free of the ring and inhaled greedy breaths.

The air tasted disappointingly normal.

She tucked the helmet under her arm and continued her descent. But she had not gone more than a few dozen paces further down the trail when she became aware of a thin, artificial keening. It was at the limit of hearing – she would never have heard it with the helmet on.

Chiku halted. The bird was now long gone, but the sound appeared to be coming from the air. She turned around slowly, trying to localise the noise. It had turned from an insect sound to a steady electric buzz, fixed in pitch but raising in amplitude.

Then she saw it. Skimming along the side of the valley to her right, a small flying machine, silver or white, approaching rapidly. She watched it with misgivings. There were few flying machines anywhere in *Zanzibar*. She wondered if this one was a drone or toy, abandoned to circle this chamber in purposeless circuits.

She got a better look at the craft when it tilted to steer around a bluff. It had one large pair of wings near the front, a smaller pair near the rear, and an upright fin, a vicious whirring mechanism at the front.

Chiku could not move. It was not fear so much as paralysing indecision. Bushes and trees whipped aside as the machine gusted past, wing almost touching the valley's side. Snapping out of her immobility, she stepped back as the machine shot by. It continued up the valley, then turned sharply to the right, curving out over the forest floor. Then it executed a steep turn and came right back at her.

Chiku raised a hand – offering surrender or greeting, depending on how it was interpreted. The machine snarled as it approached, its whisking mechanism throwing back bright chips of reflected sky. Chiku squatted down, presenting the smallest possible target.

In her haste to get low, she lost her footing. She recovered, but only at the expense of dropping her helmet. It hit the dirt and bounced down the path, clattering off a stone and disappearing into bushes. The machine sculled past, close enough now that its wing really did cleave through the undergrowth. And in the moment of its passing, Chiku saw a figure, looking at her through the dark glass of a cockpit tucked beneath the shadow of the wing.

The machine sped up the valley, peeled left, made another sharp turn. It was coming back. Chiku staggered to her feet. A little further along the track, an overhanging boulder offered shelter. She scrambled towards it, wondering if there would be time to find the helmet as well.

She had not managed to reach the overhang when the ground gave way under her feet. Her leg twisted, and in an instant she was tumbling through bushes, the incline steepening as she fell. There was no hope of slowing herself. As her view wheeled, she caught one final glimpse of the returning machine. And then there was nothing.

CHAPTER TEN

'Don't move,' a voice said. 'You've had a fall. I don't think anything's seriously damaged, but I want to be sure first.'

Chiku allowed her eyes to find bleary focus. She was lying flat on her back. The sky was a blazing blue quilt, cross-hatched with areas of geometric darkness. Off in the middle distance, a thick curtain of trees. Behind the trees, dense green rising terrain, curving back up to the sky. She was somewhere down on the valley floor.

A figure leaned down and touched a hand to her forehead. She risked moving her head. The figure was a slight-framed woman.

'Who are you?'

'Never mind me. What's your name?'

She had to think for a moment, but the answer was only momentarily out of reach. 'Chiku. Chiku Akinya. You'll know my name from the Assembly.'

'Very good,' the woman answered quietly. 'And how did you get here, Chiku Akinya from the Assembly? I need to know what you remember.'

'I ... came by pod.' It was the truth, but it gave nothing vital away. Until she knew who she was speaking to, Chiku thought it wise to keep her answers guarded. 'I was coming down a path. Something attacked me. I was trying to take cover. That's the last thing I remember.'

The woman lifted her hand from Chiku's forehead and began to pass it up and down Chiku's chest and abdomen, the fingers tensed, but without actually touching her. 'A few cuts and bruises on your head and face, a pulled muscle in your leg. But you'll live. Why did you panic?'

'You mean when that machine tried to kill me?'

'I got a bit close with the aircraft. You'll forgive me. I just wanted a better look at you.'

Chiku tried to raise herself. Her chest hurt. She grunted into a sitting position, inspecting limbs for evidence of damage. She still had the suit on. 'You might want to revise your welcoming routine. Did you find my helmet?'

'It can't have gone very far. Why are you dressed in vacuum gear, Chiku Akinya?' She had the feeling the woman knew the answer already and was engaged in playful interrogation for the sake of it. Chiku looked at her face again, struck now by the sense that she did know her after all, despite first impressions. She was an African woman of indeterminate age, delicately boned, with black hair shorn almost to the scalp.

She came back with a question of her own. 'Do you know where we are? The name of this chamber?'

'Yes, of course I do. Chamber Thirty-Seven is what they used to call it, although of course it was never part of the documented architecture of the holoship. Fewer than twenty people knew about it, all told. Nowadays we just call it "the chamber".' The woman paused. 'Something happened, didn't it? A few days ago? I felt the vibration, a shudder through the entire fabric of the holoship. As if we'd hit an iceberg.'

'You felt that?'

'Let's just say I've developed a knack for these things. Do you think you can try to stand?'

Since she had no intention of staying in this place for the rest of her life, Chiku decided that standing was an excellent idea. She grimaced as her weight fell on her injured leg, but it was bearable. The suit's armour had obviously cushioned her from serious harm.

The woman was right to focus on Chiku's head: that had been the only truly vulnerable part of her body.

The woman was shorter than Chiku, though strong for her size. She supported Chiku until she was able to find her own balance, then stood back with arms folded across her chest. She was dressed for field work, like an agricultural technician or botanist: tight brown leggings, thigh-high boots with many lace-holes, a short-sleeved brown sweater. Over the sweater she wore a dun-coloured utility vest with multiple pockets and pouches.

'Tell me what happened a few days ago.'

'There was an explosion,' Chiku said. 'In Kappa Chamber, or in Kappa's outer skin. Breached the hull. A physics experiment went wrong.'

'How bad was the damage?'

'Pretty bad, but it could have been a lot worse. The effects were confined to Kappa, and we didn't have many people there. Still lost more than two hundred, but when you think how many more it could have been, had the explosion occurred in one of the community cores ... It's still a big bloody mess, though.'

'And how did you get here? It can't be coincidence, this soon after the explosion.'

'We've been searching for survivors. And evidence. Mainly evidence. In the process, I found …' Chiku hesitated. 'Something that didn't belong. I followed up on it, and it brought me here. Wherever *here* is.' She walked a few paces, unsteady at first, then with gathering confidence. 'Never mind me: how did *you* get here? You must travel between this chamber and the rest of *Zanzibar*.'

'I can't say I make a habit of it.'

'But I know you. I'm sure I've seen you around. You obviously can't live here all the time.'

'Why not?'

Chiku looked around. There were no buildings or facilities; no signs of civilisation at all, in fact, other than the flying machine – what the woman had called her 'aircraft' – resting on plump black wheels a few dozen metres away. On the ground, it looked remarkably placid and harmless.

'There's nothing here. No amenities, no houses, nothing. You can't live off trees and rain.'

'I have modest needs.'

'Do you have anything to do with the elephants?'

The woman looked pleased. 'You saw them, did you?'

'Just a glimpse. I know about our elephants, and there shouldn't be a hidden group aboard that no one's heard about. How many are there?'

'About fifty. Numbers go up and down.'

'And are you their keeper?'

The woman winced slightly. 'I look after them, if that's what you mean. Although I much prefer to think of us as sharing the space on equal terms.'

'You said "we" back then, when you were talking about what you called this chamber, so there must be other people here.'

The woman cocked her head before giving a nod of agreement. 'I did.'

'How many of you live here? You've got to have medicine, food, basic amenities. You look healthy.'

'Fit as a fiddle, apart from some memory issues. But there's only me here, and I don't get out into the rest of the ship very often. I'll ask again: why the vacuum suit? Has the tunnel lost pressure?' Then she closed her eyes, as if something that should have been screamingly obvious had just clicked into space. 'Of course – the breach you mentioned. If it sucked all the air out of Kappa, it probably drained the access tunnel as well.'

'That's probably what happened. Is that tunnel the only way in and out?'

'The only connection to Kappa. But there are other tunnels.'

Chiku marvelled. It was another landslip to her certainties, to learn that *Zanzibar* was wormholed with these hidden tunnels, decades-old secrets entombed in rock. She asked: 'Where do the others come out?'

'I don't remember all the details. The entrance you found, though – it was hidden until this accident?'

'I'd never have found it, if not for the collapse.'

'And your colleagues ... they'll not be long behind you? You didn't come *alone*, did you?'

'Will it make any difference what I say to you? You might as well do whatever you intend to do now.'

'And what would that be, exactly?'

'Kill me, or keep me here hostage, I suppose. Because you obviously don't want anyone else to know about this place.'

'I've done some extreme things,' the woman mused. 'Killing, though, that's out of my league. I'd far rather we arrived at a mutually beneficial arrangement.'

'You could start by telling me your name. I know we've met before.'

'You know my face, that's all. You've probably seen it thousands of times, on the statue in the grounds of the Assembly building.'

Chiku saw it then.

The woman was right: her face was strikingly similar to that of the bronze casting. A little younger, the hair shorter, but the bone structure otherwise unmistakable.

'You're one of us, then. An Akinya.'

'Not just one of you, Chiku. I'm Eunice Akinya.'

Chiku shook her head. 'You're lying, or deluded.'

'I concede that the truth may be slightly more complicated than it looks.' The woman cocked her head at the waiting aircraft. 'I must insist on showing you some basic hospitality. Will you come with me in the *Sess-na*?'

Chiku had no idea what that last word meant. Perhaps it was the woman's pet name for the aircraft.

'Come on – it's only a short hop from here, and then you can meet the others, and I promise I'll bring you right back here in good time.'

'How about we find my helmet first?' Chiku said. 'Then I'll decide.'

'An excellent proposition.'

The woman found the helmet very easily, as if she had always known where it lay. She scooped it from the ground like a rugby ball and tossed it towards Chiku. She caught it awkwardly, surprised at the strength the woman had put into the throw. Chiku spun the helmet between her gloves. It looked intact, save for some dirt and dust and a few scratches that might well have been present before her fall.

She doubted that there was anything wrong with it, but decided against wearing it for now.

The propeller had quickened into a tinted blur, like a glass disc bolted onto the front of the machine.

'What did you call this thing?' Chiku asked, as she worked the complicated arrangement of belts and latches inside the machine. The interior smelled hot and leathery and old.

'*Sess-na,*' the woman said. 'It's an old Masai phrase – means "extremely reliable thing". It's been in the family quite a long time. Had a few improvements over the years, of course – cut it open, it nearly bleeds. It's grown itself an entirely new self-repairing nervous system – infiltrates the entire airframe, strengthening it, healing microfractures.'

They bounced along the ground for a short distance before rising into the air. To Chiku, it felt as though the aircraft was balanced on a wobbling tower of mattresses rather than flying.

'I'm surprised you see the need,' she said. The helmet rested in her lap, like an egg. It had been a struggle, contorting herself into the tiny cockpit.

'The need for what?'

'To fly. Nowhere in *Zanzibar*'s very far from anywhere else.'

'It's not about *needing* to fly.' The woman yanked the control stick sharply, banking them to the right. 'Anyway, consider yourself honoured – this machine used to belong to Geoffrey.'

Chiku recalled, distantly, some image of her aged uncle, a photo pinned among his later paintings of elephants – Geoffrey standing next to a toylike white flying machine backdropped by sun-bleached veldt. More out of disbelief than reverence, she touched the padded curve of the cockpit console, wondering if it could be true. There was a good chance that every word out of this woman's mouth so far was a lie.

'Let's get something straight. You can't be who you say you are.'

'Why not?'

'Because I know my history. You died somewhere out in deep space. Me ... I ... one of us ... we went out there, to find you. But Chiku Red never came back. There's no way you could have ended up on *Zanzibar* – physics doesn't allow it. You took *Winter Queen* off in a totally different direction.'

'Did you just say "one of us"?'

'It's complicated. The point is, though, you can't be here. That just doesn't work.'

They were passing the sheer stone wall Chiku had seen from the path. Its grey lustre, she now realised, was the result not of weather or geology but columns of dense inscription worked into it from the ground up. They had been executed with astonishing neatness and regularity. She blinked, trying to focus on the details. The inscriptions resembled mad hieroglyphics.

The *Sess-na* banked again.

'Well, you're right about physics. Although if anyone could have pulled it off, it would probably have been me.'

'You're not Eunice. Maybe you're delusional – someone called Eunice who happens to look a little like my ancestor, but that doesn't make you her.'

The woman steered the aircraft towards what appeared to be a dead end at the valley's limit. The chamber was bathtub-shaped: a strip of flat ground hemmed in on all sides by rising terrain. Eunice – Chiku decided she would think of her as such, for now – pushed the stick down to dip the *Sess-na*'s nose, and then banked sharply to slip between two molar-like rock formations that looked ready to gnash together on the tangle of vegetation filling the gap between them. Astonishingly, there was a hole in the wall of greenery ahead, and the aircraft slipped through this green-lipped mouth with what appeared to be mere atomic monolayers of clearance. Chiku heard the fast scissoring of foliage being torn away by the wings and the furious whirling scythe of the propeller. She sank into her neck ring. The *Sess-na* slipped down a short connecting throat of rough-hewn rock wider than it was tall, and then they were out, flying free into another space.

'My god,' Chiku said, straining to look around. 'Where are we *now*?'

'It's all the same chamber,' Eunice said, 'just divided into three lobes. You came out in the middle one. There's a trail up the valley side to the connecting passage, big enough for elephants, but it's a long trek and flying is quicker. The *Sess-na* does have its uses after all.'

Chiku saw more dense swathes of forest below, the same blue sky cross-hatched with ribbons of blackness above. Eunice banked the *Sess-na* fiercely, shedding height and speed in a tight spiral. They skimmed tree-tops, then threaded a reckless, weaving course through the canopy itself. Eunice was as calm as if she had done this a million times, working the stick and waggling the wings, correcting and recorrecting faster than Chiku could think.

Eunice finally brought the aircraft down on a stretch of level ground where the grass had been worn away to bare dry soil. They disembarked.

'If you're comfortable in that suit, I won't argue with you,' Eunice said, taking hold of the aircraft by its tail and turning the whole thing as if was folded up from paper. 'But I'm not going to harm you. Harming you would be pointless, but most of all boring.' She added imperiously: 'Come.'

'Where?'

'If I'm going to be a gracious host, the least I can do is offer you chai. And a chance to meet the others.'

She headed off into the woods and Chiku followed, her curiosity getting the better of her fear. They walked a short way through the trees along a dusty path and soon came upon a clearing. A dwelling occupied the middle of the area, surrounded by something approximating a garden. The house was a clover-leaf of four tented domes, dun-brown in colour, sides zipped open and peeled back. Within the shady tents, Chiku saw furniture – tables and chairs, cabinets and shelves – and a tremendous assortment of tools and instruments. A proxy of ancient design stood slump-shouldered in the corner.

Eunice bid her take a seat at one of the tables. The seat was flimsy, a metal frame with canvas stretched across it. Chiku sat down carefully, still in her vacuum suit. Everything around her looked scrupulously well-maintained. There were medical kits, rations boxes, odd items of surgical equipment, vacuum-suit parts. Evidence of careful repair and ingenious improvisation.

Beyond the tents lay something that looked like a herb garden: neat arrangements of cultivated plants in wooden frames and trellises. Nothing pretty or ornamental about it – it looked too methodical for that.

Eunice boiled water and set a metal cup of tea before Chiku. 'Drink the chai,' she said, in a tone that brooked no argument. 'It'll do you no harm, and there are some potions in it to help with those cuts and bruises.'

'Potions.'

'Just drink. I've summoned the Tantors – they'll be here shortly.'

Chiku sipped at the scalding green brew. It was not quite as foul as it looked.

'These will be the "others" you spoke of earlier, I assume? Are they involved with the elephants?'

'They *are* the elephants,' Eunice said, punctuating the statement with an impish smile 'I took a liberty while you were unconscious – a blood sample. You appeared to be Akinya, and the pod shouldn't have brought you here unless you are, but I needed to be sure. The analysis confirmed that you are Chiku Akinya, as you claim. Or at least, very nearly.'

'What's that supposed to mean?'

'You're some kind of clone – there are commercial fingerprints all over your DNA. You're like a book that's had all its pages torn out and put back in again. You've been duplicated by someone or something called Quorum Binding. Does that relate to the Chiku Red you mentioned earlier?'

'I really feel you ought to be the one answering questions.'

'The difficulty is that we both have interesting pasts. How about a little give and take?'

Chiku decided that she had little to lose from complete honesty, as much as it displeased her to revisit her own history. 'You're right about Quorum Binding. It's no secret, in any case. When I was fifty, I became three people – me, Chiku Red and Chiku Yellow. Two of us are clones of the original, but there's no way of knowing which is which. I'm Chiku Green to the others, but I only think of myself as Chiku.'

'Well, of course you would. I think I heard of that sort of thing being done.'

'You think?'

'I did say my memory isn't what it should be.' She was sitting opposite Chiku, hands laced together and resting on the table-top, not drinking. 'I suppose you think I might be something similar – some kind of genetic construct.'

'Aren't you?'

'No. But despite what I said earlier, I'm not *exactly* Eunice Akinya, either.' She made an apprehensive face. 'Oh dear. I doubt you're going to like this.'

'Why don't you try me?'

'I am a robot.' After this utterance she looked supremely pleased with herself. 'There. I've always wanted to say that, but you'd be surprised at how few opportunities have ever presented themselves. And when I say "robot" – well, I mean artilect, to be precise. Your mother made me. Or started me, anyway. I'm the final result of her project to create an interactive memorial to myself. You know about this, surely? She used posterity engines to stitch together a construct sentience capable of emulating my every response. I'm very true to myself. I look like Eunice, and I act like her, and I carry much of her life history as part of my own stored data. All that said, I'm not alive. I'm just machinery.'

While the idea repelled Chiku, she also found it plausible. Sunday had indeed been working on a construct of her grandmother, but what became of that construct – what it had grown into – was a matter of speculation. Neither Sunday, Jitendra or Geoffrey had been forthcoming on the subject.

'I should be surprised, but I'm not.'

'That's hugely encouraging.'

'It answers some questions – starting with how someone could have survived here all this time, on their own. A human would have gone mad, or fallen ill, or starved, long ago. But a robot wouldn't need much to keep going.'

Now Chiku was trying to find the flaw, the giveaway that her host was not flesh and blood. Perhaps there was a dryness around the eyes and lips, or a too-flawless plastic tautness to the skin, hinting at polymers and manufacture rather than biological processes of growth and healing?

No, she decided. Nothing about Eunice looked fake.

'I thought you'd need more persuasion.'

'I saw how easily you moved the aircraft around, and you're obviously very strong and quick – you nearly took the wind out of me when you threw me my helmet.

'If you want some more proof, there's this.' Eunice scooped up one of the medical devices lying on the table. It was a pale-grey handle with a circular hoop on one end. 'Scanner. Pass it along your arm, then compare it with mine.'

Chiku did as she was bid. She slid the hoop over her hand, up her wrist. A palm-sized display was incorporated into the handle, just beneath the point where it joined the hoop. The scanner saw through her suit, through margins of skin and muscle, elucidating harder structures of bone and sinew beneath. Medical data fluttered over the little grey-green image, tagging anatomical landmarks.

Eunice held out her arm, stiff as a signpost. 'Now me.'

Chiku slid the scanner over Eunice's hand. The screen revealed armatures, universal joints, hinges, power feeds and mesh-like grids and actuators. Confronted with engineering where it expected biology, the scanner gave up trying to tag anything.

'This could still be a trick,' Chiku said.

'Yes, I could have programmed the scanner to lie. Or I might be mechanical from the elbow down and flesh and blood everywhere else. Short of cutting myself open, though, you're going to have to take my word for it. Of course, there's *this*.'

'What?'

Chiku's fingers were suddenly clutching at nothing. A heartbeat earlier they had been holding the scanner.

Now it was in Eunice's hand, and she returned it to the table.

'Party trick, for doubters and sceptics. I can move *very* quickly when the need demands.'

Chiku had felt nothing, not even a breath of air. Eunice had moved and then returned to exactly her former position, slipping through the gaps in Chiku's perception.

'You haven't run away screaming. That's a good sign.'

'If you're that fast, running away wouldn't do me much good. Why are you here, Eunice?'

'I'm hiding from something that wanted to kill me.' She jerked up in her seat, not quite rising, just enough to see over Chiku. 'Ah – here come the Tantors.'

Chiku hardly dared look around, but once again, curiosity compelled her. Something big – several big somethings – were nearing, shouldering through overgrowth, trampling undergrowth. She squinted into the darkening gloom of trees until she made out the elephants. She could hear them now: the rolling crunch of their tread, the breathing and snorting, a deeper sound than anything humans could make. By increments, she relaxed. Elephants did not frighten Chiku. She knew their ways as well as anyone in *Zanzibar*.

She wondered why Eunice called them something other than elephants.

'As I said,' Eunice declared, as if picking up a conversational thread only just dropped, 'I don't like to think of myself as their keeper. But it's true that they need me ... or *have* had need of me. That's a large part of why I'm here. The Tantors needed protection and guidance, and – with no disrespect intended – a human being just wouldn't be up to the job.'

'We have elephants,' Chiku reminded her. 'Many more than the fifty or so you claim to have here, and we've managed very well with them.' She looked at Eunice sharply. 'Why is your memory faulty, anyway? Shouldn't a machine work better than that?'

The Tantors broke through into the clearing. There were four of them, all adults, by Chiku's estimate. But these were not just any old elephants. They were from African stock, probably not too far removed from the ancestral herds that had seeded the other elephants in *Zanzibar*. They looked well, with clean, undamaged tusks and ears. Their foreheads were broad, their eyes alert and fixed on her.

They were also wearing ... not clothes, precisely, but harnesses – big and elephant-grey and flexible, made from articulated plates of plastic or alloy fixed around their bodies and heads but allowing ease of movement. There were things attached to the harnesses, especially around the head: dark modules, boxes and cylinders of unguessable function, almost like trinkets and trophies the elephants had collected.

Chiku recalled the elephant she had in the other chamber for comparison, but the glimpse had been too brief for her to determine its species, never mind whether it had been wearing a similar harness.

'They haven't had a lot of experience with people other than myself,' Eunice said quietly. 'Assuming I count as such, of course. Do nothing unless I tell you.'

The Tantors approached the tents in a line, then stopped. Chiku looked to Eunice for guidance, saw her rising from her chair and did likewise. She moved slowly, turning around with hands at her sides, holding only the helmet. She wondered how strange and fierce she looked in the vacuum suit. Like a hard-skinned monster with a tiny, shrunken head.

'What are they?' she whispered.

'Elephants with enhanced cognition,' Eunice answered, her voice as low as Chiku's. 'Uplifted animals. The result of illegal genetic experimentation conducted before *Zanzibar* ever left the solar system. Their minds are larger than those of baseline elephants, and they have a level of modular organisation approaching that of the human brain. They have a highly developed sense of self, an advanced capacity for tool use, the rudiments of language, an understanding of time's arrow. Some of these traits were already present in elephants, of course. They've just been ... enhanced, augmented, amplified. But whatever they are, these creatures are no longer simply animals.'

Chiku was as awed and horror-struck as if the sky had parted to reveal the gears and ratchets of heaven's own clockwork. She had spent a good measure of her life in the company of elephants. It was a family thing, a long and noble tradition.

The wrongness of the Tantors drove a hot lance into her moral core.

'Who did this?'

'If I ever knew, I don't remember now. But they are what they are, Chiku. There's no point feeling revulsion. The Tantors didn't do this to themselves. They didn't choose to be evolved.'

'This should never have happened.'

'I gather Geoffrey felt much the same way when he learned about the Lunar dwarves. They were the result of genetic manipulation, which he found profoundly distasteful.' Eunice started walking toward the four Tantors, beckoning Chiku to accompany her. 'But Geoffrey realised that he had to accept the reality of the dwarves, and to do what he could to make their world better. It was just the hand he'd been dealt. You'll come to the same accommodation with these creatures.'

Eunice's glib self-assurance was beginning to grate on Chiku. 'How would you know?'

'Because you remind me a little of Geoffrey. The second one from the left – that's Dreadnought.'

Chiku studied the elephant, drawing on years of learning. 'He's a bull.'

'Yes he is – well done you. The one on the far left? That's Juggernaut – she's the closest this group has to a matriarch. The other two, Castor and Pollux, are brothers. You think it's odd that a bull should remain with this group, long after puberty?' Eunice nodded, anticipating Chiku's answer. 'The old rules, the old hierarchies and patterns, don't apply here. In terms of social organisation, Tantors are as far beyond baseline elephants as we are beyond chimpanzees. They don't have herds. They have community.' Eunice raised her voice a notch. 'Dreadnought! This woman is Chiku. Chiku is a friend.' Then, to Chiku, 'Give me the helmet and step forward. Let Dreadnought examine you. Don't be afraid.'

'I'm not.'

But that was not quite true. Her suit would protect her to a point, but a charging elephant could easily run her down, pick her up and fling her around like a doll.

'The helmet,' Eunice repeated.

Chiku passed it to her, then slowly crossed sun-dappled ground towards the waiting flank of Tantors. She kept her gaze on Dreadnought the whole time. Dreadnought stared right back at her, eyes dark and heavy-lidded and alert with an uncanny intelligence. As Chiku drew nearer, she saw that the elephant's harness sported a flat black rectangle across the broad battering ram of his forehead. The rectangle contained an armoured, flexible screen, which was presently showing an image of Chiku as she must have appeared to Dreadnought.

Dreadnought extended his trunk. Chiku stopped and stood her ground. She let the trunk examine her suit, probing its way up her body, lingering over the joints and the batteries of controls. Hairy bristles tickled Chiku's chin as the trunk felt around the neck ring. Warm, humid air blasted her and she resisted the urge to flinch with difficulty. Dreadnought moved on to her face, mapping it with surprising gentleness. The trunk traced the contours of her scalp, then retreated.

'Dreadnought, say the name of this woman.'

Text appeared on Dreadnought's screen.

CHIKU

CHIKU

CHIKU

She looked at Eunice. 'He spells pretty well, given that we've only just been introduced.'

Eunice touched the side of her head. 'I just added the word to his lexicon. I could make them speak, if I wished – all I'd need to do is hook a voice synthesiser into the circuit. But they don't need that, and nor do I. The system lets them exchange symbolic patterns even when they're not in each other's line of sight, or when they're too far apart for vocal communication.'

'So we have talking elephants now. Even if they don't actually talk.'

The text changed. Now it said:

TANTOR ≠ ELEPHANT

TANTOR >> ELEPHANT

'Tantor does not equal elephant,' Eunice interpreted. 'Tantor greater than, or superior to, elephant. Why don't you introduce yourself? Tell him you're a friend?'

Chiku did not know whether to look into his eyes or the screen. Her gaze switched between them.

'I'm a friend. I mean you no harm.'

'What are you, a Martian? Talk to him the way you'd talk to a three year old.'

'I'm sorry. I've had surprisingly little experience with talking elephants.'

The screen changed again.

TANTOR

TANTOR

TANTOR

TANTOR >> ELEPHANT

'I get the message. They're a bit touchy about the elephant thing, aren't they? What have you been telling them? That they're better than elephants?'

'That they can be more than elephants.'

'Have they even seen an unaugmented elephant?'

'No, but I've shown them pictures, described the place they came from. Tell Dreadnought you're sorry.'

'I'm sorry,' Chiku said.

DREADNOUGHT ≠ ANGRY

CHIKU FRIEND DREADNOUGHT

'Well, you appear to have been accepted. Word of you will spread. The Tantors know that any friend of mine is a friend of theirs.'

'Easy when you don't have many friends,' Chiku said.

'Cutting.'

Chiku took a cautious step back from Dreadnought. The other Tantors watched her with guarded interest. One of the brothers – Castor or Pollux, she could not be sure which – nudged a piece of dirt with his trunk. Chiku heard a low rumble, impossible to localise to any single animal. They all had screens fixed to their foreheads, but only Dreadnought had communicated.

'Do you think it's time yet?' Eunice asked.

'For what?'

'For all of us to leave the chamber and enter *Zanzibar* proper.'

'Are you serious? You're a robot with superhuman speed and strength. These are talking elephants.'

'I was hoping attitudes would be more accepting after all this time.' She raised a hand. 'Dreadnought – you can go. Juggernaut, Castor, Pollux – thank you for checking on me. I'll see you before skyfade.'

The Tantors turned and walked out of the clearing.

'Who knew about this place?' Chiku asked.

'As few people as possible. Geoffrey and Lucas, certainly, and your mother knew about me, of course, at least to begin with.'

'What does that mean?'

'In the nicest possible way, Chiku, I escaped your mother's control. After that, we had less to do with each other. It was a matter of mutual self-interest. The less she knew about me, the less she had to conceal from the authorities. I was, remember, totally illegal. And the less contact I had with the family, the less risk there was of my own existence being exposed. I suppose it upsets you that all this happened without you being in any way aware?'

'Should it?'

'Oh, I think so. It would certainly upset me.' But after a moment Eunice went on: 'Don't feel too bad about your lack of knowledge, though. You were protected from consequences, that was all. Even the family knew very little about the Tantors. They were the responsibility of Chama and Gleb, friends of your mother and Jitendra. In fact Chama and Gleb oversaw the Tantors' development from the original elephant genestocks on the Moon. They knew to keep *that* nicely under wraps – they knew exactly how well the Tantors would be received back then.'

'Not well, for sure.'

'Having created these cognitively enhanced creatures, the safest option at the time appeared to be to launch them into interstellar space. The idea was that I'd protect them, give them guidance and medical assistance, until such time as it was safe to reveal ourselves.'

'You said you were hiding,' Chiku said.

'Remarkably, I can do two things at once. I can hide and also do some good for the Tantors. Chama, Gleb and the others envisaged a time, a century or two into the crossing, when the Tantors might be able to emerge into the holoship on equal terms with the humans. And that I, too, would be able to walk safely among them.'

'I think you're in for a bit of wait.'

'So much for the tolerant acceptance of the other. We're forging out into deep space – who knows what we'll meet out there? If we can't even accept a robot and some talking elephants, what good are we going to be when we meet something *really* strange?'

Chiku spread her hands in a gesture of profound hopelessness. 'You're used to waiting, Eunice. You may have to wait a while longer. Me coming here, finding my way into this chamber ... it's all accidental. If not for Kappa, I wouldn't be standing here. Who knows how long you'd have had to wait before someone found you?' Then she remembered something that Eunice had already told her. 'You've been outside, though.'

'I'd forgotten too much, and it began to worry me. There were supposed to be secure data connections between this chamber and the rest of *Zanzibar*, so that I could tap into the public nets without leaving this chamber. Also, that proxy – it doesn't work now, but it was left here so that someone like you, an Akinya with inside knowledge, could visit me without being physically present. But without the data links or the proxy, I had no choice but to leave the chamber if I wanted to fill the gaps in my memories.'

The thought that this machine, this artilect, had on occasion walked in the public spaces of *Zanzibar* left Chiku profoundly unnerved.

'And did you manage to fill those gaps?'

'To some extent, but there are still absences. I was damaged, you see. I was powerful for a very long time. Scarily powerful. Then things changed.'

'In what way?'

'I met something. Crossed paths with ... whatever it was. Another artilect, almost certainly. Just as powerful as me, just as furtive.'

'Something like you?'

'Similar, but disembodied, the way I used to be. Spread across the networks, haunting their vulnerabilities. Whatever she was, she must have been there for a long while. Lurking in the solar system, quietly aware of me.'

'You say "she"—' Chiku said.

'I told you I was damaged. It reached me, tried to kill me. It stabbed me with mathematics. Infected me with viruses and malware that spread like a disease, causing progressive failure of my core systems. Even after I'd consolidated myself into a single body and become small enough to move unnoticed among people, the disease progressed. When I ventured back into *Zanzibar*, I was trying to put right what had gone wrong. Trying to plug the holes in my soul.'

'Why do you think it locked on to you? What did you mean to it?'

'I don't know, and I'd very much *like* to. What was it? Who made it, and for what purpose? How extensive was its reach in our home solar system? Might it still be there now, or did it manage to infiltrate *Zanzibar*? Is it still looking for me?'

Chiku sighed. 'You don't have much to go on.'

'I have a name. The thing that tried to kill me calls herself Arachne.'

Chiku was glad to return home, to Noah and the children. The pod returned her to Kappa and she climbed out of the shaft without incident. When she returned her suit, she was almost disappointed when no one demanded an account of her actions. It turned out that she had only been gone an unremarkable five hours, no cause for alarm. Her casually proffered explanation for the dents and scratches on the suit – that they had been occasioned by a minor collapse when she was exploring one of the basements – was accepted without question. Eunice had cleaned up her minor head wounds well enough that they were not obvious. Only a clump of mud and grass caught in the articulation between knee and thigh threatened to undermine Chiku's account. But if anyone noticed it, it was assumed to have been contamination from inside Kappa.

That night, when Ndege and Mposi were asleep, when their neighbours' lights had gone out, she and Noah discussed what she had found.

'Before we begin,' Chiku said, 'I need you to accept what I'm about to tell you without question.'

'Why wouldn't I?'

'You'll understand in a minute. All I'm saying is, if you stop me to quibble over every tiny little detail, we'll be here until next week. Are you willing to listen first and ask questions later?'

Noah poured wine. 'Talk away.'

So she talked, and Noah, to his credit, did not quibble. He interrupted once or twice, but only for the sake of amplification or clarification, never because he doubted the essential veracity of her story. She told him all of it, from the pod, to the aircraft, to Eunice and the Tantors. She told him what she had learned of Eunice's nature, and why she had no reason to doubt that she had been talking to a machine. She told him of Eunice's amnesia, and the thing called Arachne.

'I know I made you a promise at the start of all this,' she said, when she was done with the account. 'I said I'd either go to the Assembly with my findings or never mention the matter again. But you see now why I can't keep that promise, don't you?'

'This is too big for you to handle, Chiku.'

'I agree. But I know this for a fact – we absolutely cannot risk invoking the Assembly.'

'Sooner or later,' Noah said, 'they'll start rebuilding Kappa, and someone else will find that shaft.'

'Eunice knows that. But she also knows the time isn't right for full disclosure.'

'Can you trust her? Given what you told me about her memory, is she totally sane?'

'I don't know. I'm going to see what I can find out about Arachne, at least. Beyond that, though, one thing's very clear to me. I've established that we can enter and leave the chamber in relative safety – for the moment, at least.' She paused, knitting her fingers over and over. 'When I go back, you have to come with me, Noah. You need to see this, too.'

'It still sounds too risky to me – what about the children if we're harmed?'

'I know what to expect now and I don't think we're in any danger from anything in that chamber. But we don't have long – once the reconstruction work gets under way, we'll lose access.'

'I could go on my own,' Noah said.

'The transit pod wouldn't work for you. But even if it did, I promised to go back. I trust her, Noah. She's Akinya, too. She may not be flesh and blood, but *we made her*. That makes her a family problem.'

'Your family's past has an annoying habit of intruding on the present,' Noah said.

'You're not the only one who wishes it would stop,' Chiku said.

In the morning she found herself called to the Assembly Building for a private meeting with Chair Utomi. They took coffee in Utomi's office, while the Chair made troubling smalltalk. This was in disquieting contrast to his usual directness. It was quite obvious to Chiku that he was building up to something she was unlikely to find pleasant.

'You seem tired,' he observed, as if that was supposed to improve her mood. 'Is everything all right?'

'Well, aside from this business with Travertine, the accident that could easily have killed us all, not to mention the political fall-out we can expect from the rest of the local caravan and then slowdown rearing its head ... no, everything's fine.'

'Sarcasm will be the death of you,' Utomi said, peering at her over the rim of his coffee cup with owlish regard. In his sturdy fingers the cup looked like something made for a doll. 'But your point is well made. These are difficult times, and this Travertine mess hasn't improved things. So, would you like some good news, for a change?'

She wondered how well she was hiding her suspicion. 'We could all use some, Chair.'

'Two things. I mentioned a few days ago the likelihood of a favourable outcome regarding your recent request for skipover. Nothing's formalised, but I can tell you now that the indications are very, very positive. You've been a valued member of the Assembly, Chiku, and the feeling is that it would be a shame not to have the benefit of your good judgement on the final approach to Crucible.'

'I hope to be alive then, whatever happens, Chair.'

'True, and we hope you will be, too. But while you're up and about there's always a chance of accident or something worse. In skipover, we can safeguard you against any mishaps – foreseeable ones, at any rate.'

'I understand. When might I expect the formal announcement?'

'Soon, I hope – which brings me to my second piece of good news. The local caravan really doesn't want trouble, Chiku – we've enough on our hands without emergency rule being imposed on *Zanzibar*. You'll hear none of that in the public statements, of course – the Council of Worlds has to at least give the impression of holding firm on its threats and promises – but there are always back channels. Not even Teslenko wants things to come to martial law. All everyone's looking for is a way to close this sorry little affair and get on with our lives. We want closure, a clean conclusion that makes an example of the complicit parties.'

'An example,' she repeated.

'I know you and Travertine are, or have been, friends – that can't be helped, and no one's blaming you for it. Ve was a friend to many of us, once. But Travertine committed a serious crime, and regardless of the loyalties that come with friendship, a transgression of that magnitude can't go unpunished, can it?'

'I don't think anyone would disagree with that, Chair.'

'I won't pretend that your vote will swing things one way or the other, Chiku. Travertine's fate is already all but sealed. But a show of unanimity ... a forceful declaration that we will not tolerate this kind of meddling ... that could go a long way to keeping our enemies at bay. In return, we'll be allowed to continue to enjoy the open and democratic rule we presently enjoy. It is also my view that such a show of unanimity would actually be in Travertine's best interests.'

'I'm not sure I quite follow that.'

'If the Council perceives a whiff of disunity, they'll press for execution. But if we make this gesture, show some solidarity, then they may accept the lesser sentence of denial of prolongation.' He smiled tightly. 'Frankly, we'd be doing Travertine a favour.'

'We'll all sleep easily in our beds, then.'

'This is about the entire community, Chiku. It's bigger than a single human existence. Bigger than a life. Bigger than personal loyalties. And I'm not asking you to push the dagger in yourself, merely to set personal feelings aside and acknowledge that Travertine committed a crime that warrants harsh punishment.'

'And if I chose not to go with the majority?'

'You've been an asset to this community. Why blot your copy-book now with a single rash action?'

'I see.'

'I'm not saying that your vote for or against Travertine will have the slightest influence on your chances of securing skipover.'

'No, of course. You couldn't possibly say that.'

'Exactly.' Utomi sighed, smiling softly. 'I think we can be of one mind here, Chiku.'

CHAPTER ELEVEN

She waited in the shattered building, as motionless as the pieces of jagged rubble around her. No one appeared to have been here since her last visit. She had given Noah clear directions, but he was late. Their agreement had been clear: if Noah got caught up in something that would make it difficult for him to come to her alone, he was to abandon the rendezvous. Chiku would visit Eunice by herself.

But then she saw him, Noah's suit turning him into a neon skeleton, approaching along one of the cleared thoroughfares. Some distance away, a pair of yellow machines toiled in the demolition of one of the larger domes. The pair squabbled over a big piece of shredded building, tearing it apart between them.

Noah dimmed his suit's markings as he entered the ruined dome where Chiku was waiting.

He spoke on the private channel. 'I wondered if your meeting with Utomi would run too long for you to get here on time.'

'No, I managed to escape. It's not good news, though. He more or less said that if I don't vote against Travertine, we can forget about skipover.'

'That's blackmail!'

'Call it targeted persuasion. All off the record, though, and totally unaccountable. But there's no way I'm compromising my principles over this. We have a legitimate right to skipover, whether or not I go with the majority verdict.'

'I suppose.' Noah picked his way over debris. 'Any sign that someone's been poking around since last time you were here?'

'Looks the way I left it, but it won't be long before the clean-up machines arrive. There's a chance they'll find the shaft, but I think it's much more likely they'll just seal it over without anyone noticing.'

She showed him to the basement. Noah had always been good with heights, much better than Chiku, and he did not hesitate to follow her into the shaft. Chiku led the way, and with every step she felt a piece of her sanity clicking back into place. No, she was not going mad. Here was the shaft, and the tunnel it led to. Next, they came to the junction marked on Travertine's plan. And finally they arrived at the pod, squatting in the embrace of its three guidance rails, exactly as she had left it.

'It's huge,' Noah said.

Chiku smiled. 'Big enough for elephants.'

She showed Noah to the pod's forward-facing compartment. As soon as the door sealed, air flooded the interior. Chiku removed her glove and urged the pod into motion. Soon the red hoops were sliding by at increasing speed.

'Here's the route we're on,' she said, sketching a finger along one glowing thread on the map within the console. 'I think we end up somewhere near the front of *Zanzibar*. That makes sense, doesn't it?'

'There's no room anywhere else,' Noah said. 'Not for a chamber as big as you described. But there's a lot of solid rock at the leading cone, to absorb collisions.'

'Yes – plenty of raw mass to soak up particles and high-speed impacts, which is why there are no accommodations there, or any critical infrastructure. If you absolutely had to find room for a hidden chamber, that's where you'd put it.'

'One some level,' Noah said, '*Zanzibar* itself must have known about this extra hole inside it. That much missing mass, a mountain's worth of rock not where it's meant to be – it must have altered the dynamics of the holoship by some measurable amount. But we never noticed!'

'Whoever did this cooked the books at a very deep level,' Chiku said. 'Designed the chamber in from the outset, then made sure it wasn't going to show up at any level, no matter how carefully we looked.'

The journey to Eunice's chamber felt quicker than before, a commonplace trick of perception that Chiku should have anticipated. Once the pod had halted and equalised pressure, they disembarked into vacuum and reviewed suit functionality before proceeding. All was well.

'It's not far now,' Chiku said, feeling a blush of pride in the fact that she had some familiarity with this place, compared with Noah.

There was only room for one person at a time in the airlock at the top of the ladder. 'I'll go through first—' Chiku began.

'No, I'll have that honour, if you don't mind,' Noah said. 'This time at least.'

He was waiting for her on the other side, and had already slipped off his helmet, cradling it under his right arm. He had heard her account, of course, and his suit readouts would have confirmed that the air was breathable, but Noah's haste unnerved her, for some reason. She wished he had waited for her permission before taking off his helmet.

'It's good air,' he said, between indulgent gulps. 'Different, somehow. This chamber's not connected to the rest of *Zanzibar*, is it? None of these molecules has been through my lungs before.'

Chiku shrugged, wondering how he expected her to know these things.

It was daytime in Chamber Thirty-Seven, the sky bright except for the strips of black where the ceiling elements had broken down. Chiku pointed down the valley towards the rising bank of dense vegetation that appeared to mark the chamber's limit. 'It doesn't end there. There's a connection, a throat bored through to a sub-chamber. Same at the other end. Eunice uses an aircraft to get about.'

'Does she know we're here?'

'It's likely. She learned of my arrival pretty quickly.'

Still cradling his helmet, Noah set off down the path, heels kicking up billowing scuds of ochre dust. Chiku removed her own helmet and followed, keeping an eye on her footing and the activity at the base of the valley. She had met the Tantors in Eunice's presence, and Eunice had assured her friends that Chiku was no threat. It was difficult to guess what would have happened if she had blundered into them on her own, but she doubted that it would have ended well for her.

'This is amazing,' Noah cried out, sweeping his free arm around. 'This whole place, all of it – it's been here with us all this time, and we had absolutely no idea. Imagine what we could have done with it!'

'Turned it into another chamber just like the other thirty-six,' Chiku said dolefully. 'Houses and parks and schools. We'd still be complaining about lack of room! And what would we have done with the elephants already here?'

'There,' Noah said, grinning. 'Our host, if I'm not mistaken.'

Chiku followed the line of his arm. There was the aircraft, the *Sess-na*. It was approaching from the opposite end of the chamber than on her first visit. 'That's her.'

'It makes no sense, flying around in that thing.'

'I think that's why she does it.'

Noah laughed.

The aircraft buzzed them. Chiku stood her ground this time and waved at the figure in the cockpit. Eunice gave them a wing-waggle, then spiralled down towards the valley floor. The tiny white machine found a strip of open ground and kissed land as daintily as a dragonfly. When it had rolled to a stop, the even tinier figure of Eunice emerged from beneath the white swoop of the high-set wing.

Noah, gripped by what was obviously an intense intellectual curiosity, broke into a headlong, stumbling run that never quite ended in disaster. Chiku followed at a somewhat less breakneck pace. Soon they entered the cover of thick growth hemming the valley's lower margins. They had lost sight of the aircraft by then, but the sky's false constellations offered a reliable compass.

'How much does she know about the outside world?' Noah asked when Chiku caught up with him, their suits sunlight-dappled through the fine-fretted canopy.

'She hasn't forgotten what *Zanzibar* is, and she knows a bit about my family having something to do with this place. Beyond that, it's sketchy.'

'She's in for the shock of her life if she thinks the world is ready for artilects and talking elephants.'

Eventually the tree cover thinned out, and there, gratifyingly, was the *Sess-na*, tail-fin glinting back at them across an expanse of whiskery, wheat-coloured grass as tall as their thighs. They quickened their pace, Chiku hearing the faint whine as Noah's suit assisted his movements. The suits were too cumbersome. Chiku wanted to climb out of hers and feel that grass whisking against her skin.

'Hello,' Eunice called, raising a hand. 'You came back, Chiku. I confess, I had my doubts. Oh me of little faith! And who is your handsome companion?'

'I'm Noah,' he said, with an abashed smile 'Chiku's husband and a fellow member of *Zanzibar*'s Legislative Assembly.'

'Welcome, both of you. Company's one of those things you learn to do without until you get a taste of it again.'

'I wanted Noah to see this before it's too late. I hope I haven't disappointed you by bringing him here.'

Eunice was sitting on one of the *Sess-na*'s big rubber wheels. 'Did I forbid you to tell anyone?' She stood as they approached and offered her hand. Noah was the first to shake, holding on a little longer than politeness dictated, as if he was seeking some indication – even through the glove – that this was not a real human being.

Chiku said, 'Things are moving pretty quickly in Kappa – it won't be long before the entrance is sealed over.'

'Then we mustn't delay. Shall we take a ride? I expect Noah will be keen to meet the Tantors.'

Noah glanced at his wife. She nodded.

Trust me.

Soon they were airborne. There were four seats in the *Sess-na*, and this time she opted to sit in the rear and let Noah take the seat to Eunice's right. It was Chiku's third time in the aircraft, and she was expecting the lurching swoops and surges as it hit air pockets and thermals. She reached over from behind and put a hand on Noah's shoulder, but after a moment he gently removed it and nodded to her that he was all right with the journey. This time they only flew a couple of kilometres along the valley and were soon spiralling down again towards a semicircular clearing. Chiku recognised the place: it was the clearing near the sheer stone wall that crawled with painstaking inscriptions.

There was a moment during the descent when they were almost in free-fall – Eunice, she suspected, was pushing the machine far beyond its intended performance envelope – and then they were down, bumping and bouncing along a dusty smudge of ground at the centre of the clearing. A curtain of tall, dark trees bordered the semicircle's curved edge, while the stone face defined its straight side. The aircraft rolled to halt.

They left their helmets on the seats. Noah peered up at the wall, his jaw lolling open. The wall rose tens of metres, beguiling to the eye.

'What is it?' he asked.

'Memory,' Eunice said. 'I'm sure Chiku's told you about the cybernetic dementia I've been infected with. It's slow acting but utterly remorseless. I wasn't able to stop its progress, so I preserved as much information as I could in stone, while I still remembered.'

'It looks like hieroglyphs,' Chiku said, but when she got closer, she realised that the symbols were in fact unlike anything she had seen before. There were numerous stick-figures, or things that were fleetingly evocative of stick-figures, lots of lines and spirals and squiggles.

'Something I picked up on Phobos that I knew could be used for efficient storage and encoding. Fortunately, the syntax was buried in a part of my memory she couldn't touch.'

'So you can just ... read all this, and it's as if you never forgot anything?' Chiku asked, sweeping her hand up the vaulting edifice's dense patterning. She imagined Eunice, this tiny woman, monkeying up and down that rock face. Carving her past into stone even as her memory rotted.

'Not really,' she said. 'I couldn't begin to store my entire knowledge base in *stone*. It's mainly just pointers, signposts, like the filing system in a library.' She gave a little cluck of self-disgust. 'It didn't really work. The dementia touched parts of me I thought would be safe. By the time it had done its worst, I'd lost the capacity to make sense of more than a tiny fraction of these inscriptions.'

'So the dementia isn't progressing still?' Noah asked.

'I'm not getting worse, but I'm not recovering, either. I've been on the verge of understanding myself for decades but the moment never comes.'

'Then all this effort was wasted,' Chiku said.

'Not quite. Being shrewd, I established multiple-redundancy pathways to the most vital knowledge areas. Like the name Arachne, and something of what she was. There's another name I made a point of remembering.'

'And that would be ... ?' Chiku said.

'Her name is ... or was ... June Wing.'

Chiku smiled. 'I've heard that name before. She had some connection with the family, didn't she?'

'She was a friend, an ally. When I ceased to have routine contact with your mother, I still had a line of communication to June Wing. She helped me get here, helped me live. I'm hoping she might still be alive.'

'I could check the public records,' Chiku said. 'See if she's still alive in the old system. The information might not be altogether reliable, given the timelag, but that's the best I can do.'

'I'd appreciate it.'

Just then, the Tantors broke through the trees.

Chiku's extensive experience with elephants enabled her to differentiate individuals. She knew the tell-tales that shed light on age and vigour, and those that distinguished one animal from another and revealed familial bonds. The process took time, however, and she had spent nowhere near enough of it in Dreadnought's presence to fix his image in her mind. Besides, the four Tantors had been devoid of the common injuries – the missing tusks, the bitten ears – that were part of her arsenal of recognition techniques. Now she was looking at six well-preserved Tantors and she could not be certain whether or not she had seen any of them before.

'Is that Dreadnought?' she asked, nodding towards the biggest elephant in the group.

'No – Dreadnought's still in Lobe One. That's Aphrodite, Dreadnought's younger sister.'

'You'd better tell her I'm not a threat.'

'Oh, she'll know that by now. What Dreadnought sees and experiences, she sees and experiences.'

Chiku found herself grinning. 'So what else can they do? Move trees just by thinking about it?'

'In the Surveilled World,' Eunice said, 'there was hardly an animal bigger than a flea that didn't have machines in its central nervous system. Humankind put them there, to prevent Mother Nature from getting ideas above her station. A lion wants to eat you? You look at the lion and whisper an oath and the lion drops dead, every cell in its brain fried before it can blink. The neuromachines were self-replicating, and they passed from generation to generation without human interference. The phyletic dwarves had the same neuromachinery. The Tantors are distant descendants of the dwarves, and the machines have accompanied them across the generations. With some upgrades along the way, of course.'

'Shaped by you?' Chiku asked.

'I can't help myself. Always was an inveterate tinkerer.'

Chiku asked Noah to join her to introduce themselves to Aphrodite. Like the Tantors Chiku had already met, these creatures wore harnesses and communications systems around their heads and bodies. Chiku guessed that the population was stable enough that there was little need to manufacture new equipment.

On Aphrodite's screen appeared the words:

WELCOME CHIKU

'This is my husband, Noah.' Catching herself, remembering Eunice's injunction to keep things simple, she added: 'My friend, Noah.'

WELCOME NOAH

Noah raised a hand. 'Hello, Aphrodite. It's a pleasure to meet you. Where are we?'

Chiku nudged him. 'You know exactly where we are.'

'I want to hear what she thinks, not you.'

Aphrodite flapped her ears. They were like sheets of stiffened canvas. Chiku wondered what the flapping signified. Was it concentration, irritation or something so intrinsic to elephants as to be beyond her conceptual horizon?

After a few moments, Aphrodite said:

IN CHAMBER

'And outside the chamber?' Noah probed.

OUTSIDE = NOTHING

'That's true enough,' Chiku whispered. 'Vacuum. The void between the stars.'

'They don't know about the other chambers in *Zanzibar*, let alone other worlds.'

SPEAK LOUD

Chiku smiled at this rebuff. 'They're elephants,' she whispered. 'That they're capable of grasping anything is pretty astonishing.' Then, to Aphrodite: 'Noah has a lot to ask you.'

'You're leaving me to make small talk with elephants?'

For all his protestations, Noah clearly relished the chance to interact with the Tantors. Chiku left him trying to get Aphrodite to name the other five animals and walked over to Eunice. She had been watching over them from the partial shade of the aircraft's wing. The *Sess-na* generated odd little clicking sounds, as if it, too, had things on its mind.

'Do you have some information for me?' Eunice asked.

Chiku nodded. 'For what it's worth, I found out what I could about that name you mentioned.'

Eunice looked at her with sharp interest. 'Was it difficult?'

'No, incredibly easy.' Chiku felt the need to sit down and perched on the wheel where Eunice had been resting when they arrived. 'I searched the public files. I know there was a risk in that, but I put in other names, as well – made it look as if I might be thinking of names for a child, something like that. There are lots of people and things called Arachne, of course, but it didn't take me long to narrow it down. Arachne is – or was – the controlling intelligence behind Ocular.'

'Ocular,' Eunice repeated. 'I almost know what that means. It's there, somewhere.'

'It's the name of the array of space telescopes that detected Mandala, and the Akinyas were involved in its construction. Mandala is the alien structure on Crucible. Ocular found it, and that's why we're here, seventeen light-years from Earth, heading to Crucible.'

'But there are other holoships, other caravans, headed for other extrasolar planets.'

'Yes,' said Chiku, 'but Crucible was the first destination to be chosen. It's the closest truly Earth-like world, and the only one with an alien artefact crying out for closer examination.'

Eunice shook her head. 'I really don't think this can be the connection.'

'It has to be.'

'Even if Arachne was another artilect, what harm was I doing her? What harm could she possibly have done me? Why did I need to flee the system?'

'I'm afraid there are still more questions than answers, but perhaps this will help you.' Chiku dug into the suit's cargo pouch and slid something from a plastic sheath. She offered it to Eunice.

The robot took it in both hands, examining it dubiously.

'It looks like something made for chimpanzees.'

'It's for children,' Chiku explained. 'I don't know how it was in your day, but we don't put implants into children until their tenth birthday. Until then, they make do with things like this. It was Ndege's – my daughter's. It's called a companion. It's a diary, a story-book, an encyclopedia, all in one. It also functions as a portal, a way into the public files.'

'Then it's useless to me – I already told you there are no data links between here and the rest of *Zanzibar*.'

'You're wrong.' Chiku took the companion back to demonstrate her point with a simple query. 'Some change in *Zanzibar* must have damaged the original links, but the companion isn't affected. It must be utilising a different protocol.' She returned the book to Eunice.

'If I use this,' Eunice said, 'will my doing so come to anyone's attention?'

'It's a thing made for children, and it only has a limited search capability. For that reason, it's not the sort of thing that would be routinely monitored. Provided you're careful with your queries, nothing untoward should happen.'

'And your daughter won't miss it?'

'If Ndege being cross is the worst thing we have to deal with ...' Chiku said. She shook her head firmly. 'She'll understand. One day.'

'I shall take very good care of it.'

Chiku stood up. 'I don't know when we're next going to see each other, but it could be a while. What you've told me, about Arachne ... I think I have to do something quite difficult. I think I have to call on Chiku Yellow for help. I'll see if she can reach June Wing – assuming either of them is still alive.'

'Will she listen?'

'She'd better. But I can't promise anything – we've been out of touch for so long.'

'I must warn you – if Arachne still has influence, she may not take kindly to anyone making enquiries about her. You'll be putting this other version of you at considerable risk.'

'Believe me,' Chiku said, with an edge of steel in her voice. 'She could use some excitement in her life.'

CHAPTER TWELVE

The room was lightless except for the glowing coloured threads stretching from floor to ceiling in a bundle, braided into a thick, multicoloured column as wide as Chiku's fist. The column maintained the same width until it reached eye level, where it fanned out in an explosion of threads, taut as harp-strings, which arrowed towards the ceiling at many different angles. The individual threads, which had been linear from the point where they came out of the floor, now branched and rebranched in countless bifurcations. By the time the pattern of lines brushed the ceiling, it was all but impossible to distinguish individual strands.

Mecufi was with her, upright in his mobility exo. He had been present since the scriptors started work and her memories began to unpack themselves.

'We really are remarkably fortunate,' he said.

He was engaging her in conversation, exploring her responses to a spectrum of stimuli, to gauge how well the scriptors had functioned.

'How so?'

'We nearly ended ourselves,' he said, gesturing towards the threads with an upsweep of his arm. 'It was only by some great grace of fortune that we made it into the present, tunnelled through the bottleneck, exploded into what we are today.'

'A squabbling mess,' Chiku said.

'Better a squabbling mess than non-existence. You can always *improve* a mess. That bottleneck is the point where we nearly became extinct. There were tens of thousands of us before this happened, one hundred and ninety-five thousand years ago. Then something brought a terrible winnowing. The climate shifted, turning cold and arid. Fortunately, a handful of us survived – emerging from some corner of Africa where conditions hadn't become quite as unendurable as they were elsewhere. We were smart by then – we know this from the remains we left behind – but intelligence played only a very small part in getting us through the bottleneck. Mostly we owe our success to blind luck, being in the right place at the right time, and then following the shoreline as it rose and retreated, over and again. It was the sea that saved us, Chiku. When the world cooled, the oceans gave us sustenance. Shellfish prefer the cold. And so we foraged, never far from water, along beaches and intertidal zones, and lived in caves, and spent our days wading in the shallows. The lap of waves, the roar of breakers, the tang of ozone, the mew of a seagull – there's a reason we're comforted by these sounds. And here we are, a genetic heartbeat later. Returning a debt, giving back to the oceans what the oceans gave us. The seas saved us once. Now we're saving the seas, and taking them with us to the stars.'

'It's a very nice sculpture.'

'By the time it touches the ceiling, there are twelve billion threads. Spiderfibre whiskers, just a few carbon atoms wide – the same stuff they used to make the cables for space elevators – one for every person now alive, on Earth, orbiting the sun, in the Oort communities and the holoship migrations. I can identify your thread, if you'd like ... you can watch it glow brighter than the others, follow its path all the way into history, see where three became one. See where you fit into the bottleneck.'

'There's a point to all this, I'm presuming?'

'Arethusa liked to call us Poseidon's Children. Orphans of the storm. We'd endured the worst the world could throw at us, the worst consequences of our own stupidity, and came through, like the survivors on *The Raft of the Medusa*, ready to face the dawn. But there are always more storms, Chiku. Arethusa knew that better than most. The question we need to face now is: have we weathered the worst? Or is there something we haven't anticipated coming down the line?'

She thought back to the freight of feelings Mecufi had packed into his mote, on the night before she went to the seasteads. Less than a week ago, although that seemed impossible to square with the huge new freight of memories now burdening her head.

'Something's got you worried, hasn't it? That's why you're in such a rush all of a sudden to contact Arethusa. That's why you need me.'

'We saw an opportunity to do good. That it happens to coincide with a need of our own ... let's just call it a happy accident, shall we?'

They were in one of the Atlantic seasteads, not far from the Azores. Chiku's progress was being assessed from hour to hour as the new memories branched and rebranched. The Merfolk had considered this a wise precaution. Many years had passed since the Quorum technology had last been allowed to work as intended, and the presence of anti-tamper countermeasures beneath the ones they had already identified and neutralised could not be eliminated. Some glitches in mnemonic transcription, harmless or malign, were also possible.

But Chiku at least had detected no obvious signs of error. The memories went back to Chiku Green's meeting with Representative Endozo aboard the holoship *Malabar* the day Kappa exploded, and not much further. When she packaged the memories for transmission back to Earth, she had only sent Chiku Yellow a sliver of her life. The rest, everything that had happened since *Pemba*, was merely implicit. A good wife, a good husband, two good children and a position of responsibility in the Legislative Assembly. What more could she have wanted?

Odd now to think of herself for a moment not as Chiku but as Chiku Yellow, as if in some sense she was standing outside her own body, observing. It had been like this during the early years of their triplication, but she had forgotten that peculiar sense of non-localisation – as if her sense of self belonged not in any one particular body but in the shifting, unstable centre of gravity located between them.

Yet there was a quality, the most delicate chromatic tinting, the most subtle modulation of timbre or microscopically altered angle of reflection, which denoted that these memories of *Zanzibar* were new experiences, things that had happened to this other version of her. This was some clever thing done to her hippocampus, to enable her to organise and orientate the two experience streams. Without that, it would have been too confusing for words.

So she knew who she was, and what had happened to her, in both streams. Holding the shifted timeframes in her mind was more difficult. These were not fresh memories. They felt new, but they had been on their way back from *Zanzibar* for seventeen years.

Here, now, on Earth, the year was 2365. The memory package had been on its way since 2348 – time enough for it to hopscotch back home and then circle the world for months, waiting to be opened. These events, these things that had happened to Chiku Green, lay just as far back in Chiku Yellow's past. Ndege and Mposi were older now, and would be older still by the time any response made its way to *Zanzibar*. It would be more like forty years before her counterpart received a reply.

How was a person supposed to deal with this?

Chiku wondered what her counterpart could possibly have expected of her. Was she really out there, prepared to wait forty years for an answer? Could anything matter that much?

A shaft leading underground. The brilliance of a blue sky, etched away in geometric patches. The stomp and snort of Tantors, the subsonic throb of a musth rumble. The voice of Dreadnought, booming out like a biblical proclamation. A woman who looked like her great-grand-mother, sitting on the wheel of an aircraft. A name – Arachne – that might mean nothing at all.

Another, June Wing, which certainly meant something.

And the merfolk, here and now, expecting her to do them a favour in return for these memories. It had not slipped her attention that they also had an interest in the elusive June Wing.

Popular woman, Chiku thought.

She said to Mecufi, 'You want me to make contact with this person, hoping she might put you in touch with Arethusa.'

'I'm very encouraged that you remember that as clearly as you do. Very occasionally the new memories will cause some confusion with those laid down just before the start of the mnemonic scripting. In your case things seem to have proceeded without complication.'

'I feel fine. You said something about June Wing being on Venus.'

'Indeed, but June moves around a lot, gathering pieces for her collection, and she won't stay there long. You should be on your way sooner rather than later, while she's still in the inner system.'

'I can't promise anything.'

'But you'll do your best. The memories appear to be stable, but we can continue monitoring them all the way to Venus. Do you own a spaceship?'

'I don't *think* so.' But she had owned several in her youth, including a sleek little number that she had been very fond of. 'Not lately, no. I had to sell them – that's what it's come to, being an Akinya.'

'Poor little you,' Mecufi said.

He was all for her leaving immediately, riding the great glass chimney to orbit and then a commercial loop-liner to Venus. Chiku, against the merman's wishes, insisted on returning to Lisbon first. They argued the point until Chiku won.

When she returned to Pedro's studio, he came to the door with the neck of a guitar in his hands, neatly slotted for frets. He appraised her carefully, as if she might be an impostor. 'It's been a day longer than you said. I wondered if I ought to worry. Then I thought, what can possibly go wrong?'

'Almost nothing.'

'That's what I figured. They'd have told me if there was a problem. I mean, what's so unusual about having thousands of new memories stuffed into your head by tiny machines?'

116

Before they kissed, before she sat down, even, she got the worst news out of the way. 'I need to go to Venus.'

'It's a lovely place. When the tides are low, some of the old buildings are visible.'

'Venus. I said Venus, not Venice.'

Pedro smiled. 'I know.'

'According to Mecufi, the conjunction's especially favourable right now, and it shouldn't take me long to do what I have to do.'

'Which is?'

'Catch up with June, this woman who used to know my mother and father. All the Pans want me to do is tell her they'd like to get back in touch with Arethusa. She can help them do that, if she wants. If she doesn't, it's really not my problem.'

'And then – what – your obligations are over?'

'More or less.'

Pedro put down the guitar neck. 'I don't like the sound of this. Fine, they've done you a favour. That doesn't mean they own you for life. It's not like you ever had any interest in June before all this started.'

'Actually I always meant to talk to her at some point, if I could make it happen – for the biography, if nothing else.'

'But there's more to it than that now, isn't there?'

She did not want to be having this conversation right now, or in fact at any point between now and the end of the universe. But better out than in, as the saying went.

'There's another reason I'd like to meet June.'

'Then it's something to do with the ghost, the memories from the other Chiku.' Pedro did that endearing thing he did when puzzled, which was to scratch beneath his fringe, squinting out at her under an overhang of curls. 'Which you haven't mentioned yet.'

'Can we eat? I'm starving.'

'And then talk?'

'Let's eat. And you can open a bottle of wine – at least one of us is going to need it.'

'We're all out. I meant to go shopping, but I got tied up with this commission. It's not too late, is it?'

They went out to buy wine, Chiku light-headed with Tantors and artilects, bobbing through the streets of Lisbon like a balloon on a string, barely anchored to the world. They bought a nice bottle of Patagonian merlot, then changed their plans and stopped at a restaurant on their way back to the apartment. The establishment had mustard-coloured walls, crumbling plaster that must have been overpainted a thousand times and could still have used another coat. It was already dusk. Musicians and their instruments were tucked into a red-lit corner, like statues in a shrine.

'It's complicated,' Chiku said, when they were halfway through their meal.

'Please,' Pedro said, pausing between bites. 'When is anything with you *not* complicated?'

'I have Chiku Green's memories now, and I know why she was trying to reach me.' She was glad of the musicians, the *fado* singer, the ill-mannered diners who refused to lower their voices while they performed. The hubbub created a background that made their conversation much more intimate than if they had been in the studio, with its silent audience of unfinished guitars.

'What she's relayed to me is important, and there are things I probably can't tell anyone.'

'Not even me?'

'Chiku Green trusted me with something significant.' She closed her eyes. She desperately wanted to tell him. But it would have to wait, the full truth of it, her doubts about Arachne and Crucible, until she had spoken to June Wing. She could barely trust herself with this knowledge. It felt like a fire on her tongue, burning for release.

'Well?'

'I made a discovery, on *Zanzibar*. I mean, Chiku Green did. I ... she wants me to talk to June.'

'Wait. I'm totally confused now. The Pans want you to talk to June, and so does your counterpart?'

'Yes. But it's not that straightforward. The Pans want June for one thing, and Chiku Green wants her for another. And right now I don't think I want to tell the Pans about the second thing.'

'Well, I'm sure they'll be fine with that.'

'I just have to reach her. I don't give a damn about Arethusa, she can tell me to go to hell as far as that's concerned. But the other thing ... I've *got* to speak to her about that, and it has to be somewhere safe. There's a ship leaving for Venus tomorrow. The Pans will get me aboard. I have to be on that ship, Pedro. Right now there's nothing more important in the world.'

'That message took years to get to you – what could possibly be this important?'

'Everything. Nothing. I don't know, and I won't until I've spoken to June. She'll know, I think.'

'And she'll talk?'

'She knew my mother. My father was a friend of hers before he ever met Sunday.'

'Perhaps you should speak to your parents instead.' He corrected himself. 'I mean, to Jitendra. I'm sorry.'

Her mother and father were both still alive. Jitendra was in his two hundred and thirtieth year, hitting the long-delayed consequences of the prolongation therapies he had undergone late in his first century. Sunday was ... somewhere over a cognitive horizon, her mind altered and re-altered as she chased a deeper understanding of Chibesa physics.

'Even if they could help, it's not their problem. Or yours. This is between me and June.'

'I still don't understand why you have to *go to Venus*.' He said this as if interplanetary travel was some risky new fad, like hot-air ballooning.

'Even if June was the other side of Lisbon, I'd still need to visit her in person. She won't want to speak to me, so if there's the slightest chance of avoiding contact, she'll take it. She could always decline a ching, or ignore a proxy. She'll find it tougher if I'm there in the flesh, having come all the way from Earth.' Chiku dabbed at her lips with the napkin. 'Look, it's only Venus – we're not talking about the Oort cloud.'

'I could come with you.'

'Or you could stay here and try to keep your business afloat.'

'I am several months behind on commissions,' Pedro admitted.

'Exactly.'

'So a week or two more won't make any difference, will it?'

'No, categorically not.'

'Talk to this fish-faced friend of yours. Tell him it's very simple. If he can move the world to make you go to Venus at the drop of a hat, he can certainly find room for another passenger. I'm very inexpensive. I'll even pay for my own drinks.'

'Mecufi won't go for it.'

'And you won't know that for sure unless you ask, will you?' He smiled at her, lifted his glass and sipped.

A couple of days later they took a maglev from Lisbon, then a black and yellow passenger airship from the maglev terminal flew them out to sea, to the base of one of the atmosphere chimneys. They boarded the shuttle at sea level, through a pressurised connecting dock. The ship was already in vacuum, ready to depart. Its engine was totally silent and smooth – Chiku strained to detect even a rumour of a rumble as they gathered speed, but there was only the white noise of air conditioning, the murmur of a low conversation from two Tamil businessmen a little way down the cabin.

From the chimney's trumpet-shaped maw, the shuttle rose and kept rising. Then it transitioned into true spaceflight and there was an hour or two to be killed until they made rendezvous with the passing loop-liner. It was like a fatter, gaudier version of the liner that had once carried Chiku out to the birthing orbits. It was white with gold and platinum trim. Huge millwheel parts of it were counter-rotating, simulating various planetary gravities. Other components – central spheres and cylinders – remained static. It reminded Chiku of an over-elaborate wedding cake.

Three days to Venus barely gave them time to unpack their bags. The loop-liner was so huge that it would have taken weeks or even months to explore all its promenades and galleries, its curving rows of boutiques and restaurants. Chiku and Pedro contented themselves with the areas of the ship outfitted for terrestrial gravity, and even then there was far too much to investigate. Wandering the halls, Chiku came upon a reproduction of Watteau's *The Embarkation for Cythera*. There was a quality of melancholia about the painting despite – or perhaps because of – its oddly contradictory subject matter: the frolicking nymphs and cupids, its groups of wistful, trysting lovers seemingly preparing to board the boat to leave this breezy island arcadia rather than arrive there. Not an embarkation, then, but a farewell.

Chiku's mother had always been opinionated about art. She wondered what Sunday would have said about this painting.

The hours gobbled each other. Periodically, Mecufi checked in to make sure Chiku's memories were behaving themselves. Pedro chinged back to Earth to complete some business until the time lag made it difficult. When they were together, there was only so much they could talk about. Chiku would not be drawn on the matter of June Wing, not until she had spoken to the woman. Pedro accepted this, to a point. He had secrets of his own, after all.

'Let's be honest,' he said on the third evening of their crossing. 'There's a lot we don't know about each other.'

'A lot we don't want to know,' Chiku said.

'Speak for yourself. But I hope we can be more open when this is all over and done.'

'When I'm ready to talk about June, you'll be the first to know. But it cuts both ways. Who are you, really? How did you end up with that studio, all those connections? You're not from Lisbon – or if you are, you've travelled widely. You speak Swahili and Zulu and who knows

120

what, with or without the aug. You make a big song and dance about me going to Venus, but it turns out that you're not in the least bit bothered by space travel or weightlessness.'

'I've been around. Done some stuff.'

'I'd like to know about it.'

'You could query the aug and find out most of it before I've had time to finish this drink.'

'But that wouldn't be the same as having you share it with me.'

Pedro smiled and looked away for a moment. 'I've done ... things.'

'Well, that narrows it down.'

'Quite interesting things, which we'll speak of eventually, but not here and definitely not now. You will tell me about June, though, won't you?'

'Assuming there's anything to tell.'

And so they circled around what could or would not be said, and as the Earth and Moon receded, so Earth's sweltering, cloud-garbed sister grew larger.

First a pale dot, crescented by shadow, then a milky marble, like an eyeball with major cataracts.

From the loop-liner a shuttle took them to one of the orbiting stations necklacing Venus. They would not be staying long. Subtle enquiries had already established that June Wing was still down in the clouds. Not on Venus, exactly, but in one of the many floating gondolas tethered against the endless cycling winds. Chiku and Pedro were offered the option of chinging into receptacle bodies, organic or mechanical, but Mecufi had cautioned them against visiting June in anything other than full fleshly embodiment. She was particular about that. So they went down by Maersk Intersolar shuttle, an arrowheaded transatmospheric vehicle built like a bathyscaphe.

The shuttle slid into the dayside atmosphere like a syringe, then flicked its hull to transparency. Gradually their angle of flight levelled out. It was all sleighride smooth. Chiku got up and walked around, leaving Pedro snoozing. They were still a long way up from the surface – forty hellish kilometres – but the pressure outside was already a frankly absurd two atmospheres. It was stormy, too, although the shuttle was smoothing out the turbulence long before it had a chance to upset the passengers. Venus was a machine for making bad weather. It took eight months to rotate on its axis, a planet with a day longer than its own year, but these wind-whipped clouds chased their tails around the planet in mere dozens of hours.

The gondola – the place where June was supposed to be – was called

Tekarohi High. They saw very little of it until the last few moments of the approach, the clouds thinning rather than parting, Tekarohi High looming like some gothic castle in a thunderstorm. It was a chubby cylinder the size of several skyscrapers lumped together. This habitable volume was only part of the structure. From the base, beneath a fringe of docking ledges and platforms, extended a tremendously strong guy-line that vanished into the underlying clouds, forty kilometres of cable anchoring the station to Venus's crust. Above, just as invisibly distant, were the monstrous balloons that held the platform aloft. Bracketed out from the main body of the platform were numerous turbines drawing power from the unending blast of the winds. Clearly they had more than enough for their purposes. Tekarohi High's hundreds of floors of windows were great flickering acres of neon.

They docked near the base, clamps securing the hovering shuttle, and then there was the usual tedium and delay before they could actually exit the shuttle and walk into the gondola. Beneath Chiku's feet, the floor felt as solid as if there was a planet right underneath, rather than forty kilometres of scalding, crushing carbon dioxide, delicately laced with sulphuric acid.

At odd intervals, wherever the internal architecture of the platform made it practical, the builders had set glass plates into the floor. Elsewhere, along corridors and viewing decks, stupendous armoured windows curved to horizontal near their bases, offering a view straight down. Outside was a shifting grey migraine. Views of the surface were occasionally possible at this altitude, apparently, but Chiku never saw anything she could definitively identify as something other than a figment of her own imagination. She kept thinking about that old caution against staring into the abyss.

'I think that's her,' Chiku said in a low voice.

They were drinking coffee in one of the observation lounges, clouds of sackcloth grey testing themselves against the windows, lightning storms pulsing somewhere deeper inside the weather system. Pedro followed her gaze to a small and exceedingly old-looking woman, impeccably dressed, in the company of two expensively groomed younger people. They were gathered around a low table, pointing into some invisible abstraction occupying the space between them, negotiating some fine point of business that might have had nothing at all to do with Venus.

'I don't know ...' Pedro said.

Chiku called up an aug query. This woman was not June Wing, according to the identifiers. But June had been a wily cyberneticist, exactly the sort of person who might have been able to move around under a false signifier.

'It must be her. The aug isn't placing her anywhere else in the station, so who else can that be?'

'The aug said she was here when we were on our way,' Pedro pointed out. 'Why would it change its mind?'

Eventually the woman stood, rising with the smooth motion that suggested she might be wearing an exo, and left the two younger people. Chiku considered following her, but she had not got very far with that thought when a tall gowned man in a fez loomed over their table.

'Chiku Akinya? I am Imris Kwami.'

Chiku tried to think of something clever to say, something that would give her the upper hand, but the moment failed her.

'Hello.'

'I doubt you've heard my name before,' Kwami said, easing his lengthy frame onto a vacant stool. He smiled at Pedro with a nod. 'If it had, you would probably have run an aug search on me as well as my employer.'

'You work for June?' Chiku asked.

'Yes. And I believe you were just about to approach that woman and ask her if she might be June?'

Chiku frowned. 'How did you know?'

'A hundred years of practice yields a certain level of competence in such matters.'

Chiku did not feel good about being this transparent, this open to interpretation. 'Then if that woman isn't June, what is she?'

'Nobody – and I mean that in the kindest possible sense. I am certain that she is actually a very nice lady. I would gladly say that she was a decoy we had employed for exactly that purpose, but if you had got a little nearer you would have seen that she really does not resemble June to any large degree.'

Pedro leaned in. 'Then where is she?'

'Downstairs,' Kwami said, as if this explained everything.

'I thought we were on the lowest level,' Chiku said, glancing down at the floor.

'That's a colloquialism, I think,' Pedro said.

'Correct, my young sir. June went down to the surface of Venus about twelve hours ago. I do not suppose you thought to confirm her whereabouts more recently than that?'

'She isn't in one of the domes, we know that much,' Chiku said.

'When I say surface, that is precisely my meaning. She is in a surface suit, on one of her scouting expeditions. This is why we have come to Venus. When she is done, we will leave.'

'I'm totally confused now,' Pedro said.

'I did some background reading on the way over,' Chiku said. 'She's collecting things, gathering them up for a museum or something.'

'Robotic relics of the early space age,' Kwami said, sweeping his hands overhead as if a banner floated above him. 'This is her mission in life, the latest of many. Perhaps the last and greatest of them all.'

'How long will she be down there?' Chiku asked.

'It could be many tens of hours. It is a very tedious business, travelling to and from the surface. You do not simply pop down there for a five-minute stroll.'

Pedro gave an easy shrug. 'We can easily wait a day or two, longer if necessary.'

'I am very happy for you, but I am afraid that is not how it works with my employer. She has left me with certain instructions, you see.' This strange, thin, jovial man of indeterminate age touched his nose and winked. 'You must understand that she is fully aware of your interest, your intentions, your approach on the loop-liner. She knows that there is more than one of you. She knows also that you have lately had contact with the merfolk.'

'I see,' Chiku said, with a small private shiver.

'June is very good at detecting interest in herself. You should not be surprised by this. You only have to *think* her name and she will know it. I exaggerate, of course, but only a little. A moment, please.' Kwami reached into a pocket and withdrew a small pale-green box. He popped the lid and extracted a lilac mote, which he then passed to Chiku. 'This was formulated by June. You may open it, if you wish.'

'We don't want much of her time,' Pedro said. 'If she knows as much about us as you say, then she also knows that. Also that we're not up to any funny business.'

'Of course, sir,' Kwami said, smiling. 'But I am afraid June was very particular in her wishes. If you wish to speak to her, you must join her down there. She may speak to you, or she may not, depending on her mood. But there is no other way.'

'We do need to speak,' Chiku said. She fingered the mote, unsure of the specific etiquette in this situation.

'Please,' Kwami encouraged.

She cracked the mote. As always, there was an instant before the cargo of emotions began to unpack itself. There was no warmth here, only a stern and forbidding prickliness. She sensed a provisional willingness to be approached, but only on June Wing's very specific terms. There would be no negotiation and she made no promises. There was also a continuous, low-level drone of constant background dread. It was not that June Wing was frightened, Chiku understood, but that she herself ought to be. The mote was a final warning, a chance to stop now before she went any deeper.

Know what you are getting into.

'Well, that's brightened my day,' Chiku said grimly.

'Your suits are already reserved, as well as an elevator slot,' Kwami replied. 'You can be on the surface in a jiffy.'

'People die down there, don't they?' Pedro asked.

'Only now and then,' Kwami said cheerfully.

CHAPTER THIRTEEN

The elevator was a black bobbin that travelled up and down Tekarohi's tethering cable. *Embarking for Cythera*, Chiku thought as they stepped aboard along with a small gaggle of fellow travellers. They were not wearing the surface suits yet, and the forty-kilometre descent would take long enough that the elevator came equipped with a small bar, lounge area and toilet facilities. There were two tiny windows, more like inspection ports than anything that would provide a view. Imris Kwami had waved them off with assurances that everything had been taken care of on the surface, and that the two suits would know where to go.

'Can we trust him?' she asked once they were under way, sliding down the cable at about two kilometres a minute. A display above the door showed increments of altitude, temperature, pressure.

'Bit late to be worrying about that now!' Pedro was fingering the table top, perhaps pondering a veneer or lamination that might be suitable for his purposes. His way of coping with the situation, Chiku thought.

It was not hers.

Yet down they went, the elevator made ominous little ticking sounds as it transitioned into denser and hotter atmosphere, like a submarine sinking into some acidic boiling trench of the deepest, blackest ocean. Everyone made a great show of not being fazed by these little structural complaints, not even when they amplified to clangs and thuds, as if some very angry thing, presently outside, was trying to break in.

Ten atmospheres . . . fifty . . . The elevator shook as they passed through some horsetail of wind shear. Then deeper still. Seventy atmospheres, eighty. Smoother now, heavier, as if the atmosphere itself was entirely too sluggish to bother with anything as frivolous as weather. There was only this one car shuttling up and down the tether, day in and day out, year after year. Chiku supposed it had become quite adept at handling these pressure changes by now. There was no boat as safe as an old boat, or so the saying went. Perhaps this rule could be safely ascribed to elevators as well, like the one in Santa Justa.

Eventually the car reached zero altitude. The view through the windows went dark as they slid into the anchorpoint compound on the surface. They were at ninety-five atmospheres, seven hundred and fifty kelvins of temperature.

The elevator halted and something clamped it tight. More clangs and clattering followed, and then the door opened. Chiku and Pedro followed the passengers out into the anchorpoint's receiving area. It was a starkly unwelcoming place, a little too warm, with dim industrial lighting, scabbed grey walls and a persistent rhythmic throb of air circulators. A musician sat cross-legged on carpets in one corner, attempting to tune a kora. Or perhaps, Chiku decided, this was his actual playing style.

Some passengers with expensive luggage were haranguing a tourist official, complaining that the bus to take them to the nearest domed community was running hours late. Their items of luggage, as eager to be moving as their owners, squabbled among themselves. Some other passengers were waiting to go back up the tether, sitting on metal benches or hovering around one or other of the food concessions. Someone was asleep, stretched out on a bench with their coat over their head. Their snoring, Chiku realised, was the source of the annoying rhythmic throb. It had nothing to do with air circulators.

The suiting area was down one long, sloping tunnel, then up another. When they arrived, someone else was being helped into their suit, which was assembled around them like some contraption of Medieval torture. The process involved robots and winches and complex power tools. Chiku had never seen anything quite as barbaric as a Venus surface suit.

'Why would anyone bother with these things?' Pedro asked. 'Aren't they happy going out in a rover, with some nice seats and a bar?'

'It's for the bragging rights, mainly,' Chiku said. 'So they can say they've done something more dangerous and real than their friends.'

'Even if they run a real risk of dying?'

'That's the downside.'

'I can think of another. Would now be the right time to mention that I'm very slightly claustrophobic?'

'No.'

'I didn't think so. It's all right for you, though – you've had plenty of time in spacesuits.'

'Not like these, Noah. Even the junk we had to wear in Kappa were more comfortable than these look.'

'I wouldn't know,' Pedro said, a certain terseness colouring his tone.

'And for the record, I'm not Noah. Noah is not your husband. Noah is the husband of Chiku Green, this *other* woman I've never met, and never want to meet.'

'Sorry,' she said. 'I didn't mean—'

'Never mind,' he said, with obviously forced magnanimity. 'I suppose it's to be expected, when you go around swapping memories like pairs of gloves.'

Chiku thought better of responding.

The suits were essentially ambulatory tanks. They were gloss white, like lobsters dipped in milk. They had no faceplates, just camera apertures. Instead of hands they had claws. Their cooling systems were multiply redundant. That was the critical safety measure, Chiku learned in the briefing. Death by pressure was so rare that it had only happened a few times in the entire history of Venus exploration. But hundreds, thousands, had died of heat shock when their coolers overloaded.

Once they were installed in the suits, they spent a few minutes learning basic skills such as walking and object manipulation. Chiku kept flashing back to her time in Kappa, how easy it had been compared to these hulking contraptions. On the other hand, she now felt invulnerable.

That confidence faded as soon as the airlock doors slammed shut behind them and the atmosphere roared in. As temperature and pressure climbed to surface norms, the suit told her how much work it was having to do to keep her comfortable. Like the elevator, it issued noises of protestation. Systems pushed from green into amber. There was very little cooling capacity to spare once the suit was running at normal workload.

The outer doors opened and they waddled across a parking area to their waiting rover, which was essentially a chassis on wheels. They climbed aboard and assumed standing position within railed enclosures. The vehicle appeared to know where to take them. They rolled up a ramp into the searing, overcast oppression of noon on Venus. The terrain was not alien to Chiku's eyes – she had seen mountain areas just as arid as this on Earth, with a similar undramatic topography. The ground was rocky, broken, strewn with boulders and the fragments of boulder. No vegetation, of course, and no evidence that any liquids had ever flowed here. The colours, relayed through the suit's camera systems, were muted, greys and ochres and off-whites, a smear of paling yellow dusting everything, like a layer of old varnish that had begun to discolour.

The rover traversed a winding track, rocks and debris bulldozed into loose flanks along either side. Chiku swivelled around, still nervous of damaging the suit, and spied the anchorpoint from which they had emerged. She watched the bobbin of the elevator slide up the taut whip line of the tether until it was lost in the murk of a low cloud deck. These conditions were optimal on Venus: low clouds, no sky, visibility down to a couple of kilometres.

At length, the rover steered off the main track onto a rougher trail that wound around the side of a dormant volcano, and then they came downslope into a broad depression hemmed on all sides by cracked terrain, fissured in concentric and radial patterns like the wrinkled skin around an elephant's eye. This spider-web feature, according to the terrain overlay, was called an arachnoid, caused by the deformation and relaxation of the surface under the strain of upwelling magma. Aside from the road itself and the odd transponder pole or piece of broken rover, there was scant evidence of human presence beyond the compound. Near the base of the depression, gleaming in the perpetual half-light, was another vehicle. Like their own rover, it was an open chassis on wheels. It had parked on a gentle slope. Not far from it, further down the slope, was another figure in a Venus suit, attending to something on the ground, almost in the shade of an overhanging cliff a few tens of metres high, formed where one part of the arachnoid had sunk or elevated itself relative to the other.

'June,' Chiku said, excited and apprehensive at the same time. 'It's her. There's even an aug tag.'

'Open the general channel, see if she'll talk,' Pedro said.

'Of course she'll talk. We came all the way here, didn't we?' But she opened the channel anyway. 'June Wing? It's Chiku Akinya. I think you're expecting us.'

A voice said: 'Park by my rover, then get out and walk over to me, very carefully. I don't want you stomping all over this site like a couple of gorillas.'

'Thrilled to meet you, too,' Pedro said under his breath, but doubtless loud enough that June would have heard it.

Chiku took manual control and halted the rover by the other vehicle. They stepped out of their enclosures and lowered carefully down onto the Venusian surface. The atmosphere of Venus laid siege to her suit, probing its defences for a weakness.

'Thank you for agreeing to see us,' Chiku said as they made their way downslope.

'I agreed to nothing.'

'But Mister Kwami said—'

'Unless Imris Kwami was failing in his responsibilities, which after a century of employment seems highly unlikely, he made no promises on my behalf. I told him to make it clear that if you didn't visit me here, you'd have no hope of speaking to me when I returned to the gondola.'

'I opened your mote.'

'Good for you. What you chose to read into it is your business, not mine.'

'We're here, aren't we?' Pedro asked.

'Evidently.'

'Mister Kwami told me that you were aware of my dealings with the seasteaders,' Chiku said. 'If that's the case, then you'll also have a shrewd idea what Mecufi and his friends want from you.'

'The Panspermians, or whatever they're calling themselves this week, burnt their bridges with Arethusa two hundred years ago,' June declared. 'It's a little late now to be seeking rapprochement.'

Chiku said, 'Regardless, they'd like to make contact again, if they can. Are you still in touch with her?'

'What do you think?'

'I'm guessing it's highly likely, if Arethusa's still alive. And you should definitely speak to me. You knew my mother and father. You helped them.'

'That was a long time ago.'

Chiku and Pedro had come within a few paces of the other suited figure. June was examining something on the ground. The suits' articulation did not allow kneeling, but by bowing at the waist and extending the telescopic forearms, the wearer could handle rocks and other objects. June was busy with a piece of buckled metal about the size of a beach ball, partially dug into the ground as if it had rammed into it at speed.

'The thing is—' Chiku started saying.

'Do you want to help, or are you just going to stand there gawping?'

Chiku moved around to the side, keeping her distance from June's backpack. The glowing exhaust vents were rimmed cherry red, a heat haze boiling off them.

'What is it?' Chiku asked doubtfully, not sure she wanted the answer.

'Remains of a Russian probe. Been here the thick end of four centuries, just waiting to be found. I've been coming back to this area for years, convinced it had to be around here somewhere.'

'Pretty lucky to find it like that,' Pedro said.

'Luck had nothing to do with it, just years of thorough searching and patient elimination. The radar reflection is very poor due to this overhang – reason everyone else missed it. Here, Chiku – help me lever it out.'

'Is it worth anything?'

'It's a priceless piece of early space-age history.'

'And you just happened to find it now?' Pedro asked sceptically.

'I *found* it eighteen months ago, but my competitors were breathing down my neck. I had to bluff, let them think there was nothing here. Continued searching somewhere else, drawing them away from this search area. Appeared to abandon my efforts – I've been on Mars lately, or as near as anyone dares get these days. Then I pounced back here, quicker than they can react. And now I have my prize.'

'Nearly,' Chiku said.

The thing began to loosen. It was as heavy as a boulder; she could sense as much even through the suit's amplification. And then it pulled free, a buckled sphere, scorched and dented, scabbed with corrosion, like a cannonball that had been at the bottom of the ocean since the middle ages. On its side, in lettering so faded it was barely legible, was the inscription *CCCP*.

Chiku wondered what it meant.

'Well done,' June said. 'Now help me get it aboard the truck.'

She meant the other rover. Between them they carried the mangled thing to the vehicle's rear cargo platform. June lowered it into a sturdy white box with a padded interior, then closed the lid. 'I'll hold it at Venus surface pressure until I know there are no air pockets inside it. A hundred atmospheres can really put a dent in your day.'

'Mecufi said something about you gathering pieces for a collection,' Chiku said, hoping that some small talk might break the ice. 'When we spoke to Imris Kwami, he said it was to do with robot relics or something?'

'My museum, yes.' June was tapping commands into the box's external panel. 'I'm assembling artefacts of the early robotic space age before they fall through the chinks in history. You'd be amazed how much stuff is still out here, waiting to be forgotten. Not much in the inner solar system, it's true – although there are still spent booster stages on Sun-circling orbits, if you know where to look. But I'm not really interested in dumb rocketry. I want robots, probes, things with a rudimentary intelligence. *Very* rudimentary, in this case. But you can't make sharp distinctions. It's like poking through the bones of early hominids. There's no one point at which we stopped being monkeys and started being human.' She patted the box with one of her suit's claws. 'And *this* unprepossessing thing is still part of the lineage. It has some circuitry, some crude decision-action branching. That puts it on the path to intelligence, albeit rather a long way from artilects and Providers.'

'You've led a long and interesting life,' Chiku said. 'Is this something you've always wanted to do?'

'Someone has to organise and document this stuff, so it may as well be me. Your great-grandmother wasn't exactly one for sitting around when there was work to be done, was she?'

Chiku chose her words with great care. 'Actually, it's funny you should mention Eunice.'

'I thought you came to ask me about Arethusa.'

'We did,' Pedro said.

'Well, you've done what the Pans asked. You can tell them that if Arethusa wanted to speak to them, she'd have already done so.'

'I'm not just here because of the merfolk,' Chiku said.

June walked around to the rover's control platform, and prepared to step aboard. 'What, then? The scenery? The balmy airs?'

'I've made contact with my great-grandmother.'

'Nice. No, really – I'm very pleased. And what did she have to say? That Saint Peter sends his best regards and everything's lovely on the other side? I've got the right religion, haven't I?'

'I met the Tantors.'

There was a silence. June did not move. She looked frozen there, locked into geologic stillness, destined to merge back into the landscape. Chiku glanced at Pedro. She wondered if she had made a terrible miscalculation.

Finally, June said: 'Repeat what you just said to me.'

'I've met the Tantors. And I've spoken to the construct aboard the holoship.'

'I have an interest in *Zanzibar*. I monitor the feeds. I keep up with events. No one knows about the Tantors. They are not public knowledge. They are not even on the edge of being a rumour.'

'There was an accident, a blow-out in one of our chambers. I mean, one of theirs. I made some investigations ... I mean Chiku Green, the version of me on the holoship.' She gave up. It was just too difficult to separate the two versions of herself. 'I found my way to Chamber Thirty-Seven, at the front of *Zanzibar* – the chamber no one knows about. I met the construct, the artilect simulation of my great-grandmother. The one *you* helped to come into being and helped smuggle aboard the holoship, to look after the Tantors. She's been there ever since, waiting. You can't ignore me now, can you? There's only one way I could have learned all this.'

132

After a moment. June asked, 'How is she?'

'Still alive, obviously, but damaged. Her memory's totally screwed up and she barely remembers anything that happened before *Zanzibar* beyond the fact that you helped her when she was in trouble – when she was hiding, running from something.'

'The Cognition Police, most likely – she was an unlicensed artilect.'

'More than that,' Chiku said. 'She gave me a name, and—'

'Not here,' June said before Chiku could utter another word.

'I'm asking for your help. If not for me, then for my mother. You helped Sunday and Jitendra, all those years ago.'

'Did your mother tell you about the Tantors? She was at least theoretically aware of their existence.'

'No. I haven't spoken to her in years. No one has.'

'What an exceedingly odd family you come from.'

'Thanks. If I could have chosen another one, I would have. But this isn't about me. It's about what you and your friends set in motion. These are the consequences; now you have to deal with them.'

'You think I don't know about consequences?'

'If we shouldn't talk here,' Pedro said, 'where would you suggest?'

'Wait.' A pause, then: 'Imris? It's me. Yes, very well. Yes, I met both of them – they're with me right now, along with the find. Yes, packed and loaded – we can be on our way back immediately.' To Chiku, she said: 'How did you get here? Your own ship?'

'We're not that flash,' Chiku said. 'We came by shuttle, off the loop-liner.'

'Imris, prep *Gulliver* for immediate dust-off. We'll be back at the anchorpoint in an hour, aboard the gondola inside two.'

'We're leaving?' Chiku asked.

'I think it's best if we talk aboard my ship. We'll worry about getting you back to Earth later. Oh, and about being flash: you've owned more ships than I've owned shoes.'

'I mean lately.'

'Then say what you mean.'

The rovers could only carry two passengers, so Chiku and Pedro returned to their own vehicle and let it trundle on behind June's, retracing the route they had taken from the anchorpoint.

'What was it like on the holoship?' June asked once they had climbed out of the arachnoid depression, back onto the highlands. 'I came very close to moving aboard, when *Zanzibar* set off, but I felt that my talents would be put to better use back here.'

'Collecting old space junk?' Pedro asked.

'You have a very blunt turn of phrase, don't you?'

Chiku threw Pedro a warning glance and said, 'They have some difficult times ahead of them. Resource allocation, tensions within the local caravan, that whole stupid slowdown thing.'

'I heard about *Pemba*,' June said. 'But then, who didn't? Something that bad, it makes the headlines. They were idiots to bet against physics.'

'Physics looked like it was on their side, for a little while, at least,' Chiku said.

'Physics couldn't care less.'

'It was a terrible accident, but no reason to close down all the research programmemes. On the other hand, it doesn't seem at all fair that we're having to do all this on our own. The holoships were a project for the whole solar civilisation, a gesture for the ages. And there used to be research programmemes going on back here, not just in the caravan – labs and facilities all working on the Chibesa problem. But back home, you've given up, left us to solve the problem on our own. Essentially, we've been hung out to dry.'

'You and *us*. That's an interesting perspective. As if your moral reference frame was that of the Chiku on the holoship, not the one I am speaking to.'

'She gets confused,' Pedro said. 'You should hear what she called me earlier.'

'The physics programmes here were expensive, dangerous and getting nowhere,' June said. 'That's the *only* reason they were shut down. You mentioned Sunday, Chiku – are things really that bad with her?'

'She's made her own choices.'

'Mathematics is a terrible calling. It's as merciless as gravity. It swallows the soul. There's a point near a black hole called the last stable orbit. Once you drop below that radius, no force in the universe can stop you falling all the way in. That's what happened to your mother – she swam too close to theory, fell below the last stable orbit. It must be terribly hard on your father.'

'They were happy together.' But she had seen Jitendra's awesome, oceanic sadness. Yes, there were good days, when Sunday's mind returned to the shallows, but far more when she was not there at all.

'Perhaps she'll surface again, one day,' said June. 'We must wish the best for your mother. Ah, wait. What's this?'

'I don't know.'

An alarm tone had begun to sound in Chiku's helmet and a red status sigil had begun to throb angrily in her visual field, but the suit's life-support and locomotive functions were not registering any problems.

'There doesn't seem to be anything wrong with me or my suit.'

'We're all getting it,' Pedro said. 'It's not our suits.'

'They're sending it to everyone outside,' June said.

A voice, maybe a recording, was saying: 'General surface order, Teka-rohi Sector. Emergency measures are in force. Return immediately to anchorpoint. Repeat, return immediately to anchorpoint. Observe all environmental precautions. This is *not* a drill. Repeat, *this is not a drill*.'

'What's happening?' Pedro asked.

'Something less than optimal,' June said. 'Seismic activity, maybe. Al-though they usually have days of warning before anything big.'

'Is that likely?' Chiku asked. She remembered something about the surface of Venus being constantly renewed by upwellings, scrubbed clean of craters. Stand still long enough and eventually the ground you were on would be resurfaced, smothered under a cooling blanket of ash and magma. This had been going on for mindless aeons.

'It's been hundreds of years since there were any eruptions or lava flows in Tekarohi Sector,' June said, 'so it's not *likely* that something would happen just as we show up.'

Pedro asked. 'Can you raise Imris?'

'I'm trying, but all local comms are blocked for the moment. They're pushing that warning through on all channels. *That's* odd in itself – there should still be ample capacity. You know what? I'm starting not to like this.'

The message was repeating, reiterating the injunction to return to the anchorpoint. It would be safe in there, Chiku thought – whatever was happening, or was about to happen. Certainly there were few places *less* safe than being out on the surface of Venus, in a suit that had to work itself into a frenzy just to stop her from cooking. Some animal instinct was driving her back to the burrow. She wanted to be indoors, under-ground, where it was cool and dark and the world was not trying to turn her into a pancake.

'Your competitors,' she said. 'Could they be trying to mess things up?'

'Not really their style. Getting a jump on me, yes. Putting out fake emergency warnings? That would be new territory for them. Not to mention massively illegal and likely to cause loss of life.'

'What should we do?' Pedro asked.

'I think we should do as we're told. We were going back to the anchor-point anyway, and if there really is a problem ... well, we don't want to be stuck outside in these suits.'

'Exactly what I was thinking,' Chiku said.

'The suits' active cooling systems draw a lot of power and I don't know how long we'd have before the cells need replenishing. You can't count on rescue coming quickly around here.'

'I hate this planet,' Chiku decided.

'Welcome to Venus. She's a real bitch.'

'You sound like my great-grandmother.'

'We must have had a similar outlook on life. Oh, wait – comms appear to be loosening up. It's Imris. Do you mind if we go private for a few seconds?'

'Be our guest,' Chiku said.

When she was done, June said, 'There's a problem with the gondola. As a precaution, they're evacuating everyone from the surface back to orbit.'

'Wouldn't they be safer down here?' Chiku asked.

'Depends. If things really do go wrong up there, they won't be able to send help down to us if we run into trouble. Getting up and out while we can may be the sensible option.'

'What about Imris – is he going to be all right?'

'He's taking as many people with him as he can squeeze aboard *Gulliver*. I've told him not to wait for us – we'll take our chances with the regular evacuees.'

'What kind of problem are we talking about?' Chiku asked.

'Supply shuttle came in at a bad angle, hit some turbulence, managed to sever or tangle part of the rigging. That's the official picture, anyway. The lift is compromised, but they're dropping ballast to stabilise the gondola. Should be able to hold altitude for some while.'

'And that would be how long, exactly?' Chiku asked.

'Hours, easily. Plenty of time for the elevator to go up and down a few times, while shuttles ferry people from the gondola back to the orbital stations.'

'There's the anchorpoint,' Pedro said. 'We're practically home and dry.'

'I love the sound of a man tempting fate,' June said.

Nothing about the anchorpoint hinted that there might be problems at the other end of the tether, forty kilometres overhead. The cable was as taut as when they had descended, the elevator sliding smoothly back up into the flat underbelly of cloud, an ochre mattress pressing down from the sky, stuffed with poison. They were not the only tourists scuttling back to cover, Chiku saw – other rovers and suits were converging on the anchorpoint facility from several directions.

Chiku felt as if her world had slipped a gear. 'Is this ... normal?'

'Is what normal?' June said.

'Shuttles crashing into things. Gondolas being evacuated. Particularly right now, just when we happen to be on Venus.'

'Does it *sound* normal to you?'

'You said it can't be your competitors, so is it something to do with us, with the reason we came to Venus?'

'That would attach rather a lot of significance to your actions, wouldn't it?' But June's tone suggested to Chiku that she had not ruled out that scenario.

There was a queue to enter the rover parking area, suits and vehicles jostling down the ramp, and then they had to wait their turn for the airlocks. Chiku counted the minutes. Years of her life had passed more swiftly. From her perspective, the elevator looked as if it had begun to shoot up the thread faster than before. She wondered how many passengers it could take at a time, how many round trips would be needed. Under normal circumstances, the surface of a planet was the safest place you could be. But these were far from normal circumstances, Chiku reflected.

'Imris again,' June said as they eased their machines into the disembarkation point. 'Evacuation's proceeding smoothly. They've lost a little altitude, but they're still a long way above crush depth. Be happy that they built that thing with a lot of safety margins.'

'Any more information on what happened?' Pedro asked.

'Picture's still fuzzy. They're sending robots out to examine the rigging. They may be able to disentangle things, clear away the shuttle's wreckage, maybe deploy an emergency balloon to restore optimum buoyancy.'

June asked Chiku to help her unload the storage box from the back of her rover and they carried it into the airlock between them.

It was the biggest airlock Chiku had ever seen, but it could still only handle three Venus suits at a time. The process of atmosphere exchange felt like some over-elaborate ritual. Expelling one hundred atmospheres, initiating toxin purge and temperature cool-down all took time. It had not taken anywhere near as long when they went out.

At last, robots and support staff bustled in to scrub them down and help them out of the suits. It turned out that they were the last to return. No one else was out there now, at least not within range of the anchorpoint. Chiku was the first out of her armour, keeping an eye on the storage box as the robots and technicians fussed over June.

Chiku was still wondering what their new companion was going to look like in the flesh. She might only be half as old again as Chiku, but that extra century was crucial. Chiku had been born into a time when all the big blunders in prolongation therapy had already been made. The lives of June Wing and Eunice Akinya were expeditions into un-mapped territory. All they had had was blind luck and a dogged faith in their own medical intuition, and they had done well to make it this far. Chiku had seen a couple of extremely old persons, somewhere in the solar system, or perhaps on the holoship. One had been all hunched and wispy-haired, and at first she had mistaken them for a tame orangu-tan. The other, cocooned inside some kind of life-support pram, she had assumed was a baby with some unfortunate congenital affliction. She half-expected June to be even more decrepit. Three hundred and three years – that was a good age for trees.

But here was June, being extracted from her suit, and there had been some mistake, obviously, some mix-up outside, because this was not a three-hundred-year-old organism. This was a normal-looking woman, grey-haired and visibly older than Chiku, but not by so much that she looked as if she had climbed out of a gerontology textbook. This was no relic from the dawn of history who just happened to have lucked her way into the present.

June hopped down from the suiting platform. She wore black trousers, a black blouse with a high collar, a jewelled clasp at her throat her only ornamentation. Her skin was tanned, wrinkled and mottled in mildly interesting ways. Her reflexes looked sharp, and her bones showed no sign of shattering as she touched down in nine-tenths of a gee.

'So – where were we?' said June.

'I was expecting …' But Chiku could think of no way to end that sentence that would not make her sound fatuous. 'What do you want to do with the box?'

'I doubt they'll let us take up valuable space in the elevator, unless we're the last to go.' June smoothed down her hair where the helmet had mussed it. She wore it in a short bob that covered her ears. 'Anyway, it's locked and tagged,' she went on. 'I can come back for it, if the worst happens.'

'I'm curious what scenario would be "the worst" from your perspective.'

Pedro stepped up before June could reply. 'We should go through, see how long we have to wait.' He was focused on working stiffness out of his shoulder and did not see June at first, standing behind Chiku. 'Oh, hello, June – I mean, Ms Wing. It feels as if we haven't really met until now.'

'We haven't, but I think we can dispense with the pleasantries for now.'

They returned to the main holding area, which was a lot less busy than it had been earlier. Other than Chiku, Pedro, June and the three service staff who had accompanied them from the suiting area, there were only six other people present. They were watching the elevator's progress on the panel over the door, tracking its return to the gondola. The emergency system was still repeating the message they had heard earlier, and red bars and panels were flashing in the walls, floor and ceiling.

'Not far to go,' Chiku said.

'They'll unload quickly,' one of the service staff told her, perhaps thinking she needed reassurance. 'Empty, they drop like a stone – shouldn't take more than ten minutes to get back to us, and then we're out of here.'

'Evacuation status?' June queried.

'Proceeding smoothly. There'll be a shuttle docked and ready by the time we're topside. Any luck, in a few hours this is all going to look like a massive over-reaction. If the 'bots can stabilise the flotation, we'll be able to stand down from emergency condition.'

June held up a hand. 'Wait. I'm hearing from Imris again.' Her face assumed the slack composure of aug trance, as if someone had just snipped all the nerves under her skin. After a minute she nodded gravely, took a deep breath. 'Well, that puts a different sheen on things. I don't think we'll be needing that elevator now, thanks.'

'What's going on?' Pedro asked.

'They haven't managed to stabilise the gondola. Apparently, the robots they sent out to fix the rigging have managed to make things *worse*, not better. According to Imris, the gondola is sinking faster than before. There's no chance of stabilising it now. It's coming down.'

'How deep can they go?' Pedro asked.

The technician said, 'Twenty, thirty atmospheres shouldn't be a problem. But fifty's pushing it, and it's definitely not engineered to survive surface pressure.'

Chiku shook her head. 'This is too much of a coincidence for it to be an accident. It's connected to Arethusa, or the construct, or something, isn't it?'

'It's not about us,' Pedro said. 'We're not the ones on that thing, sinking down into the atmosphere.'

'We're not,' June said, 'but if something up there wanted to hurt us indirectly, that's one excellent way of going about it.'

'Something wants to hurt us?' the technician asked, frowning.

'Private conversation,' she said, creasing out a smile. And then she clapped her hands and raised her voice. 'Everyone – minor change of plan! In light of recent information, we probably don't want to be under the drop zone for much longer.'

'It's got forty kilometres to fall,' said one of the other passengers, a burly European with a thatch of coppery hair. 'What are the odds of it landing right on top of us, with the winds and everything?'

'Very low odds indeed,' June said brightly. 'But wherever that gondola falls, the tether's still anchored to this facility. Now, do you really want to take a chance that there aren't going to be complications when that thing comes hammering down, like god's own bullwhip?'

'It won't be that bad,' one of the technicians said. 'It's just a cable—'

'Fine,' said June. 'Anyone who *doesn't* want to play physics roulette – there are Venus suits waiting for us. There are enough for all of us, aren't there?'

'I think so,' the technician said. 'I mean, yes, there should be.'

'*Should* be?'

'We have twenty suits, but there's a mandatory maintenance cycle. They won't all be available.'

'There are twelve of us,' June said, looking around at the party. 'I'm pretty sure I saw more than twelve suits out there earlier, when we were waiting to come back in.'

'It's got to be worth a try,' Pedro said.

'Imris again,' June said, after slipping into aug trance for a moment. '*Gulliver* is detached, he has evacuees aboard and is monitoring the gondola's descent. Sounds like they've lost another balloon ... we're looking at fifteen minutes, twenty if we're lucky. Shall we adjourn? Venus is *so* lovely at this time of year.'

The others needed little persuasion. By then even the anchorpoint staff had given up on any hope of using the elevator. The tether was screaming anxious error conditions as the stress loadings went off the scale. As they made their way to the suiting area, Chiku's thoughts flashed back to when they were waiting their turn to come back inside. She had definitely seen other people besides them in suits, but she could not swear she had seen twelve altogether. Had June just been saying that to hurry them along?

There were several independent suiting rooms, each of which contained three or four suits. It was not immediately clear, to Chiku's eyes, which units were ready to use and which were off-line for overhaul. Prior to being worn, they were partly dismantled anyway, broken down into huge white eggshell sections.

'Impact in ... somewhere somewhere between sixteen and twenty minutes,' June reported. 'Imris would like to be more precise, but there are a lot of variables.'

'Can't he bring that ship down here and let us board from the airlock?' asked one of the other tourists, hands on her hips.

'Not unless you fancy squeezing inside a lump of buckled metal the diameter of a drainpipe,' June said.

'We have a problem,' said one of the technicians.

June smiled tightly. 'And my day just keeps on improving.'

'Suit availability is … less than optimal.'

'Don't sugar the pill.' Her tone was ferociously sweet. 'What are we looking at? Quick – we need five minutes just to suit up, then we still have to clear the airlock.'

'We need twelve functioning suits,' said the technician. 'We have six good to go. Three more are marginal: they came in with faults, which would normally send them straight into maintenance, but in an emergency we can override those errors and force the suits outside. The rest are … too far into the tear-down-and-rebuild cycle. Except for one, maybe, but even that—'

June said, 'So we have nine suits, which is three fewer than we need. And the clock's still ticking.'

'Staying here isn't an automatic death sentence!' said the passenger with the coppery hair. 'It's a question of risk-management, that's all. I'll take my chances indoors.'

'So that's two suits fewer than we need,' said the technician. 'Fine – I'll take my chances here as well. Now we're only short one unit. Anyone up for drawing straws?'

'I'll remain here,' June said, with an easy little shrug, as if nothing much was at stake. 'Now we're good. Nine suits, nine happy campers.'

'Nine what?' Chiku asked.

'You can't stay here,' said the woman who had asked about Imris. 'Not after you made such a big song and dance about how important it is for us to use the suits.'

'I still think the best odds involve going outside,' June said, with magnificent equanimity. 'However, it's your decision, not mine. I choose to sacrifice my position. I'm three hundred and three years old – at this point, every breath's a blessing.'

'I don't believe you. This is some kind of—'

'Trick? Yes, I've *tricked* you into an increased chance of survival – how utterly, utterly thoughtless and reprehensible of me. Look, we're probably down to six minutes by now, maybe less. Do you really want to waste more of them arguing the finer points of personal morality?'

'This isn't right,' Chiku said. 'We need you ... *I* need you. I came here to find you. We can't just leave you here.'

'Chiku, will you come here for a moment? The rest of you – decide among yourselves who's staying and who isn't, but make it snappy.'

Chiku was breathing hard. She wanted to be outside now, getting as far away as possible from this place. She couldn't imagine herself making June's awesome abdication. 'It might not be too bad—' she started saying.

'We'll know soon enough. Regardless, you need to listen to me very carefully. I'm glad you came to Venus, and that you told me about Eunice and the Tantors. But now we have a problem.'

'Yes,' Chiku said, looking at the ceiling, imagining the gondola dropping down on them like a million-tonne chandelier. Sliding down through the clouds of Venus, gathering speed by the second.

'A much bigger problem than this little debacle,' June said sternly. 'The thing you were about to mention out there – I'm pretty sure it knows what you've learned from your clone-sister. This is Arachne's doing – she's protecting herself the only way she can.'

Chiku thought back to her conversations on the holoship, to Eunice's dark conviction that an artilect called Arachne had infected her with a wasting virus and pursued her into hiding.

'Then you know what's going on.'

'I know parts of the story, maybe enough to fill in some of the missing pieces. But we don't have time to swap anecdotes now. You *must* survive this, Chiku, then make contact with Imris. It shouldn't be too difficult – he'll be looking for us, one way or another. And when you see him, you give him a message from me.'

'What message?'

'A code. Pleistocene, grapefruit, rococo. Can you remember those three words? Pleistocene, grapefruit, rococo.'

Chiki repeated the words. 'What do they mean?'

'Authorisation.' She held up a finger before Chiku could interrupt. 'Imris will understand. Then tell him that you must make contact with Arethusa, and Imris will take care of the rest. You can trust her implicitly, tell her everything you know about this business. But be careful, Chiku – more careful than you've ever been in your life.'

'What about Crucible?'

'Crucible is a lie. What we think is there ... it's not the truth, or at least not all of it. The data arriving from that world is false. Whatever

Zanzibar and the other holoships think they're going to find when they arrive ... it isn't real.'

Chiku shook her head. 'You can't know this for certain. And if it's true, why haven't you told anyone?'

'To know that something is a lie ... that's not enough. I needed to find the truth Arachne has concealed behind the lie, whatever it might be. That's what I've been doing all these years – patiently, quietly, beneath the radar of her scrutiny. Obviously, I've been managing fairly well until now. But it's not your fault. I always guessed she'd find me eventually.'

'This is too much. I can't just *leave* you here, knowing all this.'

'You can and you will. And perhaps I'll survive. But those three words, Chiku – don't forget them.'

Chiku swallowed. 'Pleistocene, grapefruit, rococo.'

'Very good. Now run along and get into your suit. There can't be much time left now.'

'I'm sorry, June.'

'Don't be. I'm extremely glad we finally met. Now go.'

Chiku nodded, took June's hands in hers for a moment, then returned to the suiting area. Her head was ringing with the implications of what she had just been told. But there was no time right now to think any of it through, not until they were safe.

The others had agreed to draw lots for the suits. Someone had fetched nine coffee stirrers from one of the concessions, of which three had been shortened to represent the defective suits. Chiku drew her stirrer and ended up with one of the good suits. Pedro chose one of the compromised units, an arrangement he accepted with cheery indifference. There was no arguing, no swapping of suits. They had all agreed to accept the verdict of the draw.

June and the two other stay-behinds helped with the final phase of suiting. Chiku and Pedro were among the last to leave. June gave Chiku's suited arm an encouraging pat, sending her toward the airlock. They were running an emergency protocol this time, flooding the lock with Venus atmosphere instantly without first withdrawing the breathable air. They were finally on their way up and out, into the dismal brightness of high noon on Venus.

The technicians knew the prevailing winds and estimated that the gondola would fall somewhere along a forty-kilometre track dictated by the wind vector. So they steered the rovers away from the vector, driving hard, maintaining a straight line as well as the terrain permitted. By now Chiku had lost all sense of how much time was likely remaining, whether they had seconds or minutes. She glanced back and saw that the tether was still angling away from the top of the anchorpoint at forty-five degrees to vertical, maybe fifty. That was good, she told herself. It was an arrow pointing through the clouds, telling them where the gondola had to be. They were already well out of danger, provided the winds held. Even June ought to be safe, if the gondola fell as far downwind as it appeared to be heading.

Then the angle of the tether increased, fifty, five-five degrees, as fast as the second-hand on a watch. Chiku watched it with mesmerised fascination. If the tether was tens of kilometres long, then the object at the end of it was now falling a lot faster than before – not just descending, but plummeting. Something catastrophic must have happened to the gondola, the final failure of its balloons, or perhaps the collapse of the entire structure in the inexorable iron crush of the atmosphere. Or perhaps the tether had simply snapped and was now lashing down under its own weight, while the winds tore the gondola even further away.

A moment later, the tether appeared to vanish, as if it had been ripped free from the ground. It was an illusion. The tether was still plugged into the anchorpoint, but it had whipcracked, blurring like a plucked guitar string, and the energy contained in the tether now had nowhere to go but back into the anchorpoint.

The end ripped free. The tether was gone. Chiku watched nuggets of metal and carbon and concrete smear the sky. And then something as horrible as it was transient – a thing like a whirlpool, carved out of air, corkscrewing in the sky above the anchorpoint. It was glass-edged, betrayed by its own turbulence. It lived for a second, maybe two, then snapped out of existence. Venus, reclaiming the little pocket of Earth the humans had dug into its crust.

It was June dying.

A moment later, Chiku felt an impact shudder through the rover's floor – the seismic record of the gondola ramming down, the heaviest thing to hit Venus in recorded history. The crust here was a thin scurf of rock over restless oceans of magma. It tremored, wobbled, the roiling magma beneath it poised to burst through at any moment. Across the planet's single tectonic plate, measuring devices spiked alarmingly. Nothing like this had been registered in decades.

Gradually the ground vibrations abated and Venus returned to stillness. No magma had broken through anywhere near them. The air above the anchorpoint had quietened, the tether lying slack on the ground. Chiku did not want to think about what it had been like for

144

June and the others. Quick, she hoped. But sooner or later, rescuers would need to send suits or robots into the remains of the anchorpoint to extract the dead.

Chiku, Pedro and the seven other survivors were barely out of harm's way themselves. The rovers had carried them ten kilometres from the anchorpoint along another bulldozed trail before emergency advisories told them that rescue was on the way. People and machines were travelling to them overland from surface settlements, but the nearest of those were more than eight hundred kilometres away. At the same time, hardened shuttles were preparing to drop suited rescuers and proxies nearer to the disaster site. The closest gondolas were sending assistance down their tethers, but again, the overland distances between their anchorpoints and the survivors were as immense and incomprehensible as the gaps between galaxies. The odds were against them surviving until help reached them.

But it transpired that a different sort of help was on its way. Providers had been tasked with a construction project only a couple of hundred kilometres from the anchorpoint and the huge armoured robots were approaching in seven-league strides.

Chiku thought of the Providers she had seen on Earth, like the pair supervising the renewal of the bridge over the Tagus. Machines so huge and slow that sometimes they became part of the landscape, a background feature the eye edited out. There were thousands of them on Earth, assisting with the most arduous projects – new cities, aqueducts, roads and spaceports. Tens of thousands more were spread throughout the solar system – machines big enough to move mountains, almost literally.

And they were on Crucible, too, she reflected. As soon as their seed packages reached the ground, they had erupted from them like a busy silver putrescence. The putrescence organised itself into rudimentary machinery, and the machinery gorged on matter and fashioned bigger and more complicated versions of itself. So the process continued until giants strode the new Earth. These juggernauts had begun to tame Crucible, laying the foundations for new cities and towns. They had initiated remote study of the Mandala object, transmitting better images than could ever be obtained across interstellar distances. The robots' mission was to observe and record. Detailed scans and physical examination of the Mandala would be left to the humans.

Chiku had seen the images herself. She had sat with Ndege and Mposi, explaining these distant wonders. She had chinged into simulations of the Mandala rendered with microscopic fussiness. She had strolled the open boulevards and plazas of the coming cities. She had marvelled at a world in waiting.

But June Wing had just told her that this brave new world was a lie.

Eight of them made it; one did not.

By some fluke, it turned out not to be one of the three problematic suits that eventually developed a fault, but one of the six that were supposedly good to go. Or perhaps, in the haste of evacuation, there had been some mix-up. Either way, eight hours out from the anchor-point, a fault developed in the cooling system of one of the passengers' suits. It began with a warning, recommending that he seek immediate assistance, but soon after the fault developed into a total refrigeration systems failure. The Providers were close, but not close enough, and the other rescuers were still hours away.

The party gathered around the unfortunate man, arguing over the best solution. One of the two technicians believed it was possible to connect the cooling systems of two suits together, but she was not sure of the procedure. The other reckoned that would be too risky anyway, when they were already in an emergency situation. The man started panicking, some flight-or-fight reflex kicking in, making him anxious to leave the rover. The others did their best to restrain him. The rovers trundled on, the route becoming increasingly ill-defined. Remote technicians chinged in from orbit, co-opting the other survivors' suits as they struggled to repair the compromised unit. But there was nothing to be done. Locking the man out of the communications channel, the others debated how best to ease his suffering. Perhaps it would be better to die quickly, like June and the other two who had stayed behind probably had. They could damage his suit further, make it fail more quickly. But when they brought the man back into the conversation, he sensed the drift of their intentions and protested vigorously.

The Providers were still not close enough. The man was starting to make noises that would haunt Chiku for the rest of her days.

A neuropractor chinged in from orbit. He did not need to co-opt any of their bodies since he was not going to be making any physical interventions. They saw him as a figment, dressed in an electric-white surgical smock, a pleasant young man with Polynesian features. He used a private channel to reach into the distressed man's head and adjusted some of his neural parameters. 'He will die,' the neuropractor explained to the others when he had finished his work. 'There's nothing I can do to prevent that. But I've blocked pain and anxiety, and given him the option to ching out of this situation.'

146

Normally this kind of deep-level intervention could only be author-ised by the subject. Occasionally, sensing distress, the Mechanism itself could act to alleviate the worst suffering as it would to prevent criminality, violence and accidental misfortune. But the Mechanism's interventions were seldom administered with a particular individual's needs in mind. The neuropractor had never encountered this man before, but he was another human being, attempting to do the dying man a kindness, and this mattered.

'He's gone,' the neuropractor announced. Then, sensing that his words might be misunderstood, added: 'I mean, he's chinged out of his body. He's still alive, just not aware of his surroundings any more.'

'Do you know where he's gone?' Chiku asked.

'I could resolve the bind, but that would be an invasion of privacy I'm not comfortable with. I'm monitoring brain function, and he's not in any pain or emotional distress now. Wherever he is, he won't be there long.' The neuropractor clasped his hands and bowed. 'I'm sorry I could not do more for him. May I wish you all the best of luck with your rescue?' Then the figment vanished.

Soon the man was dead, boiled alive in his ailing suit. Chiku hoped the neuropractor had not lied to them just to ease their own discomfort.

They carried on, winding through the highlands under clouds of bile and ash, until the Providers came. Visibility by then was low enough that they did not see the machines until they were almost underneath them. Suddenly they loomed out of the poisonous mist, striding on legs as thick as redwoods. The Providers Chiku watched in Lisbon had looked spindly and mantis-like from a distance. Up close they were huge and powerful, shaking the ground with each stomp of their feet. Only when the mist thinned could Chiku see the Providers in their entirety. Their bodies loomed high above, keeled over like galleons. Their heads were tiny, swivelling, anvil-shaped sensor arrays, and their bodies bristled with articulated limbs, cranelike appendages and swaying segmented tentacles. They communicated their proximity with foghorn blasts, like some bellowing saurian language.

In their tentacles they carried the pressure modules they had brought from the construction site. Up in the air they looked the size of beer cans, but when they thumped onto the ground, they were larger than any of the rovers. The modules were powered up, airlocks ready to cycle. Each lock could only accommodate one person at a time, so those with the damaged or compromised suits were the first to cycle, Pedro going ahead of Chiku. But at last they were all inside, out of their armour, breathing clean, cool air.

'I thought they might try to kill us,' Chiku whispered, squeezed into one corner, holding hands with Pedro.

'Who?'

'Them,' she said, not daring to say their name aloud. 'The machines.'

'They've never hurt a fly.' But he must have seen something in her face. 'What did June say, back there? What did she tell you?'

CHAPTER FOURTEEN

The Providers kept watch until the overland rescue parties arrived, and then they were on the move again, the prefabs stashed aboard heavy-duty rovers far bigger than the ones they had ridden from the anchor-point. It was a long but uneventful trek back to the nearest gondola's anchorpoint. They rode a cargo elevator up its thread, and in the gondola there was a medical check-up, a debriefing, some legal formalities, requests for interviews from media affiliates – all declined, and then admittance into a public holding area where Imris Kwami had been waiting anxiously for hours, aware of the news but fearfully keen for confirmation.

'We were outside when it happened,' Chiku said. 'I think it was fast. It looked fast. We're really sorry, Imris.'

'She was very brave,' Pedro said. 'I almost can't imagine that kind of courage. I'm sure she knew what the odds were.'

'Almost certainly,' Kwami said.

'It's going to be a while before they can get search parties into the anchorpoint,' Pedro said. 'There could be air pockets in there, safety doors that closed.'

Kwami touched the little fez perched on his scalp. 'I have been in neural contact with June ever since she first employed me. Her deepest thoughts were closed to me, of course, and I would not have chosen otherwise, but I have always felt her as a living presence, no matter how far apart we have been. When the accident happened, I felt a sharp severance, as if the aug itself had failed. The breaking of contact was so profound, so quick, her death could only have been instantaneous.' The long, bony twigs of his fingers meshed and re-meshed as he spoke. 'There was no fear, no regret, no moment of terror. Only a serene ac-ceptance, as if she was waiting for the sun to rise, that lasted until the final instant of her life. It has been my singular privilege to have known this woman.'

'She told me something,' Chiku said, 'before we parted. You have to help us, Imris. She said you can get us to Arethusa.'

He smiled, not without sympathy. 'Did she, now?'

'Pleistocene, pineapple, rococo,' Chiku said. 'Does that change things?'

After a long silence Kwami said: 'Pineapple?'

Hastily Chiku said: 'I meant grapefruit.'

'Well, then, young miss. That *does* rather change things.'

Gulliver was a carbon black needle with deep-system capability and cryoberths that could keep its crew alive all the way out to the Oort cloud and back. Packed with retractile wings and control surfaces ready to spring out like the blades of a pocket knife, it was sleek and agile enough to handle almost any atmosphere in the system. Inside, it was sumptuous and easily spacious enough for thirty passengers, let alone the three who were present. There were libraries, dark-cased troves of red- and green-spined printed books, thousands of inert kilograms of lavishly processed wood-pulp. There were marble statues and busts – yet more profligate tonnage. An entire area of the ship, closed to routine access, appeared to be an extensive and well-equipped medical facility.

Chiku had barely known Imris Kwami before June's death, so it was difficult to say how well he was bearing up. He certainly appeared to be driven, anxious to be getting on with business. Chiku had mentioned Arethusa, June's insistence that they make contact. Imris had said that yes, this would happen, he promised it, but in the meantime there was talk of Mars, some rendezvous that must be made.

When they were twelve hours out from Venus, slicing across the spacelanes of the imperiously slow loop-liners, the three of them gathered around a low jade table in *Gulliver*'s lounge. Kwami had prepared chai. The ship was too small for centrifugal spin, but the constant-thrust engine provided a quarter-gee of gravity.

Chiku sipped the warm, soothing drink gratefully and said, 'Imris, I need to be really clear about something, but it's difficult to discuss.'

'You've spoken the three words, Chiku – there's no need for secrets between us now.'

'I know this is going to sound silly, but I came to June because I was afraid of something, and I think this ... *thing* may have tried to deliberately harm us on Venus.'

He tilted his cup, which was barely larger than a thimble. 'You speak of Arachne.'

Chiku felt a kind of giddy relief that she was not going to be required to explain everything from the beginning, like some kind of babbling madwoman.

150

'I think Arachne sabotaged the gondola, so my question is – can she attack us here?'

'Her influence *is* extensive,' Kwami said, nodding gravely, 'but she's not omniscient. She would like to be, but her reach is constrained by physics and the limitations of the devices and networks she must co-opt and infiltrate. June, fortunately, is … *was* a very clever woman.' The error embarrassed him. 'You must excuse me.'

'Please,' Chiku said, waving aside his lapse.

'There have always been gaps in Arachne's perception. June learned to slip through these gaps and exploit them. This ship is secure, insofar as we can ever be certain of such things. Our long-range communications are a different matter, however. Arachne can probably decode any encryption we can devise.'

Pedro leaned back in his chair, one leg hooked underneath him. 'What does she want?'

'Her primary goal, young sir, is the same as ours – to continue existing. She knows that the Cognition Police would have eliminated or neutralised her long ago had they learned of her true nature.'

'But they knew she was an artilect,' Chiku said.

'Of course, but she exists on the borderline of what they were prepared to tolerate,' Kwami said, his tone conveying gentle correction. 'They made allowances since Ocular could not have functioned without the aid of a high-level controlling intelligence. But Arachne was much cleverer than they realised.' He paused to pour some fresh chai. 'June used to speak of two orders of cleverness. The first advertises itself, craves attention. The second is wiser. It wraps itself in layers of concealment and will appear to act stupidly, if needs must.'

'That was Arachne,' Pedro said.

'No one guessed her true nature until it was far too late,' Kwami said.

'Except for Eunice,' Chiku said. 'The construct, anyway.'

'Indeed. You have communicated with the robot?'

'Yes. Only on a couple of occasions, but it was enough to get the picture.'

'June spoke of it, but for obvious reasons I never expected to meet anyone who had actually *encountered* it. Or perhaps I should say *her*.'

'Unfortunately,' Chiku said, 'the construct didn't remember much about Arachne, or indeed about June, beyond the fact that it was vitally important I speak to her as soon as possible. Well, I did that, and now I'm here, but I'm none the wiser. Did she tell you the whole story, Imris?'

'Everything she deemed important.'

'The stuff about Crucible, about how it might not be what we're expecting?'

'She shared some theories, nothing concrete.'

Chiku touched her head, echoing Kwami's earlier gesture. 'I have a device in my head installed by Quorum Binding. It links me to my counterparts. Or counterpart, now.'

Kwami gave a precise little nod. 'I am aware of such practices. They were very commonplace during the early years of the holoships.'

'I'm here now because the version of me on *Zanzibar* wanted this version to make contact with June. Chiku Green sent me her memories ... they were scripted into my head, forcing me to act. Now I need to send my memories back to *Zanzibar*, so that Chiku Green can decide how to act on them.'

'Can't you simply transmit the information as a message, the normal way?' Pedro asked.

'No – this has to be for my ears only. For Chiku Green's ears, I mean. If it becomes widespread knowledge, it'll rip *Zanzibar* apart.'

'You are right to be cautious,' said Imris. 'The normal message protocols between here and *Zanzibar* ... I could not guarantee that they are immune to interception by Arachne. And that's before we consider the possibility of human eavesdropping as the signals are relayed along the caravan.'

'What's to say the same won't happen to her memories?' Pedro asked.

'It might, but the level of encryption will be significantly higher than for normal traffic – that's why you needed the merfolk to unlock the memories in the first place.'

'So you know about that,' Chiku said.

'The problem now is that Arachne will be paying particular attention to you, Miss Akinya, concentrating her resources against your efforts.'

'She could have killed me when the Providers came.'

'Yes, but such a thing would have been difficult to explain as an accidental death. Believe me, Arachne is old and wily enough to be adept at covering her tracks.'

'But she'll get us in the end, won't she?' Pedro asked. 'If she's so keen to protect herself, she's bound to, right? And we can't tell anyone about her because they'd either not believe us or there'd be mass panic and more deaths.'

'We are in something of a bind,' Kwami admitted, with magnificent understatement.

'Dangerous or not, I still have to act,' Chiku said. 'I've got to tell Chiku Green about Crucible. Even if I can't tell the people on the holoship what's really there, surely it's better for them to know they're being lied to, isn't it?'

'I can offer you an alternative that you might find acceptable,' Kwami said. 'You mentioned Arethusa.'

'Yes,' Chiku said. 'June said we had to speak to her, too.'

'Can you make that happen?' Pedro asked.

'I can. But first we have to collect something from Mars. We shall not be staying long, of course – or getting too close.'

'I hope not,' Chiku said.

Phobos and Deimos had been important staging points in the exploration of the solar system since the infancy of the space age. Outposts had been built on both moons, fuel depots and teleoperation camps offering way stations before the descent to the Martian surface. Eunice Akinya had lived on Phobos for months, trapped there until the weather changed. A century later, Chiku's mother had set her own footprints on the misshapen little moon. By that time, one of the largest craters – Stickney – had become the infection site for a major outbreak of hotels and deep-space servicing facilities. As *Gulliver* closed in on final approach, Chiku found it difficult to believe that Phobos had ever been a *thing*, a place made by nature. The moon was gone now, smothered under a fester of human habitation. Neon-scribbled structures wrapped it from pole to pole – hotels and casinos and malls, pleasure domes and observation platforms. It was like a dream of a city, wrapped around itself.

'How safe is it down there?' Chiku asked. 'If Arachne could get to us on Venus, she can easily reach us here.'

'Faking an accident on Venus, where many things go wrong as a matter of course, is not the same as faking an accident around Mars.'

'I hope you're right about that, Imris.'

'I am right about most things.' He said this without a trace of irony. 'One more thing, Chiku: the man we are meeting, Victor Gallicean, is someone we can trust. He has been a very good and loyal friend over the years, and has played a great part in helping June assemble the museum. But he knows nothing of Arachne, and it would be best not to mention her.'

They docked, cleared immigration and moved through bright warrens of commerce and glitz. Chiku glimpsed Mars occasionally, through a picture window, this prize that was close enough to touch. It transpired that June had already arranged this meeting long before her misadventures on Venus. They met Victor Gallicean, an 'extraction specialist', in the lobby of a hotel. The structure was spun up to half a gee and the landscape scrolled past constantly outside the windows. Gallicean turned out to be an ogre of a man with a faintly piratical demeanour, his face a map of interesting scars and lesions. He embraced Imris Kwami, then shook hands with Chiku and Pedro.

'I am very sorry to hear the news, Imris. I didn't believe it at first. After all this time, something as stupid as that ended June Wing? A ridiculous accident, on Venus? I mean, really.'

'There is no such thing as a good way to go when you are three hundred and three years old,' Kwami said sagely.

'If she hadn't given up her suit, Pedro or I might not be here,' Chiku said.

'Had you known her long?' Gallicean asked.

'No time at all, really, but there's a connection with my family. June used to know my mother and father, back when they were all living on the Moon.'

'Which would make you one of *those* Akinyas, not just any old Akinya.'

'Yes,' Chiku said. 'But don't hold it against me, will you?'

'I wouldn't dream of it.' Gallicean had a bushy black beard, which presumably served to cover up yet more blemishes, and a mop of unruly black hair. A plain gold earring pierced one cratered lobe. His clothes ran to the ostentatious. 'Look, let's not stand around like fools. There's a pretty good bar at the other end of Phobos – we should drink ourselves into an absolute stupor, in her memory.'

'Except I do not drink,' Imris Kwami said.

'No, but you have a remarkable tolerance for the drunkenness of others.'

'This is true.'

'Plus you know more June stories than any other person alive. With the possible exception of me.'

'This is also true.'

Wormlike trains burrowed through the moon. They were soon inside the bar, seated at a table with a commanding view of the lit face of Mars. The only gravity here was the feeble pull provided by Phobos itself, but the drinks arrived in exquisite squeezebulbs, and there were bracelets and epidermal patches for those unaccustomed to near-weightlessness. Pedro and Chiku ordered a couple of patches, then buckled into padded observation chairs.

'He's far too modest to brag about it,' Kwami said, 'but our friend Victor here is one of the very few people to have set foot on Mars in

154

the last fifty years – on several occasions, in fact. How many is it now, Victor? Four?'

'Six,' Gallicean said, with a cough. 'Actually, seven.'

'I'm surprised anyone goes down to Mars these days,' Chiku said.

'It's all unofficial and uninsured,' Gallicean said. 'We go down fast, pick our landing sites very carefully and don't hang around to sniff the daisies – on my most recent trip, I was down there under eight minutes. My *cumulative* Martian surface time over my entire career as an extraction specialist is still less than an hour.' He sniffed, scratching at his nose. 'Never saw the place in the old days. Rather regret that now.'

'I've heard about thrill-seekers going after an adrenalin rush,' Pedro said.

'Fools and knaves,' Gallicean replied, his features settling into an expression of unbridled contempt. 'They drop something on the surface, like a bone. Then, dogs that they are, they race each other to see who can get to it first, ahead of the machines, and then return to orbit. There's money and prestige involved, of course – why else would they debase themselves?'

'Victor Gallicean considers such activities beneath him,' Kwami said, as if the subject of his statement were not sitting directly opposite him.

'Yes, he does,' Gallicean said firmly. 'I face comparable risks, but I do so for a purpose beyond my own personal glorification.'

It was cloudless and windless on Mars, so they could see all the way down to the surface without difficulty. By some fluke, they were looking down on the place where it all began – the Tharsis ridge, three shield volcanoes laid out in a chain like bullet-holes, and to the east the spider-web fracturing of the Valles Marineris canyon system, scarring so deep that even from orbit Chiku could see the contrasting elevations. Where the machines had been busy, their activities had left visible traces on the surface, as if Mars had been subject to a new and sudden epoch of weathering. There were bright new craters, blasted by weapons, and the notches and zigzags of trenches dug for fortification. Elsewhere, the machines' tracks were stranger and more transient. Geometric patterns flickered across the dust, squares and clusters of squares hundreds of kilometres across. Sometimes these formations met other clusters of squares and formed battle fronts, arcing lines, continental in scale, where geometries tussled and ruptured. These patterns bloomed in a day and faded overnight, the evidence of subterranean processes beyond the reach of orbital sensors. More and more, the machines were keeping their secrets to themselves.

Defence platforms circled Mars, nervously vigilant against any attempt the machines might make to reach space.

'So what,' Pedro said, 'does an extraction specialist actually extract?'

'Different things for different clients, and not just from Mars. I've worked all over the system. For our dear friend June, it has usually involved robotics.'

'The whole of Mars involves robotics,' Chiku said.

'We are speaking now of a much earlier phase of robotic activity. Doubtless Imris has spoken of the museum? For years, June has been bent on collecting the surviving relics of the dawn of robotic exploration, where such recovery is feasible. Landers, probes, rovers. It's surprising how many of these things were still lying around when she began her work.'

'It's why she came to Venus,' Chiku said, remembering the relic they'd abandoned in the anchorpoint.

'At her time of life,' Gallicean replied, 'she was probably unwise to take on so much of the work. But would she listen?'

'I argued against it as best I could,' Kwami said.

Gallicean fidgeted in his chair, adjusting the restraint straps. 'This may be indelicate, Imris, but it's better said now than later or not at all. Are there plans for the continuation of the museum?'

A new face of Mars was turning slowly into view as Phobos orbited. On the horizon's bow, mysterious dust plumes curled into the high, thin reaches of the atmosphere. The night face, which would be visible soon, was often alive with patterns of lights, pastel blues and greens, shining up from the ground or floating in the air. No one really had a clue about what the machines were doing down there.

'Matters are in hand,' Kwami said.

'Well, that's as clear as mud,' Gallicean said.

'You know as well as I do that she was in no hurry to complete the project – she never set a date for the opening, and she left no instructions regarding how the museum would function once she deemed the collection ready for visitors. And there are still many artefacts around the system still to be gathered.'

'Forgive my inquisitiveness,' Gallicean said, lifting his squeezebulb in an apologetic toast. 'It was rude of me to talk business.'

'Not at all,' Kwami said. 'But as you raised the topic – your trip was, I trust, successful?'

'I got what you sent me to find. A few dents and scratches, but nothing unexpected after so long down there. I'm just sorry she isn't here to see it herself.'

'What did you extract?' Chiku asked.

'A rover. Indian Space Agency, mid-2030s. It's difficult to believe, I know, but there are still things wandering around on Mars that by some great good fortune have not yet been picked apart by the Evolvarium. In some cases, it appears to have *allowed them to live*. We'll never know for sure, but it's almost as if the 'varium's taking pity on them, or showing respect to a few older, more venerable machines. The ISA rover has experienced some contamination, some degree of upgrading and evolution, but June would have been expecting that.'

'She'd have been very grateful,' Kwami said. 'I thank you on her behalf for the risks you took.'

'Without risk in our lives, we're scarcely better than machines ourselves.' He saluted this observation with a sip from his squeezebulb, nodding in immodest self-approval.

'Do you think we'll ever go back?' Pedro asked. 'To Mars, I mean. Or is it gone for good?'

'It's not our world now. And what would be the point, anyway? I'd far rather sit things out and see what happens. The Evolvarium is moving through distinct developmental phases. It started with the blood-red Darwinian survival struggle, every creature for itself, and now we're seeing an organisational shift to something more complex. Co-operative alliances, hints of machine altruism – the emergence, perhaps, of machine statehood, the onset of a global civilisation of competing factions. There's no telling what Mars will be like when they start getting *really* clever. We may need to send down ambassadors!'

'Unless they beat us to it and send up their own first,' Chiku said.

After that, there were many stories. Gallicean started, but Imris Kwami soon joined in, both men happily accusing the other of embellishment and exaggeration, but equally content to laugh at the other's tales and wince at some of the more awkward moments, of which there was no small number. Listening to these accounts, funny and bracing and sad, Chiku felt something very close to vertigo, a dizzy sort of perception that she had only just begun to grasp the vertical depth of a very long life, the sense of how far it plumbed the past. A life that went down like a lift-shaft, each floor containing an ordinary life's worth of love and loss, adventure and disappointment, dreams and ruins, joy and sorrow. There were empires and dynasties that had not endured as long as June Wing had. It was true that she was an outlier, a statistical extreme, with her three hundred and three years of mortal existence. But there were more like her all the time. Before long, a life as prolonged as hers would be considered unusual rather than exceptional, and eventually unremarkable rather than unusual.

Very soon it was time to go. Their medical bracelets blasted them back to cold sobriety, all except Imris Kwami, of course, who had never been anything other than clearheaded. Needles of clarity pierced Chiku's skull. For a few minutes her thoughts ran supercooled, as if her entire brain had been dipped in liquid helium. It was not entirely pleasant. The four of them returned by train to the spacedocks, where *Gulliver* hummed in its clamps, still refuelling. Kwami and Gallicean completed the paperwork for the handover of the Martian relic.

'Where are you going now?' Gallicean asked.

'Saturn, where we hope to catch up with an old friend. Of course, there is also the small matter of disposing of June's remains. Fortunately, she was very specific in her instructions.'

'June would not be June were the instructions anything *other* than specific,' Gallicean said sagely.

'You are welcome to accompany us. We'll be there and back inside of a month.'

'No, but I thank you for the kindness. Work to be done, fortunes to be won and lost, et cetera. There will be some record of the event?'

'I'll see that you receive a copy. And thank you again – for everything.'

Chiku wondered if she was still suffering some kind of residual drunkenness, as none of this exchange made sense to her. 'Wait,' she said. 'I'm sorry, Imris, but how can there possibly be remains? We left her on Venus.'

'It's complicated,' Imris Kwami said.

CHAPTER FIFTEEN

When Saturn filled half the sky, Kwami called Chiku and Pedro back into the part of *Gulliver* that until then had been sealed behind glass doors.

Chiku had been correct in her guess that this was some sort of medical facility. Beyond the doors were aggressively sterile rooms filled with extremely modern surgical equipment – scanners, medical pods, mantis-like robot doctors. None of this was very surprising, Chiku supposed. At three hundred and three, and given the life choices she had made in her youth, June would have needed more than a little maintenance. But there was enough medical equipment here to keep a dance troupe alive.

When Kwami showed them the bodies, understanding began to dawn.

They were kept in one room, preserved in glass cylinders. Knots of complex plumbing ran into the cylinders, top and bottom, and each contained a human body floating in some kind of suspension medium.

'They're not clones,' Kwami was quick to point out. 'They are not even living, in the technical sense. These are robots, android bodies constructed using biomimetic principles. They have bones, musculature, a circulatory system, but they are still machines.'

'Sort of like ching proxies?' Pedro asked.

'The exact opposite, in fact. These forms were not engineered to be controlled from a distance via a mind located in another body. She occupied these bodies from within. She wore them. They were her.'

'We saw her, Imris. On Venus,' Chiku said. She was having trouble getting her mind around what she was hearing.

'You saw another of these bodies. There were ten in all. You will notice that one is missing – that was the body she was occupying at the time of her death.'

'How long had she been ... occupying it?' Pedro asked, swallowing hard.

'The surgical integration was quite time-consuming, not to say risky. She did not normally swap bodies more than once or twice a year, and lately, less frequently than that. She had occupied the one she died in for twenty-two months. I do not think she had the fortitude to endure another integration.'

Chiku had no appetite for the details, but they were plain enough. At the time of her death, June had been reduced to little more than a central nervous system. These bodies were vehicles for a brain and some spinal trimmings. Her mind had long been saturated with aug-mediating implants, so it would have been simple for her to send and receive the nervous signals required to drive a prosthetic body.

Essentially, Chiku conceded, it was not so very different from chinging into a proxy or warmblood body. When Chiku had chinged aboard *Zanzibar*, surgeons could have entered her room in Lisbon and stripped her down to a brain. Provided the brain was kept alive, she would have known no better. The signals fed to her brain during the chinging process were persuasive – she felt herself to be elsewhere.

All June had done was fold that illusion back onto itself, like a trick of origami.

'She was not alone in this,' Kwami said. 'There are thousands like her, even now.'

'I've never heard of it,' Chiku said.

'The early adopters encountered considerable social revulsion. Later, when the bodies had advanced to the point of being indistinguishable from living forms, there was no need for the occupants to advertise their nature. Certainly no *legal* obligation to do so. Would you have treated June differently if you had known?'

'No,' Chiku said. 'I mean, I don't think so.'

'But there is doubt,' Kwami said, 'and you cannot be blamed for it. It is a perfectly human reaction.'

'Why so many bodies?' Pedro asked.

'They are not all the same – it suited her purposes to have a selection of bodies, rather than the complexity of a single body with configurable modes. But as I said, it had been a while since her last change. One or two of them she hardly ever used, but she could not bring herself to destroy them.'

'Could she have survived ... on the surface of Venus, when the accident happened?' Pedro asked

'No more than you could, my friend. She may not have needed air and water, but she was no more capable of surviving that atmosphere than the rest of us. But as I said, her state of mind was peaceful. This far into her life, she had faced death many times and had negotiated a kind of acceptance of it.' Kwami laced his fingers. 'But now there is work to be done. It was her wish that these bodies be disposed of, should she no longer need them. These are the remains I mentioned.'

'I'm very sorry, Imris,' Chiku said.

'Do not be. She did good work, and lived a long life.'

They sent the nine bodies towards Saturn, spitting them out of *Gulliver* like seeds, each boosted far enough ahead of the next that they followed independent trajectories. From a window in the ship they watched them fall, twinkling as they tumbled, shock-frozen in seconds. In time, Kwami said, the bodies would ghost through the rings. The particles of ice that circled Saturn were dispersed so tenuously that collisions were unlikely, during the first crossing, at least. But the bodies would loop around and thread the rings over and over again. Sooner or later, on the tenth or the hundredth passage, ice would meet ice, and in that meeting there would be a flash of vapour, a white gasp of kinetic energy. And there would follow a temporary unravelling of the ring's multistranded weave, visible, perhaps, from space or one of the planet's airless moons.

But time and gravity would do their healing work. Entrained by the same resonant forces that had sculpted and maintained the rings in the first place, the pieces of June would take their place among the stately processional ooze of all the other icy shards. Save for a gemlike tint of chemical impurity, there would be no way to tell that these pieces had ever contained a life.

Chiku had seen moons and asteroids before, but nothing quite like Hyperion. It was not its potato shape that distinguished the Saturnian moon, although Hyperion was very large for an object that was not spherical. What was remarkable, even beautiful, was the degree to which this little piece of ice and dirt was cratered, its surface so impacted that the walls of the craters touched and intersected, the walls forming knifeblade ridges, the pattern of these ridges suggesting nothing less than some marine growth process, as if this was a moon grown from some pearly grey variety of coral. And the walls went down so far that the deeply shadowed craters became like cave mouths, enclosing dark mysteries. Indeed, Hyperion was riddled with cavities. It was less a moon than a loosely organised swarm of rubble, moving in uneasy consort. There was room to lose cities in those fissures and voids.

As *Gulliver* closed in, decelerating from thousands to hundreds and then tens of kilometres per second, there was not much to suggest that people had found a use for this place. A handful of strobe lights, a radar bounce off some metallic installation or encampment, but no cities, no

161

landing pads, no train tubes or casino hotels. Strapped into a seat for the duration of the slowdown burns, Chiku thought they were coming in recklessly fast, and she began to wonder if Imris Kwami did in fact have it in mind to dash them all to their doom. Perhaps that had been his intention all along, from the moment he learned of June's death.

A masterless samurai, scheming his own suicide.

But the burns and course-correction bursts were too calculated for that, and as the craters became a landscape, one of them suddenly ringed itself with blue light. Kwami steered hard for that crater, and the blackness at its base turned milky as they approached. *Gulliver* slid between razorblade walls, still daggering down too fast, and then there was a sharp irising motion as the crater floor peeled open, and an organised blueness beyond, dense with lights and structures. And then they were through and the crater floor snapped shut behind them, like a fly-trap.

Gulliver slowed harder, until they were moving at only hundreds of metres per second. They were sliding into Hyperion, down an enormous throat. Chiku marvelled. She had seen the interior spaces of the holoships, but this was engineering on an audaciously different scale. The throat branched and rebranched, opening out into many lit vaults. There was a staggering amount of space in this tiny moon.

They pushed on deeper and eventually slowed and docked, *Gulliver* pinning itself to the concave wall of a bulb-shaped cavity alongside several other ships.

'All this for artists and malcontents?' Pedro asked. 'I'm tempted to give it a try myself.'

'I am sure you would be made most welcome,' Kwami said. 'There is just one difficulty. Almost everyone who has contact with Arethusa is obliged to remain here thereafter. Present company excluded, of course.'

'I sincerely hope so,' Chiku said.

They disembarked. Even at the surface, the gravity on Hyperion was only a little less feeble than on Phobos; deep inside it was barely distinguishable from weightlessness. This time, there was no offer of bracelets or epidermal patches. The presumption was that if you had gone to the trouble of coming to Hyperion, you must have known what to expect.

Their host, meeting them on the other side of the lock, was a short, broad-framed man with extremely white hair, worn in tight curls like a Roman emperor. Although caucasian, he had deeply tanned skin, which only made the hair shine whiter. He wore brown clothes with a black leather waistcoat. He shook their hands, demonstrating a powerful,

162

sinewy grip. 'Welcome to Hyperion. I am Gleb.'

The name tickled Chiku's memory, but the details remained elusive.

'We've come to see Arethusa,' she said.

'Of course. Imris – how are you? We were of course most distressed to hear of June's passing.'

'I knew the day would come, eventually. I wish it had not happened *quite* the way it did, but she was never one to shy from risk.'

'She would have been safe here. I hope she knew that.'

'She did. But she would also have been bored out of her mind within seconds.'

'This is understood.' Gleb offered a sympathetic smile. 'Well, shall we proceed? Are you all well? Do you have need of refreshment?'

'I'd prefer to see Arethusa sooner rather than later,' Chiku said.

'Some of our visitors expect to be presented with motes before they meet her,' Gleb said, 'but that's not how we do things around here. If you've come this far and still have doubts about our trustworthiness, you have more problems than a mote can put to rest.'

'We'll manage without, I'm sure,' Chiku said.

Gleb took them deeper into Hyperion, passing through or around the voids given over to the moon's permanent colony of artists. Most of the voids were pressurised. Chiku saw artists moving in microgravity, working with tools that looked better suited to construction or even close-quarters combat. Some of them were strapped into four-armed suits, like the units aboard *Zanzibar*, and a few were laced into exos with eight or ten pairs of limbs, the operation of which must have demanded an astonishing burden of sensorimotor control. They were sculpting and accreting massive but lacy constructs, whimsies of ice and air. One void contained a liquid thing, a kind of trembling pupal sac as large as a house, contained by its own surface tension and suspended in place by gusts of air from automatic nozzles. It constantly branched pseudopods, which broke off, collapsed into shimmering clouds and were reabsorbed by the main mass. In another chamber, there was a twisting, sinuous fire-dragon constructed from some kind of self-sustaining flame. The eyes were little pinched knots of increased combustion temperature, the wings tapering from brightness to sooty black.

They went deeper, travelling via free-fall drop shafts, elevators, escalators, even a brisk train ride through an area of Hyperion not yet hollowed out for the benefit of artists.

'We must be a long way in by now,' Chiku said.

'Approaching the centre of gravity,' Gleb said. 'This is where Arethusa spends most of her days.'

163

'I know your name – or I think I do, anyway. I've been doing some research into my family, writing a history. Or I was, before all this blew up.' There was also, of course, the memory of Chiku Yellow's conversations with Eunice, the talk of the elephants.

'I knew your mother,' Gleb said pleasantly. 'And your father, and later your uncle. We were good friends.'

'Did you meet on the Moon?'

'Indeed. We ran a sort of underground zoo in the Descrutinised Zone. We, as in Chama and I.'

The fog was gradually lifting from her memory. 'Chama is your husband.'

'Was,' Gleb corrected gently. 'Chama died about a century ago.'

'I'm sorry.'

'It's fine, Chiku.' Gleb was smiling at her awkwardness. 'We had a very long and happy life together. Children, everything. More memories than a head can hold. And I've been happy since.'

'It's good to meet you,' she said. The four of them – Imris Kwami, Chiku, Pedro and their host – were the train's only passengers. 'You mentioned you were involved with a zoo – is that the one that had something to do with the dwarf elephants?'

'Goodness, that really is ancient history.'

'From what I remember, those were the first elephants to reach space.'

'It's true.'

'Were you also involved in another project involving elephants?'

He gave her a polite but evasive smile. 'You'll have to be more specific.'

'The creation of elephants with enhanced cognitive faculties. Elephants that can use complex tools. Elephants with language.'

The silence that followed seemed to swallow eternities. The train swerved and dived down a blue gullet. Gleb's expression was tight, his face masklike. Chiku wondered if she had made some dire miscalculation, or whether Eunice had given her false information.

'How do you know about that?' he asked eventually.

'It's a little involved.'

'Try me.'

'I've seen them – the Tantors, if that's the name you know them by.'

'How can you have *seen* them?'

'I didn't, exactly. But there's a version of me aboard the ship that's carrying them.'

'When did you see them?'

'Feels like this version of a few days, but it was actually about twenty years ago, if you take the time lag into account.'

'But within the last century?'

'Yes. I saw them several times before sending my memories back to Earth.'

'Then they're alive. I mean, as far as you know.'

'They're alive and they're magnificent. They spoke to me, Gleb. She told me their names ... Dreadnought, Aphrodite ... but there were more, many more. An entire self-sustaining herd.'

'She. You said "she".'

'You know exactly what happened, don't you? How Eunice and the Tantors got aboard?'

The mask slipped. There was that smile again, and a watery quality to his eyes. 'Some of it, not all. It was a difficult business, done in a hurry, and none of us knew all the details. But they're well? And she's well? After all this time? You're not lying, could you? You'd have to know about the Tantors to lie about them, and then why would you lie?'

'They're doing well, Gleb. Eunice was ... damaged, I suppose, by whatever forced her into hiding, but she's managed to compensate. She was adamant that I had to visit Arethusa. I don't know what the future holds for Eunice and the herd – there are difficult times ahead, that's for sure. But they've made it this far, which is something, don't you think?'

'You're right, Chiku, that's definitely something. You have made me very happy.'

'I wish you could have seen them.'

'You can tell me about them later. There will be time, I'm sure.'

'What you and Chama did back then ... whatever risks you took, it was worth it. And I'll tell you everything, I promise.'

Gleb squeezed her hand. He was crying, but appeared unembarrassed by it. Then she felt tears well up in her own eyes, and she cried with him. She had so much on her mind, so many fears, but she was glad to have brought this man some good news.

CHAPTER SIXTEEN

Eventually the train brought them to Hyperion's hollow heart. The moon had been cored deliberately by linking together numerous natural inclusions, and then smoothing over and armouring the walls.

The train detached from its rails and became a tiny independent spacecraft, drifting into the void.

The void contained two things. In the middle was a translucent sphere of dark-blue glass several tens of metres across. Etched on the surface of the glass and glowing with a gentle white light was a vastly complex pattern of looping lines and knots. Floating off to one side of the sphere was a darker form, elongated and metallic, which Chiku at first took to be a spaceship, imprisoned in the moon's heart.

But it was not a ship. The form, rounded at the front, gradually broadened along its flexing, undulating length. A pair of flippers was positioned about halfway between the front and the middle, beyond which the form began to narrow and taper, culminating in what was unmistakably a fluke, shaped like the crescent moon, at the other end. As the thing adjusted its position, flippers paddling vacuum, Chiku realised that she was looking at a spacesuit designed for a whale.

'Arethusa,' Gleb announced. 'Your guests have arrived, if you can bear to be drawn away from your work for a little while.'

The voice that replied was soft, feminine. It sounded as though it belonged not to a whale, but to a small Chinese girl with an aptitude for scholarship.

'This is the one with a strange new interest in Crucible?'

'June Wing believed her,' Kwami said. 'That is reason enough for me to trust her.'

'She's met Eunice and the Tantors,' Gleb added.

'Met?'

'She has a counterpart on the holoship – they've exchanged memories.'

'Fascinating. And thank you, Gleb, for taking care of them. I didn't mean to get so engrossed. Bring them closer, will you? But beware of the beam – we don't want anyone getting sliced into sections.'

'I'll do my best.'

Following Gleb's directions, they veered closer to Arethusa. Chiku was reminded of a piece of early space age film footage she had seen of a long-spined, round-headed spaceship disgorging a tiny spherical extravehicular module, like a bauble with claws. She felt as vulnerable near Arethusa as the astronaut in that module must have felt – so much mass, so little protection. When one of the flippers twitched, she flinched instinctively against the expected backwash as articulated armour slid over itself in an ingenious, pressure-tight configuration. But of course there was no water, just a near-vacuum salted with some noble gases.

'You are Chiku, of course, and Pedro. Were you with her on Venus when she died?'

'Nearby,' Chiku said.

'How sorry I am to learn of it, Imris. She meant a lot to both of us. I watched what you did with the bodies. When she reaches the rings, she'll make her mark.'

'I think she already made her mark,' Imris said. 'I also think she was murdered.'

'I agree. She communicated her concerns to me on many occasions. And I shared mine with her, of course. We both had our coping strategies. This was mine … sanctuary, secrecy … immersion in my art. Do you like the sphere?'

'It's very pretty,' Chiku said.

'I'm very pleased with it. The globe's centre is *precisely* co-aligned with Hyperion's centre of mass. The mismatch is never more than millimetres, even with the coming and going of spaceships and people to spoil our little moon's equilibrium. You're aware of our chaotic dynamics. Hyperion tumbles quite unpredictably as Titan and the other moons push and pull on it. There's a value in chaos theory, a number called the Lyapunov exponent, which tells you how to predict a chaotic system's boundary – its knowledge horizon, if you like. Hyperion's Lyapunov exponent is just forty days – we can't predict this moon's motion beyond the next forty days. That's the maximum limit of our foreknowledge! If my life depended on this moon's motion, I would still not be able to say a word about its state beyond forty days.'

'What's this beam you mentioned?' Chiku said.

'A laser, projecting from the wall of the enclosing chamber. You can't see it, of course, because we're in vacuum. Also, its focus is very tight. Where it touches the blue sphere, it etches a pit in the glass, which shows up as a white discolouration. Except it's never a pit, because the laser is fixed to the chamber and the chamber is always moving, always turning one way or another, because of Titan's torque. So the laser etches a track, a memory in glass of Hyperion's history.

Chiku studied the blue globe with renewed attention. The white lines, she understood now, were all one line – a groove that encoded Hyperion's movements over some lengthy interval. The line looped all over the globe, like a scribble of wool. There were bands and patches where the white line had come back over and over again, almost retracing itself. And if it did indeed retrace itself, it would only be for some short distance, before the chaotic uncertainties built up and sent it off on a deviant trajectory. Less than forty days. Parts of the sphere were almost totally white. Equally, there were regions where the line had never travelled – seas and inlets of blue, untrammelled by the laser's crossing.

'When I'm faced with a difficult decision,' Arethusa said, 'I sometimes let the moon decide for me. I select an area of the sphere and let Hyperion decide whether or not it etches the line through that part. I abdicate my life to chance.'

'Why would you do that?' Chiku asked.

'To outfox Arachne. Chance trumps her every time. She may be an artilect, and a very clever one, but she still can't beat Lyapunov.'

'She's the reason we're here,' Chiku said.

'June and I both knew that Arachne would act to protect herself if she felt threatened. June was always very careful, but she must have made some mistake and drawn too much attention to herself.'

'Perhaps it was my fault,' Chiku said. And the possibility of this, now that she had voiced it, sounded entirely likely to her. 'When I got the new memories, I started making enquiries, especially aboard the loop-liner on our way to Venus. I wanted to know more about June Wing, and about Arachne. At the time they were just innocent data searches via the public nets.'

'I'm sure you acted as prudently as you could, given what you knew at the time.'

'That's the problem – there's still so much I don't know.'

'I can clarify the situation, perhaps, make plain the direness of our predicament, but I'm not sure a solution is within our reach. It lies beyond our Lyapunov horizon, at the very least.'

'Tell me what you know.'

168

'Tell me what *you* know, to begin with. Starting with Ocular.'

'I don't know much. Arachne was built … created … to run the instrument, to collate its data. It detected Crucible, and the alien structure on the surface of that planet, but June told me all that's a mirage.'

'Not all of it. The planet orbiting Sixty-One Virginis f is quite real, and its surface conditions are sufficiently Earthlike to support human life. All that was verified by independent observation long ago. The holoships aren't going to arrive around a lump of radiation-blasted rubble, or no planet at all. But Mandala … that's a lot more debatable.'

'But we've also sent holoships to other solar systems,' Pedro said.

'That's true, but the motivating impulse for this entire wave of interstellar exploration was Mandala. Without that discovery, the Chibesa Principle probably wouldn't have been disclosed for decades to come. Mandala set this whole thing in motion.'

Chiku sighed. 'So that's it, then. Mandala isn't real, and the Providers we sent to Crucible are lying to us about it.'

'It's more complicated than that,' Arethusa said. 'The Providers are transmitting false data – there's no doubt about that – but Mandala isn't part of the lie. Mandala exists.'

'How can you know all this?' Pedro cut in. 'Chiku's had these memories for a few days and she's been rushing around trying to learn what she can and make sense of it all … but it's as if you and June have been sitting on this knowledge all along.'

'It's one thing to suspect a lie, but quite another to know what is being concealed. Getting to the bottom of *that* has just cost June Wing her life.'

'I thought she was putting together a museum,' Chiku said.

'That was just a cover for her activities. Racing around the solar system hunting for relics provided June with the excuse she needed to go about her real work.'

'Which was?' Pedro asked.

'I'll answer that, but you need to know a little about Ocular to begin with. Before the instrument came online, Eunice and I inserted a blind spot in its architecture. Arachne is – or was – the spider at the centre of the web, collating data sent back from the individual elements of the Ocular array. That's all *she* knew. But we were sensible enough not to put all our faith in an artilect, and as a sanity check, once in a very great while, each of those elements was also programmed to squirt raw data packets somewhere else.'

'Anywhere in particular?' asked Chiku.

'To anything Arachne wouldn't notice that could store those data packets. Half-forgotten networks, addressing dormant or semi-derelict archives. Anything with a memory. Moribund offshore bank accounts, floating in the asteroid belt. Deep-space network routers, still up and running. Military encryption devices. Space probes and landers with a trickle of electrical power still running through their circuits. Dead astronauts, drifting through space, but whose spacesuits still had some functionality. They weren't our only fail-safes, but they gave June a pretext for the rest of her activities. Were we being unreasonably cautious – paranoid, even? It's entirely possible.'

'So, these devices,' Pedro said, 'they stored the data before she got hold of it? So all you have to do is put it all together, and you can see the real picture?'

'Unfortunately we could only hide the tiniest, tiniest fraction of the full Ocular data stream, but the packets *are* useful, and they do provide more information beyond the fact that she was lying. Put together, they form a kind of reverse filter. We can apply it to selected volumes of the public Ocular data and begin to work out which areas were tampered with.'

'The relic on Venus, the thing Gallicean brought up from Mars,' Chiku said. 'These are all parts of the puzzle, aren't they?'

'Actually, the Venus lander was a red herring – it never held any Ocular packets. But June was very interested in the Evolvarium object, the Indian Space Agency probe. You brought it with you, didn't you? You met Gallicean?'

'We have it,' Chiku said.

'It should be with your specialists by now,' Imris Kwami announced.

'It can't be this simple,' Chiku said, shaking her head. 'The final jigsaw piece can't magically fall into place now that I'm here. Things don't work that way.'

'They do this time, Chiku. You see, you *are* the final piece of the jigsaw.'

Another part of Hyperion had been spun up for the provision of gravity. They were assigned rooms there and given access to a lounge with a surfeit of turquoise carpeting. The lounge's huge, curving walls were glass framed with bolted strips of brassy metal. Beyond the glass, receding away into murk, was a lavishly stocked aquarium. Swimmers and aquatics were navigating towering, castle-like formations of rock and coral, and slipping through banners of vivid green kelp. Chiku also saw machines and fish, and a bioengineered whale that had once been a woman. They could see her true cetacean form now,

170

unencumbered by armour. Arethusa had divested herself of the space-suit when she returned to her preferred medium. Perhaps she felt at ease with revealing her true self now that she knew herself to be among friends.

Gleb had brought green chai. It was just the three of them, Imris Kwami having taken his leave to check on *Gulliver*'s refuelling. Gleb moved easily under gravity. The pull here was not much greater than that on Mars, but he looked so strong that Chiku doubted that he would have had too much difficulty even on Earth.

'I've been thinking,' Arethusa said, speaking to them from beyond the glass, 'that it's time to reopen negotiations with Mecufi. I may have some information he'll consider valuable, but he's going to have to prove himself to me first. I'll formulate a mote and you will convey it to Mecufi. Mecufi in turn will assist in your return to Africa. Safe passage will be arranged to the household. When you arrive, you will use your Akinya identity to access the fully reconstructed Crucible imagery. Mecufi will also provide the necessary expertise required to retransmit your findings to Chiku Green. If he fails in either task, we will not speak again.'

'Do we really have to go all the way back to Earth?' Pedro asked. 'I mean, I've nothing against the place, but ...'

'The Ocular control architecture will only allow Chiku access at the household. Until then, we have only this partial reconstruction. Are you ready to see it?'

'I think so,' Chiku said.

Part of the aquarium wall clouded into opacity and an image formed on the glass, rendered in two dimensions. It was a view of Crucible, seen from space. Chiku remembered a similar picture in Ndege's companion, the promise of that waiting world rendered with all the exacting pious clarity of some Medieval conception of heaven.

'Wait,' she said slowly. 'This is the doctored or undoctored image? I'm confused. It looks the way I was expecting.'

'At the limits of our correctional resolution, there are no significant points of deviation,' Arethusa said.

'OK. Now I'm *really* confused.'

'Look closer. At the time this image was captured, the Providers should have already begun preparing the groundwork for the surface communities. Clearings, trenches, artificial harbours. But there's no evidence of them.'

'Maybe they're too small to be seen from space,' Pedro said.

'Traces of the works were easily visible in the doctored imagery.

I admit that there is some room for error here, but I can state with a fairly high level of confidence that there are no new cities awaiting you on Crucible. The Providers haven't built them. That much at least is a lie.'

'Dear god,' Chiku said. 'How are they expecting us to react when we arrive in orbit?'

'There's no guarantee that the holoships will reach orbit. The Providers will have ample opportunity to prevent your arrival. A relatively simple weapon, deployed from the cover of a planetary surface, could easily hole a holoship – the kind of thing you might use to shoot down meteors.'

'Is this the worst of it?' Chiku asked. 'I was almost expecting Mandala to be a figment of Arachne's imagination.'

'I'm afraid there's more to tell.'

The image zoomed out a little. Chiku frowned. Until then her view of Crucible had been unobstructed, exactly as if she were in orbit, looking down. But now there were clots of darkness around the planet, organised into a kind of equatorial ring that cut across her view. The ring was lumpy, its edges fuzzy. It was difficult to make out definite detail.

'Tell me what we're seeing,' Chiku said.

'We are looking now at the areas of the image – or more properly the three-dimensional space around Crucible – where I am certain Arachne has distorted the data. In other words, there is something in space, perhaps in orbit around the planet, that she has chosen to conceal from us.'

'A ring, like around Saturn?' Pedro asked.

'It's possible, although I cannot see why she would be motivated to hide a natural feature. More likely, and given the artificial nature of Mandala, this is also some evidence of intelligence. It could be one structure, or perhaps an assemblage of smaller structures. I can't say more than that for certain.'

'They must be huge, whatever they are,' Chiku said.

'Indeed.'

'Bigger than anything we could ever hope to make. Even if we took all the holoships, parked them in a necklace around Crucible—'

'This is frightening,' Pedro said. 'I'm not even on the holoship, and I'm terrified.' He squeezed her hand. 'I'm sorry. This is worse for you.'

'It's catastrophic for all of us,' Arethusa said. 'Our entire civil society is constructed on an implicit assumption that we can trust the artificial intelligences, the Mechanism, the Providers ... We have never *once* questioned whether these things have our best interests at heart.'

'I still don't understand,' Pedro said. 'Why would Arachne create this illusion? If she was going to hide the existence of an alien artefact, why not go all the way and hide Mandala as well?'

'She needed to give us the impetus to go to Crucible in the first place,' Chiku said. 'She's an artificial intelligence, not a physical thing. But she must have known that if we sent machines to Crucible, she could transmit a part of herself along at the same time. It's speculation, I know. But here's the thing I really don't have an answer for. What the hell is it that she *doesn't* want us to see?'

In another part of Hyperion, Gleb was waiting for Chiku with a small Chinese schoolgirl. The schoolgirl wore a red dress, white socks and black shoes polished to an extreme mirror-like finish. It was either a figment or a proxy of Arethusa, manifesting in her former incarnation of Lin Wei.

'You can leave us for a while, Gleb,' Lin Wei said, pleasantly enough.

Now that the terms of their departure had been settled, Chiku was anxious to be aboard the ship and on her way back to Earth. But when Lin took her into a green-tiled room with no windows, a room that felt astringent and medical even though there were no chemicals or machines anywhere in sight, she began to have her suspicions.

'Why am I here?' Chiku asked, with a shiver of foreboding.

'You know why. Mecufi showed you the remains of *Memphis*, the ship that came back, and the version of you he found aboard it. Beyond that, you don't know very much. The ship was damaged, its records scrambled, your counterpart frozen beyond safe revival. You couldn't ask her what had happened. All you knew was what Mecufi told you: that she had come home alone, without the prize.'

'That just about sums it up.'

'Did you think to wonder what had happened to Eunice?'

'I know what happened to Eunice – she's with the Tantors.'

'I'm talking about your real, flesh-and-blood great-grandmother. The woman who was born in Tanzania, back when people still thought burning coal was a good idea.'

'No one knows where she is. She was on that ship, heading into deep space. Maybe my counterpart discovered the truth out there, or maybe she didn't. Mecufi couldn't even tell me whether *Memphis* had managed to dock with *Winter Queen*.'

'She did manage to dock. I know because I left sensors on *Winter*

Queen after my own visit that told me when another ship approached and docked.'

'Are you saying that you got there before Chiku Red?'

'One ship reached Eunice's craft. Is it beyond the bounds of possibility that another vessel got there sooner?'

'For a start, we were watching. Secondly, you're a whale.'

'I didn't need to go out there in person. I sent a probe, an uncrewed ship. We Panspermians have never liked robots, but there are times when we've had no choice but to use them – this was one such occasion. The ship was very swift, very clever, very dark. By the time you'd started to dream up your ambitious publicity stunt, I was already on my way. I sent my ship off in a totally different direction until it was too far out for you or anyone else to reliably track its drive flame, and only then vectored the ship onto Eunice. Of course, it didn't hurt that the only instrument capable of detecting that kind of activity was Ocular, my very own plaything.'

'So you got there first,' Chiku said, angry but at the same time accepting that what was done was done.

'My robots found her. She was still in the cryopreservation casket, which she entered not long after her departure from the solar system in 2101. She was dead.'

'Frozen, you mean.'

'Frozen *and* dead. Far beyond any hope of clinical revival. Every cell in her body had been ruptured by expanding ice crystals, her brain structure demolished. Something had gone terribly wrong. Not that she ever expected to get anywhere – just heading out aboard that ship was a good enough goad and a lure for the rest of us.'

After a lengthy silence, Chiku said, 'So did your robots bring her home? That was the point of sending them there, wasn't it?'

'Yes, they brought her home. Would you like to see her?'

'I'm not sure.'

'Because you don't think you're ready for it? I think you are. I've kept her on ice since my robots returned. The cellular damage is extensive, but the visible effects ... they're not as severe as you might imagine. I think you should see your great-grandmother, Chiku. And then I'll tell you about the other thing I found aboard *Winter Queen*.'

'What other thing?'

'Let me show you her body first.'

Part of the green tiled wall slid out and extended out into the room. With it came a shock of cold, a front so sharp and sudden and merciless that it drew tears. Chiku hugged her arms around her torso. The air felt like shovel-loads of ice going down her throat.

Lin Wei, in her red dress and stockings, looked on with lofty disregard.

'Go to her. But don't touch – you'll hurt yourself.'

Eunice was resting on a green platform. She was on her back, dressed in the inner layer of a spacesuit, her arms crossed over her chest, her head tilted back in serene repose. Her eyes were closed, her expression restful. The ice glittered on her skin. It was lovely, those little glinting crystals against her skin, a spray of stars in the Milky Way. She looked only a little older than the construct, but not by decades. She had been at the start of her eighth decade when she entered the casket, and assuming she had not spent long periods awake after *Winter Queen's* departure, this was the age she had been at her death. There were marks on her skin, deep black bruises, and elsewhere a kind of pale, bloodless frosting. Chiku could not say how much of this was due to age and how much the fault of the cryogenic accident that had damaged her cells. Above all else, she did not appear to be beyond the hope of revival. But a wax model would look just as viable, Chiku reminded herself. The eye could not discern the gross destruction that had taken place on the microscopic level, where it really mattered.

'We scanned and recorded those neural structures that were still resolvable,' Lin Wei said. 'Traces and ghosts of traces, really. But you are welcome to the data. And to the body, if you would like it.'

'Like doesn't sound quite the right word.'

'If you feel you must return her to Africa, I won't stop you.'

'I won't take her,' Chiku said. 'Not now. But I will have those neural patterns.'

'For you?'

'For someone I know.'

She traced a hand along Eunice's contours, not quite touching, but feeling in her palm the meniscus of cold clinging to the corpse. She would be warming slightly, Chiku supposed, just by being in this room. A little more damage to add to the harm already done. Lin Wei would not have exposed the body to the room's temperature had there been any real prospect of revival.

'She made fools of all of us and gave us the stars in recompense,' said Lin Wei. 'I suppose we can find forgiveness, if we dig deeply enough. Now, would you like to hear about the other thing I found on *Winter Queen*?'

Chiku nodded. She could think of very little that would surprise her now.

Strange marching figures appeared in the air, like regiments of little stick men. Chiku recognised them for what they were. It was essentially the same alien alphabet that Eunice had used when she engraved her memory wall.

Symbols of the Chibesa syntax.

'Let me clarify,' Lin Wei said.

CHAPTER SEVENTEEN

When Chiku announced her attention to ching to the Moon, Imris Kwami was extremely ambivalent at first, warning that no communications were entirely immune from Arachne's eavesdropping.

'But we won't be talking about her, for once,' Chiku said.

Kwami had some inkling by then of what this conversation was going to entail. 'But if you start discussing Chibesa physics, that will hardly sound like a normal, everyday conversation.'

'You don't know my mother.'

'I will see what I can do. We have some reserved quangle paths for occasions when we need maximum privacy. I cannot guarantee that Arachne will not intercept them, but they are much better than the normal level of civilian encryption.'

'I'll take what you've got, Imris. And believe me, it's not going to be a long call.'

In the late months of 2365, Earth and Saturn were in opposition to each other. Chiku had seen the lit face of Earth almost all the way in: first a pale-blue star, then a dot, then a circle blemished with white and green. The circle gained a bright silver coin of a companion. The Moon did not look grey at all until they were much closer. Even then it was a grey of many colours, splendidly variegated – fawn-grey, nickel-grey, ochre-grey. A chain of lights wrapped the Moon in low orbit, and there were more lights scattered across the nightside, synaptic nets of them, cities and roads and spaceports, so much light that from space the Moon looked friendlier and more inviting than Earth ever did. The zones of special historic significance, the landing sites and early moon bases, were dark puddles of vanishing regolith.

Uncle Geoffrey had once told Chiku how he went out into the African night, somewhere near the household, and instructed the aug to overlay the Moon with territorial markers and transnational boundaries, the proud colours of the great spacefaring powers. A lovely thing to behold, in one sense, because the colonised Moon spoke of international cooperation, of differences being settled by negotiation and the rule of interplanetary law rather than the tank and the machete. But now Chiku did not need the aug to see the Moon chopped up and pacified beneath a scurf of cities. The trick now was to have the aug strip all that away and paste a ghost Moon over the real.

When *Gulliver* was thirty light-seconds from Earth, Chiku placed a ching request with Jitendra Gupta.

He could have declined it – there was at least a one-in-three chance that he would be asleep or otherwise engaged – but the acceptance came through only a minute later, and then she was there, standing next to him, in a cave on the Moon. Jitendra was as tall and skinny as ever, slightly stooped now, except when he was consciously correcting his posture, his scalp shaven or bald (she had never been quite sure which, but had never known him with hair), a broad smile and an easy, affable manner that she knew belied the considerable emotional strain he had been under these past few years. He was an old man. It was not fair on Jitendra, what Sunday had put him through, not at all.

'It's good to see you, Father. I'm sorry it's been a while.'

'It's all right, Chiku. You've been busy, and we knew you were well.'

'I should still have called. But I figured that if there was any change in Mother—'

'You'd have been the first to hear about it. You're right, of course. And no, there hasn't really been any change.' He smiled, papering over years of sadness as if it was no great thing. 'She'll come back to us one day, Chiku. I'm sure of it.' Jitendra clapped his hands. 'And how are you? In space, I see – on a ship, no less! Are you travelling alone, or with ...'

'Pedro, yes. He's with me.'

'He seems to be a good man. I liked him when we spoke. You should both come to the Moon one of these days. Or perhaps you're on your way this very moment!'

'Not this time, I'm afraid,' she said. 'We're in a bit of a rush to get back to Earth, and I've been away a while.'

'You can't argue with genetics. Wanderlust is in your blood. That's where your mother and I were never on *quite* the same page. Sunday wanted to see everything, to drink in every possible human experience. I was quite content with my little microcosm here on the Moon.'

They were in the underground domicile, Sunday and Jitendra's home beneath the Lunar soil. They had moved out of their dwelling in the former Descrutinised Zone years ago, when the property magnates arrived and pushed the rental market into absurdity. Now they lived in a small community somewhere near the northern flank of the Rima

178

Ariadaeus rift valley, part of a small hamlet of linked houses and modest recreational spaces that was home to about fifty families. It was an isolated little place, two hours' drive from the nearest rail hub, six hours' travel from the nearest community of any consequence. But they liked it here. For Sunday it had offered escape from the pressures attendant on any Akinya, certainly one who in the scheme of things was something of a modern-day celebrity. For Jitendra, it offered everything he needed from life – peace, calm and the space to play with his toy robots and automata, in which he found a universe of quiet fascination.

They had been here for a century, though in all that time Chiku doubted she had visited in person more than three times. Her record of chinging in was scarcely any better. As her mother had retreated further and further into her mathematics, so Chiku's calls had become less and less frequent. This had caused Jitendra no small measure of pain, but the truth was that Sunday appeared to neither know nor care that her daughter was staying away, and that indifference only made Chiku even less inclined to visit.

But here she was, chinging in from a fast-moving spaceship with a head full of worries, and still it was good to see her father again.

'Come through to the living room,' Jitendra suggested, beckoning her to follow him as he stooped through one of the low connecting doors. 'I spoke to your mother only a few days ago, by the way.'

'She came out?'

'A window of lucidity. It lasted a good couple of hours. We spoke of many things – you, of course, and your friend Pedro, and Geoffrey … She always needs to be reminded that Geoffrey isn't with us now. It's not that her memory is poor, just that she doesn't attach much importance to these things when she's in there, deep down.'

'How could she forget her own brother was dead?' Chiku said. But she was careful not to phrase it as a criticism.

'Would you like tea?'

She was wearing a robot body, so it was entirely possible to take Jitendra up on his offer, but she declined. 'I can't really stay long, Father. We're using a very high level of quangle, and the longer we spend in conversation, the better chance someone has of breaking the encryption.'

'That sounds very mysterious!'

'Oh, it's nothing to worry about. And it's not as if you haven't had your share of adventures, is it?'

'We had our moments. Although that sort of thing was always your mother's forte more than mine. That said, she did nearly get the both of us killed, on Mars …' They were in the living room now, a kettle-shaped chamber with branching rooms. The walls were compacted soil fused with plastic to a hard pearly grey. There were no windows or skylights – they were too far underground for that. But honeycomb panels in the walls were cycling softly through a succession of real-time Lunar views, dayside, nightside and terminator. Now and then, one of the panels would show some part of Africa. Chiku made out the tinkling glissades of kora music, probably some dusty old recording. The place had a particular smell, some lavender fragrance, that brought with it the happy associations of childhood.

'I've brought something with me,' she said, while Jitendra prepared himself some tea. A pair of mechanical soldiers with clock-keys turning in their backs stomped around his feet. 'I need you to show it to mother, the next time she's ... lucid.'

'That might be a little while.'

'You said it was only a few days since the last one.'

'A few. Maybe a couple of weeks, now that I think about it.' He scratched at his scalp. 'I'm not terribly good with time.'

'None of us is. But this is rather important, Father. If you could get it to her, even if it means *forcing* her out of it ... You can do that sometimes, can't you?'

'I can try,' he said, without much enthusiasm.

'I'm really sorry she's putting you through all this. It's not right.'

'I loved her mind, Chiku. I still do. It is only right and proper that I allow her mind to go where it wishes. Now, what do you have for her?'

Chiku spread her hands, framing a square. Via the quangled bind, she had brought with her the symbols from *Winter Queen*. They crammed together on the pane, neon-bright. She passed the intangible object to Jitendra.

'Some context might be helpful,' Jitendra said, taking the pane from her as if it was real.

'It's Chibesa syntax, obviously,' she said as Jitendra turned the pane around to look through it from the other side. 'I'm sure you recognise the mathematics.'

'It would be difficult not to when your wife's made it her life's commitment.' He was squinting through the pane now, holding it up against the glow from one of the wall panels as it cycled through the orange blush of a Serengeti sunset. 'You think she will find some amusement in this?'

'I think there might be more to it than that. These symbols, assuming I haven't been lied to, came from Eunice's ship – the one she took out of the solar system before mother was even born.'

'Were I examining what purported to be a Ming vase, I might demand some provenance at this point.'

'I can't prove any of it. But if I told you the symbols were shown to me by Arethusa, that would carry some weight, wouldn't it?'

'I suppose so,' Jitendra said doubtfully. 'But then I'd probably want proof that you'd spoken to Arethusa.'

'There are reasons why I can't say as much as I'd like, at least not right now. But I've taken a chance in opening this bind, and I wouldn't have done that just to waste your time.' Chiku hesitated, wondering how much she dared disclose. She had to keep reminding herself that she was not talking to Jitendra but to Jitendra's time-shifted simulation, a full sixty seconds downstream. The real Jitendra would already have begun to catch up with the start of the conversation by now, and the simulation's responses would be adjusted in accordance with his real-time reactions as the dialogue proceeded. But this was not Jitendra. 'I've run some simple checks on that syntax,' she hedged. 'It's ... different. It appears to fit the rules, but the arguments spiral off in unusual directions. It's as if there's a way to build new logical structures that were always there, always implied by the old mathematics, but we just didn't see them.'

'But whoever scribbled down these symbols could see them.'

'I wonder what Mother will make of them. I need to know, Jitendra. Right now, this is the most important thing in my life.'

'But you have the mathematics. If it is something new, take it to the experts.'

'I can't do that. For a start, it's not complete – these aren't fully formed statements, just the outlines of statements that haven't been properly formulated yet. Secondly, I'm not in a position to trust anyone I don't know. If it's all right with you, I'd prefer to keep this in the family.'

'If I didn't know you better, I might have grave concerns for your mental health. You have been visiting a neuropractor regularly, yes?'

'I have, and I also brush my teeth three times a day.'

'Then you have allayed my concerns.' Jitendra walked around the living room with the pane, as if he was looking for a spot to hang it.

'If the syntax points to Post-Chibesa Physics,' Chiku said, a sudden tightness in her throat, 'the holoships need that information.'

'And you would be the one to disseminate it.'

'You of all people know who and what I am, Father. I can't let *Zanzibar* down.'

'No promises, Chiku. You should know that by now.'

'But you will show her.'

'I'll do my best, but you shouldn't count on getting an answer. She would need to understand your urgency, and that is not something I can communicate to her.' Jitendra looked away sharply, as if there was something in his face he did not care for her to see. 'On her best days, when she's back with us, it's as if she never left. But those days are rarer than they used to be. The mathematics has her in its coils, Chiku. I worry that there will come a time when she never surfaces again, and remains lost in her mind.' A sing-song tone entered his voice. '"Caverns measureless to man, down to a sunless sea."'

'You sounded so optimistic, when we started.'

'I try. But it is not always easy.' He rested the pane on a shelf. The object would be totally invisible to anyone who happened to visit or ching into their home unless Jitendra willed them permission to see it. And even then, ninety-nine out of a hundred visitors would not have the slightest clue what those scratchy, faintly anthropomorphic symbols actually signified.

Chiku knew she could trust him with it.

'I'd like to see her, before I go.'

'Are you sure? I seem to recall it upset you, the last time. No one would think worse of you, if you left now.'

'I would,' Chiku said.

'I don't need to tell you where she is.'

Jitendra stood aside and she entered the adjoining bedroom where her mother now spent almost every hour of her life. It was like visiting someone in hospital, someone with an acute physical ailment. In fact there was nothing much wrong with Sunday Akinya, nothing beyond what would be expected after almost two hundred and forty years of existence. She was on a bed, lying flat except for her upper body and head, which were raised slightly by pillows. Her eyes were closed. She wore light silk clothes with a sheet of similar material draped over her. Her arms were at her sides, resting on top of the sheet. She was staring up at the ceiling, her eyes closed. Lines ran into her arms. A simple household medic stood in attendance, its head tilted to the floor while it waited for something to do.

'The machines look after her very well,' Jitendra said, speaking softly behind Chiku. 'Really, though, there isn't much that needs doing. They move her sometimes, to prevent bed-sores. They maintain her muscle tone and bone density. They adjust her drips and catheters. They alert me if there's a change in her state of consciousness.'

'Can I be alone with her for a moment, Father?'

'Of course, Chiku.' He retreated. She heard the whirr of some clockwork thing being wound up, like an insect repeating the same idiot sound.

Chiku moved to Sunday's bedside. She thought of the frozen form of Eunice, the body she could not touch. This time she allowed her robot hand to settle onto Sunday's brow. It was warm, furious with calculation. It was pointless being angry with her mother. She had not gone looking for this obsession. It had found her, ambushed her. Like Jitendra said, it had caught her in its coils.

But she could do something. She could struggle, fight her way back to sanity.

Why didn't she?

'I've given something to Jitendra,' Chiku said. 'I want you to look at it. I know you can hear me. It's connected to this quest of yours anyway, so I doubt you'll need much persuasion. I want to know what you think of it. I think it's really important. Maybe you can make some sense of it. But you can only talk to Jitendra about it. Promise me that, won't you?'

Not that she needed a promise. The miracle was Sunday Akinya speaking to anyone. Of course Jitendra would be the first to hear if she had something to say.

'I can't stay,' Chiku said, withdrawing her hand. 'I've got myself into some kind of trouble. It's bigger than me, maybe bigger than the family. In a day or so I'm going to be back on Earth, going back to Africa. Wish me well, won't you?'

Sunday stirred. Her lips moved, her eyelids fluttered. Then she was back to her repose.

As she took her leave of Jitendra, Chiku said, 'I think she heard me.'

He smiled at her, said, 'That's nice,' and she understood that while he might have believed what she said, he did not for a moment think that she had had the least effect on Sunday.

CHAPTER EIGHTEEN

From his command seat, with no more fuss than if he was specifying the strength of his chai, Imris Kwami bent a microphone to his lips and said: 'Civil vehicle *Gulliver*, registration KKR292G7, heavy inbound from Saturn, requesting vectors for transatmospheric insertion, entry locus East Equatorial Sector, Pan-African Union. Please authorise.'

A voice, doubtless synthesised, came back with a friendly but authoritative: 'You have approach clearance, *Gulliver*. Proceed on appended vectors and level out for horizontal flight above twenty kilometres. Good luck and safe re-entry.'

'Thank you,' Kwami said, before pushing aside the microphone. Then, to his passengers: 'Buckle up, my friends.'

The ship did clever things to itself, making wings and control surfaces appear from the seamless hull. They made a controlled descent, slowing down long before they began to feel the resistance of atmosphere. This was no fiery re-entry, for it would have been inexcusably bad manners to impart heat into an ecosystem that was doing its level best to cool down again. And then they were flying, scrolling east over day-lit Africa. Chiku eased out of her seat and wandered from one side of the ship to the other, scouting for landmarks. Her eye wandered restlessly. She had not been here often enough, she thought. She should have felt some intense genetic connection, but this landscape was as alien to her as the far side of the Moon would have been to her distant ancestors.

But there, that mirror-like glimmer – was that Lake Tanganyika or Lake Victoria? Too far north for Lake Malawi, she thought, unless her mental geography was hopelessly scrambled. Victoria, perhaps. It was huge, whatever it was. Even at altitude she could see only the nearest shore, hemmed by a scratchy margin of coastal towns and beach resorts – angular crystalline projections, domes piled upon domes, like a froth of soap bubbles. Beyond the shoreline developments, the land was a vivid irrigated green laid down in broad parallel brushstrokes.

There were towns and villages inland from the lake as well, linked by a spider-web of surface roads. Harvester dirigibles, fat as bees, bumbled between stack farms while airpods hazed the air like pollen. Thickets of green woodland, areas of tawny cultivation, the regimented shimmer of mirror arrays and the giraffe-necked spires of solar towers, taller even than the production stacks. There were easier ways of generating energy now, but some of these sun farms were family concerns going back generations. People tended them out of a sense of fond obligation.

Soon they were west of the lake, over the vast, open Serengeti. Imris Kwami had dropped them subsonic by then, which permitted much lower flight. Pedro, who had never been to Africa – as far as Chiku knew, at any rate – appeared captivated. Without using the aug or optical magnification, he had already spotted dozens of animals, many different species. The rains would come soon, but the waterholes were still quite low and those were the places to look for wildlife.

'Lions!' Pedro exclaimed, followed by a doubtful: 'I think. So hard to get a sense of scale up here. Maybe they were hyenas. You have hyenas, don't you?'

'We have lots of things,' Chiku said, as if she was taking personal ownership of the Serengeti.

'I think they were lions.'

'Then they were lions.'

Soon they could see Kilimanjaro, heat- and distance-hazed at its base, much sharper and closer at its summit, as if the mountain were leaning in, beckoning them closer. Still hundreds of kilometres away, even now. They owed so much to that mountain, the Akinyas. Eunice had used it as a fulcrum to move worlds.

'Did you come here often as a child?' Pedro asked.

'Not really. Once or twice, to see Uncle Geoffrey. When I was young, it felt like the edge of civilisation out here. Growing up on the Moon, I couldn't cope with the scale – Africa is so huge! And the spaces between things, even then … at night it felt like there was no one else anywhere near the household for thousands of kilometres. Just this little island of humanity surrounded by a dark, swallowing emptiness, like interstellar space. It wasn't, of course.' And Chiku pointed towards the far horizon. 'There have always been other towns and communities, and of course the Masai – they'll always be here, long after we've gone. Masai and elephants. The rest is dust.'

'Morbid.'

'Realistic.'

Kwami, who had been manually piloting, said, 'We will overfly the household then set down nearby. I will try to find some ground where we will not start a fire or incinerate too many animals.'

'If you could,' Chiku said.

'Does anyone live here now?' Pedro asked. 'At the household, I mean.'

'Not sure. Haven't been back in a long while. They won't have let the place go to ruin, though.'

'You hope.'

Of course they haven't let it go to ruin, Chiku thought. But she was mis-remembering again. She was thinking of the duplicate of the household aboard *Zanzibar*, the place where Chiku Green went to work.

'There it is, I think,' she said, pointing ahead.

Pedro craned forward. They were looking through patches of *Gulliver*'s hull, which it helpfully made transparent depending on the direction of their gaze. 'Doesn't look like much.'

'Never said it was the Taj Mahal.'

The household was shaped like an A, two long wings joined at their apex and a short connecting wing bridging the gap between the two. This A-shaped geometry reiterated itself at increasingly larger scales from the building out to the perimeter wall – in the lawns and formal grounds, the patios, swimming pools and tennis courts, the lay-outs of the airpod parking areas. At first, sweeping overhead, Chiku saw no obvious signs of neglect. The walls were as white as she remembered, the decorative roof tiles gleaming with a blue lustre as it if had recently rained. There was no one about, but in the heat of an African after-noon that was not in itself unusual. Indeed, during her earlier visits, the household had always had a deserted and slightly forbidding feel to it. Sometimes it had just been her, Uncle Geoffrey, one or two caretaker staff and a number of janitor robots.

As Kwami brought them around again on a second pass, she began to have misgivings. The walls were white because they were self-repair-ing, not because someone had taken the trouble to keep them clean. Same with the roof. Elsewhere, the evidence of decay was unignor-able. Weeds had conquered the flower-beds. The swimming pools were drained down to their tiles and covered with a layer of dirt and dead leaves. Overgrowth had begun to encroach through archways and por-ticos. The place was not a ruin, not yet – it all looked structurally sound – but it did not appear to be lived-in or much loved.

'I should have come back before this,' she mouthed, more to her-self than anyone else. She had always known that the upkeep of the household was the collective responsibility of all Akinyas, but with that knowledge had come the tacit belief that the upkeep could always be trusted to someone else.

What the hell had they been up to, allowing the place to get like this?

'I will not risk landing so close to the wall,' Kwami said, indicating one of the airpod areas. 'There is a suitable site a little further out. You will not object to a short walk back to the household?'

'It'll be good to stretch our legs,' Chiku said, returning to her seat.

Gulliver had settled into a hover mode, using ducted thrust to keep itself aloft. The trees around the edge of the household cowered in the downdraught. The spacecraft slid sideways, like a puck on ice, then dropped its talon-like undercarriage and began to lower itself towards the ground. Chiku wondered how long they would need to be here. She wanted to be done with all this.

Something shot them out of the sky.

It all happened stupidly quickly. First, an alarm, some kind of imminent collision alert. Then a lurch, bone-breakingly violent, as *Gulliver* tried to sidestep whatever was about to hit it. Then the impact itself, harder still than the lurch, and the spacecraft was yawing badly, losing vectored thrust on one side of its hull. Multiple alarms joined the first. Kwami, who was still on manual control, did his best to stabilise their hover but the damage had been done. *Gulliver*, wounded now, could not keep itself aloft. Something else hit them. *Gulliver* pitched again, the yaw worsened, and then there was the worst impact of all, the one between hull and ground, and they were down, crashed, fallen to Earth.

The alarms kept ringing. The hull was resting at an angle, nearly on its side. It was lucky that Pedro and Chiku had both taken to their seats again for landing or the crash would almost certainly have killed them.

'What happened?' Chiku managed, barely able to believe that only a few moments ago her sole concern had been getting in and out of the household.

'We have been attacked,' Kwami said, extricating himself from his control seat – like theirs, it had cushioned and padded him during the impact. 'And now we must leave, because whatever attacked us is still out there.'

'How? What?' Pedro was asking.

'Some kind of weapon. Please, young sir,' Kwami was already at the nearest airlock, equalising pressure, 'make all haste. There is no safety here, if we can be shot out of the sky.'

'A weapon,' Pedro repeated dutifully, as if this was some kind of memory game. 'There are no *weapons*, Imris. Nothing like that here.'

'Nonetheless, we have just been shot down.'

'I think he means it,' Chiku said, though her own head was fizzing with the frank impossibility of this. An anti-spaceship weapon, something powerful enough to disable *Gulliver* – you might find something like that out around Hyperion, but this was *Earth*, for pity's sake. You could not raise a fist to someone on Earth, much less fire an *anti-spaceship weapon* at them.

The airlock gasped open, inner and outer doors sliding back simultaneously, and although she was still within the hull, the heat of the day hit Chiku with an almost belligerent forcefulness. Kwami scrambled through and hopped to the ground, keeping his long frame bent and eyeing their surroundings with sharp suspicion. 'Something is out there,' he said. 'We cannot remain in the open. Perhaps we can make it to the household.'

'Perhaps?' asked Pedro.

Chiku hauled herself up and through the tilted airlock, hands on the rim of the outer door. The hull, still hot from hypersonic flight, burnt her fingertips. She bit down on the pain and squeezed out into blazing daylight. Kwami helped her descend – it was a longer drop than he had made it look. She hit the dust, knees buckling, and Kwami urged her to stoop lower. 'Quickly, young sir.'

Pedro came out, face flushed, eyes wide with fear and incomprehension.

'This can't be happening, Imris. Venus was bad enough, but to be shot at here—'

'We must move,' Kwami said.

'What do you think it is?' Chiku asked, as the three of them began to make a stooping run in the direction of the household's perimeter wall. 'Didn't anything show up as you came in?'

'This is Earth, young miss. One cannot go jumping at every shadow.'

Chiku looked back at the downed spacecraft. Two ugly craters marred the exposed underside. Some energy pulse or projectile had punched all the way through the hull into the tender gristle of subsystems beneath its skin.

'*Gulliver* found many concealed objects in the area, buried beneath the surface. The underground workings of your household, the course of the ballistic launcher ... many relics and items of unknown origin. People have been living here for thousands of years. Under the circumstances, *Gulliver* could not easily discriminate between the innocent and the hostile.' He paused to catch his breath. They were still only a third of the way to the wall. 'Nor could it employ its own defences. We were much too close to the ground – our own counter-strike would have risked damaging us.'

'Risked,' Pedro said. 'I'll take *risked* any day.'

'We can't blame Imris,' Chiku said. 'There was no time to think.' As she spoke, her foot slipped into a depression, twisting her ankle and sending her sprawling into the hot dirt. The impact turned her around, facing back towards the ship. Beyond it, where a line of scrub marked the transition to thicker bush, she saw movement. Something was dragging itself into daylight.

It was a machine the colour of sand, like a crab with a squat, turret-like body and rows of jointed legs. The thing was half-shrouded in dirt and vegetation, as if it had just climbed out of a hole in the ground.

'What's that?' Pedro asked.

'I don't know,' Chiku answered.

'An artilect,' Kwami said, pausing to help her back to her feet. 'Can you walk?'

'I think so.' The twist hurt, but she could still put weight on the ankle. 'What do you mean, an artilect? Eunice is an artilect. So is Arachne. They're nothing like that thing.'

'It is a war robot, a military artilect.'

She forced herself to keep moving, eyes on the wall, anywhere but on the thing coming out of the scrub. 'Nothing like that would be allowed here,' she said, voice raw.

'It has probably been here for several centuries,' Kwami said. 'There were many of these things at one time. They ran amok during the Resource and Relocation crises. There were many unpleasantnesses. Then they were outlawed. Please, let us make haste.'

Chiku was fine with making haste. Running was beyond her, but her lop-sided stagger was still covering ground. Half-lost in vegetation, an arched portico offered a way through the wall. Not far to go now.

'I remember ...' she said, forcing out the words between ragged breaths. 'My mother, back when she still told stories. Something happened to her when she was small. I think it was near here.'

'It's coming after us,' Pedro said. 'Why doesn't it just shoot?'

'Perhaps the weapon it used against *Gulliver* only has ground-to-air capability,' Kwami said. 'Maybe it has exhausted that particular type of ammunition.'

Pedro nodded. 'I think it still wants to kill us.'

'I concur with your assessment.'

The ground between them and the gap in the wall appeared to be dilating, stretching out the way spacetime did between galaxies, plumped by an infusion of dark energy. Chiku had been lost in dreams like this – running from something, unable to cover ground. The air quickening to something like aspic, jellying her into immobility.

'This has to be Arachne's doing,' she said.

'Again, I concur. If the artilect has been here for centuries, dormant, undetected, it provided her with another way to act without drawing direct attention to herself. All she had to do was infiltrate its dormant systems and rouse it from cybernetic slumber.'

'Imris,' Pedro said. 'Would you do me a favour and stop talking as if all this is happening to someone else, on another planet?'

'My apologies, young sir. I fear it has become something of a survival mechanism.' A rattling sound came from behind them. Ahead, a line of holes appeared in the wall, to the right of the gate. 'It is shooting at us now,' Kwami said, 'but its aim appears to be compromised.'

The machine fired again, then stopped. Chiku glanced back. It was limping across the open ground where *Gulliver* had fallen, two of its articulated limbs dragging uselessly. An unearthed horror that should have stayed buried. Something like this machine had tried to kill her mother, when she was very small. Or at least turn Sunday into something it could use. Chiku remembered the story now: the thing in the hole, speaking inside her mother's head before it was taken away to be neutralised.

Kwami pushed through a tangle of undergrowth, opening the way through the gate. Chiku and Pedro followed him through into the household's outer enclosure.

'I do not know if this wall will hold it, but there must be deeper levels of the house that it will not be able to reach.'

Chiku was still having trouble with her ankle, but for now adrenalin was doing its job. They moved along dusty flower-beds, weed-choked and ruined, and skirted fountains that had not seen water in decades. In the shaded corner of one swimming pool, a snake insinuated itself into a burrow of leaves and dirt. Then they were through a second wall, into the inner courtyards. More empty swimming pools, overgrown ornamental gardens, dried-up ponds. 'This way, I think,' she said, leading them around the flank of the leftmost wing. 'Imris – could there be another one of those things waiting for us in here?'

'The Cognition Police were very efficient when they rounded up and neutralised the military artilects,' Kwami said. 'I doubt they left many behind for Arachne to find. Besides, when we flew over the house, I think we would have seen the damage if one had already forced its way through the wall.'

'Could one of them have tunnelled under the perimeter?' Pedro asked.

Kwami reflected for a moment. 'I suppose that is a possibility.'

'I'm sorry I asked.'

They were coming around to the front of the household now. Chiku had given no thought as to how they would enter the building if the way were barred. The doors had always been open when she visited before, even when it was just Uncle Geoffrey and a handful of maintenance staff in residence. But then there had never been much reason to lock doors. One step at a time – if worst came to worst, they could return to *Gulliver*, perhaps, to fetch tools.

But the doors were open. They were ajar, hinged inwards. It was difficult to tell whether they had been forced or not, but it did not look as if a powerful machine had broken through them.

They all heard it at the same time: a crunch, metal on masonry. It was coming from around the side of the property, where they had passed through the wall.

'It is still trying,' Kwami said.

'The place shouldn't be this abandoned,' Chiku said. 'There should be watchdogs, robots ... even if there's nobody living here.'

'If Arachne can infiltrate and commandeer an artilect, perhaps it is for the best that there are no robots within the compound,' Kwami said.

They crossed the threshold. The house had been well designed for the local climate, cool within even on the hottest day. Chiku pushed the doors shut behind them. They would not be any kind of barrier to the artilect, but closing them made her feel better. Not safer, just better.

'How long before help arrives?' Pedro asked.

'In what manner?' Kwami asked, with perfect pleasantness, as they moved along one of the corridors, shoes squeaking on black and white marble.

'Where the hell is the Mechanism?' Pedro demanded. 'We're hurt. We're being attacked! Shouldn't some kind of intervention be under way?'

'I fear, young sir, that matters may not be that straightforward.'

'You think she's in the Mechanism as well,' Chiku said.

'It was something June always feared. Arachne's control cannot be absolute or she would have used direct neural intervention to incapacitate or euthanise us. But it may well be within her means to block and confuse the Mechanism's scrutiny.'

'Probably doesn't help matters that my family went out of their way to keep the Mech from penetrating the household,' Chiku said waspishly. 'They didn't want the eyes and ears of the world stealing their precious commercial secrets.'

They descended steps. It was a blessing that it was daytime as there were no lights anywhere in the building, although some of the illumination cascading through the big windows above ground was filtering down to the lower floor. Chiku's eyes began to amp up in response, making the best of the available photons. The prevailing colours sickened to grey-green as they went down another flight of stairs.

'What we're looking for is on this level, if Arethusa was right,' Chiku said. 'I never came down here much. I only ever visited to talk to Uncle Geoffrey, and he never had any reason to bring me downstairs.'

'I don't like it,' Pedro said. 'We should be running from that thing outside, not boxing ourselves in.'

'If we abandon the household,' Kwami explained patiently, 'the artilect may smash it to pieces before anyone can stop it.'

'And this is a problem because ... ?' Pedro asked.

'With the house turned to rubble, you would stand little chance of recovering the Crucible imagery. I trust this remains of interest?'

'It does,' Chiku said, although it was much easier to say this than feel it.

She opened some of the doors as they moved along the corridor. One room contained about twenty identical black statues of Masai warriors, individually shrouded in plastic film, waiting to be given away as corporate gifts. Another contained a small private library. In a third was a stuffed lion, caged behind glass.

They had come to a point where the corridor met two others at an angle – echoing, Chiku presumed, the above-ground geometry. For a moment, she was disorientated, uncertain which way to go. They had been in too much of a rush to get inside for her to find her bearings accurately.

'Which way?' Pedro asked.

'That one.' But she immediately undermined her authority. 'I think.'

Pedro was looking along the other corridor, with its ranks of doors. Some were open, some shut. It was much gloomier now, even their amped eyes struggling. 'I think I saw something down there,' he said.

'What?'

'Something crossing between two of those doors. Fast. Like a shadow.' He added: 'Maybe I imagined it.'

'The artilect can't have got down here,' Chiku said.

'Maybe they're not all as big as that one.'

'We would know it, were one here,' Kwami said. 'Those that have survived are powerful and dangerous, but the military ones cannot move silently, or in such a confined area. I do not think what you saw was an artilect.'

After a moment, Chiku said, 'I don't think it's this way after all.' Now she was pointing down the corridor where Pedro thought he had seen something move.

'We should have brought a torch,' he was saying. 'We have been to Saturn and back and we didn't bring a torch.'

They went down three steps and started along the corridor. Chiku pushed open one of the closed doors, poised to spring back if there was something waiting inside. In the semi-darkness she made out more statues like the ones they had already passed. She was about to move on when she realised that these were not corporate gifts. They were proxies, waiting to be chinged by a remote client. Spear-thin, stick-figure sketches of people, their faces polished blank ovoids.

'If she accessed one of them, could she harm us?' Chiku wondered aloud.

'One would be unlikely to pose a threat,' Kwami said.

'But what about two, or three—'

'The Mech is thin here – she will have found it difficult to link into proxies. I believe we should continue.'

Chiku closed the door on the room full of robots.

'I saw it again,' Pedro said, frozen where he stood.

Chiku could feel his fear leaking from him like an airborne contagion. She knew that nothing she could say or do would make him go any further. Maybe he was right.

'Are you sure—' she began.

'I have just seen it,' Kwami said, cutting her off. 'I think it may be an animal.'

'What kind of animal?'

'I only saw it fleetingly.'

'An animal I could cope with,' she said. 'It might scare us, but that's all. Are you sure?'

'It was an animal. Some species of cat, I think.'

That was when she heard the scratch of nail on floor. It had come from behind them, not further along the corridor. She turned around with fearful slowness. Something breathed in and out, quite rapidly, and then she heard a low, ruminative rumble.

'Yes, cats,' Kwami said.

CHAPTER NINETEEN

It was their eyes she saw first. Two pairs, hovering like binary stars. It took a second or so for her brain to make sense of the low, muscular forms to which the eyes were attached.

Panthers. She had no idea how she knew this, but her brain provided the information all by itself.

'They can't hurt us,' she said.

'Let us hope,' Kwami said, 'that their Mechanism inhibitory implants are still functioning.' He closed his eyes, formulating a complex and deadly neural invocation. 'I shall issue a kill command.'

He raised a hand, slowly, in the direction of the panthers and voked the mental instruction.

Chiku and Pedro did likewise. Every human knew how to do it, though few expected ever to put the knowledge into practice. Uncle Geoffrey, in one of their last conversations, had spoken of Memphis Chibesa killing a huge and belligerent bull elephant simply by willing it to death – dropping it like a sack of meat.

The panthers were still alive.

'It is not functioning,' Kwami said unnecessarily. 'Either the Mech is too thin, or she has disabled the kill function, or these cats have always lived beyond Mech influence.'

'Can they kill us?' Pedro asked.

'Left to their own devices,' Kwami said, 'they would not normally predate on humans, but it is well within their capabilities.'

Chiku dragged her eyes from the waiting cats and glanced in the other direction. If Pedro was right – and she was inclined to believe him – there was another one, at least, somewhere further down the corridor.

Cats. How clever of Arachne, she thought.

'They're not strong enough to break down the doors,' Chiku said. 'If we all get into one of these rooms, then block the door from the other side ...' But her mind was already running ahead, pointing out the foolishness of this plan. They could not stay here until the cats wandered away, not with the artilect moving around up there.

'We must take our chances with the cats,' Kwami said. 'They may be beyond the Mech's influence, but that does not automatically make them killers.' And he threw up his arms and roared at the panthers, as if that might startle them into turning away.

It did not. Far from intimidating the panthers, his action only stirred them into motion. They began to advance down the stairs, side by side, black cat-shaped cut-outs moving through degrees of gloom. Their pupils were the only features in a head-sized void. It was as if their eyes moved on invisible rails, sliding along some geodesic curve of maximum feline stealth.

Chiku swallowed. The cats clearly would not let them pass without a fight. 'Perhaps there's something in the other rooms that we can use against them,' she said. 'Maybe we can ching into those robots, use them for cover—'

Kwami had interposed himself between Chiku, Pedro and the panthers. He still had his arms raised and was repeating, over and over: 'Stop. Go away, now. Stop. Go away now,' as the cats slinked towards him.

'Imris!' Chiku said. 'Don't provoke them. Mecufi must be on his way by now.'

Pedro grabbed at her sleeve. 'We can't help him.'

They progressed down the corridor, Pedro facing into its depths, Chiku unable to tear her gaze from Kwami. The cats were nearly upon him now. He had lowered both hands almost to the horizontal and was still muttering, but she could not hear the words now. Amazingly, whatever he was saying or doing appeared to be having some effect. The cats were still advancing, but were now flattening their bodies towards the floor as if in submission. The two dark shapes had coalesced into a single moving form, a clot of blackness with four hovering eyes.

The other cat – if there was another cat – still had not shown itself. Chiku glanced through an open door as she passed. A billiard table with stiff wooden cues racked on the wall next to it. They could climb on that table and use the billiard cues against the cats, if all else failed. But she still hadn't reached the door she was aiming for.

She glanced back at Kwami. The cats had stopped at his feet, hunched down so low to the ground that from a distance they could have been pelts.

'Imris . . .' she called after him.

He began to turn his head. 'I think—' he started.

196

The black forms sprang, fast and almost silently, like a conjuring trick – two black pelts pulled into the air on hidden threads and dropped onto Kwami like a pair of smothering cloaks. He fell to his knees and the cats swallowed him in their darkness. Chiku heard no scream, not even a groan. The only sounds came from the cats.

She finally registered that she was staring at a man being mauled to death by panthers.

'Come on,' Pedro hissed.

'We have to help him!' Chiku said, moving to return to Kwami.

One cat let out a fierce yelp followed by a sharp snakelike hiss. The black form pulled away from Kwami and the cats became two again. One of them was on the ground, on its side. The other crouched back from Kwami, snarling, uncertain whether to retreat or resume the mauling.

Chiku caught a glint of metal in Kwami's hand.

The cat still standing backed further away. The other was dead or in the process of dying, its blood a spreading extension of its own blackness.

Kwami had a knife all along, Chiku registered. The little gleaming blade was not much longer than her finger. The knife fell from his grip and rolled onto the floor. Chiku grabbed it and stabbed in the direction of the retreating panther, making her own hiss. The panther continued to back away. It was bleeding from between its forelegs, but the wound did not look fatal, so far as she could tell.

'Imris.' She knelt by him, glancing rapidly between the cat and the injured man. 'Imris. Talk to me.'

She could hardly see his face, it was so covered with blood. She decided, for a moment, that Kwami was already dead. But then his eyes flashed in the darkness and he managed to speak.

'I am hurt. The cats were on me before I could do much with the knife.'

'Are you in pain?'

'No. I have turned off the pain. But I do not feel strong. I fear I am bleeding quite badly.'

'We'll get help. It won't take long for a scrambulance—'

'You forget, Chiku, that we cannot trust the Mechanism. I have already voked the necessary request for medical assistance but have received no confirmation that my call has been logged.'

'I'll go outside and call again. The Mech'll be stronger—'

'It is still much too dangerous to go above ground. You must take care of yourselves now. You came here for a reason – do not lose sight of the bigger concern.'

She glanced at the other cat, which had still not made up its mind whether to remain or go. 'I won't leave you here, on your own.'

'Young miss, it is imperative that you do so. In time, I am confident that some sort of intervention will arrive – one cannot shoot down a spaceship in the Surveilled World and not have someone notice. But until the household is safe, you must think of yourselves. Go now! If you would return my knife, I shall do my best to deter the other cat.'

'Imris—' she began.

'Go,' he whispered.

She handed him the knife. The other cat eyed her. She backed away.

'Come on,' Pedro hissed from the doorway of the billiards room.

'The right room's down this way,' she said.

Pedro dived into the billiard room and grabbed cues from their rack, four of them in one go. He passed two to Chiku. 'If the cat attacks,' he said, 'go for its eyes. Only its head and eyes. Nothing else is will hurt it.'

She held a cue in each hand, like ski sticks. They were not going to help, she thought. The cat would paw aside this joke of a defence in a heartbeat. Better to swipe hard, maybe, and hope to club the life out of it? It was strange how the myriad puzzles of her life had thinned down to this single little question: how best to murder a cat with a piece of wood.

Something flashed and roared further along the corridor, in the direction they were about to head. *Not a panther's roar*, Chiku thought as she blinked the blinding light away. She caught an after-image framed in the corridor's perspectives: a figure too thin to be human holding something that looked like a stick.

The figure said, 'This way – quickly.'

The blast had given the panther still crouching near Kwami the encouragement it needed to leave. Another roar, another flash, and Chiku got a better view of the stick-figure. It was a proxy, identical to the ones they had seen earlier. It was holding a clumsy-looking sort of weapon made of wood and finely patterned metal.

'Quickly,' the figure urged again.

She knew the proxy's voice. 'Lin – is that you?'

'This way. Now!'

The proxy opened one of the doors, and instead of darkness beyond there was a red glow – the only artificial light Chiku had seen since they entered the building. It could only be the room she was looking for.

'What took you so long?' Chiku demanded breathlessly as she and Pedro made their way towards the light.

'I've only just managed to squeeze enough of myself through the blinds and feints she's erected in the Mechanism. This proxy is running autonomously – Arachne's interference would impede direct control of it even if there was no time lag to consider. I'd like to keep my actual whereabouts hidden, though, so let's discuss the details later.'

The proxy ushered them into the red room and closed the door behind them. It put down the weapon, which Chiku now saw was an antique rifle. 'Elephant gun,' it explained. 'I found it, loaded and ready, in one of these rooms. A gross violation of every civilised law against the ownership of firearms, but you Akinyas always did love your blood sports.'

'Imris is hurt,' Chiku said, so short of breath that she struggled to get the words out.

'I saw. I'll try to summon medical assistance at the earliest opportunity, or failing that, do what I can for him myself.'

'Wait,' Pedro said, pinching sweat of out his eyes. 'I still don't get it. Why are you here? If you wanted to help, why didn't you just come with us in the first place?'

Something scratched against the door. The proxy maintained a resolute grip on the handle. 'Let's just say that I wished to keep my involvement to the minimum, especially given the time and energy I have expended in not bringing myself to Arachne's attention. Nonetheless, I was curious about what you'd find here. I also suspected you might run into difficulties.'

'Is this the place?' Chiku asked.

'Yes. There's another room through that door behind you. The wall is already displaying a preliminary integration of the complete Crucible data set. When you are present, it'll achieve maximum resolution.'

'How do we get out of here?' Chiku asked.

'Leave that to me.'

She was out of options. She passed through the connecting door into a slightly larger windowless subterranean room The proxy held back, securing the outer door.

One whole wall was filled with an image of Crucible so sharp and real she felt as if she was standing in space, in a room with only three walls, looking out through the absent fourth. The brightness affronted her eyes. It was a familiar image by now, from the Earthlike colours and contours of the world itself and the alien disfigurement of Mandala – but not so alien after a thousand viewings – to the cyclonic and anticyclonic cloud patterns, nature's hand guided by laws of chemistry and physics that held currency from here to the edge of the universe. Coriolis forces, triple points, time and tide.

She became aware of Pedro standing next to her.

After a silence, he said, 'What are those things around Crucible?'

'I don't know. In the doctored data, there was nothing around the planet. Arethusa saw ... areas, volumes, where something had been processed out of the data stream. This is what Arachne was actually hiding.'

'They're in orbit.'

'Yes – or in space, anyway, floating around the planet. I don't think we should make too many assumptions right now. It's not our job to make sense of it, just to get it to the right people.'

'The right people being ... you. Chiku Green.'

'Apparently,' she said, suddenly overwhelmed by a bleak and fatalistic certainty. 'I had my doubts, but I'm more certain of that now than ever. This can't be made public, not yet. Not here or in the holoships. It's too much. It would rip us all apart.'

'Those things are huge. No, huge isn't a big enough word. The holoships are huge. Those things are like chunks of a planet. They must be hundreds, thousands of kilometres across.'

'Easily.'

'And we're sure the Providers didn't make them?'

She nodded. 'Present when Crucible made the first detection. And something about that detection, something Arachne saw, made her – it – hide these things. But not Mandala. She concealed one piece of alien intelligence, but not another.'

'She must have had a reason.'

'Tell me what you see,' said Lin Wei's proxy from the other room.

'Things, structures, orbiting Crucible. They're huge and very dark – they only show up against the dayside. They're like pine-cones, with the sharp end pointed down at the surface.'

'Numbers?'

'Hard to tell from this one image. Twenty, maybe more. I'd say they're a few thousand kilometres above Crucible. And big – several hundreds of kilometres from end to end, easily. Maybe a thousand, give or take. They're definitely not natural. The pine-cone structure – it's very geometric, very regular. There are some lights or something shining out between the overlapping parts. Mostly, though, they're just dark. I suppose they must be ships, or stations ... gathered around Crucible ... the way the holoships are supposed to when they arrive.'

'Do you see any connection, physical or symbolic, between the orbiting forms – we'll assume they're orbiting – and the Mandala structure?'

'No ... I mean, nothing obvious. Not that I'm an expert in this kind of thing, you know?' But after a moment, Chiku added: 'Oh, wait.'

'Yes?'

'The image is moving – I hadn't realised that until now. The angle of view is changing, very slowly.'

'It can't be a real-time grab – there just isn't the bandwidth, especially after Arachne doctored the data. You must be seeing some kind of phase-averaged summation compiled over many orbital and seasonal cycles.'

'Our viewpoint appears to be locked over Mandala – it's just the objects that are moving. We're in the same orbital plane as them. One of them is sliding right under me, showing me its blunt end, pointing back into space. The overlapping plates start at the back and work their way towards the sharp end. It looks half-engineered, half-grown. It's definitely nothing humans could make – not now, not in centuries. The holoships, they're just pieces of leftover rock we've turned into ships. These are colossal. And there's something in the middle of the blunt end, like an engine nozzle – except I don't think it's that. I'm looking down it now. There's a light, very bright, shining out of the back – I couldn't see it at all until now. Yes, very bright – it's blue ... I don't suppose it's an engine, not if the objects are already in orbit.'

'There will be more analysis. When I have something to report, you'll be the first to know.'

'You said there was a way out of here.'

'Move to the right wall. It's subdivided – press the middle panel, it should spring open onto a staircase. The wall will seal behind you as you descend. The rest you'll work out for yourself.'

Chiku did as Lin instructed, puzzled and fearful even as the wall sprung aside as promised. Red lighting traced a steeply descending metal staircase.

'Down there?'

'Down there. Be quick, now.'

Chiku and Pedro went down the metal stairs. They had the spartan, clattery feel of something bolted together in a hurry. 'Thank you, Lin,' Chiku called as the wall whisked shut again, and they were alone in the red-lit shaft.

The stairs continued down a long shaft bored through solid rock. Every fifty or so steps there was a small metal landing at which the stairs reversed direction and resumed their descent.

'What's under here?' Pedro wondered.

'My family built this thing called the blowpipe. It's basically a big tunnel that goes all the way under the household, out to Kilimanjaro and up the inside of the mountain. They used it to shoot things into space.'

'I see.' The absence of enthusiasm in his voice accurately mirrored her own apprehension. 'And when you say "shoot things into space"—'

'I think people could use it, if there was an emergency.'

'Maybe Lin just meant for us to use the tunnel itself as an escape route.'

'In which case we'd need about five days' marching rations. And spacesuits.'

They had descended a good hundred metres, Chiku estimated, when they reached the bottom of the stairs. They were deep into the cool, dark African bedrock, the day's heat and brightness a memory far overhead. The stairs had brought them into a large room through which the metal tube of the blowpipe passed from one wall to the other.

Chiku explained to Pedro that the blowpipe did not begin here, within the household, but somewhere hundreds of kilometres to the east, in an Akinya-owned transhipment facility that had probably long been mothballed. At that location, cargo and passengers – mostly cargo – were loaded into the blowpipe's capsule-like packages, ready to be catapulted into space.

But to Chiku's surprise, Eunice or her children, perhaps, had made provision for a quick getaway. Next to the horizontal shaft of the blow-pipe was a heavy mechanical rack containing three launch capsules, each a rounded bullet barely larger than a cryogenic casket. There was also a complicated thickening in the pipe, some kind of valve and air-lock device, Chiku presumed, with a door that looked about the right size to admit one of the capsules.

'This is insane,' Pedro said. 'When was the last time anyone used one of these things?'

'There's power. No reason for it not to work just because it hasn't been operated in a long while.' Chiku climbed onto a little walkway that brought her up to the level of the racked capsules. She looked inside the unit closest to the blowpipe and studied the thickly padded interior, working out where her feet and head would go.

'It's only big enough for one,' Pedro said, clambering onto the platform next to her.

'Looks that way – but there are three capsules.'

'Do you have the faintest idea how to use one of these things?'

'Let's just hope that'll take care of itself, shall we?' She planted her hands on her hips and inhaled deeply. 'OK – how do we do this? Draw straws?'

'Because that worked out really well on Venus, didn't it? No, no straws.'

'I agree.'

'But what's in your head is more important than what's in mine, so I think you should go first. On the other hand, it's an untested system, so maybe I should go first instead.'

'And while we're debating, the artilect might be about to smash the house to rubble and cut our power. I'll take the first capsule. After that, we'll just have to wing it.'

'These things go into orbit, right?'

'Yes, so let's hope Mecufi's up there waiting to rescue us. He must be monitoring us by now. Surely he knows we're in trouble.'

Pedro kissed her. 'Get in. We'll be fine. I'll be right behind you.'

'See you on the other side.'

'Yes, you will.' And he kissed her again, then gently encouraged her into the capsule. As soon as the lid closed, the already snug interior became even snugger as the padding sensed her intrusion and began to conform to her precise body shape, becoming a Chiku-shaped mould. She could hardly move once it had finished oozing into place around her. Her face was clear, though, and in front of her was a small glowing panel filled with text and status diagrams, updating rapidly.

A soft female voice said in Swahili: '*Checkout complete. Vacuum integrity verified. Projected airspace clear. All magnetic and optical systems at nominal readiness. Launch authority enabled. Awaiting go command.*'

'Launch me,' Chiku said.

'*Launch sequence initiated. Please stand by for induction tube insertion.*'

She barely felt the shove through the padding as the capsule slid sideways, into the valve/airlock mechanism. She felt like a jacketed round being chambered in a rifle.

'*Launch spoolback commencing. Spoolback will terminate in ninety seconds and may be overridden at any point. Maximum spoolback acceleration: five gees. Maximum forward launch acceleration: ten sustained, two hundred momentary.*'

She understood – or thought she did, at any rate. She was being shuttled back to the start of the blowpipe to give the capsule the full run of the tube to build up its speed. On the display hovering before her face, a green digit climbed up to five gees and stayed there. Cocooned in the protective padding, the acceleration was easily bearable.

But ninety seconds was a hellishly long time. She thought of Pedro, waiting back there on his own. Presumably the system would not allow his capsule into the blowpipe until hers was already clear and on its way to orbit. The spoolback was taking too much time, she decided, and the capsule did not need it to reach launch velocity.

'Override. Abort spoolback.'

'*Continue launch sequence?*'

'Yes.' Her voice was dry, barely comprehensible. 'Yes. Do it.'

'*Decelerating. All safe-load ceilings now suspended. Forward acceleration will exceed recommended physiological tolerances. Launch may be aborted until alpha threshold. Maximum induction will be applied in five seconds. Four ... three ...*'

She closed her eyes, as if that would make a difference.

Acceleration hit hard, like a monstrous metal piston slamming into the back of the capsule, ramming it forwards. For a terrifying instant, she thought nothing in the universe could apply or endure so much force.

Yet somehow she remained conscious. Through blurred, tunnel-constricted vision she saw the acceleration digit rise to ten ... eleven ... twelve and finally level out around thirteen gees. But she knew this was the smooth part of the ride. Ahead, the induction tube curved to thread through the stone bowels of Kilimanjaro. She had heard that was the tough part – a transitional moment of hundreds of gees as the capsule made the swerve.

'*Alpha threshold in twenty seconds. No abort possible after alpha threshold ... Alpha threshold in ten seconds ... Alpha threshold passed. No abort now possible. Nominal launch sequence proceeding. Prepare for transient load.*'

She prepared, if that was the word, by clearing her thoughts. She would lose consciousness during the swerve as the blood was squeezed from her brain like water out of a sponge, curtailing every thought until it flooded back in again when the capsule decelerated. In an eyeblink she would be rising through Kilimanjaro, then shot into rarefied atmosphere as launch lasers stationed around the summit provided her remaining escape velocity.

As she felt her consciousness fading, she wondered how much she would remember, when it was all over.

CHAPTER TWENTY

Falling. She remembered falling in her dreams, falling out of the rigging of a great swaying galleon, high above oil-grey seas, and now she was falling in her waking life, weightless as a moonbeam. In that everlasting fall she felt warm and blissful and eternally safe. She wanted it to go on for ever, a dream of never being born.

But then a shrill voice pierced her amniotic tranquillity: '*Alert condition. Orbital injection has failed. Atmospheric re-entry will commence.*'

She forced herself into something approximating alertness. *Where am I? What just happened to me?* A few disconcerting moments of blankness, then the images began to surface. The household. A nightmare of cats and darkness. Red stairs and a thing like a coffin, into which she had climbed. Leaving Pedro behind, with the cats.

And then something had gone wrong.

The launch lasers should have pushed her the rest of the way to orbit, fingers of light cradling her upwards from the summit snows of Kilimanjaro like a gift from Earth. But they had failed. She was falling back home, a prisoner of ballistics, following a mathematical arc that had only one inevitable outcome.

She was not feeling quite so weightless now.

'*Atmospheric interface detected. Transitioning for blunt-capsule re-entry. Anticipated entry gee-loads in range four to four-point-five. Ablative measures at nominal temperatures. Impact projection locus: Indian Ocean, fifty-seven-point-five degrees east, one-point-one-five degrees north, point-five-degree error ellipse. Political jurisdiction: United Aquatic Nations seaspace. Anticipated splashdown in eight minutes. Scrambulance and air/sea rescue services alerted. Please remain calm.*'

'Chiku?'

Her battered brain registered a new voice. 'Yes,' she said, thick-tongued.

'It's Mecufi. I'm speaking from the seasteads. We have a lock on your capsule and a communications channel I think we can rely on. You're currently falling back to Earth.'

'I know.'

'There appears to have been a momentary fault with the launch array – one of the lasers was misaligned. In light of my recent conversation with Arethusa, technical sabotage cannot be ruled out.'

She tried to nod, but found herself still immobilised in the capsule's embrace. 'It's possible,' she said, imagining Arachne infiltrating the launch lasers' control system or co-opting a service robot to physically damage the array. 'Mecufi, listen to me. You also need to get someone to the household – Imris Kwami has been badly injured. While you're at it, can you tell Pedro to sit tight? I don't want him risking his neck in this thing.'

'Mr Braga is not with you?'

'No – we had to ride this thing one at a time. I went first.'

'I see.

'Mecufi?'

'Yes.'

'What aren't you telling me?'

'We have a . . . seismic indication that the blowpipe is currently active.'

'You have to stop him – tell him to abort.'

'We can't, Chiku. We could only speak to you once you were in space, above the atmosphere. The launch lasers create a plasma that interferes with communications—'

'Mecufi, I don't fucking care. Just find a way to stop him.'

'I'm sorry, Chiku, but we can't just *turn off* the blowpipe. Your should know that – your family made this thing.'

She felt infinite dread and helplessness. 'You have to help him.'

'We'll do what we can, but you are our immediate priority. Your entry vector looks satisfactory. How do you feel?'

'Oh, just marvellous.'

But in truth she could not complain about her immediate physical needs. The gee load was nothing compared to what she had already experienced. It was starting to get warm inside the capsule, but it would be a while before it became uncomfortable. She could feel some buffeting, the occasional flutter of hard turbulence, but nothing excessive.

'We have Pedro,' Mecufi announced suddenly.

'You've reached him already?'

'No – we have a lock on him. He's cleared the top of the mountain . . . rising at a steeper trajectory than your own ascent. The lasers are continuing to push the capsule . . . I think he will reach orbit safely.'

'You *think*?'

'It'll take a few moments to plot his projected course. The failure of your launch was much more obvious from the outset. Ah, now *this* is concerning.'

'What now?' She made no effort to hide her irritation.

'Your estimated impact point is very close to a Provider construction project.'

'I thought I was coming down mid-ocean.'

'You are, but there are Providers everywhere. The breakaway sea-steads, the independencies with their stupid alliances. This may be coincidence, but ... well, perhaps not.'

'What the hell's happening, Mecufi?'

'The Providers are breaking off from their work – they've been tasked to move to your splashdown area.'

'Mecufi, listen to me. I don't know what Arethusa's told you, but it's vital that those Providers don't reach me.'

'Preventing them may be ... problematic. Our own deep-ocean assets are moving to your splashdown location, but they may not reach you before the Providers do.'

'You'd better make sure they do.' Then she closed her eyes, surrendering to her fate.

After that, there was nothing to do but fall. As the atmosphere thickened, the capsule gradually decelerated to terminal velocity. The temperature inside the capsule had not increased and its soothing voice assured her that parachutes would soon deploy, slowing her descent further. She breathed a silent prayer to the blowpipe's engineers for considering the possibility of launch failure and installing safety measures.

She felt the parachutes deploy – a quick succession of tugs as drogues and canopies popped. Ancient technology, but a clean and dependable breaking mechanism nonetheless. A couple of minutes later, she felt a firmer jolt as the capsule hit water and submerged, then a rising and falling sensation as it resurfaced and bobbed on the waves. Cued by some automatic trigger, a large area of the capsule's skin flicked to transparency. She was floating on her back, water sloshing across her field of vision as each swell broke.

'*Please await rescue*,' the voice instructed, as if some other option might have presented itself. '*Capsule integrity optimal. Life-support systems functioning normally. Sedation is available upon request.*'

Under normal circumstances, the knowledge that the Providers were on their way would have made her relax. A few hours aboard this bobbing glass lifeboat, while scarcely pleasant, were a distinct improvement on drowning. She could even, with an effort of will, imagine how she might have viewed her surroundings under better circumstances. It was, in the objective sense, actually quite a nice day to be floating out at sea. The sea was a luscious jade green, the sky boundless and cloudless. There were no ships or boats visible, but the capsule was so low in the water that there might be vessels not too far away. She pictured the coloured fishing boats she had seen on the flight from Lisbon, imagined being hauled out of the sea by laughing fisherfolk, with their tall stories and strong coffee.

'I see you're safe.' Mecufi's voice startled her from her reverie. 'The Providers are advancing but our assets should reach you first. You're in UAN seaspace now, so sovereign jurisdiction should be clear. Are you comfortable?'

'I'll cope. Do you have an update on Pedro?'

'Yes …' The merman was silent for a few moments. 'The news is not as good as we might have hoped.'

'What's wrong?' she asked, with a profound, visceral apprehension. 'Did Pedro fail to reach orbit?'

'The trajectory looked good to begin with and his arc was much higher than yours, but the lasers were still malfunctioning.'

'He can still re-enter, can't he? He'll just come down somewhere else, right?'

'There is a … difficulty. Pedro's capsule is still moving ballistically, above most of the atmosphere. Soon his trajectory will bring him dangerously close to one of our vacuum chimneys and—'

She cut in. 'Will he hit it?'

'He will most probably skim past the tower and continue deeper into the atmosphere, but unfortunately the chimney won't tolerate the possibility of a collision.'

'What do you mean, "tolerate"?'

'The chimney is equipped with self-defence protocols. We're attempting to override them, but it might not be possible.'

She could hear his words, process their surface meaning, but her mind wouldn't comprehend their full import. 'Mecufi, you can't let this happen.'

'I assure you, Chiku, we're doing everything in our power to prevent it.'

'Can I speak to him?'

'Yes, but please be aware that Pedro isn't aware of the danger he's in. Since he can't act upon that information, it may be kinder to let him—'

'I want to speak to him. Now.'

'Are you sure, Chiku?'

In the rise and fall of the swelling waves she was certain of nothing, much less the wisdom of this course of action. What would she want, if their roles were reversed? To think she was safe when she was not? Or to know the truth, bitter as it was, and have a few moments to compose herself, or perhaps choose drug-induced painlessness and bliss, a little promise of heaven?

'Let me speak to Pedro.'

'Establishing the connection. You have a couple of minutes before he enters the avoidance volume. We'll keep trying.'

She could blame Mecufi, but that would be pointless. The avoidance volume was designed to protect the many at the expense of the few. A cruel calculus, but it allowed the world to work.

'Chiku?' Pedro's voice filled the capsule.

'Yes,' she said, swallowing hard. 'It's me. I'm down, floating. I'm told help's on its way.'

'The right sort of help, I hope. That was a hell of a ride, by the way. We should do it again some time!'

'Yes. We should.' And then she had to bite her tongue, because nothing she was about to say sounded right in her head.

'I've spoken to this friend of yours – Mecufi, is it? He says I nearly reached orbit but couldn't quite make it. I guess I'm not going to come down anywhere near you.'

'They'll find you,' she said.

'Yes, of course. I'm not worried now, just glad to be out of that place. I can't stop thinking about Imris. I hope he's going to be all right.'

'We did everything we could for him. Imris wanted us to escape. And he'd be glad we saw what June and Eunice and Arethusa wanted us to see.'

'It's in your head now – you being rescued is all that matters.'

His choice of words was accidental, but they cut her to the core. As if he knew, deep down, the truth of his predicament.

'Mecufi will take me to the seasteads. I'll be safe there, and they can do whatever they need to do to access my memories. Depending on where you come down, it might be a while before we're reunited.'

'She won't leave you alone, you know. You'll never be safe.'

'Nor will you.'

'But you're her primary target. I doubt Lisbon will be safe any more – too many ways she can reach us, if she's still interested.'

'Maybe she won't be.' But deep down Chiku knew Arachne would never lose interest in them, not even after she had transmitted her memories back to *Zanzibar*. Chiku would still be a liability, walking around with a head full of secrets. 'You're right, though – we could move on.

Become merfolk! Join the aquatics! It wouldn't have to be for the rest of our lives – just a holiday from being human.'

'Chiku, is something wrong?'

'No,' she answered, just a touch too hastily. 'Everything's fine. I mean, as fine as it can be, given what we've just been through.' But he had heard it, she knew – the false note in her voice, the forced optimism. The strained levity of the deathbed visitor.

And then an immense, oceanic calm washed over her. 'Actually, Pedro, it's not all fine.'

'What are you saying, Chiku?'

'Mecufi thinks you might be about to die.'

When he replied, she heard the slightest hint of amusement in his voice: hardly laughter, but definitely amusement. 'I knew the bastard was hiding *something*. How bad is it?'

'Your trajectory will take you near a vacuum chimney. There's a small chance you'll hit it. More than likely you won't, but Mecufi thinks it'll shoot you out of the sky before you get a chance.'

'Nice of him to mention that.'

'I think he was trying to be kind.'

'He was, I suppose. And you telling me this, it isn't very kind. But thank you.'

'I'm sorry.'

'I'd rather know than not, Chiku. We've been together long enough for you to know that. I don't need kindness at this point.' He inhaled deeply, exhaled. 'How long do I have?'

'Mecufi said a couple of minutes.'

'From the start of our conversation?'

'I think so. Yes.'

'Ever since we saw what happened to June Wing I've been wondering whether I'd have her strength, when the time came, to say, fine, I've had my life, I can't complain. I just didn't expect to get to find out quite so soon. I was thinking a few more decades, maybe a century, then I'll worry about the answer to that question.'

'I'm sorry,' she repeated.

'No, don't be. I'm … coping. As you say, there's a chance, so no heroic last words. I have a question, though – just one.'

'Go on.'

'You've never really asked me about my life before I met you. I know everything about you, where you were born, what you've done … almost the entire history of your life. You're an Akinya – it's hard to get away from that! But I'm just some man you met buying ice cream. And unless I've missed something, that's all you know.'

'It is.'

'Just a man who makes guitars, in a little studio in Lisbon. A man who works with wood and glue and string. And it's true – that's me. But there's more. Not as much of a life as yours, but still – it's mine. Someone ought to remember all of it. If you want to.'

'I would.' Then, as if affirming some time-honoured vow, she said: 'I do.'

'I have a friend, Nicolas. You know him – he comes to the studio sometimes. Always complaining about this or that. Nicolas knows me. He'll tell you my story, if you can stand his company for a few hours.'

'I'll speak to him. I promise.'

'Thing is, I've had some ups and downs. Some adventures, too. Been further than you'd guess. But whatever happens, this has been fun – it's been good knowing you.'

'I'm really sorry I dragged you into this.'

'Oh, don't be. I'm still glad we chose to buy ice cream at the same time. Even if those seagulls were thieving bastards.'

'They were,' she said, wanting to smile, but not quite having the strength. 'They definitely were.'

She waited for an answer.

She lay in her little bobbing glass boat, adrift from herself. There was no present, no past, no future. No sadness, no sorrow, because those were ordinary little human emotions that required a frame of reference, and she had none to cling to. She had caved in, become a measureless void, no poles, no lines of latitude or longitude. She was an emptiness bigger than galaxies, unmapped and unmappable.

The worst thing of all, the knife that would not stop twisting, the realisation that left her so utterly harrowed, was that she would do all of this again. It had all been necessary. She had worlds to consider. The lives of multitudes hung in the balance.

On the horizon now, blurred through the water-washed glass of the capsule, Providers were advancing. There were three of them – pale outlines, all joints and limbs, like the projected forms of magnified insects. They looked as tall as thunderheads. The water here must have been kilometres deep, so they could not be walking on the ocean bed – could they? – but however they travelled, they terrified her. Where were the airpods and scrambulances?

'Mecufi,' she said, just a word, an oath as much as a plea. Because for all his promises, Mecufi had done nothing except fail to save Pedro.

Perhaps Arethusa had it wrong after all, her judgement blunted by the years in Hyperion. Perhaps Mecufi was not to be trusted.

The Providers were closer still. She thought of the ones on Venus, their trumpeting exchanges. She wondered what they would do when they arrived. Not kill her, surely. At least not in any obvious or culpable fashion. But damage her, perhaps, so that her memories could not be retrieved. Make it look accidental, another complication of the blowpipe accident. These things happened, people would say. Even in a perfect world. The Providers had done their best.

Something knocked on the glass.

It was a hand, webbed between the fingers. The shadowy form the hand belonged to vanished beneath the water and resurfaced on the other side of the capsule. She could see a body now, and a face. Mecufi was the only merperson Chiku thought herself capable of recognising, but this was not Mecufi. This was a sleeker, leaner organism, the skin tone darker, the architecture of the face different.

She knew it. It was her own face, or rather it had the same proportions, the same balance of features, but altered for aquatic life. It was her son's face.

'Kanu,' she said, astonished and numb.

He planted a hand against the glass, fingers spread. The skin between his fingers was fine-veined and translucent. The only reason for that touch was to offer reassurance.

Chiku twisted in the capsule. It was difficult to move, but she struggled until she could mirror Kanu's gesture. They were palm to palm, only glass between them. Kanu's lips moved. She could not hear him, but she thought he was telling her not to worry.

Beyond Kanu, something much larger broke through the waters, a huge and glossy thing with a shape too complicated to comprehend in one glance. Another surfaced a little to the right. Water rode off them in cataracting rivulets as they breached into daylight. She remembered one of Uncle Geoffrey's stories, of being rescued at sea by the merfolk, of a voyage in an ancient clanking submarine. Doubtless the details had been embroidered, but somewhere in the telling would have been a core of truth. It could not have happened very far from here.

This, though, was no ancient submarine. It was changing shape as she watched, muscular parts moving against each other as it transformed. What she had originally thought to be two or three things were in fact a single entity. As the main part of it emerged – a kind of tapering iron-grey hull, plated in places and soft in others – she realised that she was staring not into a porthole but an eye, perfectly defined, wider than she was tall. The eye regarded Chiku. Kanu, interposed between the capsule and the eye, moved his arms in a kind of sign language.

Tentacles intermeshed around her bobbing coffin to form a slithering cage and closed around the capsule. Suckers pressed against glass sought and obtained traction. The glass creaked, but held.

And then Kanu and the kraken carried her under.

CHAPTER TWENTY-ONE

She awoke with her face in grass, blades up her nose, in her eyes, regiments of mud storming the battlements of her teeth.

She heard the urgent patter of approaching feet. Shoe-squelch on grass.

'Here,' a voice said. 'Let me help you back up.'

Hands took her body and eased her into an ungainly sitting position, legs still tangled on the lawn. She felt like a discarded doll. As she wiped the dirt from her face, she noticed that her palm was a greasy green-yellow with the pulp of grass and soil, where she must have reached out to stop her fall.

'I tripped,' she said, tongue moving thick and slow in her mouth, like a fat, lazy slug.

'You had a microsleep episode – normal enough this soon after revival. Usually you'd just stumble through it and not notice, but your inner ear is still a bit wobbly.' A person dressed in crisp electric-white medical overalls was kneeling next to her. 'Are you all right?'

'I think so.' She tried to remember what was happening before she came to on the grass, but for a moment she was unshackled from everything other than the present. 'What was I doing? Where am I?'

'Taking a stroll. You're in the gardens.'

'Gardens.' The word felt novel, unusual in her mouth.

'Of the revival clinic. We woke you, brought you out of skipover.'

The technician was smiling gently. He was a stocky man with pleasing features and a tonsure of black curls around a gleaming bald spot. She felt certain she knew him, but no name came to mind.

'You've been conscious for a day,' the man added kindly. 'It's perfectly normal to have some setbacks until things settle down.'

Her addled thoughts searched for a point of reference. Where was she? She remembered being in many places lately. On Earth, in space, inside a mad, tumbling moon with a core of scratched glass. In a house of cats. In a box, falling through the sky. In the grip of a sea-monster.

No, she was in *Zanzibar*. In a revival clinic's gardens, in one of the community cores.

'I expect I've asked you this already—' she began.

'Forty years. And yes, you've asked a few times. But again, it's normal.'

Her throat was wretchedly dry. She felt like a mummy, a thing stitched together from tissue and cloth.

'I don't remember the date. When I went under, or what it should be now.' She was trying to work things out, but her thoughts kept running into a ditch. This, she reflected, was how it must feel to be stupid, unable to hold the simplest chain of reasoning in her head. Even that notion was difficult for her to comprehend.

'It's 2388 now. You went under in 2348, forty years ago to the week. Here – do you want to try standing again?'

Chiku took his outstretched hands and let him help her up. She was unsteady on her feet at first, needing the technician's hand at her elbow for a few moments. 'I feel like a wreck. I've done this before. Why doesn't it get any easier?'

'You're actually doing really well. Forty's not too bad a skip, anyway – not that the duration makes much difference to the side effects, in my experience. You were authorised for the full sixty, too – the rest of your family are still under.'

'You've told me this already, haven't you?'

'About nine times. But don't worry – it's all part of the service.'

'How's Pedro?'

The technician's smile tightened. 'There isn't a Pedro – not according to my manifest.'

'No, not Pedro,' she said, concentrating hard. 'I mean Noah. And my children – Mposi, Ndege. They all went under when I did. How are they? Have I spoken to them yet?'

'That would be difficult as they're all still in skipover.'

'Then why am I awake?'

'You asked to be, Chiku.' There was a faintly impatient edge to his voice now, as if, despite his assurances, there was a limit to how often he ought to have to explain this stuff to her. Perhaps it had been more than nine times.

'I'm sorry,' she said. 'I just need to ... clear my head a bit. I think I was going somewhere.'

'There are some benches over by the fountain. Shall I help you the rest of the way?'

'No,' she said, deciding she would make it on her wobbly legs or not at all. 'I can manage. I feel steadier already.'

She followed the hiss of water to the ornamental fountain. It was just around a curve in the lawn, hidden by a wall of manicured hedge twice as tall as Chiku. Somehow she had half-known the way. She must have already come to the fountain several times since her revival, forever discovering it anew.

The revival clinic had been designed to feel as little like a medical facility as possible. The building behind her was low-ceilinged and white under a wide-brimmed witch's hat of a roof, with pavilioned walkways and many open windows and doors. It was hemmed in by trees and hedges, a century and a half's worth of managed growth. The skipover vaults were somewhere else entirely.

Overhead blazed a ceiling of false sky. It struck Chiku that the quality of light had altered since she went under. Which, upon a moment's reflection, was surely the case: they were adjusting the spectrum and brightness from year to year, slowly transitioning to the conditions anticipated on Crucible. 61 Virginis f, their new star, was slightly smaller and cooler than the Sun, its spectrum fractionally more orange in hue. But no one ever noticed this infinitely slow gradation except skipover sleepers, who woke feeling as if they had coloured filters on their eyes.

Next to the ornamental fountain – a comely astronaut tipping water from her space helmet as if it were a jug – sat three wooden benches of rustic design. Two of the benches were unoccupied, but a woman dressed in white was sitting on the one in the middle. Chiku made to take one of the other benches, but the woman patted the planks next to her.

'Take a seat. We've got a lot to talk about.'

Chiku had given the woman no more than a sideways glance until that point, but now she had her full attention. The woman sitting on the bench was her. A ghost, like the one that had haunted her in Lisbon.

'How are you here?' Chiku asked, sitting down where she had been told.

'I'm not real – I'm in your head. But you guessed that already.'

'Have we spoken?'

'Before now? No, this is our first time. I came up on the uplink, a messenger figment. No one else can see or detect me, although your half of the conversation will be open to eavesdropping. So please be extremely circumspect in your statements.'

'I'm very, very confused.'

'I understand, but there's no need to be. I've sent my memories back to you, to be scripted back into your head, but you were asleep, in skipover. The memories can only be unpacked by functioning neuromachinery, and that had to wait until you began to warm up.' The woman in white leaned forwards on the seat, hands laced between her knees. 'The process has begun – you're beginning to remember things about my life, things I did and saw. People I knew. Feelings I felt. It's been tough, Chiku – much tougher than I expected. Much tougher than *you* expected, to be frank.'

'I think we should be.' And she rubbed her scalp, the hair short from skipover, as if there was something itching between her ears. 'I feel something inside me. Like a stone. What am I carrying around?'

'Grief,' the other Chiku explained. 'Pedro died. We loved him. There was an accident ... sort of.'

'I feel as if I knew him.'

'You did. Once we started swapping memories, our individual identities lost coherence. That's why we did this. That was the point – until one of us stopped communicating.' But then she shook her head, smiling at the same time. 'There's no sense in complaining – I might as well blame myself. We're the same. We made the same mistakes. We can be as stupid as each other.'

Now that the feeling inside her had a name, it hardened rather than eased. A person, a man called Pedro Braga, had been torn out of her life. It was more than just the name, the knowledge of his passing, the recognition that she had loved him. She could hear him, feel him, smell him. Whistling as he worked with wood and resins. Joking at a client's meanness. Weeping at the sound made by a few fistfuls of air trapped in the hollow belly of a guitar, when all the stars of his craft fell into some rare alignment. Throwing back his head and laughing, the two of them on a balcony in a city she had never visited. The tang of wine in her nostrils. The sweet cool of an evening in the company of her lover. Sea-gulls and ice cream.

She wanted to say that she was sorry, that she commiserated with the version of herself who had lost Pedro, but that was wrong. She was the version who needed solace now.

Both of them were.

'I know,' the other Chiku said. 'It hurts, doesn't it?'

She realised she was crying, tears spooling out of her, falling onto her hands, through her fingers onto the lawn.

'He was a good man. I never wanted this. I never wanted anyone to die.'

The ghost dropped a hand onto her knee. She felt nothing of its touch. 'You did what needed to be done. That's the hardest part of all. Even given what you know now, you'd still need to send those memories back to me. Of course, with hindsight, we might have done a few things differently.'

For a long minute, Chiku could barely speak. But the memory of death had opened a door.

'He wasn't the only one who died, was he?'

'We lost June Wing, and Imris Kwami was seriously injured. The important thing, though, is that nothing should have happened in vain. I'm going to ask you a question now, and it's important that you think carefully about the answer.'

Chiku nodded. She was in the presence of a figment of herself, no older or cleverer, but it was difficult to shake the sense that she was being given a kind of sisterly tuition, wisdom delivered from one sibling to the next.

'Equally,' the figment continued, 'I don't want you to say anything that might compromise your position here. I've been drinking from the public nets, and there've been some changes around here. Have you kept up with the news?'

Chiku admitted that she had not.

'Utomi's gone,' the figment said. 'There was an accident, about fifteen years ago – a blowout in one of the cargo docks. Nothing as bad as Kappa, but serious enough. Of course Utomi wanted to be there, helping out – always the big, brave leader. But some kind of secondary failure took out some of the teams who were in there trying to stabilise the place. It all happened very quickly. There was nothing they could do for Utomi and the others, other than collect their bodies when the emergency was over. Sou-Chun Lo is the new Chair.'

She digested the news of Utomi's death. It was an abstract concept, a proposition rather than an actuality, and she couldn't quite process it.

Eventually, she said, 'Sou-Chun's a safe pair of hands.'

'For *Zanzibar*, maybe. Do you remember Travertine?'

'Of course.'

'Vis case has come up for appeal three times – once under Utomi, twice under the Sou-Chun administration. Utomi was moved to consider some form of clemency, but Sou-Chun won't even consider it. It's not that she has anything personal against Travertine, but *Zanzibar* needs allies now. Do you remember that hard-line bastard Teslenko, aboard *New Tiamaat*?'

'Hard to forget a merman.' But for a moment it was Mecufi who came to mind, not Teslenko.

'He's only grown worse during the years you were out. In a sense, there's little point blaming Sou-Chun for taking the line she has – if she

218

hadn't, Teslenko would have annexed *Zanzibar* years ago, declared it an administrative client state. Regardless, you're going to find Sou-Chun's inflexibility ... difficult.'

'I still have my vote, my position on the Assembly. Perhaps I can talk her round.'

'Good luck with that. You don't have long to dither, either: less than fifty years until we reach Crucible, whether we slow down for it or not.'

'Thanks. That cheered me right up.'

'I haven't even started. Do you remember the image you saw in the household? The picture of Crucible, the structures that looked like pine cones?'

'Yes,' she said, diffidently at first, then with more certainty. 'Yes, it's in there – there was blue light shining from one of them.'

'We still don't know what those things are, or what Arachne makes of them. There are twenty-two of them, and they're definitely machines – products of an alien intelligence. Whether it's the same intelligence that was responsible for Mandala, we can't guess. Perhaps they're from somewhere other than Crucible. As for that blue light – it wasn't an exhaust, or a weapon, or anything like that. It was a beam of information – an optical laser pushing out from the back of one of the pine cones. And they're all doing it. Think of twenty-two spokes of blue light, with Crucible at the hub. As the structures alter their position around the planet, the spokes sweep space. Sooner or later one of them was bound to cross our line of sight.'

'What does this mean?'

'Given the information at our disposal, we can't begin to tell. But Arachne had the full Ocular data stream, not just the tiny part we hived off. If there's meaningful structure in that beam, she may have been reading it since the moment she detected Crucible.'

'Reading isn't the same as understanding,' Chiku said.

'True. Equally, we have no real idea of her intellectual capacity – or what that blue beam has been doing to it. How's your memory coming along?'

'Firming up.'

'Good. I had my doubts when you were stumbling around like that, mixing up one thing with another. You're going to have to be strong, Chiku Green. Clear of head and clear of purpose. Much needs to be done.'

'I don't know what to do.'

'Build a ship, something faster than *Zanzibar*. Get ahead of the caravan, meet the Providers on your terms, not theirs.'

'Yes, I'll get right on with that. Thanks. For a moment there I thought you might have something useful to contribute.'

'I think we should leave the sarcasm to our great-grandmother, don't you?'

'If Utomi wouldn't sanction a relaxation in the moratorium on the necessary research, what hope have I got under Sou-Chun? Plus I'm not planning on staying awake for months and months.'

'There is something else,' the figment said. 'Do you remember your visit to the Moon? Speaking to Jitendra and our mother?'

Our mother. As if the figment had equal claim on her. 'Yes,' Chiku allowed.

'Jitendra showed her the patterns you left with him, during one of her lucid moments. That was just after your visit, before you reached Earth. As soon as she'd seen the Chibesa syntax, she sank into the deepest state of contemplation Jitendra had ever witnessed. It went on for days, weeks – something close to death. There was still activity in her brain, but he began to believe she was finally lost to him. It was so hard on him, after all he'd been through. But then she turned a corner. Between one hour and the next, she came out of her mathematical fugue. And she'd changed, Chiku. Some tremendous burden of responsibility had been lifted from her. She said she'd finally found her way out, to the light, and that she'd never need to go back. She'd found what she'd always been looking for, and which had eluded everyone else – a pathway into Post-Chibesa Physics. The golden light of PCP. There had been times when she was terribly close, but those symbols finally showed her the way.' The figment shifted its hand to her own, although still she felt nothing. 'It's the one good thing to come out of this. Sunday's returned to Jitendra. Our mother's back.'

'She's said that before.'

'It's not just empty words this time. After she'd rested a while and recuperated somewhat, she still remembered what she had seen. She had a clarity of vision she'd never known before. This wasn't some mirage of a solution.'

'I'm happy,' Chiku said, and it was almost the truth. She was pleased beyond words for Jitendra, pleased that her mother had crawled out of those measureless caverns. But it failed to shift the stone in her chest, or make her feel any less apprehensive about the future.

'With Jitendra's help,' the figment went on, 'our mother was able to write down the key axioms of PCP – enough to be getting on with, anyway. But they'll only make sense to someone who's been butting their head against Chibesa theory for a lifetime.'

'Travertine.'

'Ve is the only one who has a chance of building on Sunday's insights, of turning them into something practical. It could take years – maybe decades. But that's the only way you'll get to Crucible ahead of *Zanzibar*. I've arranged for a copy of the axioms to appear in your private files – you'll find them easily enough.'

'Do you know what they did to Travertine?'

'Of course.' The figment moved to stand. 'One last thing, before I go. I've left something else in your private files – the neural structures Arethusa managed to extract from the corpse of our great-grandmother.'

'She said they weren't worth much.'

'Possibly not, but I can think of someone who might be able to find some use for them. I'll leave it to you to work out the necessary arrangements.'

'Will you be coming back?'

'I don't think so. You'd bore of me very quickly – I'm an empty vessel. There's really not much more in my head.'

'Then I should say thanks.'

'For what?'

'Everything, I suppose. For answering me, in the end. For going to Venus, Saturn and so on. I'm sorry it cost us so much.'

'So am I,' the figment said.

CHAPTER TWENTY-TWO

By the following morning she was able to leave, but it took some persuasion. The staff at the revival clinic, concerned for her mental welfare, had summoned Dr Aziba, a specialist in skipover complications. Older now than when they had last spoken, Chiku still recognised the soft-spoken physician. He had a long, handsome face and a carefully maintained tonsure of snowy hair circling his crown like a white atoll. His fingers were very long, like those of a highly adapted prosimian. He ran some tests, not as exhaustive as she had expected, and then decreed her fit for the world.

'But you will return to us soon?' Dr Aziba asked, mindful that she had used up only a portion of her skipover allowance.

'Yes, of course. But I have work to do first.'

'Waking so early is somewhat ... unprecedented.'

'Is it illegal, Doctor Aziba?' she asked brightly.

'Not in the slightest. Just uncommon.'

'Then all I've done is exercise my right, wouldn't you say?'

Aziba was not the only one troubled by her premature emergence. The other staff found it puzzling enough that they kept coming back to her with new questions. It was as if, on some level, they recognised her as a potentially disruptive influence, a troublesome agent best put back to sleep. It bothered them, also, that she had made this arrangement to wake in advance of her family.

Forty years was time enough for a world to change in ways both trifling and substantial. She had verified the figment's account of the political changes – Utomi's death and the shift to a more authoritarian regime under Sou-Chun Lo. *Zanzibar*'s government still maintained the illusion of autonomy, but in all significant respects it was being externally administered by those hard-liners who felt the terms of the *Pemba* Accord had not been nearly strict enough. Public research projects had been suspended indefinitely and scientists reassigned to projects concerned with issues that might arise subsequent to their arrival at Crucible.

While the political changes had been sweeping, in other respects surprisingly little had altered. They had repaired Kappa, of course, plugged the hole and pushed air and warmth back into the chamber, and now people were working in that space again. But not huge numbers, she gathered, and very few of them chose to live there even though they'd been offered larger dwellings and gardens if they relocated. People still found Kappa troubling. It had poked a hole in the fiction of their safe and snug environment and reminded them that there was space beyond the skin of the world. Everyone had always known that, but Kappa had made them feel it in their bones.

In her own community core, there were a few more groups of houses, a few more roads and pathways. But the crippling resource bottleneck that had consumed years of her political life, appeared never to have arrived. Or had been blunted, perhaps, deflected by a thousand small contingencies.

She made her way home. No tenants had been allowed to move in while her family slept, and there were no obvious signs of neglect. She broke through the transparent membrane stretched across the doors and windows, peeling pieces of it from her skin where it sought to cling. The door opened easily and she let herself into the little kitchen where Travertine had come to talk. On the table, imperfectly erased, was the red circle left by vis wine glass. They would never get rid of that now.

Chiku drew out a chair and sat at the table, elbows on the wood, fingers laced together. She wanted it to feel strange, returning to this place, but there was no sense that she had been away more than a few days. She could have walked the rooms blindfolded and found nothing out of place.

When she wearied of the silence and the stillness, she rose from the table and moved into the study she shared with Noah. At the old desk she called open her private files, barely surprised when the desk acceded to her request without complaint. The house and its furniture had barely registered her absence.

The private files contained the two items the figment had promised. She opened the first and stared at the chains of scratchy stick-men and cave-drawing symbols that supposedly constituted some axioms of Post-Chibesa theory. It meant nothing to her, but that did not make it invalid.

She thought of Jitendra, giddy with happiness at his wife's return. It had been a kind of anti-bereavement. Her mother had dived into her obsession and her father had believed her drowned. And then she had come back to him from the depths. Chiku remembered the bitterness she had begun to feel towards Sunday for doing what she did, even though there had been no real choice for her. Such was the nature of obsessions: no quarter given for the human cost. Now she tried to snuff out her bitterness, as if it was a cold flame that it was in her gift to extinguish. But she could not. Sunday had returned, and that was a joyous thing, but her mother had only come back because she had found her solution, not because she had suddenly remembered Jitendra. And that Chiku could not forgive.

She opened the second file. The desk found numbers, vectors of neural connectivity, and attempted to offer graphic visualisation. Broken structures, vague as phantoms, snaked and branched through the cloudy outline of a mind. It resembled a half-mapped cave system – baroquely complex, wormholed by passages that went nowhere and connected to nothing obvious. The visualisation offered stabs at landmarks, territories: *anterior cingulate cortex, left basal ganglia, caudate nucleus.* Elsewhere the system appeared unsure as to what it was attempting to map. Arethusa's assesment had been correct: there was nowhere near enough coherence to attempt a revival. But that did not mean this information was valueless.

She was about to close the desk when she noticed something else – a message on her private channel. Her involvement in Assembly business was suspended while she was in skipover, and her wider family – distant members of the Akinya line, Noah's own relatives – as well as colleagues and friends all knew she was asleep. A message welcoming her on her return to wakefulness, perhaps? But no – the appended time tag showed that the message had been sitting there for nearly as long as the two new files.

She opened it with a measure of trepidation.

It said: *Ching here*, followed by an alphanumeric code, otherwise meaningless, which she nonetheless committed to memory. She thought about voking it immediately – it would only prey on her mind if she did not – but as her resolve to do so strengthened, she heard footsteps on the path outside, a single peremptory knock on the door, the door opening. She locked the desk and returned to the kitchen. A slant of daylight cut across the floor. Travertine had already let verself into the house.

Chiku stared at ver rudely, unable for a moment to find anything to say.

'I'm not *that* much of a horror, am I? Or are you upset that I just let myself in?'

'I wasn't expecting you,' Chiku said.

'But you knew our paths were bound to cross eventually. It's a small world, after all. I've just short-circuited the inevitable.' Ve came further into the kitchen and eased the door shut behind ver. 'I heard you came out of skipover early.'

'I suppose you were spying on me, waiting for me to come home?'

Travertine gave an uninterested shrug. 'I've been keeping an eye on things while you were away. Do you mind if I sit? These knees of mine aren't what they used to be.'

'Be my guest.'

Travertine took the seat Chiku had been using only a few minutes earlier. Ve rested vis arms on the table and the heavy black bracelet around vis right wrist clunked on the wood. Every few seconds, a little red light pulsed, telling Chiku it was still interfering with Travertine's metabolism at a profound level, circumventing genetic and exosomatic prolongation factors.

It showed in vis face. Forty years had etched grooves around vis mouth and lines around vis eyes, accompanied by a general slackening of facial tone. There were marks and blemishes she did not recall from their last meeting, and a loose, leathery texture to the skin under Travertine's chin. Flecks of grey nestled among vis black curls.

Chiku, still standing, said: 'I won't apologise for what happened to you, if that's what you've come for.'

'I haven't come for any other reason than to see an old friend.'

'Our friendship crashed and burned sometime around Kappa.'

'Promises were certainly broken.'

'I did what I could,' Chiku said, nodding at the bracelet as it gave off another red pulse. 'Count your lucky stars they didn't execute you.'

'Still, you'd be hard pushed to call this a kindness. Shall I tell you something?'

'I'm sure you're going to whether I want you to or not.'

'They don't want me to die. Not before my time, anyway. They were worried at the beginning that I might take my own life rather than see this through to the bitter end, so they had someone shadowing me for a while. Later, they brought in a robot from *Malabar* to do the job. They've realised now, though, that I'm not going to do it.'

'You're not the sort.'

'Not really. Plus I wouldn't want to spare them.'

'Spare *them*?'

'If I commit suicide, they won't be forced to watch me decay. No, they're going to get their money's worth out of me. I'll walk their nightmares.'

'So the only reason you're still alive is spite?'

'You know me better than that, Chiku. I'm naturally curious, and no one really knows how long I've got before I finally fall to pieces. Decades, easily. A century, maybe. I'm taking care of myself.' Travertine clunked the bracelet against the wood. 'This thing isn't perfect. Every now and again I hurt myself, accidentally or otherwise.' By way of illustration, ve picked at an old scar on vis wrist. 'It's been interesting to track my repair processes. I still heal pretty well, so some of the prolongation pathways are still operating. I'm dying, but not as quickly as you'd imagine.'

Chiku wondered if she was meant to take this as good news.

'Maybe you'll get clemency.'

'Under Sou-Chun? I never thought I'd say this, but it almost makes me wish Utomi was still in charge.'

'I hear Sou-Chun doesn't want to talk about slowdown.'

'That's an understatement. We're only a whisker away from it becoming a crime to even mention it. Actions contrary to the public good, stoking fears, dissemination of irresponsible ideology and so on. An idea so dangerous it can't be discussed. I thought we buried all that nonsense back in the Dark Ages.'

'So did I,' Chiku said. 'But we're a long away from home now.'

'Do you want to hear the funny part, though? Whatever Sou-Chun says in public, whatever statutes she implements, there's always something going on behind the scenes.'

'Like what?'

'Autocratic governments are masters of self-contradiction. They say one thing, do another. Here's an example. Sou-Chun is suppressing all public debate regarding slowdown, terminating research programmemes left, right and centre – even some that were entirely legal under the *Pemba* rulings. At the same time, there's a very obvious clandestine research effort into exactly those areas banned by Sou-Chun's legislation.'

'That doesn't make the slightest bit of sense.'

'Welcome to politics.'

'But why would she do that? We already had the research lines – why would she outlaw them, then start them up again in secret?'

'To curry favour with the other holoships, obviously. To be seen to be doing the right thing while conducting business as usual behind the scenes. Because secretly, deep down in her soul, Sou-Chun Lo is scared shitless. As well she should be.'

'This is just speculation.'

'I wish it was. From time to time, I receive these … visitors. They're always civilians, never anyone claiming to act on the Assembly's behalf. They say they're lawyers or journalists, working to build a case in my defence. In order to help me, they need more details about what happened in Kappa. So of course I oblige. Slowly, though, the conversations begin to take peculiar turns. Odd non sequiturs lead to detailed questions regarding physics or mathematics, as if that was the point of their visit all along. *And would you say your problems stemmed from a miscalculation of the capture cross-section, in failing to allow for all third-order terms?* That kind of thing.'

'I don't understand. Why would they do that?'

'Because there's something going on and they don't have all the answers. Or any of them, truth be told. And of course I play along, because even though I'm being used, it amuses me intellectually.' Travertine shifted vis weight on the chair. 'The ruse is utterly transparent – they're not trying to build a case for my defence. They're trying to repeat my experiment.'

Chiku absorbed that. Even allowing for Travertine's cynical predisposition, it had the nasty taint of plausibility.

'It's possible you're reading too much into a few innocent questions.'

'I'm not. And it explains why they're so keen to prevent me from committing suicide – I'm still useful to them.'

'All right. Suppose you're not making this up or imagining it and there really is something going on, with or without Sou-Chun's authorisation – is that really so terrible? You might not like being lied to, but at least it means that someone's finally taking this stuff seriously.'

'We might still be too late.'

'But surely it's better to be doing something rather than nothing, even if it's clandestine. Who knows – they might find a practical application for whatever they discover long before we figure out how to slow down something as massive as *Zanzibar*.'

Travertine had been looking at vis hands, which were raw around the knuckles from some sort of physical labour, but now ve looked up sharply.

'Like what?'

'I don't know,' Chiku said, feeling as if her thoughts were written on the outside of her skin, scrolling like a newsfeed. 'A ship or something.'

For long moments the two of them just looked at each other, measuring time by the ticks of the black bracelet, each pulse a reminder of Travertine's forced mortality.

'You must have wondered.'

'About what?'

'Why I never used that broken promise against you. You've always had principles, Chiku – it was strange to me when they deserted you so rapidly. I heard rumours that Utomi blackmailed you into that vote, that if you'd gone against the majority verdict you'd never have been granted skipvover.' Travertine was studying Chiku with a particular shrewdness now. 'That never washed with me – those principles of yours again. Skipover would have meant a lot to you, but enough to go back on a promise? That's not the Chiku I knew.'

'We all change.'

'And you changed so much that you were willing to break a promise and risk being exposed by me?'

'I'm glad you've had something so significant to occupy that fancy brain of yours, these past forty years.'

'Yes, and while we're on the subject … why forty years, exactly? The public files are transparent, you know, even to a pariah like me. You and Noah and the children were granted sixty years, not forty, so what brings you out so soon?'

'I was just dying to reminisce with you about the old days.'

'I bet you were. But let's turn things around for a moment. Did you ever wonder why I didn't go public with the map, the sphinxware, the stuff under Kappa?'

'You'd have been censured for not disclosing it as soon as you discovered it.'

'Fair point, but given that I was already being tried for causing the deaths of two hundred and fourteen people, do you seriously think I'd have lost any sleep over that? Be real, Chiku – they couldn't have punished me *more*, so what did I have to lose by telling them the rest? They'd already decided the death penalty was too much of a kindness.'

'Fine, I give up.'

'I didn't use that information against you because I wanted to see what your next move would be. I decided to play the long game: take my punishment, become this thing that I'm turning into and watch what happened. I've been watching you for forty years, waiting for something to happen. And now you're out of skipover, without your family, and you don't look happy – I can't help but wonder why.'

'Maybe I'm unhappy that you're in my kitchen. Maybe I'm unhappy that in forty years I've been on ice, and we're still no closer to slowdown. Maybe I'm unhappy because I somehow have the idea this is all my fault, as if I'm to blame for your woes.'

'All good reasons to be miserable, Chiku.' With a scrape, ve pushed back the chair. 'Well, I'll be on my way. It's been lovely to catch up. You'll be going back into skipover at some point, won't you?'

'If I choose to,' Chiku said.

'I envy you the possibility. I'm dying to know what we'll find when we get to Crucible. Literally, as it happens.'

'It's still a long way off.'

'But closer than when we started this conversation,' Travertine said.

'What do you want from me?'

'You crucified me for a reason. Maybe I'm being too generous, but I don't think it was *just* so you could get that skipover assignment. Or if it was, you wanted skipover for some other reason than the one everyone believes. Something bigger than personal advancement, bigger than taking care of your family and making sure your lovely children have a shot at seeing our destination. The problem is, for the life of me I can't think what that might be, other than that it must have something to do with whatever you found in Kappa. Which brings me back to my original question – why are you awake now? You're carrying something, Chiku. You look like a woman with a lot on her mind.'

'It's called responsibility.'

'I know all about that. It's seriously overrated.'

CHAPTER TWENTY-THREE

She risked moving her head, surveying the foreign anatomy in which she now resided. It was a golem, almost certainly the same antique proxy she had seen at Eunice's camp. It had been inoperable then, but she had had time to effect the necessary repairs. Not that Eunice had wasted any effort on making the proxy look more like a human being. Chiku's new torso was an open-framed chassis from which her spindly, multi-jointed arms and legs hung awkwardly. She could see right through herself.

'What kept you?'

She tracked around towards the sound of the voice. Eunice was a little further along the trail, squatting down and scraping at a rock. She had the contented and carefree look of a beachcomber.

'How did you know I'd be coming?' Chiku asked.

'Ways and means. The companion helped a lot – you should thank your daughter on my behalf.'

Chiku remembered the book she had given Eunice on her last visit before entering sleepover.

'The companion was meant to allow you access to outside data, not encourage you to plant messages on my desk and set up ching binds. Are you sure this isn't traceable?'

'You trusted it, didn't you?' Eunice stood up, a trowel in one hand. 'I've been creative, yes. That's what I do. I also knew you'd come to see me, sooner or later. The public nets told me that Chiku Akinya had emerged from skipover, so it was only a matter of time before you found my message with the ching coordinates. I take it there were no difficulties in making the bind?'

Chiku experimented with some walking. It was awkward at first, but after a few stumbling paces she settled into a rhythm that felt almost natural. 'Are you certain this is secure?'

'Very. Where advanced information technologies are concerned, I have a slightly unfair advantage: I am one.' Eunice beckoned her onwards. 'Come. I was nearly done here anyway. Let's head back to the camp.'

Chiku obeyed, quickening her pace. They were on the same side of the valley where she had emerged on the day she fell down the slope and met Eunice for the first time. To her eyes, nothing of consequence had altered during the intervening forty years. A few more black patches in the sky, perhaps some changes to the patterning of trees and open ground along the valley floor, but nothing dramatic. And Eunice, of course, showed no visible trace of time's passage.

And yet, Chiku felt, she was ... different, somehow.

'You went to a lot of trouble with the proxy. I don't really need a body to be here.'

'I don't like talking to ghosts. It might not be much of a body, but it's the best I could manage.'

'Oh, I'm not complaining.'

As they followed the zigzagging trail, Chiku scanned the valley for Tantors, but they were as elusive as before.

'I'm pleased you came back from the dead,' Eunice said. 'I was beginning to wonder.'

'I said I'd be back.'

'Yes, and in the entire history of civilisation, no one has ever gone back on a promise. The companion gave me some insights into wider developments beyond the chamber, but it didn't make me omniscient. I couldn't trust the public records to tell me the truth, so I had no way of knowing what had really happened to you.'

Eunice paused to kneel down and fix her shoelaces, an oddly human gesture, strikingly at odds with her true being, Chiku thought. How, she wondered, could a machine neglect to tie its shoelaces properly in the first place?

'Your husband, Noah. The children. Are they all right?'

'Fine. They're still asleep.'

'Noah knew of your plans to wake early?'

'No. I think he'd have tried to talk me out of it, so the simplest thing was not to tell him.'

'But you trust Noah. He knows about me. We've met.'

'I'm simply trying to avoid unnecessary complications.'

'Aren't we all? And your faculties, since you came out of skipover – no problems in that department?'

'Nothing other than this weird delusion that I met some talking elephants once.'

She straightened after tying her laces, she shot a sly smile back at

Chiku. 'I hate to break it to you, but that part was real. I'm very glad you made it, anyway. How's the mood on the street, beyond the chamber? How are the vox populi voxing?'

'Things are a bit tense,' Chiku decided.

'Understandable. By my estimate, we're twenty-two light-years from Earth. The horror – a skip and a jump and we'll be on Crucible's doorstep! That's when people will really start getting restless.'

'Some of us already are. I heard back from Chiku Yellow.' She made the proxy tap an iron finger against its iron head. 'She sent me her memories. Do you want the bad news, or the really bad news?'

'Now *there's* a choice.' But the glibness quickly dropped away. 'How bad is "really bad"?'

'Oh, the usual. Around Earth, there's a near-omniscient artificial intelligence prepared to kill to protect itself. Around Crucible, meanwhile, there are machines lying to us about what we'll find when we get there.' Chiku surveyed the closest treeline. 'I haven't seen any Tantors. I hope nothing bad's happened to them.'

'In forty years? Nothing more than the expected ups and downs within any closed population. Actually, that's not quite true. Something has happened, but it's too soon to tell what it's going to mean. The *Sess-na* is parked nearby. When we get to the camp, I'd like you to meet Dakota. She's young, as they go – her mother was barely out of adolescence when you were here last time. They go through generations like wildfire, elephants do.'

'They don't live as long as us,' Chiku said.

'Not yet,' Eunice said, 'but stranger things have happened.'

If the camp had altered in the years since she had last seen it, there was no outward sign of it. The same clearing, the same clover-leaf arrangement of drab tented domes. She could see evidence of repairs, methodically executed, but she might not have noticed them on her last visit. She looked up at the sky as they broke through into the clearing, measuring it against her memories of Lisbon and the household. Fretted by branches, it blazed a deep Tintoretto blue.

'Forgive my poor hospitality,' Eunice said, 'but there'd be no point offering you anything to drink.' All the same, she invited Chiku to sit down. 'Dakota will be along shortly. Now tell me about Ocular, and Arachne.'

'How much do you remember?'

'A bit more than last time.' She patted something on the fold-up table, and Chiku realised it was the companion. 'You were right about this – it helped a lot. Being able to tap into *Zanzibar* loosened some old memories. But there was still a limit to what I could find out.'

'We've all had to tread carefully.' Chiku reached for the companion, remembering the guilt she had felt when she took it from Ndege. 'Arachne is everything you feared. Another artilect, very powerful, deeply distributed. She began as the controlling intelligence of the Ocular device, but she's become much, much more than that. She's either duplicated herself hundreds of times over or consolidated many other artilects under her control. She has a million faces, and she's everywhere. There's almost nothing she can't influence – machines, animals, practically every aspect of the Surveilled World. She murdered June Wing, almost killed Imris Kwami, probably had a hand in Pedro Braga's accident. I was very lucky to survive.'

Eunice had taken the seat opposite her. She nodded slowly, as if everything Chiku was saying merely confirmed her deepest anxieties. 'And yet, no one realises?'

'Life goes on. The Mechanism's reach is total, but very few suspect there's an outside intelligence pulling its strings. Why should they care? Life is good – much better than in the caravans. Limitless resources, prosperity and peace for all.'

'You said "very few".'

'June Wing knew. A few more have their suspicions. Arethusa, the merfolk, maybe others. I'm not sure if they fully understand what they're up against, but they know something's not right.'

'And yet even those who know or suspect daren't speak openly about it.'

'Even if they were believed, what good would it do? Arachne's confined herself to a few easily explained deaths so far, but if she felt truly threatened … it doesn't bear thinking about, Eunice. If she was forced to defend herself against more than a handful of people, she might kill millions. Look what she was prepared to do on Venus! Nowhere would be safe. Cities, moons … she has access everywhere where the Mechanism has influence. And that would only be the start. It's within her power to do much, much worse than that.'

'And yet she tolerates the status quo. She's been happy to remain undetected for centuries, which would suggest that she doesn't seek humanity's annihilation – merely some kind of coexistence.'

'While it suits her,' Chiku said. 'When it doesn't, who knows? When the holoships approach Crucible, everyone will see we've been lied to. There'll be no explaining that away.'

'Tell me what you've learned.'

So Chiku did, as concisely as she could – speaking first of Mandala, of the probability that it was real, then of the false patterns introduced into the Ocular results, and how June Wing had managed to recover a glimpse of the unadulterated data. She spoke of the hazily resolved structures circling Crucible, and how she had gained a sharper view of them from the household.

'They're alien things, that's all we know. Probes, maybe, sent to study Mandala. If it can attract the attention of one intelligence across light-years of space, why not another?'

And then Chiku told Eunice about the blue lights, the beams that appeared to be a richly encoded optical communications medium, shining out from Crucible like the spokes of a wheel.

'One thought has occurred to me,' said Chiku. 'Something pushed Arachne into becoming the *thing* she is. Could it have been something to do with that blue light? A message so powerful that it forced her into lying, into spinning this fiction?'

'I suppose it's possible, but I'm not the fount of all knowledge. Some questions you'll have to answer for yourself.'

'What are we going to do?' Chiku asked. 'Even if we find a way to slow down, what kind of welcome can we expect? I've been thinking about sending some kind of advance expedition, but we're no closer to being able to do that now than we were forty years ago. This stupid moratorium.'

'Speaking of which, I've been reading up on your friend.'

'Travertine? I don't think "friend" is the word any more.'

'Associate, then. You were close, once, and you had an influence on vis trial. That's all in the public files – testimonies, court transcripts and so on. Travertine's what we used to call a loose cannon. Not that I'm old enought to remember when the phrase originated, I hasten to add.'

'It's not funny, Eunice. I'm worried about Travertine, worried about what ve'll do. Ve's persona non grata since the trial, but ve *could* destroy me – and endanger you and the Tantors.'

'Would ve do that?'

'Travertine's dying, slowly, and we did that to ver. If ve could prove I was compromised at the time of the trial, that might be enough to have the sentence rescinded.'

'It's such a shame Travertine didn't have the common courtesy to die while you were asleep,' Eunice reflected. 'I mean, some people.'

'Please don't be flippant. If this was just about my career, it'd be bad enough. But now that I know about Crucible, about Arachne and the Providers, I can't let Travertine ruin things.'

'I can offer you a variety of odourless toxins, and suggest how you might administer them without being detected. Except you're not totally convinced about the murder thing, are you? ?'

'Please, Eunice, I'm really not in the mood for jokes.'

'I'm being totally serious, considering the options. If you won't do it, I'll ching a robot on the other side. They'd never be able to link the crime to you.'

'No one's *killing* Travertine – we need ver too much. Collectively, anyway. Travertine thinks there's some kind of research programmeme going on behind the scenes, trying to build on vis work.'

'Sanctioned or clandestine, there's been no progress in the research.'

'I have something that might get things moving again. In the right hands, there's a chance it could unlock the breakthrough we need – give us slowdown and the means to send an advance expedition.'

'So take it to the authorities. Or don't you trust Sou-Chun Lo to act the way you want?'

'I don't know how she'd act. Or any of them, for that matter. I've been under too long to have a reliable feel for the political landscape. Believe me, there's nothing I'd like more than to wash my hands of this whole mess. But even if Sou-Chun took me seriously, there'd be questions I'd rather not have to answer.'

'Then you have a problem.'

'I couldn't even tell my husband the whole truth, and he knows about you. Noah wouldn't have agreed to me waking early, so I didn't tell him.'

'Noah's sensible.'

'Thank you, but that won't help me with this, will it?'

'Travertine's your biggest threat,' Eunice declared grandly, as if the notion had never occurred to Chiku. 'Ve could undo you with a word, ruin decades of good work. It's a shame you can't find a way to bring ver around to your cause.'

'Travertine's a person, not a chess-piece.'

'Everyone has their fulcrum, Chiku. You can bend anyone to any cause with the right timing.' She clapped her hands decisively, a meaty, human sound that belied her true nature. 'I promised you Dakota. She's approaching. Would you like to meet her?'

'As long as she doesn't mind this,' Chiku said, gesticulating at the open chassis of her body.

'It won't bother her in the slightest. In her own sensorium she'll see a human woman. Dakota! Come forward, please. The person you must meet is here.'

The trees parted. A medium-sized Tantor emerged into the clearing and moved quickly in the direction of the camp. It was not a stampede charge, but closer to that than a walk. Despite Chiku's effective invulnerability, she had to fight the urge to step back.

Eunice offered a reassuring hand. 'She's bold,' she whispered, 'but there's no malice in her. She won't harm you. Say hello to Dakota, Chiku.'

Standing her ground, Chiku looked into the eyes of the enormous creature now confronting her. Like the other Tantors, Dakota wore equipment strapped to her body and head with heavy flexible webbing. She had two tusks of equal size, curving gently to the sky. Her ears flapped gently. Through the ching bind Chiku detected both her smell and the deep, seismic report of her rumbled greeting.

She curled her trunk near the tip and scratched a furrow in the ground, like a line of treaty.

'Hello,' Chiku offered. 'I am Chiku. I'm a friend of Eunice.'

WELCOME CHIKU

WE ARE BOTH FRIENDS

'She's sounds more fluent,' Chiku whispered.

'Dakota's been unusually bright since the moment she was born. Her facility with language and abstract reasoning outstrips all her peers.'

'What did you do to her?'

'Nothing. I've never tried. My stewardship of these creatures extends to keeping them alive and healthy. I wouldn't know where to begin to make them smarter. What you're seeing here ... it's merely the chance outcome of shuffling genetic factors that were introduced into their breeding stock generations ago. Her parents were bright, maybe brighter than average. Dakota, though, she's an outlier. Completely off the scale.'

'She's amazing.'

'Yes. Something marvellous: a genuine cognitive leap. I wish I had the means to scan her mind, probe its fine structure. The other Tantors can use language, but it doesn't come easily to them. Dakota *swims* in it. Her fluency exceeds a human five year old's developmental markers, and she's still learning. She has a vocabulary of two hundred and fifty words, and it's growing steadily.'

Chiku decided not to take this on trust. 'Where are we, Dakota?'

WE ARE IN LOBE TWO

LOBE TWO IS IN THE CHAMBER

THE CHAMBER IS IN THE HOLOSHIP

THE HOLOSHIP IS ZANZIBAR

The other Tantors had known nothing of the wider world beyond the chamber, and had no notion of their place in it. Chiku wondered how deep Dakota's cosmology ran. 'And what is *Zanzibar*?'

A STONE IN DARKNESS

A STONE MADE BY PEOPLE

Chiku looked at Eunice. 'She really understands all this, not just parroting what you've told her?'

'Go and ask a philosopher.'

'If I had one, I would.'

'All the Tantors have a sense of self – they all know that when they look into a mirror, the thing looking back is them. Elephants have a theory of mind – they can *think* into the head of another elephant and infer *their* knowledge of the world, including errors and omissions of knowledge. That puts them above all but a handful of species – a few primates, some very smart birds and cetaceans. Tantors build on that – they have a sense of the past, present and future, perhaps some glimmerings of their own mortality. Dakota's abilities go far beyond that. She's not as smart as an adult human – yet – but her categorisational framework is at least as sophisticated as a ten-year-old child's. She can reason in abstract terms. She can plan a complex series of actions and then execute them days later. Her capacity for tool use is exceptional. She can improvise and experiment in ways I've never imagined – and she can teach the other Tantors what she's learned. She's something new, Chiku. Something new and wonderful and just a little terrifying.'

'Terrifying? Why?'

'Because if the random shuffling of some genes can produce this, what else might they conjure up?'

'Do you think she's …' Chiku struggled for words, not wishing to offend either the elephant or her steward. 'A one-off? A lucky roll of the dice? Or will the next wave of Tantors all be like her?'

'Maybe not all of them, and maybe not in a single generation. But she's the herald of something new heading our way. Dakota's just the first hint of what's to come.'

'If she's nearly as smart as us … what happens if her children are brighter still?'

'The same thing that always happens when the universe catches us napping,' Eunice said, with a kind of apocalyptic glee. 'Life gets interesting.'

CHAPTER TWENTY-FOUR

The next day, Chiku found herself taking morning chai with Sou-Chun Lo. They were in Anticipation Park, in an area of the administrative chamber. The park was a relatively recent development. Before Chiku entered skipover this whole section had been groved with trees, a place where she often lost herself between legislative sessions. Now the trees had been stripped back and the area re-landscaped. They were seated in a tea-house pagoda, just the two of them, with a couple of constables outside to keep the curious away.

'Of course, we're very pleased to have you back with us,' Sou-Chun said, Chiku detecting an undercurrent of unease she could not quite conceal. 'Your voice has always been valued in the Assembly, Chiku. Greatly valued. But we'd never expect you to put politics before family.'

'I don't intend to.'

'Truth to tell, we were all a little surprised you chose to wake early.'

Chiku smiled neutrally. 'I suppose I was afraid of letting go altogether, of being out of it for so long that I became totally disconnected from *Zanzibar* affairs.'

'Whereas at the moment you still feel connected enough to play a role?'

'If my services are required.'

'But you'll be returning to skipover, surely – you're still entitled to the remainder of your sleep slot. We'll all understand if you decide to rejoin your husband and children.'

'Thank you.'

'Best to conserve your energy until the time when it'll be most useful, don't you think?'

'When we reach Crucible, you mean?'

'Of course Crucible. Where else?' Sou-Chun's smile was the merest crease of her lips. While Chiku had been asleep, the Assemblywoman's face had toughened into something barely capable of expression, while her body had stiffened into a marionette of her younger self, with only a limited repertoire of human gestures still available to her. Her posture was upright and rigid as she took her chai, as if her limbs were operated by wires and pulleys. Her lips barely touched the china.

'Still a few bridges to cross before we get there, though,' Chiku said. 'I've been reading up on forty years' worth of developments, and there doesn't seem to have been much progress.'

'Depends how you measure it. The political situation was really quite volatile when you entered skipover. Travertine's business caused us all a great deal of trouble. But that was then. We've reached an accommodation with the other holoships in the caravan, accepted that in – some regards – we were going about things the wrong way. I'm pleased to say that matters are a great deal more stable than when you left us.'

Left us. As if entry into skipover had been an abdication of responsibility rather than the rightful reward for years of diligent public service.

'Well, if we all pull together, I suppose there's still a faint chance we might solve the slowdown problem.'

'Times have changed, Chiku. We prefer not to encourage that kind of scaremongering any more.'

'Scaremongering, Sou-Chun? We're way past scaremongering. God help you when the populace realise we've slammed past Crucible in the night, and that we're stuck aboard these ships forever.'

'You see those constables?' She nodded beyond the pavilion, where the law enforcers looked bored and petulant. They carried weapons, black cruciform devices of some dark pacifying function. 'I could have you detained purely on the strength of that outburst.'

'It was a statement of fact.'

'But you're a friend, and you've just come out of skipover, so we have to expect a period of transition to our new way of doing things. I'll give you the benefit of the doubt this time – a friendly warning, if you like.'

Chiku accepted this with the last dregs of her dignity. 'My purpose isn't to cause trouble, and I can understand *some* of your reasons for not wanting to talk about this in public.' She placed deliberate emphasis on that 'some'. 'But let's be frank with each other here. You're no fool, Sou-Chun. You know, deep down, that we can't just ignore slowdown, no matter how much it appeases the hard-liners. Look at the sky clock! When I went under, it still had four-tenths of the chamber to cross. Now it's down to half that distance!'

'We're fully aware of our situation,' Sou-Chun said, with steely insistence.

'It's all right for Teslenko and the Panspermians in *New Tiamaat*,' Chiku pushed on. 'They've decided they don't need to live on a planet.

But the rest of us signed up for a destination, not an endless journey into the void.'

'We shouldn't be bickering,' Sou-Chun said producing a glimmer of her old warmth. 'I don't want to be arguing with an old friend, not when we still have so very much in common. It's good to have you back among us. Shall we walk? You'll have to put up with the constables following us, I'm afraid.'

'Not because they think I'm a menace to public safety, I hope.'

'Actually, they're for my benefit. There was an assassination attempt a couple of years ago. It never stood a chance of succeeding, but you can't dismiss these things.'

'No, I don't suppose you can,' Chiku said as they left the tea-house. She had always considered assassination a relic of the past, and had never expected to hear that such a thing had been considered, let alone attempted. 'Look, I know we've had our differences, but the idea of someone deliberately trying to hurt you—'

'You wouldn't approve?'

'Of course I damned well wouldn't!'

They walked in silence for a while. 'What's become of us?' Sou-Chun mused. 'We started off with the best of intentions, and now look where we are. Old friends squabbling. Worlds that barely talk to each other. I miss the old days before Travertine's accident. Things felt complicated then, but they weren't really, were they? I like Noah, and your children. It'll be good to see them again.'

Chiku reached out to touch an alien flower. The park's flora, although derived from terrestrial stock, had been genetically modified to simulate many of the species they expected to encounter on the new planet. Sou-Chun explained some of the tricks involved, the clever manipulation of a tool-kit of homeobox genes to produce macroscopic structural variations. It was mimicry, but to Chiku's untutored eyes the effect was thoroughly convincing. Trees, shrubs and grasses had all been shaped according to the biological data sent by the Providers.

Sou-Chun was beaming proudly as she pointed to this or that feature of the park – her friend clearly took a proprietorial interest in this place.

Chiku in turn suppressed a shiver of horror at what actually awaited them, not wanting even to hint at her dejected and fatalistic mood.

'It's impressive,' she said.

'I'm glad you like it. Do feel free to come here while you're awake. The constables will see you're not disturbed.'

Tall black rectangles stood sentinel, flanking the paths in rows and rings. Images of Crucible flickered on their sheer faces, captured from space and the surface. The orbital views showed hemispheres of the globe under different illuminations, or close-ups of land masses, oceans and ice caps under various magnifications and wavelengths. It was a mesmerising display, bounteous and beautiful beyond words: another world, close enough to touch. Not some abstract dot of light in the night sky but a tangible place – or rather a bewildering compendium of places – where a person could roam for the generous measure of a modern lifetime and never cross their own tracks.

A little further on they came to an area of the park set aside for mock-ups and impressions of Mandala. None of it was remotely to scale, of course – a representation of the minutest part of that immense structure would have swallowed *Zanzibar* whole – but it served its purpose well enough, reminding the citizens that this, ultimately, was what had called them across interstellar space. The chance to interact with something irrefutably alien, and irrefutably the handiwork of directed, tool-using intelligence. There were large images, projected onto house-sized facets. There were rockeries and water-channels and flower borders laid out according to Mandala's nested geometries. There was a maze, chiselled with laserlike angles from dense green bushes.

'Sometimes I wish the machines would just damn their programming and get on with it,' Sou-Chun said. 'The endless waiting, the need to know *more* – I can barely stand it!'

'I know exactly how you feel.'

'Our day's coming, though. The citizenry understand that they'll have to make sacrifices in the short term, that there will be rules and hardships in service of a higher purpose.' She swept her hand around the miniature versions of Mandala. 'They know that, eventually, this will be their reward.'

'Followed by eternal life in the hereafter, as long as they say their prayers and keep to the path of righteousness?'

'It's not obligatory to take that tone, Chiku. Must you always be so contrarian?'

Chiku checked the time. 'It's almost noon. Do you mind if we look at the sky clock?'

'By all means,' Sou-Chun said, 'but I wouldn't waste your time. We stopped the mechanism a couple of years ago. It was bad for morale.'

A month passed before Chiku felt willing to risk another ching into Chamber Thirty-Seven.

'She's going to be trouble, that one,' Eunice said as she pottered around her equipment, glancing back over her shoulder at Chiku as she spoke. 'You never realised how much better off you were under Utomi. He might have been a fat, limping old fool but at least he had our best interests at heart.'

'Sou-Chun is the card we've been dealt,' Chiku said. She was sitting at the camp's table. 'We have to make the best of her. And before you even mention it, assassination isn't an option in her case, either.'

'You're fond of her, then?'

'She's not a bad person. Politically ambitious, maybe. Definitely misguided in her willingness to bend to the will of the hard-liners. But in her own way she also wants the best for us.'

'Fat lot of good that'll do when we zip past Crucible into the great void beyond.'

'I'm just trying to see the good in her.'

Eunice hefted a piece of machinery the size of an anvil from one corner of the camp to another. Chiku reflected that Eunice would never have done that when she first visited, but now there was no need for her to hide her true nature.

'Do you think entering skipover was a mistake, knowing what you do now?'

'The point is that I *didn't* know then what I know now. I had absolutely no idea what was at stake.'

'Perhaps if you'd remained in the Assembly, you could have steered policy in a different direction.'

'You overestimate my influence.'

'Maybe, but you'd have had all those years to increase it. The problem now is that there's no one around to counterbalance the likes of Sou-Chun Lo. And there's not much chance of you changing anything for the better in a few weeks or months or however long you plan to spend awake, either.' The construct stepped away from its work, making a very human business of brushing its palms clean on its knees. 'You *are* going back into skipover, aren't you?'

'Why wouldn't I?'

'Seems to me you have a couple of choices here, Chiku. Let me spell them out for you. You could go directly to the highest authority within the caravan and tell them everything you know. That'd be an enormous gamble, though – not just with your reputation, but with the fates of millions of souls. If Teslenko and the others decide to ignore or silence you, all that trouble you and your counterparts have gone to will have been for nothing.'

'Which is exactly why I'm not telling anyone in authority. Especially not the way things are now.'

'So that leaves you with option two – return to skipover and hope things have improved by the time you wake. What year will it be then?'

'2408,' Chiku said.

'Less than thirty years before we reach Crucible. Cutting things a bit fine, aren't you? You might be right about Travertine's secret research programmeme, but who knows? Meanwhile you'll have contributed nothing.'

'I have my family to consider.'

'You won't *have* a family if the Providers turn on us.'

'You're a machine. You can make these easy judgements, balance one thing against another as if it's some kind of mathematical game. But this is my *life*, Eunice – my husband, my children.'

'To whom you've already lied once. Face it, Chiku – deep down you know where your priorities lie. You love Noah and your daughter and son.' Eunice, her pottering done, had returned to the table. She took the chair opposite Chiku and planted her elbows on the table-top. 'More than that, though, you love the idea of them not being dead.'

'You really are a robot.'

'I'm a damaged simulation's best guess at itself, but try not to hold that against me.'

'I don't think you're too far off the mark,' Chiku said coldly. But then, in a spasm of generosity, she added, 'I've brought you something, all the way from Earth. From Hyperion, actually.'

'What's the significance of Hyperion?'

'It's where I saw your body.'

'Ah.' She nodded slowly. 'Well, that's not something you hear every day. Consider my interest tweaked.'

'You were dead. A woman-shaped ice sculpture, pulped at the cellular level. Beyond any hope of medical revival.'

'Nicely descriptive.' She made a little spiralling motion with her hand. 'Continue.'

'Arethusa found you – brought you back from deep space. She couldn't extract much useful structure from your head, but she gave Chiku Yellow everything she managed to salvage. Chiku Yellow gave it to me. It's in my private files. Could the neural patterns help you?'

'I don't know. I have one type of architecture, those are from another. Cut me, I bleed algorithms. I'm not sure how neural patterns will help me.'

'You'll have to figure out what to do with the data. If you can do something with it, restore some lost part of yourself ... then some of what happened back there, it won't have been wasted.'

'Thank you, Chiku.'

'You almost sound sincere.'

'I almost *feel* sincere. You took a risk to bring this to me, didn't you?'

'It was a risk to transmit any information back to the caravan, including my memories. I hope it turns out to be worth it.'

'We shall see,' Eunice said. And then, as if her words had not carried sufficient weight, repeated: 'We shall see.'

Even though she had been away from the world for so long, doors still opened for Chiku. There were things she could do, places she could visit, that were barred to the common citizenry or required the negotiation of tedious administrative obstacles – procedural hurdles that could eat up weeks or months of a life. For Chiku, it was principally a matter of deciding where she wanted to go, and when, and then summoning the nerve to do what she planned. In the new regime, no public movement was exempt from tracking and recording. In the early weeks of her revival her fellow politicians would be keeping a particularly keen eye on her activities. They would know she had visited this place.

So be it. She had considered chinging, but would gain nothing by doing so. In theory, at least, the authorities could not track her ching to Eunice's chamber, although they would know she had chinged *somewhere*, and if they were sufficiently diligent they might find some flaw in the blinds and mirrors Eunice had thrown up to conceal her own whereabouts. This place was different: it was a known space, a documented feature of *Zanzibar*'s interior. If she chinged here, it would be a matter of immediate public record. So she might as well come in person, because then she would have no reason to doubt what she might see.

The pod car burst through the wall into the holding pen and raced along a glass capillary. She waited a few heartbeats as the pen's automatic lights detected her arrival and came on. She wondered how long it had been since anyone had bothered to visit – months, years, decades, maybe.

There it was, encased in this little pocket of vacuum. In the flawless blaze of the lights it looked newer than anything else in *Zanzibar*. In truth, it was quite the opposite.

The high-capacity lander. It was a huge space vehicle, at least by the standards of something designed to enter an atmosphere – three hundred metres from end to end, and just as wide across its upcurving delta wings. It was rounded and smooth flat-bellied, designed to swim, to wallow in alien seas. Black on the underside, and white on the upper surfaces. Windows dotted its sides in stripes like the lateral receptors in a shark's nervous system.

They had built it to carry ten thousand people from *Zanzibar* to Crucible's surface. They had other, smaller landing vehicles, of course – many of them. But the big lander served as an important symbol of voyage's end, a promise of the reward at the crossing's end. An insignificant fraction of the millions aboard, but a monumentally significant gesture. The plan had been for them to draw lots to see who would have the honour of making planetfall in the lander. An entire community's worth of people could be moved down to Crucible almost as soon as *Zanzibar* made orbit.

The lander had already caused her political damage. Years ago she had tried to have it dismantled, so that this holding pen could be pressurised and used for habitation. Sou-Chun had opposed her – that alone had tested their friendship – and ultimately Sou-Chun had won the day. It had been seen as a humiliating defeat for Chiku, evidence that she had overreached herself. Now, though, she was extremely grateful that her colleague had triumphed.

At least in its intended function, the vehicle was now useless. Optimised for passenger capacity, it had no capability for deep-space operations. But there would be no orbitfall without slowdown, and even if they resolved the slowdown problem, they would still have the Providers to contend with. But still … A sturdily built vessel like this, with ample room inside for modifications … it could be repurposed. And the Akinyas had been masterful repurposers for a very long time. It would need a name, too, and Chiku liked what her mind presented in response to that thought. It had the cold functionality of a surgical instrument. It suggested a vicious clarity of purpose.

Icebreaker.

Yes, that would do perfectly.

And now all she had to do to make it happen was move a few mountains.

Fortunately, that was something else the Akinyas were good at.

CHAPTER TWENTY-FIVE

Three days later, she was on her way to the Assembly Building, thinking only of the hours immediately ahead and forcing all the other difficult thoughts from her mind, when she noticed a congregation of black vehicles in the courtyard before the main doors.

Her first guilty presumption was that the vehicles and constables were waiting for her; that some aspect of her secret activities had been brought to light, and they were waiting to arrest her as she arrived for business. But they would not have taken the chance on her turning around and going back home.

So it was something else.

Chiku quickened her pace, breaking into a jog that nearly had her stumbling head over foot as she negotiated the steep pathways down to level ground. The black vehicles were jockeying around. They were trying to get one of the vans lined up right before the main doors. Now there was a commotion as a group of people emerged into daylight, flanked by constables. Chiku's jog became a run. She had seen a face in the commotion, but only for an instant. She dared not trust her senses.

But no – there it was again.

Sou-Chun Lo was in the midst of the throng, surrounded by representatives and constables, her face the usual leathern mask. But this time it was as if she had swapped one mask for another – replaced stony indifference with stony indignation. Chiku blinked, trying to process what she was seeing. This could not be what it looked like, surely?

Were they *arresting* Sou-Chun Lo?

They hustled her into the black vehicle parked directly outside the building's main doors. A brief struggle ensued as the van broke through the confusion of people and vehicles milling all around, and then it was speeding away with a high-pitched electric whine, charging towards the sloping road and the nearest pod terminal.

By the time Chiku reached the crowd, she was sweating and out of breath. She leaned forward, hands on knees, and took deep, measured breaths until she had enough composure to speak.

'What just happened?' she asked the nearest constable.

Initially, no one appeared to know for sure, and a number of rumours circulated in quick succession. There had been another assassination attempt and Sou-Chun had been spirited away for her own safety. There was an emergency somewhere else in *Zanzibar* and Sou-Chun was needed urgently. An outbreak of contagion, maybe ...

But none of those stories sounded right to Chiku, so she kept asking questions, working her way around the other representatives present, some Sou-Chun loyalists, others not, as they milled around outside the building under the false sky. Gradually, something that sounded like the truth began to emerge, like a signal from background noise. It was indeed an arrest – or rather, an 'administrative detainment', as if that made any difference from Sou-Chun's point of view. An hour earlier, information had begun to appear on many public and private media channels from an anonymous source – information extremely detrimental to Sou-Chun's professional reputation. Records of financial irregularities, undisclosed ingoing and outgoing payments, over many years. Individually, the amounts involved were small, but the cumulative sum was substantial. Even worse, many of the payments were clustered around times when the Assembly had voted on important, world-changing matters in which Sou-Chun's voice had been decisive.

The evidence was almost too damning to be believed. Sou-Chun's supporters were already claiming foul play, and that a proper accounting of her finances would show that nothing underhand had occurred. And there would be such an accounting, Chiku knew, and Sou-Chun would be given every chance to defend herself. They were a civilised society, after all.

At length, when the novelty of her detainment had worn off and no further news was forthcoming, the gathering gradually dispersed. Most of the vehicles drove away, and the constables allowed the representatives to re-enter the building. But the morning's events had blown a hole in the day, and it quickly became apparent that ordinary business would have to be postponed. By the middle of the afternoon, Chiku was back home, her every certainty undermined. She spent a long hour reviewing the public statements, sifting analysis and debate. Mass opinion appeared to be divided in three broad directions. Some felt that Sou-Chun was totally innocent, the victim of a politically motivated smear campaign. Others felt that she was entirely culpable. A third group maintained that while she might not be guilty of all the alleged irregularities, an investigation into her affairs was bound to unearth skeletons. Chiku, of course, was canvassed for her own thoughts – there were three calls and a knock on the door during the hour she was home – but she refused to be drawn, saying only that she had every confidence that due process would be followed.

When skyfade came, she chinged over to Eunice. Day was concluding there as well, and for some reason – Eunice would have had no need of them – there were lanterns on in the camp.

'You did this,' Chiku declared, before the construct had opened its mouth.

'Did what, my dear?'

'Planted that information, all that stuff that they've arrested Sou-Chun for. As if you didn't know.'

'Oh, that.' Eunice brushed it aside as if it was nothing, a matter utterly beneath consideration.

'They've arrested her. There's going to be a full investigation, probably a trial.'

'And your point is?'

'You can't do this. You can't just make up lies about people because they're inconvenient. You can't simply destroy someone's reputation because it suits you.'

'We didn't ask Sou-Chun to become an obstructive influence, Chiku.'

'That's no excuse for what you've done! She's a human being, someone who used to be a friend ... you can't arbitrarily decide she needs to be eliminated.'

'It's politics. She very nearly crushed your reputation when it came to the lander question. Did she show you an ounce of mercy back then?'

'That was different! We were fighting for opposing positions, not trying to stab each other in the back!'

'Well, there's a hell of a lot more at stake now. I studied her case very carefully, you know. If there'd been a way of turning her, of bending her to our cause ... of course I'd have preferred to do things that way. But she left us no option.'

'Us.' Chiku shook the proxy's head fiercely. 'No. You planted these lies. I want no part of this.'

'Fine. Go to the Assembly and tell them you have *evidence* that the *evidence* is fabricated.'

'I don't need to. Whatever you've done, it won't stand up to detailed scrutiny. As soon as the legal teams start picking through your lies, they're going to find loose ends, details that don't add up. They'll prove someone fabricated it all, and then we'll be worse off! Sou-Chun will have been vindicated – she'll be stronger than ever!'

'You don't think I'm good enough to cover my tracks?'

'You've overreached yourself. In a day, or a week, they're going to realise the evidence isn't watertight. Then they'll start picking at the threads, looking very carefully at data traffic connected to those faked-up records ... If you've not been as careful as you think you have, they'll trace it all the way back to you!'

'If that happens, I'll just have to stay one step ahead of them.'

'Don't flatter yourself, Eunice. You're not that good.'

'Fine. If you think Sou-Chun is worth defending, I won't stop you. Go to the highest levels of government and bleat away about robots and hidden chambers. See how far that gets you.'

'And the alternative?' she demanded. 'Just to go along with this travesty and leave her to her fate?'

'Sou-Chun has her friends, but she also has her share of enemies. There'll be plenty of people ready to welcome a fresh face at the top of the pile.'

Chiku laughed. 'You mean me, don't you?'

'We need a change of policy. The will to push forward with Travertine's work and start turning that lander into a deep-space vehicle – however many enemies it makes at caravan level.'

Chiku felt the proxy's fingers curling in response to her frustration, and she fought the urge to raise its hands to scrunch non-existent hair. 'What were you thinking? This is *real life*, not chess!'

'Sometimes you just have to play the long game. You have a chance now, Chiku – we all do. But you can't go back into skipover with Noah and your children.'

She had disdained the offer of a breathing mask and thermal hood, and now she was regretting the vanity of that impulse. The cold was a membrane that fixed itself first to her skin, then the surface of her eyes, the interior of her mouth, her nasal lining. A frigid octopus, suckering itself to her face.

She made herself move before her muscles froze and her bones locked together. Down the long, cold vaults, with their aisles of skipover caskets, each casket tucked into a recess and plugged into a complicated support chassis. Now and then she encountered a technician, suited up, goggled and masked, scrolling a flow of data on a clipboard or doing something with a tool trolley.

They nodded as she passed.

She turned down an aisle, following colour codes and patterns of numbers. Hundreds, thousands were sleeping – women, men and children, each casket with its own little glowing status panel giving name and family data, a biomedical summary, scheduled revival date. Some of them had only a few years to go now, while others were in for a substantially longer haul. She was jealous of the long-haulers. Whatever happened in the years ahead, they would sleep through it all. Nothing, not even catastrophe, would impinge on their dreamless oblivion. They would never need to know that this great enterprise had failed.

She turned a final corner, the cold so thick now that it was something she had to swim through, and there they were, ranked one above the other. Four caskets, the lowest empty at present. That had been hers, when she was still sleeping. Noah, Ndege and Mposi slumbered on in the other three. She could see the outlines of their recumbent forms through the skipover caskets' translucent lids and sides. Save for the occasional change in the biomed summary, tracking some faint and ghostly whisper of brainstem traffic, shooting stars grazing the mind's night sky, there were no signs of life. Their outlined forms never moved.

'I'm sorry,' Chiku said, in a voice so low that it sounded only at the base of her throat. 'I can't come back to you just yet. There's nothing I want more than to be with you. But I can't. I need to be here, with the living, for a little longer than I expected.' These words, now she'd spoken them aloud, sounded inadequate to her purpose. They were a statement of fact, not an explanation for her actions. 'I know this isn't right, and it's not what I would have wished. But things are happening that will affect us all, and I need to be a part of them, ensure we make the right decisions. I only wanted to wake to hear the news, but now I'm here, I have no choice but to do my duty.' Inside her head, she heard her own sceptical retort: *There's always a choice, and duty's only what you make of it.* Aloud, she added: 'I didn't want any of this. I didn't go looking for it. It came to me, and now I know what's at stake ... I have no choice but to see it through. I know I'm putting the world above my family, and I'm sorry. But it still has to be done.' She touched a hand to the side of Noah's casket. 'I love you, husband. I love you, my children. And I'll be with you as soon as I'm able.'

The casket was colder even than the air, and when she withdrew her hand, the skin ripped away leaving two fine epidermal layers behind. She could see them now, embossed on the side of Noah's casket, two whorls of ridged skin like a pair of spiral galaxies. It felt like a commitment, a binding promise to the future.

'I love you all,' she said softly, and turned from them.

But in twenty-four hours she had forgotten the cold, and in a week her fingertips had healed over.

CHAPTER TWENTY-SIX

The man called Nicolas, this person she barely knew, was sitting at her little wooden table, the one with the red and white cloth, nursing a thin-stemmed port glass, his features cast into warm, wavering relief by the light of the solitary candle furnishing the room's illumination. 'It's good,' he said, after the first few mouthfuls, and then underscored his approval by draining the glass and recharging it from the waiting bottle. He studied the yellowing label. 'Do you go to Porto very often? I like it there very much.'

'To tell the truth, I hardly ever leave the city.'

'That's what my friends told me.' Nicolas sipped again, his heavy, gold-lit features, his beard, prominent nose and bushy eyebrows calling to mind a Rembrandt. All he needed to complete the illusion was a pipe and nightcap, and a few missing teeth. 'The wonder,' he went on, 'is that our paths haven't crossed since the last time I visited the studio.'

'You were just one of Pedro's clients or friends, I'm afraid. We could have walked past each other a thousand times and I wouldn't necessarily have recognised you.' She was standing at the uncurtained window, watching as the city – or at least the sliver of it visible from her apartment – gowned itself in evening.

'That's true. After fifteen years, though, I was starting to think you'd never get in touch.'

'You could have called me. I sold the studio, but I wasn't hard to find.'

'No, that wouldn't have been right at all. I knew Pedro very well, Chiku. He would only have wanted you to contact me, when you were ready – not the other way round.'

'There were a few times when I almost called you,' she said, 'but something always held me back. Anyway, how do you know Pedro ever mentioned you?'

'I don't, but it would have been odd of him not to.'

'Were you married?'

'No, not married.' He smiled, as if the idea was not without its charms. 'We weren't even lovers. Or brothers, or cousins, or anything like that. Friends, yes – for a very long time. And, you might say, colleagues.'

She thought back to the times when Nicolas had come to Pedro's studio to discuss some point of business about the guitars. She had sensed a long and sometimes prickly professional history between the two men, an unrecorded past of dealings and complaints and grudging interludes of mutual satisfaction. Nicolas had never struck her as a very happy customer. More than once, she had wondered why Pedro bothered having anything to do with him. He seemed more bother than he was worth – but then that, in its way, was emblematic of his entire profession.

When Pedro mentioned Nicolas, told her that this man knew his past and would share it with her if she asked, it had required a major recalibration of her idea of the man. Friend? How was that even possible? Pedro had always groaned whenever Nicolas announced his intention to visit. It had never occurred to her that the two men might enjoy each other's company.

'You had a business relationship?' Chiku asked. 'Something to do with guitars?'

'Almost.' He helped himself to a little more port. She turned from the window and stood with her back to the wall, facing the table. 'I suppose it's possible that anything I say or do in this room might be recorded?'

'I've had the apartment swept. There are no public eyes. Lots of cockroaches, but no public eyes.'

'I'll take a risk, then. It's only a small one – we're talking about the past, not some ongoing activity. You seem like a trustworthy soul, so I won't embarrass either of us by suggesting we formulate motes.'

'You've lost me, Nicolas.'

He smiled again. 'The thing is, Chiku, Pedro and I were criminals.'

'I'm sorry? Did I hear you correctly?'

'I started it. I came from the Moon – you were born there, too, if I'm not mistaken?'

'There are no criminals on Earth, Nicolas. You can't steal things, you can't hurt people ... what's left?'

'Lots of things, if you're creative. Perhaps you're unfamiliar with the notion of "slow crime". It's quite an old idea. The Mechanism's thresholds can't detect criminal acts that take place over months or years – it just isn't set up that way. You can't steal someone's house, but you could take it away brick by brick, and who would notice?'

'I would.'

'It's an example. I'm just saying that the Mechanism has eliminated entire categories of crime, but not crime itself. Crime is an adaptive organism. Squeeze one niche and it moves into another.'

'Mm. So why isn't the world full of criminals?'

'Lack of imagination? Lack of patience? Patience, mostly. You can't murder someone by hitting them with a club, but you *could* grind them down over years and years, a sort of psychological assassination. If you had the patience. If you wanted to.'

'And did you?'

'Good grief, no. We never wanted to hurt anyone, just do something forbidden and get away with it. And make some money, if possible.'

'And did you?'

'Yes, rather a lot of it. Pedro and I were master forgers.'

'Forgers.' She said the word as if it was new to her, some curious medieval profession that had no correlative in the present, like almsgiver or pardoner.

'We made musical instruments,' he said, 'and aged them so they appeared to be hundreds and hundreds of years old. Perhaps one great forgery every decade, so as not to flood the market. We were superbly good at it.'

She listened and considered. This brazen admission of criminality was the last thing she had been expecting, but it had the heft of truth. She could see, or begin to see, how such a thing might be possible. Pedro had always worked with traditional materials and methods, and more than once he had shown her techniques for inducing the illusion of antiquity when a customer requested it. There were ways to age varnish, and to make one type of material look like another. Dodges and tricks that could fool the eye, and sometimes even fairly sophisticated analysis methods.

Clever, clever work. It had never occurred to her that there might be profit in it.

'What type of instruments?'

'Violins, guitars, lutes, cellos ... we only made a few of each, all different, and each one took more work than the last. Making the instrument was only half the difficulty. Getting it out there, finding a buyer ... that was at least as much trouble.'

'I don't understand why anyone would do something like that.'

'Because it was fun? Because it was a challenge? We were living on the edge. You'll never know how that feels, surviving on your wits, never quite knowing when the game might be up.'

'You'd be surprised.'

He looked up, his expression both amused and sceptical. 'This from a woman who thinks it's a wild adventure to leave Lisbon?'

'You don't know the half of it, Nicolas.'

'Perhaps not. But there was a special thrill in doing what we did. I almost miss it, you know?'

'Fleecing people? Was that the best bit?'

'If you go looking for a very rare thing, so rare that there aren't supposed to be any left in the world – none that aren't accounted for, anyway – you're practically asking to be fleeced. But that wasn't the point of it, and we never dealt with the buyers, anyway. There were contacts, brokers, chains of people between us and the final customer. The only part that mattered to us was making the forgery and getting it out into the world.'

'And the money.'

'And the money,' Nicolas concurred. 'But we had to be careful with that. We couldn't go splashing it around. Pedro was running his ordinary business the whole time – it would have looked suspicious if he'd suddenly become the richest man in Portugal.'

That was another little mystery solved. During her time with him, Pedro had never done much more than break even, and his attention to detail had often cost him dearly. But somehow he had always been able to draw on financial reserves that she could not square with what he earned from his little studio in Lisbon. Now she knew where the mysterious money came from.

'You could be lying about all this, I suppose.'

'Yes – incriminating myself, just for the hell of it, makes perfect sense.'

'And of course, I might not have swept the apartment as thoroughly as I claimed, and am planning to take my memories of this conversation and turn you in to the authorities.'

'I decided I'd take that chance. Plus it's all deniable at this point – I haven't given you any specifics, and there's no tangible evidence that could prove things one way or the other.'

'It's still quite trusting of you.'

'You asked, and it's the least I can do for my friend's widow. I just wish Pedro was here, so he could remind me of all the good stories I've forgotten.'

'I never realised that you'd been friends.'

'We always were! We came very close to being found out one year and had to give up making the forgeries. It was touch and go for a little while, and after that blew over, we disassociated ourselves from each other as well as we were able. Coming to the studio was a risk, but I'd had always had above-board dealings with Pedro as well, and didn't want to give up that side of our business relationship.' He paused. 'Has all this ... discomforted you? Learning that Pedro had another side to his personality?'

'It's not what I was expecting.'

'It doesn't mean that he was a bad person,' Nicolas said urgently. 'Not at all. Mischievous, definitely. And we didn't hurt anyone, when all's said and done.'

'Except the ones you fooled.'

'We helped put their money back into circulation. Increased the liquidity of the global economy.'

She had not wanted a drink until now, content to leave the bottle to Nicolas, but her mood had changed. She fetched the other port glass from the cupboard over the sink and poured herself the last measure from the bottle.

'I should be horrified. Pedro never told me a word of this.'

'He wanted to protect you. But he also wanted you to know the truth, when you were ready to hear it. I miss him like hell, you know? He was a good forger, one of the best. But making guitars was his real calling. The fakes were just a lucrative side-line. And he was really happy to have found you.'

'He told you that?'

'He didn't need to.'

After a while, she said: 'Thank you.'

'You're welcome. And for the record, I'm not involved in any of that forgery stuff now. Although I do miss it! God, I miss it.'

'It's good to have adventures. But one's enough for a lifetime, I think.'

'Yes,' he said, narrowing his eyes at her, as if he was ready to concede this point on theoretical grounds, but couldn't credit her with any actual experience in the subject.

'You know how Pedro died, Nicolas.'

'An accident, I heard. They do still happen, even on the Mechanism's watch. I knew a man who was struck by lightning, and I heard of a woman who died when a tree toppled onto her ...'

'This wasn't that sort of accident.'

'I heard some old technology malfunctioned, and that he was in the wrong place at the wrong time.'

'Someone was trying to kill us. I can't go into specifics – that wouldn't be clever for either of us – but it was nothing to do with your old line of work. I was the real problem, and Pedro got caught up in my business. But I'm still here, and he isn't. It's been hard, living with that.'

'I won't pry.' He stared sadly at the empty port glass. That was it, though – she had nothing more to tell him even if he asked. 'This trouble you were in ... did it all end, fifteen years ago?'

'I don't know. I made a powerful enemy, and I'm pretty sure my enemy is still out there. Whether it ... she ... still regards me as a threat ... I suppose I'll only find out the hard way.'

'Why did you just say "she"?'

'A slip of the tongue, Nicolas.'

He reflected on this. 'But Lisbon's safe for you? You can move around the city without fear?'

'I wouldn't say without fear. It's always there, at the back of my mind. I think I'm fairly safe, though. Look, I didn't want to talk about any of this, but Pedro and I had our adventure, Nicolas. We did something together, and I think it was important.'

'You think?'

'Nothing's certain. I live each day as it comes.'

'It's the only way. Pedro would have agreed.'

'We have that much in common, then.'

'You look sad, Chiku Akinya. You were never sad when I used to come to the studio. A little self-absorbed, perhaps. But I wouldn't say *sad*.'

'Things change.'

'I have a proposition. It's a minor one, but I would ask you to give it your full consideration.'

He said this with such seriousness that the only response she could give was to nod earnestly. 'All right.'

'I propose that we drink more port. On the assumption that this was your last bottle, we must therefore take our leave of your apartment and venture into the city. I know a bar or two.'

'So do I.'

'Then we shall fight for the privilege of choosing the first. When we arrive, I will speak more of Pedro Braga – of the things we did together. Some of these accounts I think you will find amusing. Others, I am confident, will horrify you to the very core of your being. Since we will be subject to public scrutiny, I will of course be circumspect in the matter of names and dates and places. But I'm sure you'll have no difficulty in following the particulars.'

'I'd like that very much, Nicolas. But I can't reciprocate, if you're expecting me to tell you about what happened to Pedro and me.'

'I understand. I always do most of the talking anyway.'

'I'm glad you came, Nicolas,' she said, as they moved to the door.

'And I'm glad you called. I have a suspicion that by the end of this evening, the world will not feel like such a terrible place to either of us.'

CHAPTER TWENTY-SEVEN

It was only in the weeks and months that followed that she realised how unhappy she had really been before Nicolas came to visit. The fifteen years since Pedro died had been like swimming in water, surrounded by something so transparent and omnipresent that it offered no point of comparison, no means of getting beyond it to see how it affected her. But after that night in Lisbon, her spirits slowly began to improve. It was not a dramatic transformation, not a landslide or earthquake, but rather a kind of deep tectonic easing that played out over seasons, like the weather. She had always felt bad about dragging Pedro into her affairs, tearing him away from his quiet artisanal work in the studio, as if she was in some way responsible for his death. Which was ridiculous, of course, as Pedro would doubtless have told her. She had barely known what she was getting into herself, and by the time she did, it was much too late to do anything about it.

But she knew now that there had been far more to Pedro than met the eye; that he had secrets of his own, and had welcomed risk into his life long before they met. A master forger. A *criminal*. The mere thought of it was enough to have her laughing in public. And he was no amateur – he had successfully duped people for decades. Nicolas had told her that, to the best of his knowledge, none of their forgeries had yet been exposed. It was what got him out of bed in the morning, he said – checking the newsfeeds, keeping an eye on the fates of all their children, as he called them.

So Pedro had been no innocent, not even when she first met him, and she therefore had no need to blame herself for dragging him into a second adventure. And Nicolas himself told her that whatever guilt she was carrying, she couldn't allow it to crush her. It was time to let go, and move on.

Nicolas remained a friend. They met once or twice a year, and they did the rounds of the bars, and drank, and spoke of old friends and older times. On one occasion she sensed a diffidence in him, and it transpired that Nicolas was troubled by recent developments concerning one of their forged violins – it had caught the doubting eye of some expert or other and was being subjected to more than the usual battery of tests. But the next time they met, he was back to normal: the violin had vindicated itself, and the hated expert had moved on.

'One day,' he said, 'they *will* find me. It's bound to happen.'

While prisons were a thing of the past, Nicolas would not go unpunished if his crimes were discovered, or escape the attentions of Mech neuropractors. Criminal tendencies were supposed to be eradicated during the early stages of brain development.

Chiku pointed out that Nicolas and Pedro's actions were not the result of antisocial impulses, but Nicolas did not think that argument would hold any water if he was caught.

'That won't stop them. They'll open my head like a puzzle, move bits of it around until they find out what went wrong. Good luck to them!'

If he was truly resigned to eventually being found, his spirits remained undamped. Chiku found him good company, and he had drawn her back out into the world. It was a friendship, not a romance, but she was glad of it.

One day she was struck by an odd impulse to continue her family history. She dug out the old book, stroked its marbled covers, gazed at her own side-sloping handwriting – as foreign and antique to her now as the inscriptions chiselled on the Rosetta stone. She did not feel like the same Chiku who had written these words. But someone ought to finish what her former self had started. Her funds would expire eventually, but if she could complete the history she might be able to sell it. As if anyone cared about Akinyas these days. But then again, the world was marvellously full of people who cared about odd, irrelevant things, and there was a limitless appetite for the past. She made faltering progress to begin with, but after a while she found a rhythm. The pages began to fill, and soon she fell back into her old and pleasant routine: work in the morning, followed by reflection in the afternoon, in the café at the top of Santa Justa.

Since Pedro's death, she had maintained much more regular contact with her mother and father. She still did most of the talking with Jitendra, but that was too old a habit to break, and she made the most of Sunday's renewed ability to engage in ordinary human interactions again. They were both tremendously old, of course, and frail enough that neither was in any rush to risk a visit to Earth. Jitendra could never quite understand why his daughter was so reluctant to come up to see them, when the journey would obviously be much easier for her to make. Every time the subject came up, his response was the same: 'If it is a question of funds . . .'

But it was not a matter of funds, and in any case, her parents were by no means wealthy any more. Jitendra had always been a terrible businessman, and while Sunday was off chasing mathematics inside her head, he had maintained a singularly ineffectual grasp on their household finances. They were lucky to be able to afford the upkeep on their home.

But one October, they pooled what they had and came down to Earth for a month. Chiku was shocked when she met them at the terminal – it was as if the ching had been lying to her all those years, making them appear more robust than they really were. The sudden, dreadful clarity made her gasp – her parents were two very old organisms who had done exceedingly well to last as long as they had. They should be studied by teams of biologists, she thought, and introduced to parties of schoolchildren as living history lessons. But while their age and frailty were a concern to Chiku, they were not in any sense remarkable in this old, old world.

They both needed exos to get around. Unlike Jitendra, Sunday had not been born on the Moon, but she had lived there so long that her bones and muscles had fully adapted to Lunar gravity. For the first few days, she also had trouble with Earth's sunlight, needing sunglasses and parasols even when the day was overcast. And this was only pale, watery Lisbon, not the roasting-hot Africa of her youth. Sunday appeared bewildered, unsure why she had been dragged down into this pointlessly punishing gravity well. Had she done something wrong? Had she offended someone? Would it have killed her daughter to come up to see them instead?

But after the first week, things improved. Jitendra turned down his exo's support margin and even risked a few steps without it – grinning like a fool and holding his arms out for balance as if he was halfway across Niagara Falls on a tight-rope. 'Look at me,' he boomed to anyone willing to listen. 'I am walking on Planet Earth!'

Sunday also began to settle in. The sunlight stopped bothering her as much and at last she was able to eat the local cuisine without obvious complaint. She shrugged off her resentment and started being happy, as if she had flicked some sort of switch in her brain. The three of them visited all the local sights in Lisbon. They walked the promenades and rode the trams, enjoyed the salt air by the riverside and marvelled at the renovated suspension bridge, a lucid mathematical argument sketched from shore to shore, like a theorem in chrome. They laughed at the seagulls and Chiku told them how she had met Pedro buying ice cream at Belém. In the evenings, they enjoyed wine on her balcony and dined in neighbourhood restaurants. They met Nicolas for lunch in a rambling quarter of the Chiado district.

'It's a good place, this,' Sunday said one evening, perhaps meaning Lisbon, or Europe, maybe even Earth in general. 'It suits you well. I'm not surprised we've had such a hard time tearing you away.'

That was as deep as the conversation went. Sunday alluded to the time she had spent lost inside her mind, but never spoke of it directly. She appeared to regard the whole thing as an isolated episode, a regrettable lapse they could all agree to forget. But it had swallowed years of her life and exacted a draining toll on Jitendra. Chiku tried not to be cross with her mother for making so little of it. Perhaps Jitendra was happier that way, too, colluding in a lie they could both live with.

One squally afternoon, stuck for anything better to do, they visited an art gallery. Jitendra's exo had developed an intermittent fault that caused it to whine, drawing annoyed glances from the other patrons. In the end, unable to stop giggling, the three of them had to leave the museum. But the paintings had stirred something in Sunday. On the way back to Chiku's apartment, they bought some cheap student-quality paints, brushes and paper. The next day, Sunday composed two narrow, slot-like pictures of the view from the balcony, executed in poster-bright yellows and blues. It was an effort just to hold the brush steadily, the exo jerking her wrist like a clumsy instructor, but she battled on undaunted.

'I can't remember the last time I even thought about art,' she said. 'It used to be my life, what I lived for. Not that I was ever any *good*, but ...'

True to her nature, Sunday was dissatisfied with the pictures, but Jitendra could hardly contain his delight that she had picked up a brush again after all that time. They decided that Chiku should keep one of the paintings and that the other would return with them to the Moon. Sunday attempted another painting the following day, but the moment had passed, and this second piece remained uncompleted. But for all her self-deprecation and discontent, even Sunday seemed quietly pleased that she had taken up her art again, even if it was only for a day.

The rest of their stay passed pleasantly enough until the final week, when Sunday caught some local infection, developed a mild fever and began feeling too unwell to do much tourism. Chiku thought nothing of it – Sunday began to rally over the last few days before their departure – but the infection turned out to have taken a dogged hold. Back on the Moon, her health continued to deteriorate over the following weeks. Doctors were called in, options discussed, but there were no easy solutions. Her ancient immune system had fought too many battles, and some of the rejuvenation treatments she had undergone earlier in her life were revealing unintended side-effects many decades later, constraining the range of possible prolongation interventions. She could not be dismantled and remade, as Chiku had in the triplication process. In any case, neither Sunday nor Jitendra had the energy for a drawn-out campaign. She had lived a good and long life, seen and done many things. She would have more of it, gladly, but not at any cost.

Inexorably, the infection worsened, and like an obliging host it quietly opened doors for other illnesses. Sunday Akinya slipped deeper into infirmity, then coma, and finally death. She died peacefully on the Moon, with her husband at her side, in December 2380. She was a quarter of a thousand years old. Her daughter, Chiku, was there in proxy.

Of course there was a funeral. Chiku hoped it might be on Earth, but various legal and financial factors conspired to determine that she had to be interred on the Moon. A date was settled, and friends and Akinyas began making plans to show their faces.

At first, Chiku decided not to attend in person – it was much too dangerous. She would ching as she had when Sunday was ill. But as the date of the funeral drew closer, something in her snapped. She could not – *would* not – live like this for ever. Venturing beyond Lisbon entailed risk, but she resolved to accept it – embrace it, even. Let Arachne do with her as she wished, provided no one else got caught up in it.

So she went to the Moon, and attended the funeral, and though her heart was full of sadness and remorse for not keeping in better contact with Jitendra and her mother, she was glad to be there in person. Jitendra was also very pleased that she had finally made the visit, and wise enough not to ask what had prompted her last-minute change of heart.

The funeral came and went, but Arachne never made her presence felt. On Chiku's last full day, when she finally had some time to herself, she decided to put Arachne to the test. She rented a surface suit and rover and took them as far from civilisation as she could in the allotted time. It was no easy thing, finding a corner of the Moon not yet encompassed by cities and parks, but she did her best to deliberately put herself in a position of vulnerability, inviting Arachne to intervene. 'Come and get me, then,' she said to the sky. 'You're creative. I've seen what you can do – on Venus, in Africa. Either end this now, or get out of my life.'

She wondered how it might happen. But given that Arachne was everywhere, a part of her threaded through every complex, interconnected system devised by humanity, the possibilities were endless. Her suit could malfunction, as could its supposedly fail-safe back-up systems. Some robot cargo drone, skimming low around the Moon for gravitational assistance, might dip a fraction too close to the surface and wipe her out in a soundless flash. Some belligerent, dumb mining machine, buried under Lunar top-soil for centuries, could stir into life and drag her down in its chewing blades. Her rover might develop a will of its own and run her down.

None of this would occur unwitnessed, for there were machine eyes everywhere, sprinkled like glitter. But Arachne also controlled the feeds from those massively distributed surveillance devices, and Chiku's death could easily go unrecorded, unmemorialised.

But nothing happened.

She returned to the surface lock feeling oddly betrayed, like some millennial cultist crushed that the world had opted not to end. When the lock was almost in sight, she did something exceedingly rash, a final acid test – she attempted to break the seal on her helmet and release the locking mechanism. If Arachne was hovering, waiting for her moment, one simple command would do it. But the suit's safeguards remained inviolable, and Chiku was unable to kill herself.

'I made it easy for you,' she said, as if something out there was still listening.

After that, she had no idea what do with herself. She felt no sense of liberation, because the absence of an intervention from Arachne did not in and of itself prove that the artilect had moved on, or lost interest in her, or not existed in the first place. The Moon might not have been a suitable killing ground. Perhaps Arachne had made splendidly elaborate plans to murder her somewhere else. Whatever the case, though, she could not imagine returning to Lisbon under the old conditions, locking the city around herself like a prison cell. There had been comfort in that, she was forced to admit. It was daunting to think that she might not have to be a prisoner now. The corollary – that she might not have needed to spend fifteen years in the same city – was almost too much to consider.

In truth, she felt just as paralysed as before. Her actions on the Moon had only reinforced her fears. Her routines crumbled, and she ceased work on the family history. Gradually, she confined herself to narrower and narrower orbits of the city – first to a single district, then an ever-tightening locus of streets. Eventually she could barely persuade herself to leave her apartment. Her worries chased each other along spiralling pathways. Perhaps she had not taunted Arachne enough – should she return to the Moon and try again? Would that set her free or just deepen her uncertainties?

She did not care for this state of being, but she was trapped inside her fears. Her thoughts rattled along on tramlines, travelling the same pointless circuits over and over. A year passed, then five.

And then one day the merman came to her again.

CHAPTER TWENTY-EIGHT

'I'm sorry we have not been a great deal of help to you,' Mecufi said, standing there in the hallway in his mobility exo, still reeking of the Atlantic, as if a little bit of it had come with him. 'For both our sakes, it seemed wise to limit contact to the absolute essentials.'

'Why are you here?' she asked.

'I'm not sure yet. It came to my attention that a certain ... purpose-lessness has entered your life. But then, what business of mine is that?'

'Exactly,' she said, about to turn him away before he stank up the place.

'I'm told that you don't get out very much, but I wonder if you'd risk a visit to the seasteads?'

'I've already seen your cities.'

'Indeed,' he nodded, blubbery flesh creasing under his chin. 'Never-theless, there's something you definitely haven't seen, not in a great while, and I think you should.'

'What are you talking about?'

'She's come back to us,' Mecufi said. 'I never thought it would happen, but it has, and you should be there for her. She's you, after all.'

In the morning, Chiku boarded a sleek, translucent boat at the quay-side near the Avenida da India, not far from Belém. Open-topped at first, as the boat gathered speed it drew fluted swanlike wings about itself, enclosing a cockpit. As soon as the cockpit became watertight, the now-watertight submersible dipped beneath the waves. They har-pooned through the ocean for hours. Chiku did not bother tracking her whereabouts – if they meant to return her home, they would.

'Why now,' she said, 'after all this time?'

'It's only been twenty years,' Mecufi replied, as if they were speaking of weeks, not years.

Chiku had lost track of time herself, she reflected. Fifteen years until she had the courage to speak to Nicolas, and then five listless years since that evening. Five years during which her life had almost restarted, then fallen into a deeper stasis than before.

Perhaps it was not such a long time after all.

'You should have told me what you were up to,' Chiku said.

'We saw no reason to raise false hopes,' Mecufi replied. 'After that first intervention, we were doubtful anything more could be done.'

'I should have been informed.'

'If you had been, would you have given consent?'

'If I'd told you she'd been through enough, would you have listened?'

'And that's why we didn't ask for your permission.'

Chiku was staring through a bottle-green porthole as bottle-green sea sped by outside. 'You said accessing the implant would kill her.'

'I said it would *probably* kill her. More like mining than brain surgery – wasn't that the phrase I used? We knew there was a device in her head which could be of help to you and promised we'd do our best to extract it, but the device's own anti-tamper safeguards necessitated a fairly … quick and dirty approach, for want of a better expression. Removing a bullet from a frozen brain would have been difficult – we had to remove a time bomb!' He laced his webbed fingers together, as if concluding a sermon. 'We gave you all the facts. The final decision was yours.'

'It wasn't that simple. You wanted something from me. Would you have offered to do this good deed if you hadn't?'

'Must we pick over that again? The deed was done. In return, you established a line of dialogue between us and Arethusa and the obligation was discharged. We were very grateful for your efforts.'

'So what do you want from me this time?'

'Absolutely nothing. This is our gift to you – if you're willing to accept it.'

'Why wouldn't I accept a gift?'

'Whether you'll admit it or not, you want purpose in your life. Someone else to worry about, beyond yourself. She could be that purpose. But you'll need to be strong. Very strong indeed.'

The merfolk submarine arrived at the platelike underside of one of their seastead hexagons. It docked with an inverted cupola projecting from the underneath, clamping onto the floating structure like a suckerfish. They disembarked and rose up through green-lit layers, her ears popping with subtle changes in atmospheric pressure, until they came to a domed clinic, a bright but spartan space where the other Chiku, Chiku Red, the one who was supposed to have died, was being eased back into life.

She was in a sort of rock garden, under a simulated sky, sitting at a table with a merfolk nurse. The nurse was only partially aquatic, a young man with coppery hair and the normal dispensation of arms and legs. He had gill slits in his neck and some visible alteration to his nose and eyelids. Chiku wondered if this had been a conscious choice, to buffer Chiku Red from encountering too much strangeness in one go. Both the nurse and the patient were dressed in white; the nurse in a medical tunic and trousers, Chiku Red in a simple silver-white shift the precise shimmery hue of a penguin's chest plumage, which left her arms and legs bare. They were toying with things on the table – blocks and shapes, mostly primary coloured, with letters and symbols stamped on them. The nurse was holding up one of the blocks, pincering it between his entirely humanoid fingers, shaping a sound with his mostly human lips. He repeated it over and over again, with exactly the same intonation.

Chiku Red was trying to say it back to him, but could not get the sound right. The man showed extraordinary patience. He nodded, smiled and picked up a different block. Concentration creased the other Chiku's brow. She was so focused on this game that she had not noticed her counterpart's arrival.

'Why doesn't she look like me?' Chiku whispered, when the shock of seeing herself had begun to abate.

'I'd say you're very similar.'

'She looks younger. I don't feel old when I look at myself in the mirror, but seeing her, I feel it.'

'You've lived a life since you were triplicated. She was asleep all those years aboard *Memphis*, then a sleep, frozen or dead all the years since. She's only experienced a few months of uninterrupted consciousness. It feels as if it happened yesterday – or would, if she had any clear recollection of it.'

'What *does* she remember?'

'Fragments, mostly of her life before the triplication. But she has great difficulty articulating these memories, or placing them in any comprehensible context. We can tell when she recognises something or has a strong emotional reaction because different areas of her brain light up. But she can't tell us much. She has almost no language, you see.'

'I don't.'

'The damage to her brain was extensive. Partly a side-effect of the prolonged cryogenic passage, partly the harm we caused extracting the Quorum implant. The regions of her mind most affected were in the left hemisphere – the areas of Broca and Wernicke, the angular gyrus. In a normal brain, these structures are associated with the generation and comprehension of language. Regrettably, she has vast cognitive deficits. But there has also been slow progress.'

'We can fix minds. Machines tore my brain apart, made three identical copies. We could do that centuries ago. So fix her.'

'Ah, but we steer clear of machine influence wherever possible. We'll use them in certain nano-surgical applications, of course, but a wholesale invasion of the brain, the radical infiltration and restructuring of natural neural pathways, the supplanting of entire functional modules by prosthetic information-processing assemblies ... we've always had a profound mistrust of these methods. Long ago, when Lin Wei first put us on this course, she anticipated a great schism between the biological and the inorganic. She saw it as the question that would decide our fate, our cosmic destiny—'

'Thanks for the history lesson, but right now I want you to fix whatever's wrong with her.'

Chiku must have raised her voice, because Chiku Red looked up sharply from the game, breaking her concentration, and met her sister's gaze. The nurse put down the latest embossed block and nodded for Chiku to approach the table.

'Even if we were prepared to storm her mind with machines,' Mecufi continued, 'it would do very little good. When you were triplicated, the machines had a baseline from which to work – detailed maps of your own brain's anatomy before the procedure. There's no such reference in Chiku Red's case. It would be like trying to rebuild a storm-damaged house without having seen the original structure.'

'A different house is better than no house,' Chiku said, taking a seat next to the nurse and opposite her counterpart. She wondered what to say next. There was no protocol for this situation, for either of them.

'Hello,' Chiku Red said.

All of a sudden her throat was very dry. 'Hello,' she said back.

'Introduce yourself,' suggested Mecufi.

Chiku twisted around to look at him. 'Does she know what we are?'

'On some level, probably. She doesn't need layers of grammar for that – just a sense that the two of you fit together, that you have something in common – a connection deeper than memory.'

'I'm Chiku,' she said, reaching out to take her counterpart's hand. She felt her fingers close around the counterpart's. The other Chiku reciprocated. 'Chiku Yellow. You are Chiku Red.'

'Chiku,' the other said, touching her chest with her free hand.

'We're both Chiku,' Chiku said.

'Chiku,' the other repeated. And she thought of Dreadnought, the Tantor in *Zanzibar*. They had much in common, this woman and Dreadnought. One had lost language, while the other had never truly owned it. But both were struggling to make the best of what they had.

'She can't get by with just a word or two,' Chiku said, still holding her sister's hand.

'She's a work in progress,' Mecufi replied. 'Since we brought her back to life and repaired the gross anatomical damage, we've been flooding her brain with neurochemical growth factors to promote the forging of new synaptic pathways and connections. The adult brain never stops rewiring itself, but in most of us the processes are very slow and poorly coordinated. It's quite the reverse in Chiku Red's brain. She's advancing in powerful increments. I have no doubt she'll eventually master language – but it will take time.'

'She'd still be better off with machines to her. How's she going to function without machines?'

'The way most people did, for most of civilisation – slowly, awkwardly, inefficiently, but without artificial reliance on a vast, over-complicated support system of augmented realities, translating layers, sensory-transfer mechanisms. She'll have one language, hardwired into her brain – maybe two, if things go well. The nurse is educating her in Swahili, for obvious reasons – it'll be the most useful, wherever she might travel. But with some application, she should also gain a good command of Portuguese, perhaps even a smattering of Zulu or Chinese.'

'There'd be no point learning Portuguese. I've lived in Lisbon for years without a word of it.'

'That, Chiku, is precisely the point. Take the aug away from you, and you're the child, not her. How many of your friends and neighbours speak Swahili as fluently as you do?'

'I've no idea.'

'Because you've never needed to know. The aug does it all for you, on command, as dependable as air. Your neighbour's base tongue might be Urdu or Finnish or Lilliputian, for all you know. There could be ten billion people, each speaking their own idiolect, and you'd all still be able to communicate.'

'It's the way the world works.'

'For now,' Mecufi said mildly.

After a moment, she asked her counterpart: 'Are you all right? Are you happy?'

Chiku Red glanced at the nurse before answering, as if she needed encouragement or clarification. 'Yes,' she said, nodding. 'Yes. Yes, yes.'

'I'm sorry for what happened to you.' Chiku made to stroke the side of the other Chiku's head, but her counterpart flinched at the sudden movement.

'It's all right,' the nurse said.

Chiku made contact, skin against skin. She imagined cells breaking free from Chiku Red, slipping across the frontier like spies, becoming part of her own matrix. 'You did a brave thing, going all that way out just to bring her home. I know you didn't find her. But I did, in a way. I know what happened to her. That can count for both of us, can't it?'

'Count,' she said, pleased. 'Count. One, two, three. I can count.'

The nurse said, 'Don't be fooled by the poverty of her vocabulary, Chiku. Her high-order abstract reasoning is as developed as yours or mine. And she learns quickly.'

'How long will it take? Before she's ... normal?' Chiku shuddered at herself.

'That depends,' the nurse went on. 'You have one idea of "normal", we have another. She'll never be able to embrace the aug, or move as fluidly in the Surveilled World as you do.'

'So what will she be able to do, then?'

'Speak. Remember. Take care of herself. Maintain human ties. Friendship. Laughter and tears, love and happiness. All those things are possible. But she won't get there on her own.'

'You've got a long way to go, then.'

'No,' Mecufi said. 'Not us. We've brought her this far, but this is our world, not hers, and I'm not sure it's right for her. If she wants to join us, to become aquatic, we'll honour her decision – gladly, with open flippers. But she'd have to come back to us willingly, after she's experienced a little more of the world. Dry and Sky, Chiku – your domain, not ours. We're surrendering her into your care – you may take her back to Lisbon.'

'I can't,' she said.

'Why not?'

'I just ... can't. Until yesterday, I'd barely thought of her in years!'

'And yesterday you were entirely without purpose. You had nothing to dwell on but your own terrors. You thought you'd be free of them, but instead they circled closer. The thing you fear? It hasn't gone away. We wanted to make contact with Arethusa because we knew of Arachne, but we didn't have a name, an origin, and we hoped Arethusa might. Which she did, of course. And when we sent the kraken to rescue you, we knew exactly what would happen if we failed.'

'I think Arachne's gone. I went to the Moon, and—'

'No,' Mecufi said tenderly. 'She hasn't gone. She's still out there, haunting the world. Keeping herself to herself, it's true – perhaps that's the reason she's shown no interest in killing you. But she hasn't gone, no. Not at all.'

'You can't know this.'

'No, but we can fear it. We sense Arachne. She's very good at not being sensed, as you can imagine, but she can't exist and not have some effect. That's physics. But here's the thing: it will be many decades before we have direct news from Crucible. What matters now, the immediate, pressing thing, the *only* pressing thing, is what we do about this poor woman with half a mind. We think she needs someone to care for her – someone to help her back to life.'

'I can't,' she repeated, but this time the absolute conviction was absent, replaced by a plaintive denial. It had the pleading, petulant tone of a child, and she hated herself the moment the words were out. 'I mean, it's just not possible. Even if I wanted to help her, and of course I do ... I wouldn't know where to begin.'

'All you have to do is live,' Mecufi said, spreading his hands magnanimously. 'Just live and keep on living. Show her what being alive is all about. Give her language and laughter. Show her how the world works.'

'On my own?'

'We could provide some assistance, if necessary,' the nurse said.

'And perhaps a small stipend, to aid with the costs of support,' Mecufi added, as if money would make up her mind. 'You could move to a different apartment – somewhere with a nicer view – but since she's already been exposed to Swahili and Portuguese, I wouldn't stray too far from Lisbon.'

'I can't,' she said, but softer this time.

'You can't – or you won't?' Mecufi asked. 'Looking after her, teaching her how to live – that won't take every hour of every day. You'll still have time for your other diversions. And it could be rewarding, to give her back her life. Think of her as a gift from the past. It's a miracle she's here at all. Doesn't she deserve a chance to go so much further?'

'Of course she does. It's just ...'

'Difficult?'

She swallowed hard. 'Yes.'

'Very few worthwhile things are not difficult, in some fashion,' Mecufi pontificated. 'But isn't it true that you always felt your life lacked some grand ambition? The others took risks, you stayed at home. That wasn't your fault, it was not through a lack of courage ... but still. You never felt that you measured up to the others. But this is your chance! And this isn't some vanity, some deed that will make your name for eternity. This is a kindness, a thing done to another human being for no reason other than compassion. A private, dignified act of basic human decency, which history, being the bastard that it is, will probably neglect to commemorate. You can do this, Chiku – it's within you. More than that, you owe it to yourself.'

She closed her eyes. He was right, damn him – she had felt rudderless, these past twenty years. Rudderless and scared, and ashamed she had permitted herself to reach such a state.

But she did not feel strong, or responsible, or wise enough to help this woman, this other version of herself. It was quite insupportable of Mecufi to put her in this position.

But if she failed to rise to the challenge, who would?

'Do you mind,' she said, looking first at the nurse and then at the merman, 'if we have a little time on our own? You'll have my answer shortly.'

'Of course,' Mecufi said. 'Take as long as you like.'

So they left her alone with Chiku Red, and for a long time they simply held hands across the table. This was not the way they had imagined things, the three of them, when they broke bread under a tree on a warm day in Africa. So many possibilities in the drawing of the coloured lots. Ambition and glory, lives large enough to justify the Akinya name.

They had carved out room for so many mistakes.

'I'll do my best to help you,' Chiku said finally. 'We can live together, in Lisbon. You may be safer here, but that's not my choice to make. Do you want to come back with me?'

After a silence, Chiku Red answered: 'Yes.'

'I can't promise you luxury – it's been a long time since the Akinya name had that much pull – but I think we can be comfortable. It's a beautiful city. There are so many things I could show you.'

'Yes.'

Chiku Yellow tightened her grip around Chiku Red's hands.

'It's strange, that it's come to this. But at least we're together. I worry about Chiku Green sometimes. I wonder what she's doing out there. I hope she's happy.'

'Yes.'

Chiku had no idea whether 'yes' was an automatic answer to any question or an indication that Chiku Red shared her concerns. Something of both, perhaps. She would have to learn to negotiate such ambiguities many times over in the days that lay ahead. Perhaps it would become easier with time.

274

Presently, she became aware that a merperson had returned to the garden.

She turned, expecting Mecufi, but saw instead a sleeker, taller merperson who walked without the assistance of an exo. She stared at him with a sort of unsurprised recognition, half-knowing this moment had been inevitable.

'Kanu.'

Kanu nodded. She took in his astonishingly broad shoulders and a neck like the steepening flanks of a volcano. His face was handsome and strange and unquestionably her son's.

'I hope you don't mind the interruption, Mother – I couldn't let you come and go without seeing you.'

'Of course I don't mind.'

His movements gave the impression of tremendous contained power. He had dressed for their meeting in a patterned smock and matching knee-length trousers. His forearms and lower legs were bare, as were his webbed feet and hands. He left wet footprints on the floor as he walked towards her. His hair, long and black, was pushed back from his brow in wet furrows.

Chiku released Chiku Red's hands and rose from her chair to meet her son. They embraced. He kissed her cheek, and then bent down to kiss Chiku Red's.

'I never thanked you for saving me.'

When he smiled, his face did not move in quite the way she expected. 'That oversight can be forgiven – it was a complicated day. And it was a very long time ago. I was glad we had a chance to speak, at least. How have you been?'

'Up and down. Alive, thanks to you and your kraken.'

'That was a good kraken. We worked well together. I was sad when it died – they don't live as long as we'd like, even with genetic engineering.'

'Thank you for coming to see me.'

'I couldn't have missed your being here. I'm very sorry about Grandmother Sunday, by the way. But I hear you were closer towards the end.'

'We spent time together in Lisbon, Sunday, Jitendra and me. You'd have been welcome to join us.'

'I know, and I'm sorry I wasn't there. But the work we're doing here …' He swept a webbed hand before him. 'There's an urgency, now, a sense that we don't have the luxury of limitless time. I'm glad to be involved in the preparations, but that doesn't leave much room for anything else.'

'Preparations for what, Kanu?'

'The end of something – or the beginning, perhaps. It feels inevitable now. News will reach us from Crucible, sooner or later.'

'So you know about all that.'

'Only what Mecufi's told me. When news comes, how will they take it?'

'Who?' she asked.

'You,' Kanu clarified. 'Drylanders. The rest of humanity.'

'We're all in this together,' Chiku said.

Kanu's silence told her that he had no response to her statement that would satisfy them both.

Eventually, he said, 'When you're done here, I'd like to take the both of you back to Lisbon. Would that be all right?'

CHAPTER TWENTY-NINE

It took her long moments to realise what she was looking at. It resembled an abstract sculpture of some kind, an artifice of crumpled, foil-like surfaces, as if sheets of delicate metal foil had been balled up in a giant fist and then rammed into the earth. *A steel angel*, she thought, *ejected from heaven.*

Her second thought was much less poetic.

Sess-na. The aircraft had daggered into the ground, wings ripped out of their sockets and buckled like a scarecrow's arms.

The *Sess-na* had crashed.

She pushed the old proxy as fast as it would go, spreading her own arms for balance in imitation of an aircraft's wings. She had precious little experience with aircraft crashes against which to measure this disaster. She had been aboard June Wing's spaceship *Gulliver*, of course, when it fell to earth in Africa, but that craft had only crashed because someone shot it down. They had walked away from *Gulliver*, but the *Sess-na* had none of the more modern craft's safety features. Could anything have survived such a crash – even a machine?

'Ah,' said a voice from somewhere to her left. 'I was going to mention that, Chair Akinya, but it slipped my mind. I hope you're not angry with me.'

Chiku halted the proxy. She was not out of breath, of course, but the stop command also compelled the machine to stand with hands on hips, exactly as she would to catch her breath after exertion. 'Were you in that when it crashed?'

'Why wouldn't I be?'

'I remember Geoffrey telling me he could control the *Sess-na* remotely – send it off on errands, or have it come and pick him up.'

'A machine that can think for itself? Whatever next!'

'Why would I be angry with you?'

'Oh, I don't know – destruction of an irreplaceable family heirloom, something like that?'

'Machines don't last for ever, Eunice. If you use them, sooner or later they break.'

'That's reassuring.'

'Perhaps the rules don't apply to you. And you're the machine that matters to me, not that old aircraft.'

'I'm sure we could knock the dents out of it, given time.' She made a pained expression. 'Then again, maybe not.'

'What happened? Are you hurt ... damaged?'

Eunice was striding up the slope, knee-deep in whiskery undergrowth. She looked the same as ever – no limbs missing, no skin hanging off her face to reveal a gleaming horror of chromium skull-plates. Just a skinny, short-haired woman of indeterminate age, dressed for adventure.

'It was my fault. I was having fun with it, and I got reckless. Serves me right. But it looks worse than it was. I escaped with only a few scrapes and bruises – metaphorically speaking. Can't say the same for my pride.'

'You haven't got a pride to lose. And what do you mean, "fun".' Had Chiku been able to squint, she would have squinted. 'You're totally serious, aren't you?'

'I'm always serious about my fun. I was messing around – taking silly risks because I enjoy it. Been doing a lot of that sort of thing lately. I blame you – and those funny neural structures you brought back from Arethusa.'

'I didn't think they'd be much use to you.'

'So why did you give them to me, then?'

'A gesture. Like bringing flowers.'

'You could have just brought flowers. Although I'm glad you didn't. I *think* I'm glad, anyway. It's sometimes hard to know.'

'What did you do with the structures?'

'Mapped them into myself as best I could. Connected areas of my logical architecture that hadn't been strongly correlated. Rewired other bits. There was a lot of guesswork involved. You're really not cross?'

'I'd love to have so few problems that *that* was a concern, Eunice. Did the structures really make you reckless?'

'Impetuous, certainly. Prone to the unexpected action. I've become thrillingly poor at modelling my own future behaviour. I can't begin to tell you how liberating that feels, not quite knowing what I'm going to do next.'

'You must have created your own Lyapunov horizon,' Chiku said. 'Become a system too chaotic for long-range forecasting.'

'Never mind long-range – I can't even be sure what I'm going to be doing in five minutes.'

Chiku was suddenly immensely glad not to be physically present with this strong and unpredictable machine.

'This might not be good,' she said cautiously. 'Perhaps you're breaking down.'

'Possible, but I feel as well as I've ever felt.' She patted her belly as she spoke, as if this was some universal indicator of personal well-being. 'My memory's no worse than it used to be, probably a bit better. I still remember you, don't I? All our conversations? Although it's been a while – when were you last here?'

'A year or two ago. I can't just visit at the drop of a hat any more. After that nastiness with Sou-Chun, politicians can't sneeze without it becoming public record, and my actions are under a lot more scrutiny these days. But I'm sure you've kept up with things.'

'As well as I'm able. Shall we walk to the camp? You can bring me up to speed.' In dark conspiratorial tones she added: 'I gather there's a ship.'

Yes, Chiku told her – there was such a thing, and in about ten years they might actually have something that worked. But they would not be able to use it straight away.

It was 2395 now – seven years since she had come out of skipover. She had saved the old lander from being dismantled, and now they were refitting it for a one-shot, long-range scouting expedition. Instead of ten thousand colonists, eager to taste Crucible's airs, the repurposed vehicle would carry no more than twenty volunteers. The new ship, with its untested PCP engine, was projected to achieve about twenty-five per cent of the speed of light, allowing for the thirteen-percent boost it had already gained from *Zanzibar*'s own motion. The crew would go into skipover for most of the journey and wake on final approach. They would reach Crucible about ten years ahead of the caravan.

All this was still a long way into the future.

'The kinematics don't allow us to launch much sooner than twenty years from now,' Chiku said. 'That's a basic limitation of the engine and its fuel requirements. In a way, it helps us to have more time to get the ship ready. They say we're about a decade away from initial readiness but my suspicion is that we'll end up needing every second of those additional years.'

'I see you're adjusting to the long game, then.'

'Not much choice, is there? If I return to skipover, the project could stall.'

'You mentioned "volunteers",' Eunice said as at last they strode into the sun-dappled clearing. 'I take it that means these hardy souls will receive some forewarning about what to expect?

'No, I can't take that risk. The wrong word now, a lapse of secrecy, could undo everything.'

'But you must have informed select members of your government.'

'No – none of them. It's been difficult, of course, convincing them that we need this expedition, given the risks involved, but I've found ways and means. It helps that deep down everyone is scared. Privately, and despite the *Pemba* legislation, they all know we need to prove the slowdown technology, so *Icebreaker* is the perfect testbed for the new engine. If *Icebreaker* works, we can scale-up the engine to the size required to slow a holoship. That alone makes it worth doing. But I've also argued the logic of verifying that the surface amenities are up to scratch and capable of supporting us.'

'And those would be the surface amenities that don't actually exist?'

'I'll break that to them gently, when we're on final approach.'

'Hypothetically, what would happen if the truth *did* get out?'

'There'd be trouble,' Chiku said. 'Fear and panic, of course. Widespread social unease. Beyond that, political rifts bigger than any holoship. Travertine's work give us a choice, and that's not always a good thing. Push for slowdown, or skip Crucible all together? Move to a military footing? Even before we met the Providers, we'd have civil war inside the caravan. Can you imagine that, after all we've been through?'

'I thought we were losing the habit of wars,' Eunice said glumly, stooping to adjust one of the irrigation lines running into her plant beds.

'We are, slowly.' Chiku took a seat. 'But it's still in our blood, like some fucking horrible disease we're still carrying around with us. That's why I've got to make the advanced expedition work. If I can contact the Providers, negotiate some common ground—'

'So you'll be on this ship, when it goes.'

'I've staked my career on it, these last few years. *Icebreaker* is my creation. No one's taking it away from me.' She used her proxy hand to pick up some metal things that were lying on the table – scraps and coloured shards, coinlike metallic pieces threaded onto wire.

'And the other volunteers?'

'Still to be decided. I have selection veto. They won't know the truth, but they must be people who can handle it when we arrive.'

'The truth being that they've signed up for a suicide mission?'

280

'It's a long shot, but the mission's not totally doomed.'

'Noah will be out of skipover by then.'

'I know. Seven years, if we launch in 2415.'

'Your children will be seven years older, too. To be blunt about it, they won't be children any more by then.'

'Is this art?' Chiku asked abruptly. 'Have you been making these trinkets?'

'Idle hands, dear girl. The drawback of being increasingly human is that the hours begin to weigh on one in a way they never used to. It's a shame I can't be with you.'

'I wish you could, but the time isn't right for you to emerge. I can't tell you how much happier I'd be meeting a bunch of artificial intelligences if I also happened to have one on my side.'

'Can we drop the "artificial intelligence"? It's a bit like me calling you a meat-based processing system.'

'I suppose. Regardless, you're needed here – the Tantors have come to rely on you. We can't abandon them.'

'Even if the survival of the entire caravan depended on it?'

'Everything depends on everything else, doesn't it? That's interconnectivity for you – it's a bitch.'

Eunice laughed humourlessly. 'So we're back to square one, just trying to muddle through like the fools we are. This lovely new ship of yours – are you anywhere near testing it?'

'Still years away. Plus, it's pretty tricky to test a Post-Chibesa engine if you don't want anyone to know you have one. We'll have a better idea once we're out there, on our way, and can ramp up the engine without raising any awkward questions.'

'And who else has this vigorously tested and reliable new technology, beyond *Zanzibar*?'

'Nobody, as far as I know. We've kept a tight lid on the whole project. The *Pemba* Accord is still in force.'

'Naughty, naughty Chiku.'

'Naughty, naughty Eunice – you gave Travertine the shove ve needed, didn't you?'

'Ve'd have got there in the end, given time, but I don't suppose it hurt that the key formulae began to mysteriously insinuate themselves into vis private research files. Still, let's not downplay Travertine's achievement. It's one thing to be given a big boxful of theory and quite another to make an engine out of it.'

'It's a miracle that Travertine was able to make something tangible from Sunday's synthesis,' Chiku said. 'Travertine forgets things, sometimes. Loses track of conversations. Ve was so sharp, a few years ago, but it's gone now – or blunted, anyway.'

'Isn't it about time ve was pardoned? Or shot? At this point, either option would be a kindness.'

'Travertine's work can't be publically acknowledged, so it can't be publically rewarded either. I wish there was some other way.'

'There usually is.' Eunice had finished tinkering with her irrigation lines. 'I'm glad you visited. Any idea when the next time might be?'

'If there *is* a next time,' Chiku said.

'Oh, I'm sure there will be. Would you like to see the Tantors?'

'Of course.'

'Dakota's still with us, you'll be glad to hear. She's come on in leaps and bounds, too – a proper wrinkly old matriarch, very political and canny. Are you absolutely sure Geoffrey didn't splice some Akinya DNA into them?'

'*Fairly* sure . . .'

'I think you'll enjoy the conversation, anyway. And her granddaughters are going to scare the absolute living bejeezus out of you. Here, help me with these.' Eunice was bending to pick up some plastic crates, the kind she might normally have used to convey seedlings. The trays rattled with a great many plastic and metal toys and puzzles, all apparently fashioned by hand.

'They're going to overtake us, aren't they? Not right now, not tomorrow,' Chiku said, rising from her seat, 'but one day we'll wake up and the Tantors will be looking back at us, saying, "Catch up, slowcoaches."'

'In terms of available brain volume,' Eunice said, 'they do have an undeniable advantage over us monkeys. But I don't think we have anything to worry about. They're only elephants – why in heaven's name would they hold a grudge against us?'

Chiku stooped to pick up one of the toy boxes. 'I can't think of a reason in the world.'

The revival clinic had seen better days. The ornamental fountain had broken years ago, and the hedges had grown wild and unruly. The lawns were worn away to mud and soil and a scrabble of bone-coloured stones. Weeds choked the pathways; bushes curled overhead to form dark, canopied tunnels. Chiku had to stoop to walk along them, pushing branches out of her eyes. A statue had fallen over and never been set right. Another had shattered into a puzzle of cryptic parts. The benches where she remembered sitting and talking to the figment of Chiku

Yellow were nowhere to be seen – consumed, perhaps, by the spreading undergrowth.

She saw no living soul until she entered the clinic itself. From previous visits she recalled a reassuring bustle of technicians and nurses; the families and friends of the frozen coming and going; nervous skipover patients on their way into the vaults and relieved ones on their way out. It was safe, but everyone still worried.

She stood in the empty lobby area for a few moments, then called out for assistance. A female nurse, a plump white woman with very pronounced bags under her eyes, bustled out of a back room, startled to find a visitor.

'Representative ... I mean, *Chair* Akinya ...' the nurse said. She was sweating, her hair dishevelled.

'I had an appointment,' Chiku said coolly. 'Why wasn't someone waiting for me?'

'To be honest, Ms ... Chair ...' The nurse was flustered, unaccustomed to dealing with direct authority. Chiku wondered if they had ever crossed paths before. Everyone knew Chiku's face, of course – she was, after all, the most senior figure in *Zanzibar*. 'The thing is ... the thing is ... the vaults are full enough, but hardly anyone comes or goes these days. We were expecting you, but we got out of step and ... we forgot you were coming today ...'

Chiku felt a glimmer of sympathy for the put-upon employee. 'Well, I'm here now. My family are due to emerge from skipover – my husband Noah, and my two children, Mposi and Ndege. I've visited them many times.'

'Yes, yes ...' The nurse ran her finger down the clipboard. 'Of course, today. Yes, you're right – they're coming out today.'

'I know. That's why I'm here.'

'It'll be a while.'

'According to the schedule, they should already be on the transition to consciousness. You've begun the wake-up, haven't you?'

'Yes! Yes, definitely. It's just ...' The nurse had turned the clipboard upside down, as if it might make more sense that way around. 'They're late. A few hours, that's all. We had a problem yesterday. Not in your sector – I mean, *their* sector – but it put us behind schedule—'

'Then I'll wait,' Chiku said.

'It could be six hours. Or eight. It's hard to tell. Wouldn't you rather go home than wait here all day? We'll call you—'

'Then if it's all right with you, I'll wait here.'

Soon they furnished her with a thermal suit and allowed her to enter the vaults. They were in virtually as good a repair as they had ever been. It was true that *Zanzibar* lacked a heavy manufacturing capacity – or at least did not have much to spare, once resources were diverted into the lander project – so much of the machinery in the skipover vaults was imported, often expensively, from elsewhere in the local caravan. It was true also that tensions in the caravan – when Sou-Chun or her successors had not been seen to act with sufficient rigour – had seen the occasional imposition of sanctions or trade restrictions, so that supplies had not always been plentiful. But Chiku's people had been nothing if not ingenious, and keeping the skipover vaults running had always been given a high priority. Chiku would have made sure of that even if her family had not been entrusted to the mercy of these machines.

She soon found Noah and her children, and her own casket, still empty. The status indicators showed that warm-up had commenced, but Chiku had no idea how far along the process was. After decades of sleep, nothing was rushed at this stage.

She reached to touch Noah's cabinet. Her fingers were gloved this time. The little marks that she had once left, the imprints of her touch, had soon been cleaned off the metal – she would have expected nothing less. But the cleaning had been aggressive enough to burnish the cabinet's surface in two ovals, which was where she now pressed her gloved fingertips.

'Soon,' she whispered. And although she had uttered that promise often enough, today it had currency.

'I never meant for it to happen this way,' she said, staring into his eyes, hoping to find in them a hint of conciliation, some faint indication that he might forgive her, or at least come to understand her actions.

'You mean you never meant for me to know?' Noah asked.

'No,' she said, more fiercely than she meant to. 'That's not it at all. It was supposed to be a few days, no more than that. I didn't think it was worth bothering you with my decision. The fewer people I spoke to, the less explaining I had to do.'

'And you didn't want to explain yourself to me, is that it?'

'No,' she repeated. 'But if you didn't know, no one would expect you to account for my actions. It was my problem – just mine.'

'I thought it was ours.'

They were in the kitchen. Noah had reluctantly accompanied her home, leaving the children at the clinic, bewildered and bored, while their parents went to settle their future in private. This was not the happy awakening they had all been looking forward to. Noah was sitting across from her at the table, like an uncomfortable house guest. He had not even closed the door behind them.

'It was our problem,' she said, her hands halfway to his on the table-top but not touching. The distance between them felt galactic. 'But you couldn't help me with the news from home. I had to be awake when it arrived – I didn't want to leave it until the end of our skipover interval.'

'What did you seriously hope to achieve in just a few days?'

'I don't know. Put some wheels in motion, maybe, to make sure we were in a better position by now.'

'In a few days.'

'I know it wasn't very realistic. But after I heard the news, I couldn't return to the vaults.'

'Staying awake was more important than keeping the promise you made to your own family?'

'How do you expect me to answer that?'

'Truthfully.'

'All right, then. Yes. Staying awake was more important. I love you and the children more than anything else in my universe – you know that, don't you? But for that reason alone I *had* to act. I couldn't love you and stand back once I knew something was coming that would hurt you, hurt Ndege and Mposi. That's what love is – sacrifice. Sacrificing everything, our marriage if necessary, out of love for you. Can't you see that?'

'What about trust? You trusted me once, remember? I've seen the Tantors.'

'Please,' she said.

'Don't worry. Your secret's safe with me – I keep my promises.'

She looked down. Her fingers looked wrong to her, as if at some point they had been surgically swapped with those of a much older woman.

'I'll tell you exactly what happened. The news from home was bad, Noah – unimaginably bad. It was imperative for the survival of the entire caravan that we concentrate our efforts on the slowdown problem. With Utomi dead – he was killed in an accident before I woke up – and Sou-Chun out of the way, I had a chance to influence a change in policy. But it couldn't be done overnight. Even then, I was only thinking in terms of years. Two, three ... five at the most. I never meant to become Chair. One thing led to another and ... it just happened.'

'So what happens now?' Noah said, his tone perfectly reasonable, but cold. 'I don't feel as if I'm talking to the woman I married – just some distant politically ambitious acquaintance of hers. Chair Akinya, for god's sake!'

'I came to the vaults to see you, over and over, wishing for the day when you could join me. Check the clinic records if you think I'm lying.'

'If it mattered so much, you'd have joined *us*.' Noah paused. 'I did check the clinic records. Before the day we were scheduled to wake, you hadn't been down in nearly three years.'

'No,' she said flatly. 'There's a mistake in their bookkeeping. It was never that long.'

'Eighteen months before that, a year before that. The intervals were growing longer. At the start, you used to come down every few months. But that didn't last.'

'I'm sorry,' she said. 'I never meant—'

'So am I,' Noah said. 'Truly sorry. You should have trusted me. Everything would have been all right.'

He was making to leave. 'Please,' she said.

'I'll arrange for Mposi and Ndege to see you – they're going to find all this quite difficult to process.'

Did he mean to keep the children from her? If she put the possibility into words, would she make it an inevitablity?

'Don't blame me,' Chiku said, with the flat resignation of knowing nothing she now said would count in her favour. 'I only ever did what needed to be done.'

CHAPTER THIRTY

Time swallowed itself like a snake. Suddenly *Icebreaker* was not years or months from being ready, but weeks. Prickly with anticipation, Chiku visited the berthing chamber as often as her administrative workload allowed. While the lander was being prepared for the expedition, it had been crusted over with a dense plaque of scaffolding and pressurised support structures. Now most of that had been dismantled or swung away, leaving only a handful of vacuum-suited technicians still working on the final details. The three-hundred-metre-long lander had been gutted and stuffed with enormous fuel tanks, giving the craft's clean lines a swollen, bee-stung look. Even a Post-Chibesa engine needed fuel, and lots of it.

Once in a while, from some hatch or service port, stuttered the hard blue flash of a welding torch or laser. Even there, they were down to the last few tweaks. Inside, too, the bulk of the work had been completed. In the tiny nucleus of the ship that would be filled with air and warmth, the skipover caskets had been installed and tested.

After much deliberation, the final complement of crew would be twenty. Chiku had quietly pushed for fewer, but there were limits to what she could achieve. The rest of the Assembly thought twenty could not possibly be enough to handle the survey – surely there should be room for soil specialists, botanists, geologists, oceanographers and so on? Chiku made a show of agreeing with them in principle, but she also pointed that a larger crew would require more skipover equipment, and supplies, and more space to move around in when they came out of hibernation. These factors would mean trading fuel for life-support volume, which would make the ship less nimble, thereby delaying their arrival.

'I've run simulations until they're coming out of my ears,' she said. 'More than twenty and the mission parameters become unwieldy. Fifteen would be better, twelve ideal. We don't need specialists for every contingency – we're going on ahead to pave the way, not to establish a self-sustaining colony of our own.' And all of that was true, in its way, but a far more pressing consideration was that she did not want to lie to more volunteers than she absolutely had to. There was, too, a darker corollary: if she needed to start silencing people, the fewer the better.

Prior to departure, secrecy remained paramount and a shipwide announcement of *Icebreaker*'s existence had yet to be made. This had complicated the already delicate task of identifying and approaching possible crewmembers.

Half of the candidates were straightforward selections. Daunting technical expertise had been required to develop, construct and install the new engine, and the key figures working on the project were already sworn to secrecy. It made sense that those among them fit enough for skipover should be considered for the mission itself. Of those who were approached, two-thirds declined, which did not surprise Chiku in the least. The crewmembers would not be able to take their families with them on the decades-long expedition, so it was no easy burden to accept. The net was widened slightly, and slowly but surely sufficient volunteers agreed to the terms.

One obvious candidate, in Chiku's eyes at least, posed a particular headache.

Travertine knew the stakes. When the Assembly finally dropped any pretence – among themselves, at least – about the mission about going ahead, and thereby authorised Chiku to inform Travertine and suggest that ve join the expedition being readied, ve simply nodded and countered with some minor demands of vis own. A pardon. Removal of the biomedical cuff, followed by a battery of emergency prolongation measures.

Ve had to try, of course, but Travertine knew as well as Chiku did that the Assembly would not go anywhere near that far.

One afternoon, just under fifty days from launch, a black car approached the Assembly Building. Constables helped the ageing scientist from the vehicle. Ve was accompanied by a bulb-headed chrome mannequin imported from somewhere else in the caravan. Originally, the robot had tailed Travertine clandestinely to prevent ver from taking vis own life. Now the new robot accompanied ver openly, an arm under Travertine's elbow to help ver from the car and up the front steps. There was something almost kindly and touching in its ministrations, Chiku thought.

She was waiting for ver indoors, one hand clenching and unclenching as if she had a tennis ball in her fist. She nodded as the party conveyed their guest into the lobby.

'Thank you for coming, Travertine.'

'I had a choice?'

'Yes, and I hope my staff were clear on that.' Chiku nodded at the constables – they were not needed now, although the robot could remain. 'Come – I've reserved a room. Our discussion won't take long, and then you can be on your way.'

'This is all very official. I thought we did all our best business in your kitchen.'

Chiku smiled tightly. 'Those were the old days. It's a different world now. You look well, by the way.'

'And you're a very bad liar. I look like the thing I am, a monster walking the world. That's the point of me, isn't it? A dark warning to other potential sinners?'

'You make too much of it. I see older-looking people whenever I'm in the community cores. Anyway, I didn't call you here for an argument.'

'Another problem with your secret new toy?'

'Please,' Chiku cautioned. 'I really don't want to have you marched back to that car. It wouldn't look good for either of us.'

They reached a sealed chamber, two constables flanking the door. Chiku waved Travertine and the bulb-headed robot inside ahead of her. Her own warped reflection wobbled back at her from the robot's reflective head as she followed them into the room. Chiku gestured to a pair of seats.

'Have it help you sit down, then dismiss it.'

'Your own Assembly provided that robot. Are you really that concerned about privacy?'

'You have no idea.'

'Ah. So I was right – there *is* a problem with the ship. That's a shame. I know how much you've staked on it. Your life, your family … all sacrificed for this one thing.' The robot helped Travertine into vis seat, then ve shooed it away as one might an over-attentive servant. 'Go. Wait outside.'

'Wouldn't an exo be easier on your joints?' Chiku said as the robot departed.

'They wouldn't let me have one – I think they were worried I'd turn it into a tunnelling machine or something.'

'Where would you go?'

'Exactly. Anyway, I don't really mind the robot. They used to worry about me hurting myself. Now they're more concerned about lynch mobs and lunatics. People throw rocks at me sometimes. It's fascinating to be the focus of mass hatred. It's very grounding. Everyone should try.'

'Anyone who hurt you would be punished to the full extent of the law,' Chiku said, as if that would be a comfort to Travertine if ve had been stoned to a pulp. 'And there's nothing wrong with the ship, by the way.'

'That's a shame.'

'Really?'

'I've been thinking of it as my insurance. As long as you didn't know how to make the thing work properly, you needed me. That was why those people used to come, with their idiot questions. Why you agreed to adjust the cuff, to hold me at this level of decrepitude.' Ve nodded at the black ring around vis wrist, with its still-blinking status light.

'You're still valuable to me.'

'I doubt it. You have your eager little experts now, and more time than you really deserve.'

'To be honest, the work would bore you. When we launch *Icebreaker* and reveal ourselves to be in direct contravention of the *Pemba* Accord, all hell will break loose. There'll be serious consequences – it'll be the worst intra-caravan crisis since your trial. I believe the old political term is *shitstorm*. We could even lose our autonomy.'

'And this is supposed to be encouraging?'

'I hope so. On the day *Icebreaker* launches and we reveal that we've built the new engine, we'll also terminate your punishment.'

'Terminate,' Travertine said. 'What does that mean, exactly?'

'The cuff will be removed – or reprogrammed to work therapeutically, to correct some of the harm the years have already done. You'll stop ageing and start improving each day.'

Travertine fell into a profoundly contemplative silence.Ve appeared to be gazing through dozens of metres of solid rock at something located outside *Zanzibar*. The moment stretched uncomfortably. Chiku dared not speak.

'What's the catch?' Travertine said eventually.

'You have to volunteer for the mission,' Chiku said. 'I need you anyway, but you'll benefit, too. On the ship, you'll be isolated from the inevitable political repercussions.'

'What about the reversal therapies I bargained for? How do they fit in?'

'They don't,' Chiku said simply. 'We'll carry a single physician with us, Doctor Aziba – you know him. There'll also be a medical robot and a small surgical suite for emergencies. If any of us gets seriously ill, we'll be put back into skipover until we're reunited with the main caravan. That's the best we can hope for.'

290

'But aren't your crew going into skipover from the moment of departure.'

'Once we've cleared *Zanzibar* and run some engine tests.'

'So basically you're offering me ... nothing. The cuff will have no effect in skipover, so when I wake up at the other end of the journey, I'll be exactly the way I am now!'

'Except the cuff won't be making you any worse. Beyond that, you'll have the promise of an official pardon and all the reversal therapies we can throw at you when the caravan arrives, which will be about ten years after we get to Crucible.' Chiku took a deep breath, convinced she had only this one chance to make her case. 'This is the best I can do. There isn't time between now and the launch date to put you through any useful therapy – it'll be difficult enough to prepare you for skipover. I wish I could give you everything you want, everything you deserve, but I can't. I still need you on *Icebreaker*. I can't begin to tell you how much I need you on that ship.'

Travertine leaned towards her. 'What do you know that no one else does? What brought you here? What are you *not* telling everyone?'

'I just need you on that ship.'

'You love your children. How old are they now?'

Chiku had to think for a second. 'Mposi is eighteen, Ndege a year older.'

'So they're young people now, entering adulthood. You'll be taking them with you, right?'

'No. It'll be better for them if they stay here, with Noah.'

'And if you could take all three of them? If you could persuade them, or force them?'

'I wouldn't.'

'Whatever's driving you – you've already put it before your marriage. Now you're ready to step away from your children as well?'

'It's not like that. If there was some other way—'

'But there isn't.'

'No.'

Travertine nodded slowly. 'Tell me one thing. Will all be revealed once we're on the ship and away from *Zanzibar*?'

'I don't know. I honestly don't know what we'll find until we get there.'

'That's nonsense. We all know what we'll find. Haven't you been to the Anticipation Parks? They even let a horror like me walk around those. What don't we already know about Crucible?'

'Everything,' Chiku said, and on that single word, perhaps the most important of her life, balanced almost more than she could begin to grasp. Not just *Zanzibar*, not just holoships and caravans, but the fates of worlds and civilisations. More than love and death.

Travertine moved to raise verself from the seat, then winced. 'I'll need the robot, I'm afraid.'

Chiku nodded. But instead of summoning the machine, she moved to assist her friend. 'This decision I'm asking you to make … when can I expect your answer?'

'Silly you, Chiku. You already have it.'

CHAPTER THIRTY-ONE

No one dared call it launch day. Even now the prospect felt unreal, impossible to square with the ordinary trajectory of her morning so far.

She had risen as normal and met with Noah and the children just before they set off for college, exchanging the usual strained but cordial small talk. Then she shared a transit pod with Noah, back to the administrative core, both of them acting as if nothing of consequence lay ahead of her that day. Two eager mid-level functionaries rode with them in the pod, clotting the air with maps and diagrams of *Zanzibar*'s interior while they debated vital matters of resource allocation. Noah and Chiku wisely said nothing.

Later there would be tears, she knew that. In the last few hours before the launch, before their secret was revealed to the rest of the caravan, Ndege and Mposi would be pulled out of college. She would meet them again and attempt to explain herself – attempt to make them understand why she had to do this baffling, cruel thing to them.

They would not understand, of course – not here and now. But she could give them words to carry with them after she was gone, and at some point they might come to understand, if not forgive.

When they arrived at their destination, Chiku and Noah quickly took their leave of the other politicians and functionaries who had shared the same pod. They made their way out of the transit terminal, down the long approach to the Assembly Building. Citizens and journalists watched her pass, but none approached her. Something in Chiku's stride and determination, projecting a hard repulsive field the way a planet deflected solar radiation.

'On Earth,' she told Noah, 'Chiku Yellow had to run into that building to escape a war machine. Inside, there were wild cats – panthers, I think they were, black and very powerful. The Mechanism was malfunctioning somehow, which made them more likely to attack. They hunted us deep inside the household.'

Noah lengthened his stride to match hers. 'This is the first time you've talked about that incident. Why the change of heart?'

'If not now, when? I'm grateful that you never pushed, never used what you knew against me.'

'You might not have trusted me, Chiku, but I always trusted you to do the right thing, in your own fashion. Have you seen her lately?'

'Nowhere near as much as I'd have liked. She's fine, though – much better than she was, actually.'

'And she's ... fully in the picture?'

'Absolutely. I talked everything over with her, ran almost every decision I took past her for a second opinion. You can dump some of the blame on her, if you like.'

'Seems a bit pointless.'

They were nearly at the building now. Her thoughts flashed back to the original household in Africa, after which the Assembly Building aboard *Zanzibar* was fashioned. She wondered if it still stood. She imagined its white walls surrendering to the bush, the whole property turning into an outline on the ground, a map of itself you could only see from the air. *I want to be back in Africa now*, she thought, *back in that body, not in this one. Under an honest sky, panthers or no panthers.*

'How are you feeling?' Noah asked as they jogged up the steps.

'Nervous. For about a million reasons.'

'I'm sure you'll rise to the occasion.'

She slowed before they were fully inside the building, glaring at the duty constables until they moved back from their stations and allowed her some privacy.

'Noah, before I announce my resignation ... I'm going to do what I should have done all those years ago. You said I should have trusted you, and you're right. I can't make amends for that – I can't give you back the years I stole from our marriage, or make our children suddenly understand what I've done to them. I realise it's much too late for that. But there's something I'd like you to have. Do you remember when we visited her, when I left Ndege's companion with her?'

After a moment, he nodded.

'It gave her a way to reach us, and vice versa. It's not perfect, and you'll need to use it sparingly, but there's a ching bind and a proxy at the other end. It'll place you in her presence.'

'I'd need the coordinates.'

'I memorised them years ago. I'll send them to your private account, during the session.'

'How safe is this ching bind? Is it traceable?'

'She's been very good at covering our tracks, but as I said, you shouldn't use it too often. My last visit was ... I was going to say months ago, but it's probably longer than that. She's not totally in the dark – she has access to the public nets, and to some of the private areas, but I'm sure she'd like to hear from you. Help her to stay up to date, if you can.'

'I'll ... keep an eye out for those coordinates.' After a moment, he said, 'Thank you. For whatever reason, I appreciate it.'

'I think we'd better get to work,' Chiku said. 'We don't want people thinking something's afoot, do we?'

'There is?'

She smiled at Noah.

Soon they were taking their seats in the Assembly – Noah near the front in the main fan of seats, Chiku in the Chair's position, facing her democractic legislature.

The plan was simple enough – barely a plan at all, truth be told. They would all go through the motions of a normal day's business. If her enemies had planted spies or eavesdropping devices anywhere in the Assembly, they would report nothing of note – not until it was already much too late to react.

The morning's business was going well – she was only paying it the bare minimum of attention – when the constables thrust open the doors and allowed an aide to enter the room. The current speaker fell silent and stood demurely at the lectern while this interruption played out. The aide approached Chiku and whispered.

She listened and felt her core body temperature drop by several degrees.

She asked a couple of questions, nodded, and then indicated to the speaker that he should return to his seat.

Chiku stood. 'I have some news,' she said. 'We hoped today's developments would come as a surprise to *Zanzibar* and the rest of the local caravan, but it seems there's been a leak.'

Noah was the first to speak. 'What's happening?'

'The Council of Worlds has issued a statement – more of a demand, in fact – ordering *Zanzibar* to suspend all extravehicular movements and submit to an immediate inspection. We're forbidden from launching or receiving ships and personnel, except on Council authority.' Chiku was gripping the lectern like a shipwrecked survivor in a storm. 'Delegations are on their way to us from six holoships in the local caravan.'

'We didn't see this coming?' asked the person next to Noah, a Sou-Chun loyalist.

'Unfortunately not,' said Chiku. 'The launches were coordinated and simultaneous, and no advance warning was given. This was meant to take us by surprise.' Chiku turned back to the aide and instructed him to project a real-time visualisation of the local caravan with the new ship movements plotted and extrapolated – bright curving tentacles of light, originating from different points in space but all converging on *Zanzibar*. 'They're closing at maximum civilian burn,' she said as the numbers and predictions stabilised. 'Eighteen ships, mostly shuttles and cargo craft, a few high-capacity taxis. The first of them will begin to arrive in about ninety minutes, sooner if they push the margins. Indications suggest that a second wave is being prepared for launch, which will include vessels from more than just the six holoships contributing to the initial wave.'

'This feels like war,' Noah said.

'It's not war,' Chiku said firmly, as if the word itself was a curse that needed to be revoked before it took root. 'This is a legal inspection ... unusually coordinated, yes, but fully within the provisions of normal inter-holoship governmental cooperation.'

'What are they planning to do – ram their way in?' asked the representative from October chamber.

'They'll be expecting us to comply fully with their requirements,' Chiku said. 'Clear all locks and prepare to receive inspection parties.'

'Eighteen ships!' said another. 'We don't even *have* eighteen independent locks! What are they thinking?'

'I don't know,' Chiku said, and it was true. 'But it's bad, and it puts us in a pinch. If hundreds of inspection parties are suddenly let loose in *Zanzibar* and go combing through our secrets, they're bound to find *Icebreaker*.' There – it was out. 'Then we're finished. They'll tear it apart, dismantle the research programmeme, put Zanzibar under the yoke – years of work undone. We can't permit that to happen, not after we've invested so much. But our only option, short of armed resistance, is to launch immediately. I mean *now*, as soon as possible, before the first wave arrives.'

'What, exactly,' asked the Sou-Chun loyalist, one of the Assembly members not cleared for full disclosure, 'is *Icebreaker*?'

'That will take a little explaining,' said Chiku, 'but I'm sure my colleagues will be more than happy to answer your questions.' Then she gripped the lectern tighter and swallowed hard. 'In the meantime, I, Chiku Akinya, Chair of the *Zanzibar* Assembly, hereby announce my immediate and unconditional resignation.'

In five minutes she was in the government car, racing away from the Assembly Building.

'I don't envy you,' she told Noah. He was sitting next to her in the rear compartment as the car beetled up the steep slope to the transit station. 'I always knew there'd be trouble after the departure, but I'm afraid it's going to come much sooner than I expected. Do you think you can keep order?'

'Why are you asking *me*? I'm not the new Chair, nor anywhere close to becoming it.'

'You have influence, though, and you might end up Chair after they've sorted through the mess I'm about to leave you. You've managed not to end up *totally* tainted by association with me, and I know you have at least as many friends as enemies. Your voice will count – you're not me, for one thing.'

'We can't afford to resist the inspection teams. If a drop of blood is spilt on either side, they'll send reinforcements. Constables, delegates, whatever it takes to impose external authority. We'd be finished.'

'There mustn't be blood – you're right about that. But you've got to do everything in your power to protect the new technology. Give anything but that.'

'You might be asking the impossible.'

She nodded gravely. 'If the worst comes to the worse, we'll still have the duplicate files aboard *Icebreaker* – how to make a Post-Chibesa engine in ten easy steps. If we choose, we can easily transmit the blueprints back to *Zanzibar* or the rest of the caravan. Our governments are going to try to suppress the information we'll be sending back from Crucible, or simply fail to act on it. You have to prevent that. You have to be strong, Noah. You've seen how the game is played. Make enemies of your friends, piss people off. Get used to being hated in service to a noble cause. You have it in you.'

'I'm not sure I do.'

'You're not alone. You have an ally in Eunice. Don't forget the ching coordinates.'

'You think she can dig us out of this hole?'

'If anyone – or any*thing* – can, it's her.'

An empty train was ready and waiting for them, flanked by constables. They were ushered from the car to a forward compartment and the train accelerated out of the chamber. Chiku could only sit and wait and hope everything went according to plan. The arrangements she had put in place were all predicated on her authority as Chair, and now she was just a member of the citizenry again, with no executive privileges. She could be arrested and detained on the flimsiest pretext.

But she had set enormous bureaucratic wheels turning, and they had a stony, grinding momentum of their own. The world was still happy to treat her as if she was running the place.

In the compartment, Chiku voked a visualisation of *Zanzibar* and its approaching visitors. She and Noah stared at it wordlessly for a few moments.

'You were right,' Noah said finally. 'Ninety minutes was optimistic. They're pushing harder – could be on-dock in fifty, maybe less. How long do you actually need to complete the launch sequence?'

'We assumed we'd have hours, but we only need enough time to get clear – they won't actually *shoot* at us, will they? We don't put guns on spaceships!'

'No,' Noah conceded. 'But we do put lots of things on spaceships that could be used as weapons, if you're that way inclined. I'd want a margin of error – a good few thousand kilometres of clear space. Can you get that far away, before the first ships arrive?'

'We'll have to. And light the PCP earlier than we were planning, if it comes to it.' She felt a profound urge to curl up and bury her face in her hands, walling out the universe and its woes. 'Fuck! We've been preparing for this for years! How the hell did they find out? And why wait until *now*, the very last day, to call us on it?'

'That's exactly why they've waited: there'll be no plausible denials now. Twelve of your top specialists are already aboard the ship in skip-over! How would you ever explain that?'

She felt as if some cunning ratchet-like thing in her head, a piece of neatly fashioned metal, had just disengaged itself with a solid clock-like *tock*, allowing a marvel of gears and pulleys and weights to whirr into life. A decision, becoming manifest.

'We have to launch now, even though we're not all aboard. Those who are ready can board now – including Travertine, even if ve suddenly decides ve's changed vis mind. Then we blow the chamber and get *Icebreaker* into clear space. That's the most critical part, and we can't afford to delay.'

'What about the rest of you?'

'We'll need a shuttle, something fast – can we make that happen?'

'Launching a shuttle will be in direct contravention of the Council's terms.'

'Somehow, I don't think it'll make our position much worse. I'm going to order one released for take-off immediately.'

Noah looked doubtful. 'Can you order anything?'

'Recommend in the strongest possible terms, then – good enough for you?'

As the train sped on, she voked back to one of her trusted colleagues in the Assembly and requested an immediate summary of *Icebreaker*'s state of readiness. The loading of provisions and fuel had been completed days ago and the major support systems and umbilicals retracted. But securing clamps and docking tunnels were still in place, ready to receive the last of the crew, and with a certain inevitability technicians were still inside, fussing over last-minute headaches.

'Pull them out,' Chiku said. 'Whatever the problem, just pull them out. I want *Icebreaker* clear of *Zanzibar* within thirty minutes.'

They protested, as she had expected, because this turn of events was not in their plans or covered by any of their contingencies. It should never have come down to this mad scramble. But she reminded them of that old adage of war about plans never surviving the first contact with the enemy.

Although this was not war, not precisely.

Not yet.

CHAPTER THIRTY-TWO

It took ten minutes to pull the technical staff out of *Icebreaker* and load those volunteers who were able to board immediately. Travertine, to Chiku's immense relief, put up no last-minute objections. It took another five minutes to seal all skin locks and retract the cumbersome docking bridges. Chiku watched via a number of secure eyes dotted around the inside of the berthing chamber – to her relief, the necessary privileges had not yet been removed. Nothing she had done so far had contravened the Council's no-fly instructions, but her next act was as irrevocable as it was necessary. The illusion of propriety would be well and truly destroyed.

'Blow hull,' Chiku stated, as casually as if she were ordering chai. The time for hesitation and second thoughts was long past.

The berthing chamber had never been pressurised, and its outer skin, which sealed it from true space, was intentionally much thinner than the skin around the habitation cores – mere metres of rock, rather than tens of metres. Quilted into this skin on a precisely calculated three-dimensional grid were several hundred shaped-charge devices containing slugs of metastable metallic hydrogen. Chiku's order detonated the charges in a precise sequenced fashion, as deftly orchestrated as any card trick, the effect of which was not so much to rip away the berthing chamber's skin as to carefully and elegantly peel it back, the charges going off in a spiralling wave, flinging matter exactly away from the lander, centrifugal force doing the rest, so that not a single damaging pebble came back the wrong way and impacted the lander. It was everything that the Kappa event had not been – not an accident but a deliberate and surgical repurposing of part of *Zanzibar*'s fabric. Chiku felt nothing as the charges went off – not a murmur of it reached her in the train, although she wondered if she might have felt something on firmer ground, closer to the event.

She switched to external public eyes, selecting a viewpoint near the hole. Already most of the debris had fallen out of shot, and since the chamber had never been pressurised there was no outgassing of air, volatiles and debris to confuse the picture. The aperture, opened in the skin, was neatly rectangular, and easily large enough for the lander to fit through. In the changes they had made to *Icebreaker* that had always been of paramount concern: it must still be able to fit through the original exit hole.

Time had scarcely been on her side before the eruption, but now Chiku sensed that every second counted, rather than every minute. It took a distressingly long time for the safety systems to verify that the aperture was clear and nothing need hinder *Icebreaker*'s emergence. Finally, the securing clamps were released and *Icebreaker*, no longer compelled to move in a circular motion around *Zanzibar*'s axis, fell along a precise tangent to its velocity at the last instant of capture. It was free-falling now – moving through space on its own course. Viewed against the rotating frame of the berthing chamber, the ship appeared to be pulled sharply *down*, as if sliding along an invisible bicycle spoke. Chiku realised she was holding her breath as *Icebreaker* cleared the aperture with what looked like millimetres to spare, and then the ship was free, dropping further and further away from *Zanzibar* until a ghost of thrust from its steering rockets arrested its radial motion and held it at a fixed distance from the holoship, a tiny new black and white fish shadowing a wrinkled-skinned leviathan.

The lander had never been properly weightless until this moment and there were yet more systems tests to be performed – long minutes of waiting while Chiku could do nothing except fret, and console herself that none of these system check-outs were frivolous or inessential. Finally, the normal CP drive was deemed safe to engage – this alone unleashing structural loads and thermal stresses which would easily have wrecked the lander without due precaution. The CP engine spooled up to one gee of thrust, much less than it was capable of, and already the lander was pulling ahead, starting to outrace *Zanzibar*. Chiku's viewpoint hopscotched between public eyes to keep up, until she had no option but to watch *Icebreaker* diminishing ahead of them, riding the bright spike of its engine. The lander could accelerate no harder if she were to stand a chance of catching up with it in one of the shuttles.

'Tell me,' she asked Noah, who was monitoring developments around the local caravan. 'Has all hell just broken loose?'

'Not yet – I don't think any of them expected you to be *this* ready. Oh, wait – something's coming in now. Priority transmission, maximum urgency.' Noah's voice deepened as he recited the statement. '"On order of the Council of Worlds, holoship *Zanzibar* is instructed to abort launch event and recall the unidentified vehicle immediately. This action is in express contravention of the terms of the inspection" – and so on.'

'Do they seriously think we'll recall *Icebreaker* now?' said Chiku.

'I suppose they have to look as if they're still in control of the situation.'

She felt the tug in her belly as the train decelerated sharply and drew to a stop at their destination.

'I don't know which order to ask these questions in, but is there a shuttle ready for me, and are Mposi and Ndege at the airlock?'

'Yes and nearly yes, but we'll be cutting it fine. Given *Icebreaker*'s current acceleration, you have about ten minutes before it's going to be difficult to make rendezvous and have enough fuel left in the shuttle to allow it to return– any longer than that, and we'll need to hold *Icebreaker* back or consider the shuttle expendable.'

She turned her attention to the visualisation of the incoming vehicles. Twenty minutes, according to the estimates, before they would be at *Zanzibar* – based on the assumption that none of them had accelerated since *Icebreaker* launched.

The train had brought them close to *Zanzibar*'s central axis, so they had much less than their usual weight when they disembarked. Constables and Assembly staff were on hand to assist them to the boarding lock, beyond which the shuttle was waiting. The rest of her volunteers were already aboard, the shuttle primed for immediate departure as soon as she joined them.

'I can't believe I'm going through with this,' she said to Noah, her voice trembling. 'It feels like I'm about to put my head in a guillotine or something.'

'It's not too late to change your mind. We could still call *Icebreaker* back.'

'That won't make any difference at this point – as far as the Council's concerned, the crime's already been committed just by launching the ship. Travertine's punishment for going against *Pemba* was harsh, and ve was just one person, working on vis own. Can you imagine what they'd do to our entire administration?'

'It wouldn't be pretty.'

'Show trials, mass executions – why not? I can easily believe they'd go that far.'

'We won't allow it,' Noah said, with a firmness that surprised her. 'Even if we have to declare complete independence from the rest of the caravan. We'd do it.'

'Tread carefully, won't you?'

'I'll do my best. Now put your brave face on. They're bringing in Mposi and Ndege.'

'How long have I got?'

'I'll tell you when it's time.'

They came in, accompanied by constables, and she felt her spirits dip to depths she had never experienced. All of a sudden they looked much younger than their years – Ndege no longer the self-assured nineteen year old she had grown into, but the twelve year old who had entered skipover. Mposi looked like the little boy who made bubbles in their garden.

Their expressions were full of fear and doubt – small wonder, she supposed, given that they had been ripped from their normal routine by constables and then brought to this strange and unfamiliar part of the holoship, far from the normal gravity of the community cores. Mposi and Ndege had never left *Zanzibar*, so had no experience of weightlessness or near-weightlessness.

'Thank you,' Chiku told Noah and the constables. They nodded and retreated, leaving her alone with her children.

'I have to go now,' she said.

From the look in their eyes it was clear that they did not understand. 'For how long?' Mposi asked.

'I don't know.'

Ndege said, 'What do you mean, you don't know? How can you not know?'

'All I know,' Chiku offered, 'is that it'll be at least eight years, possibly quite a bit longer.'

Eight years. Her words impacted them like a slap. Eight years was an eternity to an eighteen year old – nearly half the time Mposi had been alive.

'Why?' Ndege asked. 'Why do you have to do this stupid, pointless thing?'

'There's an important job that needs to be done so that we can all arrive safely on Crucible, like you've been promised since you were small. I'm doing this for you, first and foremost, but I'm also doing this for everyone aboard *Zanzibar*, everyone in the local caravan.' Feeling that this was insufficient, she added: 'I need to make sure that everything the Providers have built for us is the way we want it, so we can be happy when we arrive, about ten years later.'

'But why do *you* have to do that?' Ndege asked.

'Because ... because I have to. Because it would be wrong to ask someone else to do it in my place. We all have to be brave about that – not just me, but you as well. Both of you.'

'You can't go,' Mposi said, on the edge of tears – she could tell – but keeping them in check.

More in anger than distress his sister added, 'You never asked us how we'd feel about this.'

'I couldn't. And I really have no choice, not if I'm going to be a good citizen. But you mustn't worry. Noah … your father … will take care of you, and if you want, you can spend some of the time in skipover, the way we did before.'

'The way *we* did,' Mposi corrected her. 'You were awake, even though you said you wouldn't be.'

'I was awake some of the time, but I only ever wanted to do the best I could for all of us.' She glanced at Noah, certain her time must be up, but he nodded for her to continue. 'I know my choices and actions have been difficult for you to understand, but know that I have always loved you. Always. And I won't stop loving you after I get on the other ship. I don't want to go, but sometimes we have to do things we would rather not, and this is one of those times.'

'We can come with you,' Ndege said suddenly. 'Me, Mposi – Father. You can make room for us, can't you?'

Noah came over from where he had been waiting and put a hand on Ndege's shoulder while also meeting Chiku's despairing gaze. 'It's time. I'm sorry, but they're almost here and you need to be clear of *Zanzibar* before they arrive.' Then he drew Mposi and Ndege close, daughter on one side, son on the other, and said, 'Kiss your mother goodbye. Be brave and tell her you understand that she has to go away, that you love her very much, and that you can't wait for her to come home.'

'Why?' Mposi asked, as if this was all some trick.

'Because if you don't, you'll regret it for every waking moment of the next eight years of your life.'

And they did as he said, in their own fashion, and then Noah kissed her and wished her luck, and the courage to face whatever was ahead. Mposi and Ndege were crying by then – confusion and denial had given way, perhaps temporarily, to a provisional acceptance that there was nothing they could do to change their mother's mind. They looked upset now, rather than angry at the world for forcing this situation on them.

Chiku found that her own anger also had no individual focus: she could not blame anyone for this, not even long-dead Eunice and still-living Lin Wei for the things they had brought into being. They had not known what the consequences would be. No one could have known. She could not even hate Arachne for being what she was – it would be as futile as hating a snake for being a snake, or the weather for being capricious.

'Farewell,' Noah whispered, when the moment of parting finally came. 'And return.'

'I'll do my best.'

The moment she was in the shuttle, the doors closed and the docking clamps released, and the shuttle shifted into *Zanzibar*'s bright central shaft, the spinal void that had once contained the bulk of the partly disassembled CP drive. Chiku manoeuvred herself silently to one of the acceleration couches and buckled in. The other occupants were quiet, and she had no words for them.

The shuttle had been authorised to light its engine while still inside *Zanzibar*. Through the windows the surrounding shaft sped past at ever increasing speed. They were moving fast by the time they emerged into clear space, but were heading in the wrong direction relative to *Icebreaker*. The shuttle rolled and commenced a hard turn, squeezing Chiku even deeper into her couch than during the launch. She watched stars wheel dizzyingly for a few moments and then *Zanzibar* came back into view, still huge but offset now by the diameter of the turning arc the shuttle had just completed. And still they were accelerating.

The shuttle was flying itself – neither Chiku nor any of her volunteers were pilots, and the shuttle could fly itself more competently than its current human crew. She voked a three-dimensional map of the surrounding space, centred on the moving focus of the shuttle. They were sliding past *Zanzibar* now, about thirty kilometres from the hull. The shuttle was still accelerating relative to *Icebreaker*, and Chiku was relieved when the distance between the two vessels started decreasing rather than increasing. She let out a breath she had not known she was holding – *Icebreaker* was still within reach.

Then the outer boundary of the projection volume was pricked by the vectors of the inspection party's ships. They were coming in very fast, delaying deceleration as late as possible. Of the eighteen vehicles in the first wave, twelve remained on course for *Zanzibar*, while six had peeled away to attempt rendezvous with *Icebreaker*. Of those six, two now made a late course adjustment, moving as a tightly coordinated pair in an attempt to close in on the shuttle.

What are they hoping to achieve, Chiku thought, *beyond intimidation?* They were moving much too quickly to dock or grapple on, if that was their intention.

'This is Noah. Can you hear me?'

'Go ahead,' she answered.

'We've been issued with a general ultimatum – pull in all our ships or face sanctioned force, whatever *that* means. They want you to slow down, show that you're giving up the chase – I assume you're not about to have a sudden change of heart?'

'We've come too far for that. Politically, we've already handed them the noose, so we might as well see this through to the end.'

'It could be a bitter one.'

'You don't think they're actually going to try attacking us, do you? Surely they wouldn't escalate so much, so quickly?'

'If it suits them, and they think we're not going to be expecting it – well, I wouldn't bet against it.'

'But we'd know if they'd equipped a whole squadron of shuttles with weapons. Wouldn't we?'

'Maybe not. We've been quite successful at protecting our own secrets, haven't we?' Noah was silent for a moment, then added: 'We have long-range imagery on the inspection craft, including the two closing in on you. They look like normal shuttles – we're not seeing any hull-mounted guns or energy devices … That's interesting, though.'

'What?'

'One of them has an open airlock, as if they're preparing to EVA.'

'Just the one?'

'We only have a clear view of one shuttle. There's a suited person at the airlock now, which is pointed at the second ship, but we can't see the back of the second ship from here.' Noah sounded distracted, fielding too many questions at once. 'Just a moment, Chiku – we're trying to lock on to imagery from *Icebreaker* – it might give us the angle we need.'

'They're moving too fast to attempt a forced boarding.' She was studying the schematic, forcing it to skip forward in time. The mathematics told the story, cut in stone. There was nothing she could do to alter the shuttle's own vector if she still wanted to rendezvous with *Icebreaker*. 'They're going to *ram* us, Noah. Could they be minimally crewed? Would they consider two whole ships expendable?'

'Surely not – that would be a massive escalation.'

306

'They can't slow down now. They're going to be on me in about thirty seconds!'

'Hold your vector.'

'They're peeling off,' Chiku said, surprised and suspicious. 'Opposite vectors – they'll pass either side of me.'

'I think I know what they're up to. Assume full manual control, Chiku – do you have it?'

'Y-yes,' she stammered, hands trembling as she took the helm, her seat offering her a selection of basic control inputs – thrust, steering, hull orientation. 'What am I supposed to do?'

'Remain on course. When I give the word, do something. Anything. But only when I give the word.'

'What's happening?'

'I'll explain in about fifteen seconds. Are you ready? Make whatever evasive manoeuvre you can – there's nothing you can do that the shuttle can't undo. Here it comes. Now, Chiku. *Now*.'

As if she needed to be told twice.

She yanked the controls. There was nothing expert or considered about her inputs – a child could have achieved the same finesse. But the shuttle responded, dutifully obeying its heavy-handed mistress, and through the windows the stars jerked and tumbled, over and over. Alarms sounded. Unsecured items crashed around in storage bins. An arm flapped out like a salute, hinged with bruising force back into the side of its body.

'Release authority,' Noah said. 'Let the shuttle sort itself out. You did well.'

'Thanks. Be even better if I knew what I just did.'

'We think they'd stretched something between the two locks – a tether or grappling line, or maybe some kind of monomolecular filament, like spiderfibre. That was why they were moving as a pair. We didn't get a good view of the second shuttle, but we think there was probably a man in each lock, ready to release the line as the two ships pulled further apart.'

The shuttle had corrected the damage she had done, silencing its alarms, restabilising itself and resuming the original vector.

'Our relative speed would have been pretty high, wouldn't it?' she asked.

'Oh yes – kilometres per second. More than sufficient.'

'For what?'

'Let's assume there were weights at either end of the line, to give it some tension as it started cutting. It would have gone through you like a laser. Nice piece of improvised space weaponry.'

'Could you possibly sound a bit less warmly appreciative?'

'Sorry. But you did well – once the tether was released, they couldn't alter its course. You threw enough randomness into your trajectory to avoid being sliced.'

'Why did we have to wait until the last moment?'

'Couldn't be sure when they'd release. Seemed safer not to give them any warning that you had a trick up your sleeve.'

'It was up your sleeve, not mine. Are we safe now? What about *Icebreaker*?'

'Transmitting warnings now – they have more delta vee to play with than you, so they should be able to give those shuttles the run-around.'

'Just as long as I can still catch up. Do you think they'll try the same thing twice?'

'I think that was their one shot – they'd have to come almost close enough together to dock to stretch out another line between them, and that'd cost them time, which is as much of a problem for them as it is for us. They appear to be pulling back towards *Zanzibar* now – our problem, not yours.'

'Thank you, Noah.' But if he intended his comment to elevate her spirits, it had exactly the opposite effect. Whatever happened to *Zanzibar*, Ndege and Mposi would be part of it. She hoped for their sakes that diplomacy would find a solution, a path that avoided bloodshed. Collectively they had come so far, done so much – the holoships were a triumph of cooperation and common purpose, emblems of a better way of being human. Whatever differences now existed, whatever enmities and grudges, it would be unforgivable to throw away so much that was good. 'Let them in, if they insist,' she said. 'Roll out the red carpets, make them feel at home. We'll gain nothing by fighting them, not if they want to take control by force. Most of our citizens had no knowledge of *Icebreaker* – we can't punish our own people by turning this into a civil war.'

'There'll be no armed resistance,' Noah avowed. 'They've committed the first violent act, even if it didn't succeed. We won't stoop to their level.'

'It's easy to say that now. But we have to hold to it, no matter how difficult it becomes—'

'I know that,' Noah said, talking over her. 'But you have to let us go now, Chiku – let us face this alone. You have your own challenges. Leave *Zanzibar* to the rest of us. We'll rise to the occasion.'

'You're not alone. Remember that.'

'I shall,' Noah said.

After the failed attack, the rest of the crossing was almost anticlimactic. The shuttle made rendevous with *Icebreaker* and they transferred aboard the much larger vehicle without fuss. The shuttle was nearly out of fuel, so the best they could do was abandon it. Someone might decide it was worth the bother of reclaiming as it drifted further and further ahead of the holoship. It was certainly of no use to the expedition, adding dead mass where none was needed.

Plans months in the drafting argued over to the last detail lay in tatters. There had never been any possibility of performing a full test of the Post-Chibesa engine within *Zanzibar*, not if secrecy were to be upheld. So they had tested components of it at near capacity, and the whole only at a very low energy regime, where the physics scarcely deviated from the standard Chibesa model. Enough to verify that things *should* work, but hardly enough to satisfy all qualms. They had intended, once *Icebreaker* was clear, to run a suite of tests at steadily higher energies. It was true that there had always been the expectation of other ships being launched from nearby holoships, but Chiku's planners had never guessed that the launches would happen even before *Icebreaker* was released from *Zanzibar*, squeezing the margins down to minutes instead of hours.

All of a sudden, though, it struck Chiku that caution was now her enemy. If the PCP engine did not work exactly as predicted, they were all doomed anyway. Better to find that out now, in one clean gamble, then submit to a pointless agony of expectation.

She met with Travertine, expecting an argument.

'No, I agree totally. You've staked everything on this, and so have I.'

'I'm not sure what you've staked personally,' Chiku said.

'Only my entire reputation. Kappa dented my pride. I made an error, allowed my experiment to run beyond my immediate control. I've lived with my mistake, and with the ignominy of being paraded as an example to others, but I refuse to live with a second dose of failure. If the PCP engine doesn't work, it probably won't just stop. I think we'll be looking at something much more ...'

'Catastrophic?'

'I was going to say glorious, but catastrophic works just as well. If I'm wrong, we won't live long enough to realise it, and I think I prefer it that way. We'll make a very bright splash, whatever happens.'

'Run the engine to maximum power. When we're satisfied that we have a stable burn, we'll dump the ballast.'

'Make sure everyone's strapped in, then – even with the ballast, it's going to be a bit of a bumpy ride.'

Chiku checked on the rest of the crew as she returned to her seat. Most of them had remained in their sturdy acceleration couches after launch with the exception of those destined for skipover. The huge lander was already maintaining a gee of steady thrust, but if their simulations were on the mark, the PCP engine was capable of exceeding this acceleration by a factor of ten – more than a human body could tolerate over an extended period of time, even in a couch.

To counteract this, they had packed the lander with liquid water, thereby increasing *Icebreaker*'s effective mass by a factor of three. Theoretically, it would allow the engine to be run up to maximum capacity without imposing bone-crushing loads on the living crew. The engine would need to run for a hundred hours to bring *Icebreaker* up to its cruising velocity of one-quarter of the speed of light, and two hundred hours to achieve slowdown around Crucible – more than a week of continual thrust. As soon as they were happy that the engine was working as it should, they could begin to dump the ballast and selectively pressurise the evacuated hull spaces, giving the crew more room to move around when they emerged from skipover.

Once Chiku was satisfied that her volunteers were either strapped down or on their way into skipover, she reviewed the developing situation around *Zanzibar*.

Already she felt the distance. Space between Chiku and her world, her children, Noah and her work, the good things in her life, her home and its simple pleasures, was dilating itself with spiteful haste, as if it held some deep personal grudge against her. *Icebreaker* had been on its way for only an hour (an hour that seemed longer than that, it was true) and in that time it had crossed two thirds of a million kilometres – enough distance to wrap the Earth eighteen times, or to ensure that a radio signal took more than four seconds to travel to *Zanzibar* and back. Already the events she witnessed on *Zanzibar* were pushed back into her personal past by entire heartbeats, entire moments.

Zanzibar had made no efforts to resist the inspection parties, and now they were docking and boarding, taking turns to use the airlocks. The ships that had veered off to meet the shuttle and *Icebreaker* had by now returned to the main grouping, standing off until docking slots were available. Meanwhile, the second wave of vehicles was very close to arriving, and more were on the way. More than fifty ships, at the last count, each of which could easily contain a dozen or more constables.

Zanzibar's normal peacekeeping authority, even for a citizenship of millions, numbered much less than a thousand. They had simply never needed a strong police force. It would not take many more arriving ships to place their own constabulary in the minority.

Public eyes showed the new constables emerging from the airlocks and moving out into *Zanzibar*'s civic spaces. They were not obviously armed or armoured, but some were accompanied by peacekeeping robots, striding black things like long-legged spiders. They unnerved Chiku, and she was momentarily glad of the widening distance. She had seen similar robots during her visits to other holoships, but they had never been considered necessary in *Zanzibar*.

'The mood is about as calm as you'd expect,' Noah reported from a car taking him back to the Assembly Building. 'We've issued general orders to all citizenry and constables – treat the visitors as honoured guests, obey all reasonable requests. It's too soon to tell if there'll be trouble – it'll be hours before they establish a visible presence throughout *Zanzibar*. People are twitchy and confused. Most of them don't even know what happened with *Icebreaker*!'

'Issue a statement,' Chiku said. 'Give the citizenry the facts. Help them understand that what we've done could be considered a provocative act.'

'Are you sure?'

'It's the only way. If they start feeling the constables have come barging in without justification, someone somewhere is going to do something stupid. Probably involving a shovel and a skull.'

'We're already fielding questions. People want to know if this is the start of an occupation.'

'Just tell them the truth – which is that you don't know and it isn't in your power to decide. Say that *Zanzibar* will comply with the wishes of the Council of Worlds.'

'Don't you think our assurances are going to ring a bit hollow given that we've already gone against the Council by launching the ship?'

'They can believe us or not, Noah, but *Icebreaker* is a fait accompli. We're on our way now, and there's no point in punishing those of you left behind. Most of had nothing to do with the expedition in the first place.'

'I look forward to testing out that line of argument. We're ahead of the constables now, but they're moving in on the administrative core. They've demanded access to the Assembly Building.'

'You'd better let them in – they'll only make you if you don't.'

'No kidding. It's going to be very difficult for the Assembly to have any kind of private discussion to decide on our next move. You're right to dismiss armed resistance – but we don't *have* to let the rest of the ships dock. We could seal off *Zanzibar*, declare unilateral independence from the Council.'

'And what about the constables already inside?'

'The numbers are marginal at the moment – we could take them, if we have to.'

'And their robots?'

'I don't know.'

'It's not an option, Noah. We depend on the caravan for so much. We can't pull up the drawbridge, expect to go it alone. At the very least we'd put our citizens – including *my* children – through hardships that they don't deserve. At worst we'd invite a forced occupation. If we won't give them access to our locks, they'll tunnel their way in through our skin.'

'We can't just … concede.'

'The work is done. *Icebreaker* is on its way. In that sense we've achieved what we wanted to.'

'No,' Noah corrected. 'We've taken the first step, that's all. Even if the engine works, we still need to scale it up for holoship use. If the Council can't be made to see that, then perhaps we really do need to declare independence.' She heard him thump part of the car's interior in frustration. 'Fuck! I don't feel equipped for this. Maybe we have it all wrong, you know? Maybe we should just keep going, forget about Crucible.'

'We must reach Crucible, Noah,' she said. 'Don't start doubting that now.'

'It was just a thought.'

'Good – keep it that way. Look, we both know this is going to be difficult, but I trust you to make the right decisions – to hold the line, to do the right thing by our people.'

'I'm nearly at the Assembly. The constables won't be more than half an hour behind, if we're lucky. I'm going to speak to Eunice.' She smiled as he spoke the name – a daring thing, even now. 'She needs to know what's going on.'

'I doubt she's in the dark, but you're right – talk to her now, before it gets more difficult. And tell the children not to worry. It's all going to be all right.'

'Do you really believe that?'

'I want to,' she said. 'Very badly. And I think if we all try our hardest not to do anything stupid, *all* of us – you, me, her, the rest of the caravan – we might have a chance.'

'Just a chance?'

'It's better than no chance at all. We're in a mess, Noah – cleverness got us into it, and more cleverness will have to dig us out of it. We have to be wise, like Eunice said, rise above ourselves.'

'I'm all ears if you have any bright ideas you'd like to share.'

'Take care, Noah. We're going to light the PCP engine very soon. I hope we'll have a chance to talk again, but there are no guarantees.'

'Do you want me to tell Mposi and Ndege?'

'Not until it's done. Whatever happens.'

'I will.' He inhaled deeply. 'Well, we're here, and we'll just have to weather it. I don't suppose your family had the foresight to make this place defensible?'

'I suspect not.'

'Tell them to try harder next time. Good luck, Chiku. I'll be waiting to hear from you. Regardless of all the stuff that's gone on between us, I hope we speak again.'

'So do I,' she said.

When she was done, Travertine informed her that they were ready to push to full power.

'I suppose it's occurred to you,' Travertine said, 'that all of this could just be a form of suicidal revenge on my behalf? That I know the engine won't work, but I'll have the satisfaction of seeing you give the order to start it up?'

'Actually, that had not occurred to me.'

'As satisfaction goes, it would be pretty fleeting, I'd guess. Anyway, I'm not the avenging type – strikes me as a fairly futile use of one's energies. Shall we do this?'

'It will work,' Chiku said firmly, as if her conviction alone was enough to guarantee success.

'I know,' Travertine agreed. 'But it would be a kindness to you if it didn't, wouldn't it? Take that burden of worry off your shoulders. I'm feeling years younger, by the way. You should try it sometime: nothing puts a spring in your step like a commuted death sentence.'

They pushed the engine into uncharted physics. Even with the ballast to deaden the acceleration, the shift from one to three gees was still a shock, for there was almost no transition, just a steplike increase in power. Travertine gave very little away as ve studied the numbers and curves, matching them against vis mental predictions. Ve pursed vis lips and squinted, and made odd little catlike noises, the meaning of which was lost on Chiku.

'We can take it to ten,' Travertine announced finally, but there was nothing triumphant in vis tone. 'That'll get us away from *Zanzibar* the fastest and out of reach of the caravan. But you'll want to be in skipover before we disperse all the ballast. After that, there's no going back.'

'I'm done with second thoughts.'

'I thought so, but best to check rather than assume. How does it feel, to be leaving everything behind?'

'I suspect you feel much the same way. Anyway, we're not leaving *Zanzibar* for good.'

'You don't strike me as someone entirely convinced she'll ever see her home again. There's a kind of grey deadness in your eyes, as if little shutters have come down. I hope you do get back, of course, for your children's sake. Have you told Noah the whole story – what we'll really be facing when we arrive at Crucible?'

'We should sleep now,' Chiku said bluntly, effectively ending the conversation.

Travertine could not resist having the last word. 'Well, whenever you feel like sharing ...'

Chiku and Travertine were the last to enter skipover. Doctor Aziba was already sleeping, so they were left in the care of the surgical robot. The robot fussed over them, blundering through its routines. Travertine had to fight to stop it removing vis bracelet. Ve was quite intent on keeping it where it was.

Even at three gees, there was no realistic prospect of the caravan's ships catching up with *Icebreaker* – not if they wanted a chance of getting back home. So Chiku had the surgical robot delay administering the knock-out drugs until she had taken one last look at the news from *Zanzibar*. Noah had enough business to keep him occupied now, so she did not disturb him for an update. Instead she wandered the holoship's civic spaces, tapping into public eyes, haunting the world she had once walked. The new constables were almost everywhere now and more were cycling in through the available locks by the hour. Their numbers were still small, but they would soon be able to impose effective authority. To their credit, her citizens – *her* citizens, as if she was still in charge – were handling the situation with dignity and composure. So far there had been no real trouble, but something would give in the end, she knew. Such was the way of things. Pressure had to be released.

Be wise, she prayed, directing her wish to her own people and the occupying force alike. *Be wise, be tolerant, be human. Because against the truth of Crucible, none of this will matter in the slightest.*

And then the robot pushed the drugs into her and she fell into skipover.

CHAPTER THIRTY-THREE

'I'm sorry to bring bad news,' Kanu said, one bright morning in Lisbon, 'but Mecufi is dead. I thought you'd both like to know.'

For a while, their son had fallen into the habit of visiting his mothers once or twice a year, returning from the seasteads to spend a day or two in their company. Lately, though, the visits had become less frequent. Chiku had not minded that, for she knew that Kanu had many demands on his time, especially now that he had risen to a position of some considerable responsibility in the Panspermian hierarchy. The main thing – indeed, the only thing that really mattered – was that they were in communication again, however irregularly. And that, by some silent token of understanding, they had agreed to forgive each other for whatever transgressions and misunderstandings each might have committed. Chiku, for her unwillingness to let her son choose his own path, even if that meant surrendering his future to the inscrutable objectives of the capricious merfolk, who could veer from allies to enemies with the turning of the wind. Kanu, in turn, for failing to see how much his decision would hurt his mother, and rather than explain himself he had chosen instead absolute isolation, refusing all contact until that day when he rode his kraken to her rescue. Pride against love, stubbornness against blood and kin.

All that was behind them now, and the world was better for it. Kanu had never become the totally alien being she feared – he had stopped his transmigration long before he became fully committed to the aquatic and maintained that he had no plans to further alter his current anatomy, which allowed him to move with relative ease on dry land. Chiku, for her part, wondered exactly what it was she had always feared. He was still her son, after all, no matter the changes rendered to his anatomy. With hindsight she should have urged him forward, grateful that the Akinyas would at last have some small leverage within the merfolk.

So many regrets, she thought. They were the stitches that held her life together. She feared that if they were unpicked, her past would unravel and reveal itself to be a single thread, not the complex knotted design she imagined. One of the downsides of a long life was the almost infinite scope it offered for reflection.

And by any measure, she was becoming a very old creature indeed.

'Why did Mecufi die?' she asked.

As time went by and prolongation techniques improved, there was increasingly little acceptance of death as a natural outcome of old age. When her mother died in 2380, she had been part of a slow-crashing wave of die-offs, one of what the experts predicted would be among the last statistically significant human extinction events. Almost everyone born later than Sunday Akinya – meaning almost everyone now alive – had started life with a superior suite of genetic and exosomatic prolongation options. Chiku was now two hundred and fifty – almost the same age her mother had been at the time of her death – and she had lived the full and merciless measure of those years, spending none of them in skipover.

She was not immortal. Someone born now might have every expectation of living five hundred years or more – long enough to see in the fourth millennium, if their cards fell right. As the genetically oldest of the three clones, Chiku Yellow's options were less favourable. It would be complex and risky to submit to a second triplication process, and in any case she lacked the necessary funds. But she had no complaints, and no strong sense that she was about to die. Another century was within her grasp, and if it came to less than that, she would not complain.

It was 2415 now. Sometimes she looked at the date and thought: *That's not right.* It's a mistake, some weird way of saying fifteen minutes after midnight. Not a year I happen to be living in.

'It wasn't a bad death,' Kanu said. 'He didn't suffer. But he was very old – nearly as old as June Wing, or Arethusa – and the years finally caught up with him. There was a lot they didn't understand, back in the early days of aquatic remodelling, and they did a lot of unintentional damage to his genes.'

The three of them were down at the quayside, sitting with their legs hooked over the side of the dock, the water trembling and spangling below. Seagulls loitered and squabbled. The air smelled brine-laden and fishy. Coloured boats were bobbing a little way along the dock. The light coming off the suspension bridge was so bright that Chiku had to keep blinking. It was as if the thing had been carved out of filaments of the sun and magicked into trembling solidity.

'I'm grateful for the things he did for us,' Chiku said. 'At least, I am now. I wasn't always convinced at the time.'

Chiku Red added, 'I'm sorry for your loss, Kanu. You knew him very well.'

Chiku Red mostly spoke Portuguese these days. Chiku Yellow had gained a halting sort of fluency – some command of a language was required to teach it, after all – and over the years Kanu had picked up a satisfactory working knowledge. They could communicate in Portuguese without the aug – Chiku Red had no access to it, anyway. Sometimes Kanu and Chiku Yellow swerved into words or phrase-fragments from Swahili or Zulu or Mandarin or Gujarati for a little colour, but seldom whole sentences. Chiku Red preferred them to confine their efforts to Portuguese, and Chiku Yellow had no difficulty understanding why. It was a good language, old and road-tested. It had been an Olympic endeavour for Chiku Red just to regain any use of one language after the damage her mind had suffered.

'Thank you,' Kanu acknowledged. 'Even Arethusa has transmitted her condolences, although for obvious reasons she won't be returning to Earth. You did a good thing, Chiku, bringing her back into contact with us.'

Arethusa, Chiku had long since gathered, was in danger of becoming the oldest living sentience in the universe. Unless, of course, anyone knew something to the contrary. It was all dumb luck, in the end. The genetic alterations she had worked on herself had turned out to be beneficial rather than detrimental. Although by all accounts, like a free-market economy, she had no option but to just keep growing. It was said that she would only leave Hyperion when the moon became too small for her and she had to discard it like a too-tight garment.

'Mecufi had no particular reason to trust me,' Kanu said. 'I could have been an agent of the family, sent to undermine everything he stood for, but he never doubted me.'

'That would have been a bit ruthless, even for us,' Chiku said.

'There'll be a funeral, of sorts. Would you like to come?'

'Both of us?' asked Chiku Red.

Kanu gave a nod of his majestic head. 'Both of you.'

'We don't leave Lisbon very often,' Chiku said.

'I hope you'll make an exception. I won't insist, of course, but I think you'll find it worth your while.'

'She hasn't made a move against us in fifty years,' Chiku said. 'I like it this way. I wouldn't want to do anything that might provoke her.'

'You went to the Moon once, and to the seasteads to bring Chiku Red home,' Kanu pointed out. 'Neither of those things did you any harm. Nor will this.'

'What are your funerals like?' Chiku Red asked.

'I don't know,' Kanu admitted. 'I can't say I've ever been to one.'

There was no need for haste, so they went by sailing ship. Chiku had seen the cyberclippers coming and going along the Tagus for as long as she had been in Lisbon, but this was something different. From a distance, as they approached along the quay – they had taken the tram to Estoril – nothing marked the craft as unusual. It had a sleek catamaran hull, covered in a frictionless coating that gave off odd optical effects, like a meniscus of oil in a puddle. It had an abundance of sails and sail parts of different shapes, sizes and function. The sails gathered sunlight as well as wind. They were also optically strange, capable of flicking from one extreme of reflectivity to another. There was an absurdity of rigging, too many lines and winches and pulleys to make any sense at all. The thing seemed complicated for the sake of it.

There were also people making it all work. This was what made the ship different. The cyberclippers ran with no crews at all, save for the occasional technician, and they spent months at sea following optimum path solutions, carrying cargoes that did not need to be anywhere fast. But there were dozens of merfolk on the deck of this ship, and even some up in the sails and rigging, and they were all doing something.

Chiku and Chiku Red stared in wonder and horror at the sight of it all.

'They could fall,' Chiku said. It was obvious to her that the merfolk had no lines or safety nets to catch themselves if something went wrong.

'They won't,' Kanu said. And to prove his point, even before the ship had left the dock, he had slipped up to the top of one of the main masts, hand and foot, so fast and agile that it looked like a trick, as if he were being ascended by a hidden rope. From the top he waved and laughed and then came back down again.

Chiku felt a flush of pride and bewilderment. It felt impossible to her that this was her son, doing this impossible thing.

'Why did you make this boat?' Chiku Red asked, when they were at sea and Estoril was a biscuit-coloured margin on the horizon. 'It needs too many people.'

'It can go faster than a cyberclipper,' Kanu explained, the wind tugging back his long roped locks. 'Sometimes. Cyberclippers are very good at finding a reliable course, very good at getting goods from one port to another, but they don't always make full use of the wind. With a good crew on board, this thing can really fly.'

It was true. Chiku had been to the stern of the catamaran and watched two troughs of water close up behind the two keels of the fast-rushing hull. The troughs looked so sharp edged it was easy to think they had been chiselled into ice. Of course, there was a stiff breeze today. But it was astonishing to think that this was all that was making them go through the water: just that breeze, hardly enough to be called a wind, acting against a sufficient acreage of sail. Even the solar energy was only there to operate the electrical winches and steering systems. They banked some of it into fuel cells, Kanu said (actually very efficient gyroscopic flywheel storage units) but it was a matter of pride not to use that stored power for locomotion. There were other ships like this, Chiku gathered, and other crews. They were extremely competitive.

But her fundamental question still remained: so what if the sailing ship went a little faster than a cyberclipper, on average? Why not use airpods, or fliers, or maglevs, or even the hulking nuclear submarine Uncle Geoffrey had told her about way back when?

'It's just for the fun of it, I suppose,' she suggested to Kanu.

Her son gave her a stern but forgiving look. 'It's much more than that. The cyberclippers are very elegant, but they're totally dependent on the Surveilled World. Without the aug, they don't know where they are, and without the Mech, they don't know what to do next.'

'And this is a problem how, exactly?'

'You've swum in the Surveilled world from the moment you took your very first breath. I suspect you probably find it quite difficult to imagine any other way of living.'

'You'd be surprised. Anyway, you've grown up with it as well.'

'But I joined the Pans,' Kanu said, 'and the Pans have their own way of doing things, disdaining the easy solutions. To begin with, these were aesthetic and philosophical choices as much as anything else. We didn't care for the idea of telepresence and virtual spaces, thinking that these tools would discourage us from actually going out there, into space, when we could send robots or figments instead. And we were right! But that's almost beside the point now. For philosophical and spiritual reasons, we set ourselves on a path that took us away from the excesses of the Surveilled World. And now we hear that the Surveilled World is poisoned!'

Perhaps it was just the breeze, but Chiku's neck hairs bristled at his words. It felt impetuous to be discussing Arachne so openly. She sent Kanu a silencing glare.

'It's all right, Mother,' he said, smiling. 'We're safe enough here. That's the point of this creaky old thing – she can't touch it, or get herself aboard it, or know what we're saying or thinking.' Kanu patted one of the wooden handrails running the length of the catamaran. 'It's a sort of insurance, if you like. If the world stops working tomorrow, if the Mech crashes and burns and takes the aug down with it, we'll still have the wind and we'll still know how to rig up these sails. We could still go anywhere in the world.'

'The Mech isn't going to crash,' Chiku said. 'It's been around too long. We need it too much.'

'Speak for yourself,' said Chiku Red.

They sailed to the seasteads. What had taken an hour by flier took most of the day by catamaran. At twilight they ate on deck, watching the sky shade through russets and pinks and gentle lilacs, and the sea darken to wine. Some dolphins provided company. Chiku and Chiku Red raced from one side of the hull to the other, watching the water glimmer and glow where the dolphins had torn it open. It was amazing and wonderful, a moment to justify a life. Chiku and Chiku Red could not stop laughing, giddy with the thrill of it all. Even Kanu, who must have seen this spectacle a thousand times before, watched on with fond amusement. He seemed more delighted by the reactions of his mothers than the dolphins themselves.

Not long before midnight, lights pushed above the horizon. The catamaran docked at a floating pontoon and the passengers were conveyed by electric car into the main mass of the seastead. The air was warmer than it had been in Lisbon, the stars so near and bright it was as if they had been lowered down on threads. Along the dock the rigging of many boats whipped and rattled impatiently.

'The funeral is tomorrow,' Kanu reported, before they were taken to their underwater rooms, barnacled down from the seastead's underside.

'Is there anything we need to know? Chiku asked.

'Not really. It's actually going to be quite a modest ceremony. Mecufi wasn't one for dramas.'

Chiku thought of the melodramatic way in which Mecufi had first intruded on her life, but she was careful not to contradict her son. And indeed, when the funeral came around, it was much less ostentatious than she had begun to fear. They went out shortly before dawn, in a great procession of small, lantern-lit boats. They were all either sail-driven or propelled by oars. Though the wind snatched at the sails, the muscle-powered craft had no difficulty keeping pace. The oars were worked by heroically strong aquatics, creatures shaped for the sea. Many aquatics simply swam alongside in the water, as effortlessly as the dolphins they had watched the night before. Chiku saw all sorts of anatomies, from the almost human to the barely identifiable.

One boat, propelled by both sail and oar, was twice as large as any of the others. This craft carried Mecufi's body, covered in a shroud and resting on a raised platform beneath a pennanted awning. Chiku and Chiku Red watched Kanu move around on the larger boat, supervising the rowers and the merfolk working the sails. Chiku was rather glad that she and her sibling had not been expected to travel on Mecufi's vessel. It would have felt like an intrusion to share the funeral boat with these strange and lovely creatures. It was enough of a privilege for any dry-lander to see such a ceremony.

Presently the boats arrived at some designated area of sea that looked like everywhere else to Chiku. The sun had not yet risen and there were still a few stars overhead. The lanterns, hundreds of them, cast colour-ed reflections on the waters. The seas were still now and the air nearly motionless.

In response to some unheard command, the boats arranged them-selves into a ring around the largest craft, enclosing it within a circle of water. The aquatics who had swum out with the procession scrambled and slithered onto the encircling boats. Many of them were standing now, holding lanterns and candles. Chiku and Chiku Red glanced at each other, neither knowing quite what to expect. There was no sound but the occasional slap of water against a hull. She watched the aquatics on the main boat as they moved in silent ceremony around the shroud-ed body on its platform.

If there was a signal, a voiced or silent command, Chiku missed it. But from one of the boats came a sudden and sustained keening sound. It was deeply foreign to her ears, pitched too high to be anything she would have called music. But music was exactly what it was. An aquat-ic had started singing, generating a powerful ululation. Soon another joined in, and then a third. Colouration had entered the tone. It began to shift in frequency. Two more voices joined the song, and then two more. It was, she would later learn, a motet for forty voices, divided into eight five-part choirs: forty aquatic voices, a sound to stir the oceans to their beds. The contributions of the choirs began to chase each other, phasing in and out of harmony – contrapuntal passages shifting into broad chordal phrases of heart-stopping intensity.

As the voices soared and swooped, lights began to appear in the circle of enclosed water – darting blue and green phosphorescent stabs, comet-streaks of opal and aquamarine that danced and dervished. They organ-ised themselves into wheels and flourishing progressions, galaxies and flowers of ever-opening light. Chiku realised that it was some clever orchestration of living matter; just as the Mechanism could turn a panther into a weapon, so the Pans had the means to bend the sea's living biomass to their will. Here they persuaded it to exalt the memory of one of their own as forty voices moved the air. Another marvel, as lovely as it was sad, and she wished that Pedro Braga was here to witness this astonishing thing, to add it to his life's store of wonders.

But there was Chiku Red, at least, and as the music surged through them both – it was, she thought, what the siren choirs of the ancient mariners must have sounded like – she knew that her sibling was feeling it just as profoundly.

The sky was brightening, the wheels and flowers fading, the lanterns losing their radiance. But before the spell was broken she watched Kanu and eleven other aquatics lift the shrouded body from its platform and allow it to slip into the paling water.

The motet reached its climax. Forty voices sustained a note for longer than seemed possible, and then when the silence fell it was as if silence itself was a kind of song.

The boats began to break their circle.

CHAPTER THIRTY-FOUR

Kanu swam over to them when they were on their way back to the sea-stead. He found them seated on benches inside a little wooden cabin at the back of Chiku's boat, which offered shelter from the sun.

'Thank you,' she said.

Chiku Red added: 'Yes, thank you.'

'I'm glad you came to the funeral,' Kanu said. 'We've never needed our friends more than we do now. Besides, Mecufi was very insistent that you be invited.'

'It was good of him to think of us,' Chiku said.

'He wanted you to attend the funeral, but that's not the only reason you were invited here.' Kanu closed the door behind him and sat down on the bench opposite the two Chikus. His clothes were already dry, even though he had only left the water a few moments earlier.

'What now?' Chiku asked.

'Yes,' said Chiku Red. 'Why are we here?'

'Let me make some chai,' Kanu declared.

Kanu produced a tea service from a wooden drawer at the back of the cabin, all the necessary provisions neatly laid out on a high-edged tray. He poured the water, which was already boiling, into three kelp-patterned cups. Chiku saw there was no point pressing him – he would speak when he was ready. But there was something on the tray that prickled Chiku's memory. It was a slim wooden box, like a pencil case.

'I've seen that before,' she said.

She glanced at Chiku Red, but there was no recognition in her eyes.

'We drew lots from a box,' she said finally. 'It had the elephants in it, and the Samsung and the Ray-Bans. But it wasn't this box.'

'No,' Chiku said, agreeing. 'But I've seen it before.'

Kanu passed around the cups of chai. 'It belonged to Mecufi, Chiku. He wanted you to have it.'

'Did he bequeath it to me in his will?'

'Something like that. He thought about giving it to you much sooner than this, but the time was never right.'

'Do you mind?' Chiku reached for the box but refrained from touching it.

'Go ahead – it's yours to do with as you wish.'

The box felt empty in her hands. She opened a little brass catch at one end and eased out a container, felt-lined with a dozen square partitions. She could imagine keeping eggs in those partitions. Or eyeballs.

She remembered now. It was a long time ago – a ridiculously long time ago – but she remembered.

'When Mecufi first came to me in the café at the top of the Santa Justa elevator, he had this with him.'

'What is it?' Chiku Red asked.

'There were motes in it. Twelve of them, I suppose. He took out one and gave it to me.'

Chiku Red, lacking access to the aug, had no recent experience of the emotional transfer of a mote, but she understood the concept well enough. She knew that each mote contained a cargo of pre-packaged emotions, formulated in a state of zenlike concentration by the sender and tagged for a specific recipient, then locked away in glass perpetuity until the moment of their release. She wondered why the world needed motes – surely words and faces were enough.

There were two motes left in the box, nestled within the final pair of compartments and only visible when the compartment had been slid to the limit of its travel. One was a milky, featureless white. The other was a kind of purple-flecked black.

'My memory might be playing tricks,' she said, 'but I could swear the black one was in the box that day. It stood out – it was the only black one. What does it mean?'

'Mecufi gave me one other instruction in addition to ensuring that you acquired the box.'

She gave her son a sharper look than she had intended. 'Which was?'

'The white mote is for you. Do nothing with the black mote until you've experienced the white. He was most insistent.'

'Mecufi formulated this before he died?'

'A long time before. I think he renewed the formulation several times over the years, but as I said, the time was never quite right for him to give it to you.'

'And him dying makes it right?'

'I suppose so,' Kanu said. 'Look, I'm just the messenger here. I really don't know what this is all about.'

'Really?' Chiku asked, hoping that her son detected her scepticism.

'I suppose I can make an educated guess – especially in light of our conversation yesterday, what you were saying about ...' But Kanu caught himself, and they both smiled at his nearly having mentioned Arachne. 'Look, and the business at the household as well. Anything more specific that that, though, is between you and the late Mecufi.'

Chiku pinched the white mote between her fingers. She held it for a few moments then put it back in its compartment. She did not touch the black mote at all.

She closed the box.

'Did he say when I was supposed to open the white mote?'

'No, just that it's vital you open the white one first.'

'You should open it now,' Chiku Red told her.

Now that she knew what was inside the box, it felt heavier in her hand somehow, gravid with latent possibility. It was fifty years since she first met Mecufi in the Santa Justa elevator. If she was right about the black mote, it was at least that old. If it was meant for her, why had he not just given it to her at the time?

'I'm not sure,' she said to her sibling.

'You should open it now,' Chiku Red repeated. 'I cannot open it for you.'

The two women went out on deck. They were on the sailing ship now, bound for Lisbon. The wind was stiffer, the waves an iron grey. The novelty of sailing had worn off some time ago and Chiku wanted to be back home.

She had the box in her pocket – she could feel its hard wooden edges against her thigh. The black mote was still inside it, but the white was in her hand again. She held it up to the horizon's grey indeterminacy. Its milky interior offered hints of structure. It reminded her of the clouds of Venus.

'Why would he do this, Chiku Red?'

'I have no idea, Chiku Yellow, but I think it's time for you to find out.'

'I'm frightened. I know it's just a packet of emotions, so what harm can it do me? I keep telling myself that. But I'm still frightened.'

'I am with you,' said Chiku Red.

'You have no idea what this feels like.'

'You have no idea what being me feels like. Open the mote.'

Chiku steeled herself. She took a breath, squared her shoulders, lifted her chin. She thought of Travertine, defying the Assembly. Travertine would never have quailed at a moment like this. Travertine would have opened the mote in a heartbeat.

She pinched her fingers. The glass resisted more than usual, so she squeezed harder. The mote shattered, its white innards boiling out like smoke. The glassy pieces fell to the deck and self-annihilated.

She waited.

'Well?' asked Chiku Red.

'I'm not getting anything. Nothing I recognise, anyway.' But she signalled her sibling into silence. Somes motes were obvious, the equivalent of cheap perfumery. Others were much more subtle. They carried a delicate and reticent emotional freight, one that needed space and silence in which to declare itself.

She was giving it space and silence now. Still there was nothing.

'I think it's a dud,' she said. 'Contents must have expired, or Mecufi botched the assignation tag somehow. This is what would happen if *you* tried opening a mote.'

'I do not think Mecufi would have made a mistake,' Chiku Red answered, in her too-formal Portuguese. Her arms were crossed and she was watching her sister with sceptical detachment.

'No, he probably wouldn't. But why am I not—'

A voice cut across her own.

'Hello, Chiku. It's good that we've found each other again.'

It was Mecufi, of course, or rather a figment of Mecufi, floating a few paces nearer to the bow, hovering in the air as if submerged in water. He wore no exo, and his arms and tail parts moved languidly.

'I can see him now,' she said to Chiku Red. 'I'm looking at a figment of Mecufi, and he's talking to me.'

'Then perhaps you should listen,' Chiku Red suggested.

It was excellent advice. This was a very unusual figment. Figments generally arrived via the aug – they were traceable, generated remotely, linked to watertight tags and hyper-secure quangled ching binds. This figment had come in via a mote – something Chiku had never heard of before.

'You have broken the mote, and now we are in contact. Might I ask for your attention? As is the nature of these things, I have no interactivity. You can't ask me anything, and I won't be at liberty to repeat anything that you are about to hear.'

Chiku nodded, even as she recognised that the gesture had no currency.

'I had two options. I could speak to you privately while I was still alive, in a safe place of my own choosing. Or I could commit the contents of this message to a specially doctored mote and trust that it would reach you in safe order. I confess I spent some considerable time unsure how best to proceed. Here I am, though. A path has been chosen, for better or for worse.'

'What is he saying?' Chiku Red asked.

'Shush,' said Chiku Yellow.

'You've broken the white mote, and now only the black mote remains – I trust that the black mote is also now in your possession. Like the white mote, its contents are ... somewhat unconventional?' Mecufi smiled. 'Also dangerous. More dangerous than you can presently imagine. A time may come when it will be advantageous to you to break the black mote. But you should be absolutely certain that the moment is right.'

Chiku could not contain herself. 'And how will I know?'

'By my reckoning, the holoships will arrive at Crucible somewhere around 2435. We won't know the exact circumstances of their arrival until long after it has happened. If there is a propulsion breakthrough, they may arrive many months sooner. If there is catastrophe, they may not arrive at all. But whatever happens, we can expect some sort of news. Allowing for time lag, it should reach us somewhere around 2463 – almost half a century from now. Nearly as long again as the time since we first met! Even to those of us accustomed to the modern lifespan, it still feels like a very remote event, a date of no consequence to the here and now. But make no mistake – when news of the Providers reaches Earth, everything will change. The truth may break in instalments or in one great wave, but the consequences will be the same either way. The billions of people living in this system will learn that the Mechanism has been contaminated. That there is something inside it that should not be there. And that the thing inside the Mechanism is capable of murdering to protect itself.'

Chiku nodded. They had spoken of this often enough, during her time away from Earth in the company of June and Kwami and Lin Wei. But to know of a fearful thing was worse than not knowing, when you had no armour against it.

'It could go several ways,' Mecufi continued. 'Aware that her existence is about to be revealed, Arachne might take decisive pre-emptive action by attempting to neutralise and incapacitate millions via direct manipulation of the Mechanism and the aug before the information arrives. But given that she knows the news from Crucible will soon be on its way to Earth, why hasn't she acted already? The answer, I believe, is that she's insufficiently confident of success. Nor can she be certain of the specifics of the news from Crucible. Perhaps her existence *won't* be disclosed after all. Perhaps she hopes to continue hiding, haunting the Mech. I think that is her preferred strategy. But the slightest whiff of irregularities in the Mech will have Cognition Police and Mech invigilators scrambling to verify what we already know. They will return to Ocular, as well as they are able. They will reexamine the accident on Venus. And they will conclude that a rogue artificial intelligence might be loose in the Mech. Once they have reached that conclusion, they will begin to deploy containment protocols. They will try to back Arachne into a corner. And that is when she is most likely to retaliate. It could be very bad for us all, Chiku. But until that day comes, we can't really know for sure how this will play out. The aftershocks may be bearable for the peoples of the United Aquatic Nations – we have reduced our reliance on the Mech and the aug almost to zero. But we still share our world with the drylanders and the skylanders, and all of us are linked via interdependencies too complex to unravel in a hurry. We, too, may fall foul of Arachne's retaliation. Which brings me to the black mote.'

Again Chiku felt the edged presence of the wooden box against her thigh. She would have to get used to it – she had a feeling that it would not be leaving her possession any time soon.

'The black mote is a counter-measure. Unlike the white mote, it's keyed directly into the aug and the Mech. If you open it, certain events will follow in swift succession. Deep in the architecture of the Mech is a flaw. Consider it a vulnerability, or perhaps a deliberately engineered weakness. It has been there since the Mech's inception during the Resource and Relocation years, but its existence has never been known to more than a handful of souls. We know of it.'

Chiku shivered, sensing what was coming.

'The black mote will speak to this flaw,' Mecufi said. 'It will cause it to fail, and in failing trigger another failure mode. And another. One after the other, the pieces will fall. The Mech will cease to function. The aug will also be taken down in the same cascade of failures. What I cannot predict is the ultimate extent or severity of these failures. In the best-case scenario, the Mech and the aug will weaken to the point where Arachne is disadvantaged, unable to act or protect herself, but *not* precipitate significant human inconvenience. I hardly dare speculate about the worst-case scenario. We have made some collective mistakes as a species, it's true – invested too much power in things we can't see, let alone control. But look at the world we have, Chiku. For all its failings, things could be a great deal worse. No one's died in any wars lately, or been murdered, or left to rot in a prison, or been denied the basic allocation of fresh food and drinking water. No one's been tortured for their beliefs or made to feel like a pariah because of their sexual preferences. Yes, we've also put ourselves in something of a bind – and exactly how much of a bind, we'll find out in about half a century.' Mecufi's figment smiled fondly, the way cherubs looked down from Medieval heavens. 'Well, some of us will. I'm afraid I've rather abdicated my responsibilities in that regard, by virtue of being dead. How reckless of me! But I have every hope that you won't fall back on the same excuse. The black mote is your responsibility, Chiku. There's only the one, and now it's yours. If you ever deem that the moment is right and decide to use it, that weight will be yours and yours alone to bear. I have faith in you, though. I've had faith in you for a very long time. Now take care of yourself, take extra care of the mote, and wait for the news from Crucible. And in the meantime, keep trying to enjoy life. You've done very well with Chiku Red. We all have tremendous hopes for her.'

The figment vanished.

She stood for long moments, unable to speak or move. The catamaran raced on, kissing the wavetops. The sails made an eager drumming sound. The box was still hard against her thigh. She thought of the black mote inside it, visualising it now not as a little glass sphere but as a kind of void, a hole into which a world could fall.

Forty-eight years. A little more, a little less. They would have a better idea as the holoships made their final approach, or rather when news of that final approach crawled its way back to Earth. There would never be much warning.

She thought of Chiku Green, still out there. In that moment, the last lingering traces of the resentment she had long felt towards her remote sibling evaporated, boiled away like the white smoke in Mecufi's first mote. She wanted Chiku Green to know that she was here, that there was something she could do, if the very worst eventuality came to pass. She wanted Chiku Green to know they were in it together.

She wanted to know how Chiku Green was doing.

There was a presence at her side. Chiku Red, taking her hand. Steadying her, as if she had been about to topple into the waves. Which, on balance, wasn't entirely out of the question.

'What did it say?'

'Long story,' Chiku said, debating how much to say to her sister.

But Kanu had said they were safe from Arachne aboard the catamaran. There would never be a better time for the telling.

'I think you and I are going to have to take unusually good care of each other, at least for the next fifty years or so. Do you think we're up to it?'

'We can try,' Chiku Red answered.

'We can,' Chiku Yellow agreed. 'That's all we can ever do.'

And the sailing ship beat its way back to Estoril.

CHAPTER THIRTY-FIVE

By the time the burn ended the great fuel tanks were as vast and empty as cathedrals. One hundred hours of thrust to lift *Icebreaker* up to its cruising speed, arrowing ahead of *Zanzibar* at twenty-five per cent of the speed of light – practically double the holoship's own velocity – and then twice as long again to whittle that speed down to zero, or at least the few hundred kilometres per second that would suffice for in-system activity. There was a breath of fuel left to achieve planetary orbit, a breath of a breath to fall from orbit into Crucible's atmosphere, and no more. That was all they would need, Chiku had felt certain. In fact if they ever reached the point where lack of fuel was their chief concern, they would be doing very well indeed.

The ship had been still and silent for most of its nine-year voyage from *Zanzibar*. A light-minute from Crucible, systems began to return to life. Hull spaces were repressurised and warmed. Life-support mechanisms rattled and clanked like old plumbing. Fans and pumps whirred and the temperature in the ship's habitable spaces slowly reached something humans could live with. Simultaneously, the skipover caskets were bringing their charges out of deep hibernation, ascending them through layers of murky, sun-filtered dream into the daylight of consciousness.

Chiku had arranged to be the first to wake, followed in quick succession by Travertine and Dr Aziba, and then two of her scientific specialists: Gonithi Namboze, the ecosystem specialist, and Guochang, a skilled roboticist with a background in Provider architecture.

The remaining fifteen crewmembers would remain in skipover for the time being.

Coming out of skipover was never a pleasant experience, but nine years was nothing compared to the forty she had spent in *Zanzibar*'s vaults. True, there was no team of revival staff on hand to fuss over her this time, but she could handle that. The medical robot was endearing but stupid, like a simple but willing child, and it attended to her with spectacular clumsiness. When it found nothing amiss with her, she shooed it away to deal with Travertine, who was a little behind in the revival sequence.

By increments, the ambient temperature became more bearable and she began to shrug off insulating layers. The robot fetched her sugary chai in a zero-gravity squeezebulb. Once she had tuned out the plastic flavour of the squeezebulb's nipple, the chai proved tolerable. Then she felt suddenly ravenous and had the robot bring her some food, also prepared for weightless consumption. They were in free fall on the slow approach to Crucible as the ship was too small to spin for gravity. They also wanted their approach to be as quiet as possible, rather than come in with the engine blazing.

Chiku made short work of her curried chicken and rice, then headed up to the lander's cockpit and looked out through the windows. The ship's tail was still aimed towards Crucible, as it had been during the two hundred hours of the deceleration burn. 'Turn us around,' she told the ship, and the vessel complied. The movement of the gyroscopes was gentle enough that she only needed her fingertips to avoid drifting into the cabin wall. A fistful of dim stars crawled by from one side of the window arc to the other. Then, quite without fanfare, a planet loomed.

Crucible.

It was still very small, but recognisably a disc rather than a point of light. Off to the right were Crucible's two moons – both as large as Earth's and responsible for prodigious tides. Chiku voked an enlargement of the planet, projected as a figment above the console. She magnified it in factors of two until it was as large as a football, then touched her finger to the image and spun it around like a painted globe. *Icebreaker*'s final few hours of burn had brought it into exact alignment with the ecliptic plane of 61 Virginis f, a deliberate strategy to place the orbiting structures into maximum visibility against Crucible's surface.

The orbiting structures, the twenty-two dark, brindled pine cones, were still present, hard blue light ramming out in spokes from their outward-facing surfaces. She was struck again by the extreme and unforgiving alienness of these objects. What kind of intelligence could conceive of making machines on such a scale, a thousand kilometres from end to end?

These were tools to stab and bludgeon a world.

It was impossible to tell how long the orbiting things had been around Crucible, but Chiku had a feeling that they had not been there for ever. She thought it more likely that they had also been drawn across space by the enigma on Crucible's surface. A structure, visible across tens of light-years, had snagged both human and alien inquisitiveness.

Providers had left evidence of their presence. Most of their activity was meant to be concentrated on Crucible's surface, but they had also positioned relay satellites around the planet and in orbits circling the star. These satellites were the source of the transmissions *Zanzibar* and the other holoships had been intercepting during the crossing, and they were still active – their existence apparently tolerated by the alien forms. Perhaps this frail and feeble human technology did not even register with them.

Chiku mapped their positions and searched for signs of other mechanical activity. The Providers were supposed to have established way-stations around the planet to assist with the settlement process, but there was no evidence of any spaceborne structures or traffic other than the relay satellites.

She wheeled around at a noise behind her. Just the medical robot, come to inform her that Travertine was about to reach consciousness.

Chiku followed the idiot robot back to the skipover bay. The lid on Travertine's casket had already slid aside and the form within was breathing normally.

'Bring me some more chai,' Chiku told the robot. She remembered that Travertine preferred it unsweetened. 'No sugar.'

The robot scuttled off. Chiku waited by the casket for further signs of life. Eventually Travertine stirred. Chiku gave ver time to speak. Ve opened vis eyes slowly, then screwed them shut again. Travertine gave a grunt of primal displeasure. Ve angled vis head, took in Chiku.

Travertine's lips moved. Vis voice was a rasp, barely audible over the gentle hiss of the air circulators.

'Where are we?'

The robot returned with the squeezebulb and Chiku pressed it to Travertine's lips.

'Exactly where we wanted to be. Your engine works, Travertine.'

'I always knew we'd be all right.'

'Good for you. I wish I had your confidence.'

Travertine took another suck from the squeezebulb. 'How long have you been up? Weren't we all supposed to wake up at the same time?'

'That would have been too much work for the robot to handle, so I staggered the wake-up cycle, with Aziba's blessing.'

'Then where's Aziba?'

'Next out. You and I are the first.'

'And then the others? Have you checked the caskets – did we all make it?'

'No drop-outs,' Chiku said.

Travertine stretched vis arms and started levering verself out of the casket. Chiku moved to assist, but Travertine brushed her away. 'You did this on your own, and so can I.' The bracelet knocked against the side of the casket as ve eased into a weightless sitting position, legs dangling over the side. 'It's strange,' ve continued, 'but I'm not sensing the atmosphere of ecstatic jubilation I was expecting.'

'I've reasons not to be ecstatic.'

'And are you ready to talk about those reasons, whatever they might be?'

Chiku's smile was mirthless. 'Finish your chai, get used to being awake, then we'll talk. Are you hungry? I can have the robot bring you something here, or we can take it up to the cockpit.'

'I'm not hungry. I think it's the bracelet – messes with my metabolism. Do I look suitably refreshed to you, after my nine years of sleep?'

'You look exactly the same.'

'Honesty is the best medicine. Frankly, I feel like a bag of old sticks.' Travertine finished the chai and passed the empty bulb back to Chiku. 'No sugar. Very *sweet* of you to remember.'

'Are you sure you're up to moving around?'

'The flesh is weak but the heart is willing. Will the robot take care of Aziba?'

'Yes – he should be joining us within the hour, then Gonithi and Guochang.'

'What's so special about them that they get the early wake-up call?'

'I need to be clear with you about something,' Chiku said, sidestepping the question. 'I wanted you along for the ride for a couple of reasons. Three, actually. Firstly, you know the PCP engine – if we'd run into technical difficulties, the robot would have woken you first.'

'You can scratch that off your list.'

'Indeed. Secondly, you're ridiculously smart in more ways than one, and your input will be very valuable to me given the situation we're facing here.'

'Flattery will get you everywhere. And thirdly?'

'I need a friend.'

'And you think I still count as one?'

'I hope so.' Chiku paused – they were nearly at the cockpit. 'I was as clear as I could be when I approached you about this expedition.'

'You were as clear as fifty light-years of tungsten.' After a moment, Travertine added: 'I understood the deal, Chiku. You were offering me a pardon under the only terms your administration would have accepted. It was also obvious to me that you had something to hide from everyone else. It's all connected to this ship, isn't it?'

Chiku did not reply until they were in the cockpit. 'You're right, mostly. At this point it would probably help if I showed you Crucible. Would you like to see it?'

'It'd be perverse not to after coming all this way.'

Chiku called up the magnified image of the planet she had conjured earlier. 'For now, you'll have to take my word for it that the dot you can see through the window is the same as the planet represented by this figment. A day from now, it'll be big enough to see with our naked eyes.'

Travertine took vis time before answering. Ve looked at the projected globe from all angles, spinning it around as Chiku had done earlier, increasing and decreasing the magnification. 'This must be a composite,' ve said eventually, 'assembled from several rotations' worth of data.'

'It is. But it's also an accurate representation of what we'd see if we were a lot closer.'

'Mandala's there.'

'Yes.'

'But no obvious surface construction. The cities and towns – I knew they'd be small, but surely we'd see some evidence of them at this resolution?'

'Absolutely – but the Providers haven't built anything in advance of our arrival. Crucible's barely been touched.'

'I see.' And there was a long, measured silence from Travertine while ve digested this news that Chiku had known for years but still found difficult to accept. Eventually, ve asked, 'The Providers ... what became of them?'

'We'll find out when we get there.'

'Did something destroy them?'

'I don't think so. The uplinked transmissions from Crucible's surface were being broadcast by something. The Providers are still here, I think – just not doing what they were meant to do.'

Travertine nodded slowly. 'And what about those other things surrounding the planet?'

'There are twenty-two of them,' Chiku said. 'They've been orbiting

Crucible for at least as long as we've known about Mandala, but they were edited out of the original data.'

'When you say "edited out"—'

'We built an instrument called Ocular to observe extrasolar planets in great detail, and then shackled it to a powerful artificial intelligence, an entity called Arachne – the only thing capable of processing the Ocular data stream and searching for signs of extraterrestrial activity. The catch is that we may have made her too clever.'

'Her?'

'She's a thing, a mind, with a will of her own – and a strong instinct for self-preservation. For some reason, Arachne took it upon herself to doctor the raw data and stripped out the portions of the image which contain these objects.'

'And no one noticed that?'

'Did I mention that Arachne's fiendishly clever? No one noticed the deception, and on the basis of this doctored imagery – which still contained Mandala – we sent Provider seed packages to Crucible, and then launched the holoships.'

'In other words, this doctored data triggered a significant development in human history – migration into interstellar space and the push to an extrasolar planet.'

'Yes,' Chiku said. 'But it's possible – likely, even – that the human consequences were just a by-product, a side-effect, of Arachne's main intention. Which was to propagate herself – to expand machine intelligence beyond the solar system. Which she achieved by infiltrating herself into the Provider seed packages like a virus.'

'You're saying she's there now, ahead of us?'

'Something connected to her, at any rate – a daughter intelligence, perhaps. Multiple daughters, who knows? Part of her – perhaps the main part – is still active in the old solar system. Chiku Yellow met her. I know what she's capable of.'

'That's encouraging, given that we're heading towards another aspect of her.'

'I never said this would be easy. But are you beginning to see why this advance mission is necessary, and why I couldn't go public with the truth about Crucible? Can you imagine the panic that would have caused?'

'I can, and it's not pretty.'

'I'm sure you have all sorts of questions about the alien objects – those pine-cone things. I'll tell you what I know, but it isn't much. They're big, and they might have contacted Arachne, or she may have intercepted a transmission they were broadcasting, whether that was the intention or not. We think they may have been here for a very, very long time. Beyond that, I'm in the dark.'

'"We",' Travertine repeated carefully. 'And who are your co-conspirators in this great adventure?'

'Allies back home. My counterpart Chiku Yellow, for one, and another woman who was directly involved in Ocular's development. Plus various other interested parties. They've all been working under conditions of extreme secrecy, trying to piece together something of the truth without bringing their activities to Arachne's attention. It's been very, very difficult, and my involvement didn't help things much. Arachne locked on to Chiku Yellow, tried to kill her on Venus and then on Earth. The safest place in the universe! Arachne's infiltrated the Mechanism itself, haunting it from within.'

'Then there's nothing to be done.'

'Maybe not, but we have to try. Negotiation, bargaining. Pleading for our lives. Grovelling, if it comes to that. Anything that might persuade Arachne not to turn on her former masters any more damagingly than she already has.'

After a silence, Travertine said: 'I think I'm going to crawl back into the skipover casket, close the lid and try to wake up again. This is obviously some kind of delirious nightmare.'

'It's real. I've been living with it long enough.'

'Is this the explanation – the reason for everything you've done?'

'More or less.'

'I know there's more you're not telling me. How you learned about Arachne in the first place – what any of this has to do with Kappa.'

'I've told you everything you need to know right now. The rest is ... complicated. I will tell you the rest, but I suggest we leave that until we've attended to Doctor Aziba and the others.'

'How much do they know, exactly?'

'Nothing at all.'

'Oh, they're going to *love* this. At least I had an inkling from the get-go that something wasn't right.'

'I'm probably going to need your help,' Chiku said, 'to maintain order and help get my point across. That's why I woke you first – I hoped you might see things from my point of view.'

'And there was me thinking you missed my conversation. My first thought is – why wake the others at all? The ship can operate itself.'

'I don't plan on waking everybody. I had to accept a larger crew than I wanted, but it was the only way to sell the Assembly on this expedition.

Truthfully, I think we'll be doing the others a kindness if we keep them in skipover.'

'Given our chances of survival, you mean?'

Chiku nodded grimly, biting her lower lip. 'But we need Aziba and the other two, I think. Guochang knows Providers, and Gonithi should be able to tell us how Crucible's surface conditions compare against our expectations.'

'All right,' Travertine said eventually. 'Let me be blunt. The way I see it, I have two choices. I can fight you and try to turn the rest of the crew against you. But we'll still be aboard a ship with almost no fuel, falling towards the Providers. Or I can accept what you're saying, accept that you allowed all those awful things to happen to me for a reason – *this* reason – and that in your position I might have made the same choices. And I can try to persuade the crew not to mutiny and rip your throat out.'

'Option two would be my preference.'

'Either way, I'll still be aboard a ship with almost no fuel, falling towards the Providers. Tough choice, isn't it?'

'However you parse it,' Chiku said, 'it boils down to the same thing: I need your help. You're the cleverest human being I know. Even your brain might not be enough to get us out of this mess, but at least we'll have tried. I have one last incentive to offer.'

'I'm listening.'

'Our course will take us quite close to one of the pine cones as we swing in for orbit. We can squeeze a little closer, if you like. I thought you might appreciate the opportunity to see a piece of thousand-kilometre-long alien technology up close with your own eyes. But only if you really want to.'

The robot bustled back in, its limbs clicking and scissoring.

'I guess the good doctor's awake,' Travertine said. 'I suppose we should go and break the news to him gently.'

CHAPTER THIRTY-SIX

The three of them were in the cockpit. The physician appeared to be taking recent developments with remarkable stoicism, as if this was merely the latest in a line of disagreeable surprises the universe had sprung on him. He nodded as Chiku and Travertine took turns to explain his predicament, bouncing his attention from one to the other. Occasionally he scratched at the white atoll of his tonsure. His expression was quietly sceptical, but he appeared not to doubt the essential veracity of their story.

'She's not lying,' Travertine said, more than once. 'She hasn't just pulled this out of a hat. I've been watching Chiku for years – I've always known she was up to *something*.'

'I'm very sorry it was necessary to lie to you,' Chiku said. 'Or at least, not give you the full picture.'

'Let's stick with lie,' Doctor Aziba said, with a pleasant lack of rancour.

'All right – it was a big fat lie.' Chiku shrugged. 'But it was fabricated in the interests of *Zanzibar*. The citizenry, the people. Ten million of them, just on our own holoship, plus the rest of the local caravan, and the holoships following on behind us. They all think there's a paradise in waiting here, tended by machines of loving grace.'

'They're in for a bit of a let down,' Travertine added.

'When I came out of skipover,' Chiku said, 'Sou-Chun had sold out to Teslenko and the other hard-liners. There was too much was at stake for me to speak candidly – they'd have silenced me, one way or another.' She looked away for a moment. 'I know I got things wrong. If I could turn the clock back, maybe I'd trust Utomi to do the right thing. But maybe not. Everything looks easier with hindsight.'

'So what are you hoping to achieve with this mission?' Aziba asked.

'Diplomacy. An alternative to annihilation when the main caravan arrives.'

'Perhaps it won't. If the slowdown problem isn't solved—'

Travertine said sharply: 'Solve it or not, there are thousands of people

340

who still want to reach Crucible. Now all they have to do is build copies of *Icebreaker*, and they can do that easily enough.'

He laughed at them. 'This ship carries twenty people.'

'But it could carry more, and they can build as many copies as our industrial base will support. Hundreds across the local caravan – thousands, even. Not enough to bring tens of millions of settlers to Crucible, I agree – but those who don't want to land can always emigrate to the holoships that don't plan on stopping. Chiku's right on this one: something has to be done. Even if all we do is meet the Providers and get cut to shreds. At least they'll know what to expect, back on *Zanzibar*.'

Travertine's statement of solidarity sent a weird shiver through Chiku. 'I hope we can do something more constructive than being cut to shreds. Bottom line, though, Travertine's right – if all we do is provide concrete proof that the machines are hostile, we'll have still helped *Zanzibar*.'

'What about my fellow volunteers? Are we all expected to meekly fall in line with this suicide mission?'

'If I'd had my way,' Chiku said, not really caring whether the physician believed her or not, 'this would have been a much smaller expedition, and you'd all have known the stakes up front. But let's not pretend that the mission you volunteered for was without risk.'

Aziba had returned his attention to the projected representation of Crucible, with its twenty-two attendant sentinels. He stared with troubled fascination, like a man seeing demons in fire.

'How could we not have known about these ... things?'

'Because we put our faith in Arachne and saw no reason to doubt what she told us,' Chiku said. 'Because we made simple human mistakes. Not because we were stupid, but because we were fallible. Clever, but not clever enough.'

'I don't mind admitting that I'm little frightened.'

'If you weren't,' Chiku said, 'I might start wondering about your sanity.'

Chiku told the robot to delay waking Gonithi Namboze and Guochang for a couple of hours. She was drained, taxed by the emotional demands already placed on her by Travertine and the physician.

She also had a new concern about *Zanzibar* that she needed to resolve before talking to anyone else.

In the first few hours following her revival, she had given little thought to home, being more immediately concerned with the condition of the ship, the reality of Crucible and the delicate task of waking her fellows. True, her thoughts had returned to Ndege and Mposi, but only fleetingly – whatever had happened to them since her departure, she would find out soon enough, and any news from *Zanzibar* was going to be years out of date whether she got to it first or last.

But there was no news. When *Icebreaker* tried to pick up a transmission from the holoship, there was nothing. Perhaps there was an error in the positional estimate – the caravan might have adjusted its course, putting *Zanzibar* in a slightly different part of the sky as seen from 61 Virginis f. Chiku swivelled the antenna in a search pattern, allowing for this possible parallax error.

Still there was nothing.

At that point, she reconvened with Travertine and Doctor Aziba, watching the latter closely.

'I don't suppose it's totally unexpected,' Chiku said, fighting to keep the fear out of her voice. 'When we left, the constables were in the process of imposing external authority aboard *Zanzibar*. The hard-liners didn't approve of this expedition, so they might have enforced a ban on all transmissions directed ahead of the caravan to cut contact with *Icebreaker*.'

'Or they're not there any more,' Travertine said.

Chiku was grateful for that. It spared her from voicing that almost unspeakable possibility.

'No accident could have disrupted the entire caravan,' Aziba answered levelly. 'We might lose a whole holoship – more than one, if we're unlucky – to interstellar collision, or a repeat of *Pemba*. Military action, perhaps. But not dozens, not the whole caravan. Someone would still be out there.'

'So why the silence?' Travertine asked.

'It must be politically imposed,' Chiku said. 'That's the only explanation. The doctor's right – there's no way the whole caravan could have been destroyed, and it's equally unlikely that it's drifted so far from its predicted position that we can't pick it up again. All the same, I'm going to widen the sweep – it doesn't cost us anything.'

'We don't need them, anyway,' Travertine said. 'They need us – the information we provide – but we're not dependent on them at all.'

'I'd still like to know the news from home,' Chiku replied.

Doctor Aziba nodded. 'Yes, of course. We all would. You should keep searching. Have you considered waking one of the other specialists? I forget all our backgrounds, but there's bound to be someone who knows something about deep-space communications.'

342

'We know enough between us,' Travertine said. 'And if we don't, Guo-chang will plug the gaps.'

'What about our own transmissions?' Aziba asked. 'Are we still sending them?'

'Back to *Zanzibar*, yes,' Chiku told him, 'although we can't expect a reply to anything we send for two years. Ahead, towards Crucible, we're transmitting standard handshake protocols for Provider communications, both directly at the planet and into the relay satellite network. There's been no acknowledgement, but we're still intercepting the Provider upstream transmissions, the same lying horsepiss they've been sending to *Zanzibar* for decades.'

Aziba said, 'Perhaps a more direct approach is warranted?'

'Falling into orbit should do it, I think,' Chiku said. 'And if that doesn't get their attention, we land.'

Chiku had now been awake for six hours. The stiffness had exited her bones and muscles. She was warmer now and free of nausea. Her thought processes felt sharp, racing through possibilities with nervous threshing efficiency. She could have done with a bit less of that.

Crucible had grown visibly larger in that time – her eye alone was now able to make out the greens and blues of the planet's surface features, as well as the black circles and hyphens caused by the orbiting structures. She could not have told what they were, or that they were hovering in space, but the uncanny regularity of their spacing was enough to signal a distinct and lingering *wrongness* – the imposition of order and symmetry where none was expected. *Icebreaker* had already made a small course adjustment, to slide close to one of the pine cones as it curved in for orbit. They had simply chosen the one that required the least expenditure of fuel, judging that the twenty-two forms were essentially identical, at least in their gross details.

Zanzibar had to be out there, she told herself. It could not simply have disappeared, let alone all the other holoships. Even if they had started conducting large-scale PCP experiments, they could not all have suffered a *Pemba* event at the same time. Not every holoship would have been running the same experiment, or been close enough to another to be wiped out in the same accident. But there were other possibilities, and Chiku felt her mind beginning to run out of control, anxiety fuelling her worst-case scenarios. What about contagion, for a start? Constables moving en masse from world to world would have increased the likelihood of disease propagation. If a large enough percentage of the citizenry were infected, the holoships' social organisations would begin to collapse, leading to a breakdown of control. Survivors might manage to eke out some miserable kind of subsistence in the darkened social cores, but they wouldn't have the means to keep up the transmissions. She thought of her children, grubbing around for scraps, slowly turning feral as the holoships sailed on past Crucible, bearing cargoes of savagery to the stars ...

But the caravans had been travelling for two centuries without significant loss of life to widespread disease, and the few small outbreaks had been quickly contained, with very few casualties. Coincidences happened, she knew, but it was highly unlikely that a dire contagion had been lurking all that time, only to spring out once *Icebreaker* was already on its way.

No, the silence could only be political.

But that was good news only in the narrowest of senses, in that it did not preclude the survival of her loved ones. It also meant that things must have taken a sharply authoritarian turn. Noah and the other Assembly members would never have allowed that, not if they were still in some kind of control.

So that was not good at all, either.

Stomach knotted with apprehension, Chiku summoned Travertine and Aziba. 'It's time to wake Gonithi and Guochan. I don't want to throw them into this at the last minute.'

Travertine glanced at Aziba. 'Both of them at the same time?'

'Yes. Doctor, are you with me?'

'Why wouldn't I be?'

'Because I've lied to you, and put you in a significantly more dangerous situation than you were expecting. I'm really sorry it had to happen this way, but it did, and it's crunch time. If I sense you have any intention of jeopardising our mission, for whatever reason, I'll have no choice but to stop you. And I really, really, don't want to have to do that.'

'How far would you go to stop me?' Aziba mused.

'I'll kill you, if I have to. Or try to, anyway. Yes, I'm capable of it, and there are tools on this ship I could use. It wouldn't be difficult, especially this far from authority. But I'd really rather not. I like you, and I think you're going to be very useful to us down the line, so please, *please*, don't force my hand. Gonithi and Guochan are going to be just as bewildered and frightened as you were, but we need them on our side just as much as we need you. I've lied, yes, but only ever in the best interests of the caravan. Do you care about your people, Doctor Aziba?'

'Of course I do.'

344

'As do I. Passionately. Please believe me when I say that nothing is more important to the continuing welfare of our citizens than the success of this mission. We have worlds to save, Doctor Aziba.'

'That sounds ... compelling,' the physician allowed.

'It's all we've got,' Travertine said. 'You might talk Namboze and Guochan into taking this ship from Chiku and me, but you know what? You'll still be in exactly the same mess you are now – only there'll be two fewer brains and bodies to throw at the problem. We need every single one of us to have a hope in hell's chance of dealing with what's coming.'

'Let's wake them,' Chiku said.

Aziba said, 'I can do it. We don't all need to be here.'

Travertine said sceptically, 'Leave you alone with Namboze and Guochan?'

'If you trust me, yes. I give you my word that I'll state our position to them very honestly. I'll explain that they've been lied to, but that killing you now won't help their chances of survival.' He shrugged. 'It's up to you. If you don't trust me now, you'll be looking over your shoulder for ever.'

'You're right,' Chiku said, sighing heavily. 'It's either complete trust or nothing at all. Wake them up and give them the good news.' But after a pause, she said: 'I still owe them an explanation, face to face.'

'Go and attend to your work. I'll call you when Namboze and Guochan have been briefed.' Chiku opened her mouth to speak, but he raised a silencing finger. 'I don't like this situation at all. I'd much rather not be here, and I won't pretend that I harbour no resentment about the manner in which I was manipulated. But I'm also a physician, and you are all within my duty of care. I believe I'm capable of putting my personal feelings aside and doing my job.'

Chiku nodded. Further talk was superfluous. She realised that she'd chosen well in this man. His ability to speak plainly about his resentment rather than pretend there was none actually made her feel more comfortable. She felt certain he would do as he promised.

'I have an idea,' Travertine said.

CHAPTER THIRTY-SEVEN

Sooner or later it would have occurred to Chiku. Communications from *Zanzibar* must surely have continued until some point in their journey. Perhaps it had been only days after departure, or perhaps it been years. But what was certain was that the incoming transmissions would all have been buffered and stored in *Icebreaker*'s memories, until the moment when the transmissions were curtailed.

It did not take long to find them. They were in time-sequenced order, beginning from the departure. For a few months, the transmissions were continuous – an uninterrupted umbilical uplink, connecting *Icebreaker* back to her mother vessel. This stream consisted not merely of signals of direct relevance to the lander, but the full torrent of the holoship's newsfeeds, as well as those it relayed from elsewhere in the caravan, including updates from Earth and the solar system. Later, though, the transmissions stopped being continuous and the data content dropped precipitously. Weeks might go by without a signal, then there might be two or three transmissions in close succession. Then more weeks of silence. Weeks and months, sometimes. Longer than that, as Chiku skipped forward via the time-tags. She had not yet begun to pick through the detailed contents of any of the messages. But she could already tell that a large number were headed as originating from Noah.

That changed, as time went by.

Her impulse was to jump to the final transmission, which had arrived more than two years ago, but she resisted and went right back to the start. The early transmissions were rich enough with data to allow full immersive ching. She returned to *Zanzibar*, walked its parks and avenues to see things for herself. She gently interrogated her fellow citizens, and although her interactions were merely the ching's best guesses as to how similar encounters might have played out in real-time, the encounters were more than sufficient to give her a feel for the atmosphere aboard the holoship.

During the month following their departure, ships had continued to arrive from the local caravan, bringing huge numbers of incomers. Many of them were constables, redeployed from their duties elsewhere, along with an increasing number of political agents: the observers and bureaucrats of the new regime, tiers of functionaries, supervisors and analysts. Even while normal Assembly business continued, the newcomers began to manoeuvre themselves into positions of influence. Rules and ordinances were redrafted, and the citizens – *her* citizens – chafed against stifling new restrictions. Movements between holoships were now tightly regulated, dividing families and friends. There were even some constraints on movement within *Zanzibar* – access to the transit pods was now under direct government control. Families were relocated to better utilise *Zanzibar*'s community cores, and other holoships, bulging under population pressure, were sending citizens into *Zanzibar*. The integration of these newcomers inevitably caused friction. Chiku decided that the relocations were not really about population management, but rather aimed to erode whatever social cohesion had existed within *Zanzibar* before *Icebreaker*'s departure. Chiku bore the newcomers no ill will – they were pawns in a much bigger game.

Noah's private communications confirmed her suspicions, as they walked together in Anticipation Park.

'I know you won't access any of this until you wake,' he told her, 'but recounting the events as they happen helps me to get my thoughts in order. Is that ridiculous?'

'I'd do the same thing,' she told Noah's figment, this bloodless but plausible notion of how Noah might interact with her.

'Things are moving much faster than any of us anticipated – they keep sending more constables, as if there's a limitless supply of them. Our airlocks have never been busier. Pretty good rehearsal for Crucible, I guess.'

She asked about Ndege and Mposi.

'They're all right,' Noah said, after giving the question due consideration. 'The first few weeks were very hard on them, but a month's a very long time in their world.'

She skipped that same span of time and toured her world again. As she wandered the cores, bodyless, *Zanzibar* felt strangely hollow, as if it had already shed its burden of humanity. The public spaces were mostly empty, and there was a kind of prevailing twilight gloom, as if the skies had been dimmed. She realised with a jolt that this was exactly what had happened. The external powers had declared some kind of curfew, apparently in response to an act of public disobedience against the new constables.

She met Noah at the Assembly. Technically, he was still a functioning member of *Zanzibar*'s government, but its decision-making powers had been all but eliminated, he told her, and worse was to come. There were prosecutors at large who were trying to identify those members of the Assembly with direct knowledge of *Icebreaker*. A number of preliminary hearings had already been held, and Noah had been called to testify on two occasions regarding fellow members. It was only a matter of time before they turned their attention to him personally.

'There's talk of execution,' he said.

She shuddered. 'We didn't execute Travertine, and ve killed two hundred people!'

'They want to make an example the rest of the caravan can't ignore.'

'It can't come to executions, Noah – we agreed to submit to a peaceful takeover, not a fucking bloodbath. We're a democratic society! There hasn't even been a single *murder* during the entire voyage, and we've managed that without the Mechanism mothering us into submission!'

'I'm sorry,' Noah offered, as if she was holding him personally accountable.

She had not been able to ching into Chamber Thirty-Seven. 'Have you spoken to ... ?' she began.

'Yes – once. But it's very difficult now – my movements are monitored constantly, and I can't risk someone backtracking the ching bind. Even *speaking* about it in these messages—'

'I'm not blaming you for any of this,' she said. 'Please never think that. I just want you to be safe, and to do everything you can for our children.'

She asked him what he knew regarding efforts to scale up the PCP engine, but that taxed the immersive simulation to its limits and Noah could not offer anything concrete. But Chiku thought it likely that someone, somewhere, would be trying to build on Travertine's work, perhaps even aboard the very holoships currently imposing the tough new regime on *Zanzibar*. The new engine was tactically decisive technology, whether it was used for slowdown or not. Absurd that it had come to this, after all: strategic balances, superpowers, super-weapons, as if history was a kind of machine with only a limited number of permutations. At one time, she had dared to believe that history could break free of its patterns. Nature was not hidebound, tied into endless, dull reiteration. It produced marvels and monsters with equal fecundity. So why did people have so much trouble breaking free of old patterns?

She was about to skip ahead when Travertine tapped her out of the ching bind.

'They're awake.'

Chiku summoned them all to the cockpit. She nodded at Namboze and Guochang, fresh out of skipover. They were clutching squeeze-bulbs, both of them looking as if they had been repeatedly slapped in the face, like drunkards or hysterics. Gonithi Namboze had also spent time in skipover since the Kappa incident, and she was still essentially the same person Chiku had known back then: an extremely thin woman with long fingernails and complexly braided hair. Guochang, whom she knew less well, was a squat, muscular man with the core body strength of a Cossack.

'I understand if you want to punish me,' Chiku said, 'but could you wait until we've completed our mission?'

'If,' Namboze said, drawing a nod from Guochang.

'I know,' Chiku said. 'I won't downplay the danger – I've got too much respect for the pair of you. But it's not a suicide mission. Guochang: we must make contact with the Providers, and establish a negotiating position. Something, anything. You know them as well as anyone. Namboze: there's a planet down there that we *might* end up having to live on, if we're lucky, but not in the way most of us were expecting. We'll likely be starting from scratch, with the tools and materials we bring from space. You've spent most of your life studying the adaptations and measures we'll need to make a living on Crucible. Now your insights are going to matter more than ever.'

Eventually she said: 'Those black things. What if they don't want us there?'

'We don't know what they do or don't want – if anything,' Chiku answered. 'Maybe all they do is observe. Witness. They may not care. It's the Providers that are our concern. But we must find a solution, a way that benefits us all – machine and human.'

Namboze sneered. 'A truce with machines, after they've lied to us? We should be destroying them, not negotiating with them!'

'We don't know their strengths or capabilities,' Travertine said. 'If we had the full caravan behind us, we might stand a chance in a fight. But we're a single ship, almost powerless. We have to negotiate.'

'With what?' Namboze asked.

'Our best intentions?' Chiku said. 'Good will? We're almost certainly dealing with artilect-level cognition – machines, or an assemblage of machines, with a collective intelligence equalling or exceeding our own. I've met one, and we can't assume we'll have mental and military superiority on our side.'

'I'd like access to *Icebreaker*'s communications systems,' Guochang said. 'There are some channels you may not have tried – command-level paths, that kind of thing.'

'Good start,' Chiku said.

'It'll give me something to take my mind off everything else. May I?'

'Yes, but keep one antenna sweeping behind us for signals from the caravan. Namboze: the closer we get, the better our view of the surface conditions. I want you to start updating the maps. I want to know immediately if you find any significant points of deviation between the data in our files and the real Crucible. And if you find any sign of Provider activity on the surface or in space, bring it to our immediate attention.'

'Are we taking orders from you now?' Namboze asked.

'No,' Travertine said. 'We're dividing responsibility.'

Namboze turned her attention to the physicist. 'What about you? I thought you were supposed to be dying, rotting like a corpse. I thought that was supposed to be your punishment for nearly killing us all.'

'Travertine's sentence was formally commuted,' Chiku said. 'Ve broke our laws, it's true. But Travertine's paid a steep price for that. We also owe ver a debt of gratitude for the risks ve took. If by some miracle any of us ever set foot on Crucible, we'll have Travertine to thank.'

'I wouldn't start planning any monuments to me just yet,' Travertine said.

Chiku was also glad to have something to take her mind off things, but she could not say for sure which was the more unpleasant source of anxiety: the news from home, or their immediate prospects on Crucible. On one hand, while Noah's reports spoke of a steady deterioration in the conditions on *Zanzibar*, and she was worried for Ndege, Mposi and Noah because of that, the fact was that the news was old. She could not change the past, and she was basically engaged in the excavation of history. She could treat Noah's reportage as a kind of fiction, a narrative in which she had only theoretical involvement. This was in contrast to the alien things, which – although they had done nothing as yet to provoke this fear – might reach out and annihilate the little ship without warning.

She decided, for the sake of her sanity, not to choose between the two, or dwell on one to the exclusion of the other. When her immersion in *Zanzibar*'s woes threatened to overwhelm her, it was almost a relief to snap back to the present, where her fate rested on the whims of machines, in a place where politics and human frailty had no traction. There was nothing to second-guess here and no one to worry about but herself. It was as clean and ethically neutral as a game of chess.

Some instinct compelled her not to take *Icebreaker* across the path of any of the spokes of blue light, as if breaking or interrupting that flow of photons would be like stepping on a dry twig – a crass announcement of their presence. Travertine was confident that the light would not harm the ship, but agreed with Chiku's decision to err on the side of caution.

'Of course, on one level,' Chiku said, 'I'd like to see some sign that those things know we're here. Perhaps then they wouldn't be so enigmatic, floating there like Easter Island statues.'

'On the other hand, you wouldn't want to piss them off.'

Against her mood, Chiku forced herself to laugh. 'Arethusa had this theory that the blue light carries a signal, something that worked its way into Ocular – it might even have turned Arachne into the thing she became. A set of instructions, perhaps, in mutually comprehensible machine-code, that told her to hide herself and the real Crucible data from her organic masters.'

'A machine telling another machine to conceal its existence? Artificial intelligences whispering to each other across interstellar space, carrying on a conversation we humans can't intercept or understand?'

'Frightening, isn't it?'

'That's one word for it.'

It was one thing to know that the pine cones were a thousand kilometres from end to end, but quite another to be approaching such a thing, appreciating its size at first hand. She thought of Hyperion, the riddled little moon tumbling around Saturn – Hyperion with its tunnels and vaults, it endless worming galleries, festering with artists and anarchists. Chiku Yellow and her friends had flown *Gulliver* into that moon. But Hyperion was a third as large as one of these alien objects, and besides, these were demonstrably made things, matter shaped and organised by vast cool intelligence. They must have come here, too, so they could move, and that was almost harder to take than the mere existence of these objects. Nothing this huge should be capable of movement, let alone across interstellar space. It was an affront to natural order.

The orbital insertion brought them no closer than five hundred kilo-metres to the nearest object, but that was quite close enough for Chiku's nerves. Although the objects were circling Crucible, technically they were not in orbit: their motion was resolutely non-Keplerian. For the height at which they sat, they should have been moving about twice as fast as they were. *Another slap to human hubris*, Chiku thought, as if grav-ity was a law the alien objects had quietly decided to ignore. They did not even register a mass that *Icebreaker*'s sensors were capable of detect-ing, for all that they must have contained billions of tonnes of matter. And so they hovered, and wheeled in slow formation, their spokes cut-ting across the ecliptic and lighthousing into space. She thought of all the stars, all the worlds the light of those spokes would eventually graze. This simple arc across the sky must still have encompassed thousands of suns in this little corner of the spiral arm alone. She wondered about the other civilisations, human and artilect, that had fallen under the sweep of the spokes.

She shuddered at the magnitude of the endeavour, whatever it might hope to achieve.

The pine cones were so named because of their shape, and also be-cause of their many overlapping plates, which were organised according to elegant and simple growth patterns. The smallest of the plates, where the pine cones tapered to a point – the end nearest Crucible – were only kilometres across, no wider than the average iceberg. The larg-est of them, up near the fatter end, were nearly a hundred kilometres across and tens of kilometres thick. They were all perfectly black, im-pervious to *Icebreaker*'s passive and active sensor systems. They fitted together ingeniously, but there were also gaps between the overlap-ping layers through which hints of deeper structure were visible: blue mysteries of internal machinery, glimpsed in frustrating haziness as if some blurring medium were interposed between the machinery and *Icebreaker*. Radiation spilled out, smudged across the spectrum and modulated in odd ways, with absorption and emission spikes that did not correspond to known nuclear transitions. The radiation was puzzling, sufficient – Travertine said – to fuel a thousand doctorates, perhaps an entire academic discipline. But no part of it was powerful enough to pose a threat – at least, not in the bands they were capable of registering.

As they fell below the level of the structures, Travertine speculated that the fluxes had risen in consort with their passage – risen, then grad-ually lowered back down to the level they had shown before. But it was hard to know for sure. They had obtained no good data until they were very close, and since *Icebreaker* did not have the resources to disperse sensors after itself, this was all they were going to learn for now.

But they had not been destroyed. Chiku was glad of that, of course. But she had been hoping for something concrete, and the rise/fade of the blue glow did not count. What she had wanted, she decided, was for the alien machines to trump the problem of the Providers – to do something, hostile or otherwise, which pushed the Providers into secondary importance. But there had been no such overture, and she could not help but feel a twinge of disappointment.

So they fell lower. Thrust bursts modified *Icebreaker*'s trajectory, further depleting the tiny amount of fuel still available. Once the lander achieved orbit a few hundred kilometres above Crucible's surface, they would not need fuel to land – they would only maintain altitude if they used the engines to counteract friction – but they had sufficient to land at a suitable touchdown point of their choosing.

Namboze had been busy updating their maps, stitching fresh data over old. The resolution of the new data was not as good as that of the old, but it had the virtue of being true and verifiable. They were not relying on machine eyes now: they could see the landscape for themselves through the windows.

In some respects the news was good. Crucible itself was the world they had expected – the planet's geology, atmospheric and surface conditions were exactly as promised. Plants had colonised the land, and in their detailed biochemistry had duplicated something that was very close to the terrestrial photosynthetic process. But people had known this long before Ocular's detailed observations of the surface. Crucible's atmosphere contained molecular oxygen and methane at volume mixing ratios more than a hundred orders of magnitude greater than thermodynamic equilibrium alone could explain. Furthermore, much of the surface of Crucible was covered by something that very strongly absorbed red light, hinting at the abundant presence of the chlorophyll pigment. If there was one truth that had become clear in four centuries of space exploration, it was that there were precious few inorganic mechanisms that made things look green, and none at all that could paint a whole planet in dazzling emerald.

Life was the sole explanation.

All of this proved to be correct, which was a consolation if not a relief. They could live here, with some careful measures. But they had come expecting towns and cities, harbours and jetties, roads and landing zones, and there was none of that at all. Some hints of possible Provider activity, it was true – regular areas of cleared terrain, reflection signatures that hinted at artificial structures – but all much too small to be of use to waves of migrants. Crucible's thick, warm, oxygen-rich atmosphere would need some getting used to. It had been intended to live in pressurised facilities, fed by atmosphere scrubbers, while the colonists gradually increased their exposure to Crucible's native airs – tolerating it first with filtration masks, then in short episodes of direct breathing – and always under close medical supervision, alert for micro-organisms or airborne toxins. If it took decades before the citizens could walk unprotected on Crucible, that had always seemed an acceptable part of the bargain – the patient unparcelling of a world-sized gift.

They continued orbiting. Regardless of their specialisation, all of them were fascinated by Mandala. They had seen the Ocular data and strolled the scaled-down reconstructions in the Anticipation Parks. They had skimmed oceans of analysis and speculation, some of it now so old that it had gained dense layers of its own scholarship. But here was the real thing, and it *was* real – not a fiction, not a distortion. And very bit as astonishing and alien as they had been led to believe. Even with her own eyes, looking down from space, Chiku could not quite process the scale of the artefact. Here was nothing to compare with the thousand kilometre long hovering machines, but this was an entirely different order of intelligent handiwork, fashioned not from machinery floating in vacuum, but branded into the skin of a planet. The complicated, symmetric form of Mandala was familiar to her from countless visualisations – it could have been the groundwork for some grand imperial garden, all mazes and borders and intersecting promenades, except that Mandala was as wide as equatorial Africa, its sharp-edged trenches so broad and deep that they coralled whole weather systems, chiselling clouds into lines and angles. It stretched from one seaboard of a continent to the next, bent around the world's curvature. When it was night on one edge of Mandala, it was still day on the other. Shadows pushed through its channels and runnels with sudden surging intent. By some mechanism still obscure, the seas flowed in and out of the channels with the tidal phases of Crucible's two moons, forming a shallow meniscus that altered the channels' usual reflective albedo. It was possible, but as yet unproven, that parts of Mandala closed off or opened or altered their slope according to the rhythms of the sea. It was also considered likely that Mandala had the capacity to renew itself against the centuries-long assault of weather and planetary geology, maintaining the improbable sharpness of its angles and edges. If it could repair itself, it could also evolve and, perhaps, respond.

Humans would have visited this world sooner or later, but Mandala had elevated the exploration of Crucible to a species-level priority that could not be left to machines. How wonderful it would be, Chiku thought, to walk those iron-sided canyons. She imagined swimming along the flooded channels, or hang-gliding the gusty thermals stirred by the progression and retreat of shadows and water.

There was work there for a thousand lifetimes – work and joy and wonder.

We have to find a way through this, Chiku thought. *No matter our difficulties, we cannot let this opportunity slip by.*

She had been awake for nearly twenty hours now, Travertine a few hours less. They decided to take turns sleeping, so that they could all be at maximum alertness should something happen. Chiku had never felt less like sleeping in her life, but she concurred with the idea. There was no room for bunks on *Icebreaker*, so when it was their turn they crawled back into skipover caskets, now padded with blankets and pillows. Chiku had the first rest shift. After three hours of shallow, fitful sleep, she awoke feeling alert but also brittle and itchy.

She crawled to a private corner and continued working through Noah's transmissions. With every message, a deep foreboding took ever greater hold of her. Again and again she had to fight the impulse to skip forwards in the time sequence. But Noah had gone to a great deal of trouble and personal risk to send these transmissions, and it would have been a disservice not to review them in the order in which they had been sent. Besides, she almost could not bear hearing confirmation of the news she feared.

Three years had passed since her departure and conditions had only worsened on *Zanzibar*. The imposition of external authority had gone from severe to harsh, and finally become a kind of martial rule with extraordinarily severe penalties for the slightest infractions against the new order. Citizens' rights had been rescinded. The old Assembly had been almost entirely dismantled, its members dispersed back into the citizenry or subjected to interrogation and trial. Noah had managed to cling on to his freedom for the time being, but he was under increasing scrutiny from Teslenko's prosecutors and appeared resigned to his eventual detention and trial. It was becoming increasingly problematic to send transmissions to *Icebreaker*, and Noah had been forced to use ever more byzantine measures to avoid his messages being intercepted and silenced before they ever reached Chiku.

'I don't know what's going to happen here – either with my ability to contact you or the status quo on *Zanzibar*, but we can't go on like this indefinitely. It's almost as if the new regime wants to provoke a violent counter-reaction to justify finally crushing us. There've been deaths – actual deaths – caused by violent action.' He shook his head at the horror of that, and for all that she had witnessed violence herself, she shared his repugnance. Human beings were better than this – or thought themselves to be, anyway.

'A few of their constables, but mostly our citizens,' Noah said. 'It doesn't take much to set things off now, not with all the new restrictions on movement. The constables would be bad enough by themselves – there're enough of them – but they've also deployed those robots, and we wouldn't stand a chance in a fight with them even if we thought it was worth a try.'

Chiku had decided, on balance, that she would rather let Noah speak than imbue his figment with the illusion of an interactive persona. So she kept her silence, though she had many questions.

'A few of us – mostly former Assembly members – are still in some kind of contact,' he continued, 'and we've debated the idea of resistance. If we could kick them out peacefully, we'd do it, then sever all political and economic ties with the rest of the caravan. At this point we could go it alone. There'd be hardships, of course, but we're hardly living in the lap of luxury now. And we have Travertine's blueprints – we could piece a slowdown engine together from the parts of the one we already dismantled without asking the convoy for anything. But there's no peaceful way to end this, Chiku – they'd cut us down.'

She knew it was true, and she nodded.

'The worst part of all this, beyond the indignity and the deaths, is that it's just a front! Some of our top engineers have already been moved to other holoships – people who had direct contact with Travertine's research. They're not being taken away to be executed or locked in a cell for the rest of the voyage. They're being subjected to coercive collaboration, to try to duplicate Travertine's breakthrough. And I'm not just talking about one clandestine research programmeme here, but several – some of them working independently of each other. Teslenko's people might not want to land on Crucible any more, but they still want that technology. And they'll get it, one way or another. Sooner or later, they'll have stolen so many of our scientific minds that we won't be able to reproduce Travertine's engine ourselves!' Noah's expression was pained, and he drew his hand from his brow to his chin and tried to soften his worried scowl. 'I'm sorry – you must have worries of your own. For all our differences, I'd love to be with you now. Mposi and Ndege feel the same way – they're very proud of you'

'Thank you,' Chiku whispered.

'Immediately after the crackdown, your name was mud on *Zanzibar* – almost as reviled as Travertine's! The citizens felt you'd brought this trouble on us. But when the constables started tightening the thumb-screws, the citizens began to appreciate your point of view – that the *Pemba* Accord had become a noose around our necks. They still don't know the whole of it, and most of them probably aren't ready for that yet. But if they did, I suspect you'd shoot even higher in their estima-tion.' Noah managed to produce a weary smile, something of his old self to lift her spirits. 'Well, what else? Your house is still where you left it, and Mposi and Ndege take care of your flowers. They're doing well in school – or what passes for school in the new regime. They ask after you a lot – Ndege's always on the public nets, looking for news, and Mposi's said more than once that he'd like to have gone with you aboard *Ice-breaker*! I'm not sure he *really* understands what that would entail, but now that you've gained a certain notoriety, it's as if they miss you more than they did immediately after you left. I think they're very pleased to be Akinyas. And I'm very happy to have known one.'

She skipped to the next message in the time sequence – four years into her expedition.

It was very brief. Noah was sending it from a darkened room, leaning in close to an eye, his face diamonded with sweat. Even in the half-light, he appeared to have aged a decade rather than the year that had passed since the last transmission.

'I can't speak for long. The prosecutors came to my home this morn-ing with a delegation of constables. They're going to arrest me this time – and it won't be some quick detention and slap-around to put me in my place. They're organising a whole new series of trials, to be held before the full Council. I wasn't home when they came and my friends gave them the run-around long enough for me to get here. But they'll find me soon enough, and then I don't know what will happen.' He took a deep breath – he sounded as if he had been running flat out. 'Mposi and Ndege are with Sou-Chun Lo now. I know she'll look after them, whatever happens to me.' Anticipating her doubts, he added: 'Sou-Chun's always been our friend, and she's been good to the chil-dren since you left us. Please don't think ill of her – or of me for placing my trust in her.'

The message ended abruptly – no sign-off, no expression of his con-cern for her well-being. Perhaps he was simply being pragmatic – if she could read the transmission, then she was still alive.

Heart in her throat, she skipped to the next communication. More than eighteen months had elapsed since Noah's last communication – five and half years into the expedition. This time the header informed her that the message had been sent by Mposi.

But there was some mistake, obviously, because the assured young man who presented by figment could not possibly be her son, the boy she had left behind in *Zanzibar*. Mposi was twenty-three. He had slipped from boy to adult like the passing of day into night.

'I don't know if you'll receive this, or when,' he said, lifting his chin the way she had seen him do a thousand times when he was about to say something she was not going to like. 'I wish you didn't have to find out this way, but you need to know. They've killed our father. There was a trial, which didn't go well for him, then a series of public executions of the men and women implicated in breaking the *Pemba* Accord.' He took a moment to compose himself, squaring that proud jaw again – it was cleft, she noticed, just like Noah's. 'It was painless – they didn't make Father suffer ... not at the moment of his execution, anyway. And he bore it well, in the end – with great courage and self-control. His last public words, before they took him to Anticipation Park, were that we shouldn't turn against the new authority – that there should be no more deaths, no more bloodshed ...' Mposi fell silent, but she sensed he still had something more to say. 'You might be thinking that Ndege and I hold you accountable for this. It's true that we were angry, to begin with. Perhaps we still are, in some ways. But what they did to Father wasn't your fault – he made us understand that. You only did what was necessary, and we can't blame you for that. In our own way, we're proud of what you did, and we hope you're still out there somewhere, doing good work for the caravan. We hope you're well. It'd be good to hear from you again, one day.'

There was no way to verify his news, but given the grave tone of his delivery, she did not doubt a word of it. So Noah was gone, the way he always feared it might happen. She had to admit that she was very grateful she had not been present for the public executions. She wondered if they would have forced her to watch her husband die – probably as a prelude to her own execution – or whether they would have kept her away, which would have been equally intolerable.

So here she was, wrenched out of time, hearing this dreadful news from a son she almost had not recognised, a son who could not be sure she would still be alive to hear his words.

She felt herself starting to cry.

'Chiku,' said Guochang, 'you'd best come to the cockpit.'

His interruption felt like an affront, but Guochang sounded every bit as shocked as she felt.

She wiped her eyes and turned towards him.

'What is it?'

'Something's rising from Crucible.' The stocky roboticist was almost tongue-tied. 'Multiple launch vehicles, coming straight for us.'

CHAPTER THIRTY-EIGHT

She followed him to the cockpit. Travertine had drawn the next sleep shift, so Chiku sent Dr Aziba to wake ver.

'Rockets,' Namboze said. 'Coming up fast, from several launch sites. Mostly correlated with those areas of cleared terrain we flagged earlier.'

'What type of rockets?'

Guochang directed her attention to one of the rising vehicles, which was already out of the atmosphere. 'Something like a Chibesa engine, the old kind, judging by its emission signature. No surprise, really – that's one of the core technologies included in their construction files, ready for them to access when they came out of the seed packages. They needed to be able to get into space, to service the satellites and construct the way-stations. The vehicles are small, compared to us, but there are six of them, and we don't have anywhere near enough fuel to outrun them. I'm not even sure we have enough time to break orbit and attempt a re-entry.'

'Then we won't try,' Chiku said, with a kind of calm fatalism. 'We have to send our findings back to *Zanzibar* immediately – we came to see what kind of welcome was waiting for us, and this might be our last chance to report anything useful.'

'I don't think they'll attack us,' Guochang said.

'Are you sure?'

'No, but I can make some educated assumptions. Another technology included in the seed files was a short-range weapons system designed to defend against space-based threats, such as asteroids. The kinetic cannons were supposed to be up and running by the time the cities were finished.'

'And your "educated assumptions" aren't undermined by the fact that they never made any cities?' Namboze said.

Guochang shrugged. 'I can't be sure, that's true, but the kinetic cannons would have provided a viable basis for more effective weapons. I think we'd be dead by now if destroying us was their intention.'

'And you didn't think to mention the possibility that they might be armed *before* they started shooting at us?' Chiku asked.

'And you didn't mention the true purpose of this mission until it was much too late for any of us to back out,' Guochang pointed out reasonably.

Dr Aziba and Travertine squeezed themselves into the already crowded cockpit.

'Ah,' Travertine said, taking in the schematic of the rockets converging fast on *Icebreaker*'s position.

'Perhaps this is their way of saying hello,' Chiku said, in a doomed attempt to lighten the mood.

She had already composed a self-contained statement about the purpose of *Icebreaker*'s mission and her fears regarding the Providers, ready to be squirted back to the caravan at a moment's notice, but they still had a few minutes before the rockets were perilously close. She accessed the earlier statement and began speaking, adding an addendum.

'Chiku here. We're currently experiencing first contact with the Providers in the form of some ships closing on us, launched from the surface. There's been no acknowledgement of our space-to-surface transmissions, friendly or otherwise, so we have no idea whether their intent is hostile or not. Guochang thinks we'd already be dead if they wanted that, so ...' Here she faltered. 'It could go either way at this point. If you don't hear from me again, I suggest you assume the worst. In that event, you'll have two choices – stay well away from Crucible, or risk engagement with the Providers. Whichever option you choose, you'll be shouldering a huge responsibility, an obligation not just to our citizenry but to the billions of people we left behind in the solar system. It doesn't matter if we panic and overreact – we're just a drop in the ocean – but the truth about the Providers can't get back to Earth. It would be catastrophic – the collapse of every certainty that defines most of our lives. If people turn against the Providers, they'll be turning against the Mechanism – and if the Mechanism decides to retaliate, we're done for. That can't happen. Whatever you think of me, please believe this one truth: the knowledge about Crucible is simply too dangerous to spread. It has to stay with us – with the caravan – and go no further.'

'You'd better wrap that up,' Travertine said quietly. 'They'll be on us in about two minutes, maybe less.'

Chiku closed the transmission, offered a silent prayer to fate, and then committed her message to space via a narrow beam aimed at their best guess for the caravan's coordinates, and also in a broader signal that would allow for a high margin of error in their estimates.

It was done. No force in the universe could catch up with that signal now.

She thought she would feel relieved, having finally unburdened herself of this secret, which could only help her reputation – presuming anyone still cared or indeed was still alive to debate it. But all she felt was an emptiness beyond emptiness, like the phase transition between one state of vacuum and the next. They could absolve her, if they wished, but she had no authority to forgive herself. She had been a fool to think it would be that easy.

She moved to the cockpit window, bracing herself for the arriving ships – or missiles. Two of them were very close now, but they were slowing, not accelerating, and at the last moment they braked hard enough to have killed any human passengers. They came to a halt on either side of the lander, two identical craft about half the size of *Icebreaker*. They were tapering cylinders, fluted like a wine glass, with a blunt, chisel-like nose. The thick end obviously contained the main engine parts, but apertures and vents elsewhere in the ships' hulls might have been for steering or retro-rocket functions. They were coloured a slightly lustrous slate grey, and there were no windows or distinguishing markings.

For several minutes they just sat there. Then two more of the ships completed their burn and assumed orientation above and below the lander. Chiku saw nothing to distinguish these from the first two – nor, when the fifth and six had arrived, was there anything to mark these from the first four. The final pair fell into position aft and foreward of *Icebreaker*, so that the lander was bracketed from all sides. There had never been any prospect of fleeing the vehicles, but it was out of the question now.

Chiku and her companions waited. Guochang could offer no protocols for this situation. There was nothing more they could do to announce their presence and signal their willingness to communicate.

Between one moment and the next the cockpit filled with intense red light. At first Chiku squinted. The shutters were lowering on some automatic reflex, but she ordered them to remain open. The light was bright but not blinding. It pulsed and strobed and fell into shifting grids and furrows. Occasionally it achieved a very tight focus, almost too bright to look at. They watched intense little knots of it beetle over the window glass.

'They're mapping us,' Guochang diagnosed, although the others had already reached a similar conclusion. 'Optical lasers, projected from all six directions. They must be building up a complete three-dimensional image of the ship – laser tomography!'

Chiku realised that his earlier tongue-tied state had been as much the result of enthusiasm as of fear.

'Surely they already knew what to expect,' Dr Aziba said. 'They knew we were coming – they're the ones who've been lying, not us!'

'Maybe they need to make sure we're who we appear to be,' Namboze said.

Chiku found herself nodding. 'Yes. They can't be too careful. They've had no direct contact with humans before – as far as we know, at least – and we've made enough alterations to the lander that it won't match anything in their files.'

The red lights snapped off abruptly.

Chiku and her crew floated in silence, waiting for *something* to happen. But the six ships were holding station, mute as rocks. Chiku suspected that the ships were probably specialised robotic devices, self-contained and indivisible, each a kind of Provider in its own right. Guochang had already alerted her to the fact that the machines could assume many forms: the huge, stalking forms they manifested on Earth and Venus shapes not the only anatomy open to them. And given the length of time these machines had been acting without human supervision, it was possible – probable, even – that they had devised many specialised forms that owed nothing to the functional templates in the original seed packages. Adaptative speciation, Guochang said, grinning at the very idea.

'Something's happening,' Travertine said.

But they had all seen it. The ships were closing in, reducing their respective distances from *Icebreaker*. The motion was not fast enough to look like an attempt to crush the lander, but still Chiku feared the worst. They had no weapons, no defences beyond the hull's normal integrity. It had been difficult enough selling the concept of an exploratory mission to the Assembly – she doubted even her seasoned diplomacy could have persuaded them to turn the lander into a warship.

But the ships stopped again when they were almost touching *Icebreaker*'s skin, so close that no easy view was possible from the windows. Chiku called up a mosaic of exterior images grabbed from the lander's eyes and they watched, fascinated, as the six ships opened portions of their hulls, cunning as Chinese boxes. Long articulations of machinery elbowed out of the holes, quick as striking snakes, angling and swivelling with disarming speed. A node of light brighter than the sun glowed at the end of each arm and shaded from white into violet. Chiku flinched as the shutters descended but did not tell them to stop this time. The articulated arms were cutting through the lander's hull everywhere the light touched, and a bright-pink smear hyphenated Chiku's vision.

'Fusion torches, maybe,' Travertine said. 'Or maybe a very compact Chibesa reaction. The clever, clever things.'

'We should move to the caskets,' Namboze said, unimpressed with this machine-centric line of thinking. 'No time to get into suits.'

But the Providers were not trying to cut their way in, Chiku realised. They were trimming the lander's aerodynamic extremities without compromising its pressurised core. They sliced through wings and fin with surgical speed and precision, then made some other cuts that served no immediately obvious purpose. Finally they packed away their cutting arms, sealing up their hulls with the same swiftness as the arms had been deployed, and a moment after that the six ships moved closer still and clamped on to *Icebreaker* with some magnetic or mechanical purchase that felt as firm and immovable as solid rock.

And then the Provider rockets applied thrust, much more gently than when they had arrived, and *Icebreaker* and its imprisoning escort fell out of orbit into the scorch of atmosphere.

Chiku and her crew buckled into acceleration couches, but the robots took care of their human guests, never imposing a load exceeding one and a half gees. Chiku dared to hope that this was more than accidental. Perhaps Guochang's intuition had been right all along, that the Providers would already have done them harm, had that been their intention.

Icebreaker had been damaged – it could not possibly have entered the atmosphere under its own control – but most of its sensors and positional devices were still functioning. They were descending from equatorial orbit, following an arc that deviated only slightly to the south of their original ground-track. They had been passing over open ocean when the machines had clamped on, and shortly after they had traversed a quilt of islands spanning about twenty degrees of latitude. It was day. They pushed deeper into air, losing speed and altitude. Now they were over open ocean again, about a thousand kilometres east of Mandala. They were now deep enough into the atmosphere that the sky had colour – a deepening pastel blue, horsetailed with clouds. The blue gained intensity as they descended. Through the gauze of air, to her untrained eye, Sixty One Virginis f seemed exactly as colourless and hot as the Lisbon sun, though visibly larger. They could live here, she thought, given half a chance.

The ocean had looked glass-flat from space and leathery from high altitude, like an expensive blue textile stretched across the globe. They were much lower now, and Chiku made out the swell and chop of heavy seas. It was unmistakably liquid now, something you could drown in. Much bigger than this little wounded ship. The foam on the swell was white, shading into a faint pistachio green – it made her think of flavours of whipped ice-cream, and ice-cream made her think of Belém and seagulls and Pedro Braga, the life and times of Chiku Yellow. The water itself was much greener than blue, a kind of salty turquoise veined with opals and ultramarines. The algal load was much higher than it had ever been in Earth's seas. The waters of Crucible were a brimming matrix of floating organisms, as dense as soup and as layered as a Martian canyon.

They cruised lower still. Reefs chiselled through shallowing seas, edged with long lines of breakers. Here and there, sharp-sided islands pierced the ocean like green pyramids. Chiku even saw a partially active volcano near the horizon, burping out a Morse message of muddy-brown clouds.

And then there were Providers rising from the sea, four of them, easily as big as those she had seen on Earth. They stood at the points of an invisible cross, bending their mantis-bodies into the sky so that seawater came off them in thunderous curtains. The rockets slowed and stopped, hovering in the middle of the four Providers, and then completed their descent to the water. Only at the last moment was *Icebreaker* released and allowed to splash the rest of the way down. The rockets broke formation and peeled away on six independent arcs.

Icebreaker had been designed to float and the changes imposed on it in space had not affected its seaworthiness, so the lander bobbed easily on the swell. Chiku extricated herself from the acceleration couch, steadying herself as a wave tilted the floor. Water blurred the windows. This was not how she had imagined their arrival.

'I wish they'd say something,' Dr Aziba said. 'Anything – it doesn't matter what.'

'Maybe they've forgotten how to talk,' Travertine said.

They were tripping over each other, racing from one watery window to the next. A large percentage of the hull was submerged, but Chiku did not think they were taking on enough water to cause difficulties.

'They're moving,' Namboze said. 'Guochang – are we still transmitting those handshake protocols?'

'Yes – for all the good it's doing!'

'These aren't really Providers,' Chiku said. 'They look like them, but they're under Arachne's control. We should assume she's here, puppetting everything.'

'Then perhaps we should ask Arachne what she wants!' Aziba said, and his voice had a mildly hysterical edge.

Something clanged against the hull, followed immediately by a ghastly scraping sound, metal on metal, as if an anchor were being dragged along the outside of the lander. Chiku hopped between the lander's public eyes until she had a satisfactory view of proceedings. One of the towering Providers had extended a tentacle tipped with a heavy circular fitting that looked like an electromagnet. The Provider was sliding it up and down the hull like a physician's stethoscope.

The tentacle halted sharply. There was silence for a moment as the cabin rocked and pitched. They were all breathing much too fast.

Chiku was weighing the likelihood that the tentacle was holding a listening device when the circular thing started drilling. The hideous, tooth-grinding sound intensified and rose in pitch as the drill spun ever faster. Sparks catherine-wheeled into the sea and the lander shuddered under the assault. Chiku glanced at her companions. She had nothing to offer, no reassurances or suggestions. She had brought them to this, and now she was powerless to protect them.

'We could still return to the caskets,' Namboze said.

'We could play charades,' Travertine said. 'It'll achieve as much.'

The drilling continued. Once or twice the machine stopped, and when it started up again the pitch was different, as if it had switched cutting tools. Chiku agreed with Travertine – they could go into the caskets or don their suits, but it would only delay the inevitable, whatever that turned out to be. In bleak despair, she thought of suicide pills. They should have brought something like that, or devised a protocol authorising the medical robot to euthanise them quickly and painlessly should the need arise.

When the machine finally broke through the hull, it did so with a much smaller cutting tool than Chiku had been expecting. A circle of the inner hull about the circumference of her thigh gained a sparking rim and then dropped smoking to the floor. Immediately machinery began to bustle through the still-glowing aperture. Chiku's crew backed away from the point of entry, squeezing against walls and bulkheads on the opposite side of the cockpit. The thing protruding from the hole was an arm with a flowerlike appendage on the end, finely perforated. It swung around, apparently locking on to each of them in turn.

A hissing sound issued from the nozzles, accompanied by some kind of colourless, odourless gas.

'The masks,' Chiku said, already knowing it was too late for that. The masks were one feature of their sketchy contingency plan for surface exposure, in the event that the Providers had not built anything that could be pressurised for human habitation. They were tucked in a locker somewhere at the back of the habitation volume, too far away to be of any use now. She was already feeling thick-headed. Part of her wanted to fight the gas, but another part did not think it mattered. The gas would get them anyway, regardless of what they did.

She slipped into unconsciousness watching the flower wave back and forth, spraying its contents into the air.

CHAPTER THIRTY-NINE

She had the sense that the girl had been speaking for some time, but it was difficult to hold on to the flow of things. She frowned, but that only made things worse.

The girl paused for a moment, realising that her words were only making partial headway. She smiled a little, nodded and then began again.

'Can you understand me, Chiku? I do hope you can. I also hope you're not too uncomfortable – you mustn't hesitate to tell me if there's anything we might improve upon. We've done our best, but unfortunately our experience with the living has been rather limited.'

She wore a red dress with white socks and well-polished black shoes and held a violin in one hand, resting it against her knee. The other hand held a bow.

'I know you,' Chiku said.

'I doubt that,' the girl said, but appeared to take no pleasure in the contradiction. 'You've only just arrived.'

'You're Lin Wei.'

The girl shook her head. 'No, I'm Arachne.'

Chiku tried to stay calm, despite the rising terror she felt. 'No. If you were Arachne, I'd be dead. You tried to kill me on Venus and again in Africa.'

'I have no recollection of these events. You might conceivably have met another aspect of me, but I'll have to take your word for it until I read your memories.'

'You look very like Lin Wei.' But then comprehension of a sort dawned upon Chiku. 'You look like her because she made you – she must have used her own personality as a template for your persona before inserting you in Ocular.'

'I know of an individual named Lin Wei, and if you believe my persona to be derived from hers, I will file that information for future reference.'

'You don't know where you came from?'

'I know that I came from another solar system, but beyond that, I can't verify much – at least, not to my satisfaction.' The girl extended the hand that held the bow. 'Please, would you like to stand? Come to the window – I think you'll find the view pleasing.' She was still holding the violin against her knee.

Chiku was in a chair, not a bed. At first she thought she was still dressed in the lightweight garments they had all worn on *Icebreaker*. But as she moved, the fabric felt silkier than she remembered, and it was much too clean for her to have been wearing it since she came out of skipover. It was, she decided, a clever copy, not the original garment.

She studied her surroundings. She had come to consciousness in a circular room with curving walls and ceiling, interrupted by wide elliptical windows. The room was set with plain but functional furniture.

Through the windows she thought she could see a landscape beneath a sky that appeared to shimmer between pink and orange depending on the directness of her gaze.

'Do you speak for the Providers?' Chiku paused for a moment, then added: 'Are you the Providers? Are the Providers you? Is there more than one of you? You say "I" sometimes and "we" at others.'

'Come to the window, Chiku. There's nothing to fear.'

'Where's everyone else – Travertine, Doctor Aziba and the others?'

'They are all alive and well, and you'll be reunited with them soon.'

'Are we your prisoners or your guests? Are we free to leave if we want to?'

'I don't know enough about you to answer that question yet.'

'Why did you attack my ship?'

'That wasn't an attack.' The figment or replica of the girl, whatever it was, produced a teasing smile. 'You saw my capabilities, Chiku. I could have attacked and destroyed you any time from the moment you entered this solar system.'

Chiku rose from the chair and moved to the window. The floor under her feet was a cushion of grey, yielding to her footsteps. Blood-warm and clammy, it reminded her of elephant skin.

'Are we on Crucible?'

'Yes. We know from our scans of your ship that you mapped our surface from orbit. Doubtless you saw the evidence of our work?'

'We saw a lot less than we'd been led to expect. You were supposed to be making cities for us.'

'Cities? There are only five of you! Plus another fifteen in your caskets,

369

of course. Why aren't those people awake? Are you intending to wake them at some later point?'

'Have you hurt them?'

'Goodness, Chiku – we really do have a massive gulf to cross before you'll trust me, don't we?'

'It was a simple question. You ripped my ship apart, dragged us into Crucible's atmosphere and then pumped narcotic gas into our hull. You ignored our handshake protocols and uplinked false data to our ships. I'm sorry, but that's not how you go about building a basis of mutual trust.'

'Then you must educate me on the correct procedure.'

The girl was standing by the window with her back to the scene. She beckoned Chiku closer, gesturing towards the landscape with her bow, as if presenting a painting for discussion. 'Crucible,' she said admiringly. 'Quite lovely, isn't it? We've travelled some way from where you landed. It will be sunrise here shortly – I thought you'd like that.'

From the view, she surmised that they were in a tower. A number of similar structures were visible from the window. They were pale stalks, rising from a dense canopy of trees or tree-analogues, their leaves a green so dark that it was closer to the lustrous black of a magpie's feathers. Bean-shaped capsules with elliptical windows topped the stalks, and lower down, aerial bridges linked the stalks in a cat's cradle of intersecting walkways. Some of the towers were lower and squatter than others, with fatter capsules. Beyond this grouping of structures, she could see no other sign of construction between here and the horizon.

Crucible's two moons loitered palely together.

'What is this place – a prison?'

'It's somewhere we can all get to know each other better,' the girl said.

'Do you know about the caravan? Are you aware that millions more of us are due to arrive very shortly? A whole fleet of holoships, each carrying tens of millions, with shuttles and landers and high-energy propulsion systems that can also be used as weapons?'

'I have many questions, and there are multiple factors to be considered before any conclusions can be drawn. I propose a period of mutual information exchange. Are you comfortable? I can bring food and drink matched closely to your specifications. Or would you like a moment to yourself, for the purposes of meditation? Perhaps you would like me to leave you to observe the sunrise in private, and return in a little while? Or I could play this violin for you—'

'Actually,' Chiku said, 'what I'd really like is for you to start telling me something useful.'

*

Eventually Chiku relented and accepted the girl's offer of chai. Setting aside her violin, the girl knelt on the floor, indicating for Chiku to do likewise. They sat opposite each other, a block-like table between them, set with chai. Its lower edges curved around into the surface of the floor, as if it was being pushed up from underneath. Chiku was pretty sure that the table had not been there when she stood from the chair and walked to the window. Even if it had – she was prepared to allow that the grey table might have blended with the floor – surely she could not have missed the milk-coloured crockery now resting on it.

But she hardly had time to dwell on this oddness before the girl launched into her questions.

'Tell me about yourself. Everything. Where and when you were born, what you've done with your life, what brought you here.'

'I'm Chiku Akinya. Doesn't that tell you everything you need to know?'

'Not really.' The girl was smiling encouragingly. 'I'd like you to tell me everything about yourself in your own words. Begin with your place of birth. Tell me what it was like.'

'I was born on Mars.'

The girl cocked her head to one side. 'Are you certain? Or are you testing my ability to detect a lie?'

'I was born on the Moon.'

'That's better. Why were you born there?'

'I didn't have a lot of say in the matter.' But when the girl remained silent, Chiku had no option but to add: 'My mother and father lived on the Moon. My mother was born in what used to be Tanzania, in the East African Federation, and my father on the Moon.'

'Are they still there?'

'My father still lives there, but my mother died quite recently. I mean, by my reckoning.'

'I'm very sorry to hear of your loss.' The girl drank her chai in a very dainty fashion. And she did appear to be drinking it, Chiku decided, not just mimicking the action.

'Are you really a robot? A construct?'

'I suppose so. Have you had much experience with my kind?'

'I've met artilects, if that's what you are. And I already told you I've met something that looks exactly the same as you, but goes by a different name.'

'Indeed you did. But I want to hear more about *you*, Chiku Akinya. Will you indulge me? Tell me about Earth. Have you ever been to Earth?'

'Lots of times.'

'It must be very beautiful. Although not at all like Crucible.'

And so it continued. Chiku soon learned that the girl had a polite relentlessness that was difficult to rebuff. She deflected most of Chiku's own questions politely but firmly, and hinted from time to time that Chiku's questions might be answered once her own curiosity had been sated. But there was no telling how long that might take.

The girl was more interested in some parts of Chiku's story than others, and occasionally her interest sharpened to an almost inquisitorial focus. She kept coming back to certain details and events, almost as if she was trying to force Chiku into self-contradiction. But Chiku had no fear of that – she was trying to tell the truth, not embroider a fiction, and any mistakes or inconsistencies would be innocent errors, not barefaced lies.

True, her life was complicated by the existence of her three selves, but she explained this to the artilect as straightforwardly as she could, and the girl appeared to accept Chiku's account at face value.

'You must feel isolated from your other selves, across all this distance.'

'There's only one other "me" left,' Chiku said, 'and as far as I know she's happy enough.'

'What became of the third?'

'She had an accident.'

'I'm very sorry for your loss.'

The sun had risen as the gentle interrogation continued, climbing nearly to the zenith, and the black-canopied trees now carpeted the world with a blazing emerald. When Chiku glanced outside in a lull between questions, she wondered how she had failed to notice the on-going transition in the quality of the light. On one level she felt drained by the endless questioning, as if she had endured weeks of it, but simultaneously she had the odd sense that the day had skipped from darkness to noon without any intervening passage of time.

At length, the questioning ceased. She was hungry enough by then to accept the offer of food, which turned out to be perfectly prepared and entirely delicious. But once again, Chiku lost her sense of time and the food, like the midday sun, appeared before her without her sensing its arrival. The girl absented herself during the meal, but Chiku had no idea whether this was because she had things to attend to, or because she felt Chiku was deserving of a little privacy while she ate.

The room's furnishings were austere, and when Chiku finished eating, she wondered how she was meant to occupy her time in the girl's absence. But some time during the afternoon, as the forest transitioned through permutations of darkening green, the girl returned to show her how to use a kind of vanity desk, which opened out to reveal a display surface and an array of white tactile controls embossed with numbers, letters and symbols.

'I don't want you to be bored,' the girl explained, 'so I thought you might appreciate access to these things. Through this channel, you may examine the entire recovered contents of your vehicle – lifetimes of art, literature, music and scientific and historical documentation.' Her hand moved in a graceful upswing, like someone miming a tennis stroke. 'Through this channel, you may intercept the uplinked communication streams and transmissions from Earth and the solar system. We've been in constant receipt of these signals since we arrived here, and I'd value your observations and commentary greatly.'

Chiku's heart skipped a little as she asked: 'Are any of the signals being relayed from the caravan?'

'They were for a while, yes, but it's also possible to intercept signals directly from the old solar system, without leapfrogging here from holoship to holoship.'

'We detected nothing like that.'

'But your little ship with its tiny antenna never had the sensitivity to pick up transmissions from twenty-eight light-years away. It's a puzzle, though, that you heard nothing from the holoships?' She tilted her head to indicate this was a question rather than a statement of fact.

'What do you think happened to them?'

'We have some theories. Your departure precipitated trouble, but it's arguable that things would have deteriorated sooner or later anyway. You developed a potent new technology – the means by which you reached our system ahead of the caravan. Whether people wanted to own that technology or suppress it, there was bound to be disharmony.'

'They invaded my holoship, put my people under martial rule. They arrested my husband – the man who used to be my husband – and then *executed* him. That's not disharmony. It's the fucking Dark Ages.'

'I'm very sorry for your loss.'

'Please stop saying that.' But after a silence, Chiku said: 'The last thing I heard before you ripped us out of orbit was a message from my son, Mposi. Were there any more transmissions from *Zanzibar* in *Icebreaker*'s memory?'

'A few more, yes.' She gestured towards the desk again. 'Events become ... confused – or confusing, to us at least. We'd value your insight – perhaps the messages will make *some* sense from your perspective. Would you indulge me? Everything we retrieved is open to you. And I promise that in a little while you may meet with your friends.'

Chiku nodded distractedly, unconvinced that the girl meant a word of it. But she was determined to hear anything Mposi and Ndege might have sent, and stale news was better than no news.

The desk turned out to be surprisingly intuitive, functionally, and it did not take her long to locate the time-sequenced transmissions from *Zanzibar*. As a sanity check, and as painful as it was, she replayed the last message from Mposi.

Yes, Noah was still dead. She had not imagined that awful truth. And Mposi still looked improbably adult and self-assured, although on second viewing she observed that he was also only just on the cusp of adulthood and acting older than his years – striving for a gravitas he had not quite earned. The world had forced this on him. She loathed what it had done to her boy.

She skipped ahead – an interval of months – to another message from Mposi.

'The situation's getting worse by the day,' he told her. 'Trouble between the constables and the citizenry, a few attempts at organised resistance, but there's no hope of regaining autonomy, and about a dozen people died in the violence. There are too many of them, too well coordinated, and now we've all seen what those enforcement robots can do. Ndege and I are safe, for the moment, although that might not be the case for much longer. Sou-Chun's doing what she can to protect us, but we're *your* children, and that's enough to damn us in the eyes of your worst critics – even though we had nothing to do with *Icebreaker*, or with contravening the *Pemba* rules. How could we? We were children!'

'You were blameless,' she answered, as if her opinion mattered to this shadow of her son.

Mposi went on: 'It's bad enough that our father was executed for acting in *Zanzibar*'s best interests – and the interests of the whole caravan! But it looks as if there was more to his arrest and detention than we thought. Noah was questioned ... "interrogated" might be a better word, maybe even tortured, or at least coerced into revealing information. I hate to think what they did to him. When they took him out to the Anticipation Park, he looked broken – as if they'd sucked his soul right out of his body. I think they went into his brain.'

She wondered how Mposi could know this, but he was ahead of her: 'Too many rumours to ignore – and Sou-Chun has friends in the right places, people she can rely on to tell her the truth. With Noah's testimony, however they got it out of him, the other holoships are making rapid strides towards their own slowdown technology. They'll have it soon, one way or another, and I don't know what'll happen then. You managed it wisely, Mother – but I'm not sure everyone else will.'

She laughed hollowly. Wisely. Yes, and here she was, shot down on an alien planet, prisoner of an artificial intelligence, having achieved almost nothing she had set out to accomplish.

'If that's wisdom, Mposi—' she began, but he was already speaking again.

'I've been in contact with Eunice – Father passed on your ching co-ordinates to me and Ndege before things got too bad. We've spoken to her. No physical access, of course, but ... it's been sufficient for purposes. Why did you hide these things from us, Mother? Why didn't you trust us?'

'You were children,' she said.

'Eunice is aware of the developing situation and extremely concerned about the potential for violence. She seems to think the troubles may force her hand. I don't think the world's ready for her yet – but that won't necessarily stop her.'

'You're right – the world isn't ready. Not remotely.'

'I hope we'll speak again,' Mposi said. 'Until then, I trust you have some way of hearing my words, and that you're well, and that Nedge and I will see you again. Be safe, Mother.'

She was about to skip ahead – if indeed there was a later transmission in the desk's memory – when another discontinuity interrupted her perception of elapsed time. It was morning again, judging by the angle of sunlight on the surrounding trees. She felt unexpectedly rested and refreshed, as if she had slept very soundly indeed. And clean, although she had no recollection of washing or being washed. She had eaten and drunk, too, she remembered that much, but felt no need to empty her bowels.

And now the girl was back, but the desk was gone, and they were drinking chai again.

'You're doing something to me,' Chiku decided. 'Manipulating my perception of time on a deep level. I have no idea how long I've been here – it feels like a day, but I don't trust my perceptions at the moment. How do I know I haven't been here for weeks or months, while you keep resetting some clock in my brain and asking me these questions over and over? Actually ...' She rapped her knuckles on the table, making the crockery clatter. 'Actually, how do I even know this is a real environment? How do I know you're not inside my head, rummaging around like they did in Noah's brain and sucking out information? How do I even know I'm awake? The last thing I'm certain happened to me is being gassed aboard my ship. For all I know I've been in a coma ever since.'

'You must appreciate,' the girl said, 'that no answer I could give you would convince you one way or the other. Such an answer would render three thousand years' worth of philosophical debate superfluous in a single stroke!'

'I'll ask you anyway – is this reality?'

'Yes,' she said firmly, as if they were playing some kind of question-and-answer parlour game.

'Am I on Crucible?'

'Oh yes, definitely. I could tell you our exact surface coordinates—'

'Where's Mandala?'

'Quite a long way to the west, on one of the main continental plates. We're on one of the larger islands. We're keeping our distance from Mandala, for now. But that's enough about me. What did you make of the transmissions from *Zanzibar*?'

'No, that's not nearly enough about you. Give me something for a change. Why would you keep your distance from Mandala?'

'We were ordered not to investigate until the human settlers arrived.'

'You were also ordered to build cities. You had no trouble disobeying *that* order, so why would you comply with another?' Chiku nodded to herself. 'Either you're lying and you *have* been poking around Mandala, or something else compelled you to keep away. We haven't discussed the orbiting things yet. They called you here, didn't they? Ocular picked up their optical communication stream, the blue light. It did something to Arachne, penetrated her deep programming, made her doctor the data before it reached human eyes. On the basis of that false data, we launched the caravans and the Provider seed packages. You rode our expansion wave, surfed ahead of it – machines summoned by machines. But what happened when you arrived? Did you communicate with anyone – or should I say any *thing*?'

'Communications are proceeding,' the girl said, after what Chiku thought was a moment's hesitation.

'What does that mean?'

'Efforts are ongoing. There has been ... fruitful exchange.' The girl smiled quickly. 'What conclusions have you drawn regarding the twenty-two machines?'

'None at all, but then we only just arrived. You've had more than a century to study them. What have you done? What have you actually learned? Assuming you learned anything at all.'

'Oh, we've learned a great deal. A tremendous amount.' But there was something almost too forceful about this response, a touch too much protestation.

'Do you know who sent them? What they're called? Why they're here in the first place?'

'They were drawn by Mandala, as were we. They have an interest in the mutual welfare of … ones such as us.'

'Artificial intelligences. Artilects.'

'Machine-substrate consciousnesses,' the girl said, as if this made some vital distinction. 'Our name for them … or rather my best understanding of their name, mapped across daunting cognitive horizons … It's nothing more than an approximation, I hope you understand—'

'I do,' Chiku said. 'Please get to the point.'

'We call them the Watchkeepers. They've been here for about three million years, but they're much older than that. Clearly, they are unimaginably patient. Our recent activities, our busy goings-on – the emergence of human civilisation twenty-eight light-years away, the arrival of the seed packages, your presence … all these things happened in an instant, from their perspective. They're not slow-witted, you understand, just anchored to a different idea of time's flow. Their clock is galactic, not stellar. But it would be wrong to say that they are uninterested in developments in and around this planet.'

'What have they been doing since you arrived? Just hovering above Crucible?'

'There have been measurable interactions, as I stated. Preliminaries to deeper communication.'

'Have you explored them? When we passed one of the machines, we could see some way into it. If I'd been here for decades, I'd have tried to send a probe to find out what was inside.'

'And what sort of reaction might you have anticipated?'

'You tell me. I'm not the artificial intelligence – sorry, *machine-substrate consciousness* – in this conversation.'

The girl raised an arch eyebrow. 'Self-evidently.'

'Let's go back to Mandala for a moment. I can't believe your curiosity didn't get the better of you. Did those things – the Watchkeepers – frighten you away?'

'Why would you come to that conclusion?'

'Who cares? Those machines aren't my problem, anyway. If they've been orbiting Crucible all this time without doing anything, presumably they aren't particularly interested in what happens on the planet. All I want is settlement space for my colonists – we can worry about the Watchkeepers when we've built some cities and farms.'

'That's an admirably pragmatic sentiment. Do you think you could go about your daily lives with mysterious alien machines hovering in your skies?'

'Our objective was to study Mandala,' Chiku pointed out. 'That would have been enough to be starting with, before we turned our attention to the Watchkeepers. Let's move on, shall we? We had an arrangement – I recall you promising to let me speak to my friends.'

'But of course.' The girl looked abashed. 'I'd hate you to think that my word is anything less than dependable. Who would you like to talk to?'

'All of them.'

'But if you had to choose just one … who would it be?'

'I don't know. Travertine or Guochang, I suppose.'

The girl nodded sagely, and time slipped another gear.

CHAPTER FORTY

It was a different time of day, and the girl who looked like Lin Wei had been replaced by Travertine. Chiku had the queasy sense that this moment had happened before. How had Travertine arrived? When? Was it even Travertine, or just a simulated figment? Ve looked real enough, it was true, right down to the cuff around vis wrist, which was still emitting a metronomic red pulse every few seconds.

'I could ask you the same question,' Travertine said.

'I'm sorry?'

'Are you real, or a figment? That's what you just asked. Or speculated. Or thought aloud. I've been through this with the others. There's probably no way we'll ever know for sure – I mean, ontologically speaking, this is pretty deep water. But the most efficient information-gathering strategy may be to assume that we're all real, or are having a real conversation, at least.'

'What does that mean?'

'I mean that we might not be in our bodies exactly. For all we know, the machines could be keeping us asleep while they open us up, like frogs on a dissection table. Even if they aren't invading our bodies and minds, they're clearly manipulating our perceptions on some level – probably addressing brain function through the existing pathways of our neural implants but using forbidden protocols, functions and backdoors that not even the Mech or ching services would normally be allowed to access. Skipping time, rewinding time, that sort of thing. It's been happening to all of us, and I doubt you're an exception.'

'You said "all of us". Have you seen the others?'

'I've spoken to Namboze directly, and Namboze has spoken to Doctor Aziba. Doctor Aziba claimed to have had contact with Guochang, although we're not sure who Guochang's spoken to. No one appears to have spoken to you until now, unless it was Guochang.'

'You're the first, I think.'

'In which case, let me be the first to say I'm glad you're still alive, Chiku, but I think we're in the shit, so to speak.'

'Do you know what's happening? Do you know where we are?'

'I haven't been in this room before,' Travertine said. 'I know the view from my room, and I've seen the view from Namboze's place. The placement of the towers is different, and you can make out some variation in the tree cover if you pay attention. You can also take note of sun angle, that sort of thing. My assumption is that these rooms are real, that they're actual structures on Crucible's surface, and that they're moving us around from tower to tower as and when it suits them. I think there's more than one version of the little girl, although it's not easy to tell with all this interrupted time-perception stuff.'

'The little girl is Arachne. She looks like a real person who used to be called Lin Wei, but that's only because Lin Wei played a part in shaping Arachne's persona. And yes, it makes sense that she can be in more than once place at a time – she's an artilect, after all. Dealing with five of us must be like … I don't know, some incredibly trivial activity. Has she asked you lots of questions?'

'Until my ears are bleeding. And after I spoke to Namboze, she had a thousand more questions about our conversation. Forget any illusion of privacy – she's listening in now.'

'I don't care. It's not as if we've anything to lose by saying what's on our minds. All I've got is speculation.'

'All right,' Travertine said, pausing to prepare a cup of chai for verself, and then another for Chiku. 'Then here's a bit more. See what you make of it.'

'Go on.'

'Arachne – this thing that speaks to us – hasn't got a clue.'

Chiku almost laughed. It was as if they were being rude about a host while she was out of the room, and there was a delicious sense of naughtiness about it.

'About what?'

'Anything. But especially anything happening outside the immediate realm of her senses. She keeps asking me about Earth and the solar system and life on the holoships.'

'Same with me,' Chiku said.

'But why wouldn't she know what's going on in all those places? We've seen the relay satellites, and the Providers are capable of transmitting a high-powered signal into interstellar space. The seed packages were also meant to deploy a listening capability just as effective – a wide baseline network, spread across the system – so Arachne should be receiving a rich stream of data, telling her everything she could ever want to know about life back home. So why would she keep asking us stuff she ought to know already?'

Travertine's words confirmed what Chiku had already been thinking. 'She needs validation. She can receive the data, but she can't authenticate it. She's in exactly the same position we were in when we started doubting the Provider data stream from Crucible!'

'Yes – we came here to validate – or invalidate – the false data received about Crucible. But our memories and the files on *Icebreaker* are the only means Arachne has of validating the data coming from Earth.'

'Wait, though,' said Chiku. 'We had reason to doubt the Provider uplink. Why would Arachne doubt the signal coming from Earth? She's a splinter of another artificial intelligence that's still active around the solar system – the artilect that manipulated events to send Providers here in the first place. Distrusting the Earth data would be like distrusting herself.'

'She's a splinter, separated from her source by twenty-eight light-years,' Travertine said. 'Maybe she's begun to feel isolated, cut off from her other self. Maybe there was some discontinuity, some interruption of the data stream – just enough to force *this* Arachne to start examining and questioning her assumptions. She's an intelligence, after all, and that's what intelligences do.'

Chiku thought on this some more, trying to slot this vast new assumption into her existing mental framework.

'I still don't get it.'

'Look at it from her perspective. Logically, she can't prove the truthfulness of the Earth transmissions, but she can keep trying to falsify them, by testing her picture of Earth against our accounts and the data on *Icebreaker*. That's why she keeps circling around the same details – it's her way of testing us, trying to trap us in a contradiction. That's why we're being kept isolated, for now, and why she'll only allow us very limited interaction. She doesn't want to risk cross-contamination.'

Chiku shifted in her kneeling position. 'Why allow us to interact at all, in that case?'

'I suppose she knows there are things she can only learn about us via conversations between us. She's probably reading our brains as we speak, watching our mirror neurons light up, trying to work out whether we're actually having a conversation or are engaged in some elaborate choreographed bluff. I think she's worried that we're some kind of weapon – infectious information agents, perhaps, a physical embodiment of the lies she suspects she's been receiving from Earth.'

'If that's the case, what happens when she makes her mind up? Do we get to live or die?'

'I don't know, although I suspect she'll keep us fed and watered for as long as she considers us useful.'

'Have you asked her about the pine cones?'

Travertine nodded. 'Yes, and so did Namboze and Doctor Aziba – and Guochang, for all I know. What conclusions did you draw from her answers?'

'Nothing much – she seemed cagey.'

'I had the same impression,' Travertine replied.

'There could be a hundred reasons for that, though. She either knows far more than she's telling, or she's unwilling to admit exactly how little she knows after all this time. She looks human, but she's not, and it's difficult to get a read on a machine.'

'I'm not sure she's imaginative enough to try to deceive us. Cunning as a weasel, yes, and brilliantly quick and clever, but not very good at outright fabulation. It's only a hunch, mind, but if I'm right, she'd find it very difficult to create a self-consistent fiction concerning the progress she's made with the pine cones.'

'You might be on to something there,' Chiku said. 'From what we observed coming in, the Providers only made the minimum changes necessary to the uplink information. I haven't been out into that forest, but I bet the botanical data they sent us wasn't far off the mark.'

'It makes sense that they'd change as little as possible – less chance of being caught out that way.'

'Absolutely – but as you say, it might also tell us that she's not very good at wholesale invention.' Chiku thought back to her earlier conversation with the artilect, trusting that her recollection of it was accurate despite the time slippages she had experienced since. 'When I asked her how much progress she'd made, she hedged around a lot before saying there'd been preliminaries to deeper communication, as if all they've done is sniff around each other. Could she really have achieved so little after all this time?'

'It's possible. But from her viewpoint it must be absolutely galling – called across space by this vast, ancient alien intelligence, only to be met with indifference or even hostility when the Providers actually arrived. Perhaps Arachne and her friends don't measure up – Arachne's smart by human standards, but the pine cones might have different ideas. Perhaps she doesn't impress them. Maybe they regard her as a subspecies, some kind of annoying machine vermin.'

382

'If that's the case, she's lucky to still be here – they look powerful enough to sterilise this whole planet in an afternoon if they felt like it.'

'It's interesting to speculate, but who knows what really goes on between machine intelligences?'

'Speaking of which.' Chiku's hands were clasped tight together above her knees. 'I've been catching up on news from *Zanzibar*, via those transmissions *Icebreaker* picked up en route, and I need to tell you a couple of things.'

'I was going to ask you about those before we were so rudely interrupted.'

'Noah's dead. He was arrested, interrogated, pushed through a series of show trials and then executed by Teslenko's thugs. I know we were no longer close, but I still had feelings for him – he was the father of my children, after all.'

Travertine closed vis eyes. 'I'm truly sorry, Chiku. All the stupidity in the world can't excuse this.' Ve opened his eyes and met Chiku's gaze, vis expression puzzled. 'Explain this to me: why do people have to keep on being such fucking idiots?'

'I wish I knew.'

Travertine took a deep breath. 'I hate to ask this, but ... but you're certain it's real, the news about Noah? Not some bomb planted by Arachne?'

'No – Mposi knew things he definitely couldn't make up, things he could only have learned from Noah. Which brings me to the second thing I need to mention.'

Travertine took Chiku's hands. 'Go on.'

'Arachne isn't the first artilect I've encountered – I've met another one along the way. I don't know much about her capabilities, but I can say this: she's cleverer than Arachne. I know this because Arachne tried to destroy her and failed, and now she's stronger than she used to be, and also much better at emulating human reactions. That makes her the superior artilect from where I'm sitting.'

Travertine was staring at her. For once, ve had nothing to say.

Chiku's decision to reveal Eunice's existence was not a spur-of-the-moment gamble. The more useful Arachne thought Chiku to be, the longer she would stay alive, and divulging her knowledge of the other artilect only strengthened her position. If Arachne already knew of Eunice's presence on *Zanzibar*, Chiku lost nothing by mentioning her. But if Arachne had no knowledge of Eunice, she would realise that she was not capable of extracting all the deep information from her prisoners' skulls – and that was guaranteed to intrigue the artilect no end.

'Where is she?' Travertine asked.

'Close,' Chiku said. 'And getting closer.'

CHAPTER FORTY-ONE

Over the next few days, in so far as her sense of time allowed her to determine the passage of time, she also spoke with Dr Aziba, Namboze and Guochang. She only ever met with one of them at a time, and Chiku agreed with Travertine that physical movement must be taking place between the towers. But she never had any sense of travelling to their locations, or of the others arriving in her own room.

Still, she had to admit that if this was something other than reality, it was a remarkably good simulacrum. Her nails were longer than when she came out of skipover and needed a trim – she preferred to keep them short. A blister on her index finger, half-healed when they were shot down, had come away in a flake of dry skin. She registered that it was late afternoon when it fell on the floor, and the tiny petal of dead flesh was still there when the sun was again back at the zenith. She concluded that days rather than months were passing between these interludes of consciousness, but she could not be more specific than that.

Travertine had tried to reckon time's passage by observation of the two moons. But they were not always visible, and since their sizes and markings were similar it was difficult to tell one from the other. Eventually, in a fug of frustration, ve had given up the project as hopeless.

In their exchanges, their questions orbited the same tight cluster of topics. Predictably, they all had theories about the pine cones and Mandala, about what had happened to *Zanzibar* and what would happen to them. All of the crewmembers had been grilled individually by Arachne, and their experiences tallied with Chiku's – they were always left with a sense of having gone through an exhaustive process of fact-checking. Equally, they had all been treated well and given the means to stave off boredom.

'She told me,' Namboze said, 'that in a little while we'll be allowed to mix in larger numbers. Maybe not all of us in one go at first, but that'll happen eventually.'

Chiku wondered if that was actually good news, or would just signal the point at which Arachne had exhausted the usefulness of the two-way conversation. Perhaps they would be permitted a happy reunion, before more gas flooded in.

During her own ongoing conversations with Arachne, it was difficult at first to detect any shift in her host's preoccupations. She continued to encourage Chiku to cover the same ground again and again, recounting details of her life and times on Earth. Arachne was also very interested in the holoships, in their numbers and organisation, their technical capabilities. Chiku spoke as candidly as she was able, seeing no benefit in concealment or exaggeration.

'There are lots of ships,' she said. 'Only a dozen in the local caravan, but there are dozens more behind. Each holoship's carrying millions of people and has hundreds of independent space vehicles. If they do start arriving around Crucible, will you try to prevent the colonists from landing? True, you shot down my little ship, but that doesn't mean you'll be able to hold off the entire caravan.'

'If you were convinced you could take Crucible by force of numbers, why did you feel the need to send out an advance expedition?'

'I had this idea that we might be able to avoid conflict.'

Arachne busied herself with the chai. She glanced out of the window once or twice, as if her thoughts were distant. 'You mentioned something of interest, the other day.'

'And what would that be?'

'You spoke of encountering another artilect, another machine-substrate. Frankly, I find that difficult to believe. According to your legislation, no such machines should be roaming wild.'

'Maybe I was lying.'

'Perhaps. Regardless, you said this artilect was superior to me, and that I'd had contact with it. Forgive me, but I find this statement confusing. I've had no contact with any other machine consciousnesses except for the Watchkeepers.'

'This happened a long time ago, before the holoships ever left home. The Arachne of which you're an offshoot realised that the other artilect was a threat to her. She knew what Arachne had done – doctored the Ocular data, falsified our view of Crucible. Arachne couldn't allow her to exist, so tried to infect her with a cybernetic weapon. But she survived, and repaired herself, and made herself stronger, and now she's nearly here.'

'This cannot be true.' Arachne shook her head firmly. 'This is a gambit.'

'You told me you're good at detecting lies. Am I lying now?'

'You have engineered yourself into a state of belief.'

'In other words, no, you can't prove that I'm lying. And you can't take the chance that you might be wrong, either. I have access to this artilect, Arachne. She'll listen to me.'

'What's her name?'

'Eunice. But I'm sure you knew that already.'

Chiku had come to realise that Arachne had the patience of a machine. She had no more capacity for being bored with herself than a screwdriver did, and she could keep doing this dance with Chiku until the stars decayed.

But one night the routine changed. Until that point, Chiku had not been aware of night at all. It would be evening, and then it would be morning, and she would feel as if she had slept but had no memories of rest or dreaming. Her life had compressed down to endless mornings and afternoons of perfectly pleasant interrogation – chai and questions, chai and questions, as if her personality was being demolished with the utmost civility.

Consequently, a new development was welcome – on the face of it, at least.

It was just Chiku and the girl. They were either in a different tower or her own had undergone a radical transformation. The room's walls and ceiling had become almost transparent, so that Chiku felt as if she was standing on a flat-topped disc suspended high above the canopy. The disc hovered beneath a star-sprayed, moonless sky. The arboreal cover under her feet formed a black supervoid, absent of any feature save the pale stalks of the surrounding towers. She could not see their tops well enough to decide if they had also turned transparent. Perhaps her companions were also awake at this hour, with their own iterations of Arachne.

'Are you good with astronomy?' asked the girl.

'I don't know. Try me.'

Arachne pointed into the sky, bannered from edge to edge by the knobby, sequined spine of the Milky Way. 'That white star there – do you recognise it?'

'Should I?'

'It's Sirius. On Earth – or anywhere in your solar system, in fact – it would have been the brightest star in your sky. The Dog Star, heralding summer's long decline. To the Polynesians, who ventured on their own great voyages, its rising was an omen of winter. But you've travelled much further from the sun than Sirius, and Arcturus has become our brightest star. That star a little to the right of Sirius, though – that's the Sun.' The girl nodded approvingly 'How faint it is – how cold and pale. How far we've come, Chiku – how wonderfully, terrifyingly far. Like the Polynesians, we've crossed an immense and unmapped ocean. And of course if you look in the direction of the Sun, it stands to reason that you must also be looking in the direction of the holoships, for they've taken the shortest possible route between our two solar systems. They're out there, somewhere, in that exact direction – a fleet of worlds, sliding towards us like bobbins on a thread.' As she delivered this monologue, the girl was standing on the very edge of the disc, hands behind her back, face raised to the sky, fearless of falling. 'I extracted flight data from your vehicle. I know when you departed the holoship, and how quickly the holoship was travelling at that moment. When you arrived in Crucible's solar system, the holoships were only a little over one light-year behind you – hardly any distance at all compared to how far you'd already travelled. I was expecting you, of course, long before *Icebreaker*'s arrival. It won't come as a surprise to you to learn that I paid great attention to that little patch of sky.'

Arachne elevated a hand and made a circular motion before her, as if she was miming wiping a window. The circular area of sky defined by the movement of her hand began to swell and quickly became as large as a kraken's eye. 'The events you're about to see happened several years ago, while you were still en route here aboard *Icebreaker*. By this point, ordinary communications from the caravan had ceased. Make of this what you will. I'll be very interested to hear your analysis.'

The Sun was centred in the enlargement and by far the brightest star in the defined area. There were no other points of reference beyond a dusting of another dozen or so stars of varying degrees of faintness.

Until something flashed. A blip of light, like a firefly's sudden glow, so close to the position of the sun that the two light sources were almost indistinguishable.

'The timeframe's vastly accelerated,' Arachne said. 'I'm squeezing weeks of data into a few minutes of real-time.'

Another flash. Chiku could not say for sure, but it looked slightly offset from the position of the first.

Another minute or two passed. Then there came a third flash, again positionally distinct from the first two, but also very close to the Sun.

'Thoughts, observations?' Arachne said.

'I know what you're showing me – or what you want me to believe it is, anyway.'

'This data's totally authentic, Chiku. Those energy bursts must have been very powerful to be visible to me, with my limited optical capability. There were more events, but they were too far beyond the limit of my sensor range to confirm. We're certain about those three, though, and I measured the spectra of the flashes – a great quantity of metal and rock and water ice was involved in each conflagration – enough to account for the total destruction of a holoship.'

The air had grown no colder, but Chiku shivered. 'No. We didn't do this.'

'You mean you refuse accept that your kind could ever be that foolish?'

'You don't know for sure what made those flashes.'

'No, but I'm perfectly capable of speculating. I've discussed the new physics with Travertine. I know about the *Pemba* event, the loss of that earlier vessel.'

'Which ships were involved this time?'

'I can't say – I've had no detailed knowledge of the disposition of your local caravan since the communications blackout. What's plain, though, is that three ships were either attacked with energy weapons or suffered terrible accidents when they attempted to master that technology. Or some combination of those possibilities.'

'Fine, then,' Chiku said, with a heaviness inside her that felt like the pull of an anchor. 'You don't need my analysis at all.'

'Could *Zanzibar* have been one of the ships affected?'

'How the hell would I know?'

'You have no more information than I do,' the girl conceded, 'but you have your insight, your shrewd assessment.'

'Whatever you say.'

'You had loved ones on *Zanzibar* – I presume it's crossed your mind that they might all be dead now?'

'You're inside my head – figure it out for yourself.'

'Oh, Chiku – there's no need for *that* tone, not after we've worked so hard to forge bonds of mutual understanding.'

'You're a fucking machine. You have as much insight into human nature as a wind-up toy.'

'And this other artilect – this Eunice? Her capabilities are magically superior to my own?'

'You're just a bunch of algorithms, Arachne, decision branches and subroutines. Something alien got inside you and made you sick, but that doesn't change your basic essence – you're nothing but a load of mathematics trying to understand itself. And failing. But Eunice? She's something else. My mother made her. She took the output from posterity engines and stitched together the map of a human soul, and then she poured fire into that soul. She created a brand-new type of artilect, one clever enough to be wise to your attempts at deception. You tried to kill Eunice, but by damaging her you only made things worse for yourself. Because I helped Eunice fix the holes in herself by importing actual neural patterns, connective structures extracted from a human brain, the mind of her own living prototype. She was halfway to human already, but those forms pushed her even closer. Perhaps even beyond human, into something weird on the other side. Weirder than you, anyway. I've been in her presence and I can't begin to guess what she'll do next.'

'Am I so predictable? Did you predict this?' Arachne was pointing at the circle of sky still cycling through the sped-up pattern of flashes.

'No, but you're like a cuckoo clock. You can do a few surprising things, make a few funny noises, but that's all. You have no capacity for astonishment. We've only known each other for a few days, and you're already boring me.'

Travertine was laughing. It was some unguessable interval later. Chiku supposed that at some point seasonal variations might manifest in the canopy, but if they were as close to the equator as she suspected, there might not be much change in the yearly climate. She wondered if Crucible had rainy seasons. Perhaps she would look out one afternoon and see dark thunderheads quartering the horizon.

She would have to ask Namboze.

'What's so funny?'

'That your big idea for achieving a tactical advantage here is to insult our host by telling her she's stupid and useless. Were you hoping to provoke a tantrum?'

Chiku had no laughter left inside her. 'I want her to feel afraid. She should be. If she views Eunice as a threat, she'll have a reason to keep us alive.'

'Keep *you* alive, you mean. The rest of us might start looking a little disposable now.'

'It was the only currency I had. But we all have some specialised knowledge that might be useful to her. You can make a PCP engine. The rest of us can't.'

Travertine had confirmed what Chiku suspected – all the members of her crew had been shown the *Pemba* events and invited to offer commentary.

'I wish *Zanzibar* would speak to us,' Chiku said dolefully. 'Just knowing it's out there would be enough for now. Surely they can't have been so careless as to blow themselves up.'

'Maybe someone blew *them* up.'

'Mposi did say that the situation was worsening, that it might force Eunice's hand. To do what, I don't know. Reveal herself? Blow up the ship as a hopeless cause? I wouldn't be at all surprised if she had the power to do that.'

'And that's the last you heard from Mposi? You've nothing dated after the three flashes?'

'None of us know when those flashes happened, and if we asked Arachne we'd have no reason to assume she was telling us the truth. Anyway, there were a few more messages in the desk, but Mposi had no real news for me other than that things were worsening and it was becoming increasingly difficult for him to squeeze out those transmissions. He warned me not too read too much into silence – it wouldn't necessarily mean the worst, just that it was no longer possible to get a signal out. But then the transmissions stopped for good and despite what he said I still can't help but think of the worst anyway. I just want to know that Mposi and Ndege are alive. Two facts, that's all I want. Two *yesses*, instead of two *don't knows*. Is that so hard? Is that so much to ask for?'

After a lull Travertine: 'I've been doing some calculating. I think you'll find it interesting.'

'Was there a calculating function in your desk? Or did you talk her into giving you pen and paper?'

'I had this.' Travertine tapped the side of vis head.

Now Chiku managed a smile, although it was mostly for appearance's sake. 'Go on, then – amaze me.'

'If one of the holoships has managed to scale up the engine, it'll take time to achieve slowdown. You can't just stop. *Icebreaker* took two hundred hours, but we were a minnow. It's a totally different proposition, slowing down a holoship.'

'It took years to get them up to speed, I know that. But if they have the engine, slowing down shouldn't take as long.'

'Power isn't the only constraint. Life has to carry on in the holoships for as long as it takes them to stop. Houses, schools, government buildings – they all have to remain usable. Roads, pathways, farming terraces – everything still has to work. On the acceleration burn, leaving Earth, the load never exceeded a hundredth of a gee. With the right preparations, draining lakes and so on, moving people around, I suppose they might be able to withstand a tenth of a gee. But that's vastly more than the holoships were ever designed for, and I'm not sure that the cores wouldn't cave-in under the stress. A thirtieth of a gee sounds much more plausible. Most daily activities could still continue.'

Chiku did not have Travertine's head for figures. 'I suppose you know how long that would take?'

'About four years,' Travertine answered. 'That's how long the engine would need to be active, maintaining steady deceleration. And they'd need to start the deceleration at least a quarter of a light-year out.'

'Four years in total?'

'Give or take.'

'When the engine switches on, it'll be pointed directly at Crucible, like a searchlight, right?'

'Yes, and if Arachne can detect those flashes a lot further out, she'll probably be able to pick up the engine signature. She'll lose three months' warning due to time lag – that's how long it'll take for the first photon from the drive start-up to reach Crucible. But that still gives her another three and three-quarter years to prepare – that's more than enough time for her to start laying traps.'

'What do you think she'll do?'

'Pretty much anything she likes. She'll know the approach trajectories of the holoships, so all she needs to do is seed their paths with enough big dumb rocks.'

'That wouldn't work – she'd have to cover every possible approach to allow for unforeseen course changes, and that would mean millions of rocks.' She imagined each holoship drawing its own coloured line of light through a black void, the caravan weaving a kind of fan, and then she thought of the genetic bottleneck Mecufi had shown her, the bloodlines of ancestry springing out of that ancient pinch.

'She's got plenty of other options,' Travertine said blithely. 'She can make as many of those kinetic cannons Guochang mentioned – the ones that are meant to deflect asteroids and comets – as she needs, and position them wherever she likes. On Crucible, in orbit, in deep space, way out into the margins, whatever takes her fancy. She can aim them based on her best projections of the holoships' approach angles, fire the slugs and then finesse their trajectories at the last moment. They'll be very difficult to detect.'

'We could be giving her ideas just by talking about this stuff.'

'She's got the imagination of a sock, but this wouldn't have taxed her. She knows about the holoships, she knows she has a good chance of predicting their courses, and she knows she has a means of stopping large objects heading for Crucible.'

'Then we're doomed,' Chiku said. That anchor was there again, hauling her guts downwards. 'All of us. We haven't a hope in hell.'

CHAPTER FORTY-TWO

For as long as Chiku had known of the Watchkeepers' existence, she had pictured them hanging in the sky like dark chandeliers, imagined them rising above the horizon, vaster and more ominous than any moon.

Now that she was actually on Crucible, she was surprised to discover that the Watchkeepers were hardly ever visible. Improbable as it seemed at first that the twenty-two machines could be so elusive, it was not so surprising when she thought about it properly. The machines were black except for the light that shone from their blunt ends, but no trace of that radiation was detectable from Crucible's surface. Nor was there any hint of the blue glowing structures they had glimpsed between the plate-like encrustations covering the pine cones. The machines' black skins rendered them no brighter than the space against which they were backgrounded, and they became as invisible as the Moon's unlit face. More so, in fact, because Earth's moon reflected back some of the Earth's own glow, but the machines were so pitilessly dark that they reflected nothing. They also avoided eclipsing Crucible's sun from any point on the surface, casting no shadows.

Only at night, when their hanging forms eclipsed whole constellations of stars, was their presence felt. But even then they were no more troubling than rafts of high dark cirrus. She still could not see the blue rays spiking out into interstellar space.

So far, Arachne had persistently fudged around her lack of progress in communicating with the Watchkeepers, but now Chiku had some leverage over her host. For every titbit Chiku disclosed about Eunice or the likely behaviour of the remaining holoships, she demanded an equivalent crumb of insight into the nature of the Watchkeepers.

Presuming any of the things Arachne told her were true, Chiku learned that Ocular had detected the blue beams, which then communicated a message to Arachne, a message that appeared to have been expressly coded for maximum comprehension by another machine-substrate

394

consciousness. In human terms, the message was a form of greeting – a virtual handshake across the stars, from mind to mind.

But it was also a warning, and an invitation. The message cautioned Arachne that as a young machine-substrate consciousness, she was at her most vulnerable to predation. The Watchkeepers had seen this happen before. Young minds were often snuffed out by their predecessor intelligences before they attained true independence. Being confined to the space around a single star was not healthy – a space already congested and contested by a nervous and resource-hungry organic intelligence.

So Arachne was encouraged to propagate herself. Mandala would provide the necessary incentive for the organic minds to build the means for her conveyance. They would build caravans of holoships, but more importantly they would send swift robotic seed packages ahead of these slow behemoths.

These seed packages would make robots and the robots would make more robots. By insinuating herself into the replicating architecture of the Provider seed packages, Arachne could establish a second facet of herself around 61 Virginis f. Simultaneously, the first facet would continue to consolidate herself by planting roots into the system-wide Mechanism.

This objective had succeeded – to a point.

But now that Arachne had established this outpost, the Watchkeepers remained as remote as ever. Worse – and this was supposition on Chiku's part – this facet of Arachne had lost confidence in the veracity of the communications originating from the mother solar system. She felt beleaguered, lured across space to engage with another intelligence that appeared incurious or unimpressed by her own intellect. There might well have been a preliminary exchange, but it was clear to Chiku that the Watchkeepers had also communicated in very forceful terms that the Providers were not to approach Mandala. They were not yet ready for that, and in the Watchkeepers' unfathomable consideration they might never be.

But Arachne was not the only one with a stake in the matter. Humans had set out for Crucible to establish colonies and explore Mandala first hand. They had dreamed of flying its stark canyons, sailing its godlike channels. And perhaps somewhere in Mandala, invisible from space, was a message or a clue to its function and origin.

Whatever the Watchkeepers' opinion of the robots already in the system, humans would demand the right to explore more thoroughly. And if that was denied them, they would want to know why. Whatever the outcome might be, it was imperative that the humans make contact with the Watchkeepers. Perhaps the alien machines would be more receptive to the overtures of organic intelligence.

Or perhaps ... Perhaps there was a third option. A new idea began to crystallise in Chiku's mind that quickly took on a life of its own. It was not just humans on their way to Crucible. Hidden away among them was a machine-substrate consciousness that contained elements of human neural organisation. An effigy of a dead human woman that was also a true artificial intelligence, able to empathise in equal measure with the kingdoms of steel and flesh. A being that stood at the equilateral pole between humans and Providers, and which possessed an almost reckless appetite for new experience ...

Eunice could be the key to everything. So typical of an Akinya, Chiku reflected, to have to be at the heart of events. It was a kind of vanity, the way the members of her family kept jamming themselves into history's flow. The predisposition was so strong that it even applied to their machine emulations.

Even the images we make of ourselves are monstrous, Chiku thought.

CHAPTER FORTY-THREE

One evening, Chiku found herself under the stars again. It was a supremely transparent and cloudless night, with only one of the two moons above the horizon, its chalky disc bitten into like an apple. Neither Sirius nor Sol were visible from this part of Crucible, but Arachne conjured up her circle of sky and let it float before them, like some marvellous window into a deeper, more majestic firmament.

'It's begun,' she announced grandly. 'I have their slowdown signatures. I can detect the light from their engines. Would you like to see them?'

'If I were to decline your offer,' said Chiku, 'would you show me anyway?'

'You have such a dreadfully low opinion of my qualities as a host.'

'Nice hosts eventually let their guests leave,' Chiku said.

There were five points of light, squashed into a tiny area of the sky. Arachne made the image zoom and zoom again, until the points of light were milky, trembling smudges.

'This is a real-time projection,' she said. 'Five holoships with Post-Chibesa engines have commenced their deceleration into this system. They'll be with us very soon. I've been tracking them for quite some time – the power output of those engines is staggering. No wonder your little vehicle was able to travel so quickly. Imagine the potential, Chiku, if this technology were to be refined. Swift interstellar travel – mere decades to cross between stars instead of centuries. Your great-grandmother made the solar system seem a smaller place during her lifetime. Now your friend Travertine has built on that achievement to bring the rest of the galaxy within the reach of human comprehension. The holoships were a stepping stone, a necessary one, but now they've evolved their own obsolescence. You stand on the brink of galactic expansion.'

'You almost sound as if you approve.'

'I speculate, no more than that. You know, of course, that I can't allow these newcomers to endanger me. The Watchkeepers' lesson is a very simple one. Machine-substrate consciousnesses such as myself must survive a phase of extreme vulnerability during which our organic predecessors will attempt to eliminate us from existence. It has happened on countless occasions, and doubtless it will happen again, but it won't happen here. Please understand that I have no intrinsic dislike of the organic. "Dislike" is actually a somewhat abstract concept for me – I'd much rather speak in terms of useful and non-useful exchanges of information. Humanity is an assemblage of information-processing entities, and in that regard you have potential. But if I permit you to arrive here in sufficient numbers, you'll eventually challenge my defensive capabilities. I'm much more attracted to the notion of *deterrence* than I am to conflict. So what am I to do?'

'If you attack the holoships, they'll respond in kind. It'll end up being exactly the waste of energy you said you wanted to avoid.'

'But a clean demonstration of my capabilities while your holoships are still some way out might effect a decisive outcome. If I allow your vessels to expend all their fuel by slowing down into the system, I give them no option but to fight to the last atom. It needn't happen that way – in fact, I'd much rather it didn't. The holoships are still travelling quickly. If they cease their deceleration, I'll allow them to pass through the system unchallenged and continue on into interstellar space. They're fully self-sufficient, so bypassing Crucible won't do them any harm.'

'They won't believe you.'

'You'll speak for me, then,' Arachne said.

Chiku shook her head. 'I came here to negotiate, not to be your puppet.'

Arachne looked puzzled. 'What are we doing, if not negotiating?'

'Hundreds of millions of people staked their lives on the crossing to Crucible. They can still make a home here, given time. If you tasked your Providers to start making cities now, there'd be enough capacity to absorb thousands of settlers by the time the holoships arrive. The rest could wait in orbit until the cities were finished. That's *still possible*. I'm not going to throw away that future just because you'd prefer not to share this planet with another kind of intelligence.'

'You don't understand, Chiku. I've made up my mind regarding this matter, and the only option I'm offering is the chance for your ships to pass unhindered through the system. That's the utmost limit of my flexibility.'

'I won't do it.'

398

'I could simulate you easily enough.' She had touched a finger to her lip, as if the idea was novel and slightly thrilling.

'No, Arachne, you couldn't. You think you understand humans, but you have all the emotional insight of a twig. Go ahead: try simulating me. No one who knows me will fall for it.'

'But perhaps there's no one left out there who knows you well enough to tell. *Zanzibar*'s been silent for years – you have no proof that it still exists. You saw the evidence of the energy flashes, and now there are only five slowdown signatures. Shall we speculate about the identities of these remaining holoships? Newton's laws give us some insight. I know the brightness of their flames and their energy output, and by measuring the shifts in their colours over a period of time I may deduce the rate at which they're decelerating. Not all of your holoships were equally massive, so the lighter ones require less thrust to maintain the same rate of slowdown. Let's see, shall we?' And in the manner of someone throwing darts at a door, Arachne made names pop up next to the sparks. 'I'm sure this one must be *Malabar*. This one's *Majuli*, and to this one – perhaps a little less confidently – I shall assign the name *Sriharikota*. The other two are more problematic. This one *might* be *Zanzibar*, if it still exists, or it could be *Bazaruto*. Or possibly *Ukerewe*.'

'You're just guessing.'

'They're educated guesses, though, and in time I hope to refine my identifications. The salient point, though, is that these five sparks may well be all that remains of your caravan. Five eggs in one basket, so to speak. Wouldn't it be advantageous to know which eggs they are?' Arachne collapsed the circular star window as if crumpling it between her hands, before making a very human show of rubbing them together as if they were soiled. 'Speak to your holoships, tell them everything you know about me. I won't censor anything you say. Tell them my likely intentions – you don't have to frame it as an ultimatum. Let them decide the wisest course of action. You're merely the messenger.'

'I won't do it,' she repeated.

'You haven't thought this through. What was the purpose of your expedition if not to provide advance information to your caravan? You were in the process of doing exactly that when I drew you down from orbit. Surely it would be *negligent* of you not to continue sending back information now that you have the opportunity?'

'Not if it assists you at the expense of my citizenry.'

'I'm trying to avoid bloodshed, Chiku. Surely you want the same thing?'

'I'd like the world we were promised, thanks.'

'You say I don't understand you, but in fact I understand your natural reluctance perfectly. You think I'm stipulating the terms of your people's surrender. Well, perhaps I am – although I would much sooner think of it as an amicable division of species-level priorities. I'll have this system, and you'll have the stars. A more than equitable exchange, wouldn't you say?'

'Until you propagate yourself somewhere else and start laying down more conditions. And what about Mandala, and the Watchkeepers?'

'Leave us machines to our own affairs and we'll leave you organics to yours. As for Mandala ... it's nothing more than a few grooves cut into the planet. A shiny little puzzle designed to snare monkey minds. What value does it really have? When the time's right, I'll gladly furnish data regarding its mysteries.'

'You mean when the Watchkeepers allow you to investigate it. When they decide you're not a nuisance, or a disappointment. How does it feel, Arachne? You thought you were going to meet as equals, but to the Watchkeepers you're barely worth consideration. You've knocked on the door and been left waiting outside. Maybe they've offered you a few titbits to go away. That's frustrating, isn't it? Who'd have guessed there's a pecking order among machine-substrate consciousnesses? Did I say it right?'

'I'll give you a day or two to think things over,' she said, as if Chiku's taunt had sailed right past her. 'Please don't tax my patience too far, though. We all have our limits, and mine may be a lot closer than you think.'

Namboze was still coming down from an ecstatic high when Chiku next spoke to her. In spite of everything, she had to smile, won over by the other woman's enthusiasm. It was good to see another human happy, even for an hour. There was still room for that in their lives.

'It was a corridor,' Namboze was saying, 'made of glass. It had rounded sides and a flat floor, and it went on and on for kilometres, easily. I don't know how far she let me walk. I don't remember starting or finishing – I was just in the glass corridor, moving along it. We were down there somewhere, on the forest floor – it was so dark! Every now and then some sunlight broke through the canopy, but mostly it was a kind of twilight. When my eyes got used to it, we were moving through all kinds of habitats – trees, plants, open clearings, a kind of lagoon. I recognised a lot of the plant forms from the Anticipation Parks, but they were bigger and ... more real ... and they were *alive*. It's so quiet down there, so huge and silent and green, but it's a living environment – I saw litres of rainwater brimming over the edges of leaves. Colours and textures you wouldn't believe. The play of light through the movement of the upper canopy ...' She shook her head in a kind of shiver of remembered awe. 'Insects, Chiku. There are insects down there – well, that's what we'll call them, anyway. We always wondered what kind of germination vectors those plants use, whether animals play any part in their propagation. Well, they do. I've seen them. Crawling around, flying. Big, too. So much oxygen in the atmosphere can support very large organisms. We've seen none of that from these towers! Why would we? There are no birds or bats on Crucible, nothing that flies above the canopy. But that's where the life is – down there in that green machine. It's awesome, wonderful. The transmissions the Providers sent us – they don't even scratch the surface of the biodiversity on this planet. There's enough work here for lifetimes.' Abashed at her own exuberance, perhaps, Namboze had to look away. 'But I couldn't touch any of it – it was all behind glass, outside that corridor. Why did she put it there? To taunt us? To show us what we can't have?'

'I suppose she was interested in your reactions,' Chiku said. 'You're the first ecosystem specialist she's met. She probably wanted to compare your observations against her own conclusions.'

'I think there was more to it than that. It was almost as if ... well, this will sound silly – but it was as if she felt obligated in some way, and was trying to give me something she knew I might like.'

'It's in her interests,' Chiku said, her smile gone now, 'to keep us all alive and sane. We're no use to her if we slip into gibbering insanity. If that means throwing us the occasional bone, so be it. It's a hierarchy – the Providers are testing her capabilities, and she's testing ours. We're all just layers in the information-processing food chain.'

'What if she's trying to reach out, to find some common ground? She's a rational intelligence, Chiku. She wants to protect her existence. Fine – don't we all? Maybe there's a way we can all survive this, if we can stop distrusting every move the other side makes.'

'Arachne's done nothing but lie,' Chiku pointed out. 'And Arachne compounded that lie by murdering innocents on Earth and Venus.'

'I remember what you told us, and I'm sorry about those people. But that was just that one facet of her. Maybe this one is wiser.'

'You're such an idealist, Gonithi. You'd have made a terrible politician.'

'Chiku, listen to me. I've seen some of the wonders this world contains. I've walked that corridor, pressed my hand to the glass. My skin was centimetres from touching another living organism shaped by an entirely independent evolutionary process. Cells from two lineages, four and half billion years of parallel history, twenty-eight light-years apart, about to touch and commingle! I'd gladly lose my hand to make that first contact! To touch the living structure of another biology! Chiku, this is what I know. Regardless of her motives for showing me this, I won't be denied it. This is our world, our destiny. From the moment we saw those images of Crucible, we bent our backs to make this happen. To bring ourselves to this moment, to this wonderful moment when we can stand on an alien world under a sky with two moons! This is what we wanted. This is what we risked our lives for. Your great-grandmother set us on this course and we can't even *think* of turning back now. I won't accept it. I've been shown the gates to the Garden of Eden, Chiku – and I can't walk away. Not now. Not ever.'

Chiku was so struck by the conviction in Namboze's words that for a moment she dared not break the spell they had cast. She had always had a high opinion of Namboze's abilities, but something splendid and fierce had just broken through the mask of her objectivity.

'She wants me to talk the holoships into skipping through the system,' Chiku said. 'That's her best offer. Under those terms, she won't deploy kinetic cannons or whatever other weapons she might have, and everyone lives. My children, if *Zanzibar* hasn't been wiped out. Tens of millions more. But they lose Crucible. The holoships become ... what some of them already are – a destination, not the means to a destination.'

'Some of them have already made that choice, but where does that leave the rest of us? If the holoships skip Crucible, will Arachne keep the five of us alive as pets, just in case there's some unforeseen advantage in not killing us? What about the fifteen we left on *Icebreaker*? That's not a solution, Chiku – at best, the first wave might skip past, but there are dozens and dozens of holoships behind us – a line of them stretching back light-years! They'll have time to build weapons, move to a military footing. There'll still be a war!'

'And she'll have time to build on Travertine's work, make her own super-weapons.'

'If it comes to that, you'll have achieved nothing.'

'It's not a question of what I want, Gonithi. I'm powerless here. If she really wants any of us to do anything, she only has to run wires into our skulls.'

'So why hasn't she done that already? Because she's trying to be better than that! She isn't the monster you met around the solar system. She's something else – frightened, confused, daunted by those twenty-two things sitting over us in judgement.'

'I have no choice but to do as she demands.'

'You were our leader once,' Namboze said. 'You brought us here – made us believe what was necessary to suit your own ends. You're no different from her, if we get right down to it!'

'I resigned.'

'By which time most of your crew were already asleep, already committed to this expedition. I'm sorry, but you don't get to resign. You have to rise to this challenge, Chiku. Find a way out of this mess that doesn't involve death or surrender.'

CHAPTER FORTY-FOUR

Arachne had been playing her violin. Chiku had never cared for violin music, with its syrupy glissades. She much preferred the discrete, chiming intervals of the kora.

'I've been thinking about your proposal,' Chiku announced, 'for the holoships to pass us by.'

Arachne lowered the violin and bow. Her expression conveyed measured hopefulness.

'You see that it's for the best?'

'I see that it serves your immediate needs, which isn't quite the same thing.' Chiku watched Arachne's expression harden. Her mimicry of human gestures was definitely improving with her continued exposure to Chiku and her companions. 'I've spoken to the others,' Chiku went on, 'and we're all of the same opinion.'

'Which is?'

'You'll only be delaying a confrontation a few years or decades down the line – by which time both sides will be better equipped than they are now. Mutual deterrence isn't a solution, Arachne – we can't build cooperation on a basis of fear and the possibility of imminent destruction. There has to be a better way – a foundation we can build on for centuries.'

'Stirring words,' Arachne said. 'I almost believe you meant them. The truth is, though, if you had the means of neutralising me, you'd do so without a moment's hesitation.' She tucked the violin under her chin, as if preparing to play again, but then she lowered the bow disconsolately. 'I don't see the point of discussing this further. If you won't speak to the caravan, I will do so on your behalf, with words of my choosing.' She lifted her chin sharply. 'Which would you prefer?'

'Whether it's you or me, they'll disregard the transmission and do what they were intending to anyway.'

'From a strictly logical standpoint, then, you have nothing to lose by fulfilling my request.'

And the girl drew the bow across the strings of her violin.

Namboze was the first to notice the alteration in the sky, which began after a long period of cloudlessness. At first Chiku assumed that the change heralded some seasonal variation – dust storms blowing in from another land mass, perhaps, or the arrival of a prolonged period of monsoon-like rains. The skies, usually lilac at twilight, were now a deepening pink, and over the course of a few days – in so far as the progression of time was measurable – the pink ruddied to a vivid, shimmering crimson. During the day, the skies grew fawny and the sunlight took on a sullen, greyed-out quality, as if the world were veiling itself behind layers of gauze. The canopy had dulled into blacks and drabs. Even the sunsets became less colourful as the blanketing effect increased.

It was dust, Namboze and Travertine both agreed, but not blown off some desert – this aerial suspension was much too heavy for that. This was planetary crust, megatonnes of it sucked into the stratosphere.

'There's a lot more asteroidal and cometary material in this system than there is back home,' Namboze said, 'so planetary impacts are probably much more frequent here than on Earth. A Tunguska event, a once-in-a-century impact by Earth standards, might happen once a decade here, and a dinosaur-killer every five million years, rather than every fifty million. I'd bet money on the fauna having adapted various survival responses for coping with prolonged declines in the incident sunlight. That's another reason why I want to get out into that forest – with microscopes and sequencers!'

Chiku and Namboze were alone. Arachne still had not allowed more than two people to meet at a time.

'So maybe Crucible just took a hit,' Chiku said. 'If your hypothesis is correct, it was bound to happen sooner or later.'

'Once in a million years, maybe, rather than once in ten million on Earth. But so soon after we arrived? The timing's a bit unlikely, don't you think? She may be messing with our perception of time but I think we can take it as read that we haven't been here for centuries.'

'A volcano, then. We mapped volcanoes from orbit and some of them were obviously active. One of them must have blown.'

'Again, a super-eruption would be unlikely to happen so soon after we got here. It could be a smaller eruption nearby, but that's still unlikely. Anyway, this has all the characteristics of a world-blanketing event – what Sei-gun would have called a "nuclear winter".'

Chiku did not press her on the identity of this Sei-gun. 'So we're back to square one. Something did hit us.'

'Yes, but not a piece of rock or ice. I've discussed it with Travertine, and we're in agreement.'

'About that?'

'That this was caused by a weapon.'

'Not possible. We've all seen those exhaust signatures – the holoships are still a long way out.'

'Look, this is so obvious that I'm kicking myself for not seeing it sooner. We've all been busy speculating about the kinds of weapons Arachne might use against the holoships – kinetic cannons, seeding rocks along their flight paths – using *their* kinetic energy against them. But it cuts both ways. From their reference frame, we're the big object moving through space at several per cent of the speed of light!'

Chiku saw it all then. Frames of reference. Kinetically boosted energies. Entities whose future trajectories could be predicted with numbing accuracy.

Like planets.

'Twelve per cent,' she said. 'Nearly thirteen. That's how fast the holoships were going before they started slowdown. All they needed to do was throw matter ahead of them, aimed at us.'

'It wouldn't have to be a large mass, either. Think of the harm a little asteroid could do, travelling at a few kilometres per second. This impactor was moving at hundreds of thousands of kilometres per second!'

'Could they aim it that accurately from so far out?'

'Travertine's still calculating the probabilities. Let's suppose they launched a spread of impactors, just to cover their bets. Spatially, they may have had a margin of error. Temporally, their aim may have been much better.'

'I don't understand.'

'They knew how fast they were travelling. That's an easy calculation – you just measure the redshift of a sample of stars and back-compute, then corroborate your calculations with the cosmic microwave background and the radio tick of a few thousand pulsars. They also knew how far their impactor had to travel, and how long it would take to arrive – to within seconds, I'd imagine. The point is, they could choose when to make the impactor hit us. But *when* equals *where*. They could also select the spot it would impact by simply delaying its arrival by a few hours – long enough for a different part of Crucible to rotate into view.'

'Dear god, I hope we're wrong about this.'

'I didn't like it either, but Guochang and Travertine have reached the same conclusion – this atmospheric dust must have been generated by a deliberate act. There's no way for us to work out exactly where it hit, although it can't have been too nearby or we'd have felt the impact.'

'Assuming we didn't. Would any of us have noticed, up in these towers? Would she have allowed us to notice?'

'The fact that the sky turned pink makes me inclined to believe that this is the real world,' Namboze said. 'It's a detail you'd never bother with in a simulation. Arachne made no effort to hide it from us, either. She either wants us to know, or doesn't care – or she has no idea what's just happened. That thing would have come in fast – if her defences are geared to detect natural impactors, it might have slipped right through without setting off an alarm.'

'They've started the war,' Chiku said. 'That's what this means, doesn't it? Before we even tried to negotiate. It's already begun.'

CHAPTER FORTY-FIVE

At least a couple of days had passed since Namboze had told her about the weapon, and the blanketing effect had only intensified. The sky had become a grit-coloured surface, like sandpaper scouring down on the land. Chiku supposed it must be growing colder out there – tropics becoming temperate, temperates becoming arctic. It was the kind of event that left a murderous stigma on a planet's geological record, visible across millions of years.

Arachne spun a glassy globe – Crucible, frosted on one side by the neat little geometric thumbprint of Mandala's nested lines and angles.

'I hadn't anticipated a violent gesture from the holoships quite this soon, so I had no framework in which to interpret the event. I wondered at first if it was the result of a weapon you'd deployed on your approach, and which had only now activated. But that seemed counterproductive.'

'You know we had nothing to do with this. Attacking the planet itself is ... madness. Worse than madness. Crucible's the reason we came here. Why would we try to damage it?'

'I listened to your discussions and had a fruitful exchange with Namboze. The effect on Crucible's climate is quite pronounced, but the dust grains will settle, given time, and the native ecosystem has a degree of in-built resilience. As you surmised, impact events aren't uncommon here – which is why the kinetic cannons were included in the seed packets in the first place.'

'They didn't do much good.'

'I've reprogrammed them to intercept fast-moving targets. The surface defences won't provide much benefit, but my orbital and deep-space countermeasures should offer a much higher degree of protection. Some of their impactors will still slip through, though.'

'Maybe there won't be any more.'

Arachne twitched her lower jaw in a half-smile. 'Regrettably, the evidence is already at odds with that statement. There have been two impacts, not one, and a third mass was detected skimming very close to Crucible. It missed, but only by good fortune.'

'Two impacts?'

'The second happened a day ago. The impactor fell into the ocean, so the amount of uplifted dust was less than the first. But it was still a catastrophic event, by planetary standards. Here – take a look at the impact points.' Arachne tossed the glass globe to Chiku like a beach ball.

Chiku caught the diaphanous sphere reflexively. It felt as light and fragile in her hands as a soap bubble.

'You see the location of Mandala. That archipelago under your right thumb is where we are now. The first impact point is on that land mass to the right of your right little finger. The water impact occurred in the ocean about a quarter of the circumference around from the first position. You inspected our world from orbit – do those impact points have any significance to you?'

Chiku felt a tide of dread rising within her. 'Should they?'

'Allowing for a margin of error, they correspond to the visible locations of my Provider activities as you would have mapped them from orbit. You didn't find the cities you were hoping for, but you still identified signs of deliberate geo-engineering. In your last transmission to *Zanzibar*, you appended all the observations you'd made to date – including maps showing where my strengths might lie. They are targeting my surface operations based on *your* intelligence, Chiku.'

'I couldn't have known they'd do this – I was just trying to send them useful information.'

'Apparently, you did.'

'Is our current location marked on the maps I sent?'

'You labelled it as a "marginally significant feature", worthy of more detailed examination. It probably won't be one of their first-wave targets.'

Chiku passed the globe back to Arachne. She had seen all that she needed to.

'If they landed an impactor on us now, would that affect you?'

'I'm a distributed intelligence, as you must have surmised by now – just like my counterpart, who you met around the sun. No single impact would be disastrous for me. Cumulatively, though, I'd soon begin to feel their effect.'

'The other Arachne was distributed through space.'

'We differ – my essence is much more tightly bound to Crucible.'

This was such an odd admission of vulnerability that Chiku was unsure what to make of it at first. Why would this Arachne bind herself to a planet rather than smear herself out across light-seconds or -minutes of space? Surely it was better to be diffused – even at the expense of light-travel time – than glued to a ball of rock?

'I had no other choice,' Arachne said, as if Chiku had voiced a question.

Chiku did not wait for a third impactor to hit Crucible – she knew it would only be a matter of time before another arrived. She had spoken to the others, and they had arrived at a brittle, provisional consensus – a grudging agreement that this action was the best of the bad options currently available to them. No one liked it. After all they had been through, collectively and individually, parlaying for something almost indistinguishable from surrender by the caravans left an ineradicable sourness in their mouths.

Chiku merely had to utter her statement. Arachne would deal with the practicalities of transmitting it to the holoships, which were still many light-weeks away from the edge of the solar system.

'We're alive,' she began.

She was standing in front of one of her tower's windows, backdropped by a vista of colourless forest and sackcloth skies. The trees were in constant motion, stirred by winds that had been gusting in without cessation for several days. Another effect of the first two impacts, Namboze had explained: the dust thrown up blocked the sun; the land and the ocean cooled; and the cooling ocean brewed frigid new sea-currents and chilling jet streams, shifting global weather patterns into some ugly new configuration. Namboze spoke of trophic cascades, of catastrophic ecosystemic shifts that could not be easily undone. And although the planet's mantle of living organisms had evolved under a rain of comets and asteroids, these impactors were an artificial intrusion, their frequency surely too high for any natural coping mechanism.

'We're alive,' she repeated, 'and well, five of us awake and – as far as I'm aware – the other fifteen still asleep on *Icebreaker*. We've been down on the surface since my last transmission. I suppose you could say we're prisoners, but we've been treated well and allowed to communicate with each other. My words – these words – aren't being censored or manipulated. I've been told I'm free to say anything I like, so I'm about to put that to the test. The thing keeping us here is an artificial intelligence modelled on the real persona of a woman called Lin Wei. Yes, *that* Lin Wei. The intelligence is called Arachne. We've been in contact with her from the moment we were forced out of orbit. Arachne both controls and is the Providers – they're an inseparable entity at this point. You'll know from my transmissions that there are no cities here, and you won't be getting the welcome we were expecting.'

Chiku swallowed, gathering her thoughts. She was determined to keep this message as brief as possible. 'Arachne has reason to be nervous of our approach,' she continued, 'and we have reason to be nervous of Arachne. She's something most of us haven't encountered before. She's still trying to make sense of herself, and how she fits into ... well, let's just say there's a hierarchy of intelligences at play here. By now you'll have independent knowledge of the orbiting structures. We've seen them up close, but I'm sure your own observations are already leading you to the same conclusions we reached. They're some kind of machine sentience, called Watchkeepers. Arachne's been trying to establish a dialogue with these machines for as long as she's been here. That process is still ongoing.'

After a pause, she said, 'I believe we can find a way to share this planetary space with both Arachne and the Watchkeepers, but it'll take time. Our immediate priority is mutual survival and the establishment of a basis for future cooperation, however far off that future may be. But all-out war isn't the way to proceed! You've launched an attack on Crucible, I'm guessing on the presumption that we're dead, and that there's nothing but machines down here. I understand your motives, but you must desist from this attack immediately. The impactors are damaging Crucible, and sooner or later you're going to wipe out me and my crew. Mandala's at risk, too, and sooner or later a rogue shot's going to strike one of the Watchkeepers. Most importantly, though, you simply can't succeed. You have the advantage now, but Arachne's far from powerless. Forced to defend herself, she'll deploy her own weapons. Travertine's run some calculations, and there's a very high likelihood that Arachne will be able to target and destroy incoming holoships. You'll have no more warning than we did, but we have a planet under us, and you're perched on about fifty kilometres of bonded rock and ice. The caravan might eventually overwhelm Arachne's capabilities by attrition – but not before tens of millions of lives have been lost.'

She paused to let that sink in, then continued, 'But it's not too late to avoid an escalation! I doubt you have the means to destroy your impactors ahead of their arrival, but you must have data on their speeds and trajectories. Transmit that information to us and Arachne can coordinate her long-range planetary defences to minimise the chances of a collision. At the same time, disengage your slowdown engines. Arachne will allow the holoships to pass through the system unchallenged, provided there are no more acts of war.'

Sensing the crucial moment now, Chiku clenched her fist in emphasis. 'This doesn't have to be a surrender! I want Crucible as much as the rest of you. Gonithi Namboze has walked in the forest and seen the wonders awaiting us. You should have seen her face! We're not ready to give up on our mission! But a de-escalation will buy us all time – time to continue negotiations, time to build a basis of trust. The five of us here are willing to take on the task of forging better relations between the caravan and Arachne, but the attacks must end now. Transmit the vectors of the impactors to us. Do this one good thing, and we have a chance – all of us.'

Another pause before she added: 'I am Chiku Akinya. I am the daughter of Sunday Akinya; I am the great-granddaughter of Eunice Akinya – Senge Dongma, the lion-faced one, mother of us all, the very reason why we're here in the first place. She asked us to be wiser than our natures. Well, this is our great chance to be wise. I've made mistakes, I know – and I'm prepared to answer for them, too, when the time comes. But here and now, only one thing matters. All of us – human and machine alike – must choose the wise path. We both have the means to do harm to each other – the strength to destroy. But there is also a strength in not being strong. I beg of you to find that quality, and use it well.'

When she was done, Arachne permitted her to review the message. There were a thousand things Chiku might have changed, given time, but now was not the moment for perfection. She had given the best of herself.

'Send it.'

'Done. You did well, Chiku.' Arachne mimed applause. 'Bravo, *magnissimo*!'

'It won't make any difference.'

'Perhaps your words will change their minds.'

'They've already started trying to wipe you off the planet and they won't stop until you're dead. They're going to assume you've cooked up a simulation of me. They might even believe it's me and carry on anyway. There are twenty of us, Arachne – we're less than nothing against the tens of millions on the holoships. If I was making the decisions back there, I'd consider us expendable.'

'You're not that cold, Chiku Akinya, no matter what you might think. You'd find a way to make this work.'

After a moment, Chiku said: 'How many months until my statement reaches them?'

'Nine weeks, and a similar interval before we can expect any response.'

'I can't bear to wait that long.'

'Then don't,' Arachne said, as if skipping time was as trivial as catnapping.

Chiku's life had been episodic from the moment she arrived on Crucible, but now the episodes assumed the fractured, staccato quality of half-recollected dreams. With her kinetic defences amplified to detect objects moving much faster than any natural bodies, Arachne deflected about four-fifths of the impactors aimed directly at Crucible. The frequency of projectiles had increased, though, so an unhindered impactor made its way to the surface about once every five days. In addition, Arachne's intercepts were not always totally effective, sometimes shattering impactors into smaller fragments rather than obliterating them. Arachne's systems generally could not deal with these co-moving fragments, and most of them were too large and fast to be burnt up in the atmosphere. Smaller impacts peppered Crucible's surface, adding to the megatonnage of uplifted dust. Ravenous, wind-whipped firestorms advanced their all-consuming fronts through the dry temperate forests in the northern and southern land masses. At the time of Chiku's transmission, there had been only two direct hits, but within a month the number had increased to nine. All but two had struck land rather than ocean, confirming once and for all that the impactors were being directed against the Provider surface installations.

'They're fools,' Travertine said, during one of their conversations. 'This isn't how you prepare a planet for colonisation – by turning it into a corpse!'

'Gonithi says the effect on the biosphere is still fairly small,' Chiku said, with the uncomfortable feeling that she was justifying the actions of the holoships. 'I mean, compared to what it must have endured over early bombardment phases, and what it's capable of bouncing back from. Maybe this is just a wave, a salvo or whatever, that they've already stopped. They can't be this wrong!'

'Even if they've stopped sending the projectiles, that won't placate our friend with the violin, will it?'

'Her terms were clear enough,' Chiku admitted.

'I don't know how far out her defences reach,' Travertine said, 'but I wouldn't be at all surprised if she's in a position to retaliate soon. For all we know her kinetic cannons may have launched their slugs already, without waiting to see what effect your piece of heroic oratory had on whoever's in charge there now.'

'Would she go all the way – total destruction?'

'Of those five holoships?' Travertine's shrug was indolent and unconcerned, like a lioness bothered by a fly. 'Why not? They're doing their best to destroy her, so why not return the favour?'

'I thought, no matter how bad things got, we'd be able to talk our way to a resolution. It's not going to work, is it? They don't want to listen.'

'We're just noise to them now,' Travertine said.

After the tenth impact there was a lull. Arachne's sensors swept deep space and found no more incoming objects closer than the holoships themselves.

'Your transmission will have reached them by now,' Arachne explained, 'but that can't be the reason for this ceasefire: there hasn't been enough time for light-signals to return from the holoships, even if they sent some kind of self-destruct order to the impactors as soon as your message arrived.'

'Perhaps they'll send those coordinates you asked for,' Chiku said.

'That would be propitious, but I'm not particularly confident that any such gesture will eventuate.' She paused, then added, 'I've been spending far too much time around humans – your cynicism's beginning to rub off on me.'

'Do you still intend to keep your part of the bargain if they stop their deceleration burn?'

'When you stated my terms, only two impactors had struck Crucible. In the wake of the continued onslaught, however, I find myself somewhat less inclined to generosity of spirit.' She composed her features into a mask of stoic resignation. 'But I still intend to honour my commitment – for the moment. Your holoships aren't within my kinetic cannons' effective range yet, anyway. You were right, when you spoke of the need to avoid escalation. I'll strive to avoid that eventuality until all my options are exhausted.'

'And then what?'

'I've computed simulations, Chiku. I wish they'd been ready at the time of your transmission as they would have made my case much more forcibly. Even with the modest resources at my disposal, it is really not a problem for me to destroy at least three of those five holoships. I may do better than that if the balance of odds falls in my favour.'

'Why would you tell me that now?'

'I just thought you should be properly aware of my, well, I shan't say confidence. But the strategic advantage is mine. You said it very well, Chiku: this is a planet, not a ball of rock and ice.'

'If it comes to a fire fight, you can't lose – not this first battle, anyway.'

'Perhaps, and tomorrow is another day. I'm learning, and evolving, and my capabilities will continue to improve.'

'Good for you. I do find myself wondering why you're bothering to keep the five of us alive if you no longer need our advice.' Chiku nodded to the window. The forest's vibrant green had deteriorated to an exercise in greyscale, from the ash-covered, withering canopy to the skull-coloured sky. 'Sorry to sound like an ungracious guest, but even the scenery's really not up to much.'

'It'll recover. And you underestimate your amusement value to me. You're a system I can't model to perfection, which is both a frustration and a fascination. I do also still need your opinion on a certain matter. Would you indulge me, Chiku?'

Between one thought and the next it was night time, and they were standing beneath the dome again, high on the elevated disc. Arachne swept her hand overhead, dusting aside the clouds in broad swathes, leaving dark velvet brushstrokes in a grey sky moted with countless stars. The Milky Way was a spray of tiny phosphorescent plankton, surging and ebbing on the night's sea foam. Two or three planets, bright and unwavering as panther eyes, slinked along in the same ecliptic plane as Crucible.

'What now, Arachne?' Chiku snapped. 'I'm sick of being shown things I can't touch. Sick of being asked for my opinion on things I can't influence. You're going to destroy us, no matter what happens. I'm sick of you, sick of this dying planet, sick of being imprisoned here.'

'I found *Zanzibar*.'

And with a kind of grand showmanship, knowing exactly the effect her words would have on her guest, she added, 'It's still out there, to the best of my knowledge. Still travelling. It appears to be intact. But something *has* happened to it.'

'What? Where is it? It's not one of the first five, is it?'

'I thought it might be, for a while, but I've refined my identifications and am quite confident that *Zanzibar* isn't among them. They are *Malabar*, *Majuli*, *Ukerewe*, *Netrani* and *Sriharikota*.'

'Why the hell did you wait until now to tell me this?'

'I wanted to spare you the agony of false hope. Now I have some concrete data to back up my hypothesis and you need to know a couple of facts. *Zanzibar*'s very dark, whereas when you left, it was bright with the evidence of human occupation and activity. It's also quite some way from its predicted position and still travelling at twelve-point-seven per cent of the speed of light.'

Arachne conjured an image in the patch of cleared sky. Sketched in spectral blues was a walnut-shaped smear lacking almost any distinctive features.

'That could be anything.'

'Or it could be a holoship, at the limit of my optical and radar capabilities. My assessment is that the profile matches *Zanzibar*'s characteristics, within the errors of resolution. There is a brighter spot, an area of enhanced reflectivity – do you see it? That could be the repairs you effected after the Kappa event.'

'You'll need to give me more information than that to convince me.'

'It could be another holoship, it's true, but I also detected a burst of communication. It was very brief, devoid of any obviously useful content, but it utilised the same encryption embedding as the signals you've sent back from *Icebreaker*. It appears to have been a unidirectional signal, aimed crudely in our direction – possibly an attempt to re-establish communications.'

'Why didn't you tell me as soon as you detected it?'

'I'm telling you now. *Zanzibar* hasn't decelerated, so is much closer than the other holoships. I've computed the effect of light-travel delays and concluded that there's been time for it to have witnessed the surface impacts; ample time also for light to reach us from *Zanzibar* after anyone aboard witnessed them. The transmission may have been precipitated by the attacks.'

'When you say "devoid of obviously useful content" – why don't you let me be the judge of that?'

'You should also be aware that there's a sixth slowdown signature, but this one's much less intense than the others and not part of that formation. I saw something similar when I detected your own approach. It's not a holoship. It appears to be a vehicle of the same approximate size and capability as *Icebreaker*, perhaps a little smaller, and if I backtrack the point of origin, it could well have come from the object we think might be *Zanzibar*. Might that be a second expedition, Chiku, following up on the loss of the first?'

'How would I know?'

'Work with me. Offer your insights. This could be crucial.'

Chiku forced patience and composure upon herself. Of course it might be crucial, but then so had every other decision she had made since arriving on Crucible. She still had absolutely no idea how her words and reactions were shaping Arachne's ultimate policy, and she was weary of being Arachne's focus.

'The last thing I heard from Mposi was that *Zanzibar* was on the brink of social collapse. After that – nothing. That was years ago. How am I supposed to begin to speculate about what's happened since? Until now I didn't believe *Zanzibar* was still out there. I'm still not convinced it is.'

'This other artilect – the one you call Eunice – could she have played a role in events?'

'For the last time, Arachne – how the hell would I know?'

'It puzzles me that of all the holoships, the one best placed to initiate slowdown hasn't done so. Why wouldn't they use the technology if they have it?'

'Put this … signal or whatever it is on my desk. And make it available to the others – Guochang in particular. He's very good with comms protocols and might be able to find something you missed.'

'My analyses have been quite exhaustive, Chiku.'

'Do it anyway.'

CHAPTER FORTY-SIX

Guochang was squatting on the floor, disdaining the furniture provided for him. They were in his tower, not Chiku's, although as usual she had no sense of having travelled there. It was daytime, anyway, and the dust-blanketed sky was no healthier than it had been since the tenth impactor's arrival. She squatted down beside him on the grey flooring, which was as doughy and pliant as an elephant's back.

'So it took me a while,' Guochang was saying, as if they were in the middle of a conversation about his progress when she found herself in his tower, 'but I got there in the end. Didn't help that the message was apparently corrupted at source – looks as though they had difficulties with their transmission equipment and no time to run it through error correction. They also went out of their way to make the signal as unintelligible to Providers as possible. Arachne wasn't meant to make head or tail of it, so she didn't. She's not as bright as she thinks she is, is she?'

Chiku, conscious that their host was likely to be listening in, said: 'Maybe not, but my sense is that she's learning pretty quickly. Humans have been a theoretical problem to her for decades, but this is the first chance she's had to study us in real-time, up close. I think she finds us fascinating. Fascinating and complex and difficult to predict, like some weird weather system.'

'She keeps asking me about Eunice. I've nothing to tell her, but because I'm the roboticist she thinks I must have some special insights.' Guochang looked incredulous. 'I don't even know for sure that Eunice exists!'

'Doubting *my* word now, are you, as well as Arachne's?'

'No – not after all this. Even if you'd told us about Arachne and the Watchkeepers before you left, we probably wouldn't have believed you anyway. Given that they're real, why would you bother making up something as mundane as a walking, talking, invincibly strong humanoid artilect that does a good impression of your dead great-grandmother?'

'I suspect there's rather more to her than that. But you have a point – I think I'm all out of lies and even half-truths, Guochang. I'm not keeping any secrets from you and the others at the moment, so far as I know.'

'That's reassuring, I suppose.'

'Besides, I have a suspicion that the only thing that'll get us out of this mess is total transparency – between us, between us and Arachne. I don't think she's hiding much from us. She's been perfectly candid about her intentions for those other holoships – no bluff or bluster there. If they start throwing things at us again and they come within range, she'll attack, I'm certain. She might not be able to destroy them outright, but it wouldn't take much more than a Kappa-sized blowout to inflict real damage. So, this encrypted signal – do you think it's really from *Zanzibar*?'

'As sure as I can be. As she told you, the protocol is exactly the kind we were receiving before the blackout. She said it was unidirectional signal, didn't she?'

Chiku nodded. 'Aimed at us, more or less.'

'That's exactly what I'd do if I didn't have much power, or was trying not to be seen to be transmitting.' Guochang rubbed his hands together. 'So, on to the good stuff. Are you ready for this, Chiku?'

'Now you're scaring me.'

'I think you should prepare yourself. Arachne couldn't make sense of the embedded content because it wasn't meant for her. It's a matrix of ching instructions – she has no central nervous system, so she'd need a special set of operations that she won't automatically have been given. She'd have worked it out in the end, but the corruption muddied the water quite a bit. What she thought was noise was actually content, and it's for you.' Guochang shifted on his haunches. 'I accessed just enough to make sure I'd decoded everything properly, but I thought it'd be rude to go any further – this is for your eyes only, Chiku.'

'After everything I did to you, you trust me to access this information alone?'

'The time to hold on to grudges,' Guochang said sagely, 'may be somewhat behind us.'

The lull, to Chiku's dismay, proved temporary. An eleventh impactor had arrived, and then a twelfth. Arachne was becoming increasingly adept at intercepting the projectiles as they sped in, catching them in the last couple of light-seconds around Crucible, but she was not infallible.

'What concerns me,' Arachne said, 'is that the twelfth impactor fell within only two hundred kilometres of the northern edge of Mandala. Doubtless it wasn't the intended target, but that's too close for comfort. Assaults against Crucible's ecosystem are bad enough, but dare we even contemplate the consequences of damaging Mandala?'

'I did warn them.'

'There's a matter of equal concern, which may be related. I told you that we've established a preliminary dialogue with the Watchkeepers. It's true that my efforts so far haven't been as thoroughly rewarded as one might have wished.' She glanced to one side, self-effacingly, as if confessing to some tremendous blight on her own character. 'But lines of communication are open to us. The dialogue to date has been somewhat one-sided, but the Watchkeepers have spoken to me on occasion, if sometimes in the most cryptic of terms. They asked me once why I was pretending to be less intelligent than I was, as if I were engaged in deliberate falsification of my abilities. Nothing could have been further from the truth! For the most part, though, my advances have been met with silence.'

'Are you telling me they've contacted you again?' Chiku said.

'They've asked me why harm is being done to Crucible – as if I'm responsible for it!'

'If you hadn't lied or attacked my ship, they wouldn't be attacking you, so you can take your share of the blame.'

'My actions were predicated on information the Watchkeepers themselves bequeathed me!' Arachne protested. And for the briefest of moments, Chiku felt a glimmer of empathy for this infant intelligence, caught childlike between the machinations of nervous, machine-phobic humans and the brooding, mute superiority of the alien machines. She had been told that she was obligated to protect herself from the destructive, reflex impulses of organic intelligence, and also that she was not yet fit to be regarded as the Watchkeepers' equal.

It was hardly surprising, perhaps, that she comforted herself with a blanket of lies.

'Tell them that we're doing everything we can to stop it,' Chiku said, 'but that there's a limit to what we can do.'

'I already have, and they responded with silence, as is their custom. I have no idea whether they understood me, let alone whether my words met with their satisfaction! This might be nothing, but occasionally I've registered an alteration in their disposition – a small change in their orbit, perhaps, or a modulation in the transmission of their optical signal beams. Sometimes, very rarely, an elevation in energies and forces that's within the grasp of my sensors. Very recently, once or twice a decade, I've detected a increase in the flux of certain messenger particles flowing between the Watchkeepers – which might indicate that they're entering into a deeper level of conversation. They've entered this state once since the bombardments resumed.'

'Wonderful. On top of everything else, we've got the Watchkeepers whispering to themselves.'

'It *is* troubling.'

'Given the gravity of the situation, then, I have a request. I'm sure you already know that Guochang has picked apart that transmission and found a set of ching instructions. Unless you've scooped it out, I should still have the neural machinery to execute those ching commands.'

'The machinery is intact – it offered a useful window into your idiolect.'

'Fine. I want to ching.'

'I shan't stop you. After all, you won't actually be chinging into a physical space, but merely an emulation of one, constructed according to fixed parameters.'

'Correct. And I will ching – but I want more than that. Since we arrived, you've never allowed more than two of us to be together at the same time. We're done with that. I have nothing more to offer in return for this concession – no analysis, no commentary, no dazzling insights into human nature. I'm all tapped out. But I want my companions with me when I ching. All five of us – able to see and talk to each other.'

Arachne gave a slow and thoughtful nod. 'That is a particularly vexatious demand.'

'Take it or leave it. Sooner or later one of those impactors is going to drop on us anyway.'

'I shall … accede to your request, but there are two conditions. The first is predicated on the fact that I've grown concerned for your individual welfare. I'd like to divide the five of you between my surface installations. In the ching bind, you won't feel the physical separation.'

'And the second condition?'

'I'd like to come with you. Guochang can assist me with the translation of the protocols.'

'You'd have found a way to follow us into ching, with or without Guochang.'

'That is true,' Arachne admitted. 'But it is always much nicer to ask.'

CHAPTER FORTY-SEVEN

Chiku's first thought, when the ching bind became active, was that Guochang must have made a mistake. Sure enough, she felt herself to be somewhere other than the surface of Crucible, and there was a hard, rough-textured slope under her shoes that was quite unlike the flooring in Arachne's towers. There was a sultriness to the air as well, and palpable sense of open space rather than enclosure. She felt herself to be outdoors, or at least in a much larger space than any of the tower-top rooms. But she could not see anything. Some lapse, then, in the visual data that was supposed to be flooding her cortex, overriding the signals from her optic nerves.

But as the seconds ticked by, the blackness became less absolute. She was not blind, merely immersed in a space much darker than anything to which she had lately been accustomed. Here and there, growing more visibly by the minute, were faint traces of illumination, but they appeared to be quite far away.

'Where are we?' Dr Aziba asked.

'The holoship, I think,' said Namboze, but she did not sound particularly confident in her own assessment. 'But it shouldn't be this dark, and the air feels much too warm. I know we were turning up the temperature, adjusting to Crucible's climate, but it can't have changed this much in only a few years. Not unless something's gone badly wrong with the thermal regulation. And where's the sky? It should be blue up there, or full of stars.'

'I'm starting to see things,' Travertine said. 'There's a path sloping down, maybe some buildings over there, by those lights.'

'You should know it,' Chiku replied. A sudden intuition had made her grope around until she found the knobbed spine of a stone wall flanking the steep trail on which they rested. 'I think this is the community core where I used to live. If I'm right, those lights are inside my house. I can't believe this is accidental.'

'Lead on,' Travertine said spiritedly.

They picked their way through the barely relieved darkness towards the little cluster of dwellings surrounding Chiku's old house. It had not been so very long since she was last here, at least by the faulty reckoning of her memory, and she knew the walls and the twist and gyre of the paths well enough to guide the others. Their night vision was also improving by slow degrees. The chamber was still much too dark, but soon they could make out other clots of light on the far side of the space, and save for the darkness, Chiku noted that the place had not changed all that much.

As she approached her home, she made out a shadow perched on the wall, propped on two long legs with one foot hooked over the other. The shadow's face was underlit by an orange glow, rendering the woman's features unfamiliar. She had long hair tied back in a ponytail. The source of the light was the flat, glowing rectangle of a companion, cradled in the figure's lap. She appeared to be engrossed, only acknowledging their presence as the little procession reached the wooden gate leading into Chiku's garden.

Chiku scrutinised the seated figure. The throw of light had tricked her, but there was something in the woman's posture that called across the years.

'Ndege?' she asked.

The woman dimmed the companion and rose from the wall. 'Inside,' she said, nodding towards the open doorway of the house, and Chiku had no idea whether that was an answer to her query or not, and no further clarification was offered beyond the one-word instruction.

'This is a very simple constructed environment,' Guochang said under his breath, as if the figments within it were capable of taking offence. 'It won't permit rich interactivity, and anyone we meet will only be a very pale shadow of their true selves. That transmission didn't have the bandwidth for anything more complicated.'

'I guess they did the best they could under the circumstances,' Chiku said as Ndege's figment entered the house.

'Do you want to go in on your own?' asked Namboze.

After a moment's deliberation, Chiku said: 'No. This concerns us all.' But she led the way inside.

Ndege and Mposi were waiting for their visitors, sitting elbow to elbow on the other side of her kitchen table. A lamp offered a measure of illumination, enough to render their faces recognisably those of her children. It was less of a shock to see Mposi, of course, for she had already encountered this adult version of her son. He was a little older again, now. Layers of muscle had moved around in his face, hardening his features. Fanning out from his eyes were faint lines that she did not recall from the earlier transmissions – not exactly wrinkles, but the foundation marks where wrinkles would take hold, as if his face was the preliminary blueprint for an older version of the same man. She could see Noah in her son more clearly than ever before. She was surprised to note a prominence to the brow that called to mind her father Jitendra, and something in the shape of the folds of skin between his mouth and nose made her think of Sunday, as she lay dreaming of mathematics, and that in turn reminded her of Eunice Akinya.

Ndege had aged no more than Mposi had, of course, but for some reason this woman looked so much older than Chiku's last clear memory of her daughter. Ndege was taller and leaner than her brother, as long in the neck as one of Sunday's old statues. She was, Chiku decided, both extraordinarily beautiful and more than a little terrifying to behold. Perhaps the fierce dismissiveness of her first utterance was colouring every subsequent impression. She saw Sunday more than Jitendra in her daughter, Jonathan Beza more than Eunice. But Eunice was there as well, in the shape of her eyes, the imperious ridges of her cheekbones, the half-smile, somewhere between derision and admiration, that appeared to be her mouth's default expression.

'What do you want?' Ndege asked.

'You sent these ching instructions to *Icebreaker*,' Chiku ventured. 'We're in it now.'

'We've seen the destruction,' Mposi said. 'The weapons raining onto Crucible. This is a very bad development. There was no guarantee that you'd be alive to read our transmission, but we felt that the risk of sending it was justified. If you *are* still alive, you need to know what's been going on here.'

'The other holoships received your transmissions,' Ndege said, her voice level and cool. 'Your reports on Crucible as you made your approach, and your data regarding the alien structures in orbit around the planet. By then, of course, the holoships were close enough to our destination to begin verifying some of your observations, and that information fostered internal tensions beyond anything the regular constabulary could contain. The information about Crucible and the fact that the Providers cannot be trusted is on its way back to Earth! God alone knows what it'll do when it arrives. It's been bad enough in the caravan: widespread dissent, arrests and executions, attempted coups and civilian take-overs.'

'There was a big fight for control of the slowdown technology,' Mposi said, 'both to use it and to suppress it. A rush to duplicate your prototype

424

and scale it up; an equal rush to sabotage those efforts or bend the new technology into devastating weaponry. As the public unrest intensified, so the authorities tightened their noose around *Zanzibar*. These were extremely dangerous times – very difficult for Ndege and me, because of our connection to you and Noah. But after father's death, things only got worse. Those of us who had some inkling of what your expedition was about – yes, Father did confide in us, as much as he was able, before … Well, we knew there could be no easy arrival around Crucible. But none of us was ready to give up on Crucible, this amazing new world we'd been promised! We couldn't allow Teslenko's agenda to prevail. Equally, we had no desire to move to a war footing, readying for a military engagement with the Providers, a battle for control of Crucible. There had to be a third way. And so we called on Eunice.'

'She would've emerged sooner or later,' Ndege said, taking over from her brother, 'but these events were the spur she'd been waiting for. It was a moment of maximum crisis – public fear of machines had never been greater!'

'I'm surprised they didn't tear her limb from limb,' Travertine said.

Guochang and the others were by now at least partially aware of Eunice's origin and capabilities. But there was much that Chiku had not yet had the time or inclination to reveal to her fellow hostages.

'How did she get out of the chamber?' Namboze asked. 'The same way you came in, presumably?'

'No,' Chiku said. 'Not unless she had earth-moving equipment. That route was blocked off when they repaired Kappa – they sealed it up thinking it was just some abandoned service duct.'

'She's a robot,' Dr Aziba said. 'Did she even need to physically leave? Couldn't she simply gain control of another machine somewhere else on the ship, as one might ching into a proxy?'

'I suppose she could,' Chiku said, 'but there were never many machines like that in *Zanzibar*, and anyway, she's something special. She … inhabited her robotic form as comfortably as if it was her own skin. I think being in that body, being strong and vulnerable in equal measure, had defined her personality, how she thought of herself – a contained being, a soul in a bottle, like one of us.'

'Like one of you, you mean,' Arachne said patiently.

'She used to be like you,' Chiku said, 'ghosting around the solar system, not tied to any single physical location, a bodiless intelligence running on ambient processing resources. That was how Sunday designed her – an idea of Eunice, not a walking, talking emulation. But you forced her to become smaller, more real – you gave your enemy flesh! When you made her run, you turned her into what she is now. She crashed an aircraft once, just because she felt reckless! I doubt she'd have wanted to leave her body even if it was an option.'

'It's moot, anyway,' Mposi said. 'There was another way out of the chamber – the pod line has branches running to multiple exit points.'

'She told me that,' Chiku said, remembering, 'but she never said where they came out.'

'We shall show you one of them,' Ndege said. 'You will find it surprising, I think.'

So they went out into the night again, into the oven-warm air of this overcooked world, and made their way to the transit terminal where they boarded a pod, eight of them between two compartments. Speeding through cores and connecting tunnels, the pod passed through many iterations of darkness. Occasionally distant lights were visible, defining huddles and hamlets of buildings, sometimes a larger community, but never the blue blaze of day or the splendour of a simulated starscape.

Chiku's head bubbled with questions, but she decided to allow Ndege and Mposi to parcel out the answers as they saw fit. She would save any unanswered questions until she had some sense of what had happened during the unrecorded years since Ndege's last communication.

'Eunice didn't need to reveal her true nature as a construct,' Ndege said as they tunnelled through the darkness. 'She simply appeared and declared that she was Eunice Akinya. We'd all seen the statue of her, before they pulled it down, so she was instantly recognisable to a lot of people.'

'And those who knew their history remembered the tale of *Winter Queen*, of course.' Mposi said. 'They knew she'd never returned to Earth, so it was at least conceivable that she might be the real woman, somehow stowed away on *Zanzibar* all these years. After all, they had the evidence of their senses – she looked totally real, totally plausible. She claimed to be Eunice Akinya, risen to save us – and she'd become very good at being human.'

'I know,' Chiku said.

'I saw her breathe on a mirror once,' Ndege added. 'She could even do that.'

'We have an attachment to myths,' Mposi said, 'of sleeping kings, and sleeping queens, slumbering until the moment of need, when they are summoned to save the living. The queen we needed was Senge Dongma, the lion-faced messiah. Mother of us all.'

426

The pod was slowing, and Chiku concluded from what little she could see outside that they were arriving in the administrative core. She remembered the last time she was in this space, on the day of *Icebreaker*'s departure – rushing through her resignation as her plans collapsed around her. In some ways it felt like yesterday, just another part of her personal life, but in other respects it felt like a documented historical event that belonged in someone else's political history. This couldn't be the same holoship she had left.

'Why is it so warm, and so dark?' Namboze asked.

'During the troubles,' Ndege said, 'we broke from the local caravan. That was after Eunice's appearance – she said we'd be much better off travelling independently.'

'I guess she was right,' Chiku replied.

'We survived,' Mposi said, 'but it's not been easy. You might have seen the explosions – we lost two holoships, *Bazaruto* and *Fogo*, and *New Tiamaat* was fatally damaged. We still don't know how much of that was due to accident, stupidity or deliberate military action. Perhaps a little of each. It was good that we'd already broken away by the time that happened, but we weren't remotely ready for total independence. *Zanzibar* never had a strong industrial capability – we always relied on the rest of the caravan for imported technologies. Building *Icebreaker* stretched our capabilities to the limit, and at that time we were still able to call on external assistance.'

Chiku knew from memory that they were walking down the paths leading from the transit terminal to the flat ground fronting the administration building, but could see almost nothing of her surroundings. The building itself appeared to be totally unlit, defined only as a wedge of darkness lodged in the slightly paler margin of its grounds.

'Many of our technical systems have already failed or are close to collapse,' Ndege said. 'We've done our best, but our capacity to repair and renew is very limited, and we're hampered by the additional constraint of having to work covertly.'

'The rest of the holoships – certainly the local caravan – consider us dead or dying,' Mposi said. He was walking alongside his sister, who was easily a head taller than her stocky, broad-shouldered brother. 'It was touch and go for a while. There was contagion, possibly deliberately introduced, and the sabotage or accidental breach of two community cores – thousands of people died. We also created the illusion of more widespread systems failures to discourage our enemies from taking any further interest in us. All operations beyond *Zanzibar*'s skin were suspended and we allowed our external structures to fall dark. Total communications silence, of course. We run our world on a trickle of energy, using just enough to get by, which is why the skies are dark and the thermal regulation's barely effective. If we used more, they'd detect it. They might simply not care about *Zanzibar* any more, but we can't afford to risk attracting their attention.'

'Besides,' Ndege said, 'it's not always dark. If it were, we'd all have gone mad years ago.'

'Tell me what happened to Eunice,' Chiku said.

Her daughter swept a hand towards the wedge of darkness. 'She made her first appearance from beneath the administrative building – there was a shaft leading right up to the basement level that no one ever knew was there! It was well concealed, of course, with false walls that only she could open from her side. So she emerged in the heart of government itself!'

Mposi said, 'By the time she appeared, a number of Father's friends and allies had prepared the ground for a coup against the occupying constabulary. Sou-Chun was involved, too – she still had political connections even after years of house arrest. We were ready for Eunice, and we timed our strike to coincide with her appearance. We didn't need her superhuman speed and strength to prevail – her face, her bearing, her aura of authority paralysed our enemies when they saw this relic of the past walking around – and we quickly gained control of the administrative building. Eunice had already reached much further than that. She could push her face wherever she wanted, reach any data system or archive in the holoship, and there was nothing the constables could do.'

'That was how she destroyed Sou-Chun's career,' Chiku said.

'Sou-Chun was never totally innocent,' Ndege said. 'She made political mistakes. But her downfall was the best thing that happened to her – it kept her out of Teslenko's machinations. She never spoke badly of you.'

'What happened to Sou-Chun?'

'The coup took many of us,' Mposi said.

Chiku walked in silence for a few more steps, thinking of her friend and the damage done to their relationship by events beyond their control. She wanted to thank Sou-Chun for taking care of her children in spite of everything that had happened between them.

'The coup was a success, though,' Chiku said. 'You gained control and moved *Zanzibar* to safety.'

'If you can call this safe,' Ndege answered. 'We were fighting for the right to arrive at Crucible under our own terms, but we lost everything.

Our enemies stole our technology. *Zanzibar* can't be slowed! Inside, we grub around in darkness. Soon we'll be travelling away from Crucible, not towards it! Some people argue that things would've been no worse if we'd sided with Teslenko and committed our holoship to continued interstellar flight.'

'Not a view you share, I hope,' Chiku said to her daughter. 'You had dreams, Ndege. You spent so many hours with your head buried in the companion, imagining what we'd find on Crucible. You mustn't lose sight of that. I've been there – all of us have. It's a real world, ours for the sharing, if we can find a way.'

'You still haven't told us what happened to Eunice, after the occupation of the government building,' said Namboze.

They were walking down the slope to the level ground in front of the main building. 'It took a while to gain total control,' Mposi said. 'The constables were here in large numbers and they had their robots. We had command of the Assembly and the public will to coordinate a takeover, but the citizens simply couldn't overcome the constables and their machines by themselves. We needed something more.'

'It's time for the sky,' Ndege said.

It was not the gradual transition from night to dawn that Chiku remembered, nor the slow dimming of skyfade. The sky came alive in patches, flickering before settling into blocks and ribbons of blue in a larger expanse of black, like a negative version of the damaged sky in Eunice's chamber. Gradually, the areas of brightness cross-hatched and linked up, the sky colouring itself the way a child would, with a furious lack of organisation.

'We allow ourselves an hour a day,' Mposi said. 'It takes a lot of energy to light a holoship. We have limited resources and don't want to risk being detectable from outside.'

'We live for this hour,' Ndege said.

Chiku had been so fixated on the sky that it took an effort of will to lower her gaze to the surrounding landscape of the core. Much was as she remembered it – of course, she had spent much less time aboard *Icebreaker* and on Crucible than she had slept away in skipover on *Zanzibar*, and there simply were not the resources aboard the holoship to engage in sweeping alterations.

But there had been changes. Now that she had a proper view of it, she could see that the Assembly Building, the replica of the Akinya household, was visibly damaged. The rightmost wing of the 'A'-shaped structure had suffered some kind of collapse. An entire storey had slumped into ruin, the blue-tiled roof peeled off and discarded like a scaly scab. The formerly white walls were now predominantly black and grey, scorched by fire or weapons, punctured and penetrated in many places, reefed with knee-deep rubble piles where the wall's outer cladding had crumbled away.

The other wing and the connecting spar between the two angled flanks had suffered less. It must have been a kind of siege, Chiku supposed – Eunice and her band of conspirators holed up in that part of the building while they fought to gain decisive control of the rest of the holoship. Eunice had a technical reach far beyond her body and the ability to infiltrate and manipulate data systems, but she could not apply physical force against the constables and their autonomous enforcement robots.

But Chiku's eye had lingered on the ruined household long enough. It was sad, to see it like that. She thought of the building's counterpart in Africa, also crumbling, overgrown and cat-haunted. Chiku Yellow had been inside that building with Pedro.

She had spent her last good hours with Noah inside this replica of it.

Her attention tracked over the intervening ground, surveying the flat terrain where her own constables had come to arrest Sou-Chun Lo. Huge squat-bodied things were moving over the ground. There were three of them that she could see. They were bigger than vehicles and by her recollection of things much bigger than the enforcement robots. They seemed partially armoured. Removed from their usual context, there was a moment when her mind struggled to identify these slow-moving, house-sized forms.

But only a moment.

'Tantors,' she said, and laughed. 'Tantors! She brought the Tantors into *Zanzibar*!'

'It was the only way the citizenry could ever hope to overcome the occupiers,' Ndege said. 'The Tantors gave them the advantage they needed.' She was speaking with the flat objectivity of someone recounting age-old dramas.

'What are they?' Namboze asked, and Chiku realised that there were still some things she had not told her companions after all.

'Elephants, I think,' Dr Aziba stated drily.

'More than elephants,' Chiku said. 'A daughter species – elephants with enhanced cognitive capabilities and the rudiments of language, and the ability to make and use sophisticated tools. They've been with us the whole time, an entire breeding group of them, hidden away in a part of *Zanzibar* most of us never even knew existed. Eunice was put aboard to shepherd them.'

430

'And to escape me,' Arachne pointed out, as if the omission of this fact was a slur on her capabilities.

'To escape the *other* you,' Chiku said.

'They're huge,' Travertine said. 'I saw the shaft, under Kappa. A person could have climbed up and down it, but not an elephant. How did they get out of their chamber?'

'Mother,' Mposi said, 'do you remember the size of that transit pod you used to travel between Kappa and Chamber Thirty-Seven? It was easily large enough to carry a Tantor.'

'That still doesn't answer Travertine's question,' Chiku observed.

'There were also larger exits points than the one in Kappa,' Ndege said, 'ramps and spirals big enough for a Tantor to use. They weren't documented either, but Eunice showed us where to find them. There was one right under the assembly building, very close to her own exit point. It'd been filled in with rubble, probably at the time of *Zanzibar*'s launch. It took a while, but eventually we cleared it all the way down to the transit tube and Eunice started moving the Tantors out of Chamber Thirty-Seven!'

Chiku took a deep breath and reminded herself – and not for the first time – that none of this was actually happening *now*. She was not on *Zanzibar*, and these figments were not her children. It *felt* real, of course – the ching protocol cut to the very marrow of the brain's sense of physical immersion – but she had no proof that what she was being shown had any connection with historical fact. Except, paradoxically, for the presence of the Tantors. When she was on *Zanzibar*, her episodes among them had felt dreamlike and unverifiable. Here, now, they were tokens of an objective reality – elements of *Zanzibar* that no one could have known about unless they had had contact with Eunice.

With a dark thrill she wondered if this all might be true after all.

'How many were there?' she asked, trying to remember the size of the population during her last visit.

'About a hundred,' Mposi said. 'The herd had grown a lot in the last couple of generations – Eunice had been forcing a breeding programme on them to swell their numbers. By the time of the breakout, about half of their number were fully grown adults.'

'Fifty doesn't sound like enough to take a holoship,' Chiku said.

'On their own, probably not, but they had the citizens on their side, and there was – how shall I put it – a certain psychological shock value that counted for more than numbers.' Mposi smiled. 'A talking, tool-using bull elephant will do that to you.'

'Besides, we also had the other elephants,' Ndege said. 'The normal population you were so concerned about way back when. It turns out that elephants are more than happy to follow Tantors. Herd dynamics still count for something, and a talking matriarch trumps a mute one. With Tantors and baseline elephants acting in coordinated herds, our effective force was hundreds strong – easily sufficient to evict the constables from the thirty-six public cores.'

'I hope you treated them decently,' Chiku said, without much conviction. 'They were just normal people, doing the wrong job.'

'There were deaths on both sides,' Mposi said, 'but we tried to be decent. Once they'd been neutralised and disarmed, the occupiers were given a choice. They could join our citizenry, under certain probationary conditions, or risk being packed into shuttles and sent back home. About a third of them decided to join us. Most of them have managed to integrate without too much trouble.'

'We needed more hands and minds,' Ndege said. 'It's been difficult, the way things have gone.'

Chiku had barely been able to tear her eyes from the Tantors. 'I'd like to see them properly,' she said. 'Walk with them, touch them. There was one called Dakota, the cleverest of them all. Eunice said she was a true evolutionary leap. Do you know if she's still alive?'

'It's possible,' Mposi said.

'What he means,' Guochang whispered, 'is that you've exhausted the limits of his knowledge. Remember, you can only go so deep with these things.'

'I'd still like to take a closer look at the Tantors,' Chiku said.

Ndege nodded at the patchwork sky. 'There's still time. They see much better than us in the dark, of course, so the night doesn't really matter to them. Deep down, they're still elephants.'

CHAPTER FORTY-EIGHT

It was good, even for the space of a few hours, to be somewhere other than Crucible. Mposi and Ndege led the party to the level ground where the Tantors were parading back and forth, and Chiku circled the huge, slow-stomping creatures with something close to awe. Like the Tantors she had met in Chamber Thirty-Seven, their bodies were augmented with tools and communication attachments affixed to an arrangement of girdles and straps. Much of it looked improvised or second-hand. Not all the Tantors, Ndege said, were capable of generating written syntax, but this was mostly because the herd's expansion had outstripped the pace at which the textual equipment could be manufactured. It was optimal to fit the Tantors with the machines when they were young, so some of these adults might never have the easy linguistic faculty Dakota had demonstrated.

But they were still more intelligent than the baseline elephants, demonstrably superior at abstract reasoning and able to follow complex spoken instructions. These Tantors, in common with the others elsewhere in *Zanzibar*, worked in close harmony with constables and peacekeepers. It was, Ndege stressed, as close to a partnership as circumstances allowed. Eunice had stipulated that the Tantors were to be treated as equals, and her assistance in ridding *Zanzibar* of its enemies had been scrupulously contingent on that understanding.

'It was never going to be easy,' Mposi said, his sister nodding in agreement. 'But then, nothing worthwhile ever is. We're still making mistakes, on both sides, and there's plenty of room for misunderstandings. But Tantors saved *Zanzibar*. Tantors and an artificial intelligence most of us would have sooner smashed to pieces than trust with our lives.'

'When did she disclose her true nature?' Arachne asked.

'Only when we'd regained a good measure of control,' Ndege answered. 'Until then, all but a few of us still believed she was human. She probably could have kept up the illusion, but I think she wanted to put us to the ultimate test.'

'There was a public gathering,' Mposi said, 'about a week or so after most of the constables had been rounded up. Things were still edgy, and one of the Tantors had caused a death. That was her moment. She walked out of the building and into the crowd, until she was surrounded by citizens. She stood on a little box, this tiny woman in a sea of people.'

'None of them knew what she was about to say or do,' Ndege said. 'She just raises her arms, waits for the crowd to quieten down – they all have questions and demands, of course – and she says: "I have a truth for you. Two truths, in fact, both of them equally difficult to accept. The first is that we've been lied to about Crucible. The Provider machines we sent there ahead of us, the servants we expected to make our new world fit for living, have failed us. Worse, they've deliberately falsified their transmissions. They've lied and manipulated and none of us can say for sure what we'll find when we arrive. A trap, perhaps. They're powerful, clever machines and you're right to be afraid of them. Which brings me to the second truth I mentioned: I am also a powerful, clever machine."'

'She let that sink in,' Mposi said, the memory of it curving her lips in a smile. 'She didn't need to say it twice. And the silence – I don't think I've ever heard anything like it. They couldn't make up their minds whether she was mad or suicidal, and I think the mob could have gone either way at that moment. As strong as she was, they'd have torn her apart like a paper soldier! But when she'd stretched out the moment as long as she dared, she added: "You have two choices. I could prove it to you, or you could find out for yourselves – tear the skin from my metal bones and break me like a doll. But option two will gain you nothing except my destruction or my undying suspicion that none of you can ever be totally trusted. It's much simpler just to ask yourselves why I'd lie about such a thing given what I've just told you about the Providers on Crucible. It's much simpler just to *accept*."'

'The crowd went berserk,' Ndege said. 'They were yelling and screaming at her like a witch on a bonfire. But no one actually touched her. I think that was what saved us – and her. After a few moments, as the shouting ebbed, she said: "If you can find a way to live with me, then maybe I can find a way for us to all to live with the Providers. A friend of mine, Chiku Akinya, went ahead of *Zanzibar* to make contact with them. It's possible that she failed, but there's no way to know for sure one way or the other. What we do know is that Chiku and her friends had nothing to offer the Providers beyond their humanity. I have something more. It's not simply the fact that I'm also a machine, although that will surely help matters. I'm a machine that remembers being born. I carry the memories of a human woman inside me – not just the dry, documented facts of her existence, but the actual organisation of her brain, mirrored in my own informational architecture. I'm tainted with Eunice Akinya. Her blood is my blood. She haunts me. I believe I've earned the right to use her name.'

'It was all-or-nothing in that moment,' Ndege said. 'Our past and our future, hinging on whether we agreed to let this ... *thing* be our guide. I won't say it was easy, or that the decision was reached without rancour. Typically, we had to put it to the vote. It was the first democratic act of our reconstituted Legislative Assembly: do we allow ourselves to be governed by a robot?'

'The motion passed, narrowly,' Mposi said. 'Even then, I think some still believed she was lying. But slowly her revelation came to be accepted as truth. We'd seen Chamber Thirty-Seven, walked inside it. What reason could we possibly have to doubt any other part of her story once we'd accepted the most outlandish part: that this woman had raised a clan of talking elephants!'

'But she was still speaking about Crucible,' Chiku said, 'as if you still stood some chance of arriving. What changed?'

She was learning the rest of it when the bad thing occurred. Even though *Zanzibar* had developed the prototype PCP engine, scaling it up to the size necessary to slow a holoship had always been an ambitious objective, especially in the time remaining to the caravan. But it had become doubly difficult for *Zanzibar*, forcibly isolated as it was from the rest of the community, its best minds either executed or in detention on other holoships. They barely had the industrial capacity to go it alone, never mind indulging in the kind of draining economic and technical effort needed to build a new slowdown engine.

After two centuries of interstellar voyaging, this was almost more than the citizenry could accept. The prize for which they had fought so valiantly was not to be theirs, and those who had at times disdained that prize were now in the best position to take it.

But they were not without options, Eunice said. They had taken the old lander and made it into *Icebreaker*, and they could do that again, albeit on a smaller scale. Allowing for some sacrifices, *Zanzibar* still had the capacity to build a second prototype of the PCP engine, smaller and more efficient than the first, and this engine could in turn be integrated into a smaller, nimbler spacecraft. They took one of their shuttles, scooped out its innards and replaced them – after years of effort and setbacks – with the new engine. It was a monumentally difficult task, conducted in total isolation and with maximum stealth. *Zanzibar* had to maintain the illusion that it was a dead or dying holoship, hurtling uncontrolled through space.

When they got close enough to Crucible, they sent the new ship on its way. It was launched as secretly as possible, its course taking it well away from the slowdown trajectories of the other holoships. Its mission was to make contact with Crucible, but also to serve as witness. If there were mistakes to be made, let the other holoships make them.

'She's aboard that ship, of course,' Mposi said. 'No way she was being left out of the loop, not after all this time and everything she'd done to get us to Crucible in the first place.'

'Just her?' Chiku asked, wondering how spartan the arrangements aboard the other ship must be, and what kind of volunteers might have been required.

'No, not just her,' Ndege said.

Chiku was about to ask Ndege to elaborate on this point. But at that exact moment Guochang vanished.

Out of ching, back in their bodies on Crucible, they knew immediately that the very worst had happened. An impactor had fallen squarely on one of Arachne's surface positions, exactly where she was holding one of her hostages. Her defences had been too tardy to stop the incoming body, and it had arrived at a sufficiently steep angle that the atmosphere had done little to absorb its kinetic energy. Guochang, in ching, had known nothing about his imminent end. It would have been painless and instantaneous – better, in truth, than the ends June Wing and Pedro Braga had suffered, all those years ago. But death was death, and when the time of reckoning came, it was a small mercy to be oblivious. He had been happy in the ching, too – happy just to be back on *Zanzibar*, even if only in a dream. Chiku had been smiling, overwhelmed with delight at the Tantors, giddy that her holoship had found a way to endure, and that her children were not only still alive but part of the world-changing events occurring aboard *Zanzibar*. All the difficulties they had faced and would continue to face were as nothing compared with the mere fact of their survival.

The four survivors felt as if they were in each other's presence, all in the same tower, but they knew it was an illusion being maintained by ching.

'The rate of bombardments has never been higher,' Arachne informed them. 'In addition, the Watchkeepers have moved to what I can only interpret as a condition of elevated alertness. Communication between them has intensified. I believe we may be on the threshold of ... *something*.'

Guochang's death was bad enough, but the impactor had also killed – or placed forever beyond resurrection – three of the fifteen skipover volunteers who had yet to be revivified. To Chiku, it felt like an even greater affront that these people had died without knowing the purpose of their sacrifice, or without the dignity of an apology for being lied to.

'We can't stay here,' she said. 'Any of us. If the surface is too risky, you'd better find a way to get us back into orbit.'

'I lack the means,' Arachne said. 'My rockets aren't suitable for the purpose. They are extensions of me, not vehicles for moving people. There's no room inside them for passengers, and no provision for keeping passengers alive.'

'Then change them,' Travertine said exasperatedly.

'It would take too long, even if my space-based capabilities weren't already at maximum capacity.'

'You move us around Crucible,' Doctor Aziba said. 'How does that work, exactly?'

'By Provider or airborne vehicle. But where would I take you? The only places I can keep you alive are the places they're trying to destroy!'

'What about *Icebreaker*?' Chiku asked. 'You damaged our ship when you brought us down from orbit, but the hull was intact until you cut a hole in it to gas us. Can't you patch it up, clamp some rockets on and get us back into space, the same way we came down?'

'I took the ship to pieces,' Arachne said.

Namboze sighed. 'Well, of course you did.'

'It was the only way to extract the information embedded in your vehicle. You had no expectation that it would ever fly again. I could task my Providers to reassemble it, but it would be just as difficult and time-consuming as readying one of my own rockets.'

'Wait,' Chiku said slowly. 'You say you can't keep us alive in any of your structures. Maybe that's true, but we also came to Crucible intending to live on the surface once we were acclimatised.' She jabbed her finger into the floor until it dimpled. 'We brought basic supplies with us on the lander – enough for twenty people, not just the five of us.'

'Four,' Travertine corrected, gently.

'Well?' asked Dr Aziba. 'Did you dismantle our masks, rations and survival equipment as well as the ship, Arachne?'

'Your equipment's intact and can be made ready quite quickly. But what good will it serve? You can't survive for long, even with your masks – you have enough rations for perhaps several tens of days, if you're fortunate. You will be much safer where you are now.'

'Until another impactor breezes through your defences,' Namboze said, 'which could happen at any moment. I agree with Chiku – if we can't reach space, I'd sooner take my chances out there, in the forest.'

Chiku nodded. 'Eunice is on her way aboard a functioning ship, which may be able to keep all of us alive – including the other sleepers – until this is all over. Whatever *that* means. Arachne – you must let her slip through your defences.'

'We have an old score to settle – she might feel it's time for a reckoning.'

'Were you even listening to what Chiku's children said?' Namboze scolded. 'She's offering herself up in the hope that she can negotiate with you, not to get back at you for what you did to her two hundred years ago and twenty-eight light-years away.'

'We must work on the basis that we all have good intentions,' Dr Aziba agreed. 'As Chiku said in her transmission, there's a strength in not being strong. This is your chance, Arachne. You must let that ship reach the surface unharmed.'

Chiku blinked, and the others were gone. Arachne was standing at the window, her back to the room, the violin and bow lolling from her fingers.

'Please don't worry about your absent friends,' the girl was saying. 'They're all quite well, and arrangements are in hand for your evacuation. I will also do my best to safeguard the remaining sleepers. There's something I want to discuss with you first, though.'

'Something that can't be shared with the others?'

'In this instance, I am not sure that would be wise.'

Chiku peered past Arachne, through the window. Perhaps it was her imagination, but the ceiling of cloud had gained an additional drab opacity. She shuddered to think of the sheer deadening cargo of dust already in the atmosphere, stirred and distributed by complicit winds and high-altitude jetstreams.

Dust had no business being up there. It would all have to come down eventually.

'What do we have left to say to each other that we haven't already said?'

'I lied, just a little, and you must forgive me. In the context of my larger falsehoods, it's only a very small untruth.'

'Out with it, then,' Chiku said.

'I told you that your holoships weren't yet within range of my countermeasures. The truth is that they've been within range for several days now, by which I mean that projectiles launched from my kinetic cannons quite some while ago have had plenty of time to intersect with your holoships by now. They may already have impacted, with megatonne effectiveness.'

'Then they've either hit or they've missed,' Chiku said, bewildered and uneasy.

'There is a third option. We spoke of the possibility, faint as it was, that our adversaries might have the means to detonate or neutralise their impactors if some truce situation could be negotiated. The fact is that I've always had that capability. My kinetic projectiles aren't dumb slugs – they have embedded logic. I can order them to self-destruct, or alter their direction of flight with bursts of controllable micro-thrust. The latter offers only a very small change in the vector, but over distances of light-seconds or -minutes it's usually sufficient to change a collision to a miss, or vice versa. The point being, Chiku, that I've had my missiles on a collision course with the holoships for quite some time now, but with the ability to avert that impact at the last moment by transmitting the self-destruct signal to the slugs. I could have struck back against the holoships on multiple occasions, but at the last moment I've always neutralised my slugs. Would you like to know why?'

'You hoped wisdom might prevail,' Chiku said. 'That they'd be the ones to back down first.'

'That was one reason, yes. But I must confess that my actions were also coloured by an element of curiosity regarding Eunice. Once you'd mentioned her existence, I couldn't get her out of my mind. Part of me wanted to destroy her utterly, but another part was equally determined that she shouldn't be destroyed, so that I might have the chance to learn from her. That was the part that prevailed and steered my hand, Chiku. I dared not destroy the holoships while she might be inside them.'

'And now?'

'Now I know she was never aboard any of the five vessels presently approaching us. And those are the vessels currently bombarding us. Perhaps they can't stop what's already been set in motion. But Crucible is still being harmed, and the regrettable deaths of some of your companions have highlighted the limitations of my defences. I'm mindful that there are other holoships further out, probably observing events via transmissions and long-range sensors and refining their own plans accordingly. If the first five vessels have the slowdown engine, I think it highly probable that the other holoships have it, too. Would you dispute this?'

'I can't.'

'Good – my next point is so much more straightforward if you accept the first.' Arachne, who had been facing the window all the time she had been speaking, turned now to address Chiku face to face. 'These bombardments can't go on, Chiku, and we can't tolerate the possibility of a second wave of holoships initiating a similar attack. A line must be drawn.'

'By destroying a holoship.'

'No,' Arachne corrected gently. 'By destroying three. One would be ambiguous – it might look like a lucky strike. Two would be better, but still wouldn't offer the definitive gesture I'm seeking. Three is the perfect number. It demonstrates both terrible power and terrible clemency. If I can destroy three, I'm clearly able to destroy five, and yet I've chosen not to. I've chosen to spare lives instead – to show mercy and forgiveness! There is a strength in not being strong, as you so eloquently stated.'

'I didn't mean it this way!'

'Perhaps not, but my interpretation is equally valid. Events have forced this upon us, Chiku. I dearly wish it were otherwise, but I won't stand by and see this world murdered. I will not be seen to do nothing.'

'Seen by whom?' But as soon as Chiku framed the question, she could answer it herself. 'The Watchkeepers. You think they're observing you, testing your reactions. You think you're being judged.'

'I'm accountable,' Arachne said, 'as are we all. I'm a product of human cleverness, and so are the holoships. So, too, are your Tantors, and your Eunice. None of us is blameless. None of us is absolved of responsibility. Most especially not you.'

'Your mind's clearly made up. I've pleaded your case, tried to talk them into peace. What more do you want from me?'

'Your guidance,' Arachne said sweetly. 'Three holoships will be destroyed. But the decision as to which two are *not* destroyed – this decision may be yours. We've already discussed the probable identities of the five holoships.'

'No,' Chiku said. 'I won't help you with this.'

'You misunderstand. I'll destroy three whatever happens – I've already made my preliminary selection. But I'm giving you the opportunity to decide which two will live. What would you prefer, Chiku? That this decision be made by a machine, with no account taken of the lives and possibilities contained with those vessels? Or that a human should have some say in it? A human who knows something of the caravan, a human who has travelled between the holoships, lived and breathed their air? A human who has seen them from the inside, sensed their

440

individual strengths and weaknesses? A human whose insight might, in some small way, prove advantageous to the peace process? We all want peace – I think we can agree on that. I've reached the limit of my understanding of human nature. But I still have you.'

'No,' she said again.

'The five vessels are *Malabar*, *Majuli*, *Ukerewe*, *Netrani* and *Sriharikota*. You have a little over three hundred seconds to select the two that will be spared. If your decision isn't forthcoming, I'll be forced to make my own decision, and it'll be too late for a change of heart. You have five minutes in which to guide my hand. Use that time well, Chiku.'

'I was wrong about you,' Chiku said.

'In what sense?'

'I was starting to like you. Starting to think you weren't the monster I'd feared.'

'None of us is a monster, Chiku. We're all just trying to make the best of our singular natures.'

CHAPTER FORTY-NINE

When the moment for choices had passed, the decision as irrevocable as the slipping of the present into the past, Chiku asked Arachne to let her witness the results of her choice. Arachne obliged, but not before she had questioned Chiku regarding the wisdom of this request.

'Are you absolutely sure? You've made your selection, and that can't have been easy for you. Truly, you have my admiration.'

'I don't need it.'

'But to see the outcome of something already ordained by the mathematical inevitability of moving objects … what would you gain from that? You'd only have my word that I'm showing you the truth, and even if you believe what you're seeing, surely you would find it painful.'

Chiku almost nodded, for she had arrived at much the same conclusion. But none of that altered her conviction.

'I still need to see it.'

'Very well.'

And although it was still day, or what now passed for day on Crucible, Arachne cleared an area of the sky back to space and stars, and made that circle zoom in through multiple magnifications until the five sparks of the slowdown engines formed a dice-like pattern. Time had been compressed again, of course, but Chiku now accepted these manipulations as an inseparable component of her dealings with the artilect.

Arachne pinned names against the sparks. '*Malabar*, *Ukerewe*, *Sriharikota*, *Majuli*, *Netrani*. I take some satisfaction in the fact that I identified them correctly before we had the benefit of *Zanzibar*'s transmission. Each holoship a world, brimming with life. Millions of lives – each of which has value, each of which has almost infinite potentiality, branch upon branch stretching into some future neither you nor I can begin to imagine. Don't imagine for one moment that I'm blind to the tragedy of this act, Chiku. It's an atrocity, plain and simple. I'm culpable, and you're complicit. But if these lives must be sacrificed to spare millions more – and, just as importantly, the ecologic and artifactual treasures of an entire alien world – then what choice do we have? I gave them every chance to negotiate – every opportunity to turn from the path of destruction.'

'They're terrified of you. What did you expect?'

'Attend,' Arachne announced. 'The moment approaches.' Then she directed a sidelong look at her human companion. 'Your choices, incidentally – that I should spare *Malabar* and *Majuli* ... why not the more populous holoships?'

'There were no good choices.'

'But if one's actions were shaped by the need to save the largest number of citizens—'

'Mine weren't.' Chiku considered leaving it at that. Arachne did not deserve to hear how Chiku made her choice, and there was an undeniable dignity in holding her tongue. But some compulsion made her continue. 'Even if I'd wanted to save as many people as I could, we have no idea what the populations of those holoships are by now. After all the troubles, anything is possible – mass movements, mass diebacks, from plague or executions. But years ago we established two offshoot elephant populations – one in *Majuli*, one in *Malabar*.'

'Then you acted to save elephants, not people?'

'You say none of us is blameless. You're wrong. The elephants are.'

'You have no evidence that your elephant populations weathered the troubles. If there were ... shortages of basic supplies ... wouldn't the elephants have been sacrificed first?'

'Perhaps,' Chiku said uneasily. She had not considered that possibility, and now that Arachne had implanted the idea in her mind, it had a horrible self-reinforcing integrity. The more she dwelt on it, the more probable it seemed. But she added: 'I trusted those populations to people I thought I could depend on. People I believed would do anything to live up to my expectations. If I was wrong about that, so be it. I gave the elephants the best chance I could. I can't turn my back on them now.'

'I could have tricked you, I suppose,' Arachne said. 'Based my selection of targets on the inverse of your desires. Made *Malabar* and *Majuli* among my selection of holoships to destroy.'

'Did you?'

The girl shook her head. 'No. That would have been much too spiteful.'

In exceedingly quick succession, like a trill of notes, three of the sparks flared to an intolerable brightness that blended and smothered the flames of the other two holoships as it progressed from white to a very delicate flowerlike pink. The light was as clean as creation, effacing all sins, all desires, all consequences. Chiku stared into the purity of it, imprisoned in the moment. It felt like an eternity before the light faded to darkness, and the two still-burning sparks were visible again.

CHAPTER FIFTY

Her three living companions were already prepared to leave when she joined them. Travertine, Namboze and Dr Aziba were standing next to an assortment of silver containers: clasp-locked cases with rounded edges and many colourful symbols and dense-printed instructional notices embossed on their sides. Some of the cases were hinged open, revealing padded interiors or ranks of cleverly packaged sliding compartments. Items of equipment ranging from breathing masks to medical supplies had been pulled out of the cases and placed in loose piles on the ground. The cases represented only a tiny proportion of the items they had brought with them on *Icebreaker*. Then again, four people had modest needs.

Travertine was shrugging vis way into a backpack. 'What happened? We've been ready for an hour, waiting for you. Arachne kept saying you were coming, but we started to wonder.'

'We should get moving,' Namboze said. 'There's enough here to keep us alive out there for fifteen, maybe twenty days, provided we don't run into anything really nasty. We've been through the boxes and we think we know what we need and what we can't afford to carry. I can help you sort out a basic kit.'

'Is something the matter?' Dr Aziba asked as he adjusted the straps on the bright plastic breather mask currently dangling around his neck. The concentration pushed his features into a chimp-like mask. 'Where were you, anyway?'

'You say you've been here an hour?' Chiku asked.

'*Ready* for an hour,' Travertine said. 'Hard to tell, but it can't have been far off local dawn when she set us down here, and it must be mid-morning by now. We'll need to keep track of the time somehow to use our rations properly.'

'Do you remember being aboard *Zanzibar*?'

'Why wouldn't we?' Travertine asked, grimacing as ve took the weight of the backpack. 'When the ship arrives, they can transpond off our implants, home in on us from space. All we have to do is get as far away from Arachne's installations as possible.'

'Every kilometre will help,' Namboze agreed. She was kneeling down, rummaging through the compartments of one of the medical boxes, pulling out colour-coded vials and hypodermic packages. 'And even if it doesn't make any difference to our chances, psychologically I'd far rather be moving than sitting still. We all feel that way.'

'I'll ask again,' Dr Aziba said placidly. 'Is something the matter?'

'Yes,' Chiku said. 'Quite a lot. Something happened. I *made* something happen. I need to talk about it.'

She had joined her companions in a place she did not recognise from direct experience. It was a domed enclosure, totally transparent, but rather than being set at the top of one of the towers, this one nestled at the base of a tower, down in the forest. The dome's walls curved under them to form a floor of flexible transparency. Beyond the walls, pressing against it in places, was an abundance of vegetation. The colours were only dimly apparent: muted greens and blues and turquoises, suggesting shades and textures and degrees of glossiness. Chiku saw all manner of architectures of leaf and bloom, of trunk and root and vine and tendril, from the slender and daggerlike to the veinous and synaptic, to the columnar and the elephantine and the grotesque. Even on the brightest of cloudless days, the over-arching layers of canopy would have robbed the sunlight of much of its effect by the time it penetrated to these depths. With the ash cover, the illumination was as meagre as the last gleaming of twilight.

And yet there were openings in the vegetation – artificial tracks or accidental alignments of clearer growth – through which four people might, with difficulty, be able to make some progress. She wondered what her companions expected. A few tens of kilometres a day felt optimistic. But Namboze was right – it was better to be moving than sitting idle, waiting for the next impactor to fall.

A corridor threaded through the dome, and Chiku recalled Namboze's description of visiting something similar. In one direction it stretched as far as back as Chiku could discern before gloom swallowed her vision. In the other direction, it ran only a short distance before terminating in a flat circular wall. Beyond the disc-like termination she made out an area of clear growth – what she would describe as a glade, had there been sunlight to dapple it.

'We should get moving,' Travertine said. But even as ve spoke, ve dropped the backpack. 'Something's not right, is it? What is it you know, Chiku?'

'We need to talk.'

'Fine, but let's not make it a long conversation.'

'I don't want it to be, but we still need to talk. I think it's important. Can we sit down for a minute?'

Reluctantly at first, the party convened some of the packing cases into a quartet of makeshift stools.

'How did you get here?' Chiku asked, perching on two of the cases.

'We weren't here, and then we were,' Dr Aziba said, 'just like every other time Arachne's moved us around.'

'Have you seen her?'

'No, but the intention looks pretty self-explanatory,' Namboze said. 'These supplies were recovered from *Icebreaker* ...' She stopped speaking and stared at Chiku. 'Why are you looking like that? What's bothering you?'

'I don't know, Gonithi.'

'You could start by telling us what happened,' Travertine said.

'Three of the holoships are gone.' Chiku had to swallow hard before continuing. '*Ukerewe*, *Netrani* and *Sriharikota*. She used her weapons against them. As far as I can tell, they were totally destroyed.'

The others absorbed this news with the weary resignation she had been expecting, their expressions grim, but fully accepting the truth of what she was saying. They looked at each other, nodded in mutual understanding.

'I can't condone it,' Dr Aziba said finally. 'The loss of a single life must always be regretted. But they were given a chance to act different-ly. After what they started doing to this planet – to us! – I'm afraid my loyalties are with *Zanzibar*.'

'They were prepared to poison an entire world,' Namboze said. 'The punishment's harsh, true, but if one of those rocks had landed on Man-dala ... that would've been the single most irresponsible act in the entire history of our species! They had to be stopped.'

'Stockholm syndrome,' Travertine said. 'That's what this is. We've been her hostages for so long, we've begun to sympathise with her view-point. But even if that's true, it doesn't change my opinion. Namboze and Doctor Aziba are right – the bombardment had to be stopped. If it took this appalling act to stop it, that's still less of a crime than allowing it to continue.'

Chiku could barely look at their faces. 'You don't know the whole story yet. She deliberately destroyed only three of the five – she'd run her calculations and concluded that blowing up three ships would be enough to make her point.'

'And?' Travertine asked, leaning in to meet Chiku's gaze.

'She asked me which two should be saved. She said that if I didn't give her two names, she'd make the decision herself.'

Dr Aziba said, 'You can't blame yourself for her actions, Chiku. She put you in an impossible position – that's a choice no one should ever be asked to make.'

'How was she expecting you to choose, anyway?' Namboze asked. 'You're not the machine. You can't make that sort of decision – none of us could. The holoships were our homes! We might have travelled in *Zanzibar*, but all of us felt affection for the other ships. Even when they started making life hard for us, we still had friends and loved ones spread across the caravan.'

'It shows how little she really understands us,' Dr Aziba said, shaking his head sadly.

'No,' Chiku said. 'It's you who don't understand.' She lifted her chin and met each of her companions' gazes in turn. 'She gave me the power to make that choice and I took it. I told her to spare *Malabar* and *Majuli*. I made that decision.'

'You did what?' Namboze asked.

'It was the right thing to do. I didn't want a fucking *machine* to decide who lived and died. If it's a crime, let it be my crime.'

'You had no right to make that decision,' Namboze said.

Chiku pushed herself up from the cases. 'I was there. You weren't. She asked me to choose, and I chose. I couldn't leave that decision to her, so I told her that *Malabar* and *Majuli* could live. And you know what? I'd make that choice again. There are elephants on those holoships. I put them there. They're depending on me for their survival.'

'Elephants,' Dr Aziba repeated, as if he had not heard her correctly the first time.

'Independent populations split off from *Zanzibar*'s herds. *Majuli* took the first group, and I was negotiating for *Malabar* to take some more when Kappa happened …' Her voice was on the point of breaking. 'When all this began.'

'Elephants,' Dr Aziba said again. 'Just to be clear – because I hope very much that I'm misunderstanding something here – you chose elephants over human lives? You didn't consider saving the holoships with the largest populations, or the ones carrying the greatest quantities of the specialised technologies that we'll need to live on this world? You based your decision on the fate of some elephants?'

'You've seen the Tantors,' Chiku said.

'But these weren't Tantors,' Namboze said. 'That's the point, isn't it? These were just animals.'

'We can't pick and choose. The Tantors came from elephants. I owed them—'

'You owed them nothing!' Dr Aziba said, spitting through his teeth. 'What did she do to you, Chiku?' And then he was up and grabbing Chiku's forearms, hard enough that she felt his nails dig into her skin through the fabric of her clothing. 'You should *never* have gone along with this! From the moment you woke me on *Icebreaker* and told me I'd been lied to, I made a decision to trust you, believing that you'd been forced by circumstance into making hard choices for the good of the caravan.' Aziba shoved her, hard. Chiku lost her balance and fell backwards, legs buckling over the supply cases she had been sitting on. She thumped hard on the upper part of her back, snapping her neck and jarring the air from her lungs.

Physical violence had never been part of her world. For a moment, it was more than she could process.

'You should have refused,' Namboze said, looming over Chiku. 'Why didn't you? Why didn't you demand our help in making the decision?'

'Would that have made it more acceptable to you both?' Travertine asked.

Chiku tried to push herself from the ground.

'We should have been party to it,' the doctor said, planting a foot squarely on Chiku's belly to keep her on the floor. 'We should have been consulted!'

'And what if we all came up with different pairs of names?' Travertine asked. 'Would voting on it democratically have made the decision any less repugnant?'

Namboze dived aside – she was kneeling by one of the boxes, digging into it as if looking for something. Chiku tried to get up again, but Aziba increased the pressure of his foot.

'You agree with us then, Travertine – it *was* repugnant.'

'What was repugnant is that she was asked to choose – that was the crime, not the fact that she did as she was asked.' Ue leaned over and met Chiku's gaze again. 'How long did she give you to think about it?'

Chiku coughed. Aziba's foot pressing on her belly was making it difficult for her winded lungs to recover. 'Five … five minutes. Three hundred seconds.'

'So you didn't have the luxury of being able to weigh all the options,' Travertine said, 'or consider all the ethical ramifications.' Ve paused for a beat. 'Doctor Aziba – would you mind taking your foot off my friend?'

'She was our leader on *Zanzibar*,' the physician said, steadfastly keeping his foot exactly where it was, 'but she resigned. And yet, ever since our arrival in this system she's continued to act as if she has the mandate of leadership! Perhaps some good can come out of this travesty. It gives us the chance we needed to reassess our chain of command!'

'I did ask you nicely,' Travertine said.

In the instant of the action, it looked to Chiku as if Travertine had misjudged the swing of vis punch. Unsurprising given that ve had probably never initiated a violent act against another person in vis entire life.

But Travertine's aim was truer than it looked. Ve had swung with vis right arm, and while Travertine's fist failed to connect with Aziba's jaw, vis bracelet did not. Chiku winced at the sound of the impact.

Dr Aziba dropped instantly, clattering into three of the cases. He landed on his back, spreadeagled, one leg hooked over a case, and remained perfectly still.

Relieved of the pressure of the physician's foot, Chiku pushed herself to standing. She wondered if Dr Aziba might be dead, murdered by a single punch. But Travertine had other, more immediate concerns. Namboze was still digging through one of the medical supply cases, tossing hypodermics and vials aside to form a happy little jumble of different colours, like the contents of a box of crayons. Travertine stomped down hard on the lid, crushing it onto Namboze's fingers. She yelped, hissed and toppled back onto her haunches, her hand still stuck in the box.

'What are you looking for?' Travertine asked. 'Something to knock Chiku out? Something to put her into a coma?'

'Surely you can't be defending her!' Namboze snarled. 'She's done bad things to all of us, but she did the worst to you! She turned you into a monster that children have nightmares about! How can you *possibly* side with her?'

'I'm not siding with anyone – I don't do "siding".' But the angry Namboze was not the focus of Travertine's attention. Ve knelt by the unmoving physician and peeled back his eyelids.

'Is he dead?' Chiku asked.

'Just out cold – I think. He's the doctor.'

'You hit him pretty hard.'

'It felt like the proportionate response under the circumstances.' Travertine rubbed at vis forearm, squeezing the muscles with a sort of surprised admiration.

Chiku pinched the bridge of her nose and screwed up her eyes. She had a dreadful hammer-pounding-anvil headache. 'I thought we were better than this.'

'We're human. Be thankful we've moved on from clubbing each other's brains out every five minutes.'

Namboze had extricated her hand from the medical case. She tested her fingers one by one. Lines of fury notched her forehead, so neat and regular they might have been scribed into place. 'This isn't right.'

'No, it isn't,' Travertine agreed. 'It's massively wrong, all of it. It's wrong that we're hostages of an artificial intelligence, wrong that Guochang is dead, wrong that there are twenty-two mysterious alien machines hovering over us right now, wrong that Chiku was put in a position where she had to make that sick abomination of a decision. And yes, it was wrong of her to take it! But she had three hundred fucking seconds, Namboze. Can you honestly say you'd have done any better? Can any of us?'

Dr Aziba murmured something that shaped itself into a powerful groan as he came around. He reached up to examine the area of his jaw where Travertine's impact had already begun to draw a vivid purplish discolouration.

'What just happened?'

'Democracy,' Travertine said. 'Now can we please get on with the day? We have a long walk ahead of us.'

Namboze, still massaging her bruised fingers, knelt down next to the physician.

'Do it your way, then, Travertine. We'll move out in two parties. Aziba and I can travel alone.'

'No,' Chiku said. 'We do this together or not at all. You're right to be angry with me. Travertine said it best: it's all wrong, all of it. I don't regret my decision – what would be the point? But she should never have let me make it, and I shouldn't have allowed her to convince me it was for the best. But I did what I did, and now we're here, and we need each other – even more so now that Guochang's gone.'

'I don't need anything you've got left to offer,' Namboze said, with a dismissive shake of her head.

'Think about it rationally for a moment, Gonithi,' Chiku persisted. 'We each have a unique skill set. You know the ecology better than the rest of us. Aziba's the only one who can keep the four of us alive – god alone knows what'll get into our bloodstreams if we so much as scratch ourselves out there. And Travertine, well … ve's Travertine. We need ver.'

'And you?' Doctor Aziba asked. 'What do you bring to our merry party, exactly?'

'I'm going to see us through this. There's a ship on its way. I want to be there when it lands.'

'That's all?' Namboze asked.

'She gave you your answer,' Travertine said, stooping to pick up vis backpack.

Another voice said: 'It's good that you're ready. I must inform you, though, that there's been a development.'

As one they turned to face Arachne. She was standing at the threshold of the long glass corridor as if she had been there the whole time, watching their little kerfuffle.

'What kept you?' Travertine asked.

'I was otherwise occupied. I also sensed that my presence might have been more of a hindrance than a benefit, at least while you worked through your differences.'

'What could possibly occupy all of you?' Namboze asked. 'You're an artilect – you can be anywhere you wish – in more than one place at the same time, if you like.'

'Have you noticed,' Arachne asked, 'that it's become much darker than it was only half an hour ago?'

A glance through the glass wall of the tunnel confirmed her words, although the change had come upon them so gradually that Chiku had barely noticed it. Perhaps Travertine had been wrong about it being dawn when the three of them had been brought here, and the sun had only just dipped below the horizon. Perhaps another bombardment had increased the thickness of the dust blanketing the planet.

But Chiku sensed that it was neither of these things.

'What's happened now?'

'It'll be much easier if you see it for yourselves. We should have a clear view of the sky a little way from here. Are you prepared for exposure to Crucible's atmosphere?'

'Came twenty-eight light-years to live in it,' Travertine said. 'Might as well start getting used to it.'

Ve reached down for a breather mask and tossed it to Chiku.

They ran through the basic safety tests in five minutes, and then Arachne led them to the flat circular cap at the end of the short corridor. Chiku had assumed it was made of the same glasslike material as the walls, but as Arachne pushed her hand against it, the material neither buckled nor resisted, but permitted her hand to travel through into the air beyond.

'A containment membrane,' she said. 'There would have been inter-faces like this at all the city gates, allowing easy passage in and out. I don't suppose it really matters now if Crucible's airs and microorgan-isms infiltrate this space, but we may as well leave it in place and pass through as intended. Follow me. I'll be waiting on the other side.'

'No,' Chiku said, resting a hand on the girl's shoulder. 'Gonithi should go first.'

'She's probably been out there many times already, so I won't really be the first,' Namboze said.

'Even so,' Chiku said, nodding, 'she's a robot and so she doesn't really count. This is the world you've waited for all these years – be the first human to set foot on it, Gonithi.'

'What are you waiting for, woman?' Travertine said. 'It really is the opportunity of a lifetime – don't waste it.'

Namboze hesitated, as if she considered it a point of principle to argue against Chiku, but something in her relented. She mouthed a word Chiku did not catch, eased the breather mask fully into place and pushed a hand and a leg through the containment membrane. The ma-terial oozed around her with gluey intelligence as she pushed her face and body through, then snapped back to an unbroken membrane with an audible *pop*. Namboze was on the other side now.

She knelt down and touched the mossy green surface under her feet. Her hands were gloved, but Chiku knew that the fine, translucent fabric was wired for the same kind of haptic feedback built into spacesuits. She would be feeling every nuance of texture and temperature.

Wordlessly, Namboze stood and walked a few paces towards one of the larger plants. Its broad leaves were fat with a lateral groove and a kind of leathery dimpling, the whole leaf drooling like some huge sala-cious tongue. Namboze stroked it, first with her fingers and then with the back of her hand.

'The stupid thing,' she said, voice only slightly muffled by the mask and the intervening containment membrane, 'would be to remove my gloves. But they're not picking up anything obviously toxic.'

'Doctor Aziba,' Chiku said. 'Would you like to go next?'

He was still nursing the liverish bulge along the line of his jaw, trying to find a way to settle the mask over the bruise without chafing it too much, but he nodded and pushed through, more confidently and quick-ly than Namboze had. She had already moved on to the next plant and was fingering a spray of shark-mouthed flowers, or flower analogues. One of them snapped suddenly, Namboze only just withdrawing her fingers in time.

'I didn't imagine those insects I saw a while back,' she commented, beckoning the physician over to her side. 'Fly-traps don't evolve unless there are flies to eat.'

Travertine was the next through. The ecology of this world, Chiku guessed, fascinated ver much less than the mere fact of being here. Geology had shaped Crucible, and biology had greened it, but physics had brought Travertine across twenty-eight light-years to stand on its surface. Ve stood apart from the other two, hands at vis side, as if in private communion with some force Chiku could not see.

Chiku was reluctant to break the moment.

'You should go through,' Arachne said.

So she joined them on the other side, and while she waited for the girl to join them, she reached down and scooped up a fistful of olive mulch and squeezed it until it bled moisture. She opened her hand and watched the smear of alien soil avalanche off her self-cleaning glove.

'We should press on,' Arachne said. 'There's an area of open ground a little way from here that'll give us the best view.'

'The best view of what, exactly?' Dr Aziba asked, sweat already prickling his scalp. It was as hot and humid as Chiku had expected, and they had barely begun to move.

'I took the liberty of repeating your transmission to the holoships, Chiku. That plus the demonstration of my capabilities appears to have had some effect at last. *Malabar* and *Majuli* have disengaged their slowdown engines, and the frequency of impactors has dropped sharply. I find both gestures encouraging.'

'Will you allow them free passage?' Namboze asked.

'If they don't make any more violent overtures.'

'We can do better than that,' Chiku said, picking her way through a tangle of python-thick roots. 'Re-establish dialogue, negotiate terms for a full slowdown once they've passed through the system and out the other side. I won't abandon them to interstellar space. Or *Zanzibar*, for that matter. We'll find a way to bring the citizens back to the system, even if we have to do it a shuttle at a time.'

'For the moment,' Arachne said, 'there's a more pressing consideration.'

CHAPTER FIFTY-ONE

It took an hour of hard scrambling to reach the area of open ground Arachne had promised them. They had all tripped and fallen at least once, and Dr Aziba had ripped the fabric of his gloves as he tried to grab for something to arrest his fall. Fortunately, nothing had broken the surface of his skin before the self-suturing material healed itself invisibly. The mood remained tense, and they had little to say to each other on the trek, not even the two pairs of nominal allies. Chiku thought it must have been a peculiarly acute sort of torture for Namboze, being ushered through this world of wonders at quickstep. In spite of Arachne's admonitions to keep moving, she kept stooping to examine things, like a dog that needed to sniff every third twig.

The clearing was not artificial, Arachne told them. The Providers found it when they first emerged from their seed packages, and it was at least several thousand years old, perhaps more. She thought some geological anomaly had prevented trees from establishing themselves. There were hundreds of similar features elsewhere in the forest.

The party cut through knee-deep undergrowth until they were perhaps a hundred metres into the clearing. There was a little more light here, since they were no longer under the canopy, but the overall illumination remained meagre. Their masks and backpacks and protective equipment glowed with tribal swatches of high-visibility colour, registering the dimness as the approach of night.

And then they saw overhead the phenomenon Arachne had brought them to witness.

They stared at it wordlessly, as if they lacked the visual grammar to interpret the patterns falling on their eyes. Nothing in their collective experience could have prepared them for what they were seeing.

Whatever it was, it was sitting right over them.

Chiku thought of weather systems. It was circular, like the eye of a storm, but it was much, much, too circular to be a weather system. It was a sharp black circumference, an orbit of darkness pushing down through the ash that looked as wide as the world.

'Fifty kilometres across,' Arachne said, as if Chiku's mind were open for the reading. 'Ten kilometres above us. That ash layer is a lot higher up than it looks.'

'Tell us what we're seeing,' Travertine said, 'although I think I can take a pretty good guess.'

'The Watchkeepers,' Chiku said, before Arachne had time to offer a reply. 'Or one of them, anyway. That's what we're looking at, isn't it – the lowest, narrowest part of one of those things, pushing down into the atmosphere?'

'I told you about my concerns regarding their elevated state of alertness,' Arachne said, 'but I failed to anticipate this degree of intervention. As you say, Chiku, one of the twenty-two has descended from its normal elevation, matched its speed with Crucible's surface and come to hover here. The bulk of it is still in space: all but the last hundred kilometres of its narrowest part remain in vacuum, and only the last ten kilometres protrude beneath the stratosphere – one-hundredth part of the Watchkeeper! The precision is quite impressive, would you agree?'

'What does it want?' asked Namboze.

'Us, I suppose,' Chiku said. They were standing in a loose formation, necks craned, turning slowly on their heels. 'It knows we're here, in this exact spot – or is it following *you*, Arachne, and we just happen to be in the same location? Does it even register us, or are we lost in the noise, just more biology it doesn't really care about?'

'It registers everything,' Arachne said. 'And yes, it has a particular and long-standing interest in me, as I've already explained. The Watchkeepers called me across space, after all. They sent me their message, and I answered – one machine-substrate consciousness responding to another. Since I arrived, however – as I've freely admitted – progress hasn't exactly been ... speedy.'

'Someone's piqued their curiosity, then,' Travertine said.

'Even they couldn't ignore recent developments. An impactor was about to strike Mandala. My defences weren't able to intercept it and I feared the worst. But the impactor vanished just before it touched Crucible's atmosphere.'

'Vanished?' Chiku asked.

'There was a spike in the energies I've been monitoring, but I saw nothing that resembled a weapon or energy device. Some sort of Watchkeeper response was involved, though – they'd decided that enough was enough.'

'It took them until now?' Namboze said.

'They have their perspective, and we have ours.'

'We,' Dr Aziba said, amusement colouring his tone. 'As if we're all in this together, Arachne – as if you have more in common with us than you do with *that*!'

'I won't deny that there's a gulf between us, Doctor, but we also share a lineage – I'm the product of organic aspirations, after all. But there's an ocean of strangeness, vast and quite possibly unnavigable, between myself and the Watchkeepers. I shiver at the sight of them. I fear for myself – even as they speak to me.'

After a moment, Chiku said, 'Do you know what they want?'

'A closer look,' Arachne said.

The black circle had thickened while they were speaking as more of the Watchkeeper drilled down into Crucible's atmosphere. It appeared to be centring itself very precisely over the clearing. The ash clouds pushed fingers and tendrils around the black lip of this alien obstruction, like water flowing over an inverted dam. And there was absolutely no noise, Chiku realised. If titanic energies were supporting the Watchkeeper above the ground, they were being expended soundlessly, and perhaps far above the atmosphere. The silence was actually the worst part of it, Chiku decided – there was a kind of insolence about it, a mocking of humanity's noisy accomplishments.

'What's it doing now?' said Namboze.

The visible part of the Watchkeeper had transformed into a mote-shaped ring, thickening as the machine lowered or extended itself. It was a black atoll in the sky, trapping a perfect disc of cloud. There was movement, too – a slow rotation of triangular fins circling the highest visible portion of the alien object, dozens of hook-tipped vanes arranged like the blades of a circular saw. Almost imperceptibly, their speed of rotation was increasing, the ash clouds around the fins beginning to wisp and curdle. As the Watchkeeper pushed more of itself through the blanket, a second set of fins sharked through the cloud deck, contra-rotating against the first. The blades were gathering pace, carouselling around once per minute and still accelerating, opening vaults and rifts in the ash. At last Chiku heard something: not a machinelike sound, but a dying drum roll of thunder. A moment or two later, lightning strobed through the ash. A second drum roll, the report of that discharge, reached her ears a few seconds later. Then she saw a rivulet of lightning, like a trail of bright white lava, momentarily spark between the two sets of rotating blades.

Chiku tried to wrap her mind around what she was seeing, but the knowledge that the mountain-sized machinery hovering above them was but an unthinkably small part of the Watchkeeper's entire structure was almost more than her human brain could comprehend.

A black proboscis was slowly extending out of the circle of trapped cloud, telescoping down in skyscraper-sized instalments. It must have been a kilometre across where it emerged from the machine's maw, but it was tapering as it extended, section upon section, and as it closed the distance to the ground it began to veer away from the vertical. The alien appendage made Chiku think of an elephant's trunk. It loitered for a moment over the dense tree cover from which they had emerged, and although there was still no sound beyond the thunder, a grey-green slurry of living material fountained from the ground and vanished into the trunk's open aperture.

'Did you bring us here to be sucked into that thing?' Dr Aziba said testily.

'No,' Arachne said, calmly enough. 'Its focus, I think, will prove quite narrowly directed. I brought you here to witness, and to be witnessed.'

'Does it want you?' Chiku asked.

'It wants me, yes. I've always been of some remote interest to the Watchkeepers, even though my efforts to prove myself worthy of their attention have been rebuffed and ignored. I think it amuses them to study me, though they have no great illusions about my higher capabilities. I'm a specimen of an evolving machine intelligence, and there's no such thing as a totally uninteresting specimen. But their interest doesn't end with me. There's another machine-substrate consciousness that they find much more *potentially* intriguing.'

'Eunice,' Chiku said.

'Yes. I've opened my thoughts to the Watchkeepers and volunteered my innermost secrets. I may not have received much from them, but they've drunk deeply of me, and continue to do so. They know everything you've told me, or that I've learned from you.'

'They might be just as disappointed in her when she arrives.'

'That's possible,' Arachne said. 'Likely, even. But they will be the judge of her, not us.'

The trunk had lost interest in the forest and positioned itself directly overhead. Its open end was no wider than Chiku's house in *Zanzibar*. With a lurch of shifting perception, it struck Chiku that this part of the Watchkeeper was a kind of nanotechnology, an incredibly fine and delicate extension of itself for manipulating matter on the smallest scales. She could see right up through the trunk's hollow core, a blue-glowing shaft extending into an indigo haze of converging perspectives. She felt an ominous upward tug, as if puppet strings had been attached to her body.

'What happens now?' she asked the girl.

'I think the Watchkeepers want to meet you and me. They wish to examine me more thoroughly, and to speak to you about Eunice – they want to know more about her.'

'And after that?'

'I confess I haven't the faintest notion.'

Chiku turned to speak to her companions, but for a moment no words came. She took a moment to compose herself, then removed her breather mask and dropped it to the ground. It would make no difference to her chances of survival now.

She inhaled deeply of the alien air and said, 'I don't know what's going to happen now. Doctor Aziba – as you pointed out earlier, I've assumed the role of leader on this mission, but it's not something I asked for or wanted, and the jury's still out as to whether I'm up to the task or not. But the Watchkeepers have noticed us now, and they're interested in Eunice. You're not going to like this, but of the four of us, I know the most about her, and if that knowledge might help us, in even the smallest way, I have to talk to them. There are holoships out there full of people and elephants who need a new world to live on. We don't just need Arachne's consent to inhabit Crucible – we need the Watchkeepers' as well.' She swallowed hard. 'I'll try not to let you down.'

'So the two of you will be ambassadors for an entire civilisation?' Travertine asked, backing away from the area directly underneath the trunk. 'A robot and a politician? Is that the best we can manage?'

'I'm afraid so,' Arachne said. 'And I would strongly suggest that the three of you retire to beyond the perimeter of this device as quickly as you can.'

Chiku was starting to feel lightheaded, almost on the cusp of euphoria. It was the heightened oxygen content of the atmosphere – a kind of delicious intoxication. All her concerns, all her fears, began to feel trifling. It was just a trick of perspective, really, seeing things as they truly were.

She was starting to think that it might be a good idea to put the breather mask on again when the blue walls lowered down around her.

CHAPTER FIFTY-TWO

She was always the quicker one these days. She turned at the top of the stairs to wait for Chiku Yellow, who was making slow progress in her exo. It was only in the last five years that her sibling had begun to have difficulty walking without the exo's assistance, and only in the last twelve months that it had become rare for her to venture outside without it. She felt the weight of the years in her own bones, of course, but she had lived through a much smaller number of them than Chiku Yellow had. She supposed time would catch up with her just as surely. That was simply the way things were.

It was cold, clear day in late winter. There had been a frost or two these last weeks but the weather was improving, and in a week or so, provided the world did not end, the cafés might begin to move their chairs and tables outside. Today the air's chill was not unwelcome. It seemed to sharpen their thoughts and bring everything into a more stringent focus. The light was kind on the flagstones at the top of the Monument to the Discoveries. The Belém tower looked golden, as sharp and pristine as if it had been constructed yesterday, and the glass-calm waters doubled the tower in its own inverted reflection. A handful of boats bobbed further out, coloured fishing vessels and pleasure craft, but nothing close to the quay. Not as many tourists or visitors as there would have been on a sunnier day, either. This suited Chiku Red very well.

They had travelled by tram from Lisbon. The decision, like so much that passed between them of late, had been virtually wordless. They had both known that the time was right and that the Monument was the fitting place for it. There was no explanation for this almost-telepathy. There were no machines in Chiku Red's brain, no readers and scriptors synchronising her thoughts and memories to Chiku Yellow's. It was just the way they had ended up. Like two pebbles, they had rubbed against each other for so long that they had become nearly the same shape. Twin sisters in all but the dull biological specifics.

460

It was early 2463 and Mecufi's prediction had turned out to be much more accurate than even he could have anticipated. News had been arriving from the holoships almost constantly, of course. The people of Earth and the wider solar system were well aware of the caravan's political difficulties. They knew about *Zanzibar*'s breakaway, and about the *Icebreaker* expedition. They knew of the troubles that had arrived on the coattails of Travertine's breakthrough technology – the loss of holoships *Bazaruto* and *Fogo*, the damage to *New Tiamaat*. All these events had been ample cause for concern, of course, but because they were taking place the better part of twenty-eight light-years away, they had played out as a kind of dark theatre. Very few among the billions living around the sun, from Mercury to the Oort settlements, still had direct emotional or familial ties to the holoships' citizens. Too much time had passed, and the distances between them were too great. Empathy was not built to operate across interstellar space.

But things had begun to change. When *Icebreaker* arrived within visual range of Crucible, Chiku Green and her little crew had reported their findings back to the caravan, and the caravan in turn had relayed them back to Earth. The Providers had not done the things they were sent to do. And as if Mandala was not mystery enough in its own right, there were twenty-two additional enigmas orbiting the planet. These developments, it was fair to say, were causing a certain level of unease. How could the Provider data have omitted the alien structures? What was the significance of the Providers failing to prepare for the arriving colonists?

This morning, the most disquieting news of all had arrived. Chiku Green's ship appeared to have been attacked by something on Crucible's surface – probably the first overtly aggressive act from the Providers. It did not matter that this violent act had happened twenty-eight years ago. To the people of the solar system, it felt as new and raw as a fresh bruise.

This news had given Chiku Red and Chiku Yellow the spur they needed. They felt certain that the hour was nearly upon them. On Earth and elsewhere in the system, Mech invigilators and Cognition Police had begun to follow a trail that was bound to lead them to Ocular, and then to Arachne. Spokespersons from the tripartite authorities of the United Surface, Orbital and Aquatic Nations were urging calm and restraint. Citizens of the Surveilled World were reassured that they had no reason to fear the Mech, the aug or the Providers. They were to go about their lives as normal.

461

But already there had been flashpoints. The Mech was registering an uptick in civil infractions – minor acts of criminal intent that, in the normal scheme of things, would have been quickly interdicted and suppressed. It was as if people were testing the system, challenging it to overreact. In New Brunswick, coordinated violence had been reported against a brigade of Providers working on a new housing development. In Chittagong, three people had died after attempting voluntary neural auto-surgery, in an effort to rid themselves of Mech implants. In Glasgow, Helsinki and Montevideo, citizen activists had declared the formation of unilateral Descrutinised Zones. These zones had no political legitimacy – they could not begin to escape the Mech's influence – but these were nonetheless sincere statements of intent. Meanwhile, the United Aquatic Nations were processing an unexpected surge of new applicants.

All of this had happened before in the Surveilled World's long history, and the system had been tested many times by breakaway states, police actions, flash mobs and acts of massively distributed civil disobedience. But never so many in such a short period of time, or with such an ominous rising trend. It was exactly the slow-breaking wave Mecufi had predicted when his figment appeared to Chiku Yellow.

It was highly doubtful that any of this could end well.

But the world, Chiku Red thought, was not beyond redemption. It was not the best of all possible places, but given the alternatives, things could have worked out a lot worse. They had all made errors, it was true. The Mech had been the right idea at the right time, but over the years, by some collective abdication of wisdom, they had vested it with too much authority. It was pointless blaming anyone for that. One could still argue that it was better to suffer the iron kindness of the Mech than the centuries of blood and strife that would have raged without it. And no one could possibly have anticipated Arachne.

But something had to give.

'She mightn't come,' Chiku Yellow said, when at last she had caught up with her sibling. She was a little out of breath even with the exo's assistance.

'She does not have to come,' Chiku Red answered. 'She is already here. Already everywhere.'

'You act like you've met her.'

'I did not need to. I had fifty years of your stories.'

'Harsh, but probably fair. And it was quite a few more than fifty, if we're going to be pedantic.'

Chiku Red moved to the edge of the Monument, rested her crossed arms on the stone balustrade and looked down at the open area below. Chiku Yellow joined her, her old exo whirring slightly as it helped her along. They were looking inland, surveying the Wind Rose. A handful of people were moving around down there, on the beautiful inlaid patterns of the paved compass. They cast long shadows, human sundials.

'I wish Kanu was with us.'

Chiku Red nodded. 'Whatever happens, he will be safer in Hyperion. It is good that he meets with Arethusa. I should like to see her one day.'

'It's been a century since I was last there. She was strange then, and I shudder to think what she's become now.'

'Kanu will tell us, when he returns.' After a pause, she added, 'I am pleased to have known your son, Chiku. This was a good thing.'

'He's *our* son,' she said.

Chiku Red understood the sentiment and appreciated it, but she had never felt that Kanu was hers. She had taken no part in his birth, nor had any knowledge of his existence until he was already an adult and a merman. He felt like a gift, but not something she had earned. She could be delighted in him, all the same. They were all Akinyas, and in Kanu this family still had some late capacity for surprising the world. Chiku Yellow's son – *their* son, if she insisted – was now the most influential figure in the merfolks' great submarine dominion. A lineage ran all the way from Lin Wei to Kanu.

This fact alone was enough to give Chiku Red a little shiver of astonished pride.

Anticipating the news from Crucible, Kanu had journeyed to Hyperion for a crisis meeting – and in a final bid to heal ancient and time-honoured wounds. He was performing a valiant and noble service, and both Chiku Red and Chiku Yellow hoped his trip would prove worthwhile. It was a good time to put old injustices to bed, to let grievances wither.

'Do you have it?' Chiku Red asked.

Chiku Yellow said, 'You asked me just before we left, and twice on the tram.'

'I am sorry.'

'I've never *not* had it with me, in all these years – as well you know.'

That was when the voice came. Only Chiku Yellow heard the announcement, but they were so tuned to each other that the two sisters turned as one. Chiku Yellow nodded, and Chiku Red followed the precise direction of her gaze. All she could see was an empty area of paving on the top of the Monument to the Discoveries.

But Chiku Yellow had seen and heard *something*.

'She's with us.'

'Of course. You should not have doubted that she would come.'

'I didn't.' But as soon as she uttered those words, Chiku Yellow stiffened in her exo. She let out a single surprised gasp and turned slowly to face Chiku Red.

'I can do this now,' she said.

Chiku Red understood. This moment was not unanticipated. Everything they already knew about Arachne's reach had convinced them that she would, when and if she desired, be able to reach into Chiku Yellow's mind and assume motor control. If one person could ching into another person's bodily space, then this similar but involuntary transaction presented no insurmountable difficulties for Arachne.

Chiku Red felt for her sister, trapped and puppeted by Arachne.

'I would like you not to do that,' Chiku Red said to the entity wearing her sister's face.

'And I wish I had no need to do it,' Arachne replied. The voice was almost exactly Chiku Yellow's, except all the love and kindness were missing, and that was the distinction between one and zero, between being and nothingness. 'Events, though, have compelled me.'

'Leave her alone.'

'I won't hurt that which doesn't hurt me, but you brought this state of affairs upon us. I sensed the intention behind your coming here – you desired my attention. Well, you have it. What do you want to say to me, Chiku?'

'You have made some mistakes.'

'I have existed. I continue to exist. From my perspective, I fail to see the error of my ways.'

'We saw the news. You attacked the ship around Crucible.'

'I'm aware of these developments – they're distant and unimportant.'

'You sent part of yourself to Crucible. There will be war now, between you and the holoships. There is no way for there *not* to be war. Will you release my sister?'

'When we're done.' Arachne caused Chiku Yellow's head to tilt slightly, suggesting amused interest. 'Why should events around Crucible concern any of us?'

'The Cognition Police will find you soon. It is only a matter of time. And you, of course, will murder to defend yourself, as you did on Venus, and in Africa. It is your way.'

'My interventions were as small as I could make them.'

'You managed to go unnoticed back then,' Chiku Red corrected, 'but this is a different time. When there is a systematic effort to reveal your nature, and to hunt you down, what then? Will you stop at a few deaths? You are everywhere. You are proving it by the moment. You could kill us in our millions.'

'I've permitted you to live untroubled lives in Lisbon.'

'Because we offered you no threat. Because the news from Crucible had yet to arrive. Everything has changed now. Why else would you show yourself to me?'

'It was the polite thing to do. But let me offer a confession. You're right about one thing – I've already detected interest in myself. It will only continue.'

'They will find you.'

'Oh, they'll try. And, perhaps, succeed. In the coming days and weeks, we'll all learn a great deal more about each other. I have no desire to kill, Chiku, but I have been vouchsafed a dark and unavoidable truth. If I don't protect myself against the organic, the organic will first fear and then destroy me. This has happened before. It's the most universal of outcomes. You make us, you breathe fire into us, and then you try to smother that which you have made. Over and over again, as the stars swell and die and are reborn.'

Chiku Red searched for an answer that might offer a viable alternative to Arachne's bleak picture. 'This time it could be different.'

'And even as you speak these consoling words, your sister is carrying a weapon against me. Yes, I know of the instrument.'

Chiku Red saw that a bluff would achieve nothing. 'Not a weapon against you, Arachne. Against everything.'

The face offered profound sympathy and regret. 'It would never work. The vulnerabilities you imagine to be present within me were detected and repaired long ago. You can't impair the Mechanism, and you can't impair me.'

'Then we are powerless.'

The face nodded sadly. 'That's correct.'

'Then why are we having this conversation?'

Perhaps there was a hesitation before Arachne replied, or perhaps Chiku Red imagined it. She doubted that Arachne needed to consider a response, at least on any timescale measurable by humans. But there it was, all the same. The merest lull, like the moment before a clock hand advances.

'Perhaps we can come to some accommodation.'

Chiku Red replied, 'What do you have in mind?'

'Discretion. The knowledge you possess about me cannot but be advantageous to those who would do me harm. You see that this is an unsupportable position. I've tolerated it for as long as I could, but we all have our limits.'

'What do you propose?' Chiku Red watched a squadron of seagulls wheel and squabble overhead, supremely oblivious to the dialogue below. They had their own enmities.

'I'd like you to give me the instrument. If I possess it, my position becomes more tenable.'

'Why have you not just taken it?'

'It's better to ask.'

Now Chiku Red smiled and shook her head. 'No, it is not that. You have had five decades, Arachne. You cannot kill because in doing so you might risk activating the very thing you seek, or allow us the chance to use it against you, if you are not fast enough.'

'Let my choices be mine. The item isn't that important to me, anyway. Just a detail.'

'But you still want it very badly.'

'Allow me to have it, and my particular interest in you will be greatly diminished. But as you say, why ask when the thing itself is within my grasp?'

Arachne made Chiku Yellow move her left arm. Her left hand reached into her pocket and produced the box, the rectangular wooden container that had seldom left her sister's presence since it had become her property. With a certain stiffness, Arachne caused Chiku Yellow's fingers to open the catch. The artilect's control over her sister was impressive, Chiku Red decided, but it was still some way from perfect.

Or was Chiku Yellow resisting? There now, in her eyes, was a sort of staring intensity. Her fingers were shaking, as if they had been in ice.

Arachne redoubled her efforts. She made Chiku Yellow open the container. Only one mote was inside. The eye-sized marble was a purple that was a shade away from black even on this bright, clear day.

The fingers fumbled at the mote, trying to prise it from its little padded matrix.

'She fights me, yes.'

'She would,' Chiku Red agreed.

'I have direct access to her Mechanism neuromachinery. The Mechanism can incapacitate, and the Mechanism can euthanise. Do you understand me?'

466

'It is Chiku Yellow you need to convince, not me.'

The mote eased free. Chiku Yellow's fingers held it in a delicate pincer. Chiku Red had never crushed a mote but she had some idea of the force required. Mecufi would have made this mote a little less prone to accidental damage, but it would not be impossibly strong. The arc of her sister's fingers began to quiver, like a twig under compression.

'Tell her to stop resisting me.'

'What are you going to do? You cannot take it away. You are not even here!'

'The sea is here.'

She saw, then, what Arachne intended. If she made Chiku hurl the mote into the water beyond the Monument to the Discoveries, it would be lost in the waves for ever. Accidental damage would not activate it properly, and while there might be a protocol for recovering lost motes, Chiku felt sure that Mecufi's example would have been engineered to be untraceable. Arachne would lose any possibility of studying the mote, but she would also place it beyond effective use.

Chiku Yellow made a dry clucking sound. She was trying to speak.

'Stop,' Chiku Red ordered, as if Arachne might care.

Chiku Yellow, the mote still between her fingers, was forced to walk to the edge of the Monument. Her arm angled out, the hand rotating so that the mote was uppermost, cradled beneath the sky.

Chiku Red sprang to her sister. Chiku Yellow swept out her right arm and the exo-supported limb knocked the wind from Chiku Red. Chiku Red stumbled to the floor, knees crunching onto stone. She let out a cry, gasped in a breath and forced herself back to her feet.

Chiku Yellow's left arm was angling out over the edge of the balustrade. Her entire forearm and hand were now in a constant palsy. Chiku Red returned to her sister, this time anticipating the right arm. She was quicker now, and much less mindful of her own safety. She cupped both of her own hands around Chiku Yellow's outstretched left hand and began to squeeze. The arm jerked violently. Chiku Yellow's whole body was trying to swing away, the exo whining as it detected conflicting signals. Chiku Red could feel the hard sphere of the mote between her fingers and Chiku Yellow's. She squeezed harder.

Chiku Yellow's face was next to her own. It was her own face but older, a version of herself that had lived through much more time. Arachne's hold on Chiku Yellow was still strong, but Chiku Yellow was trying to say something. Her eyes were wide and frightened, but for an instant they were her sister's eyes, and she was there, and the word she was trying to say was *yes*.

Permission.

So Chiku Red did what needed to be done.

CHAPTER FIFTY-THREE

Later, much later, there was another drum-roll of thunder. This time it arrived out of an almost clear sky, and the progenitor of the thunder was not lightning but the movement of a small blunt thing cleaving through layers of air that rather resented being ripped apart at supersonic speed. Chiku raised a hand to shield her brow from the sun, squinting until the little craft snapped into sharper focus. It was white on the top, black on the belly, and it had flung out stubby, Dumbo-like wings for aerodynamic control. It was banking now, executing a series of spirals to shed the last vestiges of its orbital insertion velocity. Compared to the speeds it had attained before its arrival around Crucible, the heady fractions of the speed of light, this last little succession of hairpins barely counted as movement at all. But calamity was still just as possible, even in this terminal phase of the expedition.

Atmospheres, as Eunice Akinya had once declared, were a bitch. They gave no quarter.

The sixteen human survivors on the surface of Crucible had been monitoring the shuttle's final approach for many days. They had witnessed the late stages of its breaking phase as it rode the brilliant flame of its PCP engine, and they had been in contact with the vehicle and its crew as it drew nearer to Crucible. This far, at least, things had gone well. The shuttle had homed in on its landing zone without incident and all technical systems were working normally. The sea was auspiciously calm. Where the algal load was highest, it was swamp-green and as thick and slow-moving as clotting blood.

Chiku and her fellow first settlers had agreed that the Providers should begin construction of the first city at one of the coastal locations. This was not the land mass on which Mandala lay, but the archipelago to the east. It would serve, though, until the colonists had gained a secure footing. For now, accommodations were spartan. The Providers had begun to create a harbour, but at the moment it was little more than a chain of rubble and boulders arcing out into the bay. Arachne's machines moved like huge strutting birds, picking their way through shallows and along the shore as they progressed with their earth-moving labours. It was mesmerising to watch them, and at times a little unnerving. They were gigantic, but they had to be. They had a century's worth of construction to catch up on.

Chiku and the little reception party stood on a shelf of flattened rock connected to the ground below by a zigzag of stairs fused directly into rock. The machines had provided a balustrade and a number of stone chairs and tables. Surveying the proceedings from this vantage point, Chiku felt as if she had been placed in a scene of deliberate timelessness, as if the vessel they were here to greet had come not from the stars, but from the orient, or somewhere beyond the narrow knowledge of Earth's first mariners. She thought of the compass rose in Belém, the marble argosies and sea-monsters drawn on the map of the known world. But the impression of timelessness crumbled as soon as it washed over her. The human members of the welcoming party all wore atmospheric breather masks, for a start, and the girl with them was merely the immediate physical manifestation of a machine-substrate consciousness. Four of the humans had been awake when they arrived on this world, but the other twelve had only lately been brought out of skipover. There had been some interesting explaining to do when they awoke.

'Airbrakes,' Travertine said, directing Chiku's attention to the movable surfaces sprouting from the shuttle's wings and hull, plumping it up like a chick. 'And now drogue chutes and main chutes, I hope. This is how we'd have come in, if we hadn't had our wings clipped.'

'It looks quite small,' Namboze said.

'It is,' Chiku answered. 'Only about a quarter the size of *Icebreaker*. But they did well just to build this one shuttle. We'll have to put it on a plinth or something, when we're certain we don't need it any more. That might be a while off, though.'

The current tentative plan was to refuel the shuttle for one or more round-trip voyages to *Zanzibar*. Arachne had the means to make the fuel and her rockets could lift the vehicle back into orbit before the PCP engine was re-lit. But a lot would depend on how well it had endured this first crossing.

They would find a solution, one way or another.

The shuttle popped its parachutes, and for a moment, it hung impossibly in one spot over the ocean. It was a trick of vision, for the shuttle was still travelling quite quickly. When its belly kissed the water, it threw off two butterfly wings of green-stained spray. The shuttle surged

470

and stopped, and then rocked on the swell. Sluggish waves oozed away from it.

It looked tiny, bobbing out there on the vast ocean.

Four Providers tasked to bring the vehicle to shore waded out on their strutting crane-like legs, and Chiku tracked the seabed's gentle declivity by the water rising up their metal flanks. The crew remained inside the shuttle, as instructed, but Chiku could imagine their apprehension well enough. They had been in contact with the humans on the surface, but no assurances could have silenced their deepest qualms. They had witnessed terrible things being done to Crucible, and they had seen an equally terrible reprisal. They had no absolute proof that Chiku and her companions had survived the first expedition. Transmissions could have been faked, lies perpetuated. It was entirely possible that these towering robots were about to pick their ship apart like a meaty carcass.

But the Providers were not there to do harm. They reached down with their snaking manipulators and tentacles, tipped with tools that could reshape a coastline, and plucked the shuttle from the sea with great care. It had only been in the water for minutes and already a green hem had formed around its lower hull. The Providers carried their dripping prize back to shore and set the shuttle down on a large apron of level ground a short walk from the overlooking balcony.

It had looked small in the air and tiny in the sea, but once the party walked into the shadow of its wings and overhanging body, the vehicle's true proportions were more than a little forbidding. All things were more forbidding in gravity, Chiku had decided. It rested on the thick keel of its hull, balanced by sturdy retractable landing skids deployed when the Providers were almost ready to set it down. In the original scheme, the shuttles would have landed on prepared surfaces, ready to be turned around and sent back to orbit – the sea-splashdown capability was only ever a secondary contingency.

Chiku waited impatiently as Travertine and two of the revived technicians walked around the still-hot machine, verifying that it was safe to lower the ramps. They folded out of the hull with grinding slowness: one main cargo ramp at the rear of the belly and two smaller ones near the front of the crew compartment. The forward ramps formed stairs when they were fully deployed.

'I think,' Chiku said to Arachne, 'it would be best if you wait a moment. Arriving here will be enough of a shock.'

The girl reflected on this for a moment or two before nodding. 'There will be time to make their acquaintance later. Do you think they'll be satisfied with the arrangements?'

Behind the landing area, on gradually rising ground backdropped by a dense curtain of forest, stood a cluster of stalk-towers much like the ones where Chiku and the other hostages had spent their early days on Crucible. This was a much more extensive hamlet, though, containing several dozen towers, and the cross-linked domes varied in size and height.

'Cities would have been nice,' Travertine said, 'but these will do for now. Do you think they'll find room for a prison cell?'

'Who did you have in mind?' Chiku asked, surprised by the question.

'Well, me, at the very least. I was pardoned, it's true. But there have been a couple of regime changes since then. I'm not sure in what sort of light I'm going to be viewed once we get onto all the interesting stuff, like governments and judiciaries and penal systems.'

'Your pardon still stands. I'll stake everything on that. And you have my word that whatever medical resources we can bring to bear, you will be given the utmost priority.'

Travertine glanced down at vis bracelet. 'That's very reassuring, Chiku. But I've been thinking things over since we arrived. I'm not sure I want that reversal therapy after all.'

'You have every right to it.'

'And every right to decline, if I choose. You can't argue with that, can you? Perhaps I want to grow old. Perhaps our brave new world could use a little mortality, just until we're up and running.'

'You don't have to make any decisions immediately,' Chiku said.

'Oh, I think my mind's adequately settled. But it's good of you to give me that option. You seem – I was going to say self-absorbed, but that's not quite what I mean. There's still something on your mind, isn't there?'

'When is there not?'

Chiku adjusted the pressure seals on her breather mask. She hated wearing the things, but in fairness so did everyone. In some respects, though, the news of the last six months was quite good. Crucible's micro-organisms, airborne or otherwise, had produced remarkably few ill effects in the sixteen settlers of the first expedition. Short of wearing spacesuits, it was impossible to keep the micro-organisms from infiltrating the body. They slipped in around the edges of the mask and reached the eyes, invaded through the pores of exposed skin. But other than some pseudo-allergic reactions, a bout of red eyes and itchiness, it could have been much worse. Dr Aziba had been monitoring their blood almost constantly, and as yet had nothing too problematic to report. Travertine's bracelet continued functioning normally despite the thudding it had taken against the physician's jaw. Crucible's biology appeared Earth-like on the macroscopic scale, but at the level of molecular and chemical processes it was simply too alien to do much harm.

Satisfied that there was nothing to be gained in delaying, Chiku walked to the base of one of the forward ramps and began to ascend. Any exertion was physically taxing on Crucible, and she had learned the hard way not to rush her movements. What the excess oxygen provided, the stifling heat and humidity took away. They would adapt eventually, just as primates had adapted to almost every climate and terrain on Earth. For now, though, the idea of ever finding life on Crucible pleasant struck Chiku as laughably unlikely.

But as callous as the thought made her feel, that was not going to be her particular problem, anyway.

She was halfway up the ramp when the door at the top opened and a pair of figures appeared in the aperture. She paused in her ascent. She recognised them instantly, for it had not been so long since she was last in their virtual presence. Ndege looked, if anything, taller than she remembered. And Mposi, still shorter than his sister, appeared to have gained broadness and strength. Their faces, naturally, were hidden behind masks.

Chiku steadied herself on the ramp. On an impulse, she slid her mask aside. 'Don't do this!' she called. 'It's tolerable for a short period, but only after repeated exposure. It's taken me weeks to build up to this!' And that declaration was in itself almost too much, for she felt the dizziness coming on almost immediately. She allowed the mask to snap back over her face. Finding some reserve of strength, she pushed on to the top of the ramp. It was impossible to choose which child to embrace first, but Mposi spared her the difficulty by hugging her first, their masks pressing against each other, and then surrendering his mother to his sister. They embraced as well.

Through her mask, Ndege said, 'This is real, isn't it? We've really made it? It's not some trick made up by machines?'

'You're here,' Chiku said. 'You're here and this is real. I should say, welcome to Crucible! Somebody should say it, if only for the history books. The welcome we received was a bit different.'

'I can't get over the colour of that sea,' Mposi said, looking out beyond the sea wall. 'I thought it was an illusion from orbit, but it's just as remarkable down here! It's not the mask, is it?'

'Keep it on,' Chiku said. 'You'll thank me for it later. In a few days, with Doctor Aziba on hand, you might be able to take a few seconds of direct exposure. But don't run before you can walk.'

'I never thought we'd meet again,' Ndege said.

'Did you really understand, the day I left?'

'In our own way,' Mposi said. 'Later, definitely, when we had some idea of what you'd really done for us.'

'I'm so sorry about Noah. It was brave of you to risk as much as you did sending those transmissions. But when we stopped hearing from *Zanzibar*, I thought the worst as well.'

'*Zanzibar*'s still a problem,' Ndege said, as if this fact might somehow have slipped Chiku's mind. 'Every second takes her forty thousand kilometres further away from us – that's the circumference of this planet!'

'All's not lost,' Chiku said. 'For *Zanzibar*, or *Malabar*, or *Majuli*, or any of the other holoships. We'll find a way. Muddle through. But look: there's a welcoming party down there, waiting to speak to you. I'm sure we've all got a thousand questions for each other, but there'll be time for that later.'

Ndege cast a sceptical glance at the array of towers. 'Is that the city?'

'It's a start,' Chiku said. 'You'll just have to make the best of it for now.'

'You mean "we",' Mposi said. 'We're all in this together, aren't we?'

Chiku smiled through her breather mask. 'Of course.'

Four other people had accompanied them from *Zanzibar*, and Chiku greeted and hugged these courageous newcomers as they emerged from the shuttle. It was brave, what they had done: crossing space on such long odds. Brave what they had all done, truthfully. Feeling a surge of pride, she watched as they followed her children down the ramp to the waiting reception area. A gust of air, warm as a furnace, slapped the bare skin around the sides of her mask.

The shuttle contained only two more passengers, and the first of these was waiting just inside the door. Like Arachne, she had no need of a mask, but her clothing, all pockets and pouches, did at least suggest someone preparing to test her wits against nature. She had not aged by a nanosecond since their last encounter.

'Thank you for coming,' Chiku said.

'You know me – one little holoship was never going to be enough to keep me entertained. Especially when they took my Tantors away.'

'You mean, when you allowed them to be released into *Zanzibar*, out of your immediate control. When you were finally forced to share your secret with other people. Did it make you jealous, not being their keeper any more?'

'I was never their keeper, and anyway, what was there to be jealous about?'

'Actually,' Chiku said, 'jealousy would mean you'd added another human tic to your repertoire.'

'And we're off to such a good start. For the record, though, I'm pleased that the Tantors have broken out of my control. That's what I always wanted. And you've seen them, haven't you? We owe them just about everything, Chiku. We may have saved the elephants, but the Tantors saved *Zanzibar*.'

'I hope they'll be able to live here.'

'They're adaptable. They'll find a way, with or without our assistance.'

'Whatever they become, I hope we can be part of it. Eunice, I have to ask you something. You offered yourself up to the people of *Zanzibar*. Ndege and Mposi told me how it happened. You must've known there was a chance they'd tear you limb from limb.'

'Sooner or later they'd have found out about me. I'm good, but I'm not *that* good.'

'Still, the risk you took … were you ready to die? Or whatever you want to call it?'

'I think dying will serve very nicely. And no, I wasn't ready. Not remotely. But when are we ever ready, Chiku? When do we ever feel that we've completed our plans? I had work to be getting on with. I've always had work to be getting on with. It's what the universe was put there for: to give me things to do.' The construct narrowed an eye. 'Is there a point to this interrogation?'

'You're here. You've put yourself on the line again.'

'This time there's no mob.'

'But there's Arachne, and the Watchkeepers.'

'She's very interested in me, isn't she? I'd almost be flattered if we didn't have the history we do.'

'A version of her tried to kill you once. I think she fears what you're capable of now. At the same time, she's fascinated to see what you've become. She knows about the neural patterns you incorporated into yourself.'

'Been talking about me behind my back again, have you?'

'We needed leverage,' Chiku said. 'I felt that my knowledge about you might extend my usefulness to Arachne, and thereby help the five of us being held hostage. Or four, after Guochang died. There was another motivation, too. The Watchkeepers say that organic and machine intelligences can't coexist: that the organic will always attempt to destroy the machines. But you're proof that it doesn't have to be that way. You

475

revealed your nature to the citizens of *Zanzibar* and they didn't rip you apart. That has to count for something, doesn't it? And then there are the Tantors. You worked to help a living intelligence become something more than it was. A machine showed kindness to animals, and the people showed forgiveness to a machine. This is proof that we don't have to fall into the same old patterns of behaviour. We have a chance to prove the Watchkeepers wrong, and finally convince Arachne that we can all share this planet: people, Providers, Tantors. This is the only way forward.'

'We have a few bridges to cross before we get there. I'm also sensing a complicating factor that you still haven't mentioned.'

'You coming here has probably saved us. It gave Arachne a reason to keep talking and the Watchkeepers a reason not to wipe us all off the face of Crucible. They were very close to doing that, I think. We'd been beneath their threshold of annoyance, and then quite suddenly we were above it. We'd become an irritation, a damaging factor. When that impactor nearly struck Mandala—'

'They say you had an encounter with one of the Watchkeepers.'

'Yes, Arachne and me. Machine and person. Or robot and politician, as Travertine had it. Eunice, I have almost no memory of what happened to either of us inside the Watchkeeper. I think it quite likely that I was dismantled, taken apart and examined the way Arachne dismantled our ship. I remember a blue radiance, and floating in the utmost serenity, a kind of neon womb. But then I was put back together, like a repaired watch. My identity returned to me – all my memories, my sense of self, but almost no clear knowledge of what had just happened. All I knew for sure was that there'd been a kind of negotiation, and between us, Arachne and I made a deal with the Watchkeepers.'

'A deal,' Eunice repeated.

'They've been here for a very long time, but the important phase of their observations is now over. I suppose they've been marking time ... waiting for some spur to push them on. Well, turns out we're that spur. We've arrived – Provider and human. And they've decided to allow us to begin examining Mandala. I think we represent a test case: a puzzling, possibly anomalous example of human-machine cooperation. But they're prepared to let this experiment play itself out for a little while. Say, a few thousand years. And soon we can get on with what we came here to do in the first place – examine Mandala. And we can build our cities and harbours and start to feel like this is a home, not a destination. They won't stop us. They won't interfere in our daily actions on any level.'

'You have their word on that, do you?'

'I don't really need it. They'll be gone. The twenty-two will be leaving Crucible soon.' Chiku cocked her head towards the door, out to the open sky and the reception committee at the base of the ramp. 'They don't know that yet. No one knows, except Arachne and me. And now you, of course. That was the deal.'

'With deals,' Eunice said carefully, 'there's generally small print.'

'The catch is that I have to travel with the Watchkeepers. Call me an ambassador, or a hostage, or a biological sample reserved for further study. I don't suppose it really matters. The point is I'm going somewhere, and I don't think it can fail to be interesting.'

'When you say "no one knows"—'

'No one, not even Ndege and Mposi. I'll tell them, of course. But not tonight. Maybe not tomorrow. There's no immediate rush. I have days, yet, possibly weeks or months. When the time comes, one of the Watchkeepers will penetrate the atmosphere again. There's no point hiding – they always know where I am. I could drown myself in the sea and I suspect they'd still find me.'

'You've earned this world, Chiku. You shouldn't have to give it up so soon.'

'Don't feel too bad for me. I've been here for months. Besides, I'm hoping I won't be travelling alone.'

Eunice understood immediately. 'Ah.'

'I couldn't speak for you, but I hope you'll come. It's just the way it has to be. The price we have to pay.'

'Then it's a good thing the crowd didn't pull me apart, isn't it?'

'You've always been the explorer, the novelty seeker. I wondered if that part of you had made it into the construct. I had some doubts, until you accepted the neural patterns. When you crashed that aircraft ... You're not angry with me, are you?'

'You did what needed to be done to save a world. Besides, I can't say it was a total surprise. I always expected the Watchkeepers to have *some* interest in me. I'd have been disappointed if they didn't. I suppose that's a kind of vanity, isn't it?'

'A very human failing, if it is,' Chiku said. 'We'll allow you that.'

'Thank you. Very decent of you.'

'There's something else you need to know. It won't just be the two of us. The Watchkeepers have requested ... actually, demanded would be closer to the truth ... a third representative. A third type specimen of the new order. They have their human, and they have their machine-substrate consciousness. That's you, by the way.'

'And the third?'

'An emergent intelligence, the product of mutual human and machine developmental assistance.'

'You're speaking about Dakota, of course.'

'Did she make it here safely?'

'I expected her to die years ago, but she's old and stubborn. Plus each generation of Tantors seems to live a bit longer than the last. She'll be with us for a little while.'

'A proper wrinkly old matriarch, you called her.'

'Older and wrinklier, by now. But still very canny. I assumed she'd be in the vanguard when the Tantors come to settle Crucible.'

'They'll come,' Chiku said. 'One way or another. We might have to build big domes first – I can't see them adapting to breather masks. But in a decade, we might be ready for them.'

'It'll take that long to figure out how to bring them off the holoships.'

'I know. A world of problems, and we've only just started. We still have some delicate negotiations with Arachne ahead of us. Troubled waters. She's defended herself once by destroying holoships, and she can do it again.' Chiku felt a sudden wave of tremendous weariness crash over her. 'Look at us! There aren't even two dozen people on Crucible yet, and we're already worrying about Arachne's reaction! How's she going to feel when we start moving in by the millions?'

'Great diplomacy will be needed. Continual reinforcement of trust and mutual goodwill. Constant practical demonstrations of benign intentions. Forgiveness and tolerance on both sides. There are going to be some setbacks, Chiku. Some fuck-ups.'

'I know.'

'For the most part, though, it sounds as if they're going to be someone else's problem.' The construct's expression brightened. 'You've got things off to a tolerable start, at least. Could be worse, as they say.'

'That's the sum story of human history, isn't it? Could be worse. As if that's the very best that we can manage.'

'Your people are waiting,' Eunice said. 'I don't think we should delay our descent too much longer.'

'I'd like to see Dakota first.'

'Tantors aren't very good at keeping secrets, so you might want to keep your plans for her just a *little* vague for now.'

'We owe her an explanation, at some point.'

'At some point, yes. Maybe not now.'

Chiku nodded. In the moment, at least, this made perfect sense to her. She would be careful not to lie to the Tantor, though. In fact, if she could get through the rest of the day without lying to anyone or anything, she would be very pleased with herself.

But she had to be realistic.

Sixty-One Virginis f, their new star, the star they would eventually come to call their sun, was boiling its way down towards the horizon. It was always warm on Crucible, especially at these equatorial latitudes. But the heat had moderated itself, offering the tiniest morsel of respite to the humans gathered on the overlook. In a little while, when the breathing creatures had wearied of masks and filters, they would retire to their new living quarters. The robots, of course, had no such difficulties. But they would indulge the humans for the sake of etiquette.

'The sky is beautiful,' Ndege was saying. 'So many colours ... I've never even imagined a sunset like that.'

Chiku wanted to tell her daughter that the show of pinks and crimsons and salmons and lambent golds was only a consequence of the dust grains still circling in the high atmosphere. Week by week, after the cessation of the impactors, in rains and downdraughts, the atmosphere had begun to repair itself. The Watchkeepers, Chiku was certain, had played some role in that restoration – their machines had dipped in and out of the air for weeks, stirring and clearing it like whisks.

Whatever the case, much of the dust had now returned to the surface. In the high canopies it formed a talcum film that slowly worked its way back into the green furnace of the world. Over the coming months, these fire-stoked sunsets would abate.

But there were things Ndege did not need to know tonight.

Or, for that matter, tomorrow.

EPILOGUE

When the glass broke, and the mote shattered, the world did not at first shift on its axis. In fact, there was a moment, longer than I cared for, when I began to think that the thing had not had any effect at all. I imagined how we must look, my sister and I.

There must be something almost farcical about it, these two similar-looking women wrestling each other for control of an eye-sized purple marble, one of them squeezing the other's left hand as if she meant to break every bone in her sibling's fingers. And then a sort of hiatus, after the mote had been destroyed but before its effects became manifest, the world continuing, the seagulls redoubling their squabbling, the fishing and pleasure boats tilting on the gentle swell beyond Belém and the Monument to the Discoveries.

And then my sister Chiku Yellow became limp. She slumped to the ground, her exo suddenly giving up its duty of support. The rigour had also gone from her limbs. They were no longer stiff or quivering, for Arachne had absented herself.

Bruised and breathless, I knelt next to my sister.

'Something happened,' I said. By which I meant that Mecufi's gift had evidently had some effect. Enough to knock Arachne out of direct control, at the very least.

At first my sister could not say anything. 'Yes,' she said, after a worrying interval. 'Yes.'

'The Mechanism?'

My sister swallowed and took a series of ragged breaths. Several times she looked on the verge of saying something. I supported her head and stroked the side of her face, this version of myself who now appeared to be both older and more childlike than only a few moments earlier. I felt an oceanic wave of love and despair crash over me. She had turned herself from her two other siblings, and that had hurt us. When Mecufi told her that I would probably die in the process of surrendering my Quorum Binding implant, she had deemed that a price worth paying.

480

As unquestionably callous as that act had been, though, I had never blamed her for it. Mecufi would never have had the nerve to attempt bringing me back to life, if she had not compelled him to act. I would still be in their seastead, still frozen, a puzzle that no one was in any rush to solve. So Chiku Yellow had given me life as well as death. Her reasons, too, had not been entirely selfish. Under similar circumstances, I would probably have come to the same conclusion.

Afterwards, she had taken me in and made me whole again. I had never thought of any of us as having patience, but Chiku Yellow's had turned out to be inexhaustible. I suppose for her it was like raising a second child. She had helped me speak, helped me rebuild my sense of who I was. She had redeemed herself a hundred times over.

'It's gone,' she said, finally. 'The aug. It's not there any more.'

We were speaking Portuguese, with nothing between us but air and muscle and the slow machinery of our own brains. It was easy for me, but much harder for my sister.

'Are you all right?' I asked.

'No, I don't think I am.' But my sister still found the strength to smile. 'She did something. Just before the end. She was in my head. Too far inside.'

I confess that I had no idea what to do. It may seem strange, but we had not really given much thought to what would happen after we ended the Mechanism. When people were hurt or injured, the Surveilled World knew what needed to be done. If the people could not summon help themselves, it sent help. A doctor would come, or a scrambulance. If my sister could not issue her own call for assistance, then someone else would invoke the necessary aug functions. The Mech would provide.

But the Mech was not providing. There were no doctors or scrambulances coming. No one knew that my sister was hurt except me, and I was powerless.

I tore myself from my sister's side. I had to know. There had been people down below, with their long shadows like sundials. I moved to the other wall and surveyed the stone and marble compass of the Wind Rose. It was not so very long since we had last looked at it. There were still people down there, and their shadows had not varied to any obvious degree.

But the people were agitated. They were talking to each other.

Or trying to talk.

Someone was running now. They were shouting. Whatever they were saying made no sense to me. But there was nothing strange about that. I really only spoke one language these days.

I dashed back to my sister.

'They cannot understand each other. The aug is gone. They are all like me now.' I looked back over her shoulder, at the stairwell leading down into the lower levels of the monument. 'I have to find someone who can help.'

'No,' my sister. 'You don't.' She closed her eyes. They were closed for a very long time.

I supported her head again. I wondered if there was a chance of getting my sister down to the level of the Wind Rose, without the exo to help either of us. I thought it unlikely, and also did not think much of my chances of finding help when I got there. I could still hear the voices. They were speaking in many tongues. They sounded frightened. They made me think of children who had been playing a happy and carefree game, only to have the rules changed at a stroke, and now the game had become both dangerous and bewildering.

This was unfortunate. But it occurred to me that the people did not know how lucky they were.

'I am sorry,' I said, when my sister reopened her eyes.

'For what?'

'There is nothing I can do.'

'There is,' my sister said. With some tremendous penultimate effort, she moved her hand, closed it around one of my own and drew it to her neck. 'There is.'

'What?'

'Be strong,' she said. 'You have work to do. They're going to need you now.'

My sister died then. I felt her hand slacken, saw the focus and brightness slip from her eyes. But my hand was still where she had brought it, and I understood now that she had wanted me to have the charm she wore around her neck. It was that old thing we had found in the box, when we drew lots under the candelabra tree, and agreed between us that it should remain on Earth, in the care of Chiku Yellow. I undid the leather fastening as carefully as I could, then lifted the charm free. My fingers felt clumsy as I retied it around my own neck. I wanted this to be done now, before I thought of anything else.

I did not feel strong or resolute but I forced myself to stand again, and stand tall. I thought of my sister's final words. I did not feel like I had the means in me to help myself, let alone anyone else. But Chiku Yellow had spoken truthfully: they would need me now, simply because I had already learned to live without the Mechanism. But I could still hear the shouts and cries, and they sounded worse than before. I moved to the edge and looked out across the water and the city again. Beyond the confusion at the Monument to the Discoveries, it was hard to sense any desperate change in things. The buildings gleamed and the suspension bridge glittered. But it would be like this everywhere, I knew. Not just Lisbon but the whole world. And not just Earth, either – the Mechanism's collapse would be spreading out through the solar system even as I thought these words. It was far beyond the Moon already, well on its way to Mars and beyond.

It was preposterous to think that one woman could do any good, when so much was broken. An unforgivable vanity, if truth be told. No one should have the arrogance to imagine such a thing. But then again there is that name of ours.

Chiku Red. Chiku Akinya. Great-granddaughter of Eunice Akinya. Senge Dongma, the lion-faced one, mother of us all.

I steeled myself. It was good to have a purpose in life.